OXFORD WORLD'S CLASSICS

UNCLE SILAS

JOSEPH THOMAS SHERIDAN LE FANU (1814–73) was born in Dublin, the elder son of a clergyman whose Huguenot forebears had married into the Sheridan family. His paternal grandmother was the sister of the playwright Richard Brinsley Sheridan. In 1826, the Revd Le Fanu was promoted dean of Emly, and with his family went to live at Abington, County Limerick. Educated at Trinity College and the King's Inns, Dublin, Sheridan Le Fanu began a career as a journalist and writer of fiction. By 1840 he had published a dozen or so stories (including 'A Strange Event in the Life of Schalken the Painter') in the *Dublin University Magazine*, which had been founded in 1833 by a group of young Trinity College men with strong literary interests. From 1840 onwards, he became increasingly involved in Irish journalism as editor of *The Warder* and owner or part-owner of that and other papers. In 1843 he married Susanna Bennett, the daughter of a leading Irish QC. His first two novels, *The Cock and Anchor* (1845) and *The Fortunes of Colonel Forlogh O'Brien* (1847), were historical fictions in the style of Walter Scott, expressing a fond approach to the Irish past that proved impossible to sustain following the trauma of the Great Famine. Following the deaths of his wife and mother in 1858 and 1861, Sheridan Le Fanu resumed fiction-writing with an Irish historical romance, *The House by the Churchyard* (1861–3), now remembered for its influence on James Joyce's *Finnegans Wake* (1939). *Wylder's Hand* and *Uncle Silas* both appeared in 1864. Though his subsequent novels are less achieved, *Uncle Silas* is celebrated as a chilling psychological exploration of fear, anxiety, and loss. Throughout his writing life, Le Fanu published accomplished short stories and tales, the best of which are collected *in Green Tea and Other Weird Stories* (Oxford World's Classics, 2020).

CLAIRE CONNOLLY, FLSW, MRIA, is Professor of Modern English at University College Cork in Ireland. Her book *A Cultural History of the Irish Novel, 1790–1829* (Cambridge Studies in Romanticism) won the Donald J. Murphy Prize, awarded by the American Conference for Irish Studies. With Marjorie Howes (Boston College), she is General Editor of *Irish Literature in Transition, 1700–2020* (Cambridge University Press, 2020).

OXFORD WORLD'S CLASSICS

*For over 100 years Oxford World's Classics have brought
readers closer to the world's great literature. Now with over 700
titles—from the 4,000-year-old myths of Mesopotamia to the
twentieth century's greatest novels—the series makes available
lesser-known as well as celebrated writing.*

*The pocket-sized hardbacks of the early years contained
introductions by Virginia Woolf, T. S. Eliot, Graham Greene,
and other literary figures which enriched the experience of reading.
Today the series is recognized for its fine scholarship and
reliability in texts that span world literature, drama and poetry,
religion, philosophy, and politics. Each edition includes perceptive
commentary and essential background information to meet the
changing needs of readers.*

OXFORD WORLD'S CLASSICS

SHERIDAN LE FANU

Uncle Silas

Edited with an Introduction and Notes by
CLAIRE CONNOLLY

UNIVERSITY PRESS

OXFORD
UNIVERSITY PRESS

Great Clarendon Street, Oxford, OX2 6DP,
United Kingdom

Oxford University Press is a department of the University of Oxford.
It furthers the University's objective of excellence in research, scholarship,
and education by publishing worldwide. Oxford is a registered trade mark of
Oxford University Press in the UK and in certain other countries

Published in the United States of America by Oxford University Press
198 Madison Avenue, New York, NY 10016, United States of America

British Library Cataloguing in Publication Data

Data available

Library of Congress Control Number: 2022945389

ISBN 978-0-19-886435-6

Printed and bound in the UK by
Clays Ltd, Elcograf S.p.A.

CONTENTS

UNCLE SILAS

INTRODUCTION

Readers who do not wish to learn details of the plot
will prefer to read the Introduction as an Afterword

UNCLE SILAS opens in winter, indoors, on a dark and stormy night. Candles are being lit and a substantial fire blazes inside the long, dark wood-panelled room. A violent wind screams outside. It is a liminal time of the year—the second week of November, as autumn shades into winter—and a girl is poised on the edge of adulthood. That young woman, Maud Ruthyn, is the narrator of the novel and her coming peril is already palpable. Sheridan Le Fanu's novel tracks Maud through distractions, confusions, and threats as she comes to an awareness of herself, her family history, and her friendships. In the process she has to reckon with her preoccupied and irresponsible father, a wicked governess, and the strange and enigmatic figure of her uncle Silas, a character with veiled motives and mysterious intentions. All of this is filtered via a gauzy narrative—Maud's worries accumulate 'in filmy layers, one over the other' (p. 353)—and shaped by a taut, nervy relationship between security and vulnerability.

The opening scene introduces readers to Maud's distinctive voice, marked by an uneasy tone and unsettled memories. Even as we encounter the heroine's vulnerability to her surroundings, however, there are moments of startling clarity. Seeming to hover above the domestic scene, Maud suddenly breaks with the past and declares: 'I was that girl' (p. 7). The announcement is dramatic and deliberate. But unlike Magwitch's revelation of his role in Pip's life at the end of *Great Expectations*—'It's me wot has done it'—Maud's melodramatic revelation comes at the very outset of the narrative. She is both witness to and participant in her own unfolding story, subject to vicious schemes but also possessed of the 'direful knowledge of good and evil that comes with years' (p. 47).[1] As readers, we are immersed in this divided world-view and do well to pay close attention to what

---

[1] Charles Dickens, *Great Expectations* (Oxford: Oxford University Press, 1993), 291.

Maud does and does not tell us, what she sees as well as what she fails to notice.

The shadow cast by that opening scene is a long and terrible one. What might have been a typical tale of 'The Wicked Uncle and the Endangered Heir' became, as Irish modernist writer Elizabeth Bowen described it, a novel that gains by the page in 'pressure, volume and spiritual urgency'.[2] M. R. James concurred, claiming that *Uncle Silas* was one of the few novels able to combine recognizable characters and realist settings with an intense air of mystery and 'the crescendo of impending doom'.[3] These magnetic effects were the work of Joseph Sheridan Le Fanu, a writer whose skills were honed in Ireland during the turbulent decades of the mid-nineteenth century.

Joseph Sheridan Le Fanu, novelist

When Le Fanu published *Uncle Silas* in London in December of 1864, he was already a successful novelist, journalist, and publisher. He was also a well-connected Irish Protestant whose family included the famous eighteenth-century playwright Richard Brinsley Sheridan. Le Fanu was born on 28 August 1814 at no. 45 Lower Dominick Street, Dublin. His father, the Revd Thomas Le Fanu, was appointed chaplain to the Royal Hibernian Military School in 1815, and the family moved to the village of Chapelizod, within easy reach of the fortified environs of Dublin's Phoenix Park. Ireland had been incorporated into a Union with Britain in 1800, a new stage in a centuries-old relationship between the two countries that began with the Anglo-Norman invasion in 1169. Despite the promises of the Union, a majority of Irish Catholics remained without rights in the early years of the nineteenth century while the role of Lord Lieutenant and a heavy military presence underlined Ireland's continuing status as colony. The Phoenix Park—home to the Viceregal Lodge as well as a parade ground, military barracks and hospital, a magazine fort, and from 1824 the office of the Ordnance Survey of Ireland—occupied a central role in the culture of colonial Ireland. Among the 'earliest

[2] Elizabeth Bowen, 'Introduction to *Uncle Silas*', repr. in Gary William Crawford, Jim Rockhill and Brian J. Showers (eds), *Reflections in a Glass Darkly: Essays on J. Sheridan Le Fanu* (New York: Hippocampus Press, 2011), 333–45, at 333.

[3] M. R. James, 'Introduction to *Uncle Silas*', repr. in Crawford, Rockhill and Showers (eds), *Reflections in a Glass Darkly*, 87–90, at 87.

recollections' of his brother William were 'the rejoicings, illuminations, and reviews that took place on the accession of George IV to the throne in 1820, and the excitement caused by his visit to Ireland in 1821'.[4] The Park was also a place of leisure and retreat, filled with 'green lawns and lofty trees' with a coach road running through.[5]

But Sheridan Le Fanu's youth was not entirely spent in the sheltering embrace of Anglo-Ireland. When Le Fanu senior acquired a further living at Ardnageehy, County Cork, in 1817 as well as the rectorship of Abington, County Limerick, he continued to live in Dublin as an absentee cleric. But on becoming dean of Emly in 1826, Thomas Le Fanu came into possession of a house in Abington and moved his family there. Leaving Dublin behind, the family were plunged into the inequities of rural Ireland, injustices in which Thomas Le Fanu took his part both as absentee holder of clerical posts and as the representative of a minority church that continued to collect tithes from the majority Catholic population. Speaking about Ireland in the House of Lords in 1812, Byron remarked on the 'grievance of tithes, so severely felt by the peasantry' and noted the particular 'irritation' felt in large absentee livings where 'the only resident Protestants are the tithe proctor and his family'.[6]

In 1825, Abington's Catholic priest, Father Costello, was interviewed as part of the *Third Report of the Select Committee on the State of Ireland*. Asked by the commissioners to describe the demographic make-up of the population, Costello estimated that there were around six thousand Catholics in the locality along with a passing population of 'strolling beggars who have no fixed residence'. He counted one Protestant resident to every five hundred Catholics, implying that only some half a dozen Protestants lived in this densely populated place. Of those largely impoverished Catholics, Costello noted that they lived upon a subsistence diet of 'Potatoes, and perhaps milk or

[4] William Le Fanu, *Seventy Years of Irish Life* (London: Edward Arnold, 1893), 2–3.

[5] See John Gamble, *Sketches of History, Politics and Manners, Taken in Dublin and the North of Ireland, in the Autumn of 1818*, in Gamble, *Society and Manners in Early-Nineteenth Century Ireland*, ed. Breandán MacSuibhne (Dublin: Field Day Press, 2011), 484.

[6] Lord Byron, 'Debate on the Earl of Donoughmore's Motion for a Committee on the Roman Catholic claims, April 21, 1812', in *The Parliamentary Speeches of Lord Byron* (London, 1824), 28.

herrings' while their livelihoods were subject to crop failures, typhus outbreaks, and unfair treatment:

They feel the degradation, which small as the number of persons of a different religion in the parish is, is excited by the supercilious conduct of some of those persons towards them in their transactions of life, shewing, that they feel a superiority by which the others are degraded; they are most interested also in the right of burial, in the attendance of the clergy in the churchyards at burials, of which they are deprived at present.[7]

The degradations described by Abington's Fr Costello resulted in organized forms of rural resistance, including the 'Captain Rock' campaign of 1821–4 which began near Newcastle West, County Limerick, some 50 kilometres south-west of Abington, and extended across the southern parts of Ireland. This Rockite Rebellion was succeeded by the Tithe War of 1831, which saw violent popular protests across the country. Lecturing to the National Literary Society in Dublin in 1899, on the brink of a new century, P. J. M'Donnell speculated on the likely effects on Le Fanu of living in a time and place where 'midnight attacks were frequent, when people slept with pistols at their bedsides': 'What terrible visions he must have had; what strange, wild, and mysterious pictures must have haunted his imagination. He passed through the terrible time; he was fitted to describe it.'[8] All of Le Fanu's writing can be seen to fit with that unjust and violent Munster landscape of his youth. In Abington, stones were thrown at Le Fanu's sister Elizabeth while their brother William described how he and a cousin were ambushed by 'a considerable and very threatening crowd, who saluted us with "Down with the Orangemen! Down with the tithes!" '[9] Their cousin Caroline Norton wrote from London around this time, sympathizing with the family's loss of comfort. But the detail of William Le Fanu's description is revealing: two young gentlemen on horses carrying pistols were assailed by locals on foot, armed with stones and spades. Surrounded by a populous and impoverished peasantry, the Le Fanus thought of themselves as the isolated and beleaguered victims of a diminishing income and a changing cultural world. A skewed relationship between social privilege and perilous conditions pervades the author's think-

[7] *Third Report from the Select Committee on the State of Ireland* (London, 1825), 423.
[8] *Freeman's Journal* (27 April 1899), 2.
[9] William Le Fanu, *Seventy Years of Irish Life*, 61.

ing, often realized via the image of an isolated family or house. Literary critic W. J. McCormack traces lines of connection between this Anglo-Irish background and Le Fanu's fictions of existential doubt, suggesting that the embittered, dissolving forms of authority found in *Uncle Silas* are rooted in Le Fanu's Limerick years.[10]

Even when Le Fanu commenced his degree at Trinity College Dublin in 1832, he was registered as a country scholar, meaning substantial periods spent at home in Abington. Despite being admitted to the King's Inn (Dublin) in 1836, to the Lincoln's Inn (London) in 1838, and called to the Irish Bar in 1839, Le Fanu never practised the law. Instead, he earned his money in the world of books and magazines. Le Fanu had financial interests in several Irish newspapers, including *The Warder* (Dublin) and the *Statesman and Dublin Christian Record* and from 1861 to 1869 was the owner of the *Dublin University Magazine*. In 1843 he married Susanna Bennett, the daughter of George Bennett, QC, a Dublin barrister. They had two sons and two daughters. They moved into her father's grand house on Merrion Square and lived there for the rest of their lives.

As a writer, Le Fanu is particularly associated with the *Dublin University Magazine*, a journal that he owned from 1861 to 1869, to which he began contributing in 1838, and for which he wrote his first ghost story 'The Ghost and the Bone-setter'. Founded on the principles of unionist politics and unofficially allied to the Protestant interest via Trinity College, the *Dublin University Magazine* occupied a distinctive cultural space in mid-nineteenth-century Ireland. Its overall tone was gloomy and pessimistic, expressive of failed Tory hopes in the face of Whig reforms. Even as it decried moves towards weakening of the Union and reform of the Church of Ireland, however, the magazine also published original Irish fiction and poetry by writers including Charles Lever and Samuel Ferguson. When Lever took on the editorship of the journal in 1842, he wanted Irish writers—'the acknowledged staff of periodical literature in England'—to 'unite' in a literary enterprise that would bring to Ireland 'the same proud position in public estimation, that Scotsmen have won for their magazine before the eyes of Great

[10] W. J. McCormack, *Sheridan Le Fanu and Victorian Ireland* (Dublin: Lilliput Press, 1991), 45–6.

Britain'.[11] The indirect reference to *Blackwood's Magazine* and to
Scotland spells out the unionist nature of the undertaking but such
extensive cultural ambitions meant that writers like William
Carleton and James Clarence Mangan could move between the
Dublin University Magazine and the culturally nationalist Young
Ireland publication, *The Nation*. In the traumatic aftermath of the
Great Famine (1845–8), though, what had been a broad coalition of
conservative and national interests in the politically and culturally
fluid years of the 1830s and early 1840s fell asunder. Afterwards,
divisions hardened and alliances narrowed. A moment of potential
cultural renewal closed down, not to reopen until the decades after
Le Fanu's death with the Literary Revival spearheaded by
W. B. Yeats and Lady Gregory in the 1890s.

Among Le Fanu's earliest writing is 'Passages in the Secret History
of an Irish Countess', a story that bears a close relation to the plot of
Uncle Silas. One of a series of linked stories published in the *Dublin
University Magazine* between 1838 and 1840, 'Passages in the Secret
History of an Irish Countess' was again revised as 'The Murdered
Cousin' in 1851 and later published in a book of stories given the title
The Purcell Papers. Using a device he perfected in *In A Glass Darkly*,
Le Fanu connected these fictions via the figure of 'a parish priest in
the south of Ireland' who is a 'curious and industrious collector of old
local traditions' and a compiler of stories.[12] Although it contains the
outline of *Uncle Silas*'s plot—a brother suspected of murder, a curious will, a niece in peril, an evil Frenchwoman—'Passages in the
Secret History of an Irish Countess' has a recognizably Irish topography with the brothers' houses located in Cork and Galway.

Passages through history: the publication of Uncle Silas

Uncle Silas was written and published in the aftermath of a terrible
loss. Le Fanu's wife Susanna died in 1858, having passed through
a traumatic loss of religious faith that in turn shook her husband.
Most biographies report that Susanna's death prompted Le Fanu to

---

[11] *Dublin University Magazine* 19/112 (Apr. 1842), 424; quoted in Elizabeth Tilley,
'Periodicals', in *Oxford History of the Irish Book*, iv. *The Irish Book in English, 1800–1891*,
ed. James H. Murphy (Oxford: Oxford University Press, 2011), 151–69, at 155.
[12] Sheridan Le Fanu, *The Purcell Papers* (New York: Garland, 1979), i. 1–3.

retreat to a cloistered and reclusive life, notoriously becoming the 'Invisible Prince' of Merrion Square, Dublin. Yet throughout those years and up to his death in 1873, Le Fanu continued to write, publish, and socialize while his fictions remained vividly alive to the rhythms of social, cultural, and political change. In 1867, reflecting on the threat of a Fenian uprising, Le Fanu could remark on the 'fiddlings, dancings and flirtations' of Dublin life while critic Nicholas Daly has found regular references to family social outings in the Dublin newspapers of the day.[13] Le Fanu also kept up with his brother William who was a successful railway engineer in Victorian Dublin. The wide range of contemporary cultural references found in *Uncle Silas* take in the 1859 revised edition of Thomas De Quincey's *Confessions of an English Opium Eater* along with many knowing references to contemporary print culture.

Not only was Le Fanu widowed in the 1850s but the entire face of the country changed around him. The Great Famine, caused by crop-failure but exacerbated by policies of the Government in London, was a political, social, humanitarian, and ecological disaster on an unprecedented scale, which resulted in the death of approximately one million (mainly Irish-speaking) inhabitants of Ireland. Dublin did not escape its devastating effects and many died or emigrated. For the Anglo-Irish, the political aftermath of famine saw the beginning of the break-up of their power, as bankrupt owners were forced to sell insolvent estates via the Encumbered Estates Act of 1849. Those changes had a direct impact on the writing of *Uncle Silas*. Where Le Fanu had previously penned historical novels that tried 'to gratify the new sentiment which the *Nation* had awakened' (as described by the politician and journalist Charles Gavan Duffy),[14] now he turned away from Irish topics. Prompted by his English publisher, Richard Bentley, Le Fanu began to write contemporary fiction with recognizable English settings. As a result, *Uncle Silas* offers a strange mix of Irish concerns—not least the recurrent question of a past that will not go away—with English topography. The novel's absorption in

---

[13] Nicholas Daly, *The Demographic Imagination and the Nineteenth-Century City* (Cambridge: Cambridge University Press, 2015), 84.

[14] Quoted in Melissa Fegan, 'Young Ireland and Beyond' in Matthew Campbell (ed.), *Irish Literature in Transition* (Cambridge: Cambridge University Press, 2021), 43.

a world of symbols adds a further layer to the overall atmosphere of chilling ambiguity.

Uncle Silas was published monthly from July to December 1864 in the *Dublin University Magazine*. Le Fanu seems to have already tried to interest the *Cornhill Magazine* in the story between May and July of that year and the trials and pressures of serial publication were a constant worry. Writing to his London publisher Richard Bentley, Le Fanu explained in detail how hard he worked to keep up with the pace of magazine publication, explaining that 'All then, except about 32 Magazine pages was written in 3 months only 2 thirds of which i.e. 2 months were applicable to the writing the tale. I am very tired, & claim some credit for diligence.'[15]

Exhausted as he was, Le Fanu entered into negotiations with Bentley in 1863, seeking an arrangement for a novel that would follow on from *The House by the Churchyard*, five hundred copies of which were published in London in 1863. Because of that novel's poor sales, Bentley stipulated 'the story of an English subject in modern times' for Le Fanu's next book.[16] The idea that the topic of Ireland had exhausted its audience was already suggested in 1848, at the height of the Famine, when the publisher Henry Colburn wrote to Anthony Trollope to advise him that 'readers do not like novels on Irish subjects as well as on others'.[17] And in 1853, the writer and journalist Harriet Martineau observed that 'The world is weary of the subject of Ireland; and, above all the rest, the English reading world is weary of it. The mere name brings up images of men in long coats and women in long cloaks; of mud cabins and potatoes; the conacre, the middlemen and the priest; the faction fight, and the funeral howl.' Martineau did not doubt the suffering experienced during the Famine but remarked that 'The sadness of the subject has in late years increased the weariness.' Irish difficulties, she said, were 'too real and practical to be an intellectual exercise or a pastime—to serve as knowledge or excitement. Something ought to be

[15] Le Fanu to Richard Bentley (11 October 1864); quoted in McCormack, *Sheridan Le Fanu and Victorian Ireland*, 205.

[16] Richard Bentley to Le Fanu (26 February 1863); quoted in McCormack, *Sheridan Le Fanu in Victorian Ireland*, 140.

[17] Henry Colburn to Anthony Trollope (11 November 1848); in Anthony Trollope, *An Autobiography and other Writings* (Oxford: Oxford University Press, 2016), 54.

done for Ireland; and, to readers by the fireside, it is too bewildering to say what.'[18]

Uncle Silas, *the novel*

By Christmas of 1864, *Uncle Silas* was in the hands of Le Fanu's fireside readers. Between its covers, they found no references to Irish life or history but rather a shocking tale of death and betrayal, set in contemporary England. On the sudden death of her father, Austin Ruthyn, from a heart attack, Maud is left to the care of her uncle Silas in Derbyshire, until she comes of age. Silas is suspected of having murdered (in his house) a man to whom he owed gambling debts, but he has never been brought to justice. Sinister in appearance and a consummate villain, Silas plots to marry Maud to his oafish son Dudley (who is, it emerges, already married). When this scheme fails, father and son conspire to murder the ward and so inherit her fortune. A French governess, Madame de la Rougierre, is brought in to help with the plan, in which the victim is to be killed with a spiked hammer. Amidst scenes of distress and attempted flight, the violent plot fails. The French governess is murdered in Maud's place, a sight witnessed by a petrified Maud, who looks on as Dudley drives 'a hammer, one end of which had been beaten out into a longish tapering spike' (p. 420) into the body of the shrieking woman. Though hardly rivalling the novel's lurid depiction of this 'diabolical surgery' (p. 420), Silas's own fate is also filled with menace: he takes an overdose of laudanum, leaving others to bear the brunt of the criminal plan he has masterminded. Maud ends the novel as the contented Lady Ilbury, the wife of a 'noble-hearted husband' (p. 429) but also as someone who has endured the loss of a child. It is at this later, shadowed, point in her life that she tells her story.

Uncle Silas is structured via a series of secret motives that unfold via a highly dramatic narrative that features money, violence, imprisonment, romance, and escape. The narrative hunt for clues, along with Maud's curiosity, leads literary historian Allan Hepburn to list the novel (with *Treasure Island* and *Kim*) as one among the 'Victorian precursors

[18] Harriet Martineau, *Westminster Review* 3 (1853); Deborah Ann Logan (ed.), *Harriet Martineau and the Irish Question* (Lanham, MD: Lehigh University Press, 2012), 200.

to the detective and spy novel'.[19] The account of the death of Tom Charke (a tale first heard by Maud in Knowl, then again from her aunt Monica, and finally a story that exerts a shaping force on her own destiny) turns on an inquest, clues, and signs. Where the detective novel is driven by a 'will to know', however, motivations in *Uncle Silas* remain shrouded within a mysterious plot that discovers itself only gradually as well as a series of cliffhanger endings, a mode familiar from sensation novels such as Elizabeth Braddon's *Lady Audley's Secret* (1862).

In all of this, the traditional focus on inheritance in Gothic novels proves a powerful driving force. Ann Radcliffe's *The Italian* (1797) had already explored the peculiar and unsettling threats posed by a vicious uncle. Maud, who has 'a mind very uninstructed as to the limits of the marvellous' (p. 10), is the conduit through whom the reader experiences an expansion of the boundaries of reality via such devices as her strange dreams along with the doubled relationship between the two houses of Knowl and Bartram-Haugh. The novel also makes use of Gothic themes and tropes that treat property ownership as a matter of stable patterns across the generations, even as they reduce those relationships to frayed, barely discernible connections.

Le Fanu had read widely on the supernatural and the novel references popular fiction, European folklore, and the demonology of Walter Scott as well as Irish oral tradition and Swedenborgian theology. He may also have owed a debt to a slightly earlier Catholic tradition of Irish Gothic, in particular the tales of Gerald Griffin (1803–40). Griffin had grown up on the Shannon Estuary, only a short distance from Le Fanu's childhood home in Limerick. Both writers knew not only the divided politics of the south-west of Ireland but also its supernatural stories. Among Griffin's tales can be found 'The Aylmers of Ballyaylmer', from which Le Fanu may have taken the middle name of his heroine, Maud Aylmer Ruthyn. Le Fanu's eerie tale, 'Schalken the Painter', shares with Griffin's tale 'The Brown Man' a plot, probably drawn from folklore, in which a wealthy man carries off a beautiful and vulnerable woman as his bride.

---

[19] Allan Hepburn, 'Thrillers', in Robert L Caserio and Clement Hawes (eds), *The Cambridge History of the English Novel* (Cambridge: Cambridge University Press, 2012), 693.

Much as the stories gathered by Griffin in his *Holland-Tide* and *Tales of the Munster Festivals* (1827) are explicitly framed according to a Celtic calendar, the action of *Uncle Silas* follows a traditional time frame albeit in a more discreet manner. In Griffin's *Holland-Tide* (another term for Halloween), early November is a time to retire indoors and tell stories. *Uncle Silas* opens under the shades of Samhain, signalling not only the beginning of winter in early November but also a time in pre-Christian Ireland when the line between one world and another is at its most permeable. With the plot of *Uncle Silas* concluding just as January draws to a close, the novel tracks the transition from winter to spring. Having arrived in London by train and weighed down by 'black Care' (p. 395), Maud glimpses a letter from her uncle to Madame de la Rougierre dated 30 January. The two women are to go to *Dover*, the underlined place name in the letter serving as a secret signal to the governess to return Maud to Bartram-Haugh in darkness and disguise. Passing through 'the glare of lamps' (p. 395) and a sequence of changing urban scenes, they arrive at their destination in the early hours of 31 January. As morning dawns, Maud realizes that she is not above the courtyard of a Dover hotel but rather a room overlooking the inner court of her uncle's home, to which she has been secretly returned. By late afternoon that same day, Maud knows her danger and that night she hears sounds of her grave being dug outside. Her daring rescue by Tom Brice on that same fateful night means that the novel's action closes on 1 February: in Ireland, St Brigid's Day—a Celtic fertility festival (Imbolc) to which a thin veneer of Christianity had been applied—the start of spring and the day on which the earth begins its turn towards the light.

With a narrative shaped by these threshold dates in the Celtic year—Samhain and Imbolc—the novel also recognizes the significance of Christmas, a festival made newly fashionable by the Victorians. Lady Knollys invites Maud and Milly to visit her in December when she is to spend Christmas at her home, and promises to include a gift for the loyal servant Mary Quince when she sends 'a little Christmas box' (p. 59) to Maud. Maud meanwhile is 'an admiring reader of the *Albums*, the *Souvenirs*, the *Keepsakes*, and all that flood of Christmas present lore which yearly irrigated England' (p. 67). With this reference to the Victorian seasonal fad for stories set around Christmas, Le Fanu recognizes that, as Nicholas

Daly puts it, such fashionable stories 'had a seasonal rival in the Celtic periphery: Halloween'.[20] (That intimate relationship between old and new festivals may have spurred James Joyce to trace out the overlapping territories of Christmas and Halloween in his two ghostly short stories, 'The Dead' and 'Clay'.[21])

Over these already varied supernatural influences, Le Fanu layered his interests in the life and writings of the eighteenth-century mystic Swedenborg, a visionary thinker who influenced writers from William Blake and Charles Baudelaire to William Butler Yeats and A. S. Byatt. Swedenborg lived in London from the early 1770s (having moved from his native Sweden) and his writings were available in English from the middle of the eighteenth century. His theories opened up parallels and correspondences between an earthly world and a spiritual one while the man himself was reputed to converse with angels and spirits. Le Fanu was drawn to the idea of a spiritual sphere that made itself manifest in material forms, recognizable via shapes familiar from known domestic or natural worlds: 'a world of scenery where there was a scenery like that of earth', as W. B. Yeats put it.[22] When Maud visits her mother's grave in the company of her father's Swedenborgian friend Dr Bryerly, he explains the need to look 'beyond', 'over', and '*through*' the graveyard walls in order to see her mother moving 'along an airy path' amidst 'a beautiful landscape, radiant with a wondrous light . . . peopled with human beings translated into the same image, beauty, and splendour' (p. 20). In Swedenborg's account of death, the being that passes over from mortal life retains 'an exact resemblance of themselves in face and tone of voice'.[23] Maud finds a way to reconcile this heterodox vision of life after death with her own Christianity even as the novel's use of Swedenborg extends far beyond its plot. Le Fanu took from Swedenborg a powerful symbolic language that operated via correspondences along which spiritual and natural world flowed into one another. The stories gathered in *In a Glass Darkly* (1872) find ways of opening up strange and uncanny passageways between states of consciousness but already in *Uncle Silas*

[20] Daly, *The Demographic Imagination and the Nineteenth-Century City*, 82.

[21] See Daly, *The Demographic Imagination and the Nineteenth-Century City*, 82.

[22] W. B. Yeats, *Explorations* (London: Macmillan, 1962), 72.

[23] Peter Ackroyd, *Introducing Swedenborg* (London: The Swedenborg Society, 2021), 39.

there is a close attention to symbolic patterns and equivalences, helping to shape what W. J. McCormack calls the novel's 'formal economy'.[24]

But Swedenborgianism also offered a mode of expressing extreme, barely admissible feelings, a language in which Maud becomes fluent: by the novel's conclusion she has achieved an almost writerly under-standing of the world as 'the habitation of symbols—the phantoms of spiritual things immortal shown in material shape' (p. 429). Such knowledge is achieved at the cost of a searching exploration of the nature of evil and *Uncle Silas* continues an inquiry into demonical power already found in Le Fanu's earlier fiction. Reviewing *The House by the Churchyard* in 1863, the *Dublin Evening Mail* asked of its main character, Charles Archer: 'Can a man approach so nearly to the devilish? History shows that it is possible. The records of imperial wickedness furnish ample evidence that some men want only power to develop into the Satanic.'[25] Silas Ruthyn certainly belongs to those same ranks of the wicked. His sister, Maud's Aunt Monica, expresses it best when she wonders if 'other souls than human are sometimes born into the world, and clothed in flesh' (p. 162). Maud herself experiences a dawning understanding of his nature when she identi-fies a 'semi-transparent structure' through which she could 'now and then discern the light or the glare of his inner life' (p. 341). The nature of that 'inner life' remains a question for Maud for most of the novel: 'Was, then, all his kindness but a phosphoric radiance covering some-thing colder and more awful than the grave?' (p. 342). Le Fanu's skill is to pose these terrible questions while cultivating an atmosphere of 'shadowy dread' that was, according to one contemporary review, more effective than 'fifty mortal murders'.[26]

Steeped in the experience of death and loss, the novel affords 'a peep into Pandemonium' (p. 93). Following her mother's death and her walk with the Swedenborgian Dr Bryerly to the graveyard, Maud experiences a revelation as to the location of the afterlife, shrouded in a 'strange glamour' and belonging to 'the dazzling land of ghosts' (p. 21). Even as this supernatural apprehension dawns on Maud, however, another more terrible sight materializes in the plain

---

[24] McCormack, *Sheridan Le Fanu and Victorian Ireland*, 6.

[25] *Dublin Evening Mail* (2 February 1863).

[26] Review of *Uncle Silas*, *The Athenaeum* (7 January 1865), 16–17.

light of day: 'On a sudden, on the grass before me, stood an odd
figure—a very tall woman in grey draperies, nearly white under the
moon, courtesying [*sic*] extraordinarily low, and rather fantastically'
(p. 22). The very abruptness of the arrival of the wicked French governess, Madame de la Rougierre, shifts the grounds of Le Fanu's narrative into the domain of sensation fiction. This is a move on to gory
cultural ground made familiar in the 1860s by the dominance of sensational journalism, books, and plays. The first readers of *Uncle Silas*
encountered the novel as part of a new leisure culture, within which
the drama of everyday life proved richly entertaining material for
audiences increasingly familiar with exciting and eventful popular
prints, filled with shocking tales.

While sensation might be seen both as 'updated Gothic' or 'an
aberrant strain' within domestic fiction, what was new was the focus
on 'suspense, shock and the production of physical response in the
reader or viewer'.[27] Brought up in an atmosphere of silence and 'awe',
Maud might be seen to represent a wider cultural tendency to fall
under the influence of sudden apparitions and strange sensations.
Prepared for life only by 'the three-volumed gospel of the circulating
library' (p. 47), Maud's narrative proves a powerful conduit for read-
erly immersion in a world of fearful thrills. Her susceptibility to
visual spectacles is particularly noticeable in the narrative while wider
cultural patterns of absorption and distraction are mirrored within
Le Fanu's narrative.

With suspenseful plotting second only to Wilkie Collins's *The
Woman in White* (1859) in its capacity to terrify readers, *Uncle Silas*
has been hailed as a masterpiece of the sensation genre. Its effects rely
upon the power of the insecure and uncertain voice on readers and Le
Fanu's ability to prolong states of narrative uncertainty. Given to
flights of fancy concerning all those that surround her, Maud seems
to almost delight in imagining her own victimhood: 'I could no more
stir than the bird who, cowering under its ivy, sees the white owl sailing back and forward on its predatory cruise' (p. 98). While Maud
compares herself to 'the conscientious heroine of Mrs. Ann Radcliffe'
(p. 356), however, the novel does not simply follow in Radcliffe's foot-
steps by explaining and then demystifying the dangers surrounding

---

[27] Nicholas Daly, *Sensation and Modernity* (Cambridge: Cambridge University Press,
2009), 27–8.

the imperilled heroine. Rather, Le Fanu plays out an imagined drama of victimhood that comes horribly true.

Whereas sensation fiction tended to play upon fears generated by unravelling social conventions and shifting gender roles, in contrast Le Fanu retains a traditional inheritance plot, albeit one made strange by criminal intent. The plot traces Maud's moves between family homes, affording her only a brief glimpse of urban life in London. Her fate is ultimately brought to a happy conclusion which sees her finding refuge in the home of her aunt Monica at Elverston. It is at this 'pretty gabled house, beautified with that indescribable air of shelter and comfort' which belongs to an old English residence' (p. 263) that she meets her husband Lord Ilbury, and the novel's conclusion finds her firmly fixed in the marital home. The narrative representation of domesticity is, however, considerably disturbed by the novel's absorption in mental states. Throughout *Uncle Silas*, domestic interiors framed by wild outdoor spaces lend shape and substance to an experience of interiority under threat. Literary critic Patricia Coughlan remarks that Le Fanu's chairs, tables, and portraits realize both the details of middle-class decor and the minutiae of psychic realms of 'the conscience, the mind, the consciousness'.[28] The domestic interior recalled by Maud at the novel's outset represents not only a room within a house but also a fragile state of mind that seeks shelter.

As Maud wanders through her father's parklands, coming up against the fences that surround her uncle's estate and encountering locked doors, she faces threats that are emotional, physical, financial, and sexual. These include a marauding Gypsy group, her evil governess, her leering cousin Dudley, and the menacing Dickon (also known as Pegtop) Hawkes. Worst of all though are the dangers posed by her own father and uncle. A sequence of terrible betrayals by the older generation leads Vera Kreilkamp to describe *Uncle Silas* as 'an unmerciful depiction of how a beleaguered society savagely destroys its own young, the likes of which were not seen again until Molly Keane's great novel of the Irish Big House, *Good Behaviour*'.[29] The novel's irresponsible fathers include Austin, Silas, and Dickon Hawkes.

---

[28] Patricia Coughlan, 'Doubles, Shadows, Sedan-Chairs, and the Past: The "Ghost Stories" of J. S. Le Fanu', repr. in Crawford, Rockhill and Showers (eds), *Reflections in a Glass Darkly*, 137–60, at 146.

[29] Vera Kreilkamp, *The Anglo-Irish Novel and the Big House* (Syracuse, NY: Syracuse University Press, 1998), 111.

Silas's own daughter Milly is represented as a young woman condemned to drift between class identities due to her lack of education and neglectful father. Hawkes, who lives on the estate, beats his daughter Meg and breaks her arm before conspiring in Silas's plan to murder Maud. Although not as vicious as Silas's evil schemes or as brutal as Hawkes's thuggish behaviour, Austin is explicit about his plan to put Maud in danger as part of a trial by which his reputation will be saved. 'I think little Maud would like to contribute to the restitution of her family name', says Austin, making of his daughter an 'honourable sacrifice' that will 'dispel the disgrace under which our most ancient and honourable name must otherwise continue to languish' (p. 107). Austin's intentions are made yet clearer by Dr Bryerly who explains to Maud that she has been made the ward of her uncle so as to 'purge' (p. 166) him of scandal. Maud's dream of her dead father's 'cadaverous' face with its 'unnatural expression of diabolical fury' (p. 173) seems to recognize the terrible damage done by the strange experiment in family history dreamed up by the absent Austin.

These three daughters—Maud, Milly, and Meg—are separated by class and education but come together in order to save Maud's life. Their steely nerves and clear thinking at the novel's denouement stands in contrast to their shared experience of threats and slights, lending narrative authority to women's damaged bodies and nervous feelings. But Maud's ability to recall the perils of her earlier life from her later position as a happy wife and mother relies on the conventions of the domestic novel which serve to surround and soften the chilling effects conjured up by the first-person narrative. These tensions are given a dramatic treatment in the novel's closing scenes which imagine Maud's mortal danger while according her a new power of 'terrible composure' (p. 420). Realizing her danger, she writes a letter to her aunt Monica and manages to hide it in her clothes, glad that her servant has equipped her dress with 'those capacious pockets which belonged to a former generation' (p. 372). The pocket symbolizes security as well as secrecy and confirms Maud's sense of the privileges of her class. Even in her hour of danger, her taste and wealth afford a 'Coolness' (p. 422) that screens her against harm. When she discovers that the iron bars that blocked her windows exist 'in reality' (p. 407) and not just in terrified fantasy, Maud turns resolute. Trapped in the locked chamber, she stands up 'swiftly' in order to evade her uncle: 'I often thought if I had happened to wear silk instead of the cachmere I had on that night, its rustle would have betrayed me' (p. 422).

The innermost thread

An exchange of letters between Le Fanu and Charles Dickens hints at some of the ways in which questions of class, race, and nationality are threaded through the narrative of *Uncle Silas*. Charles Dickens wrote to Le Fanu in 1870 about a story intended for his periodical, *All the Year Round*. The story in question, Dickens thought, might benefit from an Irish character, a youth who blames everything on 'his country's real or supposed wrongs' woven 'into the innermost thread of the narrative'.[30] Although Le Fanu did not follow up this hint for *The Rose and the Key*, Dickens's phrasing opens up an understanding of the crossed cultural meanings woven into the 'innermost thread' of *Uncle Silas*. In relation to Ireland, the novel's interest in possession, inheritance, and dispossession draws deeply on Irish Protestant culture, using a language and set of images that goes back to Edmund Burke and forward to W. B. Yeats. In May 1856, Friedrich Engels wrote to Karl Marx that the estates of post-Famine Ireland were 'enormous, amazingly beautiful parks, but all around is waste land, and where the money comes from is impossible to see'.[31] Irish landed estates presented an intractable political pathology in the present: a form of property that originated in colonialism and confiscation and was rapidly running into ruin and decline.

Partaking of what historian R. F. Foster calls 'Protestant insecurity and self-interrogation' and part of a broader tendency towards displaced and allegorical kinds of writing about Ireland, often with a supernatural dimension, *Uncle Silas* can be seen to address itself to post-Famine Ireland.[32] The case was best made by Elizabeth Bowen in her 1946 introduction to the novel for the Cresset Press. Where Irish critic Stephen Gwynne regretted in 1919 that Le Fanu had left

---

[30] Charles Dickens to J. S. Le Fanu (26 May 1870), in *The British Academy / The Pilgrim Edition of The Letters of Charles Dickens*, xii. *1868–1870*, ed. Graham Storey (Oxford: Oxford University Press, 2002).

[31] Engels to Marx (23 May 1853), in Karl Marx and Friedrich Engels, *Ireland and the Irish Question* (New York: International Publishers, 1972), 85.

[32] R. F. Foster, *Words Alone: Yeats and His Inheritances* (Oxford: Oxford University Press, 2011), 103.

'no memorable presentment of Irish life', caring too much in *Uncle Silas* about 'sensational incident and ingenious construction',[33] Bowen had no hesitancy in describing *Uncle Silas* as 'an Irish story transposed to an English setting'. She found her evidence in Le Fanu's background: 'The hermetic solitude and the autocracy of the great country house, the demonic power of the family myth, fatalism, feudalism and the "ascendency" outlook', all 'accepted facts of life for the race of hybrids from which Le Fanu sprang'. 'For the psychological background of *Uncle Silas*,' she wrote, 'it was necessary for him to invent nothing.'[34] In *Uncle Silas*, that 'psychological background' manifests itself in the doubt and uncertainty that pervade even the most seemingly secure houses, families, and alliances. Maud inhabits 'a sinister vacancy from which authority has withdrawn', as if to mirror the Anglo-Irish sense of authority as remote and insecure.[35]

For this, Le Fanu draws on a Big House tradition of Irish fiction that began with Maria Edgeworth's *Castle Rackrent* (1800) and was regularly revisited in the Victorian period by novelists including Anthony Trollope and Somerville and Ross. Austin's Swedenborgian views make Knowl into a mirror image of the Irish Big House with its isolated inhabitants clinging to a minority religion. Building on this understanding of the Anglo-Irish tradition 'as both sacred and fragile', Marjorie Howes makes a convincing case for the novel's Anglo-Irish resonances, arguing that along with 'genealogical decay' and 'sexual corruption', *Uncle Silas* evinces 'a preoccupation with the nature and construction of femininity indicate the text's specifically Anglo-Irish origins and concern'. Accordingly, Howes reads the novel as 'a different version of the imperial romance of reconciliation' with Maud a heroine in a line descended from Glorvina from *The Wild Irish Girl* (1806), a character whose personality is inextricably bound up with national identity.[36]

A more materially grounded understanding of the lines of connection between *Uncle Silas* and the politics of Le Fanu's day can be

[33] Stephen Gwynne, 'Novels of Irish Life in the Nineteenth Century' (1897), repr. in *Irish Books and Irish People* (New York: Frederick Stokes, 1919), 21.

[34] Elizabeth Bowen, 'Introduction to *Uncle Silas*', 334.

[35] McCormack, *Sheridan Le Fanu and Victorian Ireland*, 207.

[36] Marjorie Howes, 'Misalliance and Anglo-Irish Tradition in Le Fanu's *Uncle Silas*', *Nineteenth-Century Literature* 47/2 (1992), 173.

found in a subplot concerning the cutting of the trees on Maud's estate. Via Dr Bryerly and her aunt Monica, Maud learns that her guardian uncle has been 'cutting down and selling the timber, and the oak-bark, and burning the willows, and other trees that are turned into charcoal' (p. 269). The environmental consequences as well as legal wrong inflicted by such acts of extraction are spelled out: 'It is all *waste*, and Dr Bryerly is about to put a stop to it' (p. 269). Le Fanu here draws on a resonant arboreal language of absenteeism that stretches back to eighteenth-century Irish-language poetry. In Edgeworth's *The Absentee* (1812), the Anglo-Irish Lord Colambre spells out the link between moral authority and environmental responsibility when he informs his mother of the costs of her London lifestyle: 'For a single season . . . at the expense of a great part of your timber, the growth of a century—swallowed in the entertainments of one winter in London! Our hills to be bare for another half century to come!'[37]

The Derbyshire setting adopted in *Uncle Silas* enabled Le Fanu to examine the fate of great houses, where ownership was under threat and lineage a frail thread. Bowen suggested that Derbyshire itself exists at a distance from London that is both temporal and spatial: 'Up there, in the vast estates of the landed old stock, there appeared in the years when Le Fanu wrote (and still more in the years of which he wrote: the 1840s), a time lag—just such a time lag as, in a more marked form, separates Ireland from England more effectually than any sea.'[38] The novel's geographical framework, though, extends far beyond its Derbyshire location, taking in London and 'the Lunnon-road' (p. 190) as well as the English ports of Dover and Liverpool, France and Australia. Madame de la Rougierre, who taunts Maud with 'her ugly minstrelsy' (p. 38), is the object of hatred and suspicion among the other servants who wonder about her origins: 'Where does she come from?—is she a French or a Swiss one, or is she a Canada woman?' (p. 35). Just as Maud and her servant Mary Quince begin to approach her uncle's residence at Bartram-Haugh, they encounter a group of Gypsies who are represented as romantic outcasts from normal society: 'thievish and uncanny' in the eyes of others but 'children of mystery and liberty' (pp. 185–6) in Maud's memory.

---

[37] Maria Edgeworth, *The Absentee* (Oxford: Oxford University Press, 2001), 200.
[38] Bowen, 'Introduction to *Uncle Silas*', 334.

The presence of robbers, poachers, and Gypsies in the novel and Silas's uneasy alliance with working-class characters including Dickon Hawkes not only evokes but also accommodates the internally divided British nation of the 1860s.

Silas's own children, Milly and Dudley, are deprived of formal education while their accents and associates place them outside the social sphere of their birth. Though Silas's plan to marry Maud off to Dudley would be one that aligned her with a gentleman by birth, it is nonetheless presented in the novel in terms of the frightening prospects of cross-class union. While Milly can be saved via her marriage to a 'good little curate' (p. 278) whom she meets at Monica's house, the character of Dudley is condemned, not least by his geographical mobility within the plot. Monica reports a rumour that he has 'gone a-soldiering to India' (p. 268) even as she wishes him in Van Diemen's Land or Tasmania. He later pretends to go to Australia via Liverpool (and contemplates actually going there should Maud pay him to save her life). The novel's ending sees Meg writing to Maud from 'her Australian farm' (p. 427), to where she has travelled with capital supplied by her wealthy friend in the company of Tom Brice, her lover and Maud's saviour, and from where she reports a sighting of Dudley. The circulation of Maud's money helps smooth out these final settlements: via her own marriage, 'the capital' (p. 426) she supplies to Meg and Tom Brice to fund their emigration to Australia, and the living that she plans to endow upon Milly's husband, the Revd Sprigge Biddlepen. Her father's friend Dr Bryerly, his worth proven, enters her employ in order 'to undertake the management of the Derbyshire estates' (p. 426).

Australia also provides what Josephine McDonagh describes as 'an efficient and plausible resolution to a plot that could not end satisfactorily in England'.[39] As with Elizabeth Gaskell's decision to remove Mary and Jem to the settler colony in Canada at the conclusion of *Mary Barton* (1848), Le Fanu finds a way to acknowledge the worth of lower-class lives via a subplot of relocation within the Empire. In *Uncle Silas*, though, there are hints at a fuller reckoning with migration within the narrative: Meg Hawkes, Tom Brice, and Dudley Ruthyn are all swept up in the 'vast global redistribution of

[39] Josephine McDonagh, *Literature in a Time of Migration: British Fiction and the Movement of People, 1815–1876* (Oxford: Oxford University Press, 2021), 4.

population' that characterized colonialism in the nineteenth century.[40] As the family at home in Bartram-Haugh trace the supposed passage of Dudley's ship, the *Seamew*, in the newspaper, the novel also testifies to the role of print in shaping a quintessential nineteenth-century experience of mobility.

Unkel Silanse

According to a centenary lecture delivered in Dublin in 1943, the stories of Sheridan Le Fanu 'were the kind to float at the back of the mind'.[41] With a reputation for having influenced both Charlotte Brontë and James Joyce, Le Fanu's writing can indeed be seen to drift across the centuries and span the range of Gothic modernity. Charlotte Brontë read his 'Chapter in a History of a Tyrone Family' (in which an estranged and incarcerated wife lives on the upper floors of a Gothic mansion) in the October 1839 issue of the *Dublin University Magazine*.[42] A later novel by Le Fanu, *The Wyvern Mystery* (1869), also features bigamy alongside the so-called 'spouse-in-the-house plot' made familiar by *Jane Eyre*.[43] Meanwhile references to Le Fanu's Dublin novel, *The House by the Churchyard*, resonate throughout *Finnegans Wake*: Joyce's description of the graveyard of a 'creepered' Church of Ireland building—'the ghastcold tombshape of the quick foregone on the loftleaved elm Lefanunian abovemansioned'—gathers around itself the Gothic resonances of Le Fanu's name. Elsewhere in the *Wake*, a reference to 'Unkel Silanse' expresses an essential secrecy that both forms and deforms the novel's narrative drive towards sensational revelations.[44]

---

[40] See McDonagh, *Literature in a Time of Migration*, 5.

[41] Patrick F. Byrne, 'Joseph Sheridan Le Fanu: A Centenary Memoir', *Dublin Historical Record* 26/3 (June 1973), 80–92, at 87. The lecture was first given in 1943.

[42] See Edna Kenton, 'A Forgotten Creator of Ghosts: Joseph Sheridan Le Fanu; Possible Inspirer of the Brontës', repr. in Crawford, Rockhill and Showers (eds), *Reflections in a Glass Darkly*, 95–104; and Maia McAleavey, *The Bigamy Plot: Sensation and Convention in the Victorian Novel* (Cambridge: Cambridge University Press, 2015), 50.

[43] McAleavey, *The Bigamy Plot*, 193.

[44] James Joyce, *Finnegans Wake*, 264.29–265.06, 228.17. See Katie Mishler, ' "A phantom city, phaked of philim pholk": Spectral Topographies and Re-awakenings in James Joyce's *Finnegans Wake* and Sheridan Le Fanu's *The House by the Churchyard*', *Joyce Studies Annual* (2018), 161–94, at 163.

What one Victorian reviewer described as the 'vague and gorgeous' language of *Uncle Silas* derives much of its power from moments of hesitation and indecision whose power has not faded.[45] Le Fanu's fine-grained silences and sublimations, thought Elizabeth Bowen, made *Uncle Silas* the first great psychological novel. To grasp that compliment more fully, it is worth thinking about the ways in which nineteenth-century psychology up to Freud thought of the mind as itself a 'supernatural space'.[46] Seeking out intimate experiences via a kind of buried supernaturalism, *Uncle Silas* expresses fears at once physical and phantasmagoric. The dilemmas encountered by the main characters in the novel address themselves to the cultural predicaments of the 1860s—to be isolated in a crowd, a woman in a world made by men, Irish amidst the British Empire—but they also express a cultural pathology with continuing resonances, including the feeling of being haunted by dim apprehensions of danger. Throughout the novel, Maud imagines her predicament in terms of a creeping chill: she finds herself 'freezing with horror' (p. 27) or 'freezing with fear' (p. 98), and later experiences 'a strange freezing sensation creeping from my heels to my head and down again' (p. 369). Maud's experience of psychic alienation is so vividly physical that even when she doubts her own sanity ('Am I—am I mad?' . . . 'Is this all a dream, or is it real?', p. 417) she quickens her steps and walks into danger as a criminal might approach the hangman's drop. Yet Le Fanu also reserves for his heroine a remarkable ability to transfer her experiences of isolated terror onto the world at large: looking out the window from the room in which she is imprisoned, little knowing that her own grave lies beneath, Maud sees, 'spread on the dark azure of the night this glorious blazonry of the unfathomable Creator' (p. 416). Exterior effects of light and dark seem to express an intense sympathy with her plight while the sky unrolls as a 'dreadful scroll—inexorable eyes. The cloud of cruel witnesses looking down in freezing brightness on my prayers and agonies' (p. 416). Cold and harsh, those 'cruel witnesses' deny Maud religious consolation and remind us that even escape from immediate danger will not release

[45] Review of *Uncle Silas*, *Saturday Review* (25 November 1865); quoted in James Murphy, *Irish Novelists and the Victorian Age* (Oxford: Oxford University Press, 2011), 96.

[46] Terry Castle, 'Phantasmagoria: Spectral Technology and the Metaphorics of Modern Reverie', *Critical Inquiry* (Autumn 1998), 26–61, at 59.

her from the 'nightmare of the real'.[47] As readers, we continue to turn to *Uncle Silas* for such moments of startling symbolization, most often associated with the experience of silent terror, when we experience a sudden pause in Le Fanu's pacy plot and receive a strange and beguiling invitation to walk the dark and lonely paths along which our inner lives are made.

[47] Victor Sage, *Le Fanu's Gothic: The Rhetoric of Darkness* (Basingstoke: Macmillan 2004), 118.

A NOTE ON THE TEXT

UNCLE SILAS was serialized in the *Dublin University Magazine* for six months, beginning in July 1864 and concluding in December of that year. The first instalment bore the title *Maud Ruthyn* while subsequent episodes were titled *Maud Ruthyn and Uncle Silas: A Story of Bartram-Haugh*. An earlier version of the same plot was published as 'Passage in the Secret History of an Irish Countess' in the *Dublin University Magazine* (November 1838); later reprinted as 'The Murdered Cousin' in Le Fanu's *Ghosts Stories and Tales of Mystery* (1851). There are also a number of similarities between the plot of the novel and Le Fanu's earlier novel, *The Cock and the Anchor* (1845), a historical romance set in early eighteenth-century Dublin.

The text of this present edition is that of the first edition, published in three volumes by Richard Bentley in London to coincide with the final instalment of the novel and titled *Uncle Silas*. Bentley's edition of the novel opened with a 'Preliminary Word' which had originally appeared as the conclusion to the *Dublin University Magazine* serialization. The text was updated by W. J. McCormack for the 1981 World's Classic edition, reprinted in 1988: printing errors were corrected, accents in French words standardized, and inconsistencies of punctuation were brought into line with modern typographical practice including standardization of '-ize' endings. Chapter numbers are rendered as a single sequence, as in the serial.

SELECT BIBLIOGRAPHY

Biography

McCormack, W. J., *Sheridan Le Fanu and Victorian Ireland* (Oxford: Clarendon Press, 1980).

Criticism

Beller, Anne-Marie, 'The Fashions of the Current Season?: Recent Critical Work on Victorian Sensation Fiction', *Victorian Literature and Culture* 45/2 (2017), 461–73.

Bowen, Elizabeth, 'Introduction', *Collected Impressions* (London: Longmans, 1950), 3–17.

Brock, Marilyn (ed.), *From Wollstonecraft to Stoker: Essays on Gothic and Victorian Sensation Fiction* (Jefferson, NC, and London: McFarland, 2009).

Browne, Nelson, *Sheridan Le Fanu* (London: Barker, 1951).

Crawford, Gary William, Rockhill, Jim, and Showers, Brian J. (eds), *Reflections in a Glass Darkly: Essays on J. Sheridan Le Fanu* (New York: Hippocampo Press, 2011).

Daly, Nicholas, *Literature, Technology and Modernity, 1860–2000* (Cambridge: Cambridge University Press, 2004).

Daly, Nicholas, *Sensation and Modernity in the 1860s* (Cambridge: Cambridge University Press, 2009).

Daly, Nicholas, *The Demographic Imagination and the Nineteenth-Century City* (Cambridge: Cambridge University Press, 2015).

Ellis, S. M., *Wilkie Collins, Le Fanu and Others* (London: Constable, 1931; 2nd edn 1951).

Fantina, Richard, and Harrison, Kimberly (eds), *Victorian Sensations: Essays on a Scandalous Genre* (Athens, OH: Ohio University Press, 2006).

Garrison, Laurie, *Science, Sexuality, and Sensation Novels: Pleasures of the Senses* (New York: Palgrave Macmillan, 2011).

Gilbert, Pamela K. (ed.), *A Companion to Sensation Fiction* (Malden, MA: Wiley-Blackwell, 2011).

Killeen, Jarlath, and Cavalli, Valeria (eds), *'Inspiring a Mysterious Terror': 200 Years of Joseph Sheridan Le Fanu* (Bern: Peter Lang, 2016).

Knight, Mark, 'Figuring Out the Fascination: Recent Trends in Criticism on Victorian Sensation and Crime Fiction', *Victorian Literature and Culture* 37/1 (2009), 323–33.

Milbank, Alison, 'Joseph Sheridan Le Fanu: Gothic Grotesque and the Huguenot Inheritance', in Julia M. Wright, *A Companion to Irish Literature* (Malden, MA: Wiley-Blackwell, 2010), 362–76.

Mangham, Andrew (ed.), *The Cambridge Companion to Sensation Fiction* (Cambridge: Cambridge University Press, 2013).

O'Malley, Patrick R., *Liffey and Lethe: Paramnesiac History in Nineteenth-Century Anglo-Ireland* (Oxford: Oxford University Press, 2017).

Sage, Victor, *The Rhetoric of Darkness: Le Fanu's Gothic* (New York: Palgrave, 2004).

Tracy, Robert, *The Unappeasable Host: Studies in Irish Identities* (Dublin: UCD Press, 1998).

Walton, James, *Vision and Vacancy: The Fictions of J. S. Le Fanu* (Dublin: UCD Press, 2007).

Further Reading in Oxford World's Classics

Horror Stories from Hoffmann to Hodgson, ed. Darryl Jones.

Irish Writing, ed. Stephen Regan.

James, M. R., *Collected Stories*, ed. Darryl Jones.

Le Fanu, Sheridan, *In a Glass Darkly*, ed. Robert Tracy.

Lovecraft, H. P., *The Classic Horror Stories*, ed. Roger Luckhurst.

Machen, Arthur, *The Great God Pan and Other Horror Stories*, ed. Aaron Worth.

Poe, Edgar Allan, *The Pit and the Pendulum and Other Tales*, ed. David Van Leer.

Polidori, John, *The Vampyre and Other Tales of the Macabre*, ed. Robert Morrison and Chris Baldick.

Stoker, Bram, *Dracula*, ed. Roger Luckhurst.

A CHRONOLOGY OF SHERIDAN LE FANU

1814   (28 August) Joseph Thomas Sheridan Le Fanu born 'at about half-past five o'clock AM' at 45 Lower Dominick Street, Dublin.

1815   With the appointment of his father as chaplain to the Royal Hibernian Military School, the family move to live in the Phoenix Park, west of the city.

1826   The family move to Abington, County Limerick.

1832   Enters the University of Dublin (Trinity College), primarily as a non-residential or 'country' student.

1831–6   The Tithe War; agrarian disturbances in County Limerick.

1832–3   Cholera epidemic in Ireland.

1838   (January) 'The Ghost and the Bone-setter', Le Fanu's first published story, appears in the *Dublin University Magazine*: a further ten pieces are published before October 1840; these are posthumously collected as *The Purcell Papers* in 1880.

1839   Called to the Irish Bar but does not practise.

1838–*c*.1841   Active in the Irish Metropolitan Conservative Association with Isaac Butt.

1840–73   Involved as proprietor and editor in various Dublin newspapers, notably the *Dublin Evening Mail* and *The Warder*.

1841   (March) Death of Catherine Le Fanu, his only sister.

1843   (March–April) Publishes 'Spalatro' in the *Dublin University Magazine*.

1843   (December) Marries Susanna Bennett, daughter of George Bennett, QC.

1845   *The Cock and Anchor*.

1845–9   The Great Famine in Ireland.

1847   Promises his support to John Mitchel and Thomas Francis Meagher in their attempts to unite Irish public opinion on the topic of the Government's indifference to the Great Famine. Publishes *The Fortunes of Colonel Torlogh O'Brien*, serialized in the *Dublin University Magazine*.

1848   (March) Mitchel prosecuted for sedition: (April–June) Le Fanu publishes the three-part 'Richard Marston' in the *Dublin University Magazine*: (July) Rebellion in Ireland, led by William Smith O'Brien, MP for County Limerick.

1852 Unsuccessful attempt to get Tory nomination for County Carlow.

1856 Death of George Bennett, Le Fanu's father-in-law.

1858 Death of Susanna Le Fanu (née Bennett), Le Fanu's wife.

1861 Acquires control of the _Dublin University Magazine_, despite personal financial difficulties: the bulk of his writing from this date appears in there, including _The House by the Churchyard_ (1861–3). Death of Le Fanu's mother.

1863 Begins association with London publisher Richard Bentley.

1864 _Wylder's Hand_ and _Uncle Silas_ appear in the _Dublin University Magazine_.

1865 (September) first of a number of political articles (until September 1866) appears in the _Dublin University Magazine_.

1869 'Green Tea' serialized in Charles Dickens's _All the Year Round_. Sells the _Dublin University Magazine_.

1871–2 'Green Tea' serialized in _The Dark Blue_.

1872 Publishes _In A Glass Darkly_, including 'Green Tea' and 'Carmilla'.

1873 (7 February) dies at 18 Merrion Square South, Dublin, formerly his father-in-law's home.

1880 Posthumous publication by Bentley of _The Purcell Papers_ which collects stories formerly published in the _Dublin University Magazine_ from 1838 to 1850 with a Memoir by Alfred Perceval Graves.

UNCLE SILAS

THE writer of this tale ventures, in his own person, to address a very few words, chiefly of explanation, to his readers. A leading situation in this 'Story of Bartram-Haugh' is repeated, with a slight variation, from a short magazine tale of some fifteen pages written by him, and published long ago in a periodical under the title of 'A Passage in the Secret History of an Irish Countess', and afterwards, still anonymously, in a small volume under an altered title.* It is very unlikely that any of his readers should have encountered, and still more so that they should remember, this trifle. The bare possibility, however, he has ventured to anticipate by this brief explanation, lest he should be charged with plagiarism—always a disrespect to a reader.

May he be permitted a few words also of remonstrance against the promiscuous application of the term 'sensation' to that large school of fiction which transgresses no one of those canons of construction and morality which, in producing the unapproachable 'Waverley Novels', their great author imposed upon himself? No one, it is assumed, would describe Sir Walter Scott's romances as 'sensation novels'; yet in that marvellous series there is not a single tale in which death, crime, and, in some form, mystery, have not a place.

Passing by those grand romances of 'Ivanhoe', 'Old Mortality', and 'Kenilworth', with their terrible intricacies of crime and bloodshed, constructed with so fine a mastery of the art of exciting suspense and horror, let the reader pick out those two exceptional novels in the series which profess to paint contemporary manners and the scenes of common life; and remembering in the 'Antiquary' the vision in the tapestried chamber, the duel, the horrible secret, and the death of old Elspeth, the drowned fisherman, and above all the tremendous situation of the tide-bound party under the cliffs; and in 'St. Ronan's Well', the long-drawn mystery, the suspicion of insanity, and the catastrophe of suicide;—determine whether an epithet which it would be a profanation to apply to the structure of any, even the most exciting, of Sir Walter Scott's stories, is fairly applicable to tales which, though illimitably inferior in execution, yet observe the same limitations of incident, and the same moral aims.

The author trusts that the Press, to whose masterly criticism and generous encouragement he and other humble labourers in the art owe so much, will insist upon the limitation of that degrading term to the peculiar type of fiction which it was originally intended to indicate, and prevent, as they may, its being made to include the legitimate school of tragic English romance, which has been ennobled, and in great measure founded, by the genius of Sir Walter Scott.

December, 1864.

CHAPTER I

AUSTIN RUTHYN, OF KNOWL, AND HIS DAUGHTER

It was winter—that is, about the second week in November—and great gusts were rattling at the windows, and wailing and thundering among our tall trees and ivied chimneys—a very dark night, and a very cheerful fire blazing, a pleasant mixture of good round coal and spluttering dry wood, in a genuine old fireplace, in a sombre old room. Black wainscoting glimmered up to the ceiling, in small ebony panels; a cheerful clump of wax candles on the tea-table; many old portraits, some grim and pale, others pretty, and some very graceful and charming, hanging from the walls. Few pictures, except portraits long and short, were there. On the whole, I think you would have taken the room for our parlour. It was not like our modern notion of a drawing-room. It was a long room too, and every way capacious, but irregularly shaped.

A girl, of a little more than seventeen, looking, I believe, younger still; slight and rather tall, with a great deal of golden hair, dark grey-eyed, and with a countenance rather sensitive and melancholy, was sitting at the tea-table, in a reverie. I was that girl.

The only other person in the room—the only person in the house related to me—was my father. He was Mr. Ruthyn, of Knowl, so called in his county, but he had many other places; was of a very ancient lineage, who had refused a baronetage often, and it was said even a viscounty, being of a proud and defiant spirit, and thinking themselves higher in station and purer of blood than two-thirds of the nobility into whose ranks, it was said, they had been invited to enter. Of all this family lore I knew but little and vaguely; only what is to be gathered from the fireside talk of old retainers in the nursery.

I am sure my father loved me, and I know I loved him. With the sure instinct of childhood I apprehended his tenderness, although it was never expressed in common ways. But my father was an oddity. He had been early disappointed in Parliament, where it was his ambition to succeed. Though a clever man, he failed there, where very inferior men did extremely well. Then he went abroad, and became a connoisseur and a collector; took a part, on his return, in literary and scientific institutions, and also in the foundation and direction of some charities. But he tired of this mimic government, and gave himself up to a country life, not that of a sportsman, but rather of a student, staying sometimes at one of his places and sometimes at another, and living a secluded life.

Rather late in life he married, and his beautiful young wife died, leaving me, their only child, to his care. This bereavement, I have been told, changed him—made him more odd and taciturn than ever, and his temper also, except to me, more severe. There was also some disgrace about his younger brother—my uncle Silas—which he felt bitterly.

He was now walking up and down this spacious old room, which, extending round an angle at the far end, was very dark in that quarter. It was his wont to walk up and down, thus, without speaking—an exercise which used to remind me of Chauteaubriand's father in the great chamber of the Château de Combourg.* At the far end he nearly disappeared in the gloom, and then returning emerged for a few minutes, like a portrait with a background of shadow, and then again in silence faded nearly out of view.

This monotony and silence would have been terrifying to a person less accustomed to it than I. As it was it had its effect. I have known my father a whole day without once speaking to me. Though I loved him very much I was also much in awe of him.

While my father paced the floor, my thoughts were employed about the events of a month before. So few things happened at Knowl out of the accustomed routine, that a very trifling occurrence was enough to set people wondering and conjecturing in that serene household. My father lived in remarkable seclusion; except for a ride, he hardly ever left the grounds of Knowl, and I don't think it happened twice in the year that a visitor sojourned among us.

There was not ever that mild religious bustle which sometimes besets the wealthy and moral recluse. My father had left the Church of England for some odd sect, I forget its name, and ultimately became, I was told, a Swedenborgian.* But he did not care to trouble me upon the subject. So the old carriage brought my governess, when I had one, the old housekeeper, Mrs. Rusk, and myself to the parish church every Sunday. And my father, in the view of the honest Rector who shook his head over him—'a cloud without water, carried about of winds, and a wandering star to whom is reserved the blackness of darkness'*—corresponded with the 'minister' of his church, and was provokingly contented with his own fertility and illumination; and Mrs. Rusk, who was a sound and bitter churchwoman, said he fancied he saw visions and talked with angels like the rest of that 'rubbitch'.

I don't know that she had any better foundation than analogy and conjecture for charging my father with supernatural pretensions; and in all points when her orthodoxy was not concerned, she loved her master and was a loyal housekeeper.

I found her one morning superintending preparations for the reception of a visitor, in the hunting-room it was called, from the pieces of tapestry that covered its walls, representing scenes, *à la Wouvermans,** of falconry, and the chase, dogs, hawks, ladies, gallants, and pages. In the midst of whom Mrs. Rusk, in black silk, was rummaging drawers, counting linen, and issuing orders.

'Who is coming, Mrs. Rusk?'

Well, she only knew his name. It was a Mr. Bryerly. My papa expected him to dinner, and to stay for some days.

'I guess he's one of those creaturs, dear, for I mentioned his name just to Dr. Clay (the Rector), and he says there *is* a Doctor Bryerly, a great conjurer among the Swedenborg sect—and that's him, I do suppose.'

In my hazy notions of these sectaries there was mingled a suspicion of necromancy, and a weird freemasonry, that inspired something of awe and antipathy.

Mr. Bryerly arrived time enough to dress at his leisure, before dinner. He entered the drawing-room—a tall, lean man, all in ungainly black, with a white choker, with either a black wig, or black hair dressed in imitation of one, a pair of spectacles, and a dark, sharp, short visage, rubbing his large hands together, and with a short brisk nod to me, whom he plainly regarded merely as a child, he sat down before the fire, crossed his legs, and took up a magazine.

This treatment was mortifying, and I remember very well the resentment of which *he* was quite unconscious.

His stay was not very long; not one of us divined the object of his visit, and he did not prepossess us favourably. He seemed restless, as men of busy habits do in country houses, and took walks, and a drive, and read in the library, and wrote half a dozen letters.

His bed-room and dressing-room were at the side of the gallery, directly opposite to my father's, which had a sort of ante-room *en suite*, in which were some of his theological books.

The day after Mr. Bryerly's arrival, I was about to see whether my father's water caraffe and glass had been duly laid on the table in this ante-room, and in doubt whether he was there, I knocked at the door.

I suppose they were too intent on other matters to hear, but receiving no answer, I entered the room. My father was sitting in his chair, with his coat and waistcoat off, Mr. Bryerly kneeling on a stool beside him, rather facing him, his black scratch wig leaning close to my father's grizzled hair. There was a large tome of their divinity lore, I suppose, open on the table close by. The lank black figure of Mr. Bryerly stood up, and he concealed something quickly in the breast of his coat.

My father stood up also, looking paler, I think, than I ever saw him till then, and he pointed grimly to the door, and said, 'Go.'

Mr. Bryerly pushed me gently back with his hands to my shoulders, and smiled down from his dark features with an expression quite unintelligible to me.

I had recovered myself in a second, and withdrew without a word. The last thing I saw at the door was the tall, slim figure in black, and the dark, significant smile following me: and then the door was shut and locked, and the two Swedenborgians were left to their mysteries.

I remember so well the kind of shock and disgust I felt in the certainty that I had surprised them at some, perhaps, debasing incantation, a suspicion of this Mr. Bryerly, of the ill fitting black coat, and white choker, and a sort of fear came upon me, and I fancied he was asserting some kind of mastery over my father, which very much alarmed me.

I fancied all sorts of dangers in the enigmatical smile of the lank high-priest. The image of my father, as I had seen him, it might be, confessing to this man in black, who was I knew not what, haunted me with the disagreeable uncertainties of a mind very uninstructed as to the limits of the marvellous.

I mentioned it to no one. But I was immensely relieved when the sinister visitor took his departure the morning after, and it was upon this occurrence that my mind was now employed.

Some one said that Doctor Johnson resembled a ghost, who must be spoken to before it will speak.* But my father, in whatever else he may have resembled a ghost, did not in that particular; for no one but I in his household—and I very seldom—dare to address him until first addressed by him. I had no notion how singular this was until

I began to go out a little among friends and relations, and found no such rule in force anywhere else.

As I leaned back in my chair thinking, this phantasm of my father came, and turned, and vanished with a solemn regularity. It was a peculiar figure, strongly made, thick-set, with a face large, and very stern; he wore a loose, black velvet coat and waistcoat. It was, however, the figure of an elderly rather than an old man—though he was then past seventy—but firm, and with no sign of feebleness.

I remember the start with which, not suspecting that he was close by me, I lifted my eyes, and saw that large, rugged countenance looking fixedly on me, from less than a yard away.

After I saw him he continued to regard me for a second or two; and then, taking one of the heavy candlesticks in his gnarled hand, he beckoned me to follow him; which, in silence and wondering, I accordingly did.

He led me across the hall, where there were lights burning, and into a lobby by the foot of the back stairs, and so into his library.

It is a long, narrow room, with two tall, slim windows at the far end, now draped in dark curtains. Dusky it was with but one candle; and he paused near the door, at the left-hand side of which stood, in those days, an old-fashioned press or cabinet of carved oak. In front of this he stopped.

He had odd, absent ways, and talked more to himself, I believe, than to all the rest of the world put together.

'She won't understand,' he whispered, looking at me inquiringly. 'No, she won't. *Will* she?'

Then there was a pause, during which he brought forth from his breast pocket a small bunch of some half-dozen keys, on one of which he looked frowningly, every now and then balancing it a little before his eyes, between his finger and thumb, as he deliberated.

I knew him too well, of course, to interpose a word.

'They are easily frightened—ay, they are. I'd better do it another way.'

And pausing, he looked in my face as he might upon a picture.

'They *are*—yes—I had better do it another way—another way; yes—and she'll not suspect—she'll not suppose.'

Then he looked steadfastly upon the key, and from it to me, suddenly lifting it up, and said abruptly, 'See, child,' and after a second or two—'*Remember* this key.'

It was oddly shaped, and unlike others.

'Yes, sir.' I always called him 'sir'.

'It opens that,' and he tapped it sharply on the door of the cabinet. 'In the daytime it is always here,' at which word he dropped it into his pocket again. 'You see?—and at night under my pillow—you hear me?'

'Yes, sir.'

'You won't forget this cabinet—oak—next the door—on your left—you won't forget?'

'No, sir.'

'Pity she's a girl, and so young—ay, a girl, and so young—no sense—giddy. You say, you'll *remember*?'

'Yes, sir.'

'It behoves you.'

He turned round and looked full upon me, like a man who has taken a sudden resolution; and I think for a moment he had made up his mind to tell me a great deal more. But if so, he changed it again; and after another pause, he said slowly and sternly—

'You will tell *no*body what I have said, under pain of my displeasure.'

'Oh! no, sir.'

'Good child!'

'*Except*,' he resumed, 'under one contingency; that is, in case I should be absent, and Doctor Bryerly—you recollect the thin gentleman, in spectacles and a black wig, who spent three days here last month—should come and inquire for the key, you understand, in my absence.'

'Yes, sir.'

So he kissed me on the forehead, and said—

'Let us return.'

Which, accordingly, we did, in silence; the storm outside, like a dirge on a great organ, accompanying our flitting.

CHAPTER II

UNCLE SILAS

WHEN we reached the drawing-room, I resumed my chair, and my father his slow and regular walk to and fro, in the great room. Perhaps it was the uproar of the wind that disturbed the ordinary tenor of his thoughts; but, whatever was the cause, certainly he was unusually talkative that night.

After an interval of nearly half an hour, he drew near again, and sat down in a high-backed arm-chair, beside the fire, and nearly opposite to me, and looked at me steadfastly for some time, as was his wont, before speaking; and said he—

'This won't do—you must have a governess.'

In cases of this kind I merely set down my book or work, as it might be, and adjusted myself to listen without speaking.

'Your French is pretty well, and your Italian; but you have no German. Your music may be pretty good—I'm no judge—but your drawing might be better—yes—yes. I believe there are accomplished ladies—finishing governesses, they call them—who undertake more than any one teacher would have professed in my time, and do very well. She can prepare you, and next winter, then, you shall visit France and Italy, where you may be accomplished as highly as you please.'

'Thank you, sir.'

'You shall. It is nearly six months since Miss Ellerton left you—too long without a teacher.'

Then followed an interval.

'Dr. Bryerly will ask you about that key, and what it opens; you show all that to *him*, and no one else.'

'But,' I said, for I had a great terror of disobeying him in ever so minute a matter, 'you will then be absent, sir—how am I to find the key?'

He smiled on me suddenly—a bright but wintry smile—it seldom came, and was very transitory, and kindly though mysterious.

'True, child; I'm glad you are so wise; *that*, you will find, I have provided for, and you shall know exactly where to look. You have remarked how solitarily I live. You fancy, perhaps, I have not got a friend, and you are nearly right—*nearly*, but not altogether. I have a very sure friend—*one*—a friend whom I once misunderstood, but now appreciate.'

I wondered silently whether it could be Uncle Silas.

'He'll make me a call, some day soon; I'm not quite sure when. I won't tell you his name—you'll hear that soon enough, and I don't want it talked of; and I must make a little journey with him. You'll not be afraid of being left alone for a time?'

'And have you promised, sir?' I answered, with another question, my curiosity and anxiety overcoming my awe. He took my questioning very good-humouredly.

'Well—*promise?*—no, child; but I'm under condition; he's not to be denied. I must make the excursion with him the moment he calls. I have no choice; but, on the whole, I rather like it—remember, I say, I rather *like* it.'

And he smiled again, with the same meaning, that was at once stern and sad. The exact purport of these sentences remained fixed in my mind, so that even at this distance of time I am quite sure of them.

A person quite unacquainted with my father's habitually abrupt and odd way of talking, would have fancied that he was possibly a little disordered in his mind. But no such suspicion for a moment troubled me. I was quite sure that he spoke of a real person who was coming, and that his journey was something momentous; and when the visitor of whom he spoke did come, and he departed with him upon that mysterious excursion, I perfectly understood his language and his reasons for saying so much and yet so little.

You are not to suppose that all my hours were passed in the sort of conference and isolation of which I have just given you a specimen; and singular and even awful as were sometimes my *tête-à-têtes* with my father, I had grown so accustomed to his strange ways, and had so unbounded a confidence in his affection, that they never depressed or agitated me in the manner you might have supposed. I had a great deal of quite a different sort of chat with good old Mrs. Rusk, and very pleasant talks with Mary Quince, my somewhat ancient maid; and besides all this, I had now and then a visit of a week or so at the house of some one of our county neighbours, and occasionally a visitor—but this, I must own, very rarely—at Knowl.

There had come now a little pause in my father's revelations, and my fancy wandered away upon a flight of discovery. Who, I again thought, could this intending visitor be, who was to come, armed with the prerogative to make my stay-at-home father forthwith leave his household gods—his books and his child—to whom he clung, and set forth on an unknown knight-errantry? Who but Uncle Silas, I thought—that mysterious relative whom I had never seen—who was, it had in old times been very darkly hinted to me, unspeakably unfortunate or unspeakably vicious—whom I had seldom heard my father mention, and then in a hurried way, and with a pained, thoughtful look. Once only he had said anything from which I could gather my father's opinion of him, and then it was so slight and enigmatical that I might have filled in the character very nearly as I pleased.

It happened thus. One day Mrs. Rusk was in the oak-room, I being then about fourteen. She was removing a stain from a tapestry chair, and I watched the process with a childish interest. She sat down to rest herself—she had been stooping over her work—and threw her head back, for her neck was weary, and in this position she fixed her eyes on a portrait that hung before her.

It was a full-length, and represented a singularly handsome young man, dark, slender, elegant, in a costume then quite obsolete, though I believe it was seen at the beginning of this century—white leather pantaloons and top-boots, a buff waistcoat, and a chocolate-coloured coat, and the hair long and brushed back.

There was a remarkable elegance and a delicacy in the features, but also a character of resolution and ability that quite took the portrait out of the category of mere fops or fine men. When people looked at it for the first time, I have so often heard the exclamation—'What a wonderfully handsome man!' and then, 'What a clever face!' An Italian greyhound stood by him, and some slender columns and a rich drapery in the background. But though the accessories were of the luxurious sort, and the beauty, as I have said, refined, there was a masculine force in that slender oval face, and a fire in the large, shadowy eyes, which were very peculiar, and quite redeemed it from the suspicion of effeminacy.

'Is not that Uncle Silas?' said I.

'Yes, dear,' answered Mrs. Rusk, looking, with her resolute little face, quietly on the portrait.

'He must be a very handsome man, Mrs. Rusk. Don't you think so?' I continued.

'He *was*, my dear—yes; but it is forty years since that was painted—the date is there in the corner, in the shadow that comes from his foot, and forty years, I can tell you, makes a change in most of us'; and Mrs. Rusk laughed, in cynical good-humour.

There was a little pause, both still looking on the handsome man in top-boots, and I said—

'And why, Mrs. Rusk, is papa always so sad about Uncle Silas?'

'What's that, child?' said my father's voice, very near. I looked round, with a start, and flushed and faltered, receding a step from him.

'No harm, dear. You have said nothing wrong,' he said gently, observing my alarm. 'You said I was always sad, I think, about Uncle Silas. Well, I don't know how you gather that; but if I were, I will now tell you, it would not be unnatural. Your uncle is a man of great talents, great faults, and great wrongs. His talents have not availed him; his faults are long ago repented of; and his wrongs I believe he feels less than I do, but they are deep. Did she say any more, madam?' he demanded abruptly of Mrs. Rusk.

'Nothing, sir,' with a stiff little courtesy, answered Mrs. Rusk, who stood in awe of him.

'And there is no need, child,' he continued, addressing himself to me, 'that you should think more of him at present. Clear your head of Uncle Silas. One day, perhaps, you will know him—yes, very well—and understand how villains have injured him.'

Then my father retired, and at the door he said—

'Mrs. Rusk, a word, if you please,' beckoning to that lady, who trotted after him to the library.

I think he then laid some injunction upon the housekeeper, which was transmitted by her to Mary Quince, for from that time forth I could never lead either to talk with me about Uncle Silas. They let me talk on, but were reserved and silent themselves, and seemed embarrassed, and Mrs. Rusk sometimes pettish and angry, when I pressed for information.

Thus curiosity was piqued; and round the slender portrait in the leather pantaloons and top-boots gathered many-coloured circles of mystery, and the handsome features seemed to smile down upon my baffled curiosity with a provoking significance.

Why is it that this form of ambition—curiosity—which entered into the temptation of our first parent, is so specially hard to resist? Knowledge is power—and power of one sort or another is the secret lust of human souls; and here is, beside the sense of exploration, the undefinable interest of a story, and above all, something forbidden, to stimulate the contumacious appetite.

I THINK it was about a fortnight after that conversation in which my father had expressed his opinion, and given me the mysterious charge about the old oak cabinet in his library, as already detailed, that I was one night sitting at the great drawing-room window, lost in the melancholy reveries of night, and in admiration of the moonlighted scene. I was the only occupant of the room; and the lights near the fire, at its further end, hardly reached to the window at which I sat.

The shorn grass sloped gently downward from the windows till it met the broad level on which stood, in clumps, or solitarily scattered, some of the noblest timber in England. Hoar in the moonbeams stood those graceful trees casting their moveless shadows upon the grass, and in the background crowning the undulations of the distance, in masses, were piled those woods among which lay the solitary tomb where the remains of my beloved mother rested.

The air was still. The silvery vapour hung serenely on the far horizon, and the frosty stars blinked brightly. Every one knows the effect of such a scene on a mind already saddened. Fancies and regrets float mistily in the dream, and the scene affects us with a strange mixture of memory and anticipation, like some sweet old air heard in the distance. As my eyes rested on those, to me, funereal but glorious woods, which form the background of the picture, my thoughts recurred to my father's mysterious intimations and the image of the approaching visitor; and the thought of the unknown journey saddened me.

In all that concerned his religion, from very early association, there was to me something of the unearthly and spectral.

When my dear mamma died I was not nine years old; and I remember, two days before the funeral, there came to Knowl, where she died, a thin little man, with large black eyes, and a very grave, dark face.

He was shut up a good deal with my dear father, who was in deep affliction; and Mrs. Rusk used to say, 'It is rather odd to see him praying with that little scarecrow from London, and good Mr. Clay ready at call, in the village; much good that little black whipper-snapper will do him!'

With that little black man, on the day after the funeral, I was sent out, for some reason, for a walk; my governess was ill, I know, and there was confusion in the house, and I dare say the maids made as much of a holiday as they could.

I remember feeling a sort of awe of this little dark man; but I was not afraid of him, for he was gentle, though sad—and seemed kind. He led me into the garden—the Dutch garden, we used to call it—with a balustrade, and statues at the farther front, laid out in a carpet-pattern of brilliantly coloured flowers. We came down the broad flight of Caen stone steps* into this, and we walked in silence to the balustrade. The base was too high at the spot where we reached it for me to see over; but holding my hand, he said, 'Look through that, my child. Well, you can't; but *I* can see beyond it—shall I tell you what? I see ever so much. I see a cottage with a steep roof, that looks like gold in the sunlight; there are tall trees throwing soft shadows round it, and flowering shrubs, I can't say what, only the colours are beautiful, growing by the walls and windows, and two little children are playing among the stems of the trees, and we are on our way there, and in a few minutes shall be under those trees ourselves, and talking to those little children. Yet now to me it is but a picture in my brain, and to you but a story told by me, which you believe. Come, dear; let us be going.'

So we descended the steps at the right, and side by side walked along the grass lane between tall trim walls of evergreens. The way was in deep shadow, for the sun was near the horizon; but suddenly we turned to the left, and there we stood in rich sunlight, among the many objects he had described.

'Is this your house, my little men?' he asked of the children—pretty little rosy boys—who assented; and he leaned with his open hand against the stem of one of the trees, and with a grave smile he nodded down to me, saying—

'You see now, and hear, and *feel* for yourself that both the vision and the story were quite true; but come on, my dear, we have further to go.'

And relapsing into silence we had a long ramble through the wood, the same on which I was now looking in the distance. Every now and then he made me sit down to rest, and he in a musing solemn sort of way would relate some little story, reflecting, even to my childish mind, a strange suspicion of a spiritual meaning, but different from what honest Mrs. Rusk used to expound to me from the Parables, and, somehow, startling in its very vagueness.

Thus entertained, though a little awfully, I accompanied the dark mysterious little 'whipper-snapper' through the woodland glades. We came, to me quite unexpectedly, in the deep sylvan shadows, upon the grey, pillared temple, four-fronted, with a slanting pedestal of lichen-stained steps, the lonely sepulchre in which I had the morning before seen poor mamma laid. At the sight the fountains of my grief reopened, and I cried bitterly, repeating, 'Oh! mamma, mamma, little mamma!' and so went on weeping and calling wildly on the deaf and silent. There was a stone bench some ten steps away from the tomb.

'Sit down beside me, my child,' said the grave man with the black eyes, very kindly and gently. 'Now, what do you see there?' he asked, pointing horizontally with his stick towards the centre of the opposite structure.

'Oh, *that*—that place where poor mamma is?'

'Yes, a stone wall with pillars, too high for either you or me to see over. But'—

Here he mentioned a name which I think must have been Swedenborg, from what I afterwards learned of his tenets and revelations; I only know that it sounded to me like the name of a magician in a fairy tale; I fancied he lived in the wood which surrounded us, and I began to grow frightened as he proceeded.

'But Swedenborg sees beyond it, over, and *through* it, and has told me all that concerns us to know. He says your mamma is not there.'

'She is taken away!' I cried, starting up, and with streaming eyes, gazing on the building which, though I stamped my feet in my distraction, I was afraid to approach. 'Oh, *is* mamma taken away? Where is she? Where have they brought her to?'

I was uttering unconsciously very nearly the question with which Mary, in the grey of that wondrous morning on which she stood by the empty sepulchre, accosted the figure standing near.

'Your mamma is alive, but too far away to see or hear us; but Swedenborg, standing here, can see and hear her, and tells me all he sees, just as I told you in the garden about the little boys and the cottage, and the trees and flowers which you could not see, but believed in when *I* told you. So I can tell you now as I did then; and as we are both, I hope, walking on to the same place, just as we did to the trees and cottage, you will surely see with your own eyes how true is the description which I give you.'

I was very much frightened, for I feared that when he had done his narrative we were to walk on through the wood into that place of wonders and of shadows where the dead were visible.

He leaned his elbow on his knee, and his forehead on his hand, which shaded his downcast eyes, and in that attitude described to me a beautiful landscape, radiant with a wondrous light, in which, rejoicing, my mother moved along an airy path, ascending among mountains of fantastic height, and peaks, melting in celestial colouring into the air, and peopled with human beings translated* into the same image, beauty, and splendour. And when he had ended his relation, he rose, took my hand, and smiling gently down on my pale, wondering face, he said the same words he had spoken before—

'Come, dear, let us be going.'

'Oh! no, no, *no*—not now,' I said, resisting, and very much frightened.

'Home, I mean, dear. We cannot walk to the place I have described. We can only reach it through the gate of death, to which we are all tending, young and old, with sure steps.'

'And where is the gate of death?' I asked in a sort of whisper, as we walked together, holding his hand very fast, and looking stealthily. He smiled sadly and said—

'When, sooner or later, the time comes, as Hagar's* eyes were opened in the wilderness, and she beheld the fountain of water, so shall each of us see the door open before us, and enter in and be refreshed.'

For a long time after this walk I was very nervous; the more so for the awful manner in which Mrs. Rusk received my statement—with stern lips and upturned hands and eyes, and an angry expostulation: 'I do wonder at you, Mary Quince, letting the child walk into the wood with that limb of darkness. It is a mercy he did not show her the devil, or frighten her out of her senses, in that lonely place!'

Of these Swedenborgians, indeed, I know no more than I might learn from good Mrs. Rusk's very inaccurate talk. Two or three of them crossed in the course of my early life, like magic-lantern* figures, the disk of my very circumscribed observation. All outside was and is darkness. I once tried to read one of their books upon the future state—heaven and hell; but I grew after a day or two so nervous that I laid it aside. It is enough for me to know that their founder either saw or fancied he saw amazing visions, which, so far from superseding, confirmed, and interpreted the language of the Bible; and as dear papa accepted their ideas, I am happy in thinking that they did not conflict with the supreme authority of holy writ.

Leaning on my hand, I was now looking upon that solemn wood, white and shadowy in the moonlight, where, for a long time after that ramble with the visionary, I fancied the gate of death, hidden only by a strange glamour, and the dazzling land of ghosts, were situate; and I suppose these early associations gave to my reverie about my father's coming visitor a wilder and a sadder tinge.

CHAPTER IV

MADAME DE LA ROUGIERRE

ON a sudden, on the grass before me, stood an odd figure—a very tall woman in grey draperies, nearly white under the moon, courtesying extraordinarily low, and rather fantastically.

I stared in something like a horror upon the large and rather hollow features which I did not know, smiling very unpleasantly on me; and the moment it was plain that I saw her, the grey woman began gobbling and cackling shrilly—I could not distinctly hear *what* through the window—and gesticulating oddly with her long hands and arms.

As she drew near the window, I flew to the fireplace, and rang the bell frantically, and seeing her still there, and fearing that she might break into the room, I flew out of the door, very much frightened, and met Branston the butler in the lobby.

'There's a woman at the window!' I gasped; 'turn her away, please.'

If I had said a man, I suppose fat Branston would have summoned and sent forward a detachment of footmen. As it was, he bowed gravely, with a—

'Yes'm—shall'm.'

And with an air of authority approached the window.

I don't think that he was pleasantly impressed himself by the first sight of our visitor, for he stopped short some steps of the window, and demanded rather sternly—

'What ye doin' there, woman?'

To this summons, her answer, which occupied a little time, was inaudible to me. But Branston replied—

'I wasn't aware, ma'am; I heerd nothin'; if you'll go round *that* way, you'll see the hall-door steps, and I'll speak to the master, and do as he shall order.'

The figure said something and pointed.

'Yes, that's it, and ye can't miss of the door.'

And Mr. Branston returned slowly down the long room, and halted with out-turned pumps and a grave inclination before me, and the faintest amount of interrogation in the announcement—

'Please 'm, she says she's the governess.'

'The governess! *What* governess?'

Branston was too well-bred to smile, and he said thoughtfully—
'P'raps, 'm, I'd best ask the master?'

To which I assented, and away strode the flat pumps of the butler to the library.

I stood breathless in the hall. Every girl at my age knows how much is involved in such an advent. I also heard Mrs. Rusk, in a minute or two more, emerge I suppose from the study. She walked quickly, and muttered sharply to herself—an evil trick, in which she indulged when much 'put about'. I should have been glad of a word with her; but I fancied she was vexed, and would not have talked satisfactorily. She did not, however, come my way, merely crossing the hall with her quick, energetic step.

Was it really the arrival of a governess? Was that apparition which had impressed me so unpleasantly to take the command of me—to sit alone with me, and haunt me perpetually with her sinister looks and shrilly gabble?

I was just making up my mind to go to Mary Quince, and learn something definite, when I heard my father's step approaching from the library: so I quietly re-entered the drawing-room, but with an anxious and throbbing heart.

When he came in, as usual, he patted me on the head gently, with a kind of smile, and then began his silent walk up and down the room. I was yearning to question him on the point that just then engrossed me so disagreeably; but the awe in which I stood of him forbade.

After a time he stopped at the window, the curtain of which I had drawn, and the shutter partly opened, and he looked out, perhaps with associations of his own, on the scene I had been contemplating.

It was not for nearly an hour after, that my father suddenly, after his wont, in a few words, apprised me of the arrival of Madame de la Rougierre to be my governess, highly recommended and perfectly qualified. My heart sank with a sure presage of ill. I already disliked, distrusted, and feared her.

I had more than an apprehension of her temper and fear of possibly abused authority. The large-featured, smirking phantom, saluting me so oddly in the moonlight, retained ever after its peculiar and unpleasant hold upon my nerves.

'Well, Miss Maud, dear, I hope you'll like your new governess—for it's more than *I* do, just at present at least,' said Mrs. Rusk sharply—she was awaiting me in my room. 'I hate them Frenchwomen; they're not

natural, I think. I gave her her supper in my room. She eats like
a wolf, she does, the great raw-boned hannimal. I wish you saw her in
bed as I did. I put her next the clock-room—she'll hear the hours
betimes, I'm thinking. You never saw such a sight. The great long
nose and hollow cheeks of her, and oogh! such a mouth! I felt a'most
like little Red Riding-Hood—I did, Miss.'

Here honest Mary Quince, who enjoyed Mrs. Rusk's satire,
a weapon in which she was not herself strong, laughed outright.

'Turn down the bed, Mary. She's very agreeable—she is, just
now—all new comers is; but she did not get many compliments from
me, Miss—no, I rayther think not. I wonder why honest English girls
won't answer the gentry for governesses, instead of them gaping,
scheming, wicked furriners? Lord forgi' me, I think they're all alike.'

Next morning I made acquaintance with Madame de la Rougierre.
She was tall, masculine, a little ghastly perhaps, and draped in purple
silk, with a lace cap, and great bands of black hair, too thick and black
perhaps to correspond quite naturally with her bleached and sallow
skin, her hollow jaws, and the fine but grim wrinkles traced about her
brows and eye-lids. She smiled, she nodded, and then for a good while
she scanned me in silence with a steady, cunning eye, and a stern smile.

'And how is she named—what is Mademoiselle's name?' said the
tall stranger.

'*Maud*, Madame.'

'Maud!—what pretty name. Eh! bien. I am very sure my dear
Maud she will be very good little girl—is not so?—and I am sure
I shall love you vary moche. And what 'av you been learning, Maud,
my dear cheaile—music, French, German, eh?'

'Yes, a little; and I had just begun the use of the globes when my
governess went away.'

I nodded towards the globes, which stood near her, as I said this.

'Oh! yes—the globes;' and she spun one of them with her great
hand. 'Je vous expliquerai tout cela à fond.'*

Madame de la Rougierre, I found, was always quite ready to explain
everything 'à fond'; but somehow her 'explications', as she termed
them, were not very intelligible, and when pressed her temper woke
up, so that I preferred, after a while, accepting the expositions just as
they came.

Madame was on an unusually large scale, a circumstance which
made some of her traits more startling, and altogether rendered her,

in her strange way, more awful in the eyes of a nervous *child*, I may say, such as I was. She used to look at me for a long time sometimes, with the peculiar smile I have mentioned, and her great finger upon her lip, like the Eleusinian priestess on the vase.*

She would sit, too, sometimes for an hour together, looking into the fire or out of the window, plainly seeing nothing, and with an odd, fixed look of something like triumph—very nearly a smile—on her cunning face.

She was by no means a pleasant *gouvernante* for a nervous girl of my years. Sometimes she had accesses of a sort of hilarity which frightened me still more than her graver moods, and I will describe these by-and-by.

CHAPTER V

SIGHTS AND NOISES

THERE is not an old house in England of which the servants and young people who live in it do not cherish some traditions of the ghostly. Knowl has its shadows, noises, and marvellous records. Rachel Ruthyn, the beauty of Queen Anne's time, who died of grief for the handsome Colonel Norbrooke, who was killed in the Low Countries, walks the house by night, in crisp and sounding silks. She is not seen, only heard. The tapping of her high-heeled shoes, the sweep and rustle of her brocades, her sighs as she pauses in the galleries, near the bed-room doors; and sometimes, on stormy nights, her sobs.

There is, beside, the 'link-man',* a lank, dark-faced, black-haired man, in a sable suit, with a link or torch in his hand. It usually only smoulders, with a deep, red glow, as he visits his beat. The library is one of the rooms he sees to. Unlike 'Lady Rachel', as the maids called her, he is seen only, never heard. His steps fall noiseless as shadows on floor and carpet. The lurid glow of his smouldering torch imperfectly lights his figure and face, and, except when much perturbed, his link never blazes. On those occasions, however, as he goes his rounds, he ever and anon whirls it round his head, and it bursts into a dismal flame. This is a fearful omen, and always portends some direful crisis or calamity. It occurs, however, only once or twice in a century.

I don't know whether Madame had heard anything of these phenomena; but she did report what very much frightened me and Mary Quince. She asked us who walked in the gallery on which her bedroom opened, making a rustling with her dress, and going down the stairs, and breathing long breaths here and there. Twice, she said, she had stood at her door in the dark, listening to these sounds, and once she called to know who it was. There was no answer, but the person plainly turned back, and hurried towards her with an unnatural speed, which made her jump within her door and shut it.

When first such tales are told they excite the nerves of the young and the ignorant intensely. But the special effect, I have found, soon wears out, and the tale simply takes its place with the rest. So it was with Madame's narrative.

About a week after its relation, I had my experience of a similar sort. Mary Quince went down-stairs for a night-light, leaving me in bed, a candle burning in the room, and there, being tired, I fell asleep before her return. When I awoke the candle had been extinguished. But I heard a step softly approaching. I jumped up—quite forgetting the ghost, and thinking only of Mary Quince—and opened the door, expecting to see the light of her candle. Instead, all was dark, and near me I heard the fall of a bare foot on the oak floor. It was as if some one had stumbled. I said, 'Mary,' but no answer came, only a rustling of clothes and a breathing at the other side of the gallery, which passed off towards the upper staircase. I turned into my room, freezing with horror, and clapt my door. The noise wakened Mary Quince, who had returned and gone to her bed half-an-hour before.

About a fortnight after this Mary Quince, a very veracious spinster, reported to me, that having got up to fix the window, which was rattling, at about four o'clock in the morning, she saw a light shining from the library window. She could swear to its being a strong light, streaming through the chinks of the shutter, and moving, as no doubt the link was waved about his head by the angry 'link-man'.

These strange occurrences helped, I think, just then to make me nervous, and prepared the way for the odd sort of ascendancy which, through my sense of the mysterious and supernatural, that repulsive Frenchwoman was gradually, and it seemed without effort, establishing over me.

Some dark points of her character speedily emerged from the prismatic mist with which she had enveloped it.

Mrs. Rusk's observation about the agreeability of new-comers I found to be true, for as Madame began to lose that character, her good-humour abated very perceptibly, and she began to show gleams of another sort of temper, that was lurid and dangerous.

Notwithstanding this, she was in the habit of always having her Bible open by her, and was austerely attentive at morning and evening services, and asked my father, with great humility, to lend her some translations of Swedenborg's books, which she laid much to heart.

When we went out for our walk, if the weather were bad we generally made our promenade up and down the broad terrace in front of the windows. Sullen and malign at times she used to look, and as suddenly she would pat me on the shoulder caressingly, and smile with a grotesque benignity, asking tenderly, 'Are you fatigue, ma chère?' or 'Are you cold-a, dear Maud?'

At first these abrupt transitions puzzled me, sometimes half frightened me, savouring, I fancied, of insanity. The key, however, was accidentally supplied, and I found that these accesses of demonstrative affection were sure to supervene whenever my father's face was visible through the library windows.

I did not know well what to make of this woman, whom I feared with a vein of superstitious dread. I hated being alone with her after dusk in the school-room. She would sometimes sit for half an hour at a time, with her wide mouth drawn down at the corners, and a scowl, looking into the fire. If she saw me looking at her she would change all this on the instant, affect a sort of languor, and lean her head upon her hand, and ultimately have recourse to her Bible. But I fancied she did not read, but pursued her own dark ruminations, for I observed that the open book might often lie for half an hour or more under her eyes and yet the leaf never turned.

I should have been glad to be assured that she prayed when on her knees, or read when that book was before her; I should have felt that she was more canny and human. As it was, those external pieties made a suspicion of a hollow contrast with realities that helped to scare me; yet it was but a suspicion—I could not be certain.

Our Rector and the Curate, with whom she was very gracious, and anxious about my collects and catechism, had an exalted opinion of her. In public places her affection for me was always demonstrative.

In like manner she contrived conferences with my father. She was always making excuses to consult him about my reading, and to confide in him her sufferings, as I learned, from my contumacy and temper. The fact is, I was altogether quiet and submissive. But I think she had a wish to reduce me to a state of the most abject bondage. She had designs of domination and subversion regarding the entire household, I now believe, worthy of the evil spirit I sometimes fancied her.

My father beckoned me into the study one day, and said he—

'You ought not to give poor Madame so much pain. She is one of the few persons who take an interest in you; why should she have so often to complain of your ill-temper and disobedience?—why should she be compelled to ask my permission to punish you? Don't be afraid, I won't concede that. But in so kind a person it argues much.

Affection I can't command—respect and obedience I may—and I insist on your rendering *both* to Madame.'

'But, sir,' I said, roused into courage by the gross injustice of the charge, 'I have always done exactly as she bid me, and never said one disrespectful word to Madame.'

'I don't think, child, *you* are the best judge of that. Go, and *amend*.' And with a displeased look he pointed to the door. My heart swelled with the sense of wrong, and as I reached the door I turned to say another word, but I could not, and only burst into tears.

'There—don't cry, little Maud—only let us do better for the future. There—there—there has been enough.'

And he kissed my forehead, and gently put me out and closed the door.

In the school-room I took courage, and with some warmth upbraided Madame.

'Wat wicked cheaile!' moaned Madame, demurely. 'Read aloud those three—yes, *those* three chapters of the Bible, my dear Maud.'

There was no special fitness in those particular chapters, and when they were ended she said in a sad tone—

'Now, dear, you must commit to memory this pretty priaire for umility of art.'

It was a long one, and in a state of profound irritation I got through the task.

Mrs. Rusk hated her. She said she stole wine and brandy whenever the opportunity offered—that she was always asking her for such stimulants and pretending pains in her stomach. Here, perhaps, there was exaggeration; but I knew it was true that I had been at different times despatched on that errand and pretext for brandy to Mrs. Rusk, who at last came to her bed-side with pills and a mustard blister only, and was hated irrevocably ever after.

I felt all this was done to torture me. But a day is a long time to a child, and they forgive quickly. It was always with a sense of danger that I heard Madame say she must go and see Monsieur Ruthyn in the library, and I think a jealousy of her growing influence was an ingredient in the detestation in which honest Mrs. Rusk held her.

Two little pieces of by-play in which I detected her confirmed my unpleasant suspicion. From the corner of the gallery I one day saw her, when she thought I was out and all quiet, with her ear at the key-hole of papa's study, as we used to call the sitting-room next his bed-room. Her eyes were turned in the direction of the stairs, from which only she apprehended surprise. Her great mouth was open, and her eyes absolutely goggled with eagerness. She was devouring all that was passing there. I drew back into the shadow with a kind of disgust and horror. She was transformed into a great gaping reptile. I felt that I could have thrown something at her; but a kind of fear made me recede again toward my room. Indignation, however, quickly returned, and I came back, treading briskly as I did so. When I reached the angle of the gallery again, Madame, I suppose, had heard me, for she was halfway down the stairs.

'Ah, my dear cheaile, I am so glad to find you, and you are dress to come out. We shall have so pleasant walk.'

At that moment the door of my father's study opened, and Mrs. Rusk, with her dark energetic face very much flushed, stepped out in high excitement.

'The Master says you may have the brandy-bottle, Madame, and I'm glad to be rid of it—*I* am.'

Madame courtesied with a great smirk, that was full of intangible hate and insult.

'Better your own brandy, if drink you must!' exclaimed Mrs. Rusk. 'You may come to the store-room now, or the butler can take it.'

And off whisked Mrs. Rusk for the back stair case.

There had been no common skirmish on this occasion, but a pitched battle.

Madame had made a sort of pet of Anne Wixted, an under-chambermaid, and attached her to her interest economically by persuading me to make her presents of some old dresses and other things. Anne was such an angel!

But Mrs. Rusk, whose eyes were about her, detected Anne, with a brandy-bottle under her apron, stealing up-stairs. Anne, in a panic, declared the truth. Madame had commissioned her to buy it in the town, and convey it to her bed-room. Upon this, Mrs. Rusk impounded the flask; and with Anne beside her, rather precipitately appeared before 'the Master'. He heard, and summoned Madame. Madame was cool, frank and fluent. The brandy was purely medicinal. She produced a document in form of a note. Doctor Somebody presented his compliments to Madame de la Rougierre, and ordered her a table-spoonful of brandy and some drops of laudanum whenever the pain of stomach returned. The flask would last a whole year, perhaps two. She claimed her medicine.

Man's estimate of woman is higher than woman's own. Perhaps in their relations to man they are generally more trustworthy—perhaps woman's is the juster, and the other an appointed illusion. I don't know; but so it is ordained.

Mrs. Rusk was recalled, and I saw, as you are aware, Madame's procedure during the interview.

It was a great battle—a great victory. Madame was in high spirits. The air was sweet—the landscape charming—I, so good—every thing so beautiful! Where should we go? *this* way?

I had made a resolution to speak as little as possible to Madame, I was so incensed at the treachery I had witnessed; but such resolutions do not last long with very young people, and by the time we had reached the skirts of the wood we were talking pretty much as usual.

'I don't wish to go into the wood, Madame.'

'And for what?'

'Poor mamma is buried there.'

'Is *there* the vault?' demanded Madame, eagerly.

I assented.

'My faith, curious reason; you say because poor mamma is buried there you will not approach! Why, cheaile, what would good Monsieur Ruthyn say if he heard such thing? You are surely not so unkain', and I am with you. *Allons.* Let us come—even a little part of way.'

And so I yielded, though still reluctant.

There was a grass-grown road, which we easily reached, leading to the sombre building, and we soon arrived before it.

Madame de la Rougierre seemed rather curious. She sat down on the little bank opposite, in her most languid pose—her head leaned upon the tips of her fingers.

'How very sad—how solemn!' murmured Madame. 'What noble tomb! How triste, my dear cheaile, your visit 'ere must it be, remembering a so sweet maman. There is new inscription—is it not new?' And so, indeed, it seemed.

'I am fatigue—maybe you will read it aloud to me slowly and solemnly, my dearest Maud?'

As I approached I happened to look, I can't tell why, suddenly, over my shoulder; I was startled, for Madame was grimacing after me with a vile derisive distortion. She pretended to be seized with a fit of coughing. But it would not do; she saw that I had detected her, and she laughed aloud.

'Come here, dear cheaile. I was just reflecting how foolish is all this thing—the tomb—the epitaph. I think, I would 'av none—no, no epitaph. We regard them first for the oracle of the dead, and find them after only the folly of the living. So I despise. Do you think your house of Knowl down there is what you call haunt, my dear?'

'Why?' said I, flushing and growing pale again. I felt quite afraid of Madame, and confounded at the suddenness of all this.

'Because Anne Wixted she says there is ghost. How dark is this place, and so many of the Ruthyn family they are buried here—is not so? How high and thick are the trees all round, and nobody comes near.'

And Madame rolled her eyes awfully, as if she expected to see something unearthly, and, indeed, looked very like it herself.

'Come away, Madame,' I said, growing frightened, and feeling that if I were once, by any accident, to give way to the panic that was gathering round me I should instantaneously lose all control of myself. 'Oh, come away!—do, Madame—I'm frightened.'

'No, on the contrary, sit here by me. It is very odd you will think, ma chère—un goût bizarre vraiment!—but I love very much to be near to the dead people—in solitary place like this. I am not afraid of the dead people, nor of the ghosts. 'Av you ever see a ghost, my dear?'

'Do, Madame! *pray* speak of something else.'

'Wat little fool! But no, you are not afraid. I 'av seen the ghosts myself. I saw one, for example, last night, shape like a monkey, sitting in the corner, with his arms round his knees; very wicked, old, old man his face was like, and white eyes so large.'

'Come away, Madame! you are trying to frighten me,' I said, in the childish anger which accompanies fear.

Madame laughed an ugly laugh, and said—

'Eh, bien! little fool!—I will not tell the rest if you are really frightened; let us change to something else.'

'Yes, yes! oh, do—pray do.'

'Wat good man is your father!'

'Very—the kindest darling. I don't know why it is, Madame, I am so afraid of him, and never could tell him how much I love him.'

This confidential talking with Madame, strange to say, implied no confidence; it resulted from fear—it was deprecatory. I treated her as if she had human sympathies, in the hope that they might be generated somehow.

'Was there not a doctor from London with him a few months ago? Doctor Bryerly, I think they call him.'

'Yes, a Doctor Bryerly, who remained a few days. Shall we begin to walk towards home, Madame? Do, pray.'

'Immediately, cheaile; and does your father suffer much?'

'No—I think not.'

'And what then is his disease?'

'Disease! he has *no* disease. Have you heard anything about his health, Madame?' I said, anxiously.

'Oh, no; ma foi—I have heard nothing; but if the doctor came it was not because he was quite well.'

'But that doctor is a doctor in theology, I fancy. I know he is a Swedenborgian; and papa is so well he *could* not have come as a physician.'

'I am very glad, ma chère, to hear; but still you know your father is old man to have so young cheaile as you. Oh, yes—he is old man, and so uncertain life is. 'As he made his will, my dear? Every man so rich as he, especially so old, aught to 'av made his will.'

'There is no need of haste, Madame; it is quite time enough when his health begins to fail.'

'But has he really compose no will?'

'I really don't know, Madame.'

'Ah, little rogue! you will not tell—but you are not such fool as you feign yourself. No, no; you know everything. Come, tell me all about—it is for your advantage, you know. What is in his will, and when he wrote?'

'But, Madame, I really know nothing of it. I can't say whether there is a will or not. Let us talk of something else.'

'But, cheaile, it will not kill Monsieur Ruthyn to make his will; he will not come to lie here a day sooner by cause of that, but if he make no will you may lose a great deal of the property. Would not that be pity?'

'I really don't know anything of his will. If papa has made one, he has never spoken of it to me. I know he loves me—that is enough.'

'Ah! you are not such little goose—you do know everything, of course. Come, come, tell me, little obstinate, otherwise I will break your little finger. Tell me everything.'

'I know nothing of papa's will. You don't know, Madame, how you pain me. Do let us speak of something else.'

'You do know, and you must tell, petite dur-tête, or I will break a your leetle finger.'

With which words she seized that joint, and laughing spitefully, she twisted it suddenly back. I screamed; she continued to laugh.

'Will you tell?'

'Yes, yes! let me go'; I shrieked.

She did not release it, however, immediately, but continued her torture and discordant laughter. At last, however, she did release my finger.

'So she is going to be good cheaile, and to tell everything to her affectionate gouvernante. What do you cry for, little fool?'

'You've hurt me very much—you have broken my finger,' I sobbed.

'Rub it and blow it, and give it a kees, little fool! What cross girl! I will never play with you again—never. Let us go home.'

Madame was silent and morose all the way home. She would not answer my questions, and affected to be very lofty and offended.

This did not last very long, however, and she soon resumed her wonted ways. And she returned to the question of the will; but not so directly, and with more art.

Why should this dreadful woman's thoughts be running so continually upon my father's will? How could it concern her?

CHAPTER VII
CHURCH SCARSDALE

I THINK all the females of our household, except Mrs. Rusk, who was at open feud with her, and had only room for the fiercer emotions, were more or less afraid of this inauspicious foreigner.

Mrs. Rusk would say in her confidences in my room—

'Where does she come from?—is she a French or a Swiss one, or is she a Canada woman? I remember one of *them* when I was a girl, and a nice limb *she* was, too! And who did she live with? Where was her last family? Not one of us knows nothing about her, no more than a child; except, of course, the Master—I do suppose he made inquiry. She's always at hugger-mugger* with Anne Wixted. I'll pack that *one* about her business if she don't mind. Tattling and whispering eternally. It's not about her own business she's a-talking. Madame de la Rougepot, *I* call her. She *does* knows how to paint up to the ninety-nines—she does, the old cat. I beg your pardon, Miss, but *that* she is—a devil, and no mistake. I found her out first by her thieving the master's gin, that the doctor ordered him, and filling the decanter up with water—the old villain; but she'll be found out yet, she will; and all the maids is afraid on her. She's not right, they think—a witch or a ghost—I should not wonder. Catherine Jones found her in her bed asleep in the morning after she sulked with you, you know, Miss, with all her clothes on, whatever was the meaning; and I think she has frightened *you*, Miss, and has you as nervous as anythink—I do,' and so forth.

It was true—I *was* nervous, and growing rather more so; and I think this cynical woman perceived and intended it, and was pleased. I was always afraid of her concealing herself in my room, and emerging at night to scare me. She began sometimes to mingle in my dreams, too—always awfully; and this nourished, of course, the kind of ambiguous fear in which, in waking hours, I held her.

I dreamed one night that she led me, all the time whispering something so very fast that I could not understand her, into the library, holding a candle in her other hand above her head. We walked on tiptoe, like criminals at the dead of night, and stopped before that old oak cabinet which my father had indicated in so odd a way to me. I felt that we were about some contraband practice. There was a key in the door, which I experienced a guilty horror at turning, she whispering in the same unintelligible way, all the time, at my ear. I *did* turn it—the door opened quite softly, and within stood my father; his face white and malignant, and glaring close in mine. He cried in a terrible voice, 'Death!' Out went Madame's candle, and at the same moment, with a scream, I waked in the dark—still fancying myself in the library; and for an hour after I continued in a hysterical state.

Every little incident about Madame furnished a topic of eager discussion among the maids. More or less covertly, they nearly all hated and feared her. They fancied that she was making good her footing with 'the Master'; and that she would then oust Mrs. Rusk—perhaps usurp her place—and so make a clean sweep of them all. I fancy the honest little housekeeper did not discourage that suspicion.

About this time I recollect a pedlar, an odd, gipsified-looking man, called in at Knowl. I and Catherine Jones were in the court when he came, and set down his pack on the low balustrade beside the door.

All sorts of commodities he had—ribbons, cottons, silks, stockings, lace, and even some bad jewellery; and just as he began his display—an interesting matter in a quiet country house—Madame came upon the ground. He grinned a recognition, and hoped 'Madamasel' was well, and 'did not look to see *her* here'.

'Madamasel' thanked him—'Yes, vary well,' and looked for the first time decidedly 'put out'.

'Wat a pretty things!' she said. 'Catherine, run and tell Mrs. Rusk. She wants scissars and lace, too—I heard her say.'

So Catherine, with a lingering look, departed; and Madame said—

'Will you, dear cheaile, be so kind to bring here my purse; I forgot on the table in my room; also, I advise you, bring *your*.'

Catherine returned with Mrs. Rusk. Here was a man who could tell them something of the old Frenchwoman, at last! Slyly they dawdled over his wares, until Madame had made her market, and departed with me. But when the coveted opportunity came, the pedlar was quite impenetrable. He forgot everything—he did not believe as he ever saw the lady before. He called a Frenchwoman, all the world over, Madamasel—that wor the name on 'em all. He never seed her in partiklar afore, as he could bring to mind. He liked to see 'em always, 'cause they makes the young uns buy.

This reserve and oblivion were very provoking, and neither Mrs. Rusk nor Catherine Jones spent sixpence with him;—he was a stupid fellow, or worse.

Of course Madame had tampered with him. But truth, like murder, will out some day. Tom Williams, the groom, had seen her, when alone with him, and pretending to look at his stock, with her face almost buried in his silks and Welsh linseys, talking as fast as she could all the time, and slipping *money*, he did suppose, under a piece of stuff in his box.

In the mean time, I and Madame were walking over the wide, peaty sheepwalks that lie between Knowl and Church Scarsdale. Since our visit to the mausoleum in the wood, she had not worried me so much as before. She had been, indeed, more than usually thoughtful, very little talkative, and troubled me hardly at all about French and other accomplishments. A walk was a part of our daily routine. I now carried a tiny basket in my hand, with a few sandwiches, which were to furnish our luncheon when we reached the pretty scene, about two miles away, whither we were tending.

We had started a little too late; Madame grew unwontedly fatigued, and sat down to rest on a stile before we had got half way, and there she intoned, with a dismal nasal cadence, a quaint old Bretagne ballad, about a lady with a pig's head:—

> 'This lady was neither pig nor maid,
> And so she was not of human mould;
> Not of the living nor the dead.
> Her left hand and foot were warm to touch;
> Her right as cold as a corpse's flesh!
> And she would sing like a funeral bell, with a ding-dong tune.
> The pigs were afraid, and viewed her aloof,
> And women feared her and stood afar.
> She could do without sleep for a year and a day;
> She could sleep like a corpse, for a month and more.
> No one knew how this lady fed—
> On acorns or on flesh.
> Some say that she's one of the swine possessed,
> That swam over the sea of Genesaret.
> A mongrel body and demon soul.
> Some say she's the wife of the Wandering Jew,
> And broke the law for the sake of pork;
> And a swinish face for a token doth bear,
> That her shame is now and her punishment coming.'*

And so it went on, in a gingling rigmarole. The more anxious I seemed to go on our way, the more likely was she to loiter. I therefore showed no signs of impatience, and I saw her consult her watch in the course of her ugly minstrelsy, and slyly glance, as if expecting something, in the direction of our destination.

When she had sung to her heart's content, up rose Madame, and began to walk onward silently. I saw her glance once or twice, as before, toward the village of Trillsworth, which lay in front, a little to our left, and the smoke of which hung in a film over the brow of the hill. I think she observed me, for she inquired:

'Wat is that a smoke there?'

'That is Trillsworth, Madame; there is a railway station there.'

'Oh, le chemin de fer, so near! I did not think. Where it goes?'

I told her, and silence returned.

Church Scarsdale is a very pretty and odd scene. The slightly undulating sheep-walk dips suddenly into a wide glen, in the lap of which, by a bright, winding rill, rise from the sward the ruins of a small abbey, with a few solemn trees scattered round. The crows' nests hung untenanted in the trees; the birds were foraging far away from their roosts. The very cattle had forsaken the place. It was solitude itself.

Madame drew a long breath and smiled.

'Come down, come down, cheaile—come down to the churchyard.'

As we descended the slope which shut out the surrounding world, and the scene grew more sad and lonely, Madame's spirits seemed to rise.

'See 'ow many grave-stones—one, *two* hundred. Don't you love the dead, cheaile? I will teach you to love them. You shall see me die here to-day, for half an hour, and be among them. That is what I love.'

We were by this time at the little brook's side, and the low church-yard wall with a stile, reached by a couple of stepping-stones, across the stream, immediately at the other side.

'Come, now!' cried Madame, raising her face, as if to sniff the air; 'we are close to them. You will like them soon as I. You shall see five of them. Ah, ça ira, ça ira, ça ira! Come cross quickily! I am Madame la Morgue—Mrs. Deadhouse! I will present you my friends, Monsieur Cadavre and Monsieur Squelette. Come, come, leetle mortal, let us play. Ouaah!' And she uttered a horrid yell from her enormous mouth, and pushing her wig and bonnet back, so as to show her great, bald head. She was laughing, and really looked quite mad.

'No, Madame, I will not go with you,' I said, disengaging my hand with a violent effort, receding two or three steps.

'Not enter the churchyard! Ma foi—wat mauvais goût!* But see, we are already in shade. The sun he is setting soon—where weel you remain, cheaile? I will not stay long.'

'I'll stay here,' I said, a little angrily—for I *was* angry as well as nervous; and through my fear was that indignation at her extravagances which mimicked lunacy so unpleasantly, and were, I knew, designed to frighten me.

Over the stepping-stones, pulling up her dress, she skipped with her long, lank legs, like a witch joining a Walpurgis.* Over the stile she strode, and I saw her head wagging, and heard her sing some of her ill-omened rhymes, as she capered solemnly, with many a grin and courtesy, among the graves and headstones towards the ruin.

CHAPTER VIII

THE SMOKER

THREE years later I learned—in a way she probably little expected, and then did not much care about—what really occurred there. I learned even phrases and looks—for the story was related by one who had heard it told—and therefore I venture to narrate what at the moment I neither saw nor suspected. While I sat, flushed and nervous, upon a flat stone by the bank of the little stream, Madame looked over her shoulder, and perceiving that I was out of sight, she abated her pace, and turned sharply towards the ruin which lay at her left. It was her first visit, and she was merely exploring; but now, with a perfectly shrewd and businesslike air, turning the corner of the building, she saw, seated upon the edge of a grave-stone, a rather fat and flashily equipped young man, with large, light whiskers, a jerry hat,* green cutaway coat with gilt buttons, and waistcoat and trowsers rather striking than elegant in pattern. He was smoking a short pipe, and made a nod to Madame, without either removing it from his lips or rising, but with his brown and rather good-looking face turned up, he eyed her with something of the impudent and sulky expression that was habitual to it.

'Ha, Deedle, you are there! An' look so well. I am here, too, quite *a*lon; but my friend, she wait outside the churchyard, by-side the lee-tle river, for she must not think I know you—so I am come *a*lon.'

'You're a quarter late, and I lost a fight by you, old girl, this morning,' said the gay man, and spat on the ground; 'and I wish you would not call me Diddle. I'll call you Granny if you do.'

'Eh, bien! *Dud*, then. She is vary nice—wat you like. Slim waist, wite teeth, vary nice eyes—dark—wat you say is best—and nice lee-tle foot and ankle.'

Madame smiled leeringly.

Dud smoked on.

'Go on,' said Dud, with a nod of command.

'I am teach her to sing and play, she has such sweet voice.'

There was another interval here.

'Well, that isn't much good. I hate women's screechin' about fairies and flowers. Hang her! There's a scarecrow as sings at Curl's Divan.*

Such a caterwauling upon a stage! I'd like to put my two barrels into her.'

By this time Dud's pipe was out, and he could afford to converse.

'You shall see her and decide. You will walk down the river, and pass her by.'

'That's as may be; howsoever, it would not do, no how, to buy a pig in a poke, you know. And s'pose I shouldn't like her arter all.'

Madame sneered, with a patois ejaculation of derision.

'Vary good! Then some one else will not be so 'ard to please—as you will soon find.'

'Some one's bin a-lookin' arter her, you mean?' said the young man, with a shrewd uneasy glance on the cunning face of the French lady.

'I mean precisely—that which I mean,' replied the lady, with a teazing pause at the break I have marked.

'Come, old 'un, none of your d—— old chaff, if you want me to stay here listening to you. Speak out, can't you? There's any chap as has bin a-lookin' arter her—is there?'

'Eh, bien; I suppose some.'

'Well, you *suppose*, and *I* suppose—we may *all* suppose, I guess; but that does not make a thing be, as wasn't before; and you tell me, as how the lass is kep' private up there, and will be till *you*'re done educating her—a precious good 'un that is!' And he laughed a little lazily, with the ivory handle of his cane on his lip, and eyeing Madame with indolent derision.

Madame laughed, but looked rather dangerous.

'I'm only chaffin', you know, old girl. *You*'ve bin chaffin'—w'y shouldn't *I*? But I don't see why she can't wait a bit; and what's all the d——d hurry for? *I*'m in no hurry. I don't want a wife on my back for a while. There's no fellow marries till he's took his bit 'o fun, and seen life—is there! And why should I be driving with her to fairs, or to church, or to meeting, by jingo!—for they say she's a Quaker—with a babby on each knee, only to please them as will be dead and rotten when *I*'m only beginning?'

'Ah, you are such charming fellow; always the same—always sensible. So I and my friend we will walk home again, and you go see Maggie Hawkes. Good-a-by, Dud—good-a-by.'

'Quiet, you fool!—can't ye?' said the young gentleman, with the sort of grin that made his face vicious when a horse vexed him. 'Who ever said I wouldn't go look at the girl? Why you know that's just what I come here for—don't you? Only when I think a bit, and a notion comes across me, why shouldn't I speak out? I'm not one o' them shilly-shallies. If I like the girl I'll not be mug in and mug out about it. Only, mind ye, I'll judge for myself. Is that her a-coming?'

'No; it was a distant sound.'

Madame peeped round the corner. No one was approaching.

'Well, you go round that a-way, and you only look at her, you know, for she is such fool—so nairvous.'

'Oh, is that the way with her?' said Dud, knocking out the ashes of his pipe on a tomb-stone, and replacing the Turkish utensil in his pocket. 'Well, then, old lass, good-bye,' and he shook her hand. 'And, do ye see, don't ye come up till I pass, for I'm no hand at play-acting; an' if you called me "sir", or was coming it dignified and distant, you know, I'd be sure to laugh, a'most, and let all out. So good-bye, d'ye see, and if you want me again be sharp to time, mind.'

From habit he looked about for his dogs, but he had not brought one. He had come unostentatiously by rail, travelling in a third-class carriage, for the advantage of Jack Briderly's company, and getting a world of useful wrinkles about the steeple-chase that was coming off next week.

So he strode away, cutting off the heads of the nettles with his cane as he went; and Madame walked forth into the open space among the graves, where I might have seen her, had I stood up, looking with the absorbed gaze of an artist on the ruin.

In a little while, along the path, I heard the clank of a step, and the gentleman in the green cutaway coat, sucking his cane, and eyeing me with an offensive familiar sort of stare the while, passed me by, rather hesitating as he did so.

I was glad when he turned the corner in the little hollow close by, and disappeared. I stood up at once and was reassured by a sight of Madame, not very many yards away, looking at the ruin, and apparently restored to her right mind. The last beams of the sun were by this time touching the uplands, and I was longing to recommence our walk home. I was hesitating about calling to Madame, because that lady had a certain spirit of opposition within her, and to disclose a small wish of any sort was generally, if it lay in her power, to prevent its accomplishment.

At this moment the gentleman in the green coat returned, approaching me with a slow sort of swagger.

'I say, Miss, I dropped a glove close by here. May you have seen it?'

'No, sir,' I said, drawing back a little, and looking, I dare say, both frightened and offended.

'I do think I must 'a dropped it close by your foot, Miss.'

'No, sir,' I repeated.

'No offence, Miss; but you're sure you didn't hide it?'

I was beginning to grow seriously uncomfortable.

'Don't be frightened, Miss; it's only a bit o' chaff. I'm not going to search.'

I called aloud, 'Madame, Madame!' and he whistled through his fingers, and shouted, 'Madame, Madame,' and added, 'She's as deaf as a tombstone, or she'll hear that. Gi'e her my compliments, and say I said you're a beauty, Miss;' and with a laugh and a leer, he strode off.

Altogether this had not been a very pleasant excursion. Madame gobbled up our sandwiches, commending them every now and then to me. But I had been too much excited to have any appetite left, and very tired I was when we reached home.

'So, there is lady coming to-morrow?' said Madame, who knew everything. 'Wat is her name? I forget.'

'Lady Knollys,' I answered.

'Lady Knollys—wat odd name! She is very young—is she not?'

'Past fifty, I think.'

'Hélas! She's vary old then. Is she rich?'

'I don't know. She has a place in Derbyshire.'

'Derbyshire—that is one of your English counties, is it not?'

'Oh, yes, Madame,' I answered, laughing. 'I have said it to you twice since you came;' and I gabbled through the chief towns and rivers as catalogued in my geography.

'Bah! To be sure—of course, cheaile. And is she your relation?'

'Papa's first cousin.'

'Won't you present-a me, pray?—I would so like.'

Madame had fallen into the English way of liking people with titles, as perhaps foreigners would if titles implied the sort of power they do generally with us.

'Certainly, Madame.'

'You will not forget?'

'Oh, no.'

Madame reminded me twice, in the course of the evening, of my promise. She was very eager on this point. But it is a world of disappointment, influenza, and rheumatics, and next morning Madame was prostrate in her bed, and careless of all things but flannel and James's powder.

Madame was *désolée*; but she could not raise her head. She only murmured a question.

'For 'ow long time, dear, will Lady Knollys remain?'

'A very few days, I believe.'

'Hélas! 'ow onlucky! May be to-morrow I shall be better. Ouah! My ear. The laudanum, dear cheaile!'

And so our conversation for that time ended, and Madame buried her head in her old red cashmere shawl.

CHAPTER IX

MONICA KNOLLYS

PUNCTUALLY Lady Knollys arrived. She was accompanied by her nephew, Captain Oakley.

They arrived a little before dinner; just in time to get to their rooms and dress. But Mary Quince enlivened my toilet with eloquent descriptions of the youthful Captain whom she had met in the gallery, on his way to his room, with the servant, and told me how he stopped to let her pass, and how 'he smiled so 'ansom.'

I was very young then, you know, and more childish even than my years; but this talk of Mary Quince's interested me, I must confess, considerably. I was painting all sorts of portraits of this heroic soldier, while affecting, I am afraid, a hypocritical indifference to her narration, and I know I was very nervous and painstaking about my toilet that evening. When I went down to the drawing-room, Lady Knollys was there, talking volubly to my father as I entered—a woman not really old, but such as very young people fancy aged—energetic, bright, saucy, dressed handsomely in purple satin, with a good deal of lace, and a rich point—I know not how to call it—not a cap, a sort of head-dress—light and simple, but grand withal, over her greyish, silken hair.

Rather tall, by no means stout, on the whole a good firm figure, with something kindly in her look. She got up, quite like a young person, and coming quickly to meet me with a smile—

'My young cousin!' she cried, and kissed me on both cheeks. 'You know who I am? Your Cousin Monica—Monica Knollys—and very glad, dear, to see you, though she has not set eyes on you since you were no longer than that paper-knife. Now come here to the lamp, for I must look at you. Who is she like? Let me see. Like your poor mother, I think, my dear; but you've the Aylmer nose—yes—not a bad nose either, and come! Very good eyes, upon my life—yes, certainly—something of her poor mother—not a bit like you, Austin.'

My father gave her a look as near a smile as I had seen there for a long time, shrewd, cynical, but kindly too, and said he—

'So much the better, Monica, eh?'

'It was not for me to say—but you know, Austin, you always were an ugly creature. How shocked and indignant the little girl looks! You must not be vexed, you loyal little woman, with Cousin Monica for telling the truth. Papa was and will be ugly all his days. Come, Austin, dear, tell her—is not it so?'

'What! Depose against myself! That's not English law, Monica.'

'Well, maybe not; but if the child won't believe her own eyes, how is she to believe me? She has long, pretty hands—you have—and very nice feet too. How old is she?'

'How old, child?' said my father to me, transferring the question.

She recurred again to my eyes.

'That is the true grey—large, deep, soft—very peculiar. Yes, dear, very pretty—long lashes, and such bright tints. You'll be in the Book of Beauty, my dear, when you come out, and have all the poet people writing verses to the tip of your nose, and a very pretty little nose it is!'

I must mention here how striking was the change in my father's spirit while talking and listening to his odd and voluble old Cousin Monica. Reflected from bygone associations, there had come a glimmer of something, not gaiety, indeed, but like an appreciation of gaiety. The gloom and inflexibility were gone, and there was an evident encouragement and enjoyment of the incessant sallies of his bustling visitor.

How morbid must have been the tendencies of his habitual solitude, I think, appeared from the evident thawing and brightening that accompanied even this transient gleam of human society. I was not a companion—more childish than most girls of my age, and trained in all his whimsical ways, never to interrupt a silence, or force his thoughts by unexpected question or remark out of their monotonous or painful channel.

I was as much surprised at the good-humour with which he submitted to his cousin's saucy talk; and, indeed, just then those black-panelled and pictured walls, and that quaint, misshapen room, seemed to have exchanged their stern and awful character for something wonderfully pleasanter to me, notwithstanding the unpleasantness of the personal criticism to which the plain-spoken lady chose to subject me.

Just at that moment Captain Oakley joined us. He was my first actual vision of that awful and distant world of fashion, of whose splendours I had already read something in the three-volumed gospel of the circulating library.

Handsome, elegant, with features almost feminine, and soft, wavy, black hair, whiskers and moustache, he was altogether such a knight as I had never beheld, or even fancied, at Knowl—a hero of another species, and from the region of the demigods. I did not then perceive that coldness of the eye, and cruel curl of the voluptuous lip—only a suspicion, yet enough to indicate the profligate man, and savouring of death unto death.*

But I was young, and had not yet the direful knowledge of good and evil that comes with years, and he was so very handsome, and talked in a way that was so new to me, and was so much more charming than the well-bred converse of the humdrum county families with whom I had occasionally sojourned for a week at a time.

It came out incidentally that his leave of absence was to expire the day after to-morrow. A Lilliputian* pang of disappointment followed this announcement. Already I was sorry to lose him. So soon we begin to make a property of what pleases us.

I was shy, but not awkward. I was flattered by the attention of this amusing, perhaps rather fascinating, young man of the world; and he plainly addressed himself with diligence to amuse and please me. I dare say there was more effort than I fancied in bringing his talk down to my humble level, and interesting me and making me laugh about people whom I had never heard of before, than I then suspected.

Cousin Knollys meanwhile was talking to papa. It was just the conversation that suited a man so silent as habit had made him, for her frolic fluency left him little to supply. It was totally impossible, indeed, even in our taciturn household, that conversation should ever flag while she was among us.

Cousin Knollys and I went into the drawing-room together, leaving the gentlemen—rather ill-assorted, I fear—to entertain one another for a time.

'Come here, my dear, and sit near me,' said Lady Knollys, dropping into an easy chair with an energetic little plump, 'and tell me how you and your papa get on. I can remember him quite a cheerful man once, and rather amusing—yes, indeed—and now you see what a bore he is—all by shutting himself up and nursing his whims and fancies. Are those your drawings, dear?'

'Yes, very bad I'm afraid; but there are a few, *better* I think, in the portfolio in the cabinet in the hall.'

'They are by *no* means bad, my dear; and you play, of course?'

'Yes—that is, a little—pretty well, I hope.'

'I dare say. I must hear you by-and-by; and how does your papa amuse you? You look bewildered, dear. Well, I dare say, amusement is not a frequent word in this house. But you must not turn into a nun, or worse, into a puritan. What is he? A Fifth-Monarchy-man,* or something—I forget; tell me the name, my dear.'

'Papa is a Swedenborgian, I believe.'

'Yes, yes—I forgot the horrid name—a Swedenborgian, that is it. I don't know exactly what they think, but every one knows they are a sort of pagans, my dear. He's not making one of *you*, dear—is he?'

'I go to church every Sunday.'

'Well, that's a mercy; Swedenborgian is such an ugly name; and besides they are all likely to be damned, my dear, and that's a serious consideration. I really wish poor Austin had hit on something else; I'd much rather have no religion, and enjoy life while I'm in it, than choose one to worry me here and bedevil me hereafter. But some people, my dear, have a taste for being miserable, and provide, like poor Austin, for its gratification in the next world as well as here. Ha, ha, ha! How grave the little woman looks! Don't you think me very wicked? You know you do; and very likely you are right. Who makes your dresses, my dear? You *are* such a figure of fun!'

'Mrs. Rusk, I think, ordered *this* dress. I and Mary Quince planned it. I thought it very nice. We all like it very well.'

There was something, I dare say, very whimsical about it, probably very absurd, judged at least by the canons of fashion, and old Cousin Monica Knollys, in whose eye the London fashions were always fresh, was palpably struck by it as if it had been some enormity against anatomy, for she certainly laughed very heartily; indeed there were tears on her cheeks when she had done, and I am sure my aspect of wonder and dignity, as her hilarity proceeded, helped to revive her merriment again and again as it was subsiding.

'There, you mustn't be vexed with old Cousin Monica,' she cried, jumping up, and giving me a little hug, and bestowing a hearty kiss on my forehead, and a jolly little slap on my cheek. 'Always remember your Cousin Monica is an outspoken, wicked old fool, who likes you, and never be offended by her nonsense. A council of three—you all sat upon it—Mrs. Rusk, you said, and Mary Quince, and your wise self, the weird sisters; and Austin stepped in, as Macbeth, and said, "What is't ye do?" you all made answer together, "A something or other without a name!"* Now, seriously, my dear, it is quite unpardonable in Austin—your papa I mean—to hand you over to be robed and bedizened according to the whimsies of these wild old women—aren't they old? If they know better, it's positively *fiendish*. I'll blow him up—I will indeed, my dear. You know you're an heiress, and ought not to appear like a jack-pudding.'

'Papa intends sending me to London with Madame and Mary Quince, and going with me himself, if Doctor Bryerly says he may make the journey, and then I am to have dresses and everything.'

'Well, that is better. And who is Doctor Bryerly—is your papa ill?'

'Ill! Oh, no; he always seems just the same. You don't think him ill—*looking* ill, I mean?' I asked very eagerly and frightened.

'No, my dear, he looks very well for his time of life; but why is Doctor what's-his-name here; is he a physician, or a divine, or a horse-doctor, and why is his leave asked?'

'I—I really don't understand.'

'Is he a what d'ye call 'em—a Swedenborgian?'

'I believe so.'

'Oh, I see; ha, ha, ha! And so poor Austin must ask leave to go up to town. Well, go he shall, whether his doctor likes it or not, for it would not do to send you there in charge of your Frenchwoman, my dear. What's her name?'

'Madame de la Rougierre.'

CHAPTER X

LADY KNOLLYS REMOVES A COVERLET

LADY KNOLLYS pursued her inquiries.

'And why does not Madame make your dresses, my dear? I wager a guinea the woman's a milliner. Did not she engage to make your dresses?'

'I—I really don't know; I rather think not. She is my governess—a finishing governess, Mrs. Rusk says.'

'Finishing fiddle! Hoity-toity! And my lady's too grand to cut out your dresses and help to sew them? And what *does* she do? I venture to say she's fit to teach nothing but devilment—not that she has taught *you* much, my dear—*yet* at least. I'll see her, my dear; where is she? Come, let us visit Madame. I should so like to talk to her a little.'

'But she is ill,' I answered, and all this time I was ready to cry for vexation, thinking of my dress, which must be very absurd to elicit so much unaffected laughter from my experienced relative, and I was only longing to get away and hide myself before that handsome Captain returned.

'Ill! Is she? What's the matter?'

'A cold—feverish and rheumatic, she says.'

'Oh, a cold; is she up or in bed?'

'In her room, but not in bed.'

'I should so like to see her, my dear. It is not mere curiosity, I assure you. In fact, curiosity has nothing on earth to do with it. A governess may be a very useful or a very useless person; but she may also be about the most pernicious inmate imaginable. She may teach you a bad accent, and worse manners, and heaven knows what beside. Send the housekeeper, my dear, to tell her that I am going to see her.'

'I had better go myself, perhaps,' I said, fearing a collision between Mrs. Rusk and the bitter Frenchwoman.

'Very well, dear.'

And away I ran, not sorry somehow to escape before Captain Oakley returned.

As I went along the passage I was thinking whether my dress could be so very ridiculous as my old cousin thought it, and trying in vain to recollect any evidence of a similar contemptuous estimate on the part of that beautiful and garrulous dandy. I could not—quite the reverse, indeed. Still I was uncomfortable and feverish—girls of my then age will easily conceive how miserable, under similar circumstances, such a misgiving would make them.

It was a long way to Madame's room. I met Mrs. Rusk bustling along the passage with a housemaid.

'How is Madame?' I asked.

'Quite well, I believe,' answered the housekeeper, drily. 'Nothing the matter that *I* know of. She eat enough for two to-day. I wish *I* could sit in my room doing nothing.'

Madame was sitting, or rather reclining in a low arm-chair, when I entered the room, close to the fire, as was her wont, her feet extended near to the bars, and a little coffee equipage beside her. She stuffed a book hastily between her dress and the chair, and received me in a state of languor which, had it not been for Mrs. Rusk's comfortable assurances, would have frightened me.

'I hope you are better, Madame', I said, approaching.

'Better than I deserve, my dear cheaile, sufficiently well. The people are all so good, trying me with every little thing, like a bird; here is caffé—Mrs. Rusk-a, poor woman, I try to swallow a little, to please her.'

'And your cold, is it better?'

She shook her head languidly, her elbow resting on the chair and three finger-tips supporting her forehead, and then she made a little sigh, looking down from the corners of her eyes, in an interesting dejection.

'Je sens des lassitudes in all the members—but I am quaite 'appy, and though I suffer I am console and oblige des bontés, ma chère, que vous avez tout pour moi,'* and with these words she turned a languid glance of gratitude on me which dropped on the ground.

'Lady Knollys wishes very much to see you, only for a few minutes, if you could admit her.'

'Vous savez les malades see *never* visitors,' she replied with a startled sort of tartness, and a momentary energy. 'Besides, I cannot converse; je sens de temps en temps des douleurs de tête—of head, and of the ear, the right ear, it is parfois agony absolutely, and now it is here.'

And she winced and moaned, with her eyes closed and her hand pressed to the organ affected.

Simple as I was, I felt instinctively that Madame was shamming. She was over-acting; her transitions were too violent, and beside she forgot that I knew how well she could speak English, and must perceive that she was heightening the interest of her helplessness by that pretty tessellation of foreign idiom. I therefore said with a kind of courage which sometimes helped me suddenly—

'Oh, Madame, don't you really think you might, without much inconvenience, see Lady Knollys for a very few minutes?'

'Cruel cheaile! you know I have a pain of the ear which makes me 'orribly suffer at this moment, and you demand me whether I will not converse with strangers. I did not think you would be so unkain, Maud; but it is impossible, you must see—quaite impossible. I never, you *know*, refuse to take trouble when I am able—never— *never*.'

And Madame shed some tears, which always came at call, and with her hand pressed to her ear, said very faintly.

'Be so good to tell your friend how you see me, and how I suffer, and leave me, Maud, for I wish to lie down for a little, since the pain will not allow me to remain longer.'

So with a few words of comfort which could not well be refused, but I dare say betraying my suspicion that more was made of her sufferings than need be, I returned to the drawing-room.

'Captain Oakley has been here, my dear, and fancying, I suppose, that you had left us for the evening, has gone to the billiard-room, I think,' said Lady Knollys, as I entered.

That, then, accounted for the rumble and smack of balls which I had heard as I passed the door.

'I have been telling Maud how detestably she is got up.'

'Very thoughtful of you, Monica!' said my father.

'Yes, and really, Austin, it is quite clear you ought to marry; you want some one to take this girl out, and look after her, and who's to do it? She's a dowdy—don't you see? Such a dust! and it *is* really such a pity; for she's a very pretty creature, and a clever woman could make her quite charming.'

My father took Cousin Monica's sallies with the most wonderful good humour. She had always, I fancy, been a privileged person, and my father, whom we all feared, received her jolly attacks, as I fancy the grim Fron-de-Bœufs* of old accepted the humours and personalities of their jesters.

'Am I to accept this as an overture?' said my father to his voluble cousin.

'Yes, you may, but not for myself, Austin—I'm not worthy. Do you remember little Kitty Weadon that I wanted you to marry eight-and-twenty years ago, or more, with a hundred and twenty thousand pounds? Well, you know, she has got ever so much now, and she is really a most amiable old thing, and though *you* would not have her then, she has had her second husband since, I can tell you.'

'I'm glad I was not the first,' said my father.

'Well, they really say her wealth is absolutely immense. Her last husband, the Russian merchant, left her everything. She has not a human relation, and she is in the best set.'

'You were always a match-maker, Monica,' said my father, stopping, and putting his hand kindly on hers. 'But it won't do. No, no, Monica; we must take care of little Maud some other way.'

I was relieved. We women have all an instinctive dread of second marriages, and think that no widower is quite above or below that danger; and I remember, whenever my father, which indeed was but seldom, made a visit to town or anywhere else, it was a saying of Mrs. Rusk—

'I shan't wonder, neither need you, my dear, if he brings home a young wife with him.'

So my father, with a kind look at her, and a very tender one on me, went silently to the library, as he often did about that hour.

I could not help resenting my Cousin Knollys' officious recommendation of matrimony. Nothing I dreaded more than a step-mother. Good Mrs. Rusk and Mary Quince, in their several ways, used to enhance, by occasional anecdotes and frequent reflections, the terrors of such an intrusion. I suppose they did not wish a revolution and all its consequences at Knowl; and thought it no harm to excite my vigilance.

But it was impossible long to be vexed with Cousin Monica.

'You know, my dear, your father is an oddity,' she said, 'I don't mind him—I never did. You must not. Cracky, my dear, cracky—decidedly cracky!'

And she tapped the corner of her forehead, with a look so sly and comical, that I think I should have laughed, if the sentiment had not been so awfully irreverent.

'Well, dear, how is our friend the milliner?'

'Madame is suffering so much from pain in her ear, that she says it would be quite impossible to have the honour—'

'Honour—fiddle! I want to see what the woman's like. Pain in her ear, you say? Poor thing! Well, dear, I think I can cure that in five minutes. I have it myself, now and then. Come to my room, and we'll get the bottles.'

So she lighted her candle in the lobby, and with a light and agile step she scaled the stairs, I following; and having found the remedies, we approached Madame's room together.

I think, while we were still at the end of the gallery, Madame heard and divined our approach, for her door suddenly shut, and there was a fumbling at the handle. But the bolt was out of order.

Lady Knollys tapped at the door, saying—'We'll come in, please, and see you. I've some remedies, which I'm sure will do you good.'

There was no answer; so she opened the door, and we both entered. Madame had rolled herself in the blue coverlet, and was lying on the bed, with her face buried in the pillow, and enveloped in the covering.

'Perhaps she's asleep?' said Lady Knollys, getting round to the side of the bed, and stooping over her.

Madame lay still as a mouse. Cousin Monica set down her two little vials on the table, and, stooping again over the bed, began very gently with her fingers to lift the coverlet that covered her face. Madame uttered a slumbering moan, and turned more upon her face, clasping the coverlet faster about her.

'Madame, it is Maud and Lady Knollys. We have come to relieve your ear. Pray let me see it. She can't be asleep, she's holding the clothes so fast. Do, pray, allow me to see it.'

PERHAPS, if Madame had murmured, 'It is quite well—pray permit me to sleep,' she would have escaped an awkwardness. But having adopted the rôle of the exhausted slumberer, she could not consistently speak at the moment; neither would it do, by main force, to hold the coverlet about her face: and so her presence of mind forsook her, and Cousin Monica drew it back, and hardly beheld the profile of the sufferer, when her good-humoured face was lined and shadowed with a dark curiosity and a surprise by no means pleasant; and she stood erect beside the bed, with her mouth firmly shut and drawn down at the corners, in a sort of recoil and perturbation, looking down upon the patient.

'So, that's Madame de la Rougierre?' at length exclaimed Lady Knollys, with a very stately disdain. I think I never saw any one look more shocked.

Madame sat up, very flushed. No wonder, for she had been wrapped so close in the coverlet. She did not look quite at Lady Knollys, but straight before her, rather downward, and very luridly.

I was very much frightened and amazed, and felt on the point of bursting into tears.

'So, Mademoiselle, you have married, it seems, since I had last the honour of seeing you? I did not recognize Mademoiselle under her new name.'

'Yes—I *am* married, Lady Knollys; I thought every one who knew me had heard of that. Very respectably married, for a person of my rank. I shall not need long the life of a governess. There is no harm, I hope?'

'I hope not,' said Lady Knollys, drily, a little pale, and still looking with a dark sort of wonder upon the flushed face and forehead of the governess, who was looking downward, straight before her, very sulkily and disconcerted.

'I suppose you have explained everything satisfactorily to Mr. Ruthyn, in whose house I find you?' said Cousin Monica.

'Yes, certainly—everything he requires—in effect there is *nothing* to explain. I am ready to answer to any question. Let *him* demand me.'

'Very good, Mademoiselle.'

'*Madame*, if you please.'

'I forgot—*Madame*—yes. I shall apprise him of everything.'

Madame turned upon her a peaked and malign look, smiling askance with a stealthy scorn.

'For myself, I have nothing to conceal. I have always done my duty. What fine scene about nothing absolutely—what charming remedies for a sick person—ma foi! how much oblige I am for these so amiable attentions.'

'So far as I can see, Mademoiselle—Madame, I mean—you don't stand very much in need of remedies. Your ear and head don't seem to trouble you just now. I fancy these pains may now be dismissed.'

Lady Knollys was now speaking French.

'Mi ladi has diverted my attention for a moment, but that does not prevent that I suffer frightfully. I am, of course, only poor governess, and such people perhaps ought not to have pain—at least to show when they suffer. It is permitted us to die, but not to be sick.'

'Come, Maud, my dear, let us leave the invalid to her repose and to nature. I don't think she needs my chloroform and opium at present.'

'Mi ladi is herself a physic which chases many things, and powerfully affects the ear. I would wish to sleep, notwithstanding, and can but gain that in silence, if it pleases mi ladi.'

'Come, my dear,' said Lady Knollys, without again glancing at the scowling, smiling, swarthy face in the bed; 'let us leave your instructress to her *comforts*.'

'The room smells all over of brandy, my dear—does she drink?' said Lady Knollys, as she closed the door, a little sharply.

I am sure I looked as much amazed as I felt, at an imputation which then seemed to me so entirely incredible.

'Good little simpleton!' said Cousin Monica, smiling in my face, and bestowing a little kiss on my cheek; 'such a thing as a tipsy lady has never been dreamt of in your philosophy.* Well, we live and learn. Let us have our tea in my room—the gentlemen, I dare say, have retired.'

I assented, of course, and we had tea very cosily by her bedroom fire.

'How long have you had that woman?' she asked suddenly, after, for her, a very long rumination.

'She came in the beginning of February—nearly ten months ago—is not it?'

'And who sent her?'

'I really don't know; papa tells me so little—he arranged it all himself, I think.'

Cousin Monica made a sound of acquiescence—her lips closed, and a nod, frowning hard at the bars.

'It *is* very odd!' she said; 'how people *can* be such fools!' Here there came a little pause. 'And what sort of person is she—do you like her?'

'Very well—that is, *pretty* well. You won't tell?—but she rather frightens me. I'm sure she does not intend it, but somehow I am very much afraid of her.'

'She does not beat you?' said Cousin Monica, with an incipient frenzy in her face that made me love her.

'Oh, no!'

'Nor ill-use you in any way?'

'No.'

'Upon your honour and word, Maud?'

'No, upon my honour.'

'You know I won't tell her anything you say to me; and I only want to know, that I may put an end to it, my poor little cousin.'

'Thank you, Cousin Monica, very much; but really and truly she does not ill-use me.'

'Nor threaten you, child?'

'Well, *no*—no, she does not threaten.'

'And how the plague *does* she frighten you, child?'

'Well, I really—I'm half ashamed to tell you—you'll laugh at me—and I don't know that she wishes to frighten me. But there is something, is not there, ghosty, you know, about her?'

'*Ghosty*—is there? well, I'm sure I don't know, but I suspect there's something devilish—I mean, she seems roguish—does not she? And I really think she has had neither cold nor pain, but has just been shamming sickness, to keep out of my way.'

I perceived plainly enough that Cousin Monica's damnatory epithet referred to some retrospective knowledge, which she was not going to disclose to me.

'You knew Madame before,' I said. 'Who is she?'

'She assures me she is Madame de la Rougierre, and, I suppose, in French phrase she so calls herself,' answered Lady Knollys, with a laugh, but uncomfortably I thought.

'Oh, dear Cousin Monica, do tell me—is she—is she very wicked? I am so afraid of her.'

'How should I know, dear Maud? But I do remember her face, and I don't very much like her, and you may depend on it I will speak to your father in the morning about her, and don't, darling', ask me any more about her, for I really have not very much to tell that you would care to hear, and the fact is I *won't* say any more about her—there!'

And Cousin Monica laughed, and gave me a little slap on the cheek, and then a kiss.

'Well, just tell me this'—

'Well, I *won't* tell you this, nor anything—not a word, curious little woman. The fact is I have little to tell, and I mean to speak to your father, and he, I am sure, will do what is right; so don't ask me any more, and let us talk of something pleasanter.'

There was something indescribably winning, it seemed to me, in Cousin Monica. Old as she was, she seemed to me so girlish, compared with those slow, unexceptionable, young ladies whom I had met in my few visits at the county houses. By this time my shyness was quite gone, and I was on the most intimate terms with her.

'You know a great deal about her, Cousin Monica, but you won't tell me.'

'Nothing I should like better, if I were at liberty, little rogue; but you know, after all, I don't really say whether I *do* know anything about her or not, or what sort of knowledge it is. But tell me what you mean by ghosty, and all about it.'

So I recounted my experiences, to which, so far from laughing at me, she listened with very special gravity.

'Does she write and receive many letters?'

I had seen her write letters, and supposed, though I could only recollect one or two, that she received in proportion.

'Are *you* Mary Quince?' asked my lady cousin.

Mary was arranging the window-curtains and turned, dropping a courtesy affirmatively toward her.

'You wait on my little cousin, Miss Ruthyn, don't you?'

'Yes, 'm,' said Mary in her genteelest way.

'Does any one sleep in her room?'

'Yes 'm, *I*—please, my lady.'

'And no one else?'

'No 'm—please, my lady.'

'Not even the *governess*, sometimes?'

'No, please my lady.'

'Never, you are quite sure, my dear?' said Lady Knollys, transferring the question to me.

'Oh no, never,' I answered.

Cousin Monica mused gravely, I fancied even anxiously into the grate; then stirred her tea and sipped it, still looking into the same point of our cheery fire.

'I like your face, Mary Quince; I'm sure you are a good creature,' she said, suddenly turning toward her with a pleasant countenance. 'I'm very glad you have got her, dear. I wonder whether Austin has gone to his bed yet!'

'I think not. I am certain he is either in the library or in his private room—papa often reads or prays alone at night, and—and he does not like to be interrupted.'

'No, no; of course not—it will do very well in the morning.'

Lady Knollys was thinking deeply, as it seemed to me.

'And so you are afraid of goblins, my dear,' she said at last, with a faded sort of smile, turning toward me; 'well, if *I* were, I know what *I* should do—so soon as I and good Mary Quince here, had got into my bed-chamber for the night, I should stir the fire into a good blaze, and bolt the door—do you see, Mary Quince?—bolt the door and keep a candle lighted all night. You'll be very attentive to her, Mary Quince, for I—I don't think she is very strong, and she must not grow nervous: so get to bed early, and don't leave her alone—do you see?—and—and remember to bolt the door, Mary Quince, and I shall be sending a little Christmas box to my cousin, and I shan't forget you. Goodnight.'

And with a pleasant courtesy* Mary fluttered out of the room.

CHAPTER XII

A CURIOUS CONVERSATION

WE each had another cup of tea, and were silent for awhile.

'We must not talk of ghosts now. You are a superstitious little woman, you know, and you shan't be frightened.'

And now Cousin Monica grew silent again, and looking briskly round the room, like a lady in search of a subject, her eye rested on a small oval portrait, graceful, brightly tinted, in the French style, representing a pretty little boy, with rich golden hair, large soft eyes, delicate features, and a shy, peculiar expression.

'It is odd; I think I remember that pretty little sketch, very long ago. I think I was then myself a child, but that is a much older style of dress and of wearing the hair, too, than I ever saw. I am just forty-nine now. Oh dear, yes; that is a good while before I was *born*. What a strange, pretty little boy—a mysterious little fellow. Is he quite sincere, I wonder? What rich golden hair! It is very clever—a French artist, I dare say—and who *is* that little boy?'

'I never heard. Some one a hundred years ago, I dare say. But there is a picture down stairs I am so anxious to ask you about.'

'Oh!' murmured Lady Knollys, still gazing dreamily on the crayon.

'It is the full-length picture of Uncle Silas—I want to ask you about him.'

At mention of his name my cousin gave me a look so sudden and odd as to amount almost to a start.

'Your Uncle Silas, dear? It is very odd, I was just thinking of him'; and she laughed a little.

'Wondering whether that little boy could be he.'

And up jumped active Cousin Monica, with a candle in her hand, upon a chair, and scrutinized the border of the sketch for a name or a date.

'Maybe on the back?' said she.

And so she unhung it, and there, true enough, not on the back of the drawing, but of the frame, which was just as good, in pen and ink round Italian letters, hardly distinguishable now from the discoloured wood, we traced—

'*Silas Aylmer Ruthyn, Ætate* viii. 15 *May*, 1779.'

'It is very odd I should not have been told or remembered who it was. I think if I had *ever* been told I *should* have remembered it. I do recollect this picture, though, I am nearly certain. What a singular child's face!'

And my cousin leaned over it with a candle on each side, and her hand shading her eyes, as if seeking by aid of these fair and half-formed lineaments to read an enigma.

The childish features defied her, I suppose; their secret was unfathomable, for after a good while she raised her head, still looking at the portrait, and sighed.

'A very singular face,' she said, softly, as a person might who was looking into a coffin. 'Had not we better replace it?'

So the pretty oval, containing the fair golden hair and large eyes, the pale, unfathomable sphinx, remounted to its nail, and the *funeste* and beautiful child seemed to smile down oracularly on our conjectures.

'So is the face in the large portrait—*very* singular—more, I think, than that—handsomer too. This is a sickly child, I think; but the full length is so manly, though so slender, and so handsome too. I always think him a hero and a mystery, and they won't tell me about him, and I can only dream and wonder.'

'He has made more people than you dream and wonder, my dear Maud. I don't know what to make of him. He is a sort of idol, you know, of your father's, and yet I don't think he helps him much. His abilities were singular; so has been his misfortune; for the rest, my dear, he is neither a hero nor a wonder. So far as I know, there are very few sublime men going about the world.'

'You really must tell me all you know about him, Cousin Monica. Now don't refuse.'

'But why should you care to hear? There is really nothing pleasant to tell.'

'That is just the reason I wish it. If it were at all pleasant it would be quite commonplace. I like to hear of adventures, dangers, and misfortunes, and above all, I love a mystery. You know, papa will never tell me, and I dare not ask him; not that he is ever unkind, but, somehow, I am afraid; and neither Mrs. Rusk nor Mary Quince will tell me anything, although I suspect they know a good deal.'

'I don't see any good in telling you, dear, nor, to say the truth, any great harm either.'

'No—now that's *quite* true—no harm. There *can't* be, for I *must* know it all some day, you know, and better now, and from *you*, than perhaps from a stranger, and in a less favourable way.'

'Upon my word, it is a wise little woman; and really, that's not such bad sense after all.'

So we poured out another cup of tea each, and sipped it very comfortably by the fire, while Lady Knollys talked on, and her animated face helped the strange story.

'It is not very much, after all. Your Uncle Silas, you know, is living?'

'Oh, yes, in Derbyshire.'

'So I see you do know something of him, sly girl! but no matter. You know how very rich your father is; but Silas was the younger brother, and had little more than a thousand a year. If he had not played, and did not care to marry, it would have been quite enough—ever so much more than younger sons of dukes often have; but he was—well, a *mauvais sujet*—you know what that is. I don't want to say any ill of him—more than I really know—but he was fond of his pleasures, I suppose, like other young men, and he played, and was always losing, and your father for a long time paid great sums for him. I believe he was really a most expensive and vicious young man; and I fancy he does not deny that now, for they say he would change the past if he could.'

I was looking at the pensive little boy in the oval frame—aged eight years—who was, a few springs later, 'a most expensive and vicious young man', and was now a suffering and outcast old one, and wondering from what a small seed the hemlock or the wallflower grows, and how microscopic are the beginnings of the kingdom of God or of the mystery of iniquity in a human being's heart.

'Austin—your papa—was very kind to him—*very;* but then, you know, he's an oddity, dear—he *is* an oddity, though no one may have told you before—and he never forgave him for his marriage. Your father, I suppose, knew more about the lady than I did—I was young then—but there were various reports, none of them pleasant, and she was not visited, and for some time there was a complete estrangement between your father and your Uncle Silas; and it was made up, rather oddly, on the very occasion which some people said ought to have totally separated them. Did you ever hear anything—anything *very* remarkable—about your uncle?'

'No, never; they would not tell me, though I am sure they know. Pray go on.'

'Well, Maud, as I have begun, I'll complete the story, though perhaps it might have been better untold. It was something rather shocking—indeed, *very* shocking; in fact, they insisted on suspecting him of having committed a murder.'

I stared at my cousin for some time, and then at the little boy, so refined, so beautiful, so *funeste*, in the oval frame.

'Yes, dear,' said she, her eyes following mine; 'who'd have supposed he could ever have—have fallen under so horrible a suspicion?'

'The wretches! Of course, Uncle Silas—of course, he's innocent?' I said at last.

'Of course, my dear,' said Cousin Monica, with an odd look; 'but you know there are some things as bad almost to be suspected of as to have done, and the country gentlemen chose to suspect him. They did not like him, you see. His politics vexed them; and he resented their treatment of his wife—though I really think, poor Silas, he did not care a pin about her—and he annoyed them whenever he could. Your papa, you know, is very proud of his family—*he* never had the slightest suspicion of your uncle.'

'Oh, no!' I cried vehemently.

'That's right, Maud Ruthyn,' said Cousin Monica, with a sad little smile and a nod. 'And your papa was, you may suppose, very angry.'

'Of course he was,' I exclaimed.

'You have no idea, my dear, *how* angry. He directed his attorney to prosecute, by wholesale, all who had said a word affecting your uncle's character. But the lawyers were against it, and then your uncle tried to fight his way through it, but the men would not meet him. He was quite slurred. Your father went up and saw the Minister. He wanted to have him a Deputy-Lieutenant, or something, in his county. Your papa, you know, had a very great influence with the Government. Beside his county influence he had two boroughs* then. But the Minister was afraid, the feeling was so very strong. They offered him something in the Colonies, but your father would not hear of it—that would have been a banishment, you know. They would have given your father a peerage to make it up, but he would not accept it, and broke with the party. Except in that way—which, you know, was connected with the reputation of the family—I don't think, considering his great wealth, he has done very much for Silas. To say truth, however, he was very liberal before his marriage. Old Mrs. Aylmer says he made a vow *then* that Silas should never have more than five hundred a-year, which he still allows him. I believe, and he permits him to live in the place. But they say it is in a very wild, neglected state.'

'You live in the same county—have you seen it lately, Cousin Monica?'

'No, not very lately,' said Cousin Monica, and began to hum an air abstractedly.

NEXT morning early I visited my favourite full-length portrait in the chocolate coat and top-boots. Scanty as had been my cousin Monica's notes upon this dark and eccentric biography, they were everything to me. A soul had entered that enchanted form. Truth had passed by with her torch, and a sad light shone for a moment on that enigmatic face.

There stood the *roué*—the duellist—and, with all his faults, the hero too! In that dark large eye lurked the profound and fiery enthusiasm of his ill-starred passion. In the thin but exquisite lip I read the courage of the paladin, who would have 'fought his way', though single-handed, against all the magnates of his county, and by ordeal of battle have purged the honour of the Ruthyns. There in that delicate half-sarcastic tracery of the nostril I detected the intellectual defiance which had politically isolated Silas Ruthyn and opposed him to the landed oligarchy of his county, whose retaliation had been a hideous slander. There, too, and on his brows and lip, I traced the patience of a cold disdain. I could now see him as he was—the prodigal, the hero, and the martyr. I stood gazing on him with a girlish interest and admiration. There was indignation, there was pity, there was hope. Some day it might come to pass that I, girl as I was, might contribute by word or deed towards the vindication of that long-suffering, gallant, and romantic prodigal. It was a flicker of the Joan of Arc inspiration, common, I fancy, to many girls. I little then imagined how profoundly and strangely involved my uncle's fate would one day become with mine.

I was interrupted by Captain Oakley's voice at the window. He was leaning on the windowsill, and looking in with a smile—the window being open, the morning sunny, and his cap lifted in his hand.

'Good-morning, Miss Ruthyn. What a charming old place! quite the setting for a romance; such timber, and this really *beautiful* house. I *do* so like these white and black houses—wonderful old things. By-the-by, you treated us very badly last night—you did, indeed; upon my word, now, it really was too bad—running away, and drinking tea with Lady Knollys—so she says. I really—I should not like to tell you how very savage I felt, particularly considering how very short my time is.'

I was a shy, but not a giggling country miss. I knew I was an heiress; I knew I was somebody. I was not the least bit in the world conceited, but I think this knowledge helped to give me a certain sense of security and self-possession, which might have been mistaken for dignity or simplicity. I am sure I looked at him with a fearless inquiry, for he answered my thoughts.

'I do really assure you, Miss Ruthyn, I am quite serious; you have no idea how very much we missed you.'

There was a little pause, and, I believe, like a fool, I lowered my eyes, and blushed.

'I—I was thinking of leaving to-day; I am so unfortunate—my leave is just out—it *is* so unlucky; but I don't quite know whether my Aunt Knollys will allow me to go.'

'*I?*—certainly, my dear Charlie, *I* don't want you at all,' exclaimed a voice—Lady Knollys's—briskly, from an open window close by; 'what could put that in your head, dear?'

And in went my cousin's head, and the window shut down.

'She is *such* an oddity, poor dear Aunt Knollys,' murmured the young man, ever so little put out, and he laughed. 'I never know quite what she wishes, or how to please her; but she's *so* good-natured; and when she goes to town for the season—she does not always, you know—her house is really very gay—you can't think—'

Here again he was interrupted, for the door opened, and Lady Knollys entered. 'And you know, Charles,' she continued, 'it would not do to forget your visit to Snodhurst; you wrote, you know, and you have only to-night and to-morrow. You are thinking of nothing but that moor; I heard you talking to the gamekeeper; I know he is—is not he, Maud, the brown man with great whiskers, and leggings? I'm very sorry, you know, but I really must spoil your shooting, for they do expect you at Snodhurst, Charlie; and do not you think this window a little too much for Miss Ruthyn? Maud, my dear, the air is very sharp; shut it down, Charles, and you'd better tell them to get a fly for you from the town after luncheon. Come, dear,' she said to me. 'Was not that the breakfast bell? Why does not your papa get a gong—it is so hard to know one bell from another?'

I saw that Captain Oakley lingered for a last look, but I did not give it, and went out smiling with Cousin Knollys, and wondering why old ladies are so uniformly disagreeable.

In the lobby she said, with an odd goodnatured look—

'Don't allow any of his love-making, my dear. Charles Oakley has not a guinea, and an heiress would be very convenient. Of course, he has his eyes about him. Charles is not by any means foolish; and I should not be at all sorry to see him well married, for I don't think he will do much good any other way; but there are degrees, and his ideas are sometimes very impertinent.'

I was an admiring reader of the *Albums*, the *Souvenirs*, the *Keepsakes*,* and all that flood of Christmas present lore which yearly irrigated England, with pretty covers and engravings; and floods of elegant twaddle—the milk, not destitute of water, on which the babes of literature were then fed. On this, my genius throve. I had a little album, enriched with many gems of original thought and observation, which I jotted down in suitable language. Lately, turning over these faded leaves of rhyme and prose, I lighted, under this day's date, upon the following sage reflection, with my name appended:—

'Is there not in the female heart an ineradicable jealousy, which, if it sways the passions of the young, rules also the *advice* of the *aged?* Do they not grudge to youth the sentiments (though Heaven knows how *shadowed* with sorrow) which they can *no longer inspire*, perhaps even *experience;* and does not youth, in turn, sigh over the envy which has *power* to *blight?*
                                          'MAUD AYLMER RUTHYN.'

'He has not been making love to me,' I said, rather tartly, 'and he does not seem to me at all impertinent, and I really don't care the least whether he goes or stays.'

Cousin Monica looked in my face with her odd waggish smile, and laughed.

'You'll understand those London dandies better some day, dear Maud; they are very well, but they like money—not to keep, of course—but still they like it and know its value.'

At breakfast my father told Captain Oakley where he might have shooting, or if he preferred going to Dilsford, only half an hour's ride, he might have his choice of hunters, and find the dogs there that morning.

The Captain smiled archly at me, and looked at his aunt. There was a suspense. I hope I did not show how much I was interested—but it would not do. Cousin Monica was inexorable.

'Hunting, hawking, fishing, fiddle-de-dee! You know Charlie, my dear, it is quite out of the question. He is going to Snodhurst this afternoon, and without quite a rudeness, in which I should be involved too, he really can't—you know you can't, Charles! and—and he *must* go and keep his engagement.'

So papa acquiesced with a polite regret, and hoped another time.

'Oh, leave all that to me. When you want him only write me a note, and I'll send him or bring him if you let me. I always know where to find him—don't I, Charlie?—and we shall be only too happy.'

Aunt Monica's influence with her nephew was special, for she 'tipped' him handsomely every now and then, and he had formed for himself agreeable expectations, besides, respecting her will. I felt rather angry at his submitting to this sort of tutelage, knowing nothing of its motive; I was also disgusted by Cousin Monica's tyranny.

So soon as he had left the room Lady Knollys, not minding me, said briskly to papa, 'Never let that young man into your house again. I found him making speeches, this morning, to little Maud here; and he really has not two pence in the world—it is amazing impudence—and you know such absurd things do happen.'

'Come, Maud, what compliments did he pay you?' asked my father.

I was vexed, and therefore spoke courageously. 'His compliments were not to me; they were all to the house,' I said, drily.

'Quite as it should be—the house, of course; it is that he's in love with,' said Cousin Knollys.

"'Twas on a widow's jointure land,
The archer, Cupid, took his stand.'*

'Hey! I don't quite understand,' said my father, slily.

'Tut! Austin; you forget Charlie is my nephew.'

'So I did,' said my father.

'Therefore the literal widow in this case *can* have no interest in view but one, and that is your's and Maud's. I wish him well, but he shan't put my little cousin and her expectations into his empty pocket—*not* a bit of it. And *there's* another reason, Austin, why you should marry—you have no eye for these things—whereas a clever *woman* would see at a glance and prevent mischief.'

'So she would,' acquiesced my father, in his gloomy, amused way. 'Maud, you must try to be a clever woman.'

'So she will in her time, but that is not come yet; and I tell you, Austin Ruthyn, if you won't look about and marry somebody, somebody may possibly marry you.'

'You were always an oracle, Monica; but *here* I am lost in total per-plexity,' said my father.

'Yes; sharks sailing round you, with keen eyes and large throats; and you have come to the age precisely when men *are* swallowed up alive like Jonah.'*

'Thank you for the parallel, but you know that was not a happy union, even for the fish, and there was a separation in a few days; not that I mean to trust to that; but there's no one to throw me into the jaws of the monster, and I've no notion of jumping there; and the fact is, Monica, there's no monster at all.'

'I'm not so sure.'

'But I'm quite sure,' said my father, a little drily. 'You forget how old I am, and how long I've lived alone—I and little Maud;' and he smiled and smoothed my hair, and I thought sighed.

'No one is ever too old to do a foolish thing,' began Lady Knollys.

'Nor to say a foolish thing, Monica. This has gone on too long. Don't you see that little Maud there is silly enough to be frightened at your fun.'

So I was, but I could not divine how he guessed it.

'And well or ill, wisely or madly, I'll *never* marry; so put that out of your head.'

This was addressed rather to me, I think than to Lady Knollys, who smiled a little waggishly on me, and said—

'To be sure, Maud; maybe you are right; a stepdame is a risk, and I ought to have asked you first what you thought of it; and upon my honour,' she continued merrily but kindly, observing that my eyes, I know not exactly from what feeling, filled with tears, 'I'll never again advise your papa to marry, unless you first tell me you wish it.'

This was a great deal from Lady Knollys, who had a taste for advis-ing her friends and managing their affairs.

'I've a great respect for instinct. I believe, Austin, it is truer than reason, and yours and Maud's are both against me, though I know I have reason on my side.'

My father's brief wintry smile answered, and Cousin Monica kissed me, and said—

'I've been so long my own mistress that I sometimes forget there are such things as fear and jealousy; and are you going to your governess, Maud?'

CHAPTER XIV

ANGRY WORDS

I WAS going to my governess, as Lady Knollys said; and so I went. The undefinable sense of danger that smote me whenever I beheld that woman had deepened since last night's occurrence, and was taken out of the region of instinct or prepossession by the strange though slight indications of recognition and abhorrence which I had witnessed in Lady Knollys on that occasion.

The tone in which Cousin Monica had asked, 'are you going to your governess?' and the curious grave, and anxious look that accompanied the question disturbed me; and there was something odd and cold in the tone as if a remembrance had suddenly chilled her. The accent remained in my ear, and the sharp brooding look was fixed before me as I glided up the broad dark stairs to Madame de la Rougierre's chamber.

She had not come down to the school-room, as the scene of my studies was called. She had decided on having a relapse, and accordingly had not made her appearance down-stairs that morning. The gallery leading to her room was dark and lonely, and I grew more nervous as I approached; I paused at the door, making up my mind to knock.

But the door opened suddenly, and, like a magic-lantern figure, presented with a snap, appeared close before my eyes, the great muffled face, with the forbidding smirk, of Madame de la Rougierre.

'Wat you mean, my dear cheaile?' she inquired with a malevolent shrewdness in her eyes, and her hollow smile all the time disconcerting me more even than the suddenness of her appearance; 'wat for you approach so softly? I do not sleep, you see, but you feared, perhaps, to have the misfortune of wakening me, and so you came—is it not so?—to leesten, and looke in very gently; you want to know how I was. Vous êtes bien aimable d'avoir pensé à moi. Bah!' she cried, suddenly bursting through her irony. 'Wy could not Lady Knollys come herself and leesten to the keyhole to make her report? Fidon, wat is there to conceal? Nothing. Enter if you please. Every one they are welcome!' and she flung the door wide, turned her back upon me, and with an ejaculation which I did not understand, strode into the room.

'I did not come with any intention, Madame, to pry or to intrude—you don't think so—you *can't* think so—you can't possibly mean to insinuate anything so insulting!'

I was very angry, and my tremors had all vanished now.

'No, not for *you*, dear cheaile; I was thinking to miladi Knollys, who, without cause, is my enemy. Every one has enemy; you will learn all that so soon as you are little older, and without cause she is mine. Come, Maud, speak a the truth—was it not miladi Knollys who sent you here doucement, doucement, so quaite to my door—is not so, little rogue?'

Madame had confronted me again, and we were now standing in the middle of her floor.

I indignantly repelled the charge, and searching me for a moment with her oddly-shaped cunning eyes, she said—

'That is good cheaile, you speak a so direct—I like that, and am glad to hear; but, my dear Maud, that woman—'

'Lady Knollys is papa's cousin,' I interposed a little gravely.

'She does hate a me so, you 'av no idea. She 'as tryed to injure me several times, and would employ the most innocent person, unconsciously you know, my dear, to assist her malice.'

Here Madame wept a little. I had already discovered that she could shed tears whenever she pleased. I have heard of such persons, but I never met another before or since.

Madame was unusually frank—no one ever knew better when to be candid. At present I suppose she concluded that Lady Knollys would certainly relate whatever she knew concerning her before she left Knowl; and so Madame's reserves, whatever they might be, were dissolving, and she growing childlike and confiding.

'Et comment va monsieur votre père aujourd'hui?'

'Very well,' I thanked her.

'And how long miladi Knollys' her visit is likely to be?'

'I could not say exactly, but for some days.'

'Eh bien, my dear cheaile, I find myself better this morning, and we must return to our lessons. Je veux m'habiller, ma chère Maud, you will wait me in the school-room.'

By this time Madame, who, though lazy, could make an effort, and was capable of getting into a sudden hurry, had placed herself before her dressing-table, and was ogling her discoloured and bony countenance in the glass.

'Wat horror! I am so pale. Quel ennui! wat bore! Ow weak 'av I grow in two three days!'

And she practised some plaintive, invalid glances into the mirror. But on a sudden there came a little sharp inquisitive frown as she looked over the frame of the glass, upon the terrace beneath. It was only a glance, and she sat down languidly in her arm-chair to prepare, I suppose, for the fatigues of the toilet.

My curiosity was sufficiently aroused to induce me to ask—

'But why, Madame, do you fancy that Lady Knollys dislikes you?'

''Tis not fancy, my dear Maud. Ah, ha, no! Mais c'est toute une histoire—too tedious to tell now—some time maybe—and you will learn when you are little older, the most violent hatreds often they are the most without cause. But, my dear cheaile, the hours they are running from us, and I must dress. Vite, vite! so you run away to the school-room, and I will come after.'

Madame had her dressing-case, and her mysteries, and palpably stood in need of repairs; so away I went to my studies. The room which we called the school-room was partly beneath the floor of Madame's bed-chamber, and commanded the same view; so, remembering my governess's peering glance from her windows, I looked out, and saw Cousin Monica making a brisk promenade up and down the terrace-walk. Well, that was quite enough to account for it. I had grown very curious, and I resolved when our lessons were over to join her and make another attempt to discover the mystery.

As I sat over my books, I fancied I heard a movement outside the door. I suspected that Madame was listening. I waited for a time, expecting to see the door open, but she did not come; so I opened it suddenly myself, but Madame was not on the threshold nor on the lobby. I heard a rustling, however, and on the staircase over the banister I saw the folds of her silk dress as she descended.

She is going, I thought, to seek an interview with Lady Knollys. She intends to propitiate that dangerous lady; so I amused some eight or ten minutes in watching Cousin Monica's quick march and right-about-face upon the parade-ground of the terrace. But no one joined her.

'She is certainly talking to papa,' was my next and more probable conjecture. Having the profoundest distrust of Madame, I was naturally extremely jealous of the confidential interviews in which deceit and malice might make their representations plausibly and without answer.

'Yes, I'll run down and see—see *papa*; she shan't tell lies behind my back, horrid woman!'

At the study door I knocked, and forthwith entered. My father was sitting near the window, his open book before him, Madame standing at the other side of the table, her cunning eyes bathed in tears, and her pocket-handkerchief pressed to her mouth. Her eyes glittered stealthily on me for an instant: she was sobbing—désolé, in fact—that grim grenadier lady, and her attitude was exquisitely dejected and timid. But she was, notwithstanding, reading closely and craftily my father's face. He was not looking at her, but rather upward toward the ceiling, reflectively leaning on his hand, with an expression not angry, but rather surly and annoyed.

'I ought to have heard of this before, Madame,' my father was saying as I came in; 'not that it would have made any difference—not the least; mind that. But it was the kind of thing that I ought to have heard, and the omission was not strictly right.'

Madame, in a shrill and lamentable key opened her voluble reply, but was arrested by a nod from my father, who asked me if I wanted anything.

'Only—only that I was waiting in the school-room for Madame, and did not know where she was.'

'Well, she is here, you see, and will join you up stairs in a few minutes.'

So back I went again, huffed, angry, and curious, and sate back in my chair with a clouded countenance, thinking very little about lessons.

When Madame entered I did not lift my head or eyes.

'Good cheaile! reading,' said she, as she approached briskly and reassured.

'No,' I answered tartly; 'not good, nor a child either; I'm not reading, I've been thinking.'

'Très bien!' she said, with an insufferable smile, 'thinking is very good also; but you look unhappy—very, poor cheaile. Take care you are not grow jealous for poor Madame talking sometime to your papa; you must not, little fool. It is only for a your good, my dear Maud, and I had no objection you should stay.'

'*You!* Madame!' I said loftily; I was very angry, and showed it through my dignity, to Madame's evident satisfaction.

'No—it was your papa, Mr. Ruthyn, who weesh to speak alone; for me I do not care; there was something I weesh to tell him. I don't care who know, but Mr. Ruthyn he is deeferent.'

I made no remark.

'Come, leetle Maud, you are not to be so cross; it will be much better you and I to be good friends together. Why should a we quarrel?—wat nonsense! Do you imagine I would anywhere undertake a the education of a young person unless I could speak with her parent?—wat folly! I would like to be your friend, however, my poor Maud, if you would allow—you and I together—wat you say?'

'People grow to be friends by liking, Madame, and liking comes of itself, not by bargain; I like every one who is kind to me.'

'And so I. You are like me in so many things, my dear Maud! Are you quaite well to-day? I think you look fateague, so I feel, too, vary tire. I think we weel put off the lessons to to-morrow. Eh? and we will come to play la grâce* in the garden.'

Madame was plainly in a high state of exultation. Her audience had evidently been satisfactory, and like other people, when things went well, her soul lighted up into a sulphureous good-humour, not very genuine nor pleasant, but still it was better than other moods.

I was glad when our calisthenics* were ended, and Madame had returned to her apartment, so that I had a pleasant little walk with Cousin Monica.

We women are persevering when once our curiosity is roused, but she gaily foiled mine, and I think had a mischievous pleasure in doing so. As we were going in to dress for dinner, however, she said, quite gravely—

'I am sorry, Maud, I allowed you to see that I have any unpleasant impressions about that governess lady. I shall be at liberty some day to explain all about it, and, indeed, it will be enough to tell your father, whom I have not been able to find all day; but really we are, perhaps, making too much of the matter, and I cannot say that I know anything against Madame that is conclusive, or—or, indeed, at all; but that there are reasons, and—you must not ask any more—no, you must not.'

That evening, while I was playing the overture to Cenerentola,* for the entertainment of my cousin, there arose from the tea-table, where she and my father were sitting, a spirited and rather angry harangue from Lady Knollys' lips; I turned my eyes from the music towards the speakers, the overture swooned away with a little hesitating babble into silence, and I listened.

Their conversation had begun under cover of the music which I was making, and now they were too much engrossed to perceive its discontinuance. The first sentence I heard seized my attention; my father had closed the book he was reading, upon his finger, and was leaning back in his chair, as he used to do when at all angry; his face was a little flushed, and I knew the fierce and glassy stare which expressed pride, surprise, and wrath.

'Yes, Lady Knollys, there's an animus; I know the spirit you speak in—it does you no honour,' said my father.

'And I know the spirit *you* speak in, the spirit of *madness*,' retorted Cousin Monica, just as much in earnest. 'I can't conceive how you *can* be so *demented*, Austin. What has perverted you? are you *blind*?'

'*You* are, Monica; your own unnatural prejudice—*unnatural* prejudice, blinds you. What is it all?—*nothing*. Were I to act as you say, I should be a *coward* and a traitor. I see, I *do* see, all that's real. I'm no Quixote, to draw my sword on illusions.'*

'There should be no halting here. How *can* you—do you ever *think*? I wonder you can breathe. I feel as if the evil one were in the house.'

A stern, momentary frown was my father's only answer, as he looked fixedly at her.

'People need not nail up horseshoes, and mark their door stones with charms to keep the evil spirit out,' ran on Lady Knollys, who looked as pale and angry, in her way, 'but you open your door in the dark and invoke unknown danger. How can you look at that child that's—she's *not* playing,' said Lady Knollys, abruptly stopping.

My father rose, muttering to himself, and cast a lurid glance at me, as he went in high displeasure to the door. Cousin Monica, now flushed a little, glanced also silently at me, biting the tip of her slender gold cross, and doubtful how much I had heard.

My father opened the door suddenly, which he had just closed, and looking in said, in a calmer tone—

'Perhaps, Monica, you would come for a moment to the study; I'm sure you have none but kindly feelings towards me and little Maud, there; and I thank you for your goodwill; but you must see other things more reasonably, and I think you will.'

Cousin Monica got up silently and followed him, only throwing up her eyes and hands as she did so, and I was left alone, wondering and curious more than ever.

CHAPTER XV

A WARNING

I SATE still, listening and wondering, and wondering and listening; but I ought to have known that no sound could reach me where I was from my father's study. Five minutes passed, and they did not return. Ten, fifteen. I drew near the fire and made myself comfortable in a great arm-chair, looking on the embers, but not seeing all the scenery and *dramatis personæ* of my past life or future fortunes, in their shifting glow, as people in romances usually do; but fanciful castles and caverns in blood-red and golden glare, suggestive of dreamy fairy-land, salamanders,* sunsets, and palaces of fire-kings, and all this partly shaping and partly shaped by my fancy, and leading my closing eyes and drowsy senses off into dream-land. So I nodded and dozed, and sank into a deep slumber, from which I was roused by the voice of my Cousin Monica. On opening my eyes, I saw nothing but Lady Knollys' face looking steadily into mine, and expanding into a good-natured laugh as she watched the vacant and lack-lustre stare with which I returned her gaze.

'Come, dear Maud, it is late; you ought to have been in your bed an hour ago.'

Up I stood, and so soon as I had began to hear and see aright, it struck me that Cousin Monica was more grave and subdued than I had seen her.

'Come, let us light our candles, and go together.'

Holding hands, we ascended, I sleepy, she silent; and not a word was spoken until we reached my room. Mary Quince was in waiting, and tea made.

'Tell her to come back in a few minutes; I wish to say a word to you,' said Lady Knollys.

The maid accordingly withdrew.

Lady Knollys' eyes followed her till she closed the door behind her.

'I'm going in the morning.'

'So soon!'

'Yes, dear; I could not stay; in fact I should have gone to-night, but it was too late, and I leave instead in the morning.'

'I am so sorry—so *very* sorry,' I exclaimed, in honest disappointment, and the walls seemed to darken round me, and the monotony of the old routine loomed more terrible in prospect.

'So am I, dear Maud.'

'But can't you stay a little longer; *won't* you?'

'No, Maud, I'm vexed with Austin—very much vexed with your father; in short, I can't conceive anything so entirely preposterous, and dangerous, and insane as his conduct, now that his eyes are quite opened, and I must say a word to you before I go, and it is just this:—you must cease to be a mere child, you must try and be a woman, Maud; now don't be frightened or foolish, but hear me out. That woman—what does she call herself—Rougierre? I have reason to believe is, in fact, from circumstances, *must* be your enemy; you will find her very deep, daring, and unscrupulous, I venture to say, and you can't be too much on your guard. Do you quite understand me, Maud?'

'I do,' said I, with a gasp, and my eyes fixed on her with a terrified interest, as if on a warning ghost.

'You must bridle your tongue, mind, and govern your conduct, and command even your features. It is hard to practise reserve; but you must—you must be secret and vigilant. Try and be in appearance just as usual; don't quarrel; tell her nothing, if you do happen to know anything, of your father's business; be always on your guard when with her, and keep your eye upon her everywhere. Observe everything, disclose nothing—do you see?'

'Yes,' again I whispered.

'You have good, honest servants about you, and, thank God, they don't like her. But you must not repeat to them one word I am now saying to you. Servants are fond of dropping hints, and letting things ooze out in that way, and in their quarrels with her, would compromise you—you understand me?'

'I do,' I sighed, with a wild stare.

'And—and, Maud, don't let her meddle with your food.'

Cousin Monica gave me a pale little nod, and looked away.

I could only stare at her; and under my breath I uttered an ejaculation of terror.

'Don't be so frightened; you must not be foolish; I only wish you to be upon your guard. I have my suspicions, but I may be quite wrong; your father thinks I am a fool; perhaps I am—perhaps not; maybe he may come to think as I do. But you must not speak to him on the subject; he's an odd man, and never did and never will act wisely, when his passions and prejudices are engaged.'

'Has she ever committed any great crime?' I asked, feeling as if I were on the point of fainting.

'No, dear Maud, I never said anything of the kind; don't be so frightened: I only said I have formed, from something I know, an ill opinion of her; and an unprincipled person, under temptation, is capable of a great deal. But no matter how wicked she may be, you may defy her, simply by assuming her to be so, and acting with caution; she is cunning and selfish, and she'll do nothing desperate. But I would give her no opportunity.'

'Oh, dear! Oh, Cousin Monica, don't leave me.'

'My dear, I *can't* stay; your papa and I—we've had a quarrel. I know I'm right, and he's wrong, and he'll come to see it soon, if he's left to himself, and then all will be right. But just now he misunderstands me, and we've not been civil to one another. I could not think of staying, and he would not allow you to come away with me for a short visit, which I wished. It won't last though; and I do assure you, my dear Maud, I am quite happy about you now that you are quite on your guard. Just act respecting that person as if she were capable of any treachery, without showing distrust or dislike in your manner, and nothing will remain in her power; and write to me whenever you wish to hear from me, and if I can be of any real use, I don't care, I'll come: so there's a wise little woman; do as I've said, and depend upon it everything will go well, and I'll contrive before long to get that nasty creature away.'

Except a kiss and a few hurried words in the morning when she was leaving, and a pencilled farewell for papa, there was nothing more from Cousin Monica for some time.

Knowl was dark again—darker than ever. My father, gentle always to me, was now—perhaps it was contrast with his fitful return to something like the world's ways, during Lady Knollys' stay—more silent, sad, and isolated than before. Of Madame de la Rougierre I had nothing at first particular to remark. Only, reader, if you happen to be a rather nervous and very young girl, I ask you to conceive my fears and imaginings, and the kind of misery which I was suffering. Its intensity I cannot now even myself recall. But it overshadowed me perpetually—a care—an alarm. It lay down with me at night and got up with me in the morning, tinting and disturbing my dreams, and making my daily life terrible. I wonder now that I lived through the ordeal. The torment was secret and incessant, and kept my mind in unintermitting activity.

Externally things went on at Knowl for some weeks in the usual routine. Madame was, so far as her unpleasant ways were concerned, less tormenting than before, and constantly reminded me of 'our leetle vow of friendship you remember, dearest Maud!' and she would stand beside me, and looked from the window with her bony arm round my waist, and my reluctant hand drawn round in hers, and thus she would smile, and talk affectionately, and even play-fully; for at times she would grow quite girlish, and smile with her great carious teeth, and begin to quiz and babble about the young 'faylows', and tell bragging tales of her lovers, all of which were dreadful to me.

She was perpetually recurring, too, to the charming walk we had had together to Church Scarsdale, and proposing a repetition of that delightful excursion, which, you may be sure, I evaded, having by no means so agreeable a recollection of our visit.

One day as I was dressing to go out for a walk in came good Mrs. Rusk, the housekeeper, to my room.

'Miss Maud, dear, is not that too far for you? It is a long walk to Church Scarsdale, and you are not looking very well.'

'To Church Scarsdale?' I repeated; 'I'm not going to Church Scarsdale; who said I was going to Church Scarsdale? There is noth-ing I should so much dislike.'

'Well, I never!' exclaimed she. 'Why, there's old Madame's been down stairs with me for fruit and sandwiches, telling me you were longing to go to Church Scarsdale—'

'It's quite untrue,' I interrupted. 'She knows I hate it.'

'She does?' said Mrs. Rusk, quietly; 'and you did not tell her noth-ing about the basket? Well—if there isn't a story! Now what may she be after—what is it—what *is* she driving at?'

'I can't tell, but I won't go.'

'No, of course, dear; you won't go. But you may be sure there's some scheme in her old head. Tom Fowkes says she's bin two or three times to drink tea at Farmer Gray's—now, could it be she's thinking to marry him?' And Mrs. Rusk sat down and laughed heartily, ending with a crow of derision.

'To think of a young fellow like that, and his wife, poor thing, not dead a year—may be she's got money?'

'I don't know—I don't care—perhaps, Mrs. Rusk, you mistook Madame. I will go down; I am going out.'

Madame had a basket in her hand. She held it quietly by her capacious skirt, at the far side, and made no allusion to the preparation, neither to the direction in which she proposed walking, and prattling artlessly and affectionately she marched by my side.

Thus we reached the stile at the sheep-walk, and then I paused.

'Now, Madame, have not we gone far enough in this direction?—suppose we visit the pigeon-house in the park?'

'Wat folly! my dear a Maud—you cannot walk so far.'

'Well, towards home then.'

'And wy not a this way? We ave not walk enough, and Mr. Ruthyn he will not be pleased if you do not take proper exercise. Let us walk on by the path, and stop when you like.'

'Where do you wish to go, Madame?'

'Nowhere particular—come along; don't be fool, Maud.'

'This leads to Church Scarsdale.'

'A yes indeed! wat sweet place! bote we need not a walk all the way to there.'

'I'd rather not walk outside the grounds to-day, Madame.'

'Come, Maud, you shall not be fool—wat you mean, Mademoiselle?' said the stalworth lady, growing yellow and greenish with an angry mottling, and accosting me very gruffly.

'I don't care to cross the stile, thank you, Madame. I shall remain at this side.'

'You shall do wat I tell you!' exclaimed she.

'Let go my arm, Madame, you hurt me,' I cried.

She had griped* my arm very firmly in her great bony hand, and seemed preparing to drag me over by main force.

'Let me go,' I repeated shrilly, for the pain increased.

'La!' she cried with a smile of rage and a laugh, letting me go and shoving me backward at the same time, so that I had a rather dangerous tumble.

I stood up, a good deal hurt, and very angry, notwithstanding my fear of her.

'I'll ask papa if I am to be so ill-used.'

'Wat 'av I done?' cried Madame, laughing grimly from her hollow jaws; 'I did all I could to help you over—'ow could I prevent you to pull back and tumble if you would do so? That is the way wen you petites Mademoiselles are naughty and hurt yourself they always try to make blame other people. Tell a wat you like—you think I care?'

'Very well, Madame.'

'Are a you coming?'

'No.'

She looked steadily in my face and very wickedly. I gazed at her as with dazzled eyes—I suppose as the feathered prey do at the owl that glares on them by night. I neither moved back nor forward, but stared at her quite helplessly.

'You are nice pupil—charming young person! So polite, so obedient, so amiable! I will walk towards Church Scarsdale,' she continued, suddenly breaking through the conventionalism of her irony, and accosting me in savage accents. 'You weel stay behind if you dare. I tell you to accompany—do you hear?'

More than ever resolved against following her, I remained where I was, watching her as she marched fiercely away, swinging her basket as though in imagination knocking my head off with it.

She soon cooled, however, and looking over her shoulder, and seeing me still at the other side of the stile, she paused, and beckoned me grimly to follow her. Seeing me resolutely maintain my position, she faced about, tossed her head, like an angry beast, and seemed uncertain for a while what course to take with me.

She stamped and beckoned furiously again. I stood firm. I was very much frightened, and could not tell to what violence she might resort in her exasperation. She walked towards me with an inflamed countenance, and a slight angry wagging of the head; my heart fluttered, and I awaited the crisis in extreme trepidation. She came close, the stile only separating us, and stopped short, glaring and grinning at me like a French grenadier who has crossed bayonets, but hesitates to close.

WHAT had I done to excite this ungovernable fury? We had often before had such small differences, and she had contented herself with being sarcastic, teasing, and impertinent.

'So, for future you are gouvernante and I the cheaile for you to command—is not so?—and you must direct where we shall walk. Très bien! we shall see; Monsieur Ruthyn he shall know everything. For me I do not care—not at all—I shall be rather pleased, on the contrary. Let him decide. If I shall be responsible for the conduct and the health of Mademoiselle his daughter, it must be that I shall have authority to direct her wat she must do—it must be that she or I shall obey. I ask only witch shall command for the future—voilà tout!'

I was frightened, but resolute—I dare say I looked sullen and uncomfortable. At all events she seemed to think she might possibly succeed by wheedling; so she tried coaxing and cajoling, and patted my cheek, and predicted that I would be 'a good cheaile', and not 'vex poor Madame', but do for the future 'wat she tell a me'.

She smiled her wide wet grin, smoothed my hand, and patted my cheek, and would in the excess of her conciliatory paroxysm have kissed me; but I withdrew, and she commented only with a little laugh, and a 'Foolish little thing! but you will be quite amiable just now.'

'Why, Madame,' I asked, suddenly raising my head and looking her straight in the face, 'do you wish me to walk to Church Scarsdale so particularly to-day?'

She answered my steady look with a contracted gaze and an unpleasant frown.

'Wy do I?—I do not understand a you; there is *no* particular day—wat folly! Wy, I like Church Scarsdale? Well, it is such pretty place. There is all! Wat leetle fool! I suppose you think I want to keel a you and bury you in the churchyard?'

And she laughed, and it would not have been a bad laugh for a ghoul.

'Come, my dearest Maud, you are not a such fool to say, if *you* tell me go thees a way, I weel go that; and if you say go that a way, I weel go thees—you are rasonable leetle girl—come along—*allons donc*—we shall 'av soche agreeable walk—weel a you?'

But I was immovable. It was neither obstinacy nor caprice, but a profound fear that governed me. I was then afraid—yes, *afraid*. Afraid of *what?* Well, of going with Madame de la Rougierre to Church Scarsdale that day. That was all. And I believe that instinct was true.

She turned a bitter glance toward Church Scarsdale, and bit her lip. She saw that she must give it up. A shadow hung upon her drab features. A little scowl—a little sneer—wide lips compressed with a false smile, and a leaden shadow mottling all. Such was the countenance of the lady who only a minute or two before had been smiling and murmuring over the stile so amiably with her idiomatic 'blarney',* as the Irish call that kind of blandishment.

There was no mistaking the malignant disappointment that hooked and warped her features—my heart sank—a tremendous fear over-powered me. Had she intended poisoning me? What was in that basket? I looked in her dreadful face. I felt for a minute quite frantic. A feeling of rage with my father, with my Cousin Monica for abandoning me to this dreadful rogue, took possession of me, and I cried, helplessly wringing my hands—

'Oh! it is a shame—it is a shame—it is a shame!'

The countenance of the gouvernante relaxed. I think she in turn was frightened at my extreme agitation. It might have worked unfavourably with my father.

'Come, Maud, it is time you should try to control your temper. You shall not walk to Church Scarsdale if you do not like—I only invite. *There!* It is quite as you please, where we shall walk then? Here to the peegeon-house? I think you say. Tout bien! Remember I concede you everything. Let us go.'

We went, therefore, towards the pigeon-house, through the forest trees. I not speaking as the children in the wood did with their sinister conductor, but utterly silent and scared. She silent also, meditating, and sometimes with a sharp side glance gauging my progress towards equanimity. Her own was rapid; for Madame was a philosopher, and speedily accommodated herself to circumstances. We had not walked a quarter of an hour when every trace of gloom had left her face, which had assumed its customary brightness, and she began to sing with a spiteful hilarity as we walked forward, and indeed seemed to be approaching one of her waggish, frolicsome moods. But her fun in these moods was solitary. The joke, whatever it was, remained in her own keeping. When we approached the ruined brick tower—in old times a pigeon-house—she grew quite frisky, and twirled her basket in the air, and capered to her own singing.

Under the shadow of the broken wall, and its ivy, she sat down with a frolicsome *plump*, and opened her basket, inviting me to partake, which I declined. I must do her justice, however, upon the suspicion of poison, which she quite disposed of by gobbling up, to her own share, everything which the basket contained.

The reader is not to suppose that Madame's cheerful demeanour indicated that I was forgiven. Nothing of the kind. One syllable more, on our walk home, she addressed not to me. And when we reached the terrace, she said:—

'You will please, Maud, remain for two—three minutes in the Dutch garden, while I speak with Mr. Ruthyn in the study.'

This was spoken with a high head and an insufferable smile; and I more haughtily, but quite gravely, turned without disputing, and descended the steps to the quaint little garden she had indicated.

I was surprised, and very glad to see my father there. I ran to him, and began, 'Oh! papa!' and then stopped short, adding only, 'may I speak to you now?'

He smiled kindly and gravely on me.

'Well, Maud, say your say.'

'Oh, sir, it is only this: I entreat that our walks, mine and Madame's, may be confined to the grounds.'

'And why?'

'I—I'm afraid to go with her.'

'*Afraid!*' he repeated, looking hard at me. 'Have you lately had a letter from Lady Knollys?'

'No, papa, not for two months or more.'

There was a pause.

'And why *afraid*, Maud?'

'She brought me one day to Church Scarsdale; you know what a solitary place it is, sir; and she frightened me so that I was afraid to go with her into the churchyard. But she went and left me alone at the other side of the stream, and an impudent man passing by stopped and spoke to me, and seemed inclined to laugh at me, and altogether frightened me very much, and he did not go till Madame happened to return.'

'What kind of man—young or old?'

'A young man; he looked like a farmer's son, but very impudent, and stood there talking to me whether I would or not; and Madame did not care at all, and laughed at me for being frightened; and, indeed, I am very uncomfortable with her.'

He gave me another shrewd look, and then looked down cloudily and thought.

'You say you are uncomfortable and frightened. How is this—what causes these feelings?'

'I don't know, sir; she likes frightening me; I am afraid of her—we are all afraid of her, I think. The servants, I mean, as well as I.'

My father nodded his head contemptuously, twice or thrice, and muttered, 'A pack of fools!'

'And she was so very angry to-day with me, because I would not walk again with her to Church Scarsdale. I am very much afraid of her. I—' and quite unpremeditatedly I burst into tears.

'There, there, little Maud, you must not cry. She is here only for your good. If you are afraid—even *foolishly* afraid—it is enough. Be it as you say; your walks are henceforward confined to the grounds: I'll tell her so.'

I thanked him through my tears very earnestly.

'But, Maud, beware of prejudice; women are unjust and violent in their judgments. Your family has suffered in some of its members by such injustice. It behoves us to be careful not to practise it.'

That evening in the drawing-room my father said, in his usual abrupt way—

'About my departure, Maud; I've had a letter from London this morning, and I think I shall be called away sooner than I at first supposed, and for a little time we must manage apart from one another. Do not be alarmed. You shall not be in Madame de la Rougierre's charge, but under the care of a relation; but even so, little Maud will miss her old father, I think.'

His tone was very tender, so were his looks; he was looking down on me with a smile, and tears were in his eyes. This softening was new to me. I felt a strange thrill of surprise, delight and love, and springing up, I threw my arms about his neck and wept in silence. He, I think, shed tears also.

'You said a visitor was coming; some one you mean to go away with. Ah, yes, you love him better than me.'

'No, dear, no; but I *fear* him; and I am sorry to leave you, little Maud.'

'It won't be very long,' I pleaded.

'No, dear,' he answered with a sigh.

I was tempted almost to question him more closely on the subject, but he seemed to divine what was in my mind, for he said—

'Let us speak no more of it, but only bear in mind, Maud, what I told you about the oak cabinet, the key of which is here,' and he held it up as formerly: 'you remember what you are to do in case Doctor Bryerly should come while I am away?'

'Yes, sir.'

His manner had changed, and I had returned to my accustomed formalities.

It was only a few days later that Doctor Bryerly actually did arrive at Knowl, quite unexpectedly, except, I suppose, by my father. He was to stay only one night.

He was twice closeted in the little study up stairs with my father, who seemed to me, even for him, unusually dejected, and Mrs. Rusk inveighing against 'them rubbitch,' as she always termed the Swedenborgians, told me 'they were making him quite shakey-like, and he would not last no time, if that lankey, lean ghost of a fellow in black was to keep prowling in and out of his room like a tame cat.'

I lay awake that night, wondering what the mystery might be that connected my father and Dr. Bryerly. There was something more than the convictions of their strange religion could account for. There was something that profoundly agitated my father. It may not be reasonable, but so it is. The person whose presence, though we know nothing of the cause of that effect, is palpably attended with pain to any one who is dear to us, grows odious, and I began to detest Doctor Bryerly.

It was a grey, dark morning, and in a dark pass in the gallery, near the staircase, I came full upon the ungainly Doctor, in his glossy black suit.

I think if my mind had been less anxiously excited on the subject of his visit, or if I had not disliked him so much, I should not have found courage to accost him as I did. There was something sly, I thought, in his dark, lean face, and he looked so low, so like a Scotch artisan in his Sunday clothes, that I felt a sudden pang of indignation, at the thought that a great gentleman, like my father, should have suffered under his influence, and I stopped suddenly, instead of passing him by with a mere salutation, as he expected, 'May I ask a question, Doctor Bryerly?'

'Certainly.'

'Are you the friend whom my father expects?'

'I don't quite see.'

'The friend, I mean, with whom he is to make an expedition to some distance, I think, and for some little time?'

'No,' said the Doctor, with a shake of his head.

'And who is he?'

'I really have not a notion, Miss.'

'Why, he said that *you knew*,' I replied.

The Doctor looked honestly puzzled.

'Will he stay long away? pray tell me.'

The Doctor looked into my troubled face with inquiring and darkened eyes, like one who half reads another's meaning; and then he said a little briskly, but not sharply—

'Well, *I* don't know, I'm sure, Miss; no, indeed, you must have mistaken; there's nothing that *I* know.'

There was a little pause, and he added—

'No. He never mentioned any friend to me.' I fancied that he was made uncomfortable by my question, and wanted to hide the truth. Perhaps I was partly right.

'Oh! Doctor Bryerly, pray, *pray* who is the friend, and where is he going?'

'I do *assure* you,' he said, with a strange sort of impatience, 'I don't know; it is all nonsense.'

And he turned to go, looking, I think, annoyed and disconcerted.

A terrific suspicion crossed my brain like lightning.

'Doctor, one word,' I said, I believe, quite wildly, 'Do you—do you think his mind is at all affected?'

'Insane?' he said, looking at me with a sudden, sharp, inquisitiveness, that brightened into a smile, 'pooh, pooh! Heaven forbid; not a saner man in England.'

Then with a little nod he walked on, carrying, as I believed, notwithstanding his disclaimer, the secret with him. In the afternoon Doctor Bryerly went away.

CHAPTER XVII

AN ADVENTURE

For many days after our quarrel, Madame hardly spoke to me. As for lessons, I was not much troubled with them. It was plain, too, that my father had spoken to her, for she never after that day proposed our extending our walks beyond the precincts of Knowl.

Knowl, however, was a very considerable territory, and it was possible for a much better pedestrian than I to tire herself effectually, without passing its limits. So we took occasionally long walks.

After some weeks of sullenness, during which, for days at a time, she hardly spoke to me, and seemed lost in dark and evil abstraction, she once more, and somewhat suddenly, recovered her spirits, and grew quite friendly. Her gaieties and friendliness were not reassuring, and in my mind presaged approaching mischief and treachery. The days were shortening to the wintry span. The edge of the red sun had already touched the horizon as Madame and I, overtaken at the warren by his last beams, were hastening homeward.

A narrow carriage-road traverses this wild region of the park, to which a distant gate gives entrance. On descending into this unfrequented road I was surprised to see a carriage standing there. A thin, sly postilion, with that pert, turned-up nose which the old caricaturist Woodward* used to attribute to the gentlemen of Tewkesbury, was leaning on his horses, and looked hard at me as I passed. A lady who sat within looked out, with an extra-fashionable bonnet on, and also treated us to a stare. Very pink and white cheeks she had, very black glossy hair and bright eyes, fat, bold, and rather cross, she looked—and in her bold way, she examined us curiously as we passed.

I mistook the situation. It had once happened before that an intending visitor at Knowl, had entered the place by that park road, and lost several hours in a vain search for the house.

'Ask him, Madame, whether they want to go to the house; I dare say they have missed their way,' whispered I.

'*Eh bien*, they will find again. I do not choose to talk to post-boys; *allons!*'

But I asked the man as we passed, 'Do you want to reach the house?'

By this time he was at the horses' heads, buckling the harness.

'Noa,' he said in a surly tone, smiling oddly on the winkers; but, recollecting his politeness, he added: 'Noa, thankee, misses, it's what they calls a pic-nic; we'll be takin' the road, now.'

He was smiling now on a little buckle with which he was engaged.

'Come—nonsense!' whispered Madame, sharply in my ear, and she whisked me by the arm, so we crossed the little stile at the other side.

Our path lay across the warren, which undulates in little hillocks. The sun was down by this time, blue shadows were stretching round us, colder in the splendid contrast of the burnished sunset sky.

Descending over these hillocks we saw three figures a little in advance of us, not far from the path we were tracing. Two were standing smoking and chatting at intervals. One tall and slim, with a high chimney-pot, worn a little on one side, and a white great-coat buttoned up to the chin. The other shorter and stouter, with a dark-coloured wrapper. These gentlemen were facing rather our way as we came over the edge of the eminence, but turned their backs on perceiving our approach. As they did so I remember so well each lowered his cigar suddenly, with the simultaneousness of a drill. The third figure sustained the pic-nic character of the group, for he was repacking a hamper. He stood suddenly erect as we drew near, and a very ill-looking person he was, low-browed, square-chinned, and with a broad, broken nose. He wore gaiters, and was a little bandy, very broad, and had a closely-cropped bullet head, and deep-set little eyes. The moment I saw him, I beheld the living type of the burglars and bruisers whom I had so often beheld with a kind of scepticism in *Punch*.* He stood over his hamper and scowled sharply at us for a moment; then with the point of his foot he jerked a little fur cap that lay on the ground into his hand, drew it tight over his lowering brows, and called to his companions, just as we passed him—'Hallo! mister. How's this?'

'All right,' said the tall person in the white great-coat, who as he answered shook his shorter companion by the arm, I thought angrily.

This shorter companion turned about. He had a muffler loose about his neck and chin. I thought he seemed shy and irresolute, and the tall man gave him a great jolt with his elbow, which made him stagger, and I fancied a little angry, for he said as it seemed a sulky word or two.

The gentleman in the white surtout, however, standing direct in our way, raised his hat with a mock salutation, placing his hand on his breast, and forthwith began to advance with an insolent grin and an air of tipsy frolic.

'Jist in time, ladies; five minutes more and we'd a bin off. Thankee, Mrs. Mouser, ma'am, for the honour of the meetin', and more particular for the pleasure of making your young lady's acquaintance—niece, ma'am? daughter, ma'am? granddaughter, by Jove, is it? Hallo! there, mild 'un, I say, stop packin'.' This was to the ill-favoured person with the broken nose. 'Bring us a couple o' glasses and a bottle o' curaçoa;* what are you feard on, my dear? this is Lord Lollipop, here, a reg'lar charmer, wouldn't hurt a fly, hey Lolly? Isn't he pretty, Miss? and I'm Sir Simon Sugarstick—so called after old Sir Simon, ma'am; and I'm so tall and straight, Miss, and slim—aint I? and ever so sweet, my honey, when you come to know me, just like a sugarstick; ain't I, Lolly, boy?'

'I'm Miss Ruthyn, tell them, Madame,' I said, stamping on the ground, and very much frightened.

'Be quaite, Maud. If you are angry they will hurt us; leave me to speak,' whispered the gouvernante.

All this time they were approaching from separate points. I glanced back, and saw the ruffianly-looking man within a yard or two, with his arm raised and one finger up, telegraphing, as it seemed, to the gentlemen in front.

'Be quaite, Maud,' whispered Madame, with an awful adjuration, which I do not care to set down. 'They are teepsy; don't seem 'fraid.'

I *was* afraid—terrified. The circle had now so narrowed that they might have placed their hands on my shoulders.

'Pray, gentlemen, wat you want? *weel* a you 'av the goodness to permit us to go on?'

I now observed for the first time, with a kind of shock, that the shorter of the two men, who prevented our advance, was the person who had accosted me so offensively at Church Scarsdale. I pulled Madame by the arm, whispering, 'Let us run.'

'Be quaite, my dear Maud,' was her only reply.

'I tell you what,' said the tall man, who had replaced his high hat more jauntily than before on the side of his head, 'we've caught you now, fair game, and we'll let you off on conditions. You must not be frightened, Miss. Upon my honour and soul, I mean no mischief; do I, Lollipop? I call him Lord Lollipop, it's only chaff though; his name's Smith. Now, Lolly, I vote we let the prisoners go, when we just introduce them to Mrs. Smith; she's sitting in the carriage, and keeps Mr. S. here in precious good order, I promise you. There's easy terms for you, eh, and we'll have a glass o' curaçoa round, and so part friends. Is it a bargain? Come!'

'Yes, Maud, we must go—wat matter?' whispered Madame, vehemently.

'You shan't,' I said, instinctively terrified.

'You'll go with Ma'am, young 'un, won't you?' said Mr. Smith, as his companion called him.

Madame was holding my arm, but I snatched it from her, and would have run; the tall man, however, placed his arms round me and held me fast with an affectation of playfulness, but his grip was hard enough to hurt me a good deal. Being now thoroughly frightened, after an ineffectual struggle, during which I heard Madame say, 'You fool, Maud, weel you come with me? See wat you are doing—' I began to scream, shriek after shriek, which the man attempted to drown with loud hooting, peals of laughter, forcing his handkerchief against my mouth, while Madame continued to bawl her exhortations to 'be quaite' in my ear.

'I'll lift her, I say?' said a gruff voice behind me.

But at this instant, wild with terror, I distinctly heard other voices shouting. The men who surrounded me were instantly silent, and all looked in the direction of the sound, now very near, and I screamed with redoubled energy. The ruffian behind me thrust his great hand over my mouth.

'It is the gamekeeper,' cried Madame.

'*Two* gamekeepers—we are safe—thank Heaven!' and she began to call on Dykes by name.

I only remember, feeling myself at liberty—running a few steps—seeing Dykes' white furious face—clinging to his arm, with which he was bringing his gun to a level, and saying, 'Don't fire—they'll murder us if you do.'

Madame, screaming lustily, ran up at the same moment.

'Run on to the gate and lock it. I'll be wi' ye in a minute,' cried he to the other game-keeper; who started instantly on this mission, for the three ruffians were already in full retreat for the carriage.

Giddy—wild—fainting—still terror carried me on.

'Now, Madame Rogers—s'pose you take young Misses on—I must run and len' Bill a hand.'

'No, no; you moste not,' cried Madame. 'I am fainting myself, and more villains they may be near to us.'

But at this moment we heard a shot, and, muttering to himself and grasping his gun, Dykes ran at his utmost speed in the direction of the sound.

With many exhortations to speed, and ejaculations of alarm, Madame hurried me on toward the house, which at length we reached without further adventure.

As it happened, my father met us in the hall. He was perfectly transported with fury on hearing from Madame what had happened, and set out at once, with some of the servants, in the hope of intercepting the party at the park gate.

Here was a new agitation; for my father did not return for nearly three hours, and I could not conjecture what might be occurring during the period of his absence. My alarm was greatly increased by the arrival in the interval of poor Bill, the under-gamekeeper, very much injured.

Seeing that he was determined to intercept their retreat, the three men had set upon him, wrested his gun, which exploded in the struggle, from him, and beat him savagely. I mention these particulars because they convinced everybody that there was something specially determined and ferocious in the spirit of the party, and that the fracas was no mere frolic, but the result of a predetermined plan.

My father had not succeeded in overtaking them. He traced them to the Lugton Station, where they had taken the railway, and no one could tell him in what direction the carriage and post-horses had driven.

Madame was, or affected to be, very much shattered by what had occurred. Her recollection and mine, when my father questioned us closely, differed very materially respecting many details of the *personnel* of the villanous party. She was obstinate and clear; and although the gamekeeper corroborated my description of them, still my father was puzzled. Perhaps he was not sorry that some hesitation was forced upon him, because although at first he would have gone almost any length to detect the persons, on reflection he was pleased that there was not evidence to bring them into a court of justice, the publicity and annoyance of which would have been inconceivably distressing to me.

Madame was in a strange state—tempestuous in temper, talking incessantly—every now and then in floods of tears, and perpetually on her knees pouring forth torrents of thanksgiving to Heaven for our joint deliverance from the hands of those villains. Notwithstanding our community of danger and her thankfulness on my behalf, however, she broke forth into wrath and railing whenever we were alone together.

'Wat fool you were! so disobedient and obstinate; if you 'ad done wat *I* say, then we should 'av been quaite safe; those persons they were tipsy, and there is nothing so dangerous as to quarrel with tipsy persons; I would 'av brought you quaite safe—the lady she seem so nice and quaite, and we should 'av been safe with her—there would 'av been nothing absolutely; but instead you would scream and pooshe, and so they grow quite wild, and all the impertinence and violence follow of course; and that a poor Bill—all his beating and danger to his life it is cause entairely by you.'

And she spoke with more real virulence than that kind of upbraiding generally exhibits.

'The beast!' exclaimed Mrs. Rusk, when she, I, and Mary Quince were in my room together, 'with all her crying and praying, I'd like to know as much as she does, maybe, about them rascals. There never was sich like about the place, long as I remember it, till she came to Knowl, old witch! with them unmerciful big bones of hers, and her great bald head, grinning here, and crying there, and her nose everywhere. The old French hypocrite!'

Mary Quince threw in an observation, and I believe Mrs. Rusk rejoined, but I heard neither. For whether the housekeeper spoke with reflection or not, what she said affected me strangely. Through the smallest aperture, for a moment, I had had a peep into Pandemonium.* Were not peculiarities of Madame's demeanour and advice during the adventure partly accounted for by the suggestion? Could the proposed excursion to Church Scarsdale have had any purpose of the same sort? What was proposed? How was Madame interested in it? Were such immeasurable treason and hypocrisy possible? I could not explain nor quite believe in the shapeless suspicion that with these light and bitter words of the old housekeeper had stolen so horribly into my mind.

After Mrs. Rusk was gone I awoke from my dismal abstraction with something like a moan and a shudder, with a dreadful sense of danger.

'Oh! Mary Quince,' I cried, 'do *you* think she really knew?'

'*Who?* Miss Maud.'

'Do you think Madame knew of those dreadful people? Oh, no—say you don't—you don't believe it—tell me she did not. I'm distracted, Mary Quince, I'm frightened out of my life.'

'There now, Miss Maud, dear—there now, don't take on so—why should she?—no sich a thing. Mrs. Rusk, law bless you, she's no more meaning in what she says than the child unborn.'

But I was really frightened. I was in a horrible state of uncertainty as to Madame de la Rougierre's complicity with the party who had beset us at the warren, and afterwards so murderously beat our poor gamekeeper. How was I ever to get rid of that horrible woman? How long was she to enjoy her continual opportunities of affrighting and injuring me?

'She hates me—she hates me, Mary Quince; and she will never stop until she has done me some dreadful injury. Oh! will no one relieve me—will no one take her away? Oh, papa, papa, papa! you will be sorry when it is too late.'

I was crying and wringing my hands, and turning from side to side, at my wits' ends, and honest Mary Quince in vain endeavoured to quiet and comfort me.

CHAPTER XVIII

A MIDNIGHT VISITOR

THE frightful warnings of Lady Knollys haunted me too. Was there no escape from the dreadful companion whom fate had assigned me? I made up my mind again and again to speak to my father and urge her removal. In other things he indulged me; here, however, he met me drily and sternly, and it was plain that he fancied I was under my Cousin Monica's influence, and also that he had secret reasons for persisting in an opposite course. Just then I had a gay, odd letter from Lady Knollys, from some country house in Shropshire. Not a word about Captain Oakley. My eye skimmed its pages in search of that charmed name. With a peevish feeling I tossed the sheet upon the table. Inwardly I thought how ill-natured and unwomanly it was.

After a time, however, I read it, and found the letter very good-natured. She had received a note from papa. He had 'had the impudence to forgive *her* for *his* impertinence'. But for my sake she meant, notwithstanding this aggravation, really to pardon him; and whenever she had a disengaged week, to accept his invitation to Knowl, from whence she was resolved to whisk me off to London, where, though I was too young to be presented at Court and come out, I might yet—besides having the best masters and a good excuse for getting rid of Medusa—see a great deal that would amuse and surprise me.

'Great news, I suppose, from Lady Knollys?' said Madame, who always knew who in the house received letters by the post, and by an intuition from whom they came.

'Two letters—you and your papa. She is quite well, I hope?'

'Quite well, thank you, Madame.'

Some fishing questions, dropt from time to time, fared no better. And as usual, when she was foiled even in a trifle, she became sullen and malignant.

That night, when my father and I were alone, he suddenly closed the book he had been reading and said—

'I heard from Monica Knollys to-day. I always liked poor Monnie; and though she's no witch, and very wrong-headed at times, yet now and then she does say a thing that's worth weighing. Did she ever talk to you of a time, Maud, when you are to be your own mistress?'

'No,' I answered, a little puzzled, and looking straight in his rugged, kindly face.

'Well, I thought she might—she's a rattle, you know—always *was* a rattle, and that sort of people say whatever comes uppermost. But that's a subject for me, and more than once, Maud, it has puzzled me.'

He sighed.

'Come with me to the study, little Maud.'

So, he carrying a candle, we crossed the lobby, and marched together through the passage, which at night always seemed a little awesome, darkly wainscoted, uncheered by the cross-light from the hall, which was lost at the turn, leading us away from the frequented parts of the house to that misshapen and lonely room about which the traditions of the nursery and the servants' hall had so many fearful stories to recount.

I think my father had intended making some disclosure to me on reaching this room. If so he changed his mind, or at least postponed his intention.

He had paused before the cabinet, respecting the key of which he had given me so strict a charge, and I think he was going to explain himself more fully than he had done. But he went on, instead, to the table where his desk, always jealously locked, was placed, and having lighted the candles which stood by it, he glanced at me, and said—

'You must wait a little, Maud; I shall have something to say to you. Take this candle and amuse yourself with a book meanwhile.'

I was accustomed to obey in silence. I chose a volume of engravings, and ensconced myself in a favourite nook in which I had often passed a half-hour similarly. This was a deep recess by the fireplace, fenced on the other side by a great old escritoir. Into this I drew a stool, and, with candle and book, I placed myself snugly in the narrow chamber. Every now and then I raised my eyes and saw my father either writing or ruminating, as it seemed to me, very anxiously at his desk.

Time wore on—a longer time than he had intended, and still he continued absorbed at his desk. Gradually I grew sleepy, and as I nodded, the book and room faded away, and pleasant little dreams began to gather round me, and so I went off into a deep slumber.

It must have lasted long, for when I wakened my candle had burnt out; my father, having quite forgotten me, was gone, and the room was dark and deserted. I felt cold and a little stiff, and for some seconds did not know where I was.

I had been wakened, I suppose, by a sound which I now distinctly heard, to my great terror, approaching. There was a rustling; there was a breathing. I heard a creaking upon the plank that always creaked when walked upon in the passage. I held my breath and listened, and coiled myself up in the innermost recess of my little chamber.

Sudden and sharp, a light shone in from the nearly closed study door. It shone angularly on the ceiling like a letter L reversed. There was a pause. Then some one knocked softly at the door, which after another pause was slowly pushed open. I expected, I think, to see the dreaded figure of the linkman. I was scarcely less frightened to see that of Madame de la Rougierre. She was dressed in a sort of grey silk, which she called her Chinese silk—precisely as she had been in the daytime. In fact I do not think she had undressed. She had no shoes on. Otherwise her toilet was deficient in nothing. Her wide mouth was grimly closed, and she stood scowling into the room with a searching and pallid scrutiny, the candle held high above her head at the full stretch of her arm.

Placed as I was in a deep recess, and in a seat hardly raised above the level of the floor, I escaped her, although it seemed to me for some seconds, as I gazed on this spectre, that our eyes actually met.

I sat without breathing or winking, staring upon the formidable image which with upstretched arm, and the sharp lights and hard shadows thrown upon her corrugated features, looked like a sorceress watching for the effect of a spell.

She was plainly listening intensely. Unconsciously she had drawn her lower lip altogether between her teeth, and I well remember what a deathlike and idiotic look the contortion gave her. My terror lest she should discover me amounted to positive agony. She rolled her eyes stealthily from corner to corner of the room, and listened with her neck awry at the door.

Then to my father's desk she went. To my great relief, her back was towards me. She stooped over it, with the candle close by; I saw her try a key—it could be nothing else—and I heard her blow through the wards to clear them.

Then, again, she listened at the door, candle in hand, and then with long tip-toe steps came back, and papa's desk in another moment was open, and Madame cautiously turning over the papers it contained.

Twice or thrice she paused, glided to the door, and listened again intently with her head near the ground, and then returned and continued her search, peeping into papers one after another, tolerably methodically, and reading some quite through.

While this felonious business was going on, I was freezing with fear lest she should accidentally look round and her eyes light on me; for I could not say what she might not do rather than have her crime discovered.

Sometimes she would read a paper twice over; sometimes a whisper no louder than the ticking of a watch; sometimes a brief chuckle under her breath, bespoke the interest with which here and there a letter or a memorandum was read.

For about half an hour, I think, this went on; but at the time it seemed to me all but interminable. On a sudden she raised her head and listened for a moment, replaced the papers deftly, closed the desk without noise, except for the tiny click of the lock, extinguished the candle, and rustled stealthily out of the room, leaving in the darkness the malign and hag-like face on which the candle had just shone still floating filmy in the dark.

Why did I remain silent and motionless while such an outrage was being committed? If, instead of being a very nervous girl, preoccupied with an undefinable terror of that wicked woman, I had possessed courage and presence of mind, I dare say I might have given an alarm, and escaped from the room without the slightest risk. But so it was; I could no more stir than the bird who, cowering under its ivy, sees the white owl sailing back and forward on its predatory cruise.

Not only during her presence, but for more than an hour after, I remained cowering in my hiding-place, and afraid to stir, lest she might either be lurking in the neighbourhood, or return and surprise me.

You will not be astonished, that after a night so passed I was ill and feverish in the morning. To my horror, Madame de la Rougierre came to visit me at my bedside. Not a trace of guilty consciousness of what had passed during the night was legible in her face. She had no sign of late watching, and her toilet was exemplary.

As she sat smiling by me, full of anxious and affectionate inquiry, and smoothed the coverlet with her great felonious hand, I could quite comprehend the dreadful feeling with which the deceived husband in the 'Arabian Nights',* met his ghoul wife, after his nocturnal discovery.

Ill as I was, I got up and found my father in that room which adjoined his bedchamber. He perceived, I am sure, by my looks, that something unusual had happened. I shut the door, and came close beside his chair.

'Oh, papa, I have such a thing to tell you!' I forgot to call him 'Sir'. 'A secret; and you won't say who told you? Will you come down to the study?'

He looked hard at me, got up, and kissing my forehead, said—'Don't be frightened, Maud; I venture to say it is a mare's nest;* at all events, my child, we will take care that no danger reaches you; come, child.'

And by the hand he led me to the study. When the door was shut, and we had reached the far end of the room next the window, I said, but in a low tone, and holding his arm fast—

'Oh, sir, you don't know what a dreadful person we have living with us—Madame de la Rougierre, I mean. Don't let her in if she comes; she would guess what I am telling you, and one way or another I am sure she would kill me.'

'Tut, tut, child. You *must* know that's nonsense,' he said, looking pale and stern.

'Oh, no, papa. I am horribly frightened, and Lady Knollys thinks so too.'

'Ha! I dare say; one fool makes many. We all know what Monica thinks.'

'But I *saw* it, papa. She stole your key last night, and opened your desk, and read all your papers.'

'Stole my key!' said my father, staring at me perplexed, but at the same instant producing it. 'Stole it! Why here it is!'

'She unlocked your desk; she read your papers for ever so long. Open it now, and see whether they have not been stirred.'

He looked at me this time in silence, with a puzzled air; but he did unlock the desk, and lifted the papers curiously and suspiciously. As he did so he uttered a few of those inarticulate interjections which are made with closed lips, and not always intelligible; but he made no remark.

Then he placed me on a chair beside him, and sitting down himself, told me to recollect myself, and tell him distinctly all I had seen. This accordingly, I did, he listening with deep attention.

'Did she remove any paper?' asked my father, at the same time making a little search, I suppose, for that which he fancied might have been stolen.

'No; I did not see her take anything.'

'Well, you are a good girl, Maud. Act discreetly. Say nothing to any one—not even to your Cousin Monica.'

Directions which, coming from another person would have had no great weight, were spoken by my father with an earnest look and a weight of emphasis that made them irresistibly impressive, and I went away with the seal of silence upon my lips.

'Sit down, Maud, *there*. You have not been very happy with Madame de la Rougierre. It is time you were relieved. This occurrence decides it.'

He rang the bell.

'Tell Madame de la Rougierre that I request the honour of seeing her for a few minutes here.'

My father's communications to her were always equally ceremonious. In a few minutes there was a knock at the door, and the same figure, smiling, courtesying, that had scared me on the same threshold last night, like the spirit of evil, presented itself.

My father rose, and Madame having at his request taken a chair opposite, looking, as usual in his presence, all amiability, he proceeded at once to the point.

'Madame de la Rougierre, I have to request you that you will give me the key, now in your possession, which unlocks this desk of mine.'

With which termination he tapped his gold pencil-case suddenly on it.

Madame, who had expected something very different, became instantly so pale, with a dull purplish hue upon her forehead, that, especially when she had twice essayed with her white lips, in vain, to answer, I expected to see her fall in a fit.

She was not looking in his face; her eyes were fixed lower, and her mouth and cheek sucked in, with a strange distortion at one side.

She stood up suddenly, and staring straight in his face, she succeeded in saying, after twice clearing her throat—

'I cannot comprehend, Monsieur Ruthyn, unless you intend to insult me.'

'It won't do, Madame; I must have that *false key*. I give you the opportunity of surrendering it quietly here and now.'

'But who dares to say I possess such thing?' demanded Madame, who, having rallied from her momentary paralysis, was now fierce and voluble as I had often seen her before.

'You know, Madame, that you can rely on what I say, and I tell you that you were seen last night visiting this room, and with a key in your possession, opening this desk, and reading my letters and papers contained in it. Unless you forthwith give me that key, and any other false keys in your possession—in which case I shall rest content with dismissing you summarily—I will take a different course. You know I am a magistrate;—and I shall have you, your boxes, and places upstairs, searched forthwith, and I will prosecute you criminally. The thing is clear; you aggravate by denying; you must give me that key, if you please, instantly, otherwise I ring this bell, and you shall see that I mean what I say.'

There was a little pause. He rose and extended his hand towards the bell-rope. Madame glided round the table, extended her hand to arrest his.

'I will do everything, Monsieur Ruthyn—whatever you wish.'

And with these words Madame de la Rougierre broke down altogether. She sobbed, she wept, she gabbled piteously, all manner of incomprehensible roulades of lamentation and entreaty; coyly, penitently, in a most interesting agitation, she produced the very key from her breast, with a string tied to it. My father was little moved by this piteous tempest. He coolly took the key and tried it in the desk, which it locked and unlocked quite freely, though the wards were complicated. He shook his head and looked her in the face.

'Pray, who made this key? It is a new one, and made expressly to pick this lock.'

But Madame was not going to tell any more than she had expressly bargained for; so she only fell once more into her old paroxysm of sorrow, self-reproach, extenuation, and entreaty.

'Well,' said my father, 'I promised that on surrendering the key you should go. It is enough. I keep my word. You shall have an hour and a half to prepare in. You must then be ready to depart. I will send your money to you by Mrs. Rusk; and if you look for another situation, you had better not refer to me. Now be so good as to leave me.'

Madame seemed to be in a strange perplexity. She bridled up dried her eyes fiercely, and dropped a great courtesy, and then sailed away towards the door. Before reaching it she stopped on the way, turning half round, with a peaked, pallid glance at my father, and she bit her lip viciously as she eyed him. At the door the same repulsive pantomime was repeated, as she stood for a moment with her hand upon the handle. But she changed her bearing again with a sniff, and with a look of scorn, almost heightened to a sneer, she made another very low courtesy and a disdainful toss of her head, and so disappeared, shutting the door rather sharply behind her.

CHAPTER XIX

AU REVOIR

MRS. RUSK was fond of assuring me that Madame 'did not like a bone in my skin'. Instinctively I knew that she bore me no good-will, although I really believe it was her wish to make me think quite the reverse. At all events I had no desire to see Madame again before her departure, especially as she had thrown upon me one momentary glance in the study, which seemed to me charged with very peculiar feelings.

You may be very sure, therefore, that I had no desire for a formal leave-taking at her departure. I took my hat and cloak, therefore, and stole out quietly.

My ramble was a sequestered one, and well screened, even at this late season, with foliage; the pathway devious among the stems of old trees, and its flooring interlaced and groined with their knotted roots. Though near the house, it was a sylvan solitude; a little brook ran darkling and glimmering through it, wild strawberries and other woodland plants strewed the ground, and the sweet notes and flutter of small birds made the shadow of the boughs cheery.

I had been fully an hour in this picturesque solitude when I heard in the distance the ring of carriage-wheels, announcing to me that Madame de la Rougierre had fairly set out upon her travels. I thanked heaven; I could have danced and sung with delight; I heaved a great sigh and looked up through the branches to the clear blue sky.

But things are oddly timed. Just at this moment I heard Madame's voice close at my ear, and her large bony hand was laid on my shoulder. We were instantly face to face—I recoiling, and for a moment speechless with fright.

In very early youth we do not appreciate the restraints which act upon malignity, or know how effectually fear protects us where conscience is wanting. Quite alone, in this solitary spot, detected and overtaken with an awful instinct by my enemy, what might not be about to happen to me at that moment?

'Frightened, as usual, Maud,' she said quietly, and eyeing me with a sinister smile, 'and with cause you think, no doubt. Wat 'av you done to injure poor Madame? Well, I think I know, little girl, and have quite discover the cleverness of my sweet little Maud. Eh—is not so? Petite carogne*—ah, ha, ha!'

I was too much confounded to answer.

'You see, my dear cheaile,' she said, shaking her uplifted finger with a hideous archness at me, 'you could not hide what you 'av done from poor Madame. You cannot look so innocent but I can see your pretty little villany quite plain—you dear little diablesse.

'Wat I 'av done I 'av no reproach of myself for it. If I could explain, your papa would say I 'av done right, and you should thank me on your knees; but I cannot explain yet.'

She was speaking, as it were, in little paragraphs, with a moment-ary pause between each, to allow its meaning to impress itself.

'If I were to choose to explain, your papa he would implore me to remain. But no—I would not—notwithstanding your so cheerful house, your charming servants, your papa's amusing society, and your affectionate and sincere heart, my sweet little maraude.

'I am to go to London first, where I 'av, oh, so good friends! next I will go abroad for some time; but be sure, my sweetest Maud, wher-ever I may 'appen to be, I will remember you—ah, ha! Yes; *most cer-tainly*, I will remember you.

'And although I shall not be always near, yet I shall know everything about my charming little Maud; you will not know how, but I shall indeed, *everything*. And be sure, my dearest cheaile, I will some time be able to give you the sensible proofs of my gratitude and affec-tion—you understand.

'The carriage is waiting at the yew-tree stile, and I must go on. You did not expect to see me—here; I will appear, perhaps, as suddenly another time. It is great pleasure to us both—this opportunity to make our adieux. Farewell! my dearest little Maud. I will never cease to think of you, and of some way to recompense the kindness you 'av shown for poor Madame.'

My hand hung by my side, and she took not it, but my thumb, and shook it folded in her broad palm, and looking on me as she held it, as if meditating mischief. Then suddenly she said—

'You will always remember Madame, I *think*, and I will remind you of me beside; and for the present farewell, and I hope you may be as 'appy as you deserve.'

The large sinister face looked on me for a second with its latent sneer, and then, with a sharp nod and a spasmodic shake of my imprisoned thumb, she turned, and holding her dress together, and showing her great bony ankles, she strode rapidly away over the gnarled roots into the perspective of the trees, and I did not awake, as it were, until she had quite disappeared in the distance.

Events of this kind made no difference with my father; but every other face in Knowl was gladdened by the removal. My energies had returned, my spirits were come again. The sunlight was happy, the flowers innocent, the songs and flutter of the birds once more gay, and all nature delightful and rejoicing.

After the first elation of relief, now and then a filmy shadow of Madame de la Rougierre would glide across the sunlight, and the remembrance of her menace return with an unexpected pang of fear.

'Well, if *there* isn't impittens!' cried Mrs. Rusk. 'But never you trouble your head about it, Miss. Them sort's all alike—you never saw a rogue yet that was found out and didn't threaten the honest folk as he was leaving behind with all sorts; there was Martin, the game-keeper, and Jervis, the footman, I mind well how hard they swore all they would not do when they was a-going, and who ever heard of them since? They always threatens that way—them sort always does, and none ever the worse—not but she would if she could, mind ye, but there it is; she can't do nothing but bite her nails and cuss us—not she—ha, ha, ha!'

So I was comforted. But Madame's evil smile, nevertheless, from time to time would sail across my vision with a silent menace, and my spirits sank, and a Fate, draped in black, whose face I could not see, took me by the hand, and led me away, in the spirit, silently, on an awful exploration from which I would rouse myself with a start, and Madame was gone for a while.

She had, however, judged her little parting well. She contrived to leave her glamour over me, and in my dreams she troubled me.

I was, however, indescribably relieved. I wrote in high spirits to Cousin Monica; and wondered what plans my father might have formed about me; and whether we were to stay at home, or go to London, or go abroad. Of the last—the pleasantest arrangement, in some respects—I had nevertheless an occult horror. A secret convic-tion haunted me that were we to go abroad, we should there meet Madame, which to me was like meeting my evil genius.

I have said more than once that my father was an odd man; and the reader will, by this time, have seen that there was much about him not easily understood. I often wonder, whether if he had been franker I should have found him less odd than I supposed, or more odd still. Things that moved me profoundly did not apparently affect him at all. The departure of Madame, under the circumstances which attended it, appeared to my childish mind an event of the vastest importance. No one was indifferent to the occurrence in the house but its master. He never alluded again to Madame de la Rougierre. But whether connected with her exposure and dismissal, I could not say, there did appear to be some new care or trouble now at work in my father's mind.

'I have been thinking a great deal about you, Maud. I am anxious. I have not been so troubled for years. Why has not Monica Knollys a little more sense?'

This oracular sentence he spoke, having stopped me in the hall, and then saying 'We shall see,' he left me as abruptly as he appeared. Did he apprehend any danger to me from the vindictiveness of Madame?

A day or two afterwards, as I was in the Dutch garden, I saw him on the terrace steps. He beckoned to me, and came to meet me as I approached.

'You must be very solitary, little Maud; it is not good. I have written to Monica: in a matter of detail she is competent to advise; perhaps, she will come here for a short visit.'

I was very glad to hear this.

'*You* are more interested than for my time *I* can be, in vindicating his character.'

'Whose character, sir?' I ventured to inquire during the pause that followed.

One trick which my father had acquired from his habits of solitude and silence was this of assuming that the context of his thoughts was legible to others, forgetting that they had not been spoken.

'Whose?—your Uncle Silas's. In the course of nature he must survive me. He will then represent the family name. Would you make some sacrifice to clear that name, Maud?'

I answered briefly; but my face I believe showed my enthusiasm.

He turned on me such an approving smile as you might fancy lighting up the rugged features of a pale old Rembrandt.

'I can tell you, Maud; if my life could have done it, it should not have been undone—*ubi lapsus, quid feci*.* But I had almost made up my mind to change my plan, and leave all to time—*edax rerum**—to illuminate or to *consume*. But I think little Maud would like to contribute to the restitution of her family name. It may cost you something—are you willing to buy it at a sacrifice? Is there—I don't speak of fortune, that is not involved—but is there any other honourable sacrifice you would shrink from to dispel the disgrace under which our most ancient and honourable name must otherwise continue to languish?'

'Oh, none—none indeed, sir—I am delighted!'

Again I saw the Rembrandt smile.

'Well, Maud, I am sure there is *no* risk; but you are to suppose there is. Are you still willing to accept it?'

Again I assented.

'You are worthy of your blood, Maud Ruthyn. It will come soon, and it won't last long. But you must not let people like Monica Knollys frighten you.'

I was lost in wonder.

'If you allow them to possess you with their follies you had better recede in time—they may make the ordeal as terrible as hell itself. You have zeal—have you nerve?'

I thought in such a cause I had nerve for anything.

'Well, Maud, in the course of a few months—and it may be sooner—there must be a change. I have had a letter from London this morning that assures me of that. I must then leave you for a time; in my absence be faithful to the duties that will arise. To whom much is committed, of him will much be required.* You shall promise me not to mention this conversation to Monica Knollys. If you are a talking girl, and cannot trust yourself, say so, and we will not ask her to come. Also, don't invite her to talk about your Uncle Silas—I have reasons. Do you quite understand my conditions?'

'Yes, sir.'

'Your Uncle Silas,' he said, speaking suddenly in loud and fierce tones that sounded from so old a man almost terrible, 'lies under an intolerable slander. I don't correspond with him—I don't sympathize with him—I never quite did. He has grown religious, and that's well; but there are things in which even religion should not bring a man to acquiesce, and from what I can learn, he, the person primarily affected—the cause, though the innocent cause, of this great calamity—bears it with an easy apathy which is mistaken, and liable easily to be mistaken, and such as no Ruthyn under the circumstances ought to exhibit. I told him what he ought to do, and offered to open my purse for the purpose; but he would not, or *did* not; indeed he *never* took my advice, he followed his own, and a foul and dismal shoal he has drifted on. It is not for his sake—why should I?—that I have longed and laboured to remove the disgraceful slur under which his ill-fortune has thrown us. He troubles himself little about it, I believe—he's meek, meeker than I. He cares less about his children than I about you, Maud; he is selfishly sunk in futurity—a feeble visionary. I am not so. I believe it to be a duty to take care of others beside myself. The character and influence of an ancient family is a peculiar heritage—sacred but destructible; and woe to him who either destroys or suffers it to perish!'

This was the longest speech I ever heard my father speak before or after. He abruptly resumed—

'Yes, we will, Maud—you and I—we'll leave one proof on record, which, fairly read, will go far to convince the world.'

He looked round, but we were alone. The garden was nearly always solitary, and few visitors ever approached the house from that side.

'I have talked too long, I believe; we are children to the last. Leave me, Maud. I think I know you better than I did, and I am pleased with you. Go, child—I'll sit here.'

If he had acquired new ideas of me, so had I of him from that interview. I had no idea till then how much passion still burned in that aged frame, nor how full of energy and fire that face, generally so stern and ashen, could appear. As I left him seated on the rustic chair, by the steps, the traces of that storm were still discernible on his features. His gathered brows, glowing eyes, and strangely hectic face, and the grim compression of his mouth, still showed the agitation which, somehow, in grey old age, shocks and alarms the young.

THE REV. WILLIAM FAIRFIELD, Doctor Clay's somewhat bald curate, a mild, thin man, with a high and thin nose, who was preparing me for confirmation, came next day; and when our catechetical conference was ended, and before lunch was announced, my father sent for him to the study, where he remained until the bell rang out its summons.

'We have had some interesting—I may say *very* interesting—conversation, your papa and I, Miss Ruthyn,' said my reverend *vis-à-vis*, so soon as nature was refreshed, smiling and shining, as he leaned back in his chair, his hand upon the table, and his finger curled gently upon the stem of his wine-glass. 'It never was your privilege I believe, to see your uncle, Mr. Silas Ruthyn, of Bartram Haugh?'

'No—never—he leads so retired—so *very* retired a life.'

'Oh, no,—of course, no; but I was going to remark a likeness—I mean, of course, a *family* likeness—only *that* sort of thing—you understand—between him and the profile of Lady Margaret in the drawing-room—is not it Lady Margaret?—which you were so good as to show me on Wednesday last. There certainly *is* a likeness. I *think* you would agree with me, if you had the pleasure of seeing your uncle.'

'You know him, then? I have never seen him.'

'Oh, dear, yes—I am happy to say, I know him very well. I have that privilege. I was for three years curate of Feltram, and I had the honour of being a pretty constant visitor at Bartram Haugh during that, I may say, protracted period; and I think it really never has been my privilege and happiness, I may say, to enjoy the acquaintance and society of so very experienced a Christian, as my admirable friend, I may call him, Mr. Ruthyn, of Bartram Haugh. I look upon him, I do assure you, quite in the light of a saint; not, of course, in the Popish sense,* but in the very highest, you will understand me, which *our* Church allows—a man built up in faith—full of faith—faith and grace—altogether exemplary; and I often ventured to regret, Miss Ruthyn, that Providence in its mysterious dispensations should have placed him so far apart from his brother, your respected father. His influence and opportunities would, no doubt, we may venture to hope, at least have been blessed; and, perhaps, we—my valued rector and I—might possibly have seen more of him at church, than, I deeply regret, we *have* done.' He shook his head a little, as he smiled with a sad complacency on me through his blue steel spectacles, and then sipped a little meditative sherry.

'And you saw a good deal of my uncle?'

'Well, a *good* deal, Miss Ruthyn—I may say a *good* deal—principally at his own house. His health is wretched—miserable health—a sadly afflicted man he has been, as, no doubt, you are aware. But afflictions, my dear Miss Ruthyn, as you remember Doctor Clay so well remarked on Sunday last, though birds of ill-omen, yet spiritually resemble the ravens who supplied the prophet;* and when they visit the faithful, come charged with nourishment for the soul.

'He is a good deal embarrassed pecuniarily, I should say,' continued the curate, who was rather a good man than a very well-bred one. 'He found a difficulty—in fact it was not in his power—to subscribe generally to our little funds, and—and objects, and I used to say to him, and I really felt it, that it was more gratifying, such were his feeling and his power of expression, to be refused by him than assisted by others.'

'Did papa wish you to speak to me about my uncle?' I inquired, as a sudden thought struck me; and then I felt half ashamed of my question.

He looked surprised.

'No, Miss Ruthyn, certainly not. Oh, dear, no. It was merely a conversation between Mr. Ruthyn and me. He never suggested my opening that, or indeed any other point in my interview with you, Miss Ruthyn—not the least.'

'I was not aware before that Uncle Silas was so religious.'

He smiled tranquilly, not quite up to the ceiling, but gently upward, and shook his head in pity for my previous ignorance, as he lowered his eyes—

'I don't say that there may not be some little matters in a few points of doctrine which we could, perhaps, wish otherwise. But these you know are speculative, and in all essentials he is Church*—not in the perverted modern sense; far from it—unexceptionably Church, strictly so. Would there were more among us of the same mind that is in him! Ay, Miss Ruthyn, even in the highest places of the Church herself.'

The Rev. William Fairfield, while fighting against the Dissenters* with his right hand, was, with his left, hotly engaged with the Tractarians.* A good man I am sure he was, and I dare say sound in doctrine, though naturally, I think, not very wise. This conversation with him gave me new ideas about my Uncle Silas. It quite agreed with what my father had said. These principles and his increasing years would necessarily quiet the turbulence of his resistance to injustice, and teach him to acquiesce in his fate.

You would have fancied that one so young as I, born to wealth so vast, and living a life of such entire seclusion, would have been exempt from care. But you have seen how troubled my life was with fear and anxiety during the residence of Madame de la Rougierre, and now there rested upon my mind a vague and awful anticipation of the trial which my father had announced, without defining it.

An 'ordeal'* he called it, requiring not only zeal but nerve, which might possibly, were my courage to fail, become frightful and even intolerable. What, and of what nature, could it be? Not designed to vindicate the fair fame of the meek and submissive old man—who, it seemed, had ceased to care for his by-gone wrongs, and was looking to futurity—but the reputation of our ancient family.

Sometimes I repented my temerity in having undertaken it. I distrusted my courage. Had I not better retreat, while it was yet time? But there was shame and even difficulty in the thought. How should I appear before my father? Was it not important—had I not deliberately undertaken it—and was I not bound in conscience? Perhaps he had already taken steps in the matter which committed *him*. Besides, was I sure that, even were I free again, I would not once more devote myself to the trial, be it what it might. You perceive I had more spirit than courage. I think I had the mental attributes of courage; but then I was but a hysterical girl, and in so far neither more nor less than a coward.

No wonder I distrusted myself; no wonder also my will stood out against my timidity. It was a struggle, then; a proud, wild resolve against constitutional cowardice.

Those who have ever had cast upon them more than their strength seemed framed to bear—the weak, the aspiring, the adventurous and self-sacrificing in will, and the faltering in nerve—will understand the kind of agony which I sometimes endured.

But, again, consolation would come, and it seemed to me that I must be exaggerating my risk in the coming crisis; and certain at least, if my father believed it attended with real peril, he would never have wished to see me involved in it. But the silence under which I was bound was terrifying—double so when the danger was so shapeless and undivulged.

I was soon to understand it all—soon, too, to know all about my father's impending journey, whither—with what visitor—and why guarded from me with so awful a mystery.

That day there came a lively and good-natured letter from Lady Knollys. She was to arrive at Knowl in two or three days' time. I thought my father would have been pleased, but he seemed apathetic and dejected.

'One does not always feel quite equal to Monica. But for you—yes, thank God. I wish she could only stay, Maud, for a month or two; I may be going then, and would be glad—provided she talks about suitable things—very glad, Maud, to leave her with you for a week or so.'

There was something, I thought, agitating my father secretly that day. He had the strange hectic flush I had observed when he grew excited in our interview in the garden about Uncle Silas. There was something painful, perhaps even terrible, in the circumstances of the journey he was about to make, and from my heart I wished the suspense were over, the annoyance past, and he returned.

That night my father bid me good-night early and went up-stairs. After I had been in bed some little time, I heard his hand-bell ring. This was not usual. Shortly after I heard his man, Ridley, talking with Mrs. Rusk in the gallery. I could not be mistaken in their voices. I knew not why I was startled and excited, and had raised myself to listen on my elbow. But they were talking quietly, like persons giving or taking an ordinary direction, and not in the haste of an unusual emergency.

Then I heard the man bid Mrs. Rusk good-night and walk down the gallery to the stairs, so that I concluded he was wanted no more, and all must therefore be well. So I laid myself down again, though with a throbbing at my heart, and an ominous feeling of expectation— listening and fancying footsteps.

I was going to sleep when I heard the bell ring again; and, in a few minutes, Mrs. Rusk's energetic step passed along the gallery; and, listening intently, I heard, or fancied, my father's voice and hers in dialogue. All this was very unusual, and again I was, with a beating heart, leaning with my elbow on my pillow.

Mrs. Rusk came along the gallery in a minute or so after, and stopping at my door, began to open it gently. I was startled, and challenged my visitor with—

'Who's there?'

'It's only Rusk, Miss. Dearie me! and are you awake still?'

'Is papa ill?'

'Ill! not a bit ill, thank God. Only there's a little black book as I took for your prayer-book, and brought in here; ay, here it is, sure enough, and he wants it, and then I must go down to the study, and look out this one, "C, 15";* but I can't read the name, noways; and I was afraid to ask him again; if you be so kind to read it, Miss—I suspeck my eyes is a-going.'

I read the name; and Mrs. Rusk was tolerably expert at finding out books, as she had often been employed in that way before. So she departed.

I suppose that this particular volume was hard to find, for she must have been a long time away, and I had actually fallen into a doze when I was roused in an instant by a dreadful crash and a piercing scream from Mrs. Rusk. Scream followed scream, wilder and more terror-stricken. I shrieked to Mary Quince, who was sleeping in the room with me:—'Mary, do you hear? what is it? It is something dreadful'.

The crash was so tremendous that the solid flooring even of my room trembled under it, and to me it seemed as if some heavy man had burst through the top of the window, and shook the whole house with his descent. I found myself standing at my own door, crying, 'Help, help! murder! murder!' and Mary Quince, frightened half out of her wits, by my side.

I could not think what was going on. It was plainly something most horrible, for Mrs. Rusk's screams pealed one after the other unabated, though with a muffled sound, as if the door was shut upon her; and by this time the bells of my father's room were ringing madly.

'They are trying to murder him!' I cried, and I ran along the gallery to his door, followed by Mary Quince, whose white face I shall never forget, though her entreaties only sounded like unmeaning noises in my ears.

'Here! help, help, help!' I cried, trying to force open the door.

'Shove it, shove it, for God's sake! he's across it,' cried Mrs. Rusk's voice from within; 'drive it in. I can't move him.'

I strained all I could at the door, but ineffectually. We heard steps approaching. The men were running to the spot, and shouting as they did so—

'Never mind; hold on a bit; here we are; all right,' and the like.

We drew back, as they came up. We were in no condition to be seen. We listened, however, at my open door.

Then came the straining and bumping at the door. Mrs. Rusk's voice subsided to a sort of wailing; the men were talking all together, and I suppose the door opened, for I heard some of the voices, on a sudden, as if in the room, and then came a strange lull, and talking in very low tones, and not much even of that.

'What *is* it, Mary? what *can* it be?' I ejaculated, not knowing what horror to suppose. And now, with a counterpane about my shoulders, I called loudly and imploringly, in my horror, to know what had happened.

But I heard only the subdued and eager talk of men engaged in some absorbing task, and the dull sounds of some heavy body being moved.

Mrs. Rusk came towards us looking half wild, and pale as a spectre, and putting her thin hands to my shoulders, she said—'Now, Miss Maud, darling, you must go back again; 'tisn't no place for you; you'll see all, my darling, time enough—you will. There now, there, like a dear, do get into your room.'

What was that dreadful sound? Who had entered my father's chamber? It was the visitor whom we had so long expected, with whom he was to make the unknown journey, leaving me alone. The intruder was Death!

CHAPTER XXI

ARRIVALS

MY father was dead—as suddenly as if he had been murdered. One of those fearful aneurisms that lie close to the heart, showing no outward sign of giving way in a moment, had been detected a good time since by Doctor Bryerly. My father knew what must happen, and that it could not be long deferred. He feared to tell me that he was soon to die. He hinted it only in the allegory of his journey, and left in that sad enigma some words of true consolation that remained with me ever after. Under his rugged ways was hidden a wonderful tenderness. I could not believe that he was actually dead. Most people, for a minute or two, in the wild tumult of such a shock, have experienced the same insane scepticism. I insisted that the doctor should be instantly sent for from the village.

'Well, Miss Maud, dear, I *will* send to please you, but it is all to no use. If only you saw him yourself you'd know that. Mary Quince, run you down and tell Thomas, Miss Maud desires he'll go down this minute to the village for Doctor Elweys.'

Every minute of the interval seemed to me like an hour. I don't know what I said, but I fancied that if he were not already dead, he would lose his life by the delay. I suppose I was speaking very wildly, for Mrs. Rusk said—

'My dear child, you ought to come in and see him; indeed but you should, Miss Maud. He's quite dead an hour ago. You'd wonder all the blood that's come from him—you would indeed; it's soaked through the bed already.'

'Oh, don't, don't, *don't*, Mrs. Rusk.'

'Will you come in and see him, just?'

'Oh, no, no, no, no.'

'Well then my dear, don't, of course, if you don't like; there's no need. Would not you like to lie down, Miss Maud? Mary Quince, attend to her. I must go into the room for a minute or two.'

I was walking up and down the room in distraction. It was a cool night; but I did not feel it. I could only cry:—'Oh, Mary, Mary! what shall I do? Oh, Mary Quince! what shall I do?'

It seemed to me it must be near daylight by the time the Doctor arrived. I had dressed myself. I dared not go into the room where my beloved father lay.

I had gone out of my room to the gallery, where I awaited Dr. Elweys, when I saw him walking briskly after the servant, his coat buttoned up to his chin, his hat in his hand, and his bald head shining. I felt myself grow cold as ice, and colder and colder, and with a sudden sten* my heart seemed to stand still.

I heard him ask the maid who stood at the door, in that low, decisive, mysterious tone which doctors cultivate—

'In *here*?'

And then with a nod, I saw him enter.

'Would not you like to see the Doctor, Miss Maud?' asked Mary Quince.

The question roused me a little.

'Thank you, Mary; yes, I must see him.'

And so, in a few minutes, I did. He was very respectful, very sad, semi-undertakerlike, in air and countenance, but quite explicit. I heard that my dear father 'had died palpably from the rupture of some great vessel near the heart'. The disease had, no doubt, been 'long established, and is in its nature incurable'. It is 'consolatory in these cases that in the act of dissolution, which is instantaneous, there can be no suffering'. These, and a few more remarks, were all he had to offer; and having had his fee from Mrs. Rusk, he, with a respectful melancholy, vanished.

I returned to my room, and broke into paroxysms of grief, and after an hour or more grew more tranquil.

From Mrs. Rusk I learned that he had seemed very well; better than usual, indeed, that night, and that on her return from the study with the book he required, he was noting down, after his wont, some passages which illustrated the text on which he was employing himself. He took the book, detaining her in the room, and then mounting on a chair to take down another book from a shelf, he had fallen, with the dreadful crash I had heard, dead upon the floor. He fell across the door, which caused the difficulty in opening it. Mrs. Rusk found she had not strength to force it open. No wonder she had given way to terror. I think I should have almost lost my reason.

Every one knows the reserved aspect and the taciturn mood of the house, one of whose rooms is tenanted by that mysterious guest.

I do not know how those awful days, and more awful nights, passed over. The remembrance is repulsive. I hate to think of them. I was soon draped in the conventional black, with its heavy folds of crape. Lady Knollys came, and was very kind. She undertook the direction of all those details which were to me so inexpressibly dreadful. She wrote letters for me beside, and was really most kind and useful, and her society supported me indescribably. She was odd, but her eccentricity was leavened with strong common sense; and I have often thought since with admiration and gratitude of the tact with which she managed my grief.

There is no dealing with great sorrow as if it were under the control of our wills. It is a terrible phenomenon, whose laws we must study, and to whose conditions we must submit, if we would mitigate it. Cousin Monica talked a great deal of my father. This was easy to her, for her early recollections were full of him.

One of the terrible dislocations of our habits of mind respecting the dead is that our earthly future is robbed of them, and we thrown exclusively upon retrospect. From the long look forward they are removed, and every plan, imagination, and hope henceforth a silent and empty perspective. But in the past they are all they ever were. Now let me advise all who would comfort people in a new bereavement to talk to them, very freely, all they can, in this way of the dead. They will engage in it with interest, they will talk of their own recollections of the dead, and listen to yours, though they become sometimes pleasant, sometimes even laughable. I found it so. It robbed the calamity of something of its supernatural and horrible abruptness; it prevented that monotony of object which is to the mind what it is to the eye, and prepares the faculty for those mesmeric illusions that derange its sense.

Cousin Monica, I am sure, cheered me wonderfully. I grow to love her more and more, as I think of all her trouble, care, and kindness.

I had not forgotten my promise to dear papa about the key, concerning which he had evinced so great an anxiety. It was found in the pocket where he had desired me to remember he always kept it, except when it was placed, while he slept, under his pillow.

'And so, my dear, that wicked woman was actually found picking the lock of your poor papa's desk. I *wonder* he did not punish her—you know that is *burglary*.'

'Well, Lady Knollys, you know she is gone, and so I care no more about her—that is, I mean, I need not fear her.'

'No, my dear, but you must call me Monica—do you mind—I'm your cousin, and you call me Monica, unless you wish to vex me. No, of course, you need not be afraid of her. And she's gone. But I'm an old thing you know, and not so tender-hearted as you; and I confess I should have been very glad to hear that the wicked old witch had been sent to prison and hard labour—I should. And what do you suppose she was looking for—what did she want to steal? I think I can guess—what do *you* think?'

'To read the papers; maybe to take banknotes—I'm not sure,' I answered.

'Well, I think most likely she wanted to get at your poor papa's *will*—that's *my* idea.'

'There is nothing surprising in the supposition, dear,' she resumed. 'Did not you read the curious trial at York, the other day? There is nothing so valuable to steal as a will, when a great deal of property is to be disposed of by it. Why, you would have given her ever so much money to get it back again. Suppose you go down, dear, I'll go with you, and open the cabinet in the study.'

'I don't think I can, for I promised to give the key to Dr. Bryerly, and the meaning was that *he* only should open it.'

Cousin Monica uttered an inarticulate 'H'm!' of surprise or disapprobation.

'Has he been written to?'

'No, I do not know his address.'

'Not know his address! come, that is curious,' said Knollys, a little testily.

I could not—no one now living in the house could furnish even a conjecture. There was even a dispute as to which train he had gone by—north or south—they crossed the station at an interval of five minutes. If Doctor Bryerly had been an evil spirit, evoked by a secret incantation, there could not have been more complete darkness as to the immediate process of his approach.

'And how long do you mean to wait, my dear? No matter; at all events you may open the *desk;* you may find papers to direct you—you may find Doctor Bryerly's address—you may find, heaven knows what.'

So down we went—I assenting—and we opened the desk. How dreadful the desecration seems—all privacy abrogated—the shocking compensation for the silence of death!

Henceforward all is circumstantial evidence—all conjectural—except the *litera scripta*,* and to this evidence every note-book, and every scrap of paper and private letter, must contribute—ransacked, bare in the light of day—what it can.

At the top of the desk lay two notes sealed, one to Cousin Monica, the other to me. Mine was a gentle, and loving little farewell—nothing more—which opened afresh the fountains of my sorrow, and I cried and sobbed over it bitterly and long.

The other was for 'Lady Knollys'. I did not see how she received it, for I was already absorbed in mine. But in a while she came and kissed me in her girlish, good-natured way. Her eyes used to fill with tears at sight of my paroxysms of grief. Then she would begin, 'I remember it was a saying of his,' and so she would repeat it—something maybe wise, maybe playful, at all events consolatory—and the circumstances in which she had heard him say it, and then would follow the recollections suggested by these; and so I was stolen away half by him, and half by Cousin Monica, from my despair and lamentation.

Along with these lay a large envelope, inscribed with the words 'Directions to be complied with immediately on my death.' One of which was, 'Let the event be *forthwith* published in the *county* and principal *London* papers.' This step had been already taken. We found no record of Dr. Bryerly's address.

We made search everywhere, except in the cabinet, which I would on no account permit to be opened except according to his direction, by Dr. Bryerly's hand. But nowhere was a will, or any document resembling one, to be found. I had now, therefore, no doubt that his will was placed in that cabinet.

In the search among my dear father's papers we found two sheafs of letters, neatly tied up and labelled—these were from my Uncle Silas.

My Cousin Monica looked down upon these papers with a strange smile; was it satire—was it that indescribable smile with which a mystery which covers a long reach of years is sometimes approached?

These were odd letters. If here and there occurred passages that were querulous and even abject, there were also long passages of manly and altogether noble sentiment, and the strangest rodomontade and maunderings about religion. Here and there a letter would gradually transform itself into a prayer, and end with a doxology* and no signature; and some of them expressed such wild and disordered views respecting religion, as I imagine he can never have disclosed to good Mr. Fairfield, and which approached more nearly to the Swedenborg visions than to anything in the Church of England.

I read these with a solemn interest, but my Cousin Monica was not similarly moved. She read them with the same smile—faint, serenely contemptuous, I thought—with which she had first looked down upon them. It was the countenance of a person who amusedly traces the working of a character that is well understood.

'Uncle Silas is very religious?' I said, not quite liking Lady Knollys' looks.

'Very,' she said, without raising her eyes or abating her old bitter smile, as she glanced over a passage in one of his letters.

'You don't think he *is*, Cousin Monica?' said I. She raised her head and looked straight at me.

'Why do you say that, Maud?'

'Because you smile incredulously, I think, over his letters.'

'Do I?' said she; 'I was not thinking—it was quite an accident. The fact is, Maud, your poor papa quite mistook me. I had no prejudice respecting him—no theory. I never knew what to think about him. I do not think Silas a product of nature, but a child of the Sphinx,* and I never could understand him—that's all.'

'I always felt so too; but that was because I was left to speculation, and to glean conjectures as I might from his portrait, or anywhere. Except what you told me, I never heard more than a few sentences; poor papa did not like me to ask questions about him, and I think he ordered the servants to be silent.'

'And much the same injunction this little note lays upon me—not quite, but something like it; and I don't know the meaning of it.'

And she looked inquiringly at me.

'You are not to be *alarmed* about your Uncle Silas, because your being afraid would unfit you for an *important service* which you have undertaken for your family, the nature of which I shall soon understand, and which, although it is quite *passive*, would be made very sad if *illusory fears* were allowed to *steal into your mind*.'

She was looking into the letter in poor papa's handwriting, which she had found addressed to her in his desk, and emphasized the words, I suppose, which she quoted from it.

'Have you any idea, Maud, darling, what this *service* may be?' she inquired, with a grave and anxious curiosity in her countenance.

'None, Cousin Monica; but I have thought long over my undertaking to do it, or submit to it, be it what it may; and I will keep the promise I voluntarily made, although I know what a coward I am, and often distrust my courage.'

'Well, I am not to frighten you.'

'How could you? Why should I be afraid? *Is* there anything frightful to be disclosed? do tell me—you *must* tell me.'

'No, darling, I did not mean *that*—I don't mean that;—I could, if I would; I—I don't know exactly what I meant. But your poor papa knew him better than I—in fact I did not know him at all—that is, ever quite understood him—which your poor papa, I see, had ample opportunities of doing.' And after a little pause, she added—'So you do not know what you are expected to do or to undergo.'

'Oh! Cousin Monica, I know you think he committed that murder,' I cried, starting up, I don't know why, and I felt that I grew deadly pale.

'I don't believe any such thing, you little fool; you must not say such horrible things, Maud,' she said, rising also, and looking both pale and angry. 'Shall we go out for a little walk? Come, lock up these papers, dear, and get your things on; and if that Dr. Bryerly does not turn up to-morrow, you must send for the Rector, good Doctor Clay, and let him make search for the will—there may be directions about many things, you know; and my dear Maud, you are to remember that Silas is *my* cousin as well as your uncle. Come, dear, put on your hat.'

So we went out together for a little cloistered walk.

CHAPTER XXII

SOMEBODY IN THE ROOM WITH THE COFFIN

WHEN we returned, a 'young' gentleman had arrived. We saw him in the parlour as we passed the window. It was simply a glance, but such a one as suffices to make a photograph, which we can study afterwards, at our leisure. I remember him at this moment—a man of six-and-thirty—dressed in a grey travelling suit, not over-well made; light-haired, fat-faced, and clumsy, and he looked both dull and cunning, and not at all like a gentleman.

Branston met us, announced the arrival, and handed me the stranger's credentials. My cousin and I stopped in the passage to read them.

'*That's* your Uncle Silas's,' said Lady Knollys, touching one of the two letters with the tip of her finger.

'Shall he have lunch, Miss?'

'Certainly.' So Branston departed.

'Read it with me, Cousin Monica,' I said. And a very curious letter it was. It spoke as follows:—

'How can I thank my beloved niece for remembering her aged and forlorn kinsman at such a moment of anguish?'

I had written a note of a few, I dare say, incoherent words by the next post after my dear father's death.

'It is, however, in the hour of bereavement that we most value the ties that are broken, and yearn for the sympathy of kindred.'

Here came a little distich* of French verse, of which I could only read *ciel* and *l'amour*.*

'Our quiet household here is clouded with a new sorrow. How inscrutable are the ways of Providence! I—though a few years younger—how much the more infirm—how shattered in energy and in mind—how mere a burden—how entirely *de trop*—am spared to my sad place in a world where I can be no longer useful, where I have but one business—prayer, but one hope—the tomb; and he—apparently so robust—the centre of so much good—so necessary to you—so necessary, alas! to me—is taken! He is gone to his rest—for us, what remains but to bow our heads, and murmur, "His will be done?" I trace these lines with a trembling hand, while tears dim my old eyes. I did not think that any earthly event could have moved me so profoundly. From the world I have long stood aloof. I once led a life of pleasure—alas! of wickedness—as I now do one of austerity; but as I never was rich, so my worst enemy will allow I never was avaricious. My sins, I thank my Maker, have been of a more reducible kind, and have succumbed to the discipline which heaven has provided. To earth and its interests, as well as to its pleasures, I have long been dead. For the few remaining years of my life I ask but quiet—an exemption from the agitations and distractions of struggle and care, and I trust to the Giver of all Good for my deliverance—well knowing, at the same time, that whatever befalls will, under His direction, prove best. Happy shall I be, my dearest niece, if in your most interesting, and in some respects, forlorn situation, I can be of any use to you. My present religious adviser—of whom I ventured to ask counsel on your behalf—states that I ought to send some one to represent me at the melancholy ceremony of reading the will which my beloved and now happy brother has, no doubt, left behind; and the idea that the experience and professional knowledge possessed by the gentleman whom I have selected may possibly be of use to you, my dearest niece, determines me to place him at your disposal. He is the junior partner in the firm of Archer and Sleigh, who conduct any little business which I may have from time to time: may I entreat your hospitality for him during a brief stay at Knowl? I write, even for a moment, upon these small matters of business with an effort—a painful one, but necessary. Alas! my brother! The cup of bitterness is now full. Few and evil must the remainder of my old days be. Yet while they last, I remain always for my beloved niece, that which all her wealth and splendour cannot purchase—a loving and faithful kinsman and friend,

'SILAS RUTHYN.'

'Is not it a kind letter?' I said, while tears stood in my eyes.

'Yes,' answered Lady Knollys, drily.

'But don't you think it so, really?'

'Oh! kind, very kind,' she answered in the same tone, 'and perhaps a little cunning.'

'Cunning!—how?'

'Well, you know I'm a peevish old Tabby, and of course I scratch now and then, and see in the dark. I dare say Silas is sorry, but I don't

think he is in sackcloth and ashes. He has reason to be sorry and anxious, and I say I think he is both; and you know he pities you very
much, and also himself a good deal; and he wants money, and you—his
beloved niece—have a great deal—and altogether it is an affectionate
and prudent letter; and he has sent his attorney here to make a note of
the will; and you are to give the gentleman his meals and lodging; and
Silas, very thoughtfully, invites you to confide your difficulties and
troubles to *his* solicitor. It is very kind, but not imprudent.'

'Oh, Cousin Monica, don't you think at such a moment it is hardly
natural that he should form such petty schemes, even were he capable
at other times of practising so low? Is it not judging him hardly? and
you, you know, so little acquainted with him.'

'I told you dear, I'm a cross old thing—and there's an end; and
I really don't care two pence about him; and of the two I'd much
rather he were no relation of ours.'

Now, was not this prejudice? I dare say in part it was. So, too, was
my vehement predisposition in his favour. I am afraid we women are
factionists; we always take a side, and nature has formed us for advo-
cates rather than judges; and I think the function, if less dignified, is
more amiable.

I sat alone at the drawing-room window, at nightfall, awaiting my
Cousin Monica's entrance.

Feverish and frightened I felt that night. It was a sympathy I fancy
with the weather. The sun had set stormily. Though the air was still,
the sky looked wild and storm-swept. The crowding clouds, slanting
in the attitude of flight, reflected their own scared aspect upon my
spirits. My grief darkened with a wild presaging of danger, and
a sense of the supernatural fell upon me. It was the saddest and most
awful evening that had come since my beloved father's death.

All kinds of shapeless fears environed me in silence. For the first
time, dire misgivings about the form of faith affrighted me. Who were
these Swedenborgians who had got about him—no one could tell
how—and held him so fast to the close of his life? Who was this
bilious, bewigged, black-eyed Doctor Bryerly, whom none of us quite
liked and all a little feared; who seemed to rise out of the ground, and
came and went, no one knew whence or whither, exercising, as
I imagined, a mysterious authority over him? Was it all good and true,
or a heresy and a witchcraft? Oh, my beloved father! was it all well
with you?

When Lady Knollys entered she found me in floods of tears walking distractedly up and down the room. She kissed me in silence; she walked back and forward with me, and did her best to console me.

'I think, Cousin Monica, I would wish to see him once more. Shall we go up?'

'Unless you really wish it very much, I think, darling, you had better not mind it. It is happier to recollect them as they were; there's a change, you know, darling, and there is seldom any comfort in the sight.'

'But I do wish it *very* much. Oh! won't you come with me?'

And so I persuaded her, and up we went hand in hand, in the deepening twilight; and we halted at the end of the dark gallery, and I called Mrs. Rusk, growing frightened.

'Tell her to let us in, Cousin Monica,' I whispered.

'She wishes to see him, my lady—does she?' inquired Mrs. Rusk, in an undertone, and with a mysterious glance at me, as she softly fitted the key to the lock.

'Are you quite sure, Maud, dear?'

'Yes, yes.'

But when Mrs. Rusk entered bearing the candle, whose beam mixed dismally with the expiring twilight, disclosing a great black coffin standing upon trestles, near the foot of which she took her stand, gazing sternly into it, I lost heart again altogether and drew back.

'No, Mrs. Rusk, she won't; and I am very glad, dear,' she added to me. 'Come, Mrs. Rusk, come away. Yes, darling,' she continued to me, 'it is much better for you,' and she hurried me away, and down stairs again. But the awful outlines of that large black coffin remained upon my imagination with a new and terrible sense of death.

I had no more any wish to see him. I felt a horror even of the room, and for more than an hour after a kind of despair and terror, such as I have never experienced before or since at the idea of death.

Cousin Monica had had her bed placed in my room, and Mary Quince's moved to the dressing-room adjoining it. For the first time the superstitious awe that follows death, but not immediately, visited me. The idea of seeing my father enter the room, or open the door and look in, haunted me. After Lady Knollys and I were in bed, I could not sleep. The wind sounded mournfully outside, and the small sounds, the rattlings, and strainings that responded from within, constantly startled me, and simulated the sounds of steps, of doors opening, of knockings, and so forth, rousing me with a palpitating heart as often as I fell into a doze.

At length the wind subsided, and these ambiguous noises abated, and I, fatigued, dropped into a quiet sleep. I was awaked by a sound in the gallery—which I could not define. A considerable time had passed, for the wind was now quite lulled. I sat up in my bed a good deal scared, listening breathlessly for I knew not what.

I heard a step moving stealthily along the gallery. I called my Cousin Monica softly; and we both heard the door of the room in which my dear father's body lay unlocked, some one furtively enter, and the door shut.

'What can it be? Good Heavens, Cousin Monica, do you hear it?'

'Yes, dear; and it is two o'clock.'

Every one at Knowl was in bed at eleven. We knew very well that Mrs. Rusk was rather nervous, and would not, for worlds, go alone, and at such an hour, to the room. We called Mary Quince. We all three listened, but we heard no other sound. I set these things down here because they made so terrible an impression upon me at the time.

It ended by our peeping out, all three in a body, upon the gallery. Through each window in the perspective came its blue sheet of moonshine; but the door on which our attention was fixed was in the shade, and we thought we could discern the glare of a candle through the keyhole. While in whispers we were debating this point together, the door opened, the dusky light of a candle emerged, the shadow of a figure crossed it within, and in another moment the mysterious Doctor Bryerly—angular, ungainly, in the black cloth coat that fitted little better than a coffin—issued from the chamber, candle in hand; murmuring, I suppose, a prayer—it sounded like a farewell—as he looked back, pallid and grim, into the room; and then stepped cautiously upon the gallery floor, shutting and locking the door upon the dead; and then having listened for a second, the saturnine figure, casting a gigantic and distorted shadow upon the ceiling and side-wall from the lowered candle, strode lightly down the long dark passage, away from us.

I can only speak for myself, and I can honestly say that I felt as much frightened as if I had just seen a sorcerer stealing from his unhallowed business. I think Cousin Monica was also affected in the same way, for she turned the key on the inside of the door when we entered. I do not think one of us believed at the moment that what we had seen was a Doctor Bryerly of flesh and blood, and yet the first thing we spoke of in the morning was Doctor Bryerly's arrival. The mind is a different organ by night and by day.

CHAPTER XXIII

I TALK WITH DOCTOR BRYERLY

DOCTOR BRYERLY had, indeed, arrived at half-past twelve o'clock at night. His summons at the hall-door was little heard at our remote side of the old house of Knowl; and when the sleepy, half-dressed servant opened the door, the lank Doctor, in glossy black clothing, was standing alone, his portmanteau on its end upon the steps, and his vehicle disappearing in the shadows of the old trees.

In he came, sterner and sharper of aspect than usual.

'I've been expected? I'm Doctor Bryerly. Haven't I? So, let whoever is in charge of the body be called. I must visit it forthwith.'

So the Doctor sat in the back drawing-room, with a solitary candle; and Mrs. Rusk was called up, and, grumbling much and very peevish, dressed and went down, her ill-temper subsiding in a sort of fear as she approached the visitor.

'How do you do, Madam? a sad visit this. Is any one watching in the room where the remains of your late master are laid?'

'No.'

'So much the better; it is a foolish custom. Will you please conduct me to the room? I must pray where he lies—no longer *he*! And be good enough to show me my bedroom, and so no one need wait up, and I shall find my way.'

Accompanied by the man who carried his valise, Mrs. Rusk showed him to his apartment; but he only looked in, and then glanced rapidly about to take 'the bearings' of the door.

'Thank you—yes. Now we'll proceed, here, along here? Let me see. A turn to the right and another to the left—yes. He has been dead some days. Is he yet in his coffin?'

'Yes, sir; since yesterday afternoon.'

Mrs. Rusk was growing more and more afraid of this lean figure sheathed in shining black cloth, whose eyes glittered with a horrible sort of cunning, and whose long brown fingers groped before him, as if indicating the way by guess.

'But, of course, the lid's not on; you've not screwed him down, hey?'

'No, sir.'

'That's well. I must look on the face as I pray. He is in his place; I here on earth. He in the spirit; I in the flesh. The neutral ground lies there. So are carried the vibrations, and so the light of earth and heaven reflected back and forward—apaugasma,* a wonderful though helpless engine, the ladder of Jacob,* and behold the angels of God ascending and descending on it. Thanks, I'll take the key. Mysteries to those who *will* live altogether in houses of clay, no mystery to such as will use their eyes and read what is revealed. *This* candle, it is the longer, please; no—no need of a pair, thanks; just this, to hold in my hand. And remember, all depends upon the willing mind. Why do you look frightened? Where is your faith? Don't you know that spirits are about us at all times? Why should you fear to be near the body? The spirit is everything; the flesh profiteth nothing.'

'Yes, sir,' said Mrs. Rusk, making him a great courtesy in the threshold.

She was frightened by his eerie talk, which grew, she fancied, more voluble and energetic as they approached the corpse.

'Remember, then, that when you fancy yourself alone and wrapt in darkness, you stand, in fact, in the centre of a theatre, as wide as the starry floor of heaven, with an audience, whom no man can number, beholding you under a flood of light. Therefore, though your body be in solitude and your mortal sense in darkness, remember to walk as being in the light, surrounded with a cloud of witnesses. Thus walk; and when the hour comes, and you pass forth unprisoned from the tabernacle of the flesh, although it still has its relations and its rights'—and saying this, as he held the solitary candle aloft in the doorway, he nodded towards the coffin, whose large black form was faintly traceable against the shadows beyond—'you will rejoice; and being clothed upon with your house from on high, you will not be found naked. On the other hand, he that loveth corruption shall have enough thereof. Think upon these things. Good-night.'

And the Swedenborgian Doctor stepped into the room, taking the candle with him, and closed the door upon the shadowy still-life there, and on his own sharp and swarthy visage, leaving Mrs. Rusk in a sort of panic in the dark alone, to find her way to her room the best way she could.

Early in the morning Mrs. Rusk came to my room to tell me that Doctor Bryerly was in the parlour, and begged to know whether I had not a message for him. I was already dressed, so, though it was dreadful seeing a stranger in my then mood, taking the key of the cabinet in my hand, I followed Mrs. Rusk down stairs.

Opening the parlour door, she stepped in, and with a little courtesy said,—

'Please, sir, the young mistress—Miss Ruthyn.'

Draped in black and very pale, tall and slight, 'the young mistress' was; and as I entered I heard a newspaper rustle, and the sound of steps approaching to meet me.

Face to face we met, near the door; and, without speaking, I made him a deep courtesy.

He took my hand, without the least indication on my part, in his hard lean grasp, and shook it kindly, but familiarly, peering with a stern sort of curiosity into my face as he continued to hold it. His ill-fitting, glossy black cloth, ungainly presence, and sharp, dark, vulpine features had in them, as I said before, the vulgarity of a Glasgow artisan in his Sabbath suit. I made an instantaneous motion to withdraw my hand, but he held it firmly.

Though there was a grim sort of familiarity, there was also decision, shrewdness, and, above all, kindness, in his dark face—a gleam on the whole of the masterly and the honest—that along with a certain paleness, betraying, I thought, restrained emotion, indicated sympathy and invited confidence.

'I hope, Miss, you are pretty well?' He pronounced 'pretty' as it is spelt. 'I have come in consequence of a solemn promise exacted more than a year since by your deceased father, the late Mr. Austin Ruthyn of Knowl, for whom I cherished a warm esteem, being knit besides with him in spiritual bonds. It has been a shock to you, Miss?'

'It has, indeed, Sir.'

'I've a doctor's degree, I have—Doctor of Medicine, Miss. Like St. Luke, preacher and doctor. I was in business once, but this is better. As one footing fails, the Lord provides another. The stream of life is black and angry; how so many of us get across without drowning, I often wonder. The best way is not to look too far before—just from one stepping-stone to another; and though you may wet your feet, He won't let you drown—He has not allowed me.'

And Doctor Bryerly held up his head, and wagged it resolutely.

'You are born to this world's wealth; in its way a great blessing, though a great trial, Miss, and a great trust; but don't suppose you are destined to exemption from trouble on that account, any more than poor Emmanuel Bryerly. As the sparks fly upwards,* Miss Ruthyn! Your cushioned carriage may overturn on the high-road, as I may stumble and fall upon the foot-path. There are other troubles than debt and privation. Who can tell how long health may last, or when an accident may happen the brain; what mortifications may await you in your own high sphere; what unknown enemies may rise up in your path; or what slanders may asperse your name—ha, ha! It is a wonderful equilibrium—a marvellous dispensation—ha, ha!' and he laughed with a shake of his head, I thought a little sarcastically, as if he was not sorry my money could not avail to buy immunity from the general curse.

'But what money can't do, *prayer* can—bear that in mind, Miss Ruthyn. We can all pray; and though thorns, and snares, and stones of fire lie strewn in our way, we need not fear them. He will give His angels charge over us,* and in their hands they will bear us up, for He hears and sees everywhere, and His angels are innumerable.'

He was now speaking gently and solemnly; and paused. But another vein of thought he had unconsciously opened in my mind, and I said—

'And had my dear papa no other medical adviser?'

He looked at me sharply, and flushed a little under his dark tint. His medical skill was, perhaps, the point on which his human vanity vaunted itself, and I dare say there was something very disparaging in my tone.

'And if he *had* no other he might have done worse. I've had many critical cases in my hands, Miss Ruthyn. I can't charge myself with any miscarriage through ignorance. My diagnosis in Mr. Ruthyn's case has been verified by the result. But I was *not* alone; Sir Clayton Barrow saw him, and took my view; a note will reach him in London. But this, excuse me, is not to the present purpose. The late Mr. Ruthyn told me I was to receive a key from you, which would open a cabinet where he had placed his will—ha! thanks,—in his study. And, I think, as there may be directions about the funeral, it had better be read forthwith. Is there any gentleman—a relative or man of business—near here, whom you would wish sent for?'

'No, none, thank you; I have confidence in you, Sir.'

I think I spoke and looked frankly, for he smiled very kindly, though with closed lips.

'And you may be sure, Miss Ruthyn, your confidence shall not be disappointed.' Here was a long pause. 'But you are very young, and you must have some one by in your interest, who has some experience in business. Let me see. Is not the Rector, Dr. Clay, at hand? In the town?—very good; and Mr. Danvers, who manages the estate, *he* must come. And get Grimston—you see I know all the names—Grimston, the attorney; for though he was not employed about this will, he has been Mr. Ruthyn's solicitor a great many years; we must have Grimston; for, as I suppose you know, though it is a short will, it is a very strange one. I expostulated, but you know he was very decided when he took a view. He read it to you, eh?'

'No, sir.'

'Oh, but he told you so much as relates to you and your uncle, Mr. Silas Ruthyn, of Bartram Haugh?'

'No, indeed, Sir.'

'Ha! I wish he had.'

And with these words Doctor Bryerly's countenance darkened.

'Mr. Silas Ruthyn is a religious man?'

'Oh, *very!*' said I.

'You've seen a good deal of him?'

'No, I never saw him,' I answered.

'H'm? Odder and odder! But he's a good man, isn't he?'

'Very good indeed, Sir,—a very religious man.'

Doctor Bryerly was watching my countenance as I spoke, with a sharp and anxious eye; and then he looked down, and read the pattern of the carpet like bad news, for a while, and looking again in my face, askance, he said—

'He was very near joining *us*—on the point. He got into correspondence with Henry Voerst, one of our best men. They call us Swedenborgians, you know, but I dare say that won't go much further, now. I suppose, Miss Ruthyn, one o'clock would be a good hour, and I am sure, under the circumstances, the gentlemen will make a point of attending.'

'Yes, Dr. Bryerly, the notes shall be sent, and my cousin, Lady Knollys, would, I am sure, attend with me while the will is being read—there would be no objection to her presence?'

'None in the world. I can't be quite sure who are joined with me as executors. I'm almost sorry I did not decline; but it is too late regretting. One thing you must believe, Miss Ruthyn; in framing the provisions of the will I was never consulted—although I expostulated against the only very unusual one it contains when I heard it. I did so

strenuously; but in vain. There was one other against which I protested—having a right to do so—with better effect. In no other way
does the will in any respect owe anything to my advice or dissuasion.
You will please believe this; also that I am your friend. Yes, indeed, it
is my duty.'

The latter words he spoke looking down again, as it were in soliloquy; and thanking him, I withdrew.

When I reached the hall, I regretted that I had not asked him to
state distinctly what arrangements the will made so nearly affecting,
as it seemed, my relations with my Uncle Silas, and for a moment
I thought of returning and requesting an explanation. But then,
I bethought me, it was not very long to wait till one o'clock—so *he*, at
least, would think. I went up-stairs, therefore, to the 'school-room,'
which we used at present as a sitting-room, and there I found Cousin
Monica awaiting me.

'Are you quite well, dear?' asked Lady Knollys, as she came to meet
and kiss me.

'Quite well, Cousin Monica.'

'No nonsense, Maud! you're as white as that handkerchief—what's
the matter? Are you ill—are you frightened? Yes, you're trembling—you're terrified, child.'

'I believe I *am* afraid. There *is* something in poor papa's will about
Uncle Silas—about *me*. I don't know—Doctor Bryerly says, and he
seems so uncomfortable and frightened himself, I am sure it is some-
think very bad. I am *very* much frightened—I am—I *am*. Oh, Cousin
Monica! you won't leave me?'

So I threw my arms about her neck, clasping her very close, and we
kissed one another, I crying like a frightened child, and indeed in
experience of the world I was no more.

CHAPTER XXIV

THE OPENING OF THE WILL

PERHAPS the terror with which I anticipated the hour of one, and the disclosure of the unknown undertaking to which I had bound myself, was irrational and morbid. But, honestly, I doubt it; my tendency has always been that of many other weak characters, to act impetuously, and afterwards to reproach myself for consequences which I have, perhaps, in reality, had little or no share in producing.

It was Doctor Bryerly's countenance and manner in alluding to a particular provision in my father's will that instinctively awed me. I have seen faces in a nightmare that haunted me with an indescribable horror, and yet I could not say wherein lay the fascination. And so it was with his—an omen, a menace, lurked in its sallow and dismal glance.

'You must not be so frightened, darling,' said Cousin Monica. 'It is foolish; it *is*, *really*; they can't cut off your head, you know: they can't really harm you in any essential way. If it involved a risk of a little money you would not mind it; but men are such odd creatures; they measure all sacrifices by money. Doctor Bryerly would look just as you describe, if you were doomed to lose five hundred pounds, and yet it would not kill you.'

A companion like Lady Knollys is reassuring; but I could not take her comfort altogether to heart, for I felt that she had no great confidence in it herself.

There was a little French clock over the mantelpiece in the schoolroom, which I consulted nearly every minute. It wanted now but ten minutes of one.

'Shall we go down to the drawing-room, dear?' said Cousin Knollys, who was growing restless like me.

So down stairs we went, pausing by mutual consent at the great window at the stair-head, which looks out on the avenue. Mr. Danvers was riding his tall, grey horse at a walk, under the wide branches toward the house, and we waited to see him get off at the door. In his turn he loitered there, for the good Rector's gig, driven by the Curate, was approaching at a smart ecclesiastical trot.

Doctor Clay got down, and shook hands with Mr. Danvers; and after a word or two, away drove the Curate with that upward glance at the windows from which so few can refrain.

I watched the Rector and Mr. Danvers loitering on the steps as a patient might the gathering of surgeons who are to perform some unknown operation. They, too, glanced up at the window as they turned to enter the house, and I drew back. Cousin Monica looked at her watch.

'Four minutes only. Shall we go to the drawing-room?'

Waiting for a moment to let the gentlemen get by on the way to the study, we, accordingly, went down, and I heard the Rector talk of the dangerous state of Grindleston bridge, and wondered how he could think of such things at a time of sorrow. Everything about those few minutes of suspense remains fresh in my recollection. I remember how they loitered and came to a halt at the corner of the oak passage leading to the study, and how the Rector patted the marble head and smoothed the inflexible tresses of William Pitt, as he listened to Mr. Danvers' details about the presentment; and then, as they went on, I recollect the boisterous nose-blowing that suddenly resounded from the passage, and which I then referred, and still refer, intuitively to the Rector.

We had not been five minutes in the drawing-room when Branston entered, to say that the gentlemen I had mentioned were all assembled in the study.

'Come, dear,' said Cousin Monica; and leaning on her arm I reached the study door. I entered, followed by her. The gentlemen arrested their talk and stood up, those who were sitting, and the Rector came forward very gravely, and in low tones, and very kindly, greeted me. There was nothing emotional in this salutation, for though my father never quarrelled, yet an immense distance separated him from all his neighbours, and I do not think there lived a human being who knew him at more than perhaps a point or two of his character.

Considering how entirely he secluded himself, my father was, as many people living remember, wonderfully popular in his county. He was neighbourly in everything except in seeing company and mixing in society. He had magnificent shooting, of which he was extremely liberal. He kept a pack of hounds at Dollerton, with which all his side of the county hunted through the season. He never refused any claim upon his purse which had the slightest show of reason. He subscribed to every fund, social, charitable, sporting, agricultural, no matter what, provided the honest people of his county took an interest in it, and always with a princely hand; and although he shut himself up, no one could say that he was inaccessible, for he devoted hours daily to answering letters, and his cheque-book contributed largely in those replies. He had taken his turn long ago as High Sheriff; so there was an end of that claim before his oddity and shyness had quite secluded him. He refused the Lord-Lieutenancy of his county; he declined every post of personal distinction connected with it. He could write an able as well as a genial letter when he pleased; and his appearances at public meetings, dinners, and so forth were made in this epistolary fashion, and when occasion presented, by magnificent contributions from his purse.

If my father had been less good-natured in the sporting relations of his vast estates, or less magnificent in dealing with his fortune, or even if he had failed to exhibit the intellectual force which always characterized his letters on public matters, I dare say that his oddities would have condemned him to ridicule and possibly to dislike. But every one of the principal gentlemen of his county, whose judgment was valuable, has told me that he was a remarkably able man, and that his failure in public life was due to his eccentricities, and in no respect to deficiency in those peculiar mental qualities which make men feared and useful in Parliament.

I could not forbear placing on record this testimony to the high mental and the kindly qualities of my beloved father, who might have passed for a misanthrope or a fool. He was a man of generous nature and powerful intellect, but given up to the oddities of a shyness which grew with years and indulgence, and became inflexible with his disappointments and affliction.

There was something even in the Rector's kind and ceremonious greeting which oddly enough reflected the mixed feelings in which awe was not without a place, with which his neighbours had regarded my dear father.

Having done the honours—I am sure looking wofully pale—I had time to glance quietly at the only figure there with which I was not tolerably familiar. This was the junior partner in the firm of Archer and Sleigh who represented my Uncle Silas—a fat and pallid man of six-and-thirty, with a sly and evil countenance, and it has always seemed to me, that ill dispositions show more repulsively in a pale fat face than in any other.

Doctor Bryerly, standing near the window, was talking in a low tone to Mr. Grimston, our attorney.

I heard good Dr. Clay whisper to Mr. Danvers—

'Is not that Doctor Bryerly—the person with the black—the black—it's a wig, I think—in the window, talking to Abel Grimston?'

'Yes; that's he.'

'Odd-looking person—one of the Swedenborg people, is not he?' continued the Rector.

'So I am told.'

'Yes,' said the Rector, quietly; and he crossed one gaitered leg over the other, and with fingers interlaced, twiddled his thumbs, as he eyed the monstrous sectary under his orthodox old brows with a stern inquisitiveness. I thought he was meditating theologic battle.

But Dr. Bryerly and Mr. Grimston, still talking together, began to walk slowly from the window, and the former said in his peculiar grim tones—

'I beg pardon, Miss Ruthyn; perhaps you would be so good as to show us which of the cabinets in this room your late lamented father pointed out as that to which this key belongs.'

I indicated the oak cabinet.

'Very good ma'am—very good,' said Doctor Bryerly, as he fumbled the key into the lock.

Cousin Monica could not forbear murmuring—

'Dear! what a brute!'

The junior partner, with his dumpy hands in his pocket, poked his fat face over Mr. Grimston's shoulder, and peered into the cabinet as the door opened.

The search was not long. A handsome white paper enclosure, neatly tied up in pink tape, and sealed with large red seals, was inscribed in my dear father's hand:—'Will of Austin R. Ruthyn, of Knowl.' Then in smaller characters, the date, and in the corner a note, 'This will was drawn from my instructions by Gaunt, Hogg, and Hatchett, Solicitors, Great Woburn Street, London, A. R. R.'

'Let *me* have a squint at that indorsement, please, gentlemen,' half whispered the unpleasant person who represented my Uncle Silas.

''*Tisn't* an indorsement. There, look—a memorandum on an envelope,' said Abel Grimston, gruffly.

'Thanks—all right—that will do,' he responded, himself making a pencil-note of it, in a long clasp-book which he drew from his coat pocket.

The tape was carefully cut, and the envelope removed without tearing the writing, and forth came the will, at sight of which my heart swelled and fluttered up to my lips and then dropped down dead as it seemed into its place.

'Mr. Grimston, you will please to read it,' said Doctor Bryerly, who took the direction of the process. 'I will sit beside you, and as we go along you will be good enough to help us to understand technicalities, and give us a lift where we want it.'

'It's a short will,' said Mr. Grimston, turning over the sheets; '*very*—considering. Here's a codicil.'

'I did not see that,' said Doctor Bryerly.

'Dated only a month ago.'

'Oh!' said Doctor Bryerly, putting on his spectacles. Uncle Silas's ambassador, sitting close behind, had insinuated his face between Doctor Bryerly's and the reader's of the will.

'On behalf of the surviving brother of the testator,' interposed the delegate, just as Abel Grimston had cleared his voice to begin, 'I take leave to apply for a copy of this instrument. It will save a deal of trouble, if the young lady as represents the testator here has no objection.'

'You can have as many copies as you like when the will is proved,' said Mr. Grimston.

'I know that; but supposing as all's right, where's the objection?'

'Just the objection there always is to acting irregular,' replied Mr. Grimston.

'You don't object to act disobliging, it seems.'

'You can do as I told you,' replied Mr. Grimston.

'Thank you for nothing,' murmured Mr. Sleigh.

And the reading of the will proceeded, while he made elaborate notes of its contents in his capacious pocket-book.

'I, Austin Aylmer Ruthyn, being, I thank God, of sound mind and perfect recollection,' &c., &c.; and then came a bequest of all his estates real, chattels real, copyrights, leases, chattels, money, rights, interests, reversions, powers, plate, pictures, and estates and possessions whatsoever to four persons—Lord Ilbury, Mr. Penrose Creswell of Creswell, Sir William Aylmer, Bart., and Hans Emmanuel Bryerly, Doctor of Medicine, to have and to hold, &c., &c. Whereupon my Cousin Monica ejaculated 'Eh?' and Doctor Bryerly interposed—

'Four trustees, ma'am. We take little but trouble—you'll see; go on.'

Then it came out that all this multifarious splendour was bequeathed in trust for me, subject to a bequest of fifteen thousand

pounds to his only brother, Silas Aylmer Ruthyn, and three thousand
five hundred pounds each to the two children of his said brother; and
lest any doubt should arise by reason of his, the testator's decease as
to the continuance of the arrangement by way of lease under which he
enjoyed his present habitation and farm, he left him the use of the
mansion-house and lands of Bartram-Haugh, in the county of
Derbyshire, and of the lands of so-and-so and so-and-so, adjoining
thereto, in the said county, for the term of his natural life, on payment
of a rent of five shillings per annum, and subject to the like conditions
as to waste, &c., as are expressed in the said lease.

'By your leave, may I ask is them dispositions all the devises* to my
client, which is his only brother, as it seems to me you've seen the will
before?' inquired Mr. Sleigh.

'Nothing more, unless there is something in the codicil,' answered
Dr. Bryerly.

But there was no mention of him in the codicil.

Mr. Sleigh threw himself back in his chair, and sneered, with the
end of his pencil between his teeth. I hope his disappointment was
altogether for his client. Mr. Danvers fancied, he afterwards said, that
he had probably expected legacies which might have involved litigation, or, at all events, law costs, and perhaps a stewardship; but this
was very barren; and Mr. Danvers also remarked, that the man was
a very low practitioner, and wondered how my Uncle Silas could have
commissioned such a person to represent him.

So far the will contained nothing of which my most partial friend
could have complained. The codicil, too, devised only legacies to
servants, and a sum of £1,000, with a few kind words, to Monica,
Lady Knollys, and a further sum of £3,000 to Dr. Bryerly, stating that
the legatee had prevailed upon him to erase from the draft of his will
a bequest to him to that amount, but that, in consideration of all the
trouble devolving upon him as trustee, he made that bequest by his
codicil; and with these arrangements the permanent disposition of
his property was completed.

But that direction to which he and Doctor Bryerly had darkly
alluded, was now to come, and certainly it was a strange one. It
appointed my Uncle Silas my sole guardian, with full parental authority over me until I should have reached the age of twenty-one, up to
which time I was to reside under his care at Bartram-Haugh, and it
directed the trustees to pay over to him yearly a sum of two thousand

pounds during the continuance of the guardianship for my suitable maintenance, education, and expenses.

You have now a sufficient outline of my father's will. The only thing I painfully felt in this arrangement was the break-up—the dismay that accompanies the disappearance of home. Otherwise there was something rather pleasurable in the idea. As long as I could remember I had always cherished the same mysterious curiosity about my uncle, and the same longing to behold him. This was about to be gratified. Then there was my Cousin Milicent, about my own age. My life had been so lonely, that I had acquired none of those artificial habits that induce the fine-lady nature—a second, and not always a very amiable one. She had lived a solitary life like me. What rambles and readings we should have together! What confidences and castle-buildings! and then there was a new country and a fine old place, and the sense of interest and adventure that always accompanies change in our early youth.

There were four letters all alike with large, red seals, addressed respectively to each of the trustees named in the will. There was also one addressed to Silas Aylmer Ruthyn, Esq., Bartram-Haugh Manor, &c., &c., which Mr. Sleigh offered to deliver. But Doctor Bryerly thought the post-office was the more regular channel. Uncle Silas's representative was questioning Doctor Bryerly in an under-tone.

I turned my eyes on my Cousin Monica—I felt so inexpressibly relieved—expecting to see a corresponding expression in her countenance. But I was startled. She looked ghastly and angry. I stared in her face, not knowing what to think. Could the will have personally disappointed her? Such doubts, though we fancy in after life they belong to maturity and experience only, do sometimes cross our minds in youth. But the suggestion wronged Lady Knollys, who neither expected nor wanted anything, being rich, childless, generous, and frank. It was the unexpected character of her countenance that scared me, and for a moment the shock called up corresponding moral images.

Lady Knollys, starting up, raised her head, so as to see over Mr. Sleigh's shoulder, and biting her pale lip, she cleared her voice, and demanded—

'Doctor Bryerly, pray, Sir, is the reading concluded?'

'Concluded? Quite. Yes, nothing more,' he answered with a nod, and continued his talk with Mr. Danvers and Abel Grimston.

'And to whom,' said Lady Knollys, with an effort, 'will the property belong, in case—in case my little cousin here should die before she comes of age?'

'Eh? Well—wouldn't it go to the heir-at-law and next of kin?' said Dr. Bryerly, turning to Abel Grimston.

'Ay—to be sure,' said the attorney, thoughtfully.

'And who is that?' pursued my cousin.

'Well, her uncle, Mr. Silas Ruthyn. He's both heir-at-law and next of kin,' pursued Abel Grimston.

'Thank you,' said Lady Knollys.

Doctor Clay came forward, bowing very low, in his standing collar and single-breasted coat, and graciously folded my hand in his soft wrinkled grasp—

'Allow me, my dear Miss Ruthyn, while expressing my regret that we are to lose you from among our little flock—though I trust but for a short, a very short time—to say how I rejoice at the particular arrangement indicated by the will we have just heard read. My curate, William Fairfield, resided for some years in the same spiritual capacity in the neighbourhood of your, I will say, admirable uncle, with occasional intercourse with whom he was favoured—may I not say blessed—a true Christian Churchman—a Christian gentleman. Can I say more? A most happy, happy choice.'—A very low bow here, with eyes nearly closed, and a shake of the head.—'Mrs. Clay will do herself the honour of waiting upon you, to pay her respects, before you leave Knowl for your temporary sojourn in another sphere.'

So, with another deep bow—for I had become a great personage all at once—he let go my hand cautiously and delicately, as if he were setting down a curious china tea-cup. And I courtesied low to him, not knowing what to say, and then to the assembly generally, who all bowed. And Cousin Monica whispered, briskly, 'Come away,' and took my hand with a very cold and rather damp one, and led me from the room.

CHAPTER XXV

I HEAR FROM UNCLE SILAS

WITHOUT saying a word, Cousin Monica accompanied me to the schoolroom, and on entering she shut the door, not with a spirited clang, but quietly and determinedly.

'Well, dear,' she said, with the same pale, excited countenance, 'that certainly is a sensible and charitable arrangement. I could not have believed it possible, had I not heard it with my ears.'

'About my going to Bartram-Haugh?'

'Yes, exactly so, under Silas Ruthyn's guardianship, to spend two—*three*—of the most important years of your education and your life under that roof. Is *that*, my dear, what was in your mind when you were so alarmed about what you were to be called upon to do, or undergo?'

'No, no, indeed. I had no notion what it might be. I was afraid of something serious,' I answered.

'And my dear Maud, did not your poor father speak to you as if it *was* something serious?' said she. 'And so it *is*, I can tell you, something serious, and *very* serious; and I think it ought to be prevented, and I certainly *will* prevent it if I possibly can.'

I was puzzled utterly by the intensity of Lady Knollys' protest. I looked at her, expecting an explanation of her meaning; but she was silent, looking steadfastly on the jewels on her right-hand fingers, with which she was drumming a staccata march on the table, very pale, with gleaming eyes, evidently thinking deeply. I began to think she *had* a prejudice against my Uncle Silas.

'He is not very rich,' I commenced.

'Who?' said Lady Knollys.

'Uncle Silas,' I replied.

'No, certainly; he's in debt,' she answered.

'But then, how very highly Doctor Clay spoke of him,' I pursued.

'Don't talk of Doctor Clay, I do think that man is the greatest goose I ever heard talk. I have no patience with such men,' she replied.

I tried to remember what particular nonsense Doctor Clay had uttered, and I could recollect nothing, unless his eulogy upon my uncle were to be classed with that sort of declamation.

'Danvers is a very proper man and a good accountant, I dare say, but he is either a very deep person, or a fool—*I* believe a fool. As for your attorney, I suppose he knows his business, and also his interest, and I have no doubt he will consult it. I begin to think the best man among them, the shrewdest and the most reliable, is that vulgar visionary in the black wig. I saw him look at you, Maud, and I liked his face, though it is abominably ugly and vulgar, and cunning, too; but I think he's a just man, and I dare say with right feelings, I'm *sure* he has.'

I was quite at a loss to divine the gist of my cousin's criticism.

'I'll have some talk with Dr. Bryerly; I feel convinced he takes my view, and we must really think what had best be done.'

'Is there anything in the will, Cousin Monica, that does not appear?' I asked, for I was growing very uneasy. 'I wish you would tell me. What view do you mean?'

'No view in particular; the view that a desolate old park, and the house of a *neglected* old man, who is very poor, and has been desperately foolish, is not the right place for you, particularly at your years. It is quite shocking, and I *will* speak to Doctor Bryerly. May I ring the bell, dear?'

'Certainly;' and I rang it.

'When does he leave Knowl?'

I could not tell. Mrs. Rusk, however, was sent for, and she could tell us that he had announced his intention of taking the night train from Drackleton, and was to leave Knowl for that station at half-past six o'clock.

'May Rusk give or send him a message from me, dear?' asked Lady Knollys.

Of course she might.

'Then, please, let him know that I request he will be so good as to allow me a very few minutes, just to say a word before he goes.'

'You kind cousin!' I said, placing my two hands on her shoulders, and looking earnestly in her face; 'you are anxious about me, more than you say. Won't you tell me why? I am much more unhappy, really, in ignorance, than if I understood the cause.'

'Well, dear, haven't I told you? The two or three years of your life which are to form you, are destined to be passed in utter loneliness, and, I am sure, neglect. You can't estimate the disadvantage of such an arrangement. It is full of disadvantages. How it could have entered the head of poor Austin—although I should not say that, for I am sure I do understand it. But how he could for any purpose have directed such a measure is quite inconceivable. I never heard of anything so foolish and abominable, and I will prevent it if I can.'

At that moment Mrs. Rusk announced that Doctor Bryerly would see Lady Knollys at any time she pleased before his departure.

'It shall be this moment then,' said the energetic lady, and up she stood, and made that hasty general adjustment before the glass, which, no matter under what circumstances, and before what sort of creature one's appearance is to be made, is a duty that every woman owes to herself. And I heard her a moment after, at the stair-head, directing Branston to let Doctor Bryerly know that she awaited him in the drawing-room.

And now she was gone, and I began to wonder and speculate. Why should my Cousin Monica make all this fuss about, after all, a very natural arrangement? My uncle, whatever he might have been, was now a good man—a religious man—perhaps a little severe, and with this thought a dark streak fell across my sky.

A cruel disciplinarian! had I not read of such characters?—lock and key, bread and water, and solitude! To sit locked up all night in a dark out-of-the-way room, in a great, ghosty old-fashioned house, with no one nearer than the other wing. What years of horror in one such night! Would not this explain my poor father's hesitation, and my Cousin Monica's apparently disproportioned opposition? When an idea of terror presents itself to a young person's mind, it transfixes and fills the vision, without respect of probabilities or reason.

My uncle was now a terrible old martinet, with long Bible lessons, lectures, pages of catechism, sermons to be conned by rote, and an awful catalogue of punishments for idleness, and what would seem to him impiety. I was going, then, to a frightful isolated reformatory, where for the first time in my life I should be subjected to a rigorous and perhaps barbarous discipline.

All this was an exhalation of fancy, but it quite overcame me. I threw myself, in my solitude, on the floor, upon my knees, and prayed for deliverance, prayed that Cousin Monica might prevail with Doctor Bryerly, and both on my behalf with the Lord Chancellor* or the High Sheriff, or whoever else my proper deliverer might be; and when my cousin returned, she found me quite in an agony.

'Why, you little fool! what fancy has taken possession of you now?' she cried.

And when my new terror came to light, she actually laughed a little to reassure me, and she said—

'My dear child, your Uncle Silas will never put you through your duty to your neighbour;* all the time you are under his roof you'll have idleness and liberty enough, and too much I fear. It is neglect, my dear, not discipline, that I'm afraid of.'

'I think, dear Cousin Monica, you are afraid of something more than neglect,' I said, relieved, however.

'I *am* afraid of more than neglect,' she replied promptly; 'but I hope my fears may turn out illusory, and that possibly they may be avoided. And now, for a few hours at least, let us think of something else. I rather like that Doctor Bryerly. I could not get him to say what I wanted. I don't think he's Scotch, but he is very cautious, and I am sure, though he would not say so, that he thinks of the matter exactly as I do. He says that those fine people, who are named as his co-trustees, won't take any trouble, and will leave everything to him, and I am sure he is right. So we must not quarrel with him, Maud, nor call him hard names, although he certainly is intolerably vulgar and ugly, and at times very nearly impertinent—I suppose without knowing, or indeed very much caring.'

We had a good deal to think of, and talked incessantly. There were bursts and interruptions of grief, and my kind cousin's consolations. I have often since been so lectured for giving way to grief, that I wonder at the patience exercised by her during this irksome visit. Then there was some reading of that book whose claims are always felt in the terrible days of affliction. After that we had a walk in the yew garden, that quaint little cloistered quadrangle—the most solemn, sad, and antiquated of gardens.

'And now, my dear, I must really leave you for two or three hours. I have ever so many letters to write, and my people must think I'm dead by this time.'

So till tea-time I had poor Mary Quince, with her gushes of simple prattle and her long fits of vacant silence, for my companion. And such a one, who can con over by rote the old friendly gossip about the dead, talk about their ways, and looks, and likings, without much psychologic refinement, but with a simple admiration and liking that never measured them critically, but always with faith and love, is in general about as comfortable a companion as one can find for the common moods of grief.

It is not easy to recall in calm and happy hours the sensations of an acute sorrow that is past. Nothing, by the merciful ordinance of God, is more difficult to remember than pain. One or two great agonies of that time I do remember, and they remain to testify of the rest, and convince me, though I can see it no more, how terrible all that period was.

Next day was the funeral, that appalling necessity; smuggled away in whispers, by black familiars, unresisting, the beloved one leaves home, without a farewell, to darken those doors no more; hence-forward to lie outside, far away, and forsaken, through the drowsy heats of summer, through days of snow and nights of tempest, without light or warmth, without a voice near. Oh, Death, king of terrors!* The body quakes, and the spirit faints before thee. It is vain, with hands clasped over our eyes, to scream our reclamation; the horrible image will not be excluded. We have just the word spoken eighteen hundred years ago, and our trembling faith. And through the broken vault the gleam of the Star of Bethlehem.*

I was glad in a sort of agony when it was over. So long as it remained to be done, something of the catastrophe was still suspended. Now it was all over.

The house so strangely empty. No owner—no master! I with my strange momentary liberty, bereft of that irreplaceable love, never quite prized until it is lost. Most people have experienced the dismay that underlies sorrow under such circumstances.

The apartment of the poor outcast from life is now dismantled. Bed and curtains taken down, and furniture displaced; carpets removed, windows open and doors locked, the bedroom and ante-room were henceforward, for many a day, uninhabited. Every shocking change smote my heart like a reproach.

I saw that day that Cousin Monica had been crying for the first time, I think, since her arrival at Knowl, and I loved her more for it, and felt consoled. My tears have often been arrested by the sight of another person weeping, and I never could explain why. But I believe that many persons experience the same odd reaction.

The funeral was conducted, in obedience to his brief but peremp-tory direction, very privately and with little expense. But, of course, there was an attendance, and the tenants of the Knowl estate also followed the hearse to the mausoleum, as it is called, in the park, where he was laid beside my dear mother. And so the repulsive ceremonial of that dreadful day was over. The grief remained, but there was rest from the fatigue of agitation, and a comparative calm supervened.

It was now the stormy equinoctial weather that sounds the wild dirge of autumn, and marches the winter in. I love, and always did, that grand undefinable music, threatening and bewailing, with its strange soul of liberty and desolation.

By this night's mail, as we sat listening to the storm, in the drawing-room at Knowl, there reached me a large letter with a great black seal, and a wonderfully deep-black border, like a widow's crape. I did not recognize the handwriting, but on opening the funereal missive, it proved to be from my Uncle Silas, and was thus expressed.

'MY DEAREST NIECE,—This letter will reach you, probably, on the day which consigns the mortal remains of my beloved brother, Austin, your dear father, to the earth. Sad ceremony! from taking my mournful part in which I am excluded by years, distance, and broken health. It will, I trust, at this season of desolation, be not unwelcome to remember that a substitute, imperfect—unworthy—but most affectionately zealous, for the honoured parent whom you have just lost, has been appointed, in me, your uncle, by his will. I am aware that you were present during the reading of it, but I think it will be for our mutual satisfaction that our new and more affectionate relations should be forthwith entered upon. My conscience and your safety, and I trust convenience, will thereby be consulted. You will, my dear niece, remain at Knowl, until a few simple arrangements shall have been completed for your reception at this place. I will then settle the details of your little journey to us, which shall be performed as comfortably and easily as possible. I humbly pray that this affliction may be sanctified to us all, and that in our new duties we may be supported, comforted, and directed. I need not remind you that I now stand to you in *loco parentis*, which means in the relation of father, and you will not forget that you are to remain at Knowl until you hear further from me.

'I remain, my dear niece, your most affectionate uncle and guardian,
'SILAS RUTHYN.

'P.S.—Pray present my respects to Lady Knollys, who, I understand, is sojourning at Knowl. I would observe that a lady who cherishes, I have reason to fear, unfriendly feelings against your uncle is not the most desirable companion for his ward. But upon the express condition that I am not made the subject of your discussions—a distinction which could not conduce to your forming a just and respectful estimate of me—I do not interpose my authority to bring your intercourse to an immediate close.'

As I read this postscript my cheek tingled as if I had received a box on the ear. Uncle Silas was as yet a stranger. The menace of authority was new and sudden, and I felt with a pang of mortification the full force of the position in which my dear father's will had placed me.

I was silent, and handed the letter to my cousin, who read it with a kind of smile until she came, as I supposed, to the postscript, when her countenance, on which my eyes were fixed, changed, and with flushed cheeks she knocked the hand that held the letter on the table before her, and exclaimed—

'Did I ever hear! Well, if this isn't impertinence! *What* an old man that is!'

There was a pause, during which Lady Knollys held her head high with a frown, and sniffed a little.

'I did not intend to talk about him, but now I *will*. I'll talk away just whatever I like; and I'll stay here just as long as you let me, Maud, and you need not be one atom afraid of him. Our intercourse to an "immediate close", indeed! I only wish he were here. He should hear something!'

And Cousin Monica drank off her entire cup of tea at one draught, and then she said, more in her own way—

'I'm better!' and drew a long breath, and then she laughed a little in a waggish defiance. 'I wish we had him here, Maud, and *would* not we give him a bit of our minds? And this before the poor will is so much as proved!'

'I am almost glad he wrote that postscript, for although I don't think he has any authority in that matter while I am under my own roof,' I said, extemporizing a legal opinion, 'and therefore, shan't obey him, it has somehow opened my eyes to my real situation.'

I sighed, I believe, very desolately, for Lady Knollys came over and kissed me very gently and affectionately.

'It really seems, Maud, as if he had a supernatural sense, and heard things through the air over fifty miles of heath and hill. You remember how, just as he was probably writing that very postscript yesterday, I was urging you to come and stay with me, and planning to move

Dr. Bryerly in our favour. And so I will, Maud, and to me you *shall* come—my guest, mind—I should be so delighted; and really if Silas is under a cloud, it has been his own doing, and I don't see that it is your business to fight his battles. He can't live very long. The suspicion, whatever it is, dies with him, and what could poor dear Austin prove by his will but what everybody knew quite well before—his own strong belief in Silas's innocence. What an awful storm! The room trembles. Don't you like the sound! What they used to call "wolving"* in the old organ at Dorminster!'

END OF VOL. I.

CHAPTER XXVI

AND so it was like the yelling of phantom hounds and hunters, and the thunder of their coursers in the air—a furious, grand, and super-natural music, which in my fancy made a suitable accompaniment to the discussion of that enigmatical person—martyr—angel—demon—Uncle Silas—with whom my fate was now so strangely linked, and whom I had begun to fear.

'The storm blows from that point,' I said, indicating it with my hand and eye, although the window shutters and curtains were closed. 'I saw all the trees bend that way this evening. That way stands the great lonely wood, where my darling father and mother lie. Oh, how dreadful on nights like this, to think of them—a vault!—damp, and dark, and solitary—under the storm.'

Cousin Monica looked wistfully in the same direction, and with a short sigh she said—

'We think too much of the poor remains, and too little of the spirit which lives for ever. I am sure they are happy.' And she sighed again. 'I wish I dare hope as confidently for myself. Yes, Maud, it is sad. We are such materialists, we can't help feeling so. We forget how well it is for us that our present bodies are not to last always. They are constructed for a time and place of trouble—plainly mere temporary machines that wear out, constantly exhibiting failure and decay, and with such tremendous capacity for pain. The body lies alone, and so it ought, for it is plainly its good Creator's will; it is only the tabernacle, not the person, who is clothed upon after death, Saint Paul says, "with a house which is from heaven".* So Maud, darling, although the thought will trouble us again and again, there is nothing in it; and the poor mortal body is only the cold ruin of a habitation which *they* have forsaken before we do. So this great wind, you say, is blowing toward us from the wood there. If so, Maud, it is blowing from Bartram-Haugh, too, over the trees and chimneys of that old place, and the mysterious old man, who is quite right in thinking I don't like him; and I can fancy him an old enchanter in his castle, waving his familiar spirits on the wind to fetch and carry tidings of our occupations here.'

I lifted up my head and listened to the storm, dying away in the distance sometimes. Sometimes swelling and pealing around and above us, and through the dark and solitude my thoughts sped away to Bartram-Haugh and Uncle Silas.

'This letter,' I said at last, 'makes me feel differently. I think he is a stern old man—is he?'

'It is twenty years, now, since I saw him,' answered Lady Knollys. 'I did not choose to visit at his house.'

'Was that before the dreadful occurrence at Bartram-Haugh?'

'Yes—before, dear. He was not a reformed rake, but only a ruined one then. Austin was very good to him. Mr. Danvers says it is quite unaccountable how Silas can have made away with the immense sums he got from his brother from time to time without benefiting himself in the least. But, my dear, he played; and trying to help a man who plays, and is unlucky—and some men are, I believe, habitually unlucky—is like trying to fill a vessel that has no bottom. I think, by-the-by, my hopeful nephew, Charles Oakley, plays. Then Silas went most unjustifiably into all manner of speculations, and your poor father had to pay everything. He lost something quite astounding in that bank that ruined so many country gentlemen—poor Sir Harry Shackleton, in Yorkshire, had to sell half his estate. But your kind father went on helping him, up to his marriage—I mean in that extravagant way which was really totally useless.'

'Has my aunt been long dead?'

'Twelve or fifteen years—more, indeed—she died before your poor mamma. She was very unhappy, and I am sure would have given her right hand she had never married Silas.'

'Did you like her?'

'No, dear; she was a coarse, vulgar woman.'

'Coarse and vulgar, and Uncle Silas's wife?' I echoed in extreme surprise, for Uncle Silas was a man of fashion—a beau in his day—and might have married women of good birth and fortune, I had no doubt, and so I expressed myself.

'Yes, dear; so he might, and poor dear Austin was very anxious he should, and would have helped him with a handsome settlement, I dare say, but he chose to marry the daughter of a Denbigh inn-keeper.'

'How utterly incredible!' I exclaimed.

'Not the least incredible, dear—a kind of thing not at all so uncommon as you fancy.'

'What!—a gentleman of fashion and refinement marry a person—'

'A barmaid!—just so,' said Lady Knollys. 'I think I could count half a dozen men of fashion who, to my knowledge, have ruined themselves just in a similar way.'

'Well, at all events, it must be allowed that in this he proved himself altogether unworldly.'

'Not a bit unworldly, but very vicious,' replied Cousin Monica, with a careless little laugh. 'She was very beautiful, curiously beautiful, for a person in her station. She was very like that Lady Hamilton who was Nelson's sorceress—elegantly beautiful, but perfectly low and stupid. I believe, to do him justice, he only intended to ruin her, but she was cunning enough to insist upon marriage. Men who have never in all their lives denied themselves the indulgence of a single fancy, cost what it may, will not be baulked even by that condition if the *penchant* be only violent enough.'

I did not half understand this piece of worldly psychology, at which Lady Knollys seemed to laugh.

'Poor Silas, he certainly struggled honestly against the consequences, for he tried after the honeymoon to prove the marriage bad.* But the Welsh parson and the innkeeper papa were too strong for him, and the young lady was able to hold her struggling swain fast in that respectable noose—and a pretty prize he proved.'

'And she died, poor thing, broken-hearted, I heard.'

'She died, at all events, about ten years after her marriage; but I really can't say about her heart. She certainly had enough ill-usage, I believe, to kill her, but I don't know that she had feeling enough to die of it, if it had not been that she drank; I am told that Welsh women often do.* There was jealousy, of course, and brutal quarrelling, and all sorts of horrid stories. I visited at Bartram-Haugh for a year or two, though no one else would. But when that sort of thing began, of course I gave it up; it was out of the question. I don't think poor Austin ever knew how bad it was. And then came that odious business about wretched Mr. Charke. You know he—he committed suicide at Bartram.'

'I never heard about that,' I said; and we both paused, and she looked sternly at the fire, and the storm roared and ha-ha-ed till the old house shook again.

'But Uncle Silas could not help that,' I said at last.

'No, he could not help it,' she acquiesced unpleasantly.

'And Uncle Silas was'—I paused in a sort of fear.

'He was suspected by some people of having killed him'—she completed the sentence.

There was another long pause here, during which the storm outside bellowed and hooted like an angry mob roaring at the windows for a victim. An intolerable and sickening sensation over-powered me.

'But *you* did not suspect him, Cousin Knollys?' I said, trembling very much.

'No,' she answered very sharply. 'I told you so before. Of course I did not.'

There was another silence.

'I wish, Cousin Monica,' I said, drawing close to her, 'you had not said *that* about Uncle Silas being like a wizard, and sending his spirits on the wind to listen. But I'm very glad you never suspected him.' I insinuated my cold hand into hers, and looked into her face I know not with what expression. She looked down into mine with a hard, haughty stare, I thought.

'Of *course* I never suspected him; and *never* ask me *that* question again, Maud Ruthyn.'

Was it family pride, or what was it, that gleamed so fiercely from her eyes as she said this? I was frightened—I was wounded—I burst into tears.

'What is my darling crying for? I did not mean to be cross. *Was* I cross?' said this momentary phantom of a grim Lady Knollys, in an instant translated again into kind, pleasant Cousin Monica, with her arms about my neck.

'No, no, indeed—only I thought I had vexed you; and, I believe, thinking of Uncle Silas makes me nervous, and I can't help thinking of him nearly always.'

'Nor can I, although we might both easily find something better to think of. Suppose we try?' said Lady Knollys.

'But, first, I must know a little more about that Mr. Charke, and what circumstances enabled Uncle Silas's enemies to found on his death that wicked slander, which has done no one any good, and caused some persons so much misery. There is Uncle Silas, I may say, ruined by it; and we all know how it darkened the life of my dear father.'

'People will talk, my dear. Your Uncle Silas had injured himself before that in the opinion of the people of his county. He was a black sheep, in fact. Very bad stories were told and believed of him. His marriage certainly was a disadvantage, you know, and the miserable scenes that went on in his disreputable house—all that predisposed people to believe ill of him.'

'How long is it since it happened?'

'Oh, a long time; I think before you were born,' answered she.

'And the injustice still lives—they have not forgotten it yet?' said I, for such a period appeared to me long enough to have consigned anything in its nature perishable to oblivion.

Lady Knollys smiled.

'Tell me, like a darling cousin, the whole story as well as you can recollect it. Who was Mr. Charke?'

'Mr. Charke, my dear, was a gentleman on the turf—that is the phrase, I think—one of those London men, without birth or breeding, who merely in right of their vices and their money are admitted to associate with young dandies who like hounds and horses, and all that sort of thing. That set knew him very well, but of course no one else. He was at the Matlock races, and your uncle asked him to Bartram-Haugh; and the creature, Jew or Gentile, whatever he was, fancied there was more honour than, perhaps, there really was in a visit to Bartram-Haugh.'

'For the kind of person you describe, it *was*, I think, a rather unusual honour to be invited to stay in the house of a man of Uncle Ruthyn's birth.'

'Well, so it was perhaps; for though they knew him very well on the course, and would ask him to their tavern dinners, they would not, of course, admit him to the houses where ladies were. But Silas's wife was not much regarded at Bartram-Haugh. Indeed, she was very little seen, for she was every evening tipsy in her bedroom, poor woman!'

'How miserable!' I exclaimed.

'I don't think it troubled Silas very much, for she drank gin, they said, poor thing, and the expense was not much; and, on the whole, I really think he was glad she drank, for it kept her out of his way, and was likely to kill her. At this time your poor father, who was thoroughly disgusted at his marriage, had stopped the supplies, you know, and Silas was very poor, and as hungry as a hawk, and they said he pounced upon this rich London gamester, intending to win his money. I am telling you now all that was said afterwards. The races lasted I forget how many days, and Mr. Charke stayed at Bartram-Haugh all this time and for some days after. It was thought that poor

Austin would pay all Silas's gambling debts, and so this wretched Mr. Charke made heavy wagers with him on the races, and they played very deep, besides, at Bartram. He and Silas used to sit up at night at cards. All these particulars, as I told you, came out afterwards, for there was an inquest, you know, and then Silas published what he called his "statement", and there was a great deal of most distressing correspondence in the newspapers.'

'And why did Mr. Charke kill himself?' I asked.

'Well, I will tell you first what all are agreed about. The second night after the races, your uncle and Mr. Charke sat up till between two and three o'clock in the morning, quite by themselves, in the parlour. Mr. Charke's servant was at the Stag's Head Inn at Feltram, and therefore could throw no light upon what occurred at night at Bartram-Haugh; but he was there at six o'clock in the morning, and very early at his master's door by his direction. He had locked it, as was his habit, upon the inside, and the key was in the lock, which turned out afterwards a very important point. On knocking he found that he could not awaken his master, because, as it appeared when the door was forced open, his master was lying dead at his bedside, not in a pool, but a perfect pond of blood, as they described it, with his throat cut.'

'How horrible!' cried I.

'So it was. Your Uncle Silas was called up, and greatly shocked of course, and he did what I believe was best. He had everything left as nearly as possible in the exact state in which it had been found, and he sent his own servant forthwith for the coroner, and, being himself a justice of the peace, he took the depositions of Mr. Charke's servant while all the incidents were still fresh in his memory.'

'Could anything be more straightforward, more right and wise?' I said.

'Oh, nothing of course,' answered Lady Knollys, I thought a little drily.

So the inquest was held, and Mr. Manwaring, of Wail Forest, was the only juryman who seemed to entertain the idea during the inquiry that Mr. Charke had died by any hand but his own.

'And how *could* he fancy such a thing?' I exclaimed indignantly.

'Well, you will see the result was quite enough to justify them in saying as they did, that he died by his own hand. The window was found fastened with a screw on the inside, as it had been when the chambermaid had arranged it at nine o'clock; no one could have entered through it. Besides, it was on the third story, and the rooms are lofty, so it stood at a great height from the ground, and there was no ladder long enough to reach it. The house is built in the form of a hollow square, and Mr. Charke's room looked into the narrow court-yard within. There is but one door leading into this, and it did not show any sign of having been open for years. The door was locked upon the inside, and the key in the lock, so that nobody could have made an entrance that way either, for it was impossible, you see, to unlock the door from the outside.'

'And how could they affect to question anything so clear?' I asked.

'There did come, nevertheless, a kind of mist over the subject, which gave those who chose to talk unpleasantly an opportunity of insinuating suspicions, though they could not themselves find the clue of the mystery. In the first place, it appeared that he had gone to bed very tipsy, and that he was heard singing and noisy in his room while getting to bed—not the mood in which men make away with themselves. Then, although his own razor was found in that dreadful blood (it is shocking to have to hear all this) near his right hand, the fingers of his left were cut to the bone. Then the memorandum book in which his bets were noted was nowhere to be found. That, you know, was very odd. His keys were there attached to a chain. He wore a great deal of gold and trinkets. I saw him, wretched man, on the course. They had got off their horses. He and your uncle were walking on the course.'

'Did he look like a gentleman?' I inquired, as, I dare say, other young ladies would.

'He looked like a Jew, my dear. He had a horrid brown coat with a velvet cape, curling black hair over his collar, and great whiskers, very high shoulders, and he was puffing a cigar straight up into the air. I was shocked to see Silas in such company.'

'And did his keys discover anything?' I asked.

'On opening his travelling desk and a small japanned box within it a vast deal less money was found than was expected—in fact, very little. Your uncle said that he had won some of it the night before at play, and that Charke complained to him when tipsy of having had severe losses to counterbalance his gains on the races. Besides, he had been paid but a small part of those gains. About his book it appeared that there were little notes of his bets on the backs of letters, and it was said that he sometimes made no other memorandum of his wagers—but this was disputed—and among those notes there was not one referring to Silas. But, then, there was an omission of all allusion to his transactions with two other well-known gentlemen. So that was not singular.'

'No, certainly; that was quite accounted for,' said I.

'And then came the question,' continued she, 'what motive could Mr. Charke possibly have had for making away with himself.'

'But is not that very difficult to make out in many cases?' I interposed.

'It was said that he had some mysterious troubles in London, at which he used to hint. Some people said that he really was in a scrape, but others that there was no such thing, and that when he talked so he was only jesting. There was no suspicion during the inquest that your Uncle Silas was involved, except those questions of Mr. Manwaring's.'

'What were they?' I asked.

'I really forget; but they greatly offended your uncle, and there was a little scene in the room. Mr. Manwaring seemed to think that some one had somehow got into the room. Through the door it could not be, nor down the chimney, for they found an iron bar across the flue, near the top in the masonry. The window looked into a courtyard no bigger than a ball-room. They went down and examined it, but, though the ground beneath was moist, they could not discover the slightest trace of a footprint. So far as they could make out, Mr. Charke had hermetically sealed himself into his room, and then cut his throat with his own razor.'

'Yes,' said I, 'for it was all secured—that is, the window and the door—upon the inside, and no sign of any attempt to get in.'

'Just so; and when the walls were searched, and, as your Uncle Silas directed, the wainscoting removed, some months afterwards, when the scandal grew loudest, then it was evident that there was no concealed access to the room.'

'So the answer to all those calumnies was simply that the crime was impossible,' said I. 'How dreadful that such a slander should have required an answer at all!'

'It was an unpleasant affair even then, although I cannot say that any one supposed Silas guilty; but you know the whole thing was disreputable, that Mr. Charke was a discreditable inmate, the occurrence was horrible, and there was a glare of publicity which brought into relief the scandals of Bartram-Haugh. But in a little time it became, all on a sudden, a great deal worse.'

My cousin paused to recollect exactly.

'There were very disagreeable whispers among the sporting people in London. This person, Charke, had written two letters. Yes—two. They were published about two months after, by the villain to whom they were written; he wanted to extort money. They were first talked of a great deal among that set in town; but the moment they were published they produced a sensation in the country, and a storm of newspaper commentary. The first of these was of no great consequence, but the second was very startling, embarrassing, and even alarming.'

'What was it, Cousin Monica?' I whispered.

'I can only tell you in a general way, it is so very long since I read it; but both were written in the same kind of slang, and parts as hard to understand as a prize fight. I hope you never read those things.'

I satisfied this sudden educational alarm, and Lady Knollys proceeded.

'I am afraid you hardly hear me, the wind makes such an uproar. Well, listen. The letter said distinctly, that he, Mr. Charke, had made a very profitable visit to Bartram-Haugh, and mentioned in exact figures for how much he held your Uncle Silas's I.O.U.s, for he could not pay him. I can't say what the sum was. I only remember that it was quite frightful. It took away my breath when I read it.'

'Uncle Silas had lost it?' I asked.

'Yes, and owed it; and had given him those papers called I.O.U.s, promising to pay, which, of course, Mr. Charke had locked up with his money; and the insinuation was that Silas had made away with him, to get rid of this debt, and that he had also taken a great deal of his money.

'I just recollect these points which were exactly what made the impression,' continued Lady Knollys, after a short pause; 'the letter was written in the evening of the last day of the wretched man's life, so that there had not been much time for your Uncle Silas to win back his money; and he stoutly alleged that he did not owe Mr. Charke a guinea. It mentioned an enormous sum as being actually owed by Silas; and it cautioned the man, an agent, to whom he wrote, not to mention the circumstance, as Silas could only pay by getting the money from his wealthy brother, who would require management; and he distinctly said that he had kept the matter very close at Silas's request. That, you know, was a very awkward letter, and all the worse that it was written in brutally high spirits, and not at all like a man meditating an exit from the world. You can't imagine what a sensation the publication of these letters produced. In a moment the storm was up, and certainly Silas did meet it bravely—yes, with great courage and ability. What a pity he did not early enter upon some career of ambition! Well, well, it is idle regretting. He suggested that the letters were forgeries. He alleged that Charke was in the habit of boasting, and telling enormous false-hoods about his gambling transactions, especially in his letters. He reminded the world how often men affect high animal spirits at the very moment of meditating suicide. He alluded, in a manly and grace-ful way, to his family and their character. He took a high and menacing tone with his adversaries, and he insisted that what they dared to insinuate against him was physically impossible.'

I asked in what form this vindication appeared.

'It was a letter, printed as a pamphlet; everybody admired its abil-ity, ingenuity, and force, and it was written with immense rapidity.'

'Was it at all in the style of his letters?' I innocently asked.

My cousin laughed.

'Oh, dear, no! Ever since he avowed himself a religious character, he has written nothing but the most vapid and nerveless twaddle. Your poor dear father used to send his letters to me to read, and I sometimes really thought that Silas was losing his faculties; but I believe he was only trying to write in character.'

'I suppose the general feeling was in his favour?' I said.

'I don't think it was, anywhere; but in his own county it was certainly unanimously against him. There is no use in asking why; but so it was, and I think it would have been easier for him with his unaided strength to uproot the Peak than to change the convictions of the Derbyshire gentlemen. They were all against him. Of course there were predisposing causes. Your uncle published a very bitter attack upon them, describing himself as the victim of a political conspiracy: and I recollect he mentioned that from the hour of the shocking catastrophe in his house, he had foresworn the turf and all pursuits and amusements connected with it. People sneered, and said he might as well go as wait to be kicked out.'

'Were there law-suits about all this?' I asked.

'Everybody expected that there would, for there were very savage things printed on both sides, and I think, too, that the persons who thought worst of him expected that evidence would yet turn up to convict Silas of the crime they chose to impute; and so years have glided away, and many of the people who remembered the tragedy of Bartram-Haugh, and took the strongest part in the denunciation, and ostracism that followed, are dead, and no new light has been thrown upon the occurrence, and your Uncle Silas remains an outcast. At first he was quite wild with rage, and would have fought the whole county, man by man, if they would have met him. But he has since changed his habits and, as he says, his aspirations altogether.'

'He has become religious.'

'The only occupation remaining to him. He owes money; he is poor; he is isolated; and he says, sick and religious. Your poor father, who was very decided and inflexible, never helped him beyond the limit he had prescribed, after Silas's *mésalliance*. He wanted to get him into Parliament, and would have paid his expenses, and made him an allowance; but either Silas had grown lazy, or he understood his position better than poor Austin, or he distrusted his powers, or possibly he really is in ill-health; but he objected his religious scruples. Your poor papa thought self-assertion possible, where an injured man has right to rely upon; but he had been very long out of the world, and the theory won't do. Nothing is harder than to get a person who has once been effectually slurred, received again. Silas, I think, was right. I don't think it was practicable.

'Dear child, how late it is!' exclaimed Lady Knollys suddenly, looking at the Louis Quatorze clock, that crowned the mantelpiece.

It was near one o'clock. The storm had a little subsided, and I took a less agitated and more confident view of Uncle Silas, than I had at an earlier hour of that evening.

'And what do you think of him?' I asked.

Lady Knollys drummed on the table with her finger points as she looked into the fire.

'I don't understand metaphysics, my dear, nor witchcraft. I sometimes believe in the supernatural, and sometimes I don't. Silas Ruthyn is himself alone, and I can't define him, because I don't understand him. Perhaps other souls than human are sometimes born into the world, and clothed in flesh. It is not only about that dreadful occurrence, but nearly always throughout his life; early and late he has puzzled me. I have tried in vain to understand him. But at one time of his life I am sure he was awfully wicked—eccentric indeed in his wickedness—gay, frivolous, secret, and dangerous. At one time I think he could have made poor Austin do almost anything; but his influence vanished with his marriage, never to return again. No; I don't understand him. He always bewildered me, like a shifting face, sometimes smiling, but always sinister, in an unpleasant dream.'

CHAPTER XXVIII
I AM PERSUADED

So now at last I had heard the story of Uncle Silas's mysterious disgrace. We sat silent for a while, and I, gazing into vacancy, sent him in a chariot of triumph, chapletted,* ringed, and robed through the city of imagination, crying after him, 'Innocent! innocent! martyr and crowned!' All the virtues and honesties, reason and conscience, in myriad shapes—tier above tier of human faces—from the crowded pavement, crowded windows, crowded roofs, joined in the jubilant acclamation, and trumpeters trumpeted, and drums rolled, and great organs and choirs through open cathedral gates, rolled anthems of praise and thanksgiving, and bells rang out, and cannons sounded, and the air trembled with the roaring harmony; and Silas Ruthyn, the full-length portrait, stood in the burnished chariot, with a proud, sad, clouded face, that rejoiced not with the rejoicers, and behind him the slave, thin as a ghost, white-faced, and sneering something in his ear: While I and all the city went on crying 'Innocent! innocent! martyr and crowned!' And now the reverie was ended; and there were only Lady Knollys' stern, thoughtful face, with the pale light of sarcasm on it, and the storm outside, thundering and lamenting desolately.

It was very good of Cousin Monica to stay with me so long. It must have been unspeakably tiresome. And now she began to talk of business at home, and plainly to prepare for immediate flight, and my heart sank.

I know that I could not then have defined my feelings and agitations. I am not sure that I even now could. Any misgiving about Uncle Silas was, in my mind, a questioning the foundations of my faith, and in itself an impiety. And yet I am not sure that some such misgiving, faint, perhaps, and intermittent, may not have been at the bottom of my tribulation.

I was not very well. Lady Knollys had gone out for a walk. She was not easily tired, and sometimes made a long excursion. The sun was setting now, when Mary Quince brought me a letter which had just arrived by the post. My heart throbbed violently. I was afraid to break the broad black seal. It was from Uncle Silas. I ran over in my mind all the unpleasant mandates which it might contain, to try and prepare myself for a shock. At last I opened the letter. It directed me to hold myself in readiness for the journey to Bartram-Haugh. It stated that I might bring two maids with me if I wished so many, and that his next letter would give me the details of my route, and the day of my departure for Derbyshire; and he said that I ought to make arrangements about Knowl during my absence, but that he was hardly the person properly to be consulted on that matter. Then came a prayer that he might be enabled to acquit himself of his trust to the full satisfaction of his conscience, and that I might enter upon my new relations in a spirit of prayer.

I looked round my room, so long familiar, and now so endeared by the idea of parting and change. The old house—dear, dear Knowl, how could I leave you and all your affectionate associations, and kind looks and voices for a strange land!

With a great sigh I took Uncle Silas's letter, and went down stairs to the drawing-room. From the lobby window, where I loitered for a few moments, I looked out upon the well-known forest-trees. The sun was down. It was already twilight, and the white vapours of coming night were already filming their thinned and yellow foliage. Everything looked melancholy. How little did those who envied the young inheritrex of a princely fortune suspect the load that lay at her heart, or bating* the fear of death, how gladly at that moment she would have parted with her life!

Lady Knollys had not yet returned, and it was darkening rapidly; a mass of black clouds stood piled in the west, through the chasms of which was still reflected a pale metallic lustre.

The drawing-room was already very dark; but some streaks of this cold light fell upon a black figure, which would otherwise have been unseen, leaning beside the curtains against the window frame.

It advanced abruptly, with creaking shoes; it was Doctor Bryerly.

I was startled and surprised, not knowing how he had got there. I stood staring at him in the dusk rather awkwardly, I am afraid.

'How do you do, Miss Ruthyn?' said he, extending his hand, long, hard, and brown as a mummy's, and stooping a little so as to approach more nearly, for it was not easy to see in the imperfect light. 'You're surprised, I dare say, to see me here so soon again?'

'I did not know you had arrived. I am glad to see you, Dr. Bryerly. Nothing unpleasant, I hope, has happened?'

'No, nothing unpleasant, Miss. The will has been lodged, and we shall have probate in due course; but there has been something on my mind, and I'm come to ask you two or three questions which you had better answer very considerately. Is Lady Knollys still here?'

'Yes, but she is not returned from her walk.'

'I am glad she is here. I think she takes a sound view, and women understand one another better. As for me, it is plainly my duty to put it before you as it strikes me, and to offer all I can do in accomplishing, should you wish it, a different arrangement. You don't know your uncle, you said the other day?'

'No, I've never seen him.'

'You understand your late father's intention in making you his ward?'

'I suppose he wished to show his high opinion of my uncle's fitness for such a trust.'

'That's quite true; but the nature of the trust in this instance is extraordinary.'

'I don't understand.'

'Why, if you die before you come to the age of twenty-one, the entire of the property will go to him—do you see?—and he has the custody of your person in the meantime; you are to live in his house, under his care and authority. You see now, I think, how it is; and I did not like it when your father read the will to me, and I said so. Do *you*?'

I hesitated to speak, not sure that I quite comprehended him.

'And the more I think of it, the less I like it, Miss,' said Dr. Bryerly, in a calm, stern tone.

'Merciful Heaven! Doctor Bryerly, you can't suppose that I should not be as safe in my uncle's house as in the Lord Chancellor's?' I ejaculated, looking full in his face.

'But don't you see, Miss, it is not a fair position to put your uncle in,' replied he, after a little hesitation.

'But suppose *he* does not think so. You know if he does, he may decline it.'

'Well, that's true—but he won't. Here is his letter'—and he produced it—'announcing officially that he means to accept the office; but I think he ought to be told it is not *delicate*, under all circumstances. You know, Miss, that your uncle, Mr. Silas Ruthyn, was talked about unpleasantly once.'

'You mean'—I began.

'I mean about the death of Mr. Charke, at Bartram-Haugh.'

'Yes, I have heard that,' I said; he was speaking with a shocking *aplomb*.

'We assume, of course, *unjustly*; but there are many who think quite differently.'

'And possibly, Doctor Bryerly, it was for that very reason that my dear papa made him my guardian.'

'There can be no doubt of that, Miss; it was to purge him of that scandal.'

'And when he has acquitted himself honourably of that trust, don't you think such a proof of confidence so honourably fulfilled must go far to silence his traducers?'

'Why, if all goes well, it may do a little; but a great deal less than you fancy. But take it that you happen to *die*, Miss, during your minority. We are all mortal, and there are three years and some months to go; how will it be then? Don't you see? Just fancy how people will talk.'

'I think you know that my uncle is a religious man?' said I.

'Well, Miss, what of that?' he asked again.

'He is—he has suffered intensely,' I continued. 'He has long retired from the world; he is very religious. Ask our curate, Mr. Fairfield, if you doubt it.'

'But I am not disputing it, Miss; I'm only supposing what may happen—an accident, we'll call it small-pox, diphtheria, *that's* going very much. Three years and three months, you know, is a long time. You proceed to Bartram-Haugh, thinking you have much goods laid up for many years; but your Creator, you know, may say, "Thou fool, this day is thy soul required of thee."* You go—and what pray is thought of your uncle, Mr. Silas Ruthyn, who walks in for the entire inheritance, and who has long been abused like a pickpocket, or worse, in his own county, I'm told?'

'You are a religious man, Doctor Bryerly, according to your lights?' I said.

The Swedenborgian smiled.

'Well, knowing that he is so too, and having yourself experienced the power of religion, do not you think him deserving of every confidence? Don't you think it well that he should have this opportunity of exhibiting both his own character and the reliance which my dear papa reposed on it, and that we should leave all consequences and contingencies in the hands of Heaven.'

'It appears to have been the will of Heaven hitherto,' said Doctor Bryerly—I could not see with what expression of face, but he was looking down, and drawing little diagrams with his stick on the dark carpet, and spoke in a very low tone—'that your uncle should suffer under this ill report. In countervailing the appointment of Providence, we must employ our reason, with conscientious diligence, as to the means, and if we find that they are as likely to do mischief as good, we have no right to expect a special interposition to turn our experiment into an ordeal. I think you ought to weigh it well—I am sure there are reasons against it. If you make up your mind that you would rather be placed under the care, say of Lady Knollys, I will endeavour all I can to effect it.'

'That could not be done without his consent, could it?' said I.

'No, but I don't despair of getting that—on terms, of course,' remarked he.

'I don't quite understand,' I said.

'I mean, for instance, if he were allowed to keep the allowance for your maintenance—eh?'

'I mistake my Uncle Silas very much,' I said, 'if that allowance is any object whatever to him compared with the moral value of the position. If he were deprived of that, I am sure he would decline the other.'

'We might try him at all events,' said Doctor Bryerly, on whose dark sinewy features, even in this imperfect light, I thought I detected a smile.

'Perhaps,' said I, 'I appear very foolish in supposing him actuated by any but sordid motives; but he is my near relation, and I can't help it, sir.'

'This is a very serious thing, Miss Ruthyn,' he replied. 'You are very young, and cannot see it at present, as you will hereafter. He is very religious, you say, and all that, but his house is not a proper place for you. It is a solitude—its master an outcast, and it has been the repeated scene of all sorts of scandals, and of one great crime; and Lady Knollys thinks your having been domesticated there, will be an injury to you all the days of your life.'

'So I do, Maud,' said Lady Knollys, who had just entered the room unperceived,—'How do you do, Doctor Bryerly?—a serious injury. You have no idea how entirely that house is condemned and avoided, and the very name of its inmates tabooed.'

'How monstrous—how cruel!' I exclaimed.

'Very unpleasant, my dear, but perfectly natural. You are to recollect that quite independently of the story of Mr. Charke, the house was talked about, and the county people had cut your Uncle Silas long before that adventure was dreamed of; and as to the circumstance of your being placed in his charge by his brother, who took, from strong family feeling, a totally one-sided view of the affair from the first, having the slightest effect in restoring his position in the county, you must quite give that up. Except me, if he will allow me, and the clergyman, not a soul in the country will visit at Bartram-Haugh. They may pity you, and think the whole thing the climax of folly and cruelty; but they won't visit at Bartram, or know Silas, or have anything to do with his household.'

'They will see, at all events, what my dear papa's opinion was.'

'They know that already,' answered she, 'and it has not, and ought not to have, the slightest weight with them. There are people there who think themselves just as great as the Ruthyns, or greater; and your poor father's idea of carrying it by a demonstration was simply the dream of a man who had forgotten the world and learned to exaggerate himself in his long seclusion. I know he was beginning himself to hesitate; and I think if he had been spared another year that provision of his will would have been struck out.'

Doctor Bryerly nodded, and he said—

'And if he had the power to dictate *now*, would he insist on that direction? It is a mistake every way, injurious to you, his child; and should you happen to die during your sojourn under your uncle's care, it would wofully defeat the testator's object, and raise such a storm of surmise and inquiry as would awaken all England, and send the old scandal on the wing through the world again.'

'Doctor Bryerly will, I have no doubt, arrange it all. In fact, I do not think it would be very difficult to bring Silas to terms; and if you do not consent to his trying, Maud, mark my words, you will live to repent it.'

Here were two persons, viewing the question from totally different points; both perfectly disinterested; both in their different ways, I believed, shrewd and even wise; and both honourable, urging me against it, and in a way that undefinably alarmed my imagination, as well as moved my reason. I looked from one to the other—there was a silence. By this time the candles had come, and we could see one another.

'I only wait your decision, Miss Ruthyn,' said the trustee, 'to see your uncle. If his advantage was the chief object contemplated in this arrangement, he will be the best judge whether his interest *is* really best consulted by it or no; and I think he will clearly see that it is *not* so, and will answer accordingly.'

'I cannot answer now—you must allow me to think it over—I will do my best. I am *very* much obliged, my dear Cousin Monica, you are so very good, and you too, Doctor Bryerly.'

Doctor Bryerly by this time was looking into his pocket-book, and did not acknowledge my thanks even by a nod.

'I must be in London the day after to-morrow. Bartram-Haugh is nearly sixty miles from here, and only twenty of that by rail, I find. Forty miles of posting over those Derbyshire mountains is slow work; but if you say *try*, I'll see him to-morrow morning.'

'You must say try—you *must*, my dear Maud.'

'But how can I decide in a moment? Oh, dear Cousin Monica, I am so distracted!'

'But *you* need not decide at all; the decision rests with *him*. Come; he is more competent than you. You *must* say yes.'

Again I looked from her to Doctor Bryerly, and from him to her again. I threw my arms about her neck, and hugging her closely to me, I cried—

'Oh, Cousin Monica, dear Cousin Monica, advise me. I am a wretched creature. You must advise me.'

I did not know till now how irresolute a character was mine.

I knew somehow by the tone of her voice that she was smiling as she answered—

'Why, dear, I have advised you; I *do* advise you;' and then she added, impetuously, 'I entreat and implore, if you really think I love you, that you will *follow* my advice. It is your duty to leave your Uncle Silas, whom you believe to be more competent than you are, to decide, after full conference with Doctor Bryerly, who knows more of your poor father's views and intentions in making that appointment than either you or I.'

'Shall I say, yes?' I cried, drawing her close, and kissing her, helplessly. 'Oh, tell me—tell me to say, yes.'

'Yes, of course, *yes*. She agrees, Doctor Bryerly, to your kind proposal.'

'I am to understand so?' he asked.

'Very well—yes, Dr. Bryerly,' I replied.

'You have resolved wisely and well,' said he, briskly, like a man who has got a care off his mind.

'I forgot to say, Doctor Bryerly—it was very rude—that you must stay here to-night.'

'He *can't*, my dear,' interposed Lady Knollys; 'it is a long way.'

'He will dine. Won't you, Doctor Bryerly?'

'No; he can't. You know you can't, sir,' said my cousin, peremptorily. 'You must not worry him, my dear, with civilities he can't accept. He'll bid us good-bye this moment. Good-bye, Doctor Bryerly. You'll write immediately; don't wait till you reach town. Bid him good-bye, Maud. I'll say a word to you in the hall.'

And thus she literally hurried him out of the room, leaving me in a state of amazement and confusion, not able to review my decision—unsatisfied, but still unable to recall it.

I stood where they had left me, looking after them, I suppose, like a fool.

Lady Knollys returned in a few minutes. If I had been a little cooler I was shrewd enough to perceive that she had sent poor Doctor Bryerly away upon his travels, to find board and lodging half-way to Bartram, to remove him forthwith from my presence, and thus to make my decision—if mine it was—irrevocable.

'I applaud you, my dear,' said Cousin Knollys, in her turn embracing me heartily. 'You are a sensible little darling, and have done exactly what you ought to have done.'

'I hope I have,' I faltered.

'Hope? fiddle! stuff! the thing's as plain as a pikestaff.'

And in came Branston to say that dinner was served.

CHAPTER XXIX

LADY KNOLLYS, I could plainly see, when we got into the brighter lights at the dinner table, was herself a good deal excited; she was relieved and glad, and was garrulous during our meal, and told me all her early recollections of dear papa. Most of them I had heard before; but they could not be told too often.

Notwithstanding my mind sometimes wandered, *often* indeed, to the conference so unexpected, so suddenly decisive, possibly so momentous; and with a dismayed uncertainty, the question—had I done right?—was always before me.

I dare say my cousin understood my character better, perhaps, after all my honest self-study, than I do even now. Irresolute, suddenly reversing my own decisions, impetuous in action as she knew me, she feared, I am sure, a revocation of my commission to Doctor Bryerly, and thought of the countermand I might send galloping after him.

So, kind creature, she laboured to occupy my thoughts, and when one theme was exhausted found another, and had always her parry prepared as often as I directed a reflection or an inquiry to the reopening of the question which she had taken so much pains to close.

That night I was troubled. I was already upbraiding myself. I could not sleep, and at last sat up in bed, and cried. I lamented my weakness in having assented to Doctor Bryerly's and my cousin's advice. Was I not departing from my engagement to my dear papa? Was I not consenting that my Uncle Silas should be induced to second my breach of faith by a corresponding perfidy?

Lady Knollys had done wisely in despatching Doctor Bryerly so promptly; for, most assuredly, had he been at Knowl next morning when I came down I should have recalled my commission.

That day in the study I found four papers which increased my perturbation. They were in dear papa's handwriting, and had an indorsement in these words—'Copy of my letter addressed to ——, one of the trustees named in my will.' Here, then, were the contents of those four sealed letters which had excited mine and Lady Knollys' curiosity on the agitating day on which the will was read.

It contained these words:—

'I name my oppressed and unhappy brother, Silas Ruthyn, residing at my house of Bartram-Haugh, as guardian of the person of my beloved child, to convince the world if possible, and failing that, to satisfy at least all future generations of our family that his brother, who knew him best, had implicit confidence in him, and that he deserved it. A cowardly and preposterous slander, originating in political malice, and which would never have been whispered had he not been poor and imprudent, is best silenced by this ordeal of puri-fication. All I possess goes to him if my child dies under age; and the custody of her person I commit meanwhile to him alone, knowing that she is as safe in his as she could have been under my own care. I rely upon your remembrance of our early friendship to make this known wherever an opportunity occurs, and also to say what your sense of justice may warrant.'

The other letters were in the same spirit. My heart sank like lead as I read them. I quaked with fear. What had I done? My father's wise and noble vindication of our dishonoured name I had presumed to frustrate. I had, like a coward, receded from my easy share in the task; and, merciful Heaven, I had broken my faith with the dead!

With these letters in my hand, white with fear, I flew like a shadow to the drawing-room where Cousin Monica was, and told her to read them. I saw by her countenance how much alarmed she was by my looks, but she said nothing, only read the letters hurriedly, and then exclaimed—

'Is this all, my dear child? I really fancied you had found a second will, and had lost everything. Why, my dearest Maud, we knew all this before. We quite understood poor dear Austin's motive. Why are you so easily disturbed?'

'Oh, Cousin Monica, I think he was right; it all seems quite reason-able now; and I—oh, what a crime!—it must be stopped.'

'My dear Maud, listen to reason. Doctor Bryerly has seen your uncle at Bartram at least two hours ago. You *can't* stop it, and why on earth should you if you could? Don't you think your uncle should be consulted?' said she.

'But he has *decided*. I have his letter speaking of it as settled; and Doctor Bryerly—oh, Cousin Monica, he's gone *to tempt him*.'

'Nonsense, girl! Doctor Bryerly is a good and just man, I do believe, and has, beside, no imaginable motive to pervert either his conscience or his judgment. He's not gone to tempt him—stuff!—but to unfold the facts and invite his consideration; and I say, considering how thoughtlessly such duties are often undertaken, and how long Silas has been living in lazy solitude, shut out from the world, and unused to discuss anything, I do think it only conscientious and honourable that he should have a fair and distinct view of the matter in all its bearings submitted to him before he indolently incurs what may prove the worst danger he was ever involved in.'

So Lady Knollys argued, with feminine energy, and I must confess, with a good deal of the repetition which I have sometimes observed in logicians of my own sex, and she puzzled without satisfying me.

'I don't know why I went to that room,' I said, quite frightened; 'or why I went to that press; how it happened that these papers, which we never saw there before, were the first things to strike my eye to-day.'

'What do you mean, dear?' said Lady Knollys.

'I mean this—I think I was *brought* there, and that *there* is poor papa's appeal to me, as plain as if his hand came and wrote it upon the wall.' I nearly screamed the conclusion of this wild confession.

'You are nervous, my darling; your bad nights have worn you out. Let us go out; the air will do you good; and I do assure you that you will very soon see that we are quite right, and rejoice conscientiously that you have acted as you did.'

But I was not to be satisfied, although my first vehemence was quieted. In my prayers that night my conscience upbraided me. When I lay down in bed my nervousness returned four-fold. Everybody at all nervously excitable has suffered some time or another by the appearance of ghastly features presenting themselves in every variety of contortion, one after another, the moment the eyes are closed. This night my dear father's face troubled me—sometimes white and sharp as ivory, sometimes strangely transparent like glass, sometimes all hanging in cadaverous folds, always with the same unnatural expression of diabolical fury.

From this dreadful vision I could only escape by sitting up and staring at the light. At length, worn out, I dropped asleep, and in a dream I distinctly heard papa's voice say sharply outside the bed-curtain:—'Maud, we shall be late at Bartram-Haugh.'

And I awoke in a horror, the walls, as it seemed, still ringing with the summons, and the speaker, I fancied, standing at the other side of the curtain.

A miserable night I passed. In the morning, looking myself like a ghost, I stood in my nightdress by Lady Knollys' bed.

'I have had my warning,' I said. 'Oh, Cousin Monica, papa has been with me, and ordered me to Bartram-Haugh; and go I will.'

She stared in my face uncomfortably, and then tried to laugh the matter off; but I know she was troubled at the strange state to which agitation and suspense had reduced me.

'You're taking too much for granted, Maud,' said she; 'Silas Ruthyn, most likely, will refuse his consent, and insist on your going to Bartram-Haugh.'

'Heaven grant!' I exclaimed; 'but if he doesn't, it is all the same to me, go I will. He may turn me out, but I'll go, and try to expiate the breach of faith that I fear is so horribly wicked.'

We had several hours still to wait for the arrival of the post. For both of us the delay was a suspense; for me an almost agonizing one. At length, at an unlooked-for moment, Branston did enter the room with the post-bag. There was a large letter, with the Feltram postmark, addressed to Lady Knollys—it was Doctor Bryerly's despatch; we read it together. It was dated on the day before, and its purport was thus:—

'RESPECTED MADAM,

'I this day saw Mr. Silas Ruthyn, at Bartram-Haugh, and he peremptorily refuses, on any terms, to vacate the guardianship or to consent to Miss Ruthyn's residing anywhere but under his own immediate care. As he bases his refusal, first upon a conscientious difficulty, declaring that he has no right, through fear of personal contingencies, to abdicate an office imposed in so solemn a way, and so naturally devolving on him as only brother to the deceased; and secondly upon the effect such a withdrawal, at the instance of the acting trustee, would have upon his own character, amounting to a public self-condemnation; and as he refused to discuss these positions with me, I could make no way whatsoever with him. Finding, therefore, that his mind was quite made up, after a short time I took my leave. He mentioned that preparations for his niece's reception are being completed, and that he will send for her in a few days; so that I think it will be advisable that I should go down to Knowl, to assist Miss Ruthyn with any advice she may require before her departure, to dis-

charge servants, get inventories made, and provide for the care of the
place and grounds during her minority.

'I am, respected Madam, yours truly,

'HANS E. BRYERLY.'

I can't describe to you how chapfallen and angry my cousin looked.
She sniffed once or twice, and then said, rather bitterly, in a subdued
tone:—

'Well, *now*; I hope you are pleased?'

'No, no, no; you *know* I'm not—grieved to the heart, my only
friend, my dear Cousin Monica; but my conscience is at rest; you
don't know what a sacrifice it is; I am a most unhappy creature. I feel
an indescribable foreboding. I am frightened; but you won't forsake
me, Cousin Monica.'

'No, darling, never,' she said, sadly.

'And you'll come and see me, won't you, as often as you can?'

'Yes, dear; that is if Silas allows me; and I'm sure he will,' she added
hastily, seeing, I suppose, my terror in my face. 'All I can do, you may be
sure I will, and perhaps he will allow you to come to me, now and then,
for a short visit. You know I am only six miles away—little more than
half an hour's drive, and though I hate Bartram, and detest Silas—Yes,
I *detest Silas*,' she repeated in reply to my surprised gaze—'I *will* call at
Bartram—that is, I say, if he allows me; for, you know, I haven't been
there for a quarter of a century; and though I never understood Silas,
I fancy he forgives no sins, whether of omission or commission.'

I wondered what old grudge could make my cousin judge Uncle
Silas always so hardly—I could not suppose it was justice. I had seen
my hero indeed lately so disrespectfully handled before my eyes, that
he had, as idols will, lost something of his sacredness. But as an article
of faith, I still cultivated my trust in his divinity, and dismissed every
intruding doubt with an exorcism, as a suggestion of the evil one. But
I wronged Lady Knollys in suspecting her of pique, or malice, or
anything more than that tendency to take strong views which some
persons attribute to my sex.

So then, the little project of Cousin Monica's guardianship, which,
had it been poor papa's wish, would have made me so very happy, was
quite knocked on the head, to revive no more. I comforted myself,
however, with her promise to re-open communications with Bartram-
Haugh, and we grew resigned.

I remember, next morning, as we sat at a very late breakfast, Lady Knollys, reading a letter, suddenly made an exclamation and a little laugh, and read on with increased interest for a few minutes, and then, with another little laugh, she looked up, placing her hand, with the open letter in it, beside her tea-cup.

'You'll not guess whom I've been reading about,' said she, with her head the least thing on one side, and an arch smile.

I felt myself blushing—cheeks, forehead, even down to the tips of my fingers. I anticipated the name I was to hear. She looked very much amused. Was it possible that Captain Oakley was married?

'I really have not the least idea,' I replied, with that kind of over-done carelessness which betrays us.

'No, I see quite plainly you have not; but you can't think how prettily you blush,' answered she, very much diverted.

'I really don't care,' I replied, with some little dignity, and blushing deeper and deeper.

'Will you make a guess?' she asked.

'I *can't* guess.'

'Well, shall I tell you?'

'Just as you please.'

'Well, I will—that is, I'll read a page of my letter, which tells it all. Do you know Georgina Fanshawe?' she asked.

'Lady Georgina? No.'

'Well, no matter; she's in Paris now, and this letter is from her, and she says—let me see the place—"Yesterday, what do you think?—quite an apparition!—you shall hear. My brother Craven yesterday insisted on my accompanying him to Le Bas' shop in that odd little antique street near the Grève; it is a wonderful old curiosity shop.* I forget what they call them here. When we went into this place it was very nearly deserted, and there were so many curious things to look at all about, that for a minute or two I did not observe a tall woman, in a grey silk and a black velvet mantle, and quite a nice new Parisian bonnet. You will be *charmed*, by-the-by, with the new shape—it is only out three weeks, and is quite *indescribably* elegant, *I* think, at least. They have them, I am sure, by this time at Molnitz's, so I need say no more. And now that I am on this subject of dress, I have got your lace; and I think you will be very ungrateful if you are not *charmed* with it." Well, I need not read all that—here is the rest;' and she read—

' "But you'll ask about my mysterious *dame* in the new bonnet and velvet mantle: she was sitting on a stool at the counter, not buying, but evidently selling a quantity of stones and trinkets which she had in a card-box, and the man was picking them up one by one, and, I suppose, valuing them. I was near enough to see such a darling little pearl cross, with at least half a dozen really good pearls in it, and had begun to covet them for my set, when the lady glanced over my shoulder, and she knew me—in fact, we knew one another—and who do you think she was? Well—you'll not guess in a week, and I can't wait so long; so I may as well tell you at once—she was that horrid old Mademoiselle Blassemare whom you pointed out to me at Elverston; and I never forgot her face since—nor she, it seems, mine, for she turned away very quickly, and when I next saw her her veil was down."

'Did not you tell me, Maud, that you had lost your pearl cross while that dreadful Madame de la Rougierre was here?'

'Yes; but—'

'I know; but what has she to do with Mademoiselle de Blassemare, you were going to say—they are one and the same person.'

'Oh, I perceive,' answered I, with that dim sense of danger and dismay with which one hears suddenly of an enemy of whom one has lost sight of for a time.

'I'll write and tell Georgie to buy that cross. I wager my life it is yours,' said Lady Knollys, firmly.

The servants, indeed, made no secret of their opinion of Madame de la Rougierre, and frankly charged her with a long list of larcenies. Even Anne Wixted, who had enjoyed her barren favour while the gouvernante was here, hinted privately that she had bartered a missing piece of lace belonging to me with a gipsy pedlar, for French gloves and an Irish poplin.

'And so surely as I find it is yours, I'll set the police in pursuit.'

'But you must not bring me into court,' said I, half amused and half alarmed.

'No occasion, my dear; Mary Quince and Mrs. Rusk can prove it perfectly.'

'And why do you dislike her so very much?' I asked.

Cousin Monica leaned back in her chair, and searched the cornice from corner to corner with upturned eyes for the reason, and at last laughed a little, amused at herself.

'Well, really, it is not easy to define, and, perhaps, it is not quite charitable; but I know I hate her, and I know, you little hypocrite, you hate her as much as I;' and we both laughed a little.

'But you must tell me all you know of her history.'

'Her history?' echoed she. 'I really know next to nothing about it; only that I used to see her sometimes about the place that Georgina mentions, and there were some unpleasant things said about her; but you know they may be all lies. The worst I *know* of her is her treatment of you, and her robbing the desk,'—(Cousin Monica always called it her *robbery*)—'and I think that's enough to hang her. Suppose we go out for a walk?'

So together we went, and I resumed about Madame; but no more could I extract—perhaps there was not much more to hear.

ALL at Knowl was indicative of the break-up that was so near at hand. Doctor Bryerly arrived according to promise. He was in a whirl of business all the time. He and Mr. Danvers conferred about the management of the estate. It was agreed that the grounds and gardens should be let, but not the house, of which Mrs. Rusk was to take the care. The gamekeeper remained in office, and some other out-door servants. But the rest were to go, except Mary Quince, who was to accompany me to Bartram-Haugh as my maid.

'Don't part with Quince,' said Lady Knollys, peremptorily: 'they'll want you, but *don't*.'

She kept harping on this point, and recurred to it half a dozen times every day.

'They'll say, you know, that she is not fit for a lady's maid, as she certainly is *not*, if it in the least signified in such a wilderness as Bartram-Haugh; but she is attached, trustworthy, and honest; and those are qualities valuable everywhere, especially in a solitude. Don't allow them to get you a wicked young French milliner in her stead.'

Sometimes she said things that jarred unpleasantly on my nerves, and left an undefined sense of danger. Such as:—

'I know she's true to you, and a good creature; but is she shrewd enough?'

Or, with an anxious look:—

'I hope Mary Quince is not easily frightened.'

Or, suddenly:—

'Can Mary Quince write, in case you were ill?'

Or,

'Can she take a message exactly?'

Or,

'Is she a person of any enterprise and resource, and cool in an emergency?'

Now, these questions did not come all in a string, as I write them down here, but at long intervals, and were followed quickly by ordinary talk; but they generally escaped from my companion after silence and gloomy thought; and though I could extract nothing more defined than these questions, yet they seemed to me to point at some possible danger contemplated in my good cousin's dismal ruminations.

Another topic that occupied my cousin's mind a good deal was obviously the larceny of my pearl cross. She made a note of the description furnished by the recollection, respectively, of Mary Quince, Mrs. Rusk, and myself. I had fancied her little vision of the police was no more than the result of a momentary impulse; but really to judge by her methodical examinations of us, I should have fancied that she had taken it up in downright earnest.

Having learned that my departure from Knowl was to be so very soon, she resolved not to leave me before the day of my journey to Bartram-Haugh; and as day after day passed by, and the hour of our leave-taking approached, she became more and more kind and affectionate. A feverish and sorrowful interval it was to me.

Of Doctor Bryerly, though staying in the house, we saw almost nothing, except for an hour or so at tea-time. He breakfasted very early, and dined solitarily, and at uncertain hours, as business permitted.

The second evening of his visit, Cousin Monica took occasion to introduce the subject of his visit to Bartram-Haugh.

'You saw him, of course?' said Lady Knollys.

'Yes, he saw me; he was not well. On hearing who I was, he asked me to go to his room, where he sat in a silk dressing-gown and slippers.'

'About business principally,' said Cousin Monica, laconically.

'That was despatched in very few words; for he was quite resolved, and placed his refusal upon grounds which it was difficult to dispute. But difficult or no, mind you, he intimated that he would hear nothing more on the subject—so that was closed.'

'Well; and what is his religion now?' inquired she, irreverently.

'We had some interesting conversation on the subject. He leans much to what we call the doctrine of correspondents.* He is read rather deeply in the writings of Swedenborg, and seemed anxious to discuss some points with one who professes to be his follower. To say truth, I did not expect to find him either so well read or so deeply interested in the subject.'

'Was he angry when it was proposed that he should vacate the guardianship?'

'Not at all. Contrariwise, he said he had at first been so minded himself. His years, his habits, and something of the unfitness of the situation, the remoteness of Bartram-Haugh from good teachers, and all that, had struck him, and nearly determined him against accepting the office. But then came the views which I stated in my letter, and they governed him; and nothing could shake them, he said, or induce him to re-open the question in his own mind.'

All the time Doctor Bryerly was relating his conference with the head of the family at Bartram-Haugh, my cousin commented on the narrative with a variety of little 'pishes' and sneers, which I thought showed more of vexation than contempt.

I was glad to hear all that Doctor Bryerly related. It gave me a kind of confidence; and I experienced a momentary reaction. After all, could Bartram-Haugh be more lonely than I had found Knowl? Was I not sure of the society of my Cousin Millicent, who was about my own age? Was it not quite possible that my sojourn in Derbyshire might turn out a happy though very quiet remembrance through all my after-life? Why should it not? What time or place would be happy if we gave ourselves over to dismal imaginations?

So the summons reached me from Uncle Silas. The hours at Knowl were numbered.

The evening before I departed I visited the full-length portrait of Uncle Silas, and studied it for the last time carefully, with deep interest, for many minutes; but with results vaguer than ever.

With a brother so generous and so wealthy, always ready to help him forward; with his talents; with his lithe and gorgeous beauty, the shadow of which hung on that canvas—what might he not have accomplished? whom might he not have captivated? And yet where and what was he? A poor and shunned old man, occupying a lonely house and place that did not belong to him, married to degradation, with a few years of suspected and solitary life before him, and then swift oblivion his best portion.

I gazed on the picture, to fix it well and vividly in my remembrance. I might still trace some of its outlines and tints in its living original, whom I was next day to see for the first time in my life.

So the morning came—my last for many a day at Knowl—a day of partings, a day of novelty and regrets. The travelling carriage and post horses were at the door. Cousin Monica's carriage had just carried her away to the railway. We had embraced with tears; and her kind face was still before me, and her words of comfort and promise in my ears. The early sharpness of morning was still in the air; the frosty dew still glistened on the window-panes. We had made a hasty breakfast, my share of which was a single cup of tea. The aspect of the house how strange! Uncarpeted, uninhabited, doors for the most part locked, all the servants but Mrs. Rusk and Branston departed. The drawing-room door stood open, and a charwoman was washing the bare floor. I was looking my last—for who could say how long?—on the old house, and lingered. The luggage was all up. I made Mary Quince get in first, for every delay was precious; and now the moment was come. I hugged and kissed Mrs. Rusk in the hall.

'God bless you, Miss Maud, darling. You must not fret; mind, the time won't be long going over—*no* time at all; and you'll be bringing back a fine young gentleman—who knows? as great as the Duke of Wellington, for your husband; and I'll take the best of care of everything, and the birds and dogs, till you come back; and I'll go and see you and Mary, if you'll allow, in Derbyshire;' and so forth.

I got into the carriage, and bid Branston, who shut the door, good-bye, and kissed hands to Mrs. Rusk, who was smiling and drying her eyes and courtesying on the hall-door steps. The dogs who had started gleefully with the carriage, were called back by Branston, and driven home, wondering and wistful, looking back with ears oddly cocked and tails dejected. My heart thanked them for their kindness, and I felt like a stranger, and very desolate.

It was a bright, clear morning. It had been settled that it was not worth the trouble changing from the carriage to the railway for sake of five-and-twenty miles, and so the entire journey of sixty miles was to be made by the post road—the pleasantest travelling, if the mind were free. The grander and more distant features of the landscape we may see well enough from the window of the railway-carriage; but it is the foreground that interests and instructs us, like a pleasant gossiping history; and *that* we had, in old days, from the post-chaise window. It was more than travelling picquet.* Something of all conditions of life—luxury and misery—high spirits and low;—all sorts of costume, livery, rags, millinery; faces buxom, faces wrinkled, faces kind, faces wicked;—no end of interest and suggestion, passing in a procession silent and vivid, and all in their proper scenery. The golden corn-sheafs—the old dark-alleyed orchards, and the high streets of antique towns. There were few dreams brighter, few books so pleasant.

We drove by the dark wood—it always looked dark to me—where the 'mausoleum' stands—where my dear parents both lay now.

I gazed on its sombre masses not with a softened feeling, but a peculiar sense of pain, and was glad when it was quite past.

All the morning I had not shed a tear. Good Mary Quince cried at leaving Knowl; Lady Knollys' eyes were not dry as she kissed and blessed me, and promised an early visit; and the dark, lean, energetic face of the housekeeper was quivering, and her cheeks wet, as I drove away. But I, whose grief was sorest, never shed a tear. I only looked about from one familiar object to another, pale, excited, not quite apprehending my departure, and wondering at my own composure.

But when we reached the old bridge, with the tall osiers standing by the buttress, and looked back at poor Knowl—the places we love and are leaving look so fairy-like and so sad in the clear distance, and this is the finest view of the gabled old house, with its slanting meadow-lands and noble timber reposing in solemn groups—I gazed at the receding vision, and the tears came at last, and I wept in silence long after the fair picture was hidden from view by the intervening uplands.

I was relieved, and when we had made our next change of horses, and got into a country that was unknown to me, the new scenery and the sense of progress worked their accustomed effects on a young traveller who had lived a particularly secluded life, and I began to experience, on the whole, a not unpleasurable excitement.

Mary Quince and I, with the hopefulness of inexperienced travellers, began already to speculate about our proximity to Bartram-Haugh, and were sorely disappointed when we heard from the nondescript courier—more like an ostler than a servant, who sat behind in charge of us and the luggage, and represented my guardian's special care—at nearly one o'clock, that we had still forty miles to go, a considerable portion of which was across the high Derbyshire mountains, before we reached Bartram-Haugh.

The fact was, we had driven at a pace accommodated rather to the convenience of the horses than to our impatience; and finding at the quaint little inn where we now halted, that we must wait for a nail or two in a loose shoe of one of our relay, we consulted, and being both hungry, agreed to beguile the time with an early dinner, which we enjoyed very sociably in a queer little parlour with a bow window, and commanding, with a little garden for foreground, a very pretty landscape.

Good Mary Quince, like myself, had quite dried her tears by this time, and we were both highly interested, and I a little nervous, too,

about our arrival and reception at Bartram. Some time, of course, was
lost in this pleasant little parlour, before we found ourselves once
more pursuing our way.

The slowest part of our journey was the pull up the long mountain
road, ascending zig-zag, as sailors make way against a head-wind, by
tacking. I forget the name of the pretty little group of houses—it did
not amount to a village—buried in trees, where we got our *four*
horses and two postilions, for the work was severe. I can only desig-
nate it as the place where Mary Quince and I had our tea, very comfortably, and bought some gingerbread, very curious to look upon,
but quite uneatable.

The greater portion of the ascent when we were fairly upon the
mountain, was accomplished at a walk, and at some particularly steep
points we had to get out and go on foot. But this to me was quite
delightful. I had never scaled a mountain before, and the ferns and
heath, the pure boisterous air, and above all the magnificent view of
the rich country we were leaving behind, now gorgeous and misty in
sunset tints, stretching in gentle undulations far beneath us, quite
enchanted me.

We had just reached the summit when the sun went down. The low
grounds at the other side were already lying in cold gray shadow, and
I got the man who sat behind to point out as well as he could the site
of Bartram-Haugh. But mist was gathering over all by this time. The
filmy disk of the moon which was to light us on, so soon as twilight
faded into night, hung high in air. I tried to see the sable mass of wood
which he described. But it was vain, and to acquire a clear idea of the
place, as of its master, I must only wait that nearer view which an hour
or two more would afford me.

And now we rapidly descended the mountain side. The scenery
was wilder and bolder than I was accustomed to. Our road skirted the
edge of a great heathy moor. The silvery light of the moon began to
glimmer, and we passed a gipsy bivouac with fires alight and caldrons
hanging over them. It was the first I had seen. Two or three low tents;
a couple of dark, withered crones, veritable witches; a graceful girl
standing behind, gazing after us; and men in odd-shaped hats, with
gaudy waist-coats and bright-coloured neck-handkerchiefs and gaitered legs, stood lazily in front. They had all a wild tawdry display of
colour; and a group of alders in the rear made a background of shade
for tents, fires, and figures.

I opened a front window of the chariot, and called to the post-boys to stop. The groom from behind came to the window.

'Are not those gipsies?' I inquired.

'Yes, please'm, them's gipsies, sure, Miss,' he answered, glancing with that odd smile, half contemptuous, half superstitious, with which I have since often observed the peasants of Derbyshire eyeing those thievish and uncanny neighbours.

CHAPTER XXXI

BARTRAM-HAUGH

In a moment a tall, lithe girl, black-haired, black-eyed, and, as I thought, inexpressibly handsome, was smiling, with such beautiful rings of pearly teeth, at the window; and in her peculiar accent, with a suspicion of something foreign in it, proposing with many courtesies to tell the lady her fortune.

I had never seen this wild tribe of the human race before—children of mystery and liberty. Such vagabondism and beauty in the figure before me! I looked at their hovels and thought of the night, and wondered at their independence, and felt my inferiority. I could not resist. She held up her slim oriental hand.

'Yes, I'll hear my fortune,' I said, returning the sibyl's smile instinctively.

'Give me some money, Mary Quince. No, *not* that,' I said, rejecting the thrifty sixpence she tendered, for I had heard that the revelations of this weird sisterhood were bright in proportion to the kindness of their clients, and was resolved to approach Bartram with cheerful auguries. 'That five-shilling piece,' I insisted; and honest Mary reluctantly surrendered the coin.

So the feline beauty took it, with courtesies and 'thankees', smiling still, and hid it away as if she stole it, and looked on my open palm still smiling; and told me, to my surprise, that there was *somebody* I liked very much, and I was almost afraid she would name Captain Oakley; that he would grow very rich, and that I should marry him; that I should move about from place to place a great deal for a good while to come. That I had some enemies, who should be sometimes so near as to be in the same room with me, and yet they should not be able to hurt me. That I should see blood spilt and yet not my own, and finally be very happy and splendid, like the heroine of a fairy tale.

Did this strange, girlish charlatan see in my face some signs of shrinking when she spoke of enemies, and set me down for a coward whose weakness might be profitable? Very likely. At all events she plucked a long brass pin, with a round bead for a head, from some part of her dress, and holding the point in her fingers, and exhibiting the treasure before my eyes, she told me that I must get a charmed pin like that, which her grandmother had given to her, and she ran glibly through a story of all the magic expended on it, and told me she could not part with it; but its virtue was that you were to stick it through the blanket, and while it was there neither rat, nor cat, nor snake—and then came two more terms in the catalogue, which I suppose belonged to the gipsy dialect, and which she explained to mean, as well as I could understand, the first, a malevolent spirit, and the second 'a cove to cut your throat,' could approach or hurt you.

A charm like that, she gave me to understand, I must by hook or by crook obtain. She had not a second. None of her people in the camp over there possessed one. I am ashamed to confess that I actually paid her a pound for this brass pin! The purchase was partly an indication of my temperament, which could never let an opportunity pass away irrevocably without a struggle, and always apprehended 'some day or other I'll reproach myself for having neglected it?' and partly a record of the trepidations of that period of my life. At all events I had her pin, and she my pound, and I venture to say I was the gladder of the two.

She stood on the road-side bank curtesying and smiling, the first enchantress I had encountered with, and I watched the receding picture, with its patches of firelight, its dusky groups, and donkey carts, white as skeletons in the moonlight, as we drove rapidly away.

They, I suppose, had a wild sneer and a merry laugh over my purchase, as they sat and ate their supper of stolen poultry, about their fire, and were duly proud of belonging to the superior race.

Mary Quince, shocked at my prodigality, hinted a remonstrance.

'It went to my heart, Miss, it did. They're such a lot, young and old, all alike thieves and vagabonds, and many a poor body wanting.'

'Tut, Mary, never mind. Everyone has her fortune told some time in her life, and you can't have a good one without paying. I think, Mary, we must be near Bartram now.'

The road now traversed the side of a steep hill, parallel to which, along the opposite side of a winding river, rose the dark steeps of a corresponding upland, covered with forest that looked awful and dim in the deep shadow, while the moonlight rippled fitfully upon the stream beneath.

'It seems to be a beautiful country,' I said to Mary Quince, who was munching a sandwich in the corner, and thus appealed to, adjusted her bonnet and made an inspection from *her* window, which, however, commanded nothing but the heathy slope of the hill whose side we were traversing.

'Well, Miss, I suppose it is; but there's a deal o' mountains—is not there?'

And so saying, honest Mary leaned back again, and went on with her sandwich.

We were now descending at a great pace. I knew we were coming near. I stood up as well as I could in the carriage to see over the postilions' heads. I was eager, but frightened too; agitated as the crisis of the arrival and meeting approached. At last, a long stretch of comparatively level country below us, with masses of wood as well as I could see irregularly overspreading it, became visible as the narrow valley through which we were speeding made a sudden bend.

Down we drove, and now I did perceive a change. A great grass-grown park-wall, over-topped with mighty trees; but still on and on we came at a canter that seemed almost a gallop. The old grey park wall flanking us at one side, and a pretty pastoral hedgerow of ash-trees, irregularly on the other.

At last the postilions began to draw bridle, and at a slight angle, the moon shining full upon them, we wheeled into a wide semicircle formed by the receding park walls, and halted before a great fantastic iron gate, and a pair of tall fluted piers, of white stone, all grass-grown and ivy-bound, with great cornices, surmounted with shields and supporters, the Ruthyn bearings washed by the rains of Derbyshire for many a generation of Ruthyns, almost smooth by this time, and looking bleached and phantasmal, like giant sentinels, with each a hand clasped in his comrade's, to bar our passage to the enchanted castle—the florid tracery of the iron gate showing like the draperies of white robes hanging from their extended arms to the earth.

Our courier got down and shoved the great gate open, and we entered between sombre files of magnificent forest trees, one of those very broad straight avenues, whose width measures the front of the house. This was all built of white stone, resembling that of Caen, which parts of Derbyshire produce in such abundance.

So this was Bartram, and here was Uncle Silas. I was almost breathless as I approached. The bright moon shining full on the white front of the old house revealed not only its highly decorated style, its fluted pillars and doorway, rich and florid carving, and balustraded summit, but also its stained and moss-grown front. Two giant trees, over-thrown at last by the recent storm, lay with their upturned roots, and their yellow foliage still flickering on the sprays that were to bloom no more, where they had fallen, at the right side of the court-yard, which, like the avenue, was studded with tufted weeds and grass.

All this gave to the aspect of Bartram a forlorn character of desertion and decay, contrasting almost awfully with the grandeur of its proportions and richness of its architecture.

There was a ruddy glow from a broad window in the second row, and I thought I saw some one peep from it and disappear; at the same moment there was a furious barking of dogs, some of whom ran scampering into the court-yard from a half-closed side door; and amid their uproar, the bawling of the man in the back seat, who jumped down to drive them off, and the crack of the postilions' whips, who struck at them, we drew up before the lordly door-steps of this melancholy mansion.

Just as our attendant had his hand on the knocker the door opened, and we saw, by a not very brilliant candle-light, three figures— a shabby, little old man, thin, and very much stooped, with a white cravat, and looking as if his black clothes were too large, and made for some one else, stood with his hand upon the door; a young, plump, but very pretty female figure, in unusually short petticoats, with fattish legs, and nice ankles, in boots, stood in the centre; and a dowdy maid, like an old charwoman behind her.

The household paraded for welcome was not certainly very brilliant. Amid the riot the trunks were deliberately put down by our attendant, who kept shouting to the old man at the door, and to the dogs in turn; and the old man was talking and pointing stiffly and tremulously, but I could not hear what he said.

'Was it possible—could that mean-looking old man be Uncle Silas?'

The idea stunned me; but I almost instantly perceived that he was much too small, and I was relieved, and even grateful. It was certainly an odd mode of procedure to devote primary attention to the trunks and boxes, leaving the travellers still shut up in the carriage, of which they were by this time pretty well tired. I was not sorry for the reprieve, however: being nervous about first impressions, and willing to defer mine, I sate shyly back, peeping at the candle and moonlight picture before me, myself unseen.

'Will you tell—yes or no—is my cousin in the coach?' screamed the plump young lady, stamping her stout black boot, in a momentary lull.

Yes, I was there, sure.

'And why the puck* don't you let her out, you stupe, you?'

'Run down, Giblets, you never do nout without driving, and let Cousin Maud out. You're very welcome to Bartram.' This greeting was screamed at an amazing pitch, and repeated before I had time to drop the window, and say 'thank you'. 'I'd a let you out myself—there's a good dog, you would na' bite Cousin'—(the parenthesis was to a huge mastiff, who thrust himself beside her, by this time quite pacified)—'only I daren't go down the steps, for the governor said I shouldn't.'

The venerable person who went by the name of Giblets had by this time opened the carriage door, and our courier, or 'boots', he looked more like the latter functionary, had lowered the steps, and in greater trepidation than I experienced when in after-days I was presented to my sovereign, I glided down, to offer myself to the greeting and inspection of the plain-spoken young lady, who stood at the top of the steps to receive me.

She welcomed me with a hug and a hearty buss, as she called that salutation, on each cheek, and pulled me into the hall, and was evidently glad to see me.

'And you're tired a bit, I warrant; and who's the old 'un, who?' she asked eagerly, in a stage whisper, which made my ear numb for five minutes after. 'Oh, oh, the maid! and a precious old 'un—ha, ha, ha! But hawk! how grand she is, with her black silk cloak and crape, and I only in twilled cotton, and rotten old Coburg* for Sundays. Odds! it's a shame; but you'll be tired, you will. It's a smartish pull, they do say from Knowl. I know a spell of it, only so far as the "Cat and Fiddle", near the Lunnon-road. Come up, will you? Would you like to come in first and talk a bit wi' the governor? Father, you know, he's a bit silly, he is, this while.' I found that the phrase meant only *bodily* infirmity. 'He took a pain o' Friday, newralgie—something or other he calls it—rheumatics it is when it takes old "Giblets" there; and he's sitting in his own room; or maybe you'd like better to come to your bedroom first, for it is dirty work travelling, they do say.'

Yes; I preferred the preliminary adjustment. Mary Quince was standing behind me; and as my voluble kinswoman talked on, we had each ample time and opportunity to observe the personnel of the other; and she made no scruple of letting me perceive that she was improving it, for she stared me full in the face, taking in evidently feature after feature; and she felt the material of my mantle pretty carefully between her finger and thumb, and manually examined my chain and trinkets, and picked up my hand as she might a glove, to con over my rings.

I can't say, of course, exactly what impression I may have produced on her. But in my Cousin Milly I saw a girl who looked younger than her years, plump, but with a slender waist, with light hair, lighter than mine, and very blue eyes, rather round; on the whole very good-looking. She had an odd swaggering walk, a toss of her head, and a saucy and imperious, but rather good-natured and honest countenance. She talked rather loud, with a good ringing voice, and a boisterous laugh when it came.

If *I* was behind the fashion, what would Cousin Monica have thought of her? She was arrayed, as she had stated, in black twilled cotton expressive of her affliction; but it was made almost as short in the skirt as that of the prints of the Bavarian broom girls.* She had white cotton stockings, and a pair of black leather boots, with leather buttons, and, for a lady, prodigiously thick soles, which reminded me of the navvy boots I had so often admired in *Punch*. I must add that the hands with which she assisted her scrutiny of my dress, though pretty, were very much sunburnt indeed.

'And what's *her* name?' she demanded, nodding to Mary Quince, who was gazing on her awfully with round eyes, as an inland spinster might upon a whale beheld for the first time.

Mary courtesied, and I answered.

'Mary Quince,' she repeated. 'You're welcome, Quince. What shall I call her? I've a name for all o' them. Old Giles there, is Giblets. He did not like it first, but he answers quick enough now; and Old Lucy Wyat there,' nodding toward the old woman, 'is Lucia de l'Amour.' A slightly erroneous reading of Lammermoor,* for my cousin sometimes made mistakes, and was not much versed in the Italian opera. 'You know it's a play, and I call her l'Amour for shortness;' and she laughed hilariously, and I could not forbear joining; and, winking at me, she called aloud, 'l'Amour.'

To which the crone, with a high-cauled cap, resembling Mother Hubbard, responded with a courtesy and 'Yes 'm.'

'Are all the trunks and boxes took up?'

They were.

'Well, we'll come now; and what shall I call you, Quince? Let me see.'

'According to your pleasure, Miss,' answered Mary, with dignity, and a dry courtesy.

'Why you're as horase as a frog, Quince. We'll call you Quinzy for the present. That'll do. Come along, Quinzy.'

So my Cousin Milly took me under the arm, and pulled me forward; but as we ascended, she let me go, leaning back to make inspection of my attire from a new point of view.

'Hallo, cousin,' she cried, giving my dress a smack with her open hand. 'What a plague do you want of all that bustle: you'll leave it behind, lass, the first bush you jump over.'

I was a good deal astounded. I was also very near laughing, for there was a sort of importance in her plump countenance, and an indescribable grotesqueness in the fashion of her garments, which heightened the outlandishness of her talk, in a way which I cannot at all describe.

What palatial wide stairs those were which we ascended, with their prodigious carved banisters of oak, and each huge pillar on the landing-place crowned with a shield and carved heraldic supporters; florid oak panelling covered the walls. But of the house I could form no estimate, for Uncle Silas's housekeeping did not provide light for hall and passages, and we were dependent on the glimmer of a single candle; but there would be quite enough of this kind of exploration in the daylight.

So along dark oak flooring we advanced to my room, and I had now an opportunity of admiring, at my leisure, the lordly proportions of the building. Two great windows, with dark and tarnished curtains, rose half as high again as the windows of Knowl; and yet Knowl, in its own style, is a fine house. The door-frames, like the window-frames, were richly carved; the fireplace was in the same massive style, and the mantelpiece projected with a mass of very rich carving. On the whole I was surprised. I had never slept in so noble a room before.

The furniture, I must confess, was by no means on a par with the architectural pretensions of the apartment. A French bed, a piece of carpet about three yards square, a small table, two chairs, a toilet table—no wardrobe—no chest of drawers. The furniture painted white, and of the light and diminutive kind, was particularly ill adapted to the scale and style of the apartment, one end only of which it occupied, and that but sparsely, leaving the rest of the chamber in the nakedness of a stately desolation. My Cousin Milly ran away to report progress to 'the Governor', as she termed Uncle Silas.

'Well, Miss Maud, I never did expect to see the like o' that!' exclaimed honest Mary Quince. 'Did you ever see such a young lady? She's no more like one o' the family than I am—Law bless us! and what's she dressed like? Well, well, well!' And Mary, with a rueful shake of her head, clicked her tongue pathetically to the back of her teeth, while I could not forbear laughing.

'And such a scrap o' furniture! Well, well, well!' and the same ticking of the tongue followed.

But, in a few minutes, back came Cousin Milly, and, with a barbarous sort of curiosity, assisted in unpacking my trunks, and stowing away the treasures on which she ventured a variety of admiring criticisms, in the presses which, like cupboards, filled recesses in the walls, with great oak doors, the keys of which were in them.

As I was making my hurried toilet, she entertained me now and then with more strictly personal criticisms.

'Your hair's a shade darker than mine—it's none the better o' that though—is it? Mine's said to be the right shade. I don't know—what do you say?'

I conceded the point with a good grace.

'I wish my hands was as white though—you do lick me there; but it's all gloves, and I never could abide 'em. I think I'll try though—they *are* very white, sure.'

'I wonder which is the prettiest, you or me? *I* don't know, *I*'m sure—which do *you* think?'

I laughed outright at this challenge, and she blushed a little, and for the first time seemed for a moment a little shy.

'Well, you *are* a half an inch longer than me, I think—don't you?'

I was fully an inch taller, so I had no difficulty in making the proposed admission.

'Well, you do look handsome! doesn't she, Quinzy, lass? but your frock comes down almost to your heels—it does.'

And she glanced from mine to hers, and made a little kick up with the heel of the navvy boot to assist her in measuring the comparative distance.

'Maybe mine's a thought too short?' she suggested. 'Who's there? Oh! it's you, is it?' she cried, as Mother Hubbard appeared at the door. 'Come in, L'Amour—don't you know, lass, you're always welcome?'

She had come to let us know that Uncle Silas would be happy to see me whenever I was ready; and that my Cousin Millicent would conduct me to the room where he awaited me.

In an instant all the comic sensations awakened by my singular cousin's eccentricities vanished, and I was thrilled with awe. I was about to see in the flesh—faded, broken, aged, but still identical—that being who had been the vision and the problem of so many years of my short life.

CHAPTER XXXII
UNCLE SILAS

I THOUGHT my odd cousin was also impressed with a kind of awe, though different in degree from mine, for a shade overcast her face, and she was silent as we walked side by side along the gallery, accompanied by the crone who carried the candle which lighted us to the door of that apartment, which I may call Uncle Silas's presence chamber.

Milly whispered to me as we approached—

'Mind how you make a noise, the Governor's as sharp as a weasel, and nothing vexes him like that.'

She was herself toppling along on tiptoe. We paused at a door near the head of the great staircase, and L'Amour knocked timidly with her rheumatic knuckles.

A voice, clear and penetrating, from within summoned us to enter. The old woman opened the door, and the next moment I was in the presence of Uncle Silas.

At the far end of a handsome wainscoted room, near the hearth in which a low fire was burning, beside a small table on which stood four waxlights, in tall silver candlesticks, sat a singular-looking old man.

The dark wainscoting behind him, and the vastness of the room, in the remoter parts of which the light which fell strongly upon his face and figure expended itself with hardly any effect, exhibited him with the forcible and strange relief of a finely painted Dutch portrait.* For some time I saw nothing but him.

A face like marble, with a fearful monumental look, and, for an old man, singularly vivid strange eyes, the singularity of which rather grew upon me as I looked; for his eyebrows were still black, though his hair descended from his temples in long locks of the purest silver and fine as silk, nearly to his shoulders.

He rose, tall and slight, a little stooped, all in black, with an ample black velvet tunic, which was rather a gown than a coat, with loose sleeves, showing his snowy shirt some way up the arm, and a pair of wrist buttons, then quite out of fashion, which glimmered aristocratically with diamonds.

I know I can't convey in words an idea of this apparition, drawn as it seemed in black and white, venerable, bloodless, fiery-eyed, with its singular look of power, and an expression so bewildering—was it derision, or anguish, or cruelty, or patience?

The wild eyes of this strange old man were fixed upon me as he rose; an habitual contraction which in certain lights took the character of a scowl, did not relax as he advanced toward me with his thin-lipped smile. He said something in his clear, gentle, but cold voice, the import of which I was too much agitated to catch, and he took both my hands in his, welcomed me with a courtly grace which belonged to another age, and led me affectionately, with many inquiries which I only half comprehended, to a chair near his own.

'I need not introduce my daughter; she has saved me that mortification. You'll find her, I believe, good-natured and affectionate; *au reste*, I fear a very rustic Miranda, and fitted rather for the society of Caliban than of a sick, old Prospero.* Is it not so, Millicent?'

The old man paused sarcastically for an answer, with his eyes fixed severely on my odd cousin, who blushed and looked uneasily to me for a hint.

'I don't know who they be—neither one nor t'other.'

'Very good, my dear,' he replied, with a little mocking bow. 'You see, my dear Maud, what a Shakesperean you have got for a cousin. It's plain, however, she has made acquaintance with some of our dramatists: she has studied the rôle of *Miss Hoyden** so perfectly.'

It was not a reasonable peculiarity of my uncle that he resented, with a good deal of playful acrimony, my poor cousin's want of education, for which, if he were not to blame, certainly neither was she.

'You see her, poor thing, a result of all the combined disadvantages of want of refined education, refined companionship, and, I fear, naturally, of refined tastes; but a sojourn at a good French conventual school will do wonders, and that I hope to manage by-and-by. In the meantime we jest at our misfortunes, and love one another, I hope, cordially.'

He extended his thin, white hand with a chilly smile towards Milly, who bounced up, and took it with a frightened look; and he repeated, holding her hand rather slightly, I thought, 'Yes, I hope, very cordially,' and then turning again to me, he put it over the arm of his chair, and let it go, as a man might drop something he did not want from a carriage window.

Having made this apology for poor Milly, who was plainly bewildered, he passed on, to her and my relief, to other topics, every now and then expressing his fears that I was fatigued, and his anxiety that I should partake of some supper or tea; but these solicitudes somehow seemed to escape his remembrance almost as soon as uttered; and he maintained the conversation, which soon degenerated into a close, and to me a painful examination, respecting my dear father's illness and its symptoms, upon which I could give no information, and his habits, upon which I could.

Perhaps he fancied that there might be some family predisposition to the organic disease, of which his brother died, and that his questions were directed rather to the prolonging of his own life than to the better understanding of my dear father's death.

How little was there left to this old man to make life desirable, and yet how keenly, I afterwards found, he clung to it. Have we not all of us seen those to whom life was not only *undesirable*, but positively painful—a mere series of bodily torments, yet hold to it with a desperate and pitiable tenacity—old children or young, it is all the same.

See how a sleepy child will put off the inevitable departure for bed. The little creature's eyes blink and stare, and it needs constant jogging to prevent his nodding off into the slumber which nature craves. His waking is a pain; he is quite worn out, and peevish, and stupid, and yet he implores a respite, and deprecates repose, and vows he is not sleepy, even to the moment when his mother takes him in her arms, and carries him, in a sweet slumber, to the nursery. So it is with us old children of earth and the great sleep of death, and nature our kind mother. Just so reluctantly we part with consciousness, the picture is, even to the last, so interesting; the bird in the hand, though sick and moulting, so inestimably better than all the brilliant tenants of the bush. We sit up, yawning, and blinking, and stupid, the whole scene swimming before us, and the stories and music humming off into the sound of distant winds and waters. It is not time yet; we are not fatigued; we are good for another hour still, and so protesting against bed, we falter and drop into the dreamless sleep which nature assigns to fatigue and satiety.

He then spoke a little eulogy of his brother, very polished, and, indeed, in a kind of way, eloquent. He possessed in a high degree that accomplishment too little cultivated, I think, by the present generation, of expressing himself with perfect precision and fluency. There was, too, a good deal of slight illustrative quotation, and a sprinkling of French flowers, over his conversation, which gave to it a character at once elegant and artificial. It was all easy, light, and pointed, and being quite new to me, had a wonderful fascination.

He then told me that Bartram was the temple of liberty, that the health of a whole life was founded in a few years of youth, air, and exercise, and that accomplishments, at least, if not education, should wait upon health. Therefore while at Bartram I should dispose of my time quite as I pleased, and the more I plundered the garden and gipsied in the woodlands, the better.

Then he told me what a miserable invalid he was, and how the doctors interfered with his frugal tastes. A glass of beer and a mutton chop—his ideal of a dinner—he dared not touch. They made him drink light wines, which he detested, and live upon those artificial abominations, all liking for which vanishes with youth.

There stood on a side-table, in its silver coaster, a long-necked Rhenish bottle, and beside it a thin pink glass, and he quivered his fingers, in a peevish way toward them.

But unless he found himself better very soon, he would take his case into his own hands, and try the dietary to which nature pointed.

He waved his fingers toward his bookcases, and told me his books were altogether at my service during my stay; but this promise ended, I must confess, disappointingly. At last, remarking that I must be fatigued, he rose, and kissed me with a solemn tenderness, placed his hand upon what I now perceived to be a large Bible, with two broad silk markers, red and gold, folded in it—the one, I might conjecture, indicating the place in the Old, the other in the New Testament. It stood on the small table that supported the waxlights, with a handsome cut bottle of eau-de-cologne, his gold and jewelled pencil-case, and his chased repeater,* chain, and seals, beside it. There certainly were no indications of poverty in Uncle Silas's room; and he said impressively—

'Remember that book; in it your father placed his trust, in it he found his reward, in it lives my only hope; consult it, my beloved niece, day and night, as the oracle of life.'

Then he laid his thin hand on my head, and blessed me, and then kissed my forehead.

'No—a!' exclaimed Cousin Milly's lusty voice. I had quite forgotten her presence, and looked at her with a little start. She was seated on a very high old-fashioned chair; she had palpably been asleep; her round eyes were blinking and staring glassily at us; and her white legs and navvy boots were dangling in the air.

'Have you anything to remark about Noah?' inquired her father, with a polite inclination and an ironical interest.

'No—a,' she repeated in the same blunt accents; 'I didn't snore; did I? No—a.'

The old man smiled and shrugged a little at me—it was the smile of disgust.

'Good night, my dear Maud;' and turning to her, he said, with a peculiar gentle sharpness, 'Had not you better wake, my dear, and try whether your cousin would like some supper?'

So he accompanied us to the door, outside which we found L'Amour's candle awaiting us.

'I'm awful afraid of the Governor, I am. Did I snore that time?'

'No, dear; at least, I did not hear it,' I said, unable to repress a smile.

'Well, if I didn't, I was awful near it,' she said, reflectively.

We found poor Mary Quince dozing over the fire; but we soon had tea and other good things, of which Milly partook with a wonderful appetite.

'I *was* in a qualm about it,' said Milly, who by this time was quite herself again. 'When he spies me a napping, maybe he don't fetch me a prod with his pencil-case over the head. Odd! girl, it *is* sore.'

When I contrasted the refined and fluent old gentleman whom I had just left with this amazing specimen of young ladyhood, I grew sceptical almost as to the possibility of her being his child.

I was to learn, however, how little she had, I won't say of his society, but even of his presence—that she had no domestic companion of the least pretensions to education—that she ran wild about the place—never, except in church, so much as saw a person of that rank to which she was born—and that the little she knew of reading and writing had been picked up, in desultory half-hours, from a person who did not care a pin about her manners or decorum, and perhaps rather enjoyed her grotesqueness—and that no one who was willing to take the least trouble about her was competent to make her a particle more refined than I saw her—the wonder ceased. We don't know how little is heritable, and how much simply training, until we encounter some such spectacle as that of my poor Cousin Milly.

When I lay down in my bed and reviewed the day, it seemed like a month of wonders. Uncle Silas was always before me; the voice so silvery for an old man—so preternaturally soft; the manners so sweet, so gentle; the aspect, smiling, suffering, spectral. It was no longer a shadow; I had now seen him in the flesh. But after all, was he more than a shadow to me? When I closed my eyes I saw him before me still, in necromantic black, ashy with a pallor on which I looked with fear and pain, a face so dazzlingly pale, and those hollow, fiery, awful eyes! It sometimes seemed as if the curtain opened, and I had seen a ghost.

I had seen him; but he was still an enigma and a marvel. The living face did not expound the past, any more than the portrait portended the future. He was still a mystery and a vision; and thinking of these things I fell asleep.

Mary Quince, who slept in the dressing-room, the door of which was close to my bed, and lay open to secure me against ghosts, called me up; and the moment I knew where I was I jumped up, and peeped eagerly from the window. It commanded the avenue and courtyard; but we were many windows removed from that over the hall-door, and immediately beneath ours lay the two giant lime trees, prostrate and uprooted, which I had observed as we drove up the night before.

I saw more clearly in the bright light of morning the signs of neglect and almost of dilapidation which had struck me as I approached. The courtyard was tufted over with grass, seldom from year to year crushed by the carriage-wheels, or trodden by the feet of visitors. This melancholy verdure thickened where the area was more remote from the centre; and under the windows, and skirting the walls to the left, was reinforced by a thick grove of nettles. The avenue was all grass-grown, except in the very centre, where a narrow track still showed the roadway. The handsome carved balustrade of the court-yard was discoloured with lichens, and in two places gapped and broken; and the air of decay was heightened by the fallen trees, among whose sprays and yellow leaves the small birds were hopping.

Before my toilet was completed, in marched my Cousin Milly. We were to breakfast alone that morning, 'and so much the better,' she told me. Sometimes the Governor ordered her to breakfast with him, and 'never left off chaffing her' till his newspaper came, and 'sometimes he said such things he made her cry,' and then he only 'boshed her more,' and packed her away to her room; but she was by chalks nicer than him, talk as he might. '*Was* not she nicer? was not she? was not she?' Upon this point she was so strong and urgent that I was obliged to reply by a protest against awarding the palm of elegance between parent and child, and declaring I liked her very much, which I attested by a kiss.

'I know right well which of us you do think's the nicest, and no mistake, only you're afraid of him; and he had no business boshing me last night before you. I knew he was at it, though I couldn't twig him altogether; but wasn't he a sneak, now, wasn't he?'

This was a still more awkward question; so I kissed her again, and said she must never ask me to say of my uncle in his absence anything I could not say to his face.

At which speech she stared at me for a while, and then treated me to one of her hearty laughs, after which she seemed happier, and gradually grew into better humour with her father.

'Sometimes, when the curate calls, he has me up—for he's as religious as six, he is—and they read Bible and prays, ho—don't they? You'll have that, lass, like me, to go through; and maybe I don't hate it; oh, no!'

We breakfasted in a small room, almost a closet, off the great parlour, which was evidently quite disused. Nothing could be homelier than our equipage, or more shabby than the furniture of the little apartment. Still, somehow, I liked it. It was a total change; but one likes 'roughing it'* a little at first.

CHAPTER XXXIII

THE WINDMILL WOOD

I HAD not time to explore this noble old house as my curiosity prompted; for Milly was in such a fuss to set out for the 'blackberry dell' that I saw little more than just so much as I necessarily traversed in making my way to and from my room.

The actual decay of the house had been prevented by my dear father; and the roof, windows, masonry, and carpentry had all been kept in repair. But short of indications of actual ruin, there are many manifestations of poverty and neglect which impress with a feeling of desolation. It was plain that not nearly a tithe of this great house was inhabited; long corridors and galleries stretched away in dust and silence, and were crossed by others, whose dark arches inspired me in the distance with an awful sort of sadness. It was plainly one of those great structures in which you might easily lose yourself, and with a pleasing terror it reminded me of that delightful old abbey in Mrs. Radcliffe's romance, among whose silent staircases, dim passages, and long suites of lordly, but forsaken chambers, begirt without by the sombre forest, the family of La Mote* secured a gloomy asylum.

My Cousin Milly and I, however, were bent upon an open-air ramble, and traversing several passages, she conducted me to a door which led us out upon a terrace overgrown with weeds, and by a broad flight of steps we descended to the level of the grounds beneath. Then on, over the short grass, under the noble trees, we walked; Milly in high good humour, and talking away volubly, in her short garment, navvy boots, and a weather-beaten hat. She carried a stick in her gloveless hand. Her conversation was quite new to me, and resembled very much what I would have fancied the holiday recollections of a schoolboy; and the language in which it was sustained was sometimes so outlandish, that I was forced to laugh outright—a demonstration which she plainly did not like.

Her talk was about the great jumps she had made—how she 'snowballed the chaps' in winter—how she could slide twice the length of her stick beyond 'Briddles, the cowboy'.

With this and similar conversation she entertained me.

The grounds were delightfully wild and neglected. But we had now passed into a vast park beautifully varied with hollows and uplands, and such glorious old timber massed and scattered over its slopes and levels. Among these, we got at last into a picturesque dingle; the gray rocks peeped from among the ferns and wild flowers, and the steps of soft sward along its sides were dark in the shadows of silver-stemmed birch, and russet thorn, and oak, under which, in the vaporous night, the erl-king* and his daughter might glide on their aërial horses.

In the lap of this pleasant dell were the finest blackberry bushes, I think, I ever saw, bearing fruit quite fabulous; and plucking these, and chatting, we rambled on very pleasantly.

I had first only thought of Milly's absurdities, to which, in description, I cannot do justice, simply because so many details have, by distance of time, escaped my recollection. But her ways and her talk were so indescribably grotesque that she made me again and again quiver with suppressed laughter.

But there was a pitiable and even a melancholy meaning underlying the burlesque.

This creature, with no more education than a dairy-maid, I gradually discovered had fine natural aptitudes for accomplishment—a very sweet voice, and wonderfully delicate ear, and a talent for drawing which quite threw mine into the shade. It was really astonishing.

Poor Milly, in all her life, had never read three books, and hated to think of them. One, over which she was wont to yawn and sigh, and stare fatiguedly for an hour every Sunday, by command of the Governor, was a stout volume of sermons, of the earlier school of George III, and a dryer collection you can't fancy. I don't think she read anything else. But she had, notwithstanding, ten times the cleverness of half the circulating library misses one meets with. Besides all this, I had a long sojourn before me at Bartram-Haugh, and I had learned from Milly, as I had heard before, what a perennial solitude it was, with a ludicrous fear of learning Milly's preposterous dialect, and turning at last into something like her. So I resolved to do all I could for her—teach her whatever I knew, if she would allow me—and gradually, if possible, effect some civilizing changes in her language, and, as they term it in boarding-schools, her demeanour.

But I must pursue at present our first day's ramble in what was called Bartram Chase. People can't go on eating blackberries always; so after a while we resumed our walk along this pretty dell, which gradually expanded into a wooded valley—level beneath and enclosed by irregular uplands, receding, as it were, in mimic bays and harbours at some points, and running out at others into broken promontories, ending in clumps of forest trees.

Just where the glen which we had been traversing expanded into this broad, but wooded valley, it was traversed by a high and close paling, which although it looked decayed, was still very strong.

In this there was a wooden gate, rudely but strongly constructed, and at the side we were approaching stood a girl, who was leaning against the post, with one arm resting on the top of the gate.

This girl was neither tall nor short—taller than she looked at a distance; she had not a slight waist; sooty black was her hair, with a broad forehead, perpendicular but low; she had a pair of very fine, dark, lustrous eyes, and no other good feature—unless I may so call her teeth, which were very white and even. Her face was rather short, and swarthy as a gipsy's; observant and sullen too; and she did not move, only eyed us negligently from under her dark lashes as we drew near. Altogether a not unpicturesque figure, with a dusky, red petticoat of drugget,* and tattered red jacket of bottle green stuff, with short sleeves, which showed her brown arms from the elbow.

'That's Pegtop's daughter,' said Milly.

'Who is Pegtop?' I asked.

'He's the miller—see, yonder it is,' and she pointed to a very pretty feature in the landscape, a windmill, crowning the summit of a hillock which rose suddenly above the level of the tree-tops, like an island in the centre of the valley.

'The mill not going to-day, Beauty?' bawled Milly.

'No—a, Beauty; it baint,' replied the girl, loweringly, and without stirring.

'And what's gone with the stile?' demanded Milly, aghast. 'It's tore away from the paling!'

'Well, so it be,' replied the wood nymph in the red petticoat, showing her fine teeth with a lazy grin.

'Who's a bin and done all that?' demanded Milly.

'Not you nor me, lass,' said the girl.

''Twas old Pegtop, your father, did it,' cried Milly, in rising wrath.

''Appen it wor,' she replied.

'And the gate locked.'

'That's it—the gate locked,' she repeated, sulkily, with a defiant side-glance at Milly.

'And where's Pegtop?'

'At t'other side, somewhere; how should I know where he be?' she replied.

'Who's got the key?'

'Here it be, lass,' she answered, striking her hand on her pocket.

'And how durst you stay us here! Unlock it, huzzy, this minute!' cried Milly, with a stamp.

Her answer was a sullen smile.

'Open the gate this instant!' bawled Milly.

'Well, I *won't*.'

I expected that Milly would have flown into a frenzy at this direct defiance, but she looked instead puzzled and curious—the girl's unexpected audacity bewildered her.

'Why, you fool, I could get over the paling as soon as look at you, but I won't. What's come over you? Open the gate, I say, or I'll make you.'

'Do let her alone, dear,' I entreated, fearing a mutual assault. 'She has been ordered, may be, not to open it. Is it so, my good girl?'

'Well, thou'rt not the biggest fool o' the two,' she observed, commendatively, 'thou'st hit it, lass.'

'And who ordered you?' exclaimed Milly.

'Fayther.'

'Old Pegtop. Well, *that's* summat to laugh at, it is—our servant a-shutting us out of our own grounds.'

'No servant o' yourn!'

'Come, lass, what do you mean?'

'He be old Silas's miller, and what's that to thee?'

With these words the girl made a spring on the hasp of the padlock, and then got easily over the gate.

'Can't you do that, cousin?' whispered Milly to me, with an impatient nudge. 'I *wish* you'd try.'

'No, dear—come away, Milly,' and I began to withdraw.

'Lookee, lass, 'twill be an ill day's work for thee when I tell the Governor,' said Milly, addressing the girl, who stood on a log of timber at the other side, regarding us with a sullen composure.

'We'll be over in spite o' you,' cried Milly.

'You lie!' answered she.

'And why not, huzzy?' demanded my cousin, who was less incensed at the affront than I expected. All this time I was urging Milly in vain to come away.

'Yon lass is no wild cat, like thee—that's why,' said the sturdy portress.

'If I cross, I'll give you a knock,' said Milly.

'And I'll gi' thee another,' she answered, with a vicious wag of the head.

'Come, Milly, *I'll* go if *you* don't,' I said.

'But we must not be beat,' whispered she, vehemently, catching my arm; 'and ye *shall* get over, and *see* what I will gi' her!'

'I'll *not* get over.'

'Then I'll break the door, for ye *shall* come through,' exclaimed Milly, kicking the stout paling with her ponderous boot.

'Purr it, purr it, purr it!' cried the lass in the red petticoat, with a grin.

'Do you know who this lady is?' cried Milly, suddenly.

'She is a prettier lass than thou,' answered Beauty.

'She's *my* Cousin Maud—Miss Ruthyn of Knowl—and she's a deal richer than the Queen; and the Governor's taking care of her, and he'll make old Pegtop bring you to reason.'

The girl eyed me with a sulky listlessness, a little inquisitively I thought.

'See if he don't,' threatened Milly.

'You positively *must* come,' I said, drawing her away with me.

'Well, shall we come in?' cried Milly, trying a last summons.

'You'll not come in that much,' she answered, surlily, measuring an infinitesimal distance on her finger with her thumb, which she pinched against it, the gesture ending with a snap of defiance, and a smile that showed her fine teeth.

'I've a mind to shy a stone at you,' shouted Milly.

'Faire away; I'll shy wi' ye as long as ye like, lass; take heed o' yerself;' and Beauty picked up a round stone as large as a cricket ball.

With difficulty I got Milly away without an exchange of missiles, and much disgusted at my want of zeal and agility.

'Well, come along, cousin, I know an easy way by the river, when it's low,' answered Milly. 'She's a brute—is not she?'

As we receded, we saw the girl slowly wending her way toward the old thatched cottage, which showed its gable from the side of a little rugged eminence embowered in spreading trees, and dangling and twirling from its string on the end of her finger the key for which a battle had so nearly been fought.

The stream was low enough to make our flank movement round the end of the paling next it quite easy, and so we pursued our way, and Milly's equanimity returned, and our ramble grew very pleasant again.

Our path lay by the river bank, and as we proceeded the dwarf timber was succeeded by grander trees, which crowded closer and taller, and, at last, the scenery deepened into solemn forest, and a sudden sweep in the river revealed the beautiful ruin of a steep old bridge, with the fragments of a gate-house on the farther side.

'Oh, Milly darling!' I exclaimed, 'what a beautiful drawing this would make! I should so like to make a sketch of it.'

'So it would. *Make* a picture—*do!*—here's a stone that's pure and flat to sit upon, and you look very tired. Do make it, and I'll sit by you.'

'Yes, Milly, I *am* tired, a little, and I *will* sit down; but we must wait for another day to make the picture, for we have neither pencil nor paper. But it is much too pretty to be lost; so let us come again to-morrow.'

'To-morrow be hanged! you'll do it to-day, bury-me-wick, but you *shall*; I'm wearying to see you make a picture, and I'll fetch your conundrums out o' your drawer, for do't you shall.'

CHAPTER XXXIV

ZAMIEL

IT was all vain my remonstrating. She vowed that by crossing the stepping-stones close by she could, by a short cut, reach the house, and return with my pencils and block-book in a quarter of an hour. Away then, with many a jump and fling, scampered Milly's queer white stockings and navvy boots across the irregular and precarious stepping-stones, over which I dared not follow her; so I was fain to return to the stone so 'pure and flat', on which I sat, enjoying the grand sylvan solitude, the dark background and the gray bridge mid-way, so tall and slim, across whose ruins a sunbeam glimmered, and the gigantic forest trees that slumbered round, opening here and there in dusky vistas, and breaking in front into detached and solemn groups. It was the setting of a dream of romance.

It would have been the very spot in which to read a volume of German folk-lore,* and the darkening colonnades and silent nooks of the forest seemed already haunted with the voices and shadows of those charming elves and goblins.

As I sat here enjoying the solitude and my fancies among the low branches of the wood, at my right I heard a crashing, and saw a squat broad figure in a stained and tattered military coat, and loose short trousers, one limb of which flapped about a wooden leg. He was for-cing himself through. His face was rugged and wrinkled, and tanned to the tint of old oak; his eyes black, bead-like, and fierce, and a shock of sooty hair escaped from under his battered wide-awake nearly to his shoulders. This forbidding-looking person came stumping and jerking along toward me, whisking his stick now and then viciously in the air, and giving his fell of hair a short shake, like a wild bull prepar-ing to attack.

I stood up involuntarily with a sense of fear and surprise, almost fancying I saw that wooden-legged old soldier, who was the forest demon Der Freischütz.*

So he approached shouting—

'Hollo! you—how came you here? Dost 'eer?'

And he drew near panting, and sometimes tugging angrily in his haste at his wooden leg, which sunk now and then deeper than was convenient in the sod. This exertion helped to anger him, and when he halted before me, his dark face smirched with smoke and dust, and the nostrils of his flat drooping nose expanded and quivered as he panted, like the gills of a fish; an angrier or uglier face it would not be easy to fancy.

'Ye'll all come when ye like, will ye? and do nout but what pleases yourselves, won't you? And who'rt thou? Dost 'eer—who *are* ye, I say; and what the deil seek ye in the woods here? Come, bestir thee!'

If his wide mouth and great tobacco-stained teeth, his scowl, and loud discordant tones were intimidating, they were also extremely irritating. The moment my spirit was roused, my courage came.

'I am Miss Ruthyn of Knowl, and Mr. Silas Ruthyn, your master, is my uncle.'

'Hoo!' he exclaimed more gently, 'an' if Silas be thy uncle, thou'lt be come to live wi' him, and thou'rt she as come over night—eh?'

I made no answer, but I believe I looked both angrily and disdainfully.

'And what make ye alone here? and how was I to know't, an Milly not wi' ye, nor no one? But Maud or no Maud, I wouldn't let the Dooke hisself set foot inside the palin' without Silas said let him. And you may tell Silas them's the words o' Dickon Hawkes, and I'll stick to 'm—and what's more I'll tell him *myself*—I will; I'll tell him there be no use o' my striving and straining hee, day an' night and night and day, watchin' again poachers, and thieves, and gipsies, and they robbing lads, if rules won't be kep, and folk do jist as they pleases. Dang it, lass, thou'rt in luck I didn't heave a brick at thee when I saw thee first.'

'I'll complain of you to my uncle,' I replied.

'So do, and 'appen thou'lt find thyself in the wrong box, lass; thou canst na' say I set the dogs arter thee, nor cau'd thee so much as a wry name, nor heave a stone at thee—did I? Well and where's the complaint then?'

I simply answered, rather fiercely,

'Be good enough to leave me.'

'Well, I make no objections, mind. I'm takin' thy word—thou'rt Maud Ruthyn—'appen thou be'st and 'appen thou baint I'm not aweer on't, but I takes thy word, and all I want to know's just this, did Meg open the gate to thee?'

I made him no answer, and to my great relief I saw Milly striding and skipping across the unequal stepping-stones.

'Hallo, Pegtop! what are you after now?' she cried, as she drew near.

'This man has been extremely impertinent. You know him, Milly?' I said.

'Why that's Pegtop Dickon Dirty old Hawkes that never was washed. I tell you, lad, ye'll see what the Governor thinks o't—a-ha! He'll talk to you.'

'I done or said nout—not but I *should*, and there's the fack—she can't deny't; she hadn't a hard word from I; and I don't care the top o' that thistle what no one says—not I. But I tell thee, Milly, I stopped *some* o' thy pranks, and I'll stop more. Ye'll be shying no more stones at the cattle.'

'Tell your tales, and welcome,' cried Milly. 'I wish I was here when you jawed cousin. If Winny was here she'd catch you by the timber toe and put you on your back.'

'Ay, she'll be a good 'un yet if she takes arter thee,' retorted the old man with a fierce sneer.

'Drop it, and get away wi' ye,' cried she, 'or maybe I'd call Winny to smash your timber leg for you.'

'A-ha! there's more on't. She's a sweet 'un. Isn't she?' he replied sardonically.

'You did not like it last Easter, when Winny broke it with a kick.'

'Twas a kick o' a horse,' he growled with a glance at me.

'Twas no such thing—'twas Winny did it—and he laid on his back for a week while carpenter made him a new one.' And Milly laughed hilariously.

'I'll fool no more wi' ye, losing my time; I won't; but mind ye, I'll speak wi' Silas.' And going away he put his hand to his crumpled wide-awake, and said to me with a surly deference—

'Good evening, Miss Ruthyn—good evening, ma'am—and ye'll please remember, I did not mean nout to vex thee.'

And so he swaggered away, jerking and waddling over the sward, and was soon lost in the wood.

'It's well he's a little bit frightened—I never saw him so angry, I think; he is awful mad.'

'Perhaps he really is not aware how very rude he is,' I suggested.

'I hate him. We were twice as pleasant with poor Tom Driver—he never meddled with any one, and was always in liquor; Old Gin was the name he went by. But this brute—I do hate him—he comes from Wigan, I think, and he's always spoiling sport—and he whops

Meg—that's Beauty, you know, and I don't think she'd be half as bad only for him. Listen to him whistlin'.'

'I did hear whistling at some distance among the trees.'

'I declare if he isn't callin' the dogs! Climb up here I tell ye,' and we climbed up the slanting trunk of a great walnut tree, and strained our eyes in the direction from which we expected the onset of Pegtop's vicious pack.

But it was a false alarm.

'Well, I don't think he *would* do that, after all—*hardly*; but he is a brute, sure!'

'And that dark girl who would not let us through, is his daughter, is she?'

'Yes, that's Meg—Beauty, I christened her, when I called him Beast;* but I call him Pegtop now, and she's Beauty still, and that's the way o't.'

'Come, sit down now, an' make your picture,' she resumed so soon as we had dismounted from our position of security.

'I'm afraid I'm hardly in the vein. I don't think I could draw a straight line. My hand trembles.'

'I wish you could, Maud,' said Milly, with a look so wistful and entreating, that considering the excursion she had made for the pencils, I could not bear to disappoint her.

'Well, Milly, we must only try; and if we fail we can't help it. Sit you down beside me and I'll tell you why I begin with one part and not another, and you'll see how I make trees and the river, and—yes *that* pencil, it is hard and answers for the fine light lines; but we must begin at the beginning, and learn to copy drawings before we attempt real views like this. And if you wish it, Milly, I'm resolved to teach you everything I know, which, after all, is not a great deal, and we shall have such fun making sketches of the same landscapes, and then comparing.'

And so on, Milly, quite delighted, and longing to begin her course of instruction, sat down beside me in a rapture, and hugged and kissed me so heartily that we were very near rolling together off the stone on which we were seated. Her boisterous delight and good-nature helped to restore me, and both laughing heartily together, I commenced my task.

'Dear me! who's that?' I exclaimed suddenly, as looking up from my block-book I saw the figure of a slight man in the careless morning-dress of a gentleman, crossing the ruinous bridge in our direction, with considerable caution, upon the precarious footing of the battlement, which alone offered an unbroken passage.

This was a day of apparitions! Milly recognized him instantly. The gentleman was Mr. Carysbroke. He had taken The Grange only for a year. He lived quite to himself, and was very good to the poor, and was the only gentleman, for ever so long, who had visited at Bartram, and oddly enough nowhere else. But he wanted leave to cross through the grounds, and having obtained it, had repeated his visit, partly induced, no doubt, by the fact that Bartram boasted no hospitalities, and that there was no risk of meeting the county folk there.

With a stout walking-stick in his hand, and a short shooting-coat, and a wide-awake hat in much better trim than Zamiel's, he emerged from the copse that covered the bridge, walking at a quick but easy pace.

'He'll be goin' to see old Snoddles, I guess,' said Milly, looking a little frightened and curious; for Milly, I need not say, was a bumpkin, and stood in awe of this gentleman's good-breeding, though she was as brave as a lion, and would have fought the Philistines at any odds, with the jawbone of an ass.*

''Appen he won't see us,' whispered Milly, hopefully.

But he did, and raising his hat, with a cheerful smile, that showed very white teeth, he paused.

'Charming day, Miss Ruthyn.'

I raised my head suddenly as he spoke, from habit appropriating the address; it was so marked that he raised his hat respectfully to me, and then continued to Milly—

'Mr. Ruthyn, I hope, quite well? but I need hardly ask, you seem so happy. Will you kindly tell him, that I expect the book I mentioned in a day or two, and when it comes I'll either send or bring it to him immediately?'

Milly and I were standing, by this time, but she only stared at him, tongue-tied, her cheeks rather flushed, and her eyes very round, and to facilitate the dialogue, as I suppose he said again—

'He's quite well, I hope?'

Still no response from Milly, and I, provoked, though myself a little shy, made answer—

'My uncle, Mr. Ruthyn, is very well, thank you,' and I felt that I blushed as I spoke.

'Ah, pray excuse me, may I take a great liberty? you are Miss Ruthyn, of Knowl? Will you think me very impertinent—I'm afraid you will—if I venture to introduce myself. My name is Carysbroke, and I had the honour of knowing poor Mr. Ruthyn when I was quite a little boy, and he has shown a kindness for me since, and I hope you will pardon the liberty I fear I've taken. I think my friend, Lady Knollys, too, is a relation of yours; what a charming person she is!'

'Oh, is not she? such a darling!' I said, and then blushed at my outspoken affection.

But he smiled kindly, as if he liked me for it; and he said—

'You know whatever I think, I dare not quite say that; but frankly I can quite understand it. She preserves her youth so wonderfully, and her fun and her good-nature are so entirely girlish. What a sweet view you have selected,' he continued, changing all at once. 'I've stood just at this point so often to look back at that exquisite old bridge. Do you observe—you're an artist, I see—something very peculiar in the tint of the gray, with those odd cross stains of faded red and yellow?'

'I do, indeed; I was just remarking the peculiar beauty of the colouring—was not I, Milly?'

Milly stared at me, and uttered an alarmed 'Yes,' and looked as if she had been caught in a robbery.

'Yes, and you have so very peculiar a background,' he resumed. 'It was better before the storm though; but it is very good still.'

Then a little pause, and 'Do you know this country at all?' rather suddenly.

'No, not in the least—that is I've only had the drive to this place; but what I did see interested me very much.'

'You will be charmed with it when you know it better—the very place for an artist. I'm a wretched scribbler myself, and I carry this little book in my pocket,' and he laughed deprecatingly while he drew forth a thin fishing-book,* as it looked. 'They are mere memoranda, you see. I walk so much and come unexpectedly on such pretty nooks and studies, I just try to make a note of them, but it is really more writing than sketching; my sister says it is a cipher which nobody but myself understands. However, I'll try and explain just two—because you really ought to go and see the places. Oh, no; not that,' he laughed, as accidentally the page blew over, 'that's the Cat and Fiddle, a curious little pot-house, where they gave me some very good ale one day.'

Milly at this exhibited some uneasy tokens of being about to speak, but not knowing what might be coming, I hastened to observe on the spirited little sketches to which he meant to draw my attention.

'I want to show you only the places within easy reach—a short ride or drive.'

So he proceeded to turn over two or three, in addition to the two he had at first proposed, and then another; then a little sketch just tinted, and really quite a charming little gem, of Cousin Monica's pretty gabled old house; and every subject had its little criticism, or its narrative, or adventure.

As he was about returning this little sketchbook to his pocket still chatting to me, he suddenly recollected poor Milly, who was looking rather lowering; but she brightened a good deal as he presented it to her, with a little speech which she palpably misunderstood, for she made one of her odd courtesies, and was about I thought to put it into her large pocket, and accept it as a present.

'Look at the drawings, Milly, and then return it,' I whispered.

At his request I allowed him to look at my unfinished sketch of the bridge, and while he was measuring distances and proportions with his eye, Milly whispered rather angrily to me,

'And why should I?'

'Because he wants it back, and only meant to lend it to you,' whispered I.

'*Lend* it to me—and after you! Bury-me-wick if I look at a leaf of it,' she retorted in high dudgeon. 'Take it, lass; give it him yourself—I'll not,' and she popped it into my hand, and made a sulky step back.

'My cousin is very much obliged,' I said, returning the book, and smiling for her, and he took it smiling also and said—

'I think if I had known how very well you draw, Miss Ruthyn, I should have hesitated about showing you my poor scrawls. But these are not my best, you know; Lady Knollys will tell you that I can really do better—a great deal better, I think.'

And then with more apologies for what he called his impertinence, he took his leave, and I felt altogether very much pleased and flattered.

He could not be more than twenty-nine or thirty, I thought, and he was decidedly handsome—that is, his eyes and teeth, and clear brown complexion were—and there was something distinguished and graceful in his figure and gesture; and altogether there was the indescribable attraction of intelligence; and I fancied—though this, of course, was a secret—that from the moment he spoke to us he felt an interest in me. I am not going to be vain. It was a *grave* interest, but still an interest, for I could see him studying my features while I was turning over his sketches, and he thought I saw nothing else. It was flattering, too, his anxiety that I should think well of his drawing, and referring me to Lady Knollys. Carysbroke—had I ever heard my dear father mention that name? I could not recollect it. But then he was habitually so silent, that his not doing so argued nothing.

CHAPTER XXXV

WE VISIT A ROOM IN THE SECOND STORY

Mr. Carysbroke amused my fancy sufficiently to prevent my observing Milly's silence, till we had begun our return homeward.

'The Grange must be a pretty house, if that little sketch be true; is it far from this?'

''Twill be two mile.'

'Are you vexed, Milly?' I asked, for both her tone and looks were angry.

'Yes, I am vexed; and why not, lass?'

'What has happened?'

'Well, now, that is rich! Why look at that fellow, Carysbroke: he took no more notice to me than a dog, and kep' talking to you all the time of his pictures, and his walks, and his people. Why a pig's better manners than that.'

'But, Milly dear, you forget, he tried to talk to you, and you would not answer him,' I expostulated.

'And is not that just what I say—I can't talk like other folk—ladies, I mean. Every one laughs at me; an' I'm dressed like a show, I am. It's a shame! I saw Polly Shives—what a lady she is, my eyes!—laughing at me in church last Sunday. I was minded to give her a bit of my mind. An' I know I'm queer. It's a shame, it is. Why should *I* be so rum? it is a shame! I don't want to be so, nor it isn't my fault.'

And poor Milly broke into a flood of tears, and stamped on the ground, and buried her face in her short frock, which she whisked up to her eyes; and an odder figure of grief I never beheld.

'And I could not make head or tail of what he was saying,' cried poor Milly through her buff cotton, with a stamp; 'and you twigged every word o't. An' why am I so? It's a shame—a shame! Oh, ho, ho! it's a shame!'

'But, my dear Milly, we were talking of *drawing*, and you have not learned yet, but you shall—I'll teach you; and then you'll understand all about it.'

'An' every one laughs at me—even you; though you try, Maud, you can scarce keep from laughing sometimes. I don't blame you, for I know I'm queer; but I can't help it; and it's a shame.'

'Well, my dear Milly, listen to me: if you allow me, I assure you, I'll teach you all the music and drawing I know. You have lived very much alone; and as you say, ladies have a way of speaking of their own that is different from the talk of other people.'

'Yes, that they have, an' gentlemen too—like the Governor, and that Carysbroke; and a precious lingo it is—dang it—why the devil himself could not understand it; an' I'm like a fool among you. I could 'most drown myself. It's a shame! It is—you know it is.—It's a shame!'

'But I'll teach you that lingo too, if you wish it, Milly; and you shall know everything that I know; and I'll manage to have your dresses better made.'

By this time she was looking very ruefully, but attentively, in my face, her round eyes and nose swelled, and her cheeks all wet.

'I think if they were a little longer—yours is longer, you know;' and the sentence was interrupted by a sob.

'Now, Milly, you must not be crying; if you choose you may be just the same as any other lady—and you shall; and you will be very much admired, I can tell you, if only you will take the trouble to quite unlearn all your odd words and ways, and dress yourself like other people; and I will take care of that if you let me; and I think you are very clever, Milly; and I know you are very pretty.'

Poor Milly's blubbered face expanded into a smile in spite of herself; but she shook her head, looking down.

'Noa, noa, Maud, I fear 'twon't be.' And indeed it seemed I had proposed to myself a labour of Hercules.*

But Milly was really a clever creature, could see quickly, and when her ungainly dialect was mastered, describe very pleasantly; and if only she would endure the restraint, and possessed the industry requisite, I did not despair, and was resolved at least to do my part.

Poor Milly! she was really very grateful, and entered into the project of her education with great zeal, and with a strange mixture of humility and insubordination.

Milly was in favour of again attacking 'Beauty's' position on our return, and forcing a passage from this side; but I insisted on following the route by which we had arrived, and so we got round the paling by the river, and were treated to a provoking grin of defiance by 'Beauty,' who was talking across the gate to a slim young man, arrayed in fustian, and with an odd-looking cap of rabbit-skin on his head, which, on seeing us, he pulled sheepishly to the side of his face next to us, as he lounged, with his arm under his chin, on the top bar of the gate.

After our encounter of to-day, indeed, it was Miss 'Beauty's' wont to exhibit a kind of jeering disdain in her countenance whenever we passed.

I think Milly would have engaged her again, had I not reminded her of her undertaking, and exerted my new authority.

'Look at that sneak, Pegtop, there, going up the path to the mill. He makes belief now he does not see us; but he does, though, only he's afraid we'll tell the Governor, and he thinks Governor won't give him his way with you. I hate that Pegtop: he stopped me o' riding the cows a year ago, he did.'

I thought Pegtop might have done worse. Indeed it was plain that a total reformation was needed here; and I was glad to find that poor Milly seemed herself conscious of it; and that her resolution to become more like other people of her station was not a mere spasm of mortification and jealousy, but a genuine and very zealous resolve.

I had not half seen this old house of Bartram Haugh yet. At first, indeed, I had but an imperfect idea of its extent. There was a range of rooms along one side of the great gallery, with closed window-shutters, and the doors generally locked. Old L'Amour grew cross when we went into them, although we could see nothing; and Milly was afraid to open the windows—not that any Bluebeard* revelations were apprehended, but simply because she knew that Uncle Silas's order was that things should be left undisturbed; and this boisterous spirit stood in awe of him to a degree which his gentle manners and apparent quietude rendered quite surprising.

There were in this house, what certainly did not exist at Knowl, and what I have never observed, though they may possibly be found in other old houses—I mean, here and there, very high hatches, which we could only peep over by jumping in the air. They crossed the long corridors and great galleries; and several of them were turned across and locked, so as to intercept the passage, and interrupt our explorations.

Milly, however, knew a queer little, very steep and dark back stair, which reached the upper floor; so she and I mounted, and made a long ramble through rooms much lower and ruder in finish than the lordly chambers we had left below. These commanded various views of the beautiful, though neglected grounds; but on crossing a gallery we entered suddenly a chamber, which looked into a small and dismal quadrangle, formed by the inner walls of this great house, and of course designed only by the architect to afford the needful light and air to portions of the structure.

I rubbed the window-pane with my handkerchief and looked out. The surrounding roof was steep and high. The walls looked soiled and dark. The windows lined with dust and dirt, and the window-stones were in places tufted with moss, and grass, and groundsel. An arched doorway had opened from the house into this darkened square, but it was soiled and dusty; and the damp weeds that over-grew the quad-rangle drooped undisturbed against it. It was plain that human foot-steps tracked it little, and I gazed into that blind and sinister area with a strange thrill and sinking.

'This is the second floor—there is the enclosed courtyard'—I, as it were, soliloquized.

'What are you afraid of, Maud? you look as ye'd seen a ghost,' exclaimed Milly, who came to the window and peeped over my shoulder.

'It reminded me suddenly, Milly, of that frightful business.'

'What business, Maud?—what a plague are ye thinking on?' demanded Milly, rather amused.

'It was in one of these rooms—maybe this—yes it certainly *was* this—for see, the panelling has been pulled off the wall—that Mr. Charke killed himself.'

I was staring ruefully round the dim chamber, in whose corners the shadows of night were already gathering.

'Charke!—what about him?—who's Charke?' asked Milly.

'Why, you must have heard of him,' said I.

'Not as I'm aware on,' answered she. 'And he killed himself, did he, hanged himself, eh, or blowed his brains out?'

'He cut his throat in one of these rooms—*this* one, I'm sure—for your papa had the wainscoting stripped from the wall to ascertain whether there was any second door through which a murderer could have come; and you see these walls are stripped, and bear the marks of the woodwork that has been removed,' I answered.

'Well! that *was* awful! I don't know how they have pluck to cut their throats; if I was doing it, I'd like best to put a pistol to my head and fire, like the young gentleman did, they say, in Deadman's Hollow.

But the fellows that cut their throats, they must be awful game lads, I'm thinkin', for it's a long slice, you know.'

'Don't, don't, Milly dear. Suppose we come away,' I said, for the evening was deepening rapidly into night.

'Hey and bury-me-wick, but here's the blood; don't you see a big black cloud all spread over the floor hereabout, don't ye see?' Milly was stooping over the spot, and tracing the outline of this, perhaps, imaginary mapping, in the air with her finger.

'No, Milly, you could not see it: the floor is too dark, and it's all in shadow. It must be fancy; and perhaps, after all, this is not the room.'

'Well—I think, I'm *sure* it *is*. Stand—just look.'

'We'll come in the morning, and if you are right we can see it better then. Come away,' I said, growing frightened.

And just as we stood up to depart, the white high-cauled cap and large sallow features of old L'Amour peeped in at the door.

'Lawk! what brings you here?' cried Milly, nearly as much startled as I at the intrusion.

'What brings *you* here, Miss?' whistled L'Amour through her gums.

'We're looking where Charke cut his throat,' replied Milly.

'Charke the devil!' said the old woman, with an odd mixture of scorn and fury. ''Tisn't his room; and come ye out of it, please. Master won't like when he hears how you keep pulling Miss Maud from one room to another, all through the house, up and down.'

She was gabbling sternly enough, but dropped a low courtesy as I passed her, and with a peaked and nodding stare round the room, the old woman clapped the door sharply, and locked it.

'And who has been a talking about Charke—a pack o' lies, I warrant. I s'pose you want to frighten Miss Maud here' (another crippled courtesy) 'wi' ghosts and like nonsense.'

'You're out there: 'twas she told me; and much about it. Ghosts, indeed! I don't vally them, not I; if I did, I know who'd frighten me,' and Milly laughed.

The old woman stuffed the key in her pocket, and her wrinkled mouth pouted and receded with a grim uneasiness.

'A harmless brat, and kind she is; but wild—wild—she will be wild.'

So whispered L'Amour in my ear, during the silence that followed, nodding shakily toward Milly over the banister, and she courtesied again as we departed, and shuffled off toward Uncle Silas's room.

'The Governor is queerish this evening,' said Milly, when we were seated at our tea.

'You never saw him queerish, did you?'

'You must say what you mean, more plainly, Milly. You don't mean ill, I hope?'

'Well! I don't know what it is; but he does grow very queer some-times—you'd think he was dead a'most, maybe two or three days and nights together. He sits all the time like an old woman in a swound. Well, well, it is awful!'

'Is he insensible when in that state?' I asked, a good deal alarmed.

'I don't know; but it never signifies anything. It won't kill him, I do believe; but old L'Amour knows all about it. I hardly ever go into the room when he's so, only when I'm sent for; and he sometimes wakes up and takes a fancy to call for this one or that. One day he sent for Pegtop all the way to the mill; and when he came, he only stared at him for a minute or two, and ordered him out o' the room. He's like a child a'most, when he's in one o' them dazes.'

I always knew when Uncle Silas was 'queerish', by the injunctions of old L'Amour, whistled and spluttered over the banister as we came up stairs, to mind how we made a noise passing Master's door; and by the sound of mysterious to-ings and fro-ings about his room.

I saw very little of him. He sometimes took a whim to have us breakfast with him, which lasted perhaps for a week; and then the order of our living would relapse into its old routine.

I must not forget two kind letters from Lady Knollys, who was detained away, and delighted to hear that I enjoyed my quiet life; and promised to apply, in person, to Uncle Silas, for permission to visit me.

She was to be for the Christmas at Elverston, and that was only six miles away from Bartram-Haugh, so I had the excitement of a pleas-ant look forward.

She also said that she would include poor Milly in her invitation; and a vision of Captain Oakley rose before me, with his handsome gaze turned in wonder on poor Milly, for whom I had begun to feel myself responsible.

I HAVE sometimes been asked why I wear an odd little tourquoise ring—which to the uninstructed eye appears quite valueless and altogether an unworthy companion of those jewels which flash insultingly beside it. It is a little keepsake, of which I became possessed about this time.

'Come, lass, what name shall I give you,' cried Milly, one morning, bursting into my room in a state of alarming hilarity.

'My own, Milly.'

'No, but you must have a nickname, like every one else.'

'Don't mind it, Milly.'

'Yes, but I will. Shall I call you Mrs. Bustle?'

'You shall do no such thing.'

'But you must have a name.'

'I refuse a name.'

'But I'll give you one, lass.'

'And *I* won't have it.'

'But you can't help me christening you.'

'I can decline answering.'

'But I'll make you,' said Milly, growing very red.

Perhaps there was something provoking in my tone, for I certainly was very much disgusted at Milly's relapse into barbarism.

'You can't,' I retorted quietly.

'See if I don't, and I'll give ye one twice as ugly.'

I smiled, I fear disdainfully.

'And I think you're a minx, and a slut, and a fool,' she broke out, flushing scarlet.

I smiled in the same unchristian way.

'And I'd give ye a smack o' the cheek as soon as look at you.'

And she gave her dress a great slap, and drew near me, in her wrath. I really thought she was about tendering the ordeal of single combat.

I made her, however, a paralysing courtesy, and, with immense dignity, sailed out of the room, and into Uncle Silas's study, where it happened we were to breakfast that morning, and for several subsequent ones.

During the meal we maintained the most dignified reserve; and I don't think either so much as looked at the other.

We had no walk together that day.

I was sitting in the evening, quite alone, when Milly entered the room. Her eyes were red, and she looked very sullen.

'I want your hand, Cousin,' she said, at the same time taking it by the wrist, and administering with it a sudden slap on her plump cheek, which made the room ring, and my fingers tingle; and before I had recovered from my surprise, she had vanished.

I called after her, but no answer; I pursued, but she was running too; and I quite lost her at the cross galleries.

I did not see her at tea, nor before going to bed; but after I had fallen asleep I was awakened by Milly, in floods of tears.

'Cousin Maud, will ye forgi' me—you'll never like me again, will ye? No—I know ye won't—I'm such a brute—I hate it—it's a shame. And here's a Banbury cake* for you—I sent to the town for it, and some taffy*—won't ye eat it? and here's a little ring—'tisn't as pretty as your own rings; and ye'll wear it, maybe, for my sake—poor Milly's sake, before I was so bad to ye—if ye forgi' me; and I'll look at breakfast, and if it's on your finger I'll know you're friends wi' me again; and if ye don't, I won't trouble you no more; and I think I'll just drown myself out o' the way, and you'll never see wicked Milly no more.'

And without waiting a moment, leaving me only half awake, and with the sensations of dreaming, she scampered from the room, in her bare feet, with a petticoat about her shoulders.

She had left her candle by my bed, and her little offerings on the coverlet by me. If I had stood an atom less in terror of goblins than I did, I should have followed her, but I was afraid. I stood in my bare feet at my bed-side, and kissed the poor little ring and put it on my finger, where it has remained ever since and always shall. And when I lay down, longing for morning, the image of her pale, imploring, penitential face was before me for hours; and I repented bitterly of my cool provoking ways, and thought myself, I dare say justly, a thousand times more to blame than Milly.

I searched in vain for her before breakfast. At that meal, however, we met, but in the presence of Uncle Silas, who, though silent and apathetic, was formidable; and we, sitting at a table disproportionably large, under the cold, strange gaze of my guardian, talked only what was inevitable, and that in low tones; for whenever Milly for a moment raised her voice, Uncle Silas would wince, place his thin white fingers quickly over his ear, and look as if a pain had pierced his brain, and then shrug and smile piteously into vacancy. When Uncle Silas, therefore, was not in the talking vein himself—and that was not often—you may suppose there was very little spoken in his presence.

When Milly, across the table, saw the ring upon my finger, she, drawing in her breath, said 'Oh!' and, with round eyes and mouth, she looked so delighted; and she made a little motion, as if she was on the point of jumping up; and then her poor face quivered, and she bit her lip; and staring imploringly at me, her eyes filled fast with tears, which rolled down her round penitential cheeks.

I am sure I felt more penitent than she. I know I was crying and smiling, and longing to kiss her. I suppose we were very absurd; but it is well that small matters can stir the affections so profoundly at a time of life when great troubles seldom approach us.

When at length the opportunity did come, never was such a hug out of the wrestling ring as poor Milly bestowed on me, swaying me this way and that, and burying her face in my dress, and blubbering—

'I was so lonely before you came, and you so good to me, and I such a devil; and I'll never call you a name, but Maud—my darling Maud.'

'You must, Milly—Mrs. Bustle. I'll be Mrs. Bustle, or anything you like. You must.' I was blubbering like Milly, and hugging my best; and, indeed, I wonder how we kept our feet.

So Milly and I were better friends than ever.

Meanwhile, the winter deepened, and we had short days and long nights, and long fireside gossipings at Bartram-Haugh. I was frightened at the frequency of the strange collapses to which Uncle Silas was subject. I did not at first mind them much, for I naturally fell into Milly's way of talking about them.

But one day, while in one of his 'queerish' states, he called for me, and I saw him, and was unspeakably scared.

In a white wrapper, he lay coiled in a great easy chair. I should have thought him dead had I not been accompanied by old L'Amour, who knew every gradation and symptom of these strange affections.

She winked and nodded to me with a ghastly significance, and whispered—

'Don't make no noise, Miss, till he talks; he'll come to for a bit, anon.'

Except that there was no sign of convulsions, the countenance was like that of an epileptic* arrested in one of its contortions.

There was a frown and smirk like that of idiotcy, and a strip of white eyeball was also disclosed.

Suddenly, with a kind of chilly shudder, he opened his eyes wide, and screwed his lips together, and blinked and stared on me with a fatuized uncertainty, that gradually broke into a feeble smile.

'Ah! the girl—Austin's child. Well, dear, I'm hardly able—I'll speak to-morrow—next day—it is tic—neuralgia,* or something—*torture*—tell her.'

So, huddling himself together, he lay again in his great chair, with the same inexpressible helplessness in his attitude, and gradually his face resumed its dreadful cast.

'Come away, Miss: he's changed his mind; he'll not be fit to talk to you noways all day, maybe,' said the old woman, again in a whisper.

So forth we stole from the room, I unspeakably shocked. In fact he looked as if he were dying, and so, in my agitation, I told the crone, who, forgetting the ceremony with which she usually treated me, chuckled out derisively,

'A dying is he? Well, he be like Saint Paul—he's bin a dying daily this many a day.'*

I looked at her with a chill of horror. She did not care, I suppose, what sort of feelings she might excite, for she went on mumbling sarcastically to herself. I had paused, and overcame my reluctance to speak to her again, for I was really very much frightened.

'Do you think he is in danger? Shall we send for a doctor?' I whispered.

'Law bless ye, the doctor knows all about it, Miss.' The old woman's face had a gleam of that derision which is so shocking in the features of feebleness and age.

'But it is a *fit*, it is paralytic,* or something horrible—it can't be *safe* to leave him to chance or nature to get through these terrible attacks.'

'There's no fear of him, 'tisn't no fits at all, he's nout the worse o't. Jest silly a bit now and again. It's been the same a dozen year and more; and the doctor knows all about it,' answered the old woman sturdily. 'And ye'll find he'll be as mad as bedlam* if ye make any stir about it.'

That night I talked the matter over with Mary Quince.

'They're very dark, Miss; but I think he takes a deal too much laud-lum,'* said Mary.

To this hour I cannot say what was the nature of those periodical seizures. I have often spoken to medical men about them, since, but never could learn that excessive use of opium could altogether account for them. It was, I believe, certain, however, that he did use that drug in startling quantities. It was, indeed, sometimes a topic of complaint with him that his neuralgia imposed this sad necessity upon him.

The image of Uncle Silas, as I had seen him that day, troubled and affrighted my imagination, as I lay in my bed; I had slept very well since my arrival at Bartram. So much of the day was passed in the open air, and in active exercise, that this was but natural. But that night I was nervous and wakeful, and it was past two o'clock when I fancied I heard the sound of horses and carriage-wheels on the avenue.

Mary Quince was close by, and therefore, I was not afraid to get up and peep from the window. My heart beat fast as I saw a post-chaise approach the court-yard. A front window was let down, and the postilion pulled up for a few seconds.

In consequence of some directions received by him, I fancied he resumed his route at a walk, and so drew up at the hall-door, on the steps of which a figure awaited its arrival. I think it was old L'Amour, but I could not be quite certain. There was a lantern on the top of the balustrade, close by the door. The chaise-lamps were lighted, for the night was rather dark.

A bag and valise, as well as I could see, were pulled from the interior by the post-boy, and a box from the top of the vehicle, and these were carried into the hall.

I was obliged to keep my cheek against the window-pane to command a view of the point of debarkation, and my breath upon the glass, which dimmed it again almost as fast as I wiped it away, helped to obscure my vision. But I saw a tall figure, in a cloak, get down and swiftly enter the house, but whether male or female I could not discern.

My heart beat fast. I jumped at once to a conclusion. My uncle was worse—was, in fact, dying; and this was the physician, too late summoned to his bedside.

I listened for the ascent of the doctor, and his entrance at my uncle's door, which, in the stillness of the night, I thought I might easily hear, but no sound reached me. I listened so for fully five minutes, but without result. I returned to the window, but the carriage and horses had disappeared.

I was strongly tempted to wake Mary Quince, and take counsel with her, and persuade her to undertake a reconnoissance. The fact is, I was persuaded that my uncle was in extremity, and I was quite wild to know the doctor's opinion. But after all, it would be cruel to summon the good soul from her refreshing nap. So, as I began to feel very cold, I returned to my bed, where I continued to listen and conjecture until I fell asleep.

In the morning, as was usual, before I was dressed, in came Milly.

'How is Uncle Silas?' I eagerly inquired.

'Old L'Amour says he's queerish still; but he's not so dull as yesterday,' answered she.

'Was not the doctor sent for?' I asked.

'Was he? Well that's odd; and she said never a word o't to me,' answered she.

'I'm asking only,' said I.

'I don't know whether he came or no,' she replied; 'but what makes you take that in your head?'

'A chaise arrived here between two and three o'clock last night.'

'Hey! and who told you?' Milly seemed all on a sudden highly interested.

'I saw it, Milly; and some one, I fancy the doctor, came from it into the house.'

'Fudge, lass! who'd send for the doctor? 'Twasn't he, I tell you. What was he like?' said Milly.

'I could only see clearly that he, or *she*, was tall, and wore a cloak,' I replied.

'Then 'twasn't him nor t'other I was thinking on, neither; and I'll be hanged but I think it will be Cormoran,' cried Milly, with a thoughtful rap with her knuckle on the table.

Precisely at this juncture a tapping came to the door.

'Come in,' said I.

And old L'Amour entered the room, with a courtesy.

'I came to tell Miss Quince her breakfast's ready,' said the old lady.

'Who came in the chaise, L'Amour?' demanded Milly.

'What chaise?' spluttered the beldame tartly.

'The chaise that came last night, past two o'clock,' said Milly.

'That's a lie, and a damn lie!' cried the beldame. 'There worn't no chaise at the door since Miss Maud there come from Knowl.'

I stared at the audacious old menial who could utter such language.

'Yes, there was a chaise, and Cormoran, as I think, be come in it,' said Milly, who seemed accustomed to L'Amour's daring address.

'And there's another damn lie, as big as the t'other,' said the crone, her haggard and withered face flushing orange all over.

'I beg you will not use such language in my room,' I replied, very angrily. 'I *saw* the chaise at the door; your untruth signifies very little, but your impertinence, here, I will not permit. Should it be repeated, I will assuredly complain to my uncle.'

The old woman flushed more fiercely as I spoke, and fixed her bleared glare on me, with a compression of her mouth that amounted to a wicked grimace. She resisted her angry impulse, however, and only chuckled a little spitefully, saying,

'No offence, Miss: it be a way we has in Derbyshire o' speaking our minds. No offence, Miss, were meant, and none took, as I hopes,' and she made me another courtesy.

'And I forgot to tell you, Miss Milly, the Master wants you this minute.'

So Milly, in mute haste, withdrew, followed closely by L'Amour.

CHAPTER XXXVII

DOCTOR BRYERLY EMERGES

WHEN Milly joined me at breakfast, her eyes were red and swollen. She was still sniffing with that little sobbing hiccough, which betrays, even were there no other signs, recent violent weeping. She sat down quite silent.

'Is he worse, Milly?' I inquired, anxiously.

'No, nothing's wrong wi' him; he's right well,' said Milly, fiercely.

'What's the matter then, Milly dear?'

'The poisonous old witch! 'Twas just to tell the gov'nor how I'd said 'twas Cormoran that came by the po'-shay last night.'

'And who is Cormoran?' I inquired.

'Ay, there it is, I'd like to tell, and you want to hear—and I just daren't, for he'll send me off right to a French school—hang it—hang them all!—if I do.'

'And why should Uncle Silas care?' said I, a good deal surprised.

'They're a tellin' lies.'

'Who?' said I.

'L'Amour—that's who. So soon as she made her complaint of me, the Gov'nor asked her, sharp enough, did any one come last night, or a po'shay; and she was ready to swear there was no one. Are ye quite sure, Maud, you really did see aught, or 'appen 'twas all a dream?'

'It was no dream, Milly; so sure as you are there, I saw exactly what I told you,' I replied.

'Gov'nor won't believe it anyhow; and he's right mad wi' me; and he threatens me he'll have me off to France; I wish 'twas under the sea. I hate France—I do—like the devil. Don't you? They're always a-threatening me wi' France, if I dare say a word more about the po'shay, or—or anyone.'

I really was curious about Cormoran; but Cormoran was not to be defined to me by Milly; nor did she, in reality, know more than I respecting the arrival of the night before.

One day I was surprised to see Doctor Bryerly on the stairs, I was standing in a dark gallery as he walked across the floor of the lobby to my uncle's door, his hat on, and some papers in his hand.

He did not see me; and when he had entered Uncle Silas's door, I went down and found Milly awaiting me in the hall.

'So Doctor Bryerly is here,' I said.

'That's the thin fellow, wi' the sharp look, and the shiny black coat, that went up just now?' asked Milly.

'Yes, he's gone into your papa's room,' said I.

''Appen 'twas he come 'tother night. He may be staying here, though we see him seldom, for it's a barrack of a house—it is.'

The same thought had struck me for a moment, but was dismissed immediately. It certainly was *not* Doctor Bryerly's figure which I had seen.

So, without any new light gathered from this apparition, we went on our way, and made our little sketch of the ruined bridge. We found the gate locked as before; and, as Milly could not persuade me to climb it, we got round the paling by the river's bank.

While at our drawing, we saw the swarthy face, sooty locks, and old weather-stained red coat of Zamiel, who was glowering malignly at us from among the trunks of the forest trees, and standing motionless as a monumental figure in the side aisle of a cathedral. When we looked again he was gone.

Although it was a fine mild day for the wintry season, we yet, cloaked as we were, could not pursue so still an occupation as sketching for more than ten or fifteen minutes. As we returned, in passing a clump of trees, we heard a sudden outbreak of voices, angry and expostulatory; and saw, under the trees, the savage old Zamiel strike his daughter with his stick two great blows, one of which was across the head. 'Beauty' ran only a short distance away, while the swart old wood-demon stumped lustily after her, cursing and brandishing his cudgel.

My blood boiled. I was so shocked that for a moment I could not speak; but in a moment more I screamed—

'You brute! How dare you strike the poor girl?'

She had only run a few steps, and turned about confronting him and us, her eyes gleaming fire, her features pale and quivering to suppress a burst of weeping. Two little rivulets of blood were trickling over her temple.

'I say, fayther, look at that,' she said, with a strange tremulous smile, lifting her hand, which was smeared with blood.

Perhaps he was ashamed, and the more enraged on that account, for he growled another curse, and started afresh to reach her, whirling his stick in the air. Our voices, however, arrested him.

'My uncle shall hear of your brutality. The poor girl!'

'Strike him, Meg, if he does it again; and pitch his leg into the river to-night, when he's asleep.'

'I'd serve *you* the same;' and out came an oath. 'You'd have her lick her fayther, would ye? Look out!'

And he wagged his head, with a scowl at Milly, and a flourish of his cudgel.

'Be quiet, Milly,' I whispered, for Milly was preparing for battle; and I again addressed him with the assurance that, on reaching home, I would tell my uncle how he had treated the poor girl.

''Tis you she may thank for't, a wheedling o' her to open that gate,' he snarled.

'That's a lie; we went round by the brook,' cried Milly.

I did not think proper to discuss the matter with him; and looking very angry, and, I thought, a little put out, he jerked and swayed himself out of sight. I merely repeated my promise of informing my uncle as he went, to which, over his shoulder, he bawled—

'Silas won't mind ye *that*;' snapping his horny finger and thumb.

The girl remained where she had stood, wiping the blood off roughly with the palm of her hand, and looking at it before she rubbed it on her apron.

'My poor girl,' I said, 'you must not cry. I'll speak to my uncle about you.'

But she was not crying. She raised her head, and looked at us a little askance, with a sullen contempt, I thought.

'And you must have these apples—won't you?' We had brought in our basket two or three of those splendid apples for which Bartram was famous.

I hesitated to go near her, these Hawkeses, Beauty and Pegtop, were such savages. So I rolled the apples gently along the ground to her feet.

She continued to look doggedly at us with the same expression, and kicked away the apples sullenly that approached her feet. Then, wiping her temple and forehead in her apron, without a word, she turned and walked slowly away.

'Poor thing! I'm afraid she leads a hard life. What strange, repulsive people they are!'

When we reached home, at the head of the great staircase old L'Amour was awaiting me; and with a courtesy, and very respectfully, she informed me that the Master would be happy to see me.

Could it be about my evidence as to the arrival of the mysterious chaise that he summoned me to this interview? Gentle as were his ways, there was something undefinable about Uncle Silas which inspired fear; and I should have liked few things less than meeting his gaze in the character of a culprit.

There was an uncertainty, too, as to the state in which I might find him, and a positive horror of beholding him again in the condition in which I had last seen him.

I entered the room, then, in some trepidation, but was instantly relieved. Uncle Silas was in the same health apparently, and, as nearly as I could recollect it, in precisely the same rather handsome though negligent garb in which I had first seen him.

Doctor Bryerly—what a marked and vulgar contrast, and yet, somehow, how reassuring!—sat at the table near him, and was tying up papers. His eyes watched me, I thought, with an anxious scrutiny, as I approached; and I think it was not until I had saluted him that he recollected suddenly that he had not seen me before at Bartram, and stood up and greeted me in his usual abrupt and somewhat familiar way. It was vulgar and not cordial, and yet it was honest and indefinably kind.

Up rose my uncle, that strangely venerable pale portrait, in his loose Rembrandt black velvet. How gentle, how benignant, how unearthly, and inscrutable!

'I need not say how she is. Those lilies and roses, Doctor Bryerly, speak their own beautiful praises of the air of Bartram. I almost regret that her carriage will be home so soon. I only hope it may not abridge her rambles. It positively does me good to look at her. It is the glow of flowers in winter, and the fragrance of a field which the Lord hath blessed.'

'Country air, Miss Ruthyn, is a right good kitchen to country fare. I like to see young women eat heartily. You have had some pounds of beef and mutton since I saw you last,' said Doctor Bryerly.

And this sly speech made, he scrutinized my countenance in silence rather embarrassingly.

'My system, Doctor Bryerly, as a disciple of Æsculapius* you will approve—health first, accomplishment afterwards. The Continent is the best field for elegant instruction, and we must see the world a little, by-and-by, Maud; and to me, if my health be spared, there would be an unspeakable, though a melancholy charm in the scenes where so many happy, though so many wayward and foolish young days were passed; and I think I should return to these picturesque solitudes, with, perhaps, an increased relish. You remember old Chaulieu's sweet lines—

> "Désert, aimable solitude,
> Séjour du calme et de la paix,
> Asile où n'entrèrent jamais
> Le tumulte et l'inquiétude."*

I can't say that care and sorrow have not sometimes penetrated these sylvan fastnesses; but the tumults of the world, thank Heaven!—never.'

There was a sly scepticism, I thought, in Doctor Bryerly's sharp face; and hardly waiting for the impressive 'never', he said—

'I forgot to ask, who is your banker?'

'Oh! Bartlet and Hall, Lombard-street,' answered Uncle Silas, dryly and shortly.

Dr. Bryerly made a note of it, with an expression of face which seemed, with a sly resolution, to say, 'You shan't come the anchorite over me.'

I saw Uncle Silas's wild and piercing eye rest suspiciously on me for a moment, as if to ascertain whether I felt the spirit of Doctor Bryerly's almost interruption; and, nearly at the same moment, stuffing his papers into his capacious coat pockets, Doctor Bryerly rose and took his leave.

When he was gone, I bethought me that now was a good opportunity of making my complaint of Dickon Hawkes. Uncle Silas having risen, I hesitated, and began,

'Uncle, may I mention an occurrence—which I witnessed?'

'Certainly, child,' he answered, fixing his eye sharply on me. I really think he fancied that the conversation was about to turn upon the phantom chaise.

So I described the scene which had shocked Milly and me, an hour or so ago, in the Windmill Wood.

'You see, my dear child, they are rough persons; their ideas are not ours; their young people must be chastised, and in a way and to a degree that we would look upon in a serious light. I've found it a bad plan interfering in strictly domestic misunderstandings, and should rather not.'

'But he struck her violently on the head, Uncle, with a heavy cudgel, and she was bleeding very fast.'

'Ah?' said my uncle, dryly.

'And only that Milly and I deterred him by saying that we would certainly tell you, he would have struck her again; and I really think if he goes on treating her with so much violence and cruelty he may injure her very seriously, or perhaps kill her.'

'Why, you romantic little child, people in that rank of life think absolutely nothing of a broken head,' answered Uncle Silas, in the same way.

'But is it not horrible brutality, Uncle?'

'To be sure it is brutality; but then you must remember they are brutes, and it suits them,' said he.

I was disappointed. I had fancied that Uncle Silas's gentle nature would have recoiled from such an outrage with horror and indignation; and instead, here he was, the apologist of that savage ruffian, Dickon Hawkes.

'And he is always so rude and impertinent to Milly and to me,' I continued.

'Oh! impertinent to you—that's another matter. I must see to that. Nothing more, my dear child?'

'Well, there *was* nothing more.'

'He's a useful servant, Hawkes; and though his looks are not prepossessing, and his ways and language rough, yet he is a very kind father, and a most honest man—a thoroughly moral man, though severe—a very rough diamond though, and has no idea of the refinements of polite society. I venture to say he honestly believes that he has been always unexceptionably polite to you, so we must make allowances.'

And Uncle Silas smoothed my hair with his thin aged hand, and kissed my forehead.

'Yes, we must make allowances, we must be kind. What says the Book?—"Judge not, that ye be not judged."* Your dear father acted upon that maxim—so noble and so awful—and I strive to do so. Alas! dear Austin, *longo intervallo*,* far behind! and you are removed—my example and my help; you are gone to your rest, and I remain beneath my burden, still marching on by bleak and alpine paths, under the awful night.

> "O nuit, nuit douloureuse! O toi, tardive aurore.
> Viens-tu? vas-tu venir? es-tu bien loin encore." '*

And repeating these lines of Chenier, with upturned eyes, and one hand lifted, and an indescribable expression of grief and fatigue, he sank stiffly into his chair, and remained mute, with eyes closed for some time. Then applying his scented handkerchief to them hastily, and looking very kindly at me, he said—

'Anything more, dear child?'

'Nothing, Uncle, thank you, very much, only about that man, Hawkes; I dare say that he does not mean to be so uncivil as he is, but I am really afraid of him, and he makes our walks in that direction quite unpleasant.'

'I understand quite, my dear. I will see to it; and you must remember that nothing is to be allowed to vex my beloved niece and ward during her stay at Bartram—nothing that her old kinsman, Silas Ruthyn, can remedy.'

So with a tender smile, and a charge to shut the door 'perfectly, but without clapping it,' he dismissed me.

Doctor Bryerly had not slept at Bartram, but at the little inn in Feltram, and he was going direct to London, as I afterwards learned.

'Your ugly Doctor's gone away in a fly,' said Milly, as we met on the stairs, she running up, I down.

On reaching the little apartment which was our sitting-room, however, I found that she was mistaken, for Doctor Bryerly, with his hat and a great pair of woollen gloves on, and an old Oxford gray surtout that showed his lank length to advantage, buttoned all the way up to his chin, had set down his black leather bag on the table, and was reading at the window a little volume which I had borrowed from my uncle's library.

It was Swedenborg's account of the other worlds, Heaven and Hell.*

He closed it on his finger as I entered, and without recollecting to remove his hat, he made a step or two toward me with his splay, creaking boots. With a quick glance at the door, he said—

'Glad to see you alone for a minute—very glad.'

But his countenance, on the contrary, looked very anxious.

'I'M going this minute—I—I want to know'—another glance at the door—'are you really quite comfortable here?'

'Quite,' I answered promptly.

'You have only your cousin's company?' he continued, glancing at the table, which was laid for two.

'Yes; but Milly and I are very happy together.'

'That's very nice; but I think there are no teachers, you see—painters, and singers, and that sort of thing that is usual with young ladies. No teachers of that kind—of *any* kind—are there?'

'No; my uncle thinks it better I should lay in a store of health, he says.'

'I know; and the carriage and horses have not come; how soon are they expected?'

'I really can't say, and I assure you I don't much care. I think running about great fun.'

'You walk to church?'

'Yes, Uncle Silas's carriage wants a new wheel, he told me.'

'Ay, but a young woman of your rank, you know, it is not usual she should be without the use of a carriage. Have you horses to ride?'

I shook my head.

'Your uncle, you know, has a very liberal allowance for your maintenance and education.'

I remembered something in the will about it, and Mary Quince was constantly grumbling that 'he did not spend a pound a week on our board.'

I answered nothing, but looked down.

Another glance at the door from Doctor Bryerly's sharp black eyes.

'Is he kind to you?'

'Very kind—most gentle and affectionate.'

'Why doesn't he keep company with you? Does he ever dine with you, or drink tea, or talk to you? Do you see much of him?'

'He is a miserable invalid—his hours and regimen are peculiar. Indeed I wish very much you would consider his case; he is, I believe, often insensible for a long time, and his mind in a strange feeble state sometimes.'

'I dare say—worn out in his young days; and I saw that preparation of opium in his bottle—he takes too much.'

'Why do you think so, Doctor Bryerly?'

'It's made on water: the spirit interferes with the use of it beyond a certain limit. You have no idea what those fellows can swallow. Read the "Opium Eater".* I knew two cases in which the quantity exceeded De Quincy's. Aha! it's new to you?' and he laughed quietly at my simplicity.

'And what do you think his complaint is?' I asked.

'Pooh! I haven't a notion; but, probably, one way or another, he has been all his days working on his nerves and his brain. These men of pleasure, who have no other pursuit, use themselves up mostly, and pay a smart price for their sins. And so he's kind and affectionate. but hands you over to your cousin and the servants. Are his people civil and obliging?'

'Well, I can't say much for them; there is a man named Hawkes, and his daughter, who are very rude, and even abusive sometimes, and say they have orders from my uncle to shut us out from a portion of the grounds; but I don't believe that, for Uncle Silas never alluded to it when I was making my complaint of them to-day.'

'From what part of the grounds is that?' asked Doctor Bryerly, sharply.

I described the situation as well as I could.

'Can we see it from this?' he asked, peeping from the window.

'Oh, no.'

Doctor Bryerly made a note in his pocket-book here, and I said—

'But I am really quite sure it was a story of Dickon's, he is such a surly, disobliging man.'

'And what sort is that old servant that came in and out of his room?'

'Oh, that is old L'Amour,' I answered, rather indirectly, and forgetting that I was using Milly's nickname.

'And is *she* civil?' he asked.

No, she certainly was not; a most disagreeable old woman, with a vein of wickedness. I thought I had heard her swearing.

'They don't seem to be a very engaging lot,' said Doctor Bryerly; 'but where there's one, there will be more. See here, I was just reading a passage,' and he opened the little volume at the place where his finger marked it, and read for me a few sentences, the purport of which I well remember, although, of course, the words have escaped me.

It was in that awful portion of the book which assumes to describe the condition of the condemned; and it said, that independently of the physical causes in that state operating to enforce community of habitation, and an isolation from superior spirits, there exist sympathies, aptitudes, and necessities which would, of themselves, induce that depraved gregariousness, and isolation too.

'And what of the rest of the servants, are they better?' he resumed.

We saw little or nothing of the others, except of old 'Giblets', the butler, who went about like a little automaton of dry bones, poking here and there, and whispering and smiling to himself as he laid the cloth; and seeming otherwise quite unconscious of an external world.

'This room is not got up like Mr. Ruthyn's: does he talk of furnishing and making things a little smart? No! Well, I must say, I think he might.'

Here there was a little silence, and Doctor Bryerly, with his accustomed simultaneous glance at the door, said in low, cautious tones, very distinctly—

'Have you been thinking at all over that matter again, I mean about getting your uncle to forego his guardianship? I would not mind his first refusal. You could make it worth his while, unless he—that is—unless he's very unreasonable indeed; and I think you would consult your interest, Miss Ruthyn, by doing so, and, if possible, getting out of this place.'

'But I have not thought of it at all; I am much happier here than I had at all expected, and I am very fond of my Cousin Milly.'

'How long have you been here exactly?'

I told him. It was some two or three months.

'Have you seen your other cousin, yet—the young gentleman?'

'No.'

'H'm! Aren't you very lonely?' he inquired.

'We see no visitors here; but that, you know, I was prepared for.'

Doctor Bryerly read the wrinkles on his splay boot intently and peevishly, and tapped the sole lightly on the ground.

'Yes, it is very lonely, and the people a bad lot. You'd be pleasanter somewhere else—with Lady Knollys, for instance, eh?'

'Well, *there* certainly. But I am very well here; really the time passes very pleasantly; and my uncle is so kind. I have only to mention anything that annoys me, and he will see that it is remedied, he is always impressing that on me.'

'Yes, it is not a fit place for you,' said Doctor Bryerly. 'Of course, about your uncle,' he resumed, observing my surprised look, 'it is all right; but he's quite helpless, you know. At all events, *think* about it. Here's my address—Hans Emmanuel Bryerly, M.D., 17, King-street, Covent Garden, London—don't lose it, mind,' and he tore the leaf out of his note-book.

'Here's my fly at the door, and you must—you must' (he was looking at his watch)—'mind you *must* think of it seriously; and so, you see, don't let anyone see that. You'll be sure to leave it throwing about. The best way will be just to scratch it on the door of your press, inside, you know; and don't put my name—you'll remember that—only the rest of the address; and burn this. Quince is with you?'

'Yes,' I answered, glad to have a satisfactory word to say.

'Well, don't let her go; it's a bad sign if they wish it. Don't consent, mind; but just tip me a hint, and you'll have me down. And any letters you get from Lady Knollys, you know, for she's very plain-spoken, you'd better burn them off-hand. And I've stayed too long, though; mind what I say, scratch it with a pin, and burn that, and not a word to a mortal about it. Good-bye; oh, I was taking away your book.'

And so, in a fuss, with a slight shake of the hand, getting up his umbrella, his bag, and tin box, he hurried from the room; and in a minute more, I heard the sound of his vehicle as it drove away.

I looked after it with a sigh: the uneasy sensations which I had experienced respecting my sojourn at Bartram-Haugh were reawakened.

My ugly, vulgar, true friend was disappearing beyond those gigantic lime trees which hid Bartram from the eyes of the outer world. The fly, with the Doctor's valise on top, vanished, and I sighed an anxious sigh. The shadow of the over-arching trees contracted, and I felt helpless and forsaken; and glancing down the torn leaf, Doctor Bryerly's address met my eye, between my fingers.

I slipt it into my breast, and ran up-stairs stealthily, trembling lest the old woman should summon me again, at the head of the stairs, into Uncle Silas's room, where under his gaze, I fancied, I should be sure to betray myself.

But I glided unseen and safely by, entered my room, and shut my door. So, listening and working, I, with my scissors' point, scratched the address where Doctor Bryerly had advised. Then, in positive terror, lest some one should even knock during the operation, I, with a match, consumed to ashes the tell-tale bit of paper.

Now, for the first time, I experienced the unpleasant sensations of having a secret to keep. I fancy the pain of this solitary liability was disproportionately acute in my case, for I was naturally very open and very nervous. I was always on the point of betraying it *apropos des bottes**—always reproaching myself for my duplicity; and in constant terror when honest Mary Quince approached the press, or good-natured Milly made her occasional survey of the wonders of my wardrobe. I would have given anything to go and point to the tiny inscription, and say:—'This is Doctor Bryerly's address in London. I scratched it with my scissors' point, taking every precaution lest any one—you, my good friends, included—should surprise me. I have ever since kept this secret to myself, and trembled whenever your frank kind faces looked into the press. There—you at last know all about it. Can you ever forgive my deceit?'

But I could not make up my mind to reveal it; nor yet to erase the inscription, which was my alternative thought. Indeed I am a wavering, irresolute creature as ever lived, in my ordinary mood. High excitement or passion only can inspire me with decision. Under the inspiration of either, however, I am transformed, and often both prompt and brave.

'Some one left here last night, I think, Miss,' said Mary Quince, with a mysterious nod, one morning. ''Twas two o'clock, and I was bad with the tooth-ache, and went down to get a pinch o' red pepper—leaving the candle a-light here lest you should awake. When I was coming up—as I was crossing the lobby, at the far end of the long gallery—what should I hear, but a horse snorting, and some people a-talking, short and quiet like. So I looks out o' the window; and there surely I did see two horses yoked to a shay, and a fellah a pullin' a box up o' top; and out comes a walise and a bag; and I think it was old Wyat, please 'm, that Miss Milly calls L'Amour, that stood in the doorway a-talking to the driver.'

'And who got into the chaise, Mary?' I asked.

'Well, Miss, I waited as long as I could; but the pain was bad, and me so awful cold; I gave it up at last, and came back to bed, for I could not say how much longer they might wait. And you'll find, Miss, 'twill be kep' a secret, like the shay as you saw'd, Miss, last week. I hate them dark ways, and secrets; and old Wyat—she does tell stories, don't she?—and she as ought to be partickler, seein' her time be short now, and she so old. It is awful, an old 'un like that telling such crams* as she do.'

Milly was as curious as I, but could throw no light on this. We both agreed, however, that the departure was probably that of the person whose arrival I had accidentally witnessed. This time the chaise had drawn up at the side door, round the corner of the left side of the house; and, no doubt, driven away by the back road.

Another accident had revealed this nocturnal move. It was very provoking, however, that Mary Quince had not had resolution to wait for the appearance of the traveller. We all agreed, however, that we were to observe a strict silence, and that even to Wyat—L'Amour I had better continue to call her—Mary Quince was not to hint what she had seen. I suspect, however, that injured curiosity asserted itself, and that Mary hardly adhered to this self-denying resolve.

But cheerful wintry suns and frosty skies, long nights, and brilliant starlight, with good homely fires in our snuggery—gossipings, stories, short readings now and then, and brisk walks through the always beautiful scenery of Bartram-Haugh, and, above all, the unbroken tenor of our life, which had fallen into a serene routine, foreign to the idea of danger or misadventure, gradually quieted the qualms and misgivings which my interview with Doctor Bryerly had so powerfully resuscitated.

My Cousin Monica, to my inexpressible joy, had returned to her country house; and an active diplomacy, through the post-office, was negotiating the re-opening of friendly relations between the courts of Elverston and of Bartram.

At length, one fine day, Cousin Monica, smiling pleasantly, with her cloak and bonnet on, and her colour fresh from the shrewd air of the Derbyshire hills, stood suddenly before me in our sitting-room. Our meeting was that of two school-companions, long separated. Cousin Monica was always a girl in my eyes.

What a hug it was; what a shower of kisses and ejaculations, inquiries and caresses! At last I pressed her down into a chair, and, laughing, she said—

'You have no idea what self-denial I have exercised to bring this visit about. I, who detest writing, have actually written five letters to Silas; and I don't think I said a single impertinent thing in one of them! What a wonderful little old thing your butler is! I did not know what to make of him on the steps. Is he a struldbrug,* or a fairy, or only a ghost? Where on earth did your uncle pick him up? I'm sure he came in on All Hallows E'en,* to answer an incantation—not your future husband, I hope—and he'll vanish some night into gray smoke, and whisk sadly up the chimney. He's the most venerable little thing I ever beheld in my life. I leaned back in the carriage and thought I should absolutely die of laughing. He's gone up to prepare your uncle for my visit; and I really am very glad, for I'm sure I shall look as young as Hebe* after *him*. But who is this? Who are you, my dear?'

This was addressed to poor Milly, who stood at the corner of the chimney-piece, staring with her round eyes and plump cheeks in fear and wonder upon the strange lady.

'How stupid of me,' I exclaimed. 'Milly, dear, this is your cousin, Lady Knollys.'

'And so *you* are Millicent. Well, dear, I am very glad to see you.' And Cousin Monica was on her feet again in an instant, with Milly's hand very cordially in hers; and she gave her a kiss upon each cheek, and patted her head.

Milly, I must mention, was a much more presentable figure than when I had first encountered her. Her dresses were at least a quarter of a yard longer. Though very rustic, therefore, she was not so barbarously grotesque, by any means.

COUSIN MONICA, with her hands upon Milly's shoulders, looked amusedly and kindly in her face. 'And,' said she, 'we must be very good friends—you funny creature, you and I. I'm allowed to be the most saucy old woman in Derbyshire—quite incorrigibly privileged; and nobody is ever affronted with me, so I say the most shocking things constantly.'

'I'm a bit that way, myself; and I think,' said poor Milly, making an effort, and growing very red; she quite lost her head at that point, and was incompetent to finish the sentiment she had prefaced.

'You think? Now, take my advice, and never wait to think, my dear; talk first, and think afterwards, that is my way; though, indeed, I can't say I ever think at all. It is a very cowardly habit. Our cold-blooded Cousin Maud, there, thinks sometimes; but it is always such a failure that I forgive her. I wonder when your little pre-Adamite butler will return. He speaks the language of the Picts and Ancient Britons,* I dare say, and your father requires a little time to translate him. And, Milly dear, I am very hungry, so I won't wait for your butler, who would give me, I suppose, one of the cakes baked by King Alfred,* and some Danish beer in a skull;* but I'll ask you for a little of that nice bread and butter.'

With which accordingly Lady Knollys was quickly supplied, but it did not at all impede her utterance.

'Do you think, girls, you could be ready to come away with me, if Silas gives leave, in an hour or two? I should so like to take you both home with me to Elverston.'

'How delightful! you darling,' cried I, embracing and kissing her; 'for my part, I should be ready in five minutes; what do you say, Milly?'

Poor Milly's wardrobe, I am afraid, was more portable than handsome; and she looked horribly affrighted, and whispered in my ear—

'My best petticoat is away at the laundress; say in a week, Maud.'

'What does she say?' asked Lady Knollys.

'She fears she can't be ready,' I answered, dejectedly.

'There's a deal of my slops in the wash,' blurted out poor Milly, staring straight at Lady Knollys.

'In the name of wonder, what does my cousin mean?' asked Lady Knollys.

'Her things have not come home yet from the laundress,' I replied; and at this moment our wondrous old butler entered to announce to Lady Knollys that his master was ready to receive her, whenever she was disposed to favour him; and also to make polite apologies for his being compelled, by his state of health, to give her the trouble of ascending to his room.

So Cousin Monica was at the door in a moment, over her shoulder calling to us, 'Come, girls.'

'Please, not yet, my lady—you alone; and he requests the young ladies will be in the way, as he will send for them presently.'

I began to admire poor 'Giblets' as the wreck of a tolerably respectable servant.

'Very good; perhaps it *is* better we should kiss and be friends in private first,' said Cousin Knollys, laughing; and away she went under the guidance of the mummy,

I had an account of this *tête-à-tête* afterwards from Lady Knollys.

'When I saw him, my dear,' she said, 'I could hardly believe my eyes—such white hair—such a white face—such mad eyes—such a death-like smile. When I saw him last, his hair was dark; he dressed himself like a modern Englishman; and he really preserved a likeness to the full-length portrait at Knowl, that you fell in love with, you know; but, angels and ministers of grace!* such a spectre! I asked myself is it necromancy, or is it delirium tremens* that has reduced him to this? And said he, with that odious smile, that made me fancy myself half insane—

' "You see a change, Monica."

'What a sweet, gentle, insufferable voice he has! Somebody once told me about the tone of a glass flute that made some people hysterical to listen to, and I was thinking of it all the time. There was always a peculiar quality in his voice.

' "I do see a change, Silas," I said at last; "and, no doubt, so do you in me—a great change."

' "There has been time enough to work a greater than I observe in you since you last honoured me with a visit," said he.

'I think he was at his old sarcasms, and meant that I was the same impertinent minx he remembered long ago, uncorrected by time; and so I am, and he must not expect compliments from old Monica Knollys.

' "It is a long time, Silas; but that, you know, is not my fault," said I.

' "Not your fault, my dear—your instinct. We are all imitative creatures: the great people ostracized me, and the small ones followed. We are very like turkeys, we have so much good sense and so much generosity. Fortune, in a freak, wounded my head, and the whole brood were upon me, pecking and gobbling, gobbling and pecking, and you among them, dear Monica. It wasn't your fault, only your instinct, so I quite forgive you; but no wonder the peckers wear better than the pecked. You are robust; and I, what I am."

' "Now, Silas, I have not come here to quarrel. If we quarrel now, mind, we can never make it up—we are too old, so let us forget all we can, and try to forgive something; and if we can do neither, at all events let there be truce between us while I am here."

' "My personal wrongs I can quite forgive, and I do, Heaven knows, from my heart; but there are things which ought not to be forgiven. My children have been ruined by it. I may, by the mercy of Providence, be yet set right in the world, and so soon as that time comes, I will remember, and I will act; but my children—you will see that wretched girl, my daughter—education, society, all would come too late—my children have been ruined by it."

' "I have not done it; but I know what you mean," I said. "You menace litigation whenever you have the means; but you forget that Austin placed you under promise, when he gave you the use of this house and place, never to disturb my title to Elverston. So there is my answer, if you mean that."

' "I mean what I mean," he replied, with his old smile.

' "You mean then," said I, "that for the pleasure of vexing me with litigation, you are willing to forfeit your tenure of this house and place."

' "Suppose I *did* mean precisely that, why should I forfeit anything? My beloved brother, by his will, has given me a right to the use of Bartram-Haugh for my life, and attached no absurd condition of the kind you fancy to his gift."

'Silas was in one of his vicious old moods, and liked to menace me. His vindictiveness got the better of his craft; but he knows as well as I do that he never could succeed in disturbing the title of my poor dear Harry Knollys; and I was not at all alarmed by his threats; and I told him so, as coolly as I speak to you now.

'"Well, Monica," he said, "I have weighed you in the balance, and you are not found wanting. For a moment the old man possessed me: the thought of my children, of past unkindness, and present affliction and disgrace, exasperated me, and I was mad. It was but for a moment—the galvanic spasm of a corpse. Never was breast more dead than mine to the passions and ambitions of the world. They are not for white locks like these, nor for a man who, for a week in every month, lies in the gate of death. Will you shake hands? *Here*—I *do* strike a truce; and I *do* forget and forgive *everything*."

'I don't know what he meant by this scene. I have no idea whether he was acting, or lost his head, or, in fact, why or how it occurred; but I am glad, darling, that, unlike myself, I was calm, and that a quarrel has not been forced upon me.'

When our turn came and we were summoned to the presence, Uncle Silas was quite as usual; but Cousin Monica's heightened colour, and the flash of her eyes, showed plainly that something exciting and angry had occurred.

Uncle Silas commented in his own vein upon the effect of Bartram air and liberty, all he had to offer; and called on me to say how I liked them. And then he called Milly to him, kissed her tenderly, smiled sadly upon her, and turning to Cousin Monica, said—

'This is my daughter, Milly—oh! she has been presented to you down stairs, has she? You have, no doubt, been interested by her. As I told her Cousin Maud, though I am not yet quite a Sir Tunbelly Clumsy,* she is a very finished Miss Hoyden. Are not you, my poor Milly? You owe your distinction, my dear, to that line of circumvallation* which has, ever since your birth, intercepted all civilization on its way to Bartram. You are much obliged, Milly, to everybody who, whether naturally or *un*-naturally, turned a sod in that invisible but impenetrable work. For your accomplishments—rather singular than fashionable—you are indebted, in part, to your cousin, Lady Knollys. Is not she, Monica? *Thank* her, Milly.'

'This is your *truce*, Silas,' said Lady Knollys, with a quiet sharpness. 'I think, Silas Ruthyn, you want to provoke me to speak in a way before these young creatures which we should all regret.'

'So my badinage excites your temper, Monnie. Think how you would feel, then, if I had found you by the highway side, mangled by robbers, and set my foot upon your throat, and spat in your face. But—stop this. Why have I said this? Simply to emphasize my forgiveness. See, girls, Lady Knollys and I, cousins long estranged, forget and forgive the past, and join hands over its buried injuries.'

'Well, *be* it so; only let us have done with ironies and covert taunts.'

And with these words their hands were joined; and Uncle Silas, after he had released hers, patted and fondled it with his, laughing icily and very low all the time.

'I wish so much, dear Monica,' he said, when this piece of silent byplay was over, 'that I could ask you to stay to-night; but absolutely I have not a bed to offer, and even if I had, I fear my suit would hardly prevail.'

Then came Lady Knollys' invitation for Milly and me. He was very much obliged; he smiled over it a great deal, meditating. I thought he was puzzled; and amid his smiles, his wild eyes scanned Cousin Monica's frank face once or twice suspiciously.

There was a difficulty—an *undefined* difficulty—about letting us go that day; but on a future one—soon—*very* soon—he would be most happy.

Well, there was an end of that little project, for to-day at least; and Cousin Monica was too well-bred to urge it beyond a certain point.

'Milly, my dear, will you put on your hat and show me the grounds about the house? May she, Silas? I should like to renew my acquaintance.'

'You'll see them sadly neglected, Monnie. A poor man's pleasure grounds must rely on Nature, and trust to her for effects. Where there is fine timber, however, and abundance of slope, and rock, and hollow, we sometimes gain in picturesqueness what we lose by neglect in luxury.'

Then, as Cousin Monica said she would cross the grounds by a path, and meet her carriage at a point to which we would accompany her, and so make her way home, she took leave of Uncle Silas; a ceremony whereat—without, I thought, much zeal at either side—a kiss took place.

'Now, girls!' said Cousin Knollys, when we were fairly in motion over the grass, 'what do you say—will he let you come—yes or no? I can't say, but I think, dear,'—this to Milly—'he ought to let you see a little more of the world than appears among the glens and bushes of Bartram. Very pretty they are, like yourself; but very wild, and very little seen. Where is your brother, Milly; is not he older than you?'

'I don't know where; and he is older by six years and a bit.'

By-and-by, when Milly was gesticulating to frighten some herons by the river's brink into the air, Cousin Monica said confidentially to me—

'He has run away, I'm told—I wish I could believe it—and enlisted in a regiment going to India, perhaps the best thing for him. Did you see him here before his judicious self-banishment?'

'No.'

'Well, I suppose you have had no loss. Doctor Bryerly says from all he can learn he is a very bad young man. And now tell me, dear, *is* Silas kind to you?'

'Yes, always gentle, just as you saw him to-day; but we don't see a great deal of him—very little, in fact.'

'And how do you like your life and the people?' she asked.

'My life, very well; and the people, *pretty* well. There's an old woman we don't like, old Wyat, she is cross and mysterious, and tells untruths; but I don't think she is dishonest—so Mary Quince says—and that, you know, is a point; and there is a family, father and daughter, called Hawkes, who live in the Windmill Wood, who are perfect savages, though my uncle says they don't mean it; but they are very disagreeable, rude people; and except them we see very little of the servants or other people. But there has been a mysterious visit, some one came late at night, and remained for some days, though Milly and I never saw them, and Mary Quince saw a chaise at the side-door at two o'clock at night.'

Cousin Monica was so highly interested at this that she arrested her walk and stood facing me, with her hand on my arm, questioning and listening, and lost, as it seemed, in dismal conjecture.

'It is not pleasant, you know,' I said.

'No, it is not pleasant,' said Lady Knollys, very gloomily.

And just then Milly joined us, shouting to us to look at the herons flying; so Cousin Monica did, and smiled and nodded in thanks to Milly, and was again silent and thoughtful as we walked on.

'You are to come to me, mind, both of you, girls,' she said, abruptly; 'you *shall*. I'll manage it.'

When silence returned, and Milly ran away once more to try whether the old gray trout was visible in the still water under the bridge, and Cousin Monica said to me in a low tone, looking hard at me—

'You've not seen anything to frighten you, Maud? Don't look so alarmed, dear,' she added with a little laugh, which was not very merry however. 'I don't mean frighten in any awful sense—in fact,

I did not mean frighten at all. I meant—I can't exactly express it—anything to vex, or make you uncomfortable, have you?'

'No, I can't say I have, except that room in which Mr. Charke was found dead.'

'Oh! you saw that, did you?—I should like to see it so much. Your bedroom is not near it?'

'Oh, no; on the floor beneath, and looking to the front. And Doctor Bryerly talked a little to me, and there seemed to be something on his mind more than he chose to tell me; so that for some time after I saw him I really was, as you say, frightened; but, except that, I really have had no cause. And what was in your mind when you asked me?'

'Well, you know, Maud, you are afraid of ghosts, banditti, and *every*thing; and I wished to know whether you were uncomfortable, and what your particular bogle* was just now—that, I assure you, was all; and I know,' she continued, suddenly changing her light tone and manner, for one of pointed entreaty, 'what Doctor Bryerly said; and I *implore* of you, Maud, to think of it seriously; and when you come to me, you shall do so with the intention of remaining at Elverston.'

'Now, Cousin Monica, is this fair? You and Doctor Bryerly both talk in the same awful way to me: and, I assure you, you don't know how nervous I am sometimes, and yet you won't, either of you, say what you mean. Now, Monica, dear cousin, won't you tell me?'

'You see, dear, it is so lonely; it's a strange place, and he so odd. I don't like the place, and I don't like him. I've tried, but I can't, and I think I never shall. He may be a very—what was it that good little silly curate at Knowl used to call him?—a very advanced Christian—that is it, and I hope he is; but if he is only what he used to be, his utter seclusion from society removes the only check, except personal fear—and he never had much of that—upon a very bad man. And you must know, my dear Maud, what a prize you are, and what an immense trust it is.'

Suddenly Cousin Monica stopped short, and looked at me as if she had gone too far.

'But you know, Silas may be very good *now*, although he was wild and selfish in his young days. Indeed I don't know what to make of him; but I am sure when you have thought it over, you will agree with me and Doctor Bryerly, that you must not stay here.'

It was vain trying to induce my cousin to be more explicit.

'I hope to see you at Elverston in a very few days. I will *shame* Silas into letting you come. I don't like his reluctance.'

'But don't you think he must know that Milly would require some little outfit before her visit?'

'Well, I can't say. I hope that is all; but be it what it may, I'll *make* him let you come, and *immediately* too.'

After she had gone, I experienced a repetition of those undefined doubts, which had tortured me for some time after my conversation with Doctor Bryerly. I had truly said, however, I was well enough contented with my mode of life here, for I had been trained at Knowl to a solitude very nearly as profound.

CHAPTER XL

IN WHICH I MAKE ANOTHER COUSIN'S ACQUAINTANCE

MY correspondence about this time was not very extensive. About once a fortnight a letter from honest Mrs. Rusk conveyed to me how the dogs and ponies were, in queer English, oddly spelt; some village gossip, a critique upon Doctor Clay's or the Curate's last sermon, and some severities generally upon the dissenters' doings, with loves to Mary Quince, and all good wishes to me. Sometimes a welcome letter from cheerful Cousin Monica; and now, to vary the series, a copy of complimentary verses, with a signature, very adoring—very like Byron, I then fancied, and now, I must confess, rather vapid. Could I doubt from whom they came?

I had received, about a month after my arrival, a copy of verses in the same hand, in a plaintive ballad style, of the soldierly sort, in which the writer said, that as living his sole object was to please me, so dying I should be his latest thought; and some more poetic impieties, asking only in return, that when the storm of battle had swept over, I should 'shed a tear' on seeing 'the *oak lie*, where it fell.' Of course, about this lugubrious pun, there could be no misconception. The Captain was, unmistakably, indicated; and I was so moved that I could no longer retain my secret; but walking with Milly that day, confided the little romance to that unsophisticated listener, under the chestnut trees. The lines were so amorously dejected, and yet so heroically redolent of blood and gunpowder, that Milly and I agreed that the writer must be on the verge of a sanguinary campaign.

It was not easy to get at Uncle Silas's 'Times' or 'Morning Post,' which we fancied would explain these horrible allusions; but Milly bethought her of a sergeant in the militia, resident in Feltram, who knew the destination and quarters of every regiment in the service; and circuitously, from this authority, we learned, to my infinite relief, that Captain Oakley's regiment had still two years to sojourn in England.

I was summoned one evening by old L'Amour to my uncle's room. I remember his appearance that evening so well, as he lay back in his chair: the pillow; the white glare of his strange eye; his feeble, painful smile.

'You'll excuse my not rising, dear Maud, I am so miserably ill this evening.'

I expressed my respectful condolence.

'Yes; I *am* to be pitied; but pity is of no use, dear,' he murmured, peevishly. 'I sent for you to make you acquainted with your cousin, my son. Where are you, Dudley?'

A figure seated in a low lounging chair, at the other side of the fire, and which till then I had not observed, at these words, rose up a little slowly, like a man stiff after a day's hunting; and I beheld with a shock that held my breath, and fixed my eyes upon him in a stare, the young man whom I had encountered at Church Scarsdale, on the day of my unpleasant excursion there with Madame, and who, to the best of my belief, was also one of that ruffianly party who had so unspeakably terrified me in the warren at Knowl.

I suppose I looked very much affrighted. If I had been looking at a ghost I could not have felt much more scared and incredulous.

When I was able to turn my eyes upon my uncle he was not looking at me, but with a glimmer of that smile with which a father looks on a son whose youth and comeliness he admires, his white face was turned towards the young man, in whom I beheld nothing but the image of odious and dreadful associations.

'Come, sir,' said my uncle, 'we must not be too modest. Here's your Cousin Maud—what do you say?'

'How are ye, Miss?' he said, with a sheepish grin.

'Miss! Come, come. Miss us no Misses,' said my uncle; 'she is Maud, and you Dudley, or I mistake; or we shall have you calling Milly, madame. She'll not refuse you her hand, I venture to think. Come, young gentleman, speak for yourself.'

'How are ye, Maud?' he said, doing his best, and drawing near, he extended his hand. 'You're welcome to Bartram-Haugh, Miss.'

'Kiss your cousin, sir. Where's your gallantry? On my honour, I disown you,' exclaimed my uncle, with more energy than he had shown before.

With a clumsy effort, and a grin that was both sheepish and impudent, he grasped my hand and advanced his face. The imminent salute gave me strength to spring back a step or two, and he hesitated.

My uncle laughed peevishly.

'Well, well, that will do, I suppose. In my time first-cousins did not meet like strangers; but perhaps we were wrong; we are learning modesty from the Americans, and old English ways are too gross for us.'

'I have—I've seen him before—that is;' and at this point I stopped.

My uncle turned his strange glare, in a sort of scowl of inquiry, upon me.

'Oh!—hey! why this is news. You never told me. Where have you met, eh, Dudley?'

'Never saw her in my days, so far as I'm aweer on,' said the young man.

'No! Well, then, Maud, will *you* enlighten us?' said Uncle Silas, coldly.

'I *did* see that young gentleman before,' I faltered.

'Meaning *me*, ma'am?' he asked, coolly.

'Yes—certainly *you*. I *did*, Uncle,' answered I.

'And where was it, my dear? Not at Knowl, I fancy. Poor dear Austin did not trouble me or mine much with his hospitalities.'

This was not a pleasant tone to take in speaking of his dead brother and benefactor; but at the moment I was too much engaged upon the one point to observe it.

'I met'—I could not say my cousin—'I met him, Uncle—your son—that young gentleman—I *saw* him, I should say, at Church Scarsdale, and afterwards with some other persons in the warren at Knowl. It was the night our gamekeeper was beaten.'

'Well, Dudley, what do you say to that?' asked Uncle Silas.

'I never *was* at them places, so help me. I don't know where they be; and I never set eyes on the young lady before, as I hope to be saved, in all my days,' said he, with a countenance so unchanged and an air so confident that I began to think I must be the dupe of one of those strange resemblances which have been known to lead to positive identification in the witness-box, afterwards proved to be utterly mistaken.

'You look so—so *uncomfortable*, Maud, at the idea of having seen him before, that I hardly wonder at the vehemence of his denial. There was plainly something disagreeable; but you see as respects him it is a total mistake. My boy was always a truth-telling fellow—you may rely implicitly on what he says. You were *not* at those places?'

'I wish I may—' began the ingenuous youth, with increased vehemence.

'There, there—that will do; your honour and word as a gentle-
man—and *that* you are, though a poor one—will quite satisfy your
Cousin Maud. Am I right, my dear? I do assure you, as a gentleman,
I never knew him to say the thing that was not.'

So Mr. Dudley Ruthyn began, not to curse, but to swear, in the
prescribed form, that he had never seen me before, or the places I had
named, 'since I was weaned, by—'

'That's enough—now, shake hands, if you won't kiss, like cousins,'
interrupted my uncle.

And very uncomfortably I did lend him my hand to shake.

'You'll want some supper, Dudley, so Maud and I will excuse your
going. Good night, my dear boy,' and he smiled and waved him from
the room.

'That's as fine a young fellow, I think, as any English father can
boast for his son—true, brave, and kind, and quite an Apollo. Did you
observe how finely proportioned he is, and what exquisite features the
fellow has? He's rustic and rough, as you see; but a year or two in
the militia—I've a promise of a commission for him—he's too old for
the line—will form and polish him. He wants nothing but manner;
and I protest when he has had a little drilling of that kind, I do believe
he'll be as pretty a fellow as you'd find in England.'

I listened with amazement. I could discover nothing but what was
disagreeable in the horrid bumpkin, and thought such an instance of
the blindness of parental partiality was hardly credible.

I looked down, dreading another direct appeal to my judgment;
and Uncle Silas, I suppose, referred those downcast looks to maiden
modesty, for he forbore to task mine by any new interrogatory.

Dudley Ruthyn's cool and resolute denial of ever having seen me
or the places I had named, and the inflexible serenity of his countenance while doing so, did very much shake my confidence in my own
identification of him. I could not be *quite* certain that the person I had
seen at Church Scarsdale was the very same whom I afterwards saw at
Knowl. And now, in this particular instance, after the lapse of a still
longer period, could I be perfectly certain that my memory, deceived
by some accidental points of resemblance, had not duped me, and
wronged my cousin, Dudley Ruthyn?

I suppose my uncle had expected from me some signs of acquiescence in his splendid estimate of his cub, and was nettled at my
silence. After a short interval he said—

'I've seen something of the world in my day, and I can say, without a misgiving of partiality, that Dudley is the material of a perfect English gentleman. I'm not blind, of course—the training must be supplied; a year or two of good models, active self-criticism, and good society. I simply say that the *material* is there.'

Here was another interval of silence.

'And now tell me, child, what these recollections of Church—Church—*what?*'

'Church Scarsdale,' I replied.

'Yes, thank you—Church Scarsdale and Knowl—are?'

So I related my stories as well as I could.

'Well, dear Maud, the adventure of Church Scarsdale is hardly so terrific as I expected,' said Uncle Silas, with a cold little laugh; 'and I don't see, if he had really been the hero of it, why he should shrink from avowing it. I know I should not. And I really can't say that your pic-nic party in the grounds of Knowl has frightened me much more. A lady waiting in the carriage, and two or three tipsy young men. Her presence seems to me a guarantee that no mischief was meant; but champagne is the soul of frolic, and a row with the gamekeepers a natural consequence. It happened to me once—forty years ago, when I was a wild young buck—one of the worst rows I ever was in.'

And Uncle Silas poured some eau-de-cologne over the corner of his handkerchief, and touched his temples with it.

'If my boy had been there, I do assure you—and I know him—he would say so at once. I fancy he would rather *boast* of it. I never knew him utter an untruth. When you know him a little you'll say so.'

With these words Uncle Silas leaned back exhausted, and languidly poured some of his favourite eau-de-cologne over the palms of his hands, nodded a farewell, and, in a whisper, wished me good-night.

'Dudley's come,' whispered Milly, taking me under the arm as I entered the lobby. 'But I don't care: he never gives me nout; and he gets money from Governor, as much as he likes, and I never a sixpence. It's a shame!'

So there was no great love between the only son and only daughter of the younger line of the Ruthyns.

I was curious to learn all that Milly could tell me of this new inmate of Bartram-Haugh; and Milly was communicative without having a great deal to relate, and what I heard from her tended to confirm my own disagreeable impressions about him. She was afraid of him. He

was 'a woundy ugly customer in a wax, she could tell me.' He was the
only one 'she ever knowed as had pluck to jaw the Governor.' But he
was 'afeard on the Governor, too.'

His visits to Bartram-Haugh, I heard, were desultory; and this, to
my relief, would probably not outlast a week or a fortnight. 'He *was*
such a fashionable cove;' he was always 'a gadding about, mostly to
Liverpool or Birmingham, and sometimes to Lunnun, itself.' He was
'keeping company one time with Beauty, Governor thought, and he
was awfully afraid he'd a married her; but that was all bosh and nonsense; and Beauty would have none of his chaff and wheedling, for
she liked Tom Brice'; and Milly thought that Dudley never 'cared
a crack of a whip for her'. He used to go to the Windmill to have 'a
smoke with Pegtop'; and he was a member of the Feltram Club, that
met at the 'Plume o' Feathers'. He was 'a rare good shot', she heard:
and 'he was before the justices for poaching, but they could make
nothing of it'. And the Governor said 'it was all through spite of
him—for they hate us for being better blood than they.' And 'all but
the squires and those upstart folk loves Dudley, he is so handsome
and gay—though he be a bit cross at home.' And, 'Governor says,
he'll be a Parliament man yet, spite o' them all.'

Next morning, when our breakfast was nearly ended, Dudley tapped
at the window with the end of his clay pipe—a 'churchwarden' Milly
called it—just such a long curved pipe as Joe Willet is made to hold
between his lips in those charming illustrations of 'Barnaby
Rudge'*—which we all know so well—and lifting his 'wide-awake'
with a burlesque salutation, which, I suppose, would have charmed the
'Plume of Feathers', he dropped, kicked and caught his 'wide-awake',
with an agility and a gravity as he replaced it, so inexpressibly humor-
ous, that Milly went off in a loud fit of laughter, with the ejaculation—

'Did you ever!'

It was odd how repulsively my confidence in my original identification always revived on unexpectedly seeing Dudley after an interval.

I could perceive that this piece of comic by-play was meant to make
a suitable impression upon me. I received it, however, with a killing
gravity; and after a word or two to Milly, he lounged away, having first
broken his pipe, bit by bit, into pieces, which he balanced in turn on
his nose and on his chin, from which features he jerked them into his
mouth, with a precision which, along with his excellent pantomime of
eating them, highly excited Milly's mirth and admiration.

GREATLY to my satisfaction this engaging person did not appear again that day. But next day Milly told me that my uncle had taken him to task for the neglect with which he was treating us.

'He did pitch into him, sharp and short, and not a word from him, only sulky like; and I so frightened, I durst not look up almost; and they said a lot I could not make head or tail of; and Governor ordered me out o' the room, and glad I was to go; and so they had it out between them.'

Milly could throw no light whatsoever upon the adventures at Church Scarsdale and Knowl; and I was left still in doubt, which sometimes oscillated one way and sometimes another. But, on the whole, I could not shake off the misgivings which constantly recurred and pointed very obstinately to Dudley as the hero of those odious scenes.

Oddly enough, though, I now felt far less confident upon the point than I did at first sight. I had begun to distrust my memory, and to suspect my fancy; but of this there could be no question, that between the person so unpleasantly linked in my remembrance with those scenes, and Dudley Ruthyn, a striking, though possibly only a general resemblance did exist.

Milly was certainly right as to the gist of Uncle Silas's injunctions, for we saw more of Dudley henceforward.

He was shy; he was impudent; he was awkward; he was conceited;— altogether a most intolerable bumpkin. Though he sometimes flushed and stammered, and never for a moment was at his ease in my presence, yet, to my inexpressible disgust, there was a self-complacency in his manner, and a kind of triumph in his leer, which very plainly told me how satisfied he was as to the nature of the impression he was making upon me.

I would have given worlds to tell him how odious I thought him. Probably, however, he would not have believed me. Perhaps he fancied that 'ladies' affected airs of indifference and repulsion to cover their real feelings. I never looked at or spoke to him when I could avoid either, and then it was as briefly as I could. To do him justice, however, he seemed to have no liking for our society, and certainly never seemed altogether comfortable in it.

I find it hard to write quite impartially even of Dudley Ruthyn's personal appearance; but, with an effort, I confess that his features were good, and his figure not amiss, though a little fattish. He had light whiskers, light hair, and a pink complexion, and very good blue eyes. So far my uncle was right; and if he had been perfectly gentlemanlike he really might have passed for a handsome man in the judgment of some critics.

But there was that odious mixture of *mauvaise honte* and impudence, a clumsiness, a slyness, and a consciousness in his bearing and countenance, not distinctly boorish, but *low*, which turned his good looks into an ugliness more intolerable than that of feature; and a corresponding vulgarity pervading his dress, his demeanour, and his very walk, marred whatever good points his figure possessed. If you take all this into account, with the ominous and startling misgivings constantly recurring, you will understand the mixed feelings of anger and disgust with which I received the admiration he favoured me with.

Gradually he grew less constrained in my presence, and certainly his manners were not improved by his growing ease and confidence.

He came in while Milly and I were at luncheon, jumped up, with a 'right-about face' performed in the air, sitting on the sideboard, whence grinning slyly and kicking his heels, he leered at us.

'Will you have something, Dudley?' asked Milly.

'No, lass; but I'll look at ye, and maybe drink a drop for company.'

And with these words, he took a sportsman's flask from his pocket; and helping himself to a large glass and a decanter, he compounded a glass of strong brandy and water, as he talked, and refreshed himself with it from time to time.

'Curate's up wi' the Governor,' he said, with a grin. 'I wanted a word wi' him; but I s'pose I'll hardly git in this hour or more; they're a praying and disputing, and a Bible chopping as usual. Ha, ha! But 'twont hold much longer, old Wyat says, now that Uncle Austin's dead; there's nout to be made o' praying and that work no longer, and it don't pay of itself.'

'O fie! For shame, you sinner!' laughed Milly. 'He wasn't in a church these five years, he says, and then only to meet a young lady. Now, isn't he a sinner, Maud—isn't he?'

Dudley, grinning, looked with a languishing slyness at me, biting the edge of his wide-awake, which he held over his breast.

Dudley Ruthyn probably thought there was a manly and desperate sort of fascination in the impiety he professed.

'I wonder, Milly,' said I, 'at your laughing. How *can* you laugh?'

'You'd have me cry, would ye?' answered Milly.

'I certainly would not have you laugh,' I replied.

'I know I wish *some* one 'ud cry for me, and I know who,' said Dudley, in what he meant for a very engaging way, and he looked at me as if he thought I must feel flattered by his caring to have my tears.

Instead of crying, however, I leaned back in my chair, and began quietly to turn over the pages of Walter Scott's poems,* which I and Milly were then reading in the evenings.

The tone in which this odious young man spoke of his father, his coarse mention of mine, and his low boasting of his irreligion, disgusted me more than ever with him.

'They parsons be slow coaches—awful slow. I'll have a good bit to wait, I s'pose. I should be three miles away and more by this time—drat it!' He was eyeing the legging of the foot which he held up while he spoke, as if calculating how far away that limb should have carried him by this time. 'Why can't folk do their Bible and prayers o' Sundays, and get it off their stomachs? I say, Milly lass, will ye see if Governor be done wi' the Curate? Do. I'm a losing the whole day along o' him.'

Milly jumped up, accustomed to obey her brother, and as she passed me, whispered, with a wink—

'*Money.*'

And away she went. Dudley whistled a tune, and swung his foot like a pendulum, as he followed her with his side glance.

'I say, it is a hard case, Miss, a lad o' spirit should be kept so tight. I haven't a shilling but what comes through his fingers; an' drat the tizzy he'll gi' me till he knows the reason why.'

'Perhaps,' I said, 'my uncle thinks you should earn some for yourself.'

'I'd like to know how a fella's to earn money now-a-days. You wouldn't have a gentleman to keep a shop, I fancy. But I'll ha' a fistful jist now, and no thanks to he. Them executors, you know, owes me a deal o' money. Very honest chaps, of course; but they're cursed slow about paying, I know.'

I made no remark upon this elegant allusion to the executors of my dear father's will.

'An' I tell ye, Maud, when I git the tin, I know who I'll buy a farin' for. I do, lass.'

The odious creature drawled this with a side-long leer, which, I suppose, he fancied quite irresistible.

I am one of those unfortunate persons who always blushed when I most wished to look indifferent; and now, to my inexpressible chagrin, with its accustomed perversity, I felt the blush mount to my cheeks, and glow even on my forehead.

I saw that he perceived this most disconcerting indication of a sentiment the very idea of which was so detestable, that, equally enraged with myself and with him, I did not know how to exhibit my contempt and indignation.

Mistaking the cause of my discomposure, Mr. Dudley Ruthyn laughed softly, with an insufferable suavity.

'And there's some'at, lass, I must have in return. Honour thy father, you know; you would not ha' me disobey the Governor? No, you wouldn't—would ye?'

I darted at him a look which I hoped would have quelled his impertinence; but I blushed most provokingly—more violently than ever.

'I'd back them eyes again' the county, I would,' he exclaimed, with a condescending enthusiasm. 'You're awful pretty, you are, Maud. I don't know what came over me t'other night when Governor told me to buss ye; but, dang it, ye shan't deny now, and I'll have a kiss, lass, in spite o' thy blushes.'

He jumped from his elevated seat on the sideboard, and came swaggering toward me, with an odious grin, and his arms extended. I started to my feet, absolutely transported with fury.

'Drat me, if she baint agoing to fight me!' he chuckled humorously.

'Come, Maud, you would not be ill-natured, sure? Arter all, it's only our duty. Governor bid us kiss, didn't he?'

'Don't—*don't*, sir. Stand back, or I'll call the servants.'

And as it was I began to scream for Milly.

'There's how it is wi' all they cattle! You never knows your own mind—ye don't,' he said, surlily. 'You make such a row about a bit o' play. Drop it, will you? There's no one a harming you—is there? *I*'m not, for sartain.'

And, with an angry chuckle, he turned on his heel, and left the room.

I think I was perfectly right to resist, with all the vehemence of which I was capable, this attempt to assume an intimacy which, notwithstanding my uncle's opinion to the contrary, seemed to me like an outrage.

Milly found me alone—not frightened, but very angry. I had quite made up my mind to complain to my uncle, but the Curate was still with him; and, by the time he had gone, I was cooler. My awe of my uncle had returned. I fancied that he would treat the whole affair as a mere playful piece of gallantry. So, with the comfortable conviction that he had had a lesson, and would think twice before repeating his impertinence, I resolved, with Milly's approbation, to leave matters as they were.

Dudley, greatly to my comfort, was huffed with me, and hardly appeared, and was sulky and silent when he did. I lived then in the pleasant anticipation of his departure, which, Milly thought, would be very soon.

My uncle had his Bible and his consolations; but it cannot have been pleasant to this old *roué*, converted though he was—this refined man of fashion—to see his son grow up an outcast, and a Tony Lumpkin;* for whatever he may have thought of his natural gifts, he must have known how mere a boor he was.

I try to recall my then impressions of my uncle's character. Grizzly and chaotic the image rises—silver head—feet of clay. I as yet knew little of him.

I began to perceive that he was what Mary Quince used to call 'dreadful particular'—I suppose a little selfish and impatient. He used to get cases of turtle from Liverpool.* He drank claret and hock for his health, and ate woodcock and other light and salutary dainties for the same reason; and was petulant and vicious about the cooking of these and the flavour and clearness of his coffee.

His conversation was easy, polished, and, with a sentimental glazing, cold; but across this artificial talk, with its French rhymes, racy phrases, and fluent eloquence, like a streak of angry light, would, at intervals, suddenly gleam some dismal thought of religion. I never could quite satisfy myself whether they were affectations or genuine, like intermittent thrills of pain.

The light of his large eyes was very peculiar. I can liken it to nothing but the sheen of intense moonlight on burnished metal. But that cannot express it. It glared white and suddenly—almost fatuous. I thought of Moore's lines whenever I looked on it:—

'Oh, ye dead! oh, ye dead! whom we know by the light you give
From your cold gleaming eyes, though you move like men who live.'*

I never saw in any other eye the least glimmer of the same baleful effulgence. His fits, too—his hoverings between life and death—between intellect and insanity—a dubious, marsh-fire existence, horrible to look on!

I was puzzled even to comprehend his feelings toward his children. Sometimes it seemed to me that he was ready to lay down his soul for them; at others, he looked and spoke almost as if he hated them. He talked as if the image of death was always before him, yet he took a terrible interest in life, while seemingly dozing away the dregs of his days in sight of his coffin.

Oh! Uncle Silas, tremendous figure in the past, burning always in memory in the same awful lights; the fixed white face of scorn and anguish! It seems as if the Woman of Endor* had led me to that chamber and showed me a spectre.

Dudley had not left Bartram-Haugh when a little note reached me from Lady Knollys. It said—

'DEAREST MAUD,—I have written by this post to Silas, beseeching a loan of you and my Cousin Milly. I see no reason your uncle can possibly have for refusing me; and, therefore, I count confidently on seeing you both at Elverston to-morrow, to stay for at least a week. I have hardly a creature to meet you. I have been disappointed in several visitors; but, another time, we shall have a gayer house. Tell Milly—with my love—that I will not forgive her if she fails to accompany you.

'Believe me ever your affectionate cousin,
'MONICA KNOLLYS.'

Milly and I were both afraid that Uncle Silas would refuse his consent, although we could not divine any sound reason for his doing so, and there were many in favour of his improving the opportunity of allowing poor Milly to see some persons of her own sex above the rank of menials.

At about twelve o'clock my uncle sent for us, and, to our great delight, announced his consent, and wished us a very happy excursion.

CHAPTER XLII

ELVERSTON AND ITS PEOPLE

So Milly and I drove through the gabled high street of Feltram next day. We saw my gracious cousin smoking with a man like a groom, at the door of the 'Plume of Feathers'. I drew myself back as we passed, and Milly popped her head out of the window.

'I'm blessed,' said she, laughing, 'if he hadn't his thumb to his nose, and winding up his little finger, the way he does with old Wyat—L'Amour, ye know; and you may be sure he said something funny, for Jim Jolliter was laughin', with his pipe in his hand.'

'I wish I had not seen him, Milly. I feel as if it were an ill omen. He always looks so cross; and I dare say he wished us some ill,' I said.

'No, no, you don't know Dudley; if he were angry he'd say nothing that's funny; no, he's not vexed, only shamming vexed.'

The scenery through which we passed was very pretty. The road brought us through a narrow and wooded glen. Such studies of ivied rocks and twisted roots! A little stream tinkled lonely through the hollow. Poor Milly! In her odd way she made herself companionable. I have sometimes fancied an enjoyment of natural scenery not so much a faculty as an acquirement. It is so exquisite in the instructed, so strangely absent in uneducated humanity. But certainly with Milly it was inborn and hearty; and so she could enter into my raptures, and requite them.

Then over one of those beautiful Derbyshire moors we drove, and so into a wide wooded hollow, where was our first view of Cousin Monica's pretty gabled house, beautified with that indescribable air of shelter and comfort which belongs to an old English residence, with old timber grouped round it, and something in its aspect of the quaint old times and bygone merrymakings, saying sadly, but genially, 'Come in: I bid you welcome. For two hundred years, or more, have I been the home of this beloved old family, whose generations I have seen in the cradle and in the coffin, and whose mirth and sorrows and hospitalities I remember. All their friends, like you, were welcome; and you, like them, will here enjoy the warm illusions that cheat the sad conditions of mortality; and like them you will go your way, and others succeed you, till at last I, too, shall yield to the general law of decay, and disappear.'

By this time poor Milly had grown very nervous, a state which she described in such very odd phraseology as threw me, in spite of myself—for I affected an impressive gravity in lecturing her upon her language—into a hearty fit of laughter.

I must mention, however, that in certain important points Milly was very essentially reformed. Her dress, though not very fashionable, was no longer absurd. And I had drilled her into speaking and laughing quietly; and for the rest I trusted to the indulgence which is always, I think, more honestly and easily obtained from well-bred than from under-bred people.

Cousin Monica was out when we arrived; but we found that she had arranged a double-bedded room for me and Milly, greatly to our content; and good Mary Quince was placed in the dressing-room beside us.

We had only just commenced our toilet when our hostess entered, as usual in high spirits, welcomed and kissed us both again and again. She was, indeed, in extraordinary delight, for she had anticipated some stratagem or evasion to prevent our visit; and in her usual way spoke her mind as frankly about Uncle Silas to poor Milly as she used to do of my dear father to me.

'I did not think he would let you come without a battle; and you know if he chose to be obstinate it would not have been easy to get you out of the enchanted ground, for so it seems to be with that awful old wizard in the midst of it. I mean, Silas, your papa, my dear. Honestly, is not he very like Michael Scott?'*

'I never saw him,' answered poor Milly. 'At least, that I'm aware of,' she added, perceiving us smile. 'But I do think he's a thought like old Michael Dobbs, that sells the ferrets, maybe you mean him?'

'Why, you told me, Maud, that you and Milly were reading Walter Scott's poems. Well, no matter. Michael Scott, my dear, was a dead wizard, with ever so much silvery hair, lying in his grave for ever so many years, with just life enough to scowl when they took his book; and you'll find him in the "Lay of the Last Minstrel",* exactly like your papa, my dear. And my people tell me that your brother Dudley has been seen drinking and smoking about Feltram this week. How long does he remain at home? Not very long, eh? And, Maud, dear, he has not been making love to you? Well, I see; of course he has. And *apropos* of love-making, I hope that impudent creature, Charles Oakley, has not been teazing you with notes or verses.

'Indeed but he has though,' interposed Miss Milly; a good deal to my chagrin, for I saw no particular reason for placing his verses in Cousin Monica's hands. So I confessed the two little copies of verses, with the qualification, however, that I did not know from whom they came.

'Well now, dear Maud, have not I told you fifty times over to have nothing to say to him? I've found out, my dear, he plays, and he is very much in debt. I've made a vow to pay no more for him. I've been such a fool, you have no notion; and I'm speaking, you know, against myself; it would be such a relief if he were to find a wife to support him; and he has been, I'm told, very sweet upon a rich old maid— a button-maker's sister, in Manchester.'

This arrow was well shot.

'But don't be frightened: you are richer as well as younger; and, no doubt, will have your chance first, my dear; and in the meantime, I dare say, those verses, like Falstaff's *billet-doux*,* you know, are doing double duty.'

I laughed, but the button-maker was a secret trouble to me; and I would have given I know not what that Captain Oakley were one of the company, that I might treat him with the refined contempt which his deserts and my dignity demanded.

Cousin Monica busied herself about Milly's toilet, and was a very useful lady's maid, chatting in her own way all the time; and, at last, tapping Milly under the chin with her finger, she said, very complacently—

'I think I have succeeded, Miss Milly; look in the glass. She really is a very pretty creature.'

And Milly blushed, and looked with a shy gratification, which made her still prettier, on the mirror.

Milly indeed was very pretty. She looked much taller now that her dresses were made of the usual length. A little plump she was, beautifully fair, with such azure eyes, and rich hair.

'The more you laugh the better, Milly, for you've got very pretty teeth—very pretty; and if you were my daughter, or if your father would become president of a college of magicians, and give you up to me, I venture to say I would place you very well; and even as it is we must try, my dear.'

So down to the drawing-room we went; and Cousin Monica entered, leading us both by the hands.

By this time the curtains were closed, and the drawing-room dependent on the pleasant glow of the fire, and the slight provisional illumination usual before dinner.

'Here are my two cousins,' began Lady Knollys: 'this is Miss Ruthyn, of Knowl, whom I take the liberty of calling Maud; and this is Miss Millicent Ruthyn, Silas's daughter, you know, whom I venture to call Milly; and they are very pretty, as you will see, when we get a little more light, and they know it very well themselves.'

And as she spoke, a frank-eyed, gentle, prettyish lady, not so tall as I, but with a very kind face, rose up from a book of prints, and, smiling, took our hands.

She was by no means young, as I then counted youth—past thirty, I suppose—and with an air that was very quiet, and friendly, and engaging. She had never been a mere fashionable woman plainly; but she had the ease and polish of the best society, and seemed to take a kindly interest both in Milly and me; and Cousin Monica called her Mary, and sometimes Polly. That was all I knew of her for the present.

So very pleasantly the time passed by till the dressing-bell rang, and we ran away to our room.

'Did I say anything very bad?' asked poor Milly, standing exactly before me, so soon as our door was shut.

'Nothing, Milly; you are doing admirably.'

'And I do look a great fool, don't I?' she demanded.

'You look extremely pretty, Milly; and not a bit like a fool.'

'I watch everything. I think I'll learn it at last; but it comes a little troublesome at first; and they do talk different from what I used—you were quite right there.'

When we returned to the drawing-room, we found the party already assembled, and chatting, evidently with spirit.

The village doctor, whose name I forget, a small man, grey, with shrewd grey eyes, sharp and mulberry nose, whose conflagration extended to his rugged cheeks, and touched his chin and forehead, was conversing, no doubt agreeably, with Mary, as Cousin Monica called her guest.

Over my shoulder Milly whispered—

'Mr. Carysbroke.'

And Milly was quite right: that gentleman chatting with Lady Knollys, his elbow resting on the chimney-piece, was, indeed, our acquaintance of the Windmill Wood. He instantly recognized us, and met us with his pleased and intelligent smile.

'I was just trying to describe to Lady Knollys the charming scenery of the Windmill Wood, among which I was so fortunate as to make your acquaintance, Miss Ruthyn. Even in this beautiful county I know of nothing prettier.'

Then he sketched it, as it were, with a few light but glowing words.

'What a sweet scene!' said Cousin Monica: 'only think of her never bringing me through it. She reserves it, I fancy, for her romantic adventures; and you, I know, are very benevolent, Ilbury, and all that kind of thing; but I am not quite certain that you would have walked along that narrow parapet, over a river, to visit a sick old woman, if you had not happened to see two very pretty demoiselles on the other side.'

'What an ill-natured speech! I must either forfeit my character for disinterested benevolence, so justly admired, or disavow a motive that does such infinite credit to my taste,' exclaimed Mr. Carysbroke. 'I think a charitable person would have said that a philanthropist, in prosecuting his virtuous, but perilous vocation, was unexpectedly *rewarded* by a vision of angels.'

'And with these angels loitered away the time which ought to have been devoted to good Mother Hubbard, in her fit of lumbago, and returned without having set eyes on that afflicted Christian, to amaze his worthy sister with poetic babblings about wood-nymphs and such pagan impieties,' rejoined Lady Knollys.

'Well, be just,' he replied, laughing: 'did not I go next day and see the patient?'

'Yes; next day you went by the same route—in quest of the dryades,* I am afraid, and were rewarded—by the spectacle of Mother Hubbard.'

'Will nobody help a humane man in difficulties?' Mr. Carysbroke appealed.

'I do believe,' said the lady whom as yet I knew only as Mary, 'that every word that Monica says is perfectly true.'

'And if it be so, am I not all the more in need of help? Truth is simply the most dangerous kind of defamation, and I really think I'm most cruelly persecuted.'

At this moment dinner was announced, and a meek and dapper little clergyman, with smooth pink cheeks, and tresses parted down the middle, whom I had not seen before, emerged from shadow.

This little man was assigned to Milly, Mr. Carysbroke to me, and I know not how the remaining ladies divided the doctor between them.

That dinner, the first at Elverston, I remember as a very pleasant repast. Everyone talked—it was impossible that conversation should flag where Lady Knollys was; and Mr. Carysbroke was very agreeable and amusing. At the other side of the table the little pink curate, I was happy to see, was prattling away, with a modest fluency, in an under tone to Milly, who was following my instructions most conscientiously, and speaking in so low a key that I could hardly hear at the opposite side one word she was saying.

That night Cousin Monica paid us a visit, as we sat chatting by the fire in our room; and I told her—

'I have just been telling Milly what an impression she has made. The pretty little clergyman—*il en est épris**—he has evidently quite lost his heart to her. I dare say he'll preach next Sunday on some of King Solomon's wise sayings about the irresistible strength of women.'

'Yes,' said Lady Knollys; 'or maybe on the sensible text, "Whoso findeth a wife findeth a good thing, and obtaineth favour,"* and so forth. At all events, I may say, Milly, whoso findeth a husband such as he findeth a tolerably good thing. He is an exemplary little creature, second son of Sir Harry Biddlepen, with a little independent income of his own, beside his church revenues of ninety pounds a year; and I don't think a more harmless and docile little husband could be found anywhere; and I think, Miss Maud, *you* seemed a good deal interested too.'

I laughed and blushed, I suppose; and Cousin Monica, skipping after her wont to quite another matter, said in her odd frank way—

'And how has Silas been?—not cross, I hope, or very odd. There was a rumour that your brother, Dudley, had gone a-soldiering to India, Milly, or somewhere; but that was all a story, for he has turned up, just as usual. And what does he mean to do with himself? He has got some money now—your poor father's will, Maud. Surely he doesn't mean to go on lounging and smoking away his life among poachers, and prizefighters, and worse people. He ought to go to Australia, like Thomas Swain, who, they say, is making a fortune— a great fortune—and coming home again. That's what your brother Dudley should do, if he has either sense or spirit; but I suppose he won't—too long abandoned to idleness and low company—and he'll not have a shilling left in a year or two. Does he know, I wonder, that his father has served a notice or something on Dr. Bryerly, telling him to pay sixteen hundred pounds of poor Austin's legacy to *him*, and saying that he has paid debts of the young man, and holds his acknowledgments to that amount. He won't have a guinea in a year if he stays here. I'd give fifty pounds he was in Van Diemen's Land*—not that I care for the cub, Milly, any more than you do; but I really don't see any honest business he has in England.'

Milly gaped in a total puzzle as Lady Knollys rattled on.

'You know, Milly, you must not be talking about this when you go home to Bartram, because Silas would prevent your coming to me any more if he thought I spoke so freely: but I can't help it; so you must promise to be more discreet than I. And I am told that all kinds of claims are about to be pressed against him, now that he is thought to have got some money; and he has been cutting down oak and selling the bark, Doctor Bryerly has been told, in that Windmill Wood; and he has kilns there for burning charcoal, and got a man from Lancashire who understands it. Hawk, or something like that.'

'Ay, Hawkes—Dickon Hawkes; that's Pegtop, you know, Maud,' said Milly.

'Well, I dare say; but a man of very bad character, Dr. Bryerly says; and he has written to Mr. Danvers about it—for that is what they call waste, cutting down and selling the timber, and the oak-bark, and burning the willows, and other trees that are turned into charcoal. It is all *waste*, and Dr. Bryerly is about to put a stop to it.'

'Has he got your carriage for you, Maud, and your horses?' asked Cousin Monica, suddenly.

'They have not come yet, but in a few weeks, Dudley says, positively'—

Cousin Monica laughed a little and shook her head.

'Yes, Maud, the carriage and horses will always be coming in a few weeks, till the time is over; and meanwhile the old travelling chariot and post horses will do very well,' and she laughed a little again.

'That's why the stile's pulled away at the paling, I suppose; and Beauty—Meg Hawkes, that is—is but there to stop us going through; for I often spied the smoke beyond the windmill,' observed Milly.

Cousin Monica listened with interest and nodded silently.

I was very much shocked. It seemed to me quite incredible. I think Lady Knollys read my amazement, and my exalted estimate of the heinousness of the procedure in my face, for she said—

'You know we can't quite condemn Silas till we have heard what he has to say. He may have done it in ignorance; or, it is just possible, he may have the right.'

'Quite true. He may have the right to cut down trees at Bartram-Haugh. At all events, I am sure he thinks he has,' I echoed.

The fact was that I would not avow to myself a suspicion of Uncle Silas. Any falsehood there opened an abyss beneath my feet into which I dared not look.

'And now, dear girls, good-night. You must be tired. We breakfast at a quarter past nine—not too early for you, I know.'

And so saying she kissed us, smiling, and was gone.

I was so unpleasantly occupied, for some time after her departure, with the knaveries said to be practised among the dense cover of the Windmill Wood, that I did not immediately recollect that we had omitted to ask her any particulars about her guests.

'Who can Mary be?' said Milly.

'Cousin Monica says she's engaged to be married, and I think I heard the Doctor call her *Lady* Mary, and I intended asking her ever so much about her; but what she told us about cutting down the trees, and all that, quite put it out of my head. We shall have time enough to-morrow, however, to ask questions. I like her very much, I know.'

'And I think,' said Milly, 'it is to Mr. Carysbroke she's to be married.'

'Do you?' said I, remembering that he had sat beside her for more than a quarter of an hour after tea in very close and low-toned conversation; 'and have you any particular reason?' I asked.

'Well, I heard her once or twice call him "dear", and she called him his Christian name, just like Lady Knollys did—Ilbury, I think—and I saw him gi' her a sly kiss as she was going up stairs.'

I laughed.

'Well, Milly,' I said, 'I remarked something myself, I thought, like confidential relations; but if you really saw them kiss on the staircase, the question is pretty well settled.'

'Ay, lass.'

'You're not to say *lass*.'

'Well, *Maud, then*. I did see them with the corner of my eye, and my back turned, when they did not think I could spy anything, as plain as I see you now.'

I laughed again; but I felt an odd pang—something of mortification—something of regret; but I smiled very gaily, as I stood before
the glass, un-making my toilet preparatory to bed.

'Maud—Maud—fickle Maud!—What, Captain Oakley already
superseded! and Mr. Carysbroke—oh! humiliation—engaged.' So
I smiled on, very much vexed; and being afraid lest I had listened with
too apparent an interest to this impostor, I sang a verse of a gay little
chanson, and tried to think of Captain Oakley, who somehow had
become rather silly.

MILLY and I, thanks to our early Bartram hours, were first down next morning; and so soon as Cousin Monica appeared we attacked her.

'So Lady Mary is the *fiancée* of Mr. Carysbroke,' said I, very cleverly; 'and I think it was very wicked of you to try and involve me in a flirtation with him yesterday.'

'And who told you that, pray?' asked Lady Knollys, with a pleasant little laugh.

'Milly and I discovered it, simple as we stand here,' I answered.

'But you did not flirt with Mr. Carysbroke, Maud, did you?' she asked.

'No, certainly not; but that was not your doing, wicked woman, but my discretion. And now that we know your secret, you must tell us all about her, and all about him; and in the first place, what is her name—Lady Mary what?' I demanded.

'Who would have thought you so cunning? Two country misses—two little nuns from the cloisters of Bartram! Well, I suppose I must answer. It is vain trying to hide anything from you; but how on earth did you find it out?'

'We'll tell you that presently, but you shall first tell us who she is,' I persisted.

'Well, that I will, of course, without compulsion. She is Lady Mary Carysbroke,' said Lady Knollys.

'A relation of Mr. Carysbroke's,' I asserted.

'Yes, a relation; but who told you he was Mr. Carysbroke?' asked Cousin Monica.

'Milly told me, when we saw him in the Windmill Wood.'

'And who told you, Milly?'

'It was L'Amour,' answered Milly, with her blue eyes very wide open.

'What does the child mean? L'Amour! You don't mean *love*?' exclaimed Lady Knollys, puzzled in her turn.

'I mean old Wyat; *she* told me, and the Governor.'

'You're *not* to say that,' I interposed.

'You mean your father?' suggested Lady Knollys.

'Well, yes; father told her, and so I knew him.'

'What could he mean?' exclaimed Lady Knollys, laughing, as it were in soliloquy; 'and I did not mention his name. I recollect now. He recognized you, and you him, when you came into the room yesterday; and now you must tell me how you discovered that he and Lady Mary were to be married?'

So Milly restated her evidence, and Lady Knollys laughed unaccountably heartily; and she said—

'They *will* be *so* confounded! but they deserve it; and, remember, *I* did not say so.'

'Oh! we acquit you.'

'All I say is, such a deceitful, dangerous pair of girls—all things considered—I never heard of before,' exclaimed Lady Knollys. 'There's no such thing as conspiring in your presence.'

'Good morning. I hope you slept well.' She was addressing the lady and gentleman who were just entering the room from the conservatory. 'You'll hardly sleep so well tonight, when you have learned what eyes are upon you. Here are two very pretty detectives who have found out your secret, and entirely by your imprudence and their own cleverness have discovered that you are a pair of betrothed lovers, about to ratify your vows at the hymeneal altar. I assure you I did not tell of you; you betrayed yourselves. If you will talk in that confidential way on sofas, and call one another stealthily by your Christian names, and actually kiss at the foot of the stairs, while a clever detective is scaling them, apparently with her back toward you, you must only take the consequences, and be known prematurely as the hero and heroine of the forthcoming paragraph in the *Morning Post*.'

Milly and I were horribly confounded, but Cousin Monica was resolved to place us all upon the least formal terms possible, and I believe she had set about it in the right way.

'And now, girls, I am going to make a counter-discovery, which, I fear, a little conflicts with yours. This Mr. Carysbroke is Lord Ilbury, brother of this Lady Mary; and it is all my fault for not having done my honours better; but you see what clever match-making little creatures they are.'

'You can't think how flattered I am at being made the subject of a theory, even a mistaken one, by Miss Ruthyn.'

And so, after our modest fit was over, Milly and I were very merry, like the rest, and we all grew a great deal more intimate that morning.

I think altogether those were the pleasantest and happiest days of my life: gay, intelligent, and kindly society at home; charming excursions—sometimes riding—sometimes by carriage—to distant points of beauty in the county. Evenings varied with music, reading, and spirited conversation. Now and then a visitor for a day or two, and constantly some neighbour from the town, or its dependencies, dropt in. Of these I but remember tall old Miss Wintletop, most entertaining of rustic old maids, with her nice lace and thick satin, and her small, kindly round face—pretty, I dare say, in other days, and now frosty, but kindly—who told us such delightful old stories of the county in her father's and grandfather's time; who knew the lineage of every family in it, and could recount all its duels and elopements; give us illustrative snatches from old election squibs, and lines from epitaphs, and tell exactly where all the old-world highway robberies had been committed: how it fared with the chief delinquents after the assizes; and, above all, where, and of what sort, the goblins and elves of the county had made themselves seen, from the phantom post-boy, who every third night crossed Windale moor, by the old coach-road, to the fat old ghost, in mulberry velvet, who showed his great face, crutch, and ruffles, by moonlight, at the bow window of the old court-house that was taken down in 1803.

You cannot imagine what agreeable evenings we passed in this society, or how rapidly my good Cousin Milly improved in it. I remember well the intense suspense in which she and I awaited the answer from Bartram Haugh to kind Cousin Monica's application for an extension of our leave of absence.

It came, and with it a note from Uncle Silas, which was curious, and, therefore, is printed here—

'MY DEAR LADY KNOLLYS,—To your kind letter I say yes (that is, for another week, not a fortnight), with all my heart. I am glad to hear that my starlings chatter so pleasantly; at all events the refrain is not that of Sterne's.* They can get out; and do get out; and shall get out as much as they please. I am no gaoler, and shut up nobody but myself. I have always thought that young people have too little liberty. My principle has been to make little free men and women of them from the first. In morals, altogether—in intellect, more than we allow—*self*-education is that which abides; and *it* only begins where constraint ends. Such is my theory. My practice is consistent. Let them remain for a week longer, as you say. The horses shall be at Elverston on Tuesday, the 7th. I shall be more than usually sad and solitary till their return; so pray, I selfishly entreat, do not extend their absence. You will smile, remembering how little my health will allow me to see of them, even when at home; but as Chaulieu so prettily says*—I stupidly forget the words, but the sentiment is this—"although concealed by a sylvan wall of leaves, impenetrable—(he is pursuing his favourite nymphs through the alleys and intricacies of a rustic labyrinth)—yet, your songs, your prattle, and your laughter, faint and far away, inspire my fancy; and, through my ears, I see your unseen smiles, your blushes, your floating tresses, and your ivory feet; and so, though sad, am happy; though alone, in company;"—and such is my case.

'One only request, and I have done. Pray remind them of a promise made to me. The Book of Life—the fountain of life—it must be drunk of, night and morning, or their spiritual life expires.

'And now, Heaven bless and keep you, my dear cousin; and with all assurances of affection to my beloved niece and my child, believe me ever yours affectionately,

'Silas Ruthyn.'

Said Cousin Monica, with a waggish smile—

'And so, girls, you have Chaulieu and the evangelists; the French rhymester in his alley, and Silas in the valley of the shadow of death; perfect liberty, and a peremptory order to return in a week;—all illustrating one another. Poor Silas! old as he is, I don't think his religion fits him.'

I really rather liked his letter. I was struggling hard to think well of him, and Cousin Monica knew it; and I really think if I had not been by, she would often have been less severe on him.

As we were all sitting pleasantly about the breakfast table a day or two after, the sun shining on the pleasant wintry landscape, Cousin Monica suddenly exclaimed—

'I quite forgot to tell you that Charles Oakley has written to say he is coming on Wednesday. I really don't want him. Poor Charlie! I wonder how they manage those doctors' certificates. I know nothing ails him, and he'd be much better with his regiment.'

Wednesday!—how odd. Exactly the day after my departure. I tried to look perfectly unconcerned. Lady Knollys had addressed herself more to Lady Mary and Milly than to me, and nobody in particular was looking at me. Notwithstanding, with my usual perversity, I felt myself blushing with a brilliancy that may have been very becoming, but which was so intolerably provoking that I would have risen and left the room but that matters would have been so infinitely worse. I could have boxed my odious ears. I could almost have jumped from the window.

I felt that Lord Ilbury saw it. I saw Lady Mary's eyes for a moment resting gravely on my tell-tale—my lying cheeks—for I really had begun to think much less celestially of Captain Oakley. I was angry with Cousin Monica, who, knowing my blushing infirmity, had mentioned her nephew so suddenly while I was strapped by etiquette in my chair, with my face to the window, and two pair of most disconcerting eyes, at least, opposite. I was angry with myself—generally angry—refused more tea rather dryly, and was laconic to Lord Ilbury, all which, of course, was very cross and foolish; and afterwards, from my bed-room window, I saw Cousin Monica and Lady Mary among the flowers, under the drawing-room window, talking, as I instinctively knew, of that little incident. I was standing at the glass.

'My odious, stupid, *perjured* face,' I whispered, furiously, at the same time stamping on the floor, and giving myself quite a smart slap on the cheek. 'I *can't* go down—I'm ready to cry—I've a mind to return to Bartram to-day; I am *always* blushing; and I wish that impudent Captain Oakley was at the bottom of the sea.'

I was, perhaps, thinking more of Lord Ilbury than I was aware; and I am sure if Captain Oakley had arrived that day I should have treated him with most unjustifiable rudeness.

Notwithstanding this unfortunate blush, the remainder of our visit passed very happily for me. No one who has not experienced it can have an idea how intimate a small party, such as ours, will grow in a short time in a country house.

Of course, a young lady of a well-regulated mind cannot possibly care a pin about any one of the opposite sex until she is well assured that he is beginning, at least, to like her better than all the world beside; but I could not deny to myself that I was rather anxious to know more about Lord Ilbury than I actually did know.

There was a 'Peerage', in its bright scarlet and gold uniform, corpulent and tempting, upon the little marble table in the drawing-room. I had many opportunities of consulting it, but I never could find courage to do so.

For an inexperienced person it would have been a matter of several minutes, and during those minutes what awful risk of surprise and detection. One day, all being quiet, I did venture, and actually, with a beating heart, got so far as to find out the letters 'Il', when I heard a step outside the door, which opened a little bit, and I heard Lady Knollys, luckily arrested at the entrance, talk some sentences outside, her hand still upon the door-handle. I shut the book, as Mrs. Bluebeard might the door of the chamber of horrors at sound of her husband's step, and skipped to a remote part of the room, where Cousin Knollys found me, in a mysterious state of agitation.

On any other subject I would have questioned Cousin Monica unhesitatingly; upon this, somehow, I was dumb. I distrusted myself, and dreaded my odious habit of blushing, and knew that I should look so horribly guilty, and become so agitated and odd, that she would have reasonably concluded that I had quite lost my heart to him.

After the lesson I had received, and my narrow escape of detection in the very act, you may be sure I never trusted myself in the vicinity of that fat and cruel 'Peerage', which possessed the secret, but would not disclose without compromising me.

In this state of tantalizing darkness and conjecture I should have departed, had not Cousin Monica quite spontaneously relieved me.

The night before our departure she sat with us in our room, chatting a little farewell gossip.

'And what do you think of Ilbury?' she asked.

'I think him clever and accomplished, and amusing; but he sometimes appears to me very melancholy—that is, for a few minutes together—and then, I fancy, with an effort, re-engages in our conversation.'

'Yes, poor Ilbury! He lost his brother only about five months since, and is only beginning to recover his spirits a little. They were very much attached, and people thought that he would have succeeded to the title, had he lived, because Ilbury is *difficile*—or a philosopher—or a *Saint Kevin*;* and, in fact, has begun to be treated as a premature old bachelor.'

'What a charming person his sister, Lady Mary, is. She has made me promise to write to her,' I said, I suppose—such hypocrites are we—to prove to Cousin Knollys that I did not care particularly to hear anything more about him.

'Yes, and so devoted to him. He came down here, and took The Grange, for change of scene, and solitude—of all things the worst for a man in grief—a morbid whim, as he is beginning to find out; for he is very glad to stay here, and confesses that he is much better since he came. His letters are still addressed to him as Mr. Carysbroke; for he fancied if his rank were known that the county people would have been calling upon him, and so he would have found himself soon involved in a tiresome round of dinners, and must have gone somewhere else. You saw him, Milly, at Bartram, before Maud came?'

Yes, she had, when he called there to see her father.

'He thought, as he had accepted the trusteeship, that he could hardly, residing so near, omit to visit Silas. He was very much struck and interested by him, and he has a better opinion of him—you are not angry, Milly—than some ill-natured people I could name; and he says that the cutting down of the trees will turn out to have been a mere slip. But these slips don't occur with clever men in other things; and some persons have a way of always making them in their own favour. And, to talk of other things, I suspect that you and Milly will probably see Ilbury at Bartram; for I think he likes you very much.'

You; did she mean *both*, or only me?

So our pleasant visit was over. Milly's good little curate had been much thrown in her way by our deep and dangerous Cousin Monica. He was most laudably steady; and his flirtation advanced upon the field of theology, where, happily, Milly's little reading had been concentrated. A mild and earnest interest in poor, pretty Milly's orthodoxy was the leading feature of his case; and I was highly amused at her references to me, when we had retired at night, upon the points which she had disputed with him, and her anxious reports of their low-toned conferences, carried on upon a sequestered ottoman, where he patted and stroked his crossed leg, as he smiled tenderly and shook his head at her questionable doctrine. Milly's reverence for her instructor and his admiration, grew daily; and he was known among us as Milly's confessor.

He took luncheon with us on the day of our departure, and with an adroit privacy, which in a layman would have been sly, presented her, in right of his holy calling, with a little book, the binding of which was mediæval and costly, and whose letter-press dealt in a way which he commended, with some points on which she was not satisfactory; and she found on the fly-leaf this little inscription:—'Presented to Miss Millicent Ruthyn by an earnest well-wisher, 1st December, 1844.' A text, very neatly penned, followed this; and the 'presentation' was made unctuously indeed, but with a blush, as well as the accustomed smile, and with eyes that were lowered.

The early crimson sun of December had gone down behind the hills before we took our seats in the carriage.

Lord Ilbury leaned with his elbow on the carriage window, looking in, and he said to me—

'I really don't know what we shall do, Miss Ruthyn; we shall all feel so lonely. For myself, I think I shall run away to Grange.'

This appeared to me as nearly perfect eloquence as human lips could utter.

His hand still rested on the window, and the Rev. Sprigge Biddle-pen was standing with a saddened smirk on the door steps, when the whip smacked, the horses scrambled into motion, and away we rolled down the avenue, leaving behind us the pleasantest house and hostess in the world, and trotting fleetly into darkness toward Bartram-Haugh.

We were both rather silent. Milly had her book in her lap, and I saw her every now and then try to read her 'earnest well-wisher's' little inscription, but there was not light to read by.

When we reached the great gate of Bartram-Haugh it was dark. Old Crowl, who kept the gate, I heard enjoining the postilion to make no avoidable noise at the hall-door, for the odd but startling reason that he believed my uncle 'would be dead by this time.'

Very much shocked and frightened we stopped the carriage, and questioned the tremulous old porter.

Uncle Silas, it seemed, had been 'silly-ish' all yesterday, and 'could not be woke this morning,' and 'the doctor had been here twice, being now in the house.'

'Is he better?' I asked tremblingly.

'Not as I'm aweer on, Miss; he lay at God's mercy two hours agone; 'appen he's in heaven be this time.'

'Drive on—drive fast,' I said to the driver. 'Don't be frightened, Milly; please heaven we shall find all going well.'

After some delay, during which my heart sank, and I quite gave up Uncle Silas, the aged little servant-man opened the door, and trotted shakily down the steps to the carriage side.

Uncle Silas had been at death's door for hours; the question of life had trembled in the scale; but now the Doctor said 'he might do.'

'Where was the Doctor?'

'In master's room; he blooded him three hours agone.'

I don't think that Milly was so much frightened as I. My heart beat, and I was trembling so that I could hardly get upstairs.

CHAPTER XLIV

A FRIEND ARISES

AT the top of the great staircase I was glad to see the friendly face of Mary Quince, who stood, candle in hand, greeting us with many little courtesies, and a very haggard and pallid smile.

'Very welcome Miss, hoping you are very well.'

'All well, and you are well, Mary? and oh! tell us quickly how is Uncle Silas.'

'We thought he was gone, Miss, this morning, but doing fairly now; Doctor says in a trance like. I was helping old Wyat most of the day, and was there when Doctor blooded him, an' he spoke at last; but he must be awful weak, he took a deal o' blood from his arm, Miss; I held the basin.'

'And he's better—decidedly better?' I asked.

'Well, he's better, Doctor says; he talked some, and Doctor says if he goes off asleep again, and begins a-snoring like he did before, we're to loose the bandage, and let him bleed till he comes to his self again; which, it seems to me and Wyat, is the same thing a'most as saying he's to be killed off-hand, for I don't believe he has a drop to spare, as you'll say likewise, Miss, if you'll please look in the basin.'

This was not an invitation with which I cared to comply. I thought I was going to faint. I sat on the stairs and sipped a little water, and Quince sprinkled a little in my face, and my strength returned.

Milly must have felt her father's danger more than I, for she was affectionate, and loved him from habit and relation, although he was not kind to her. But I was more nervous and more impetuous, and my feelings both stimulated and overpowered me more easily. The moment I was able to stand I said—thinking of nothing but the one idea—

'We must see him—*come*, Milly.'

I entered his sitting room; a common 'dip' candle hanging like the tower of Pisa all to one side, with a dim, long wick, in a greasy candle-stick profaned the table of the fastidious invalid. The light was little better than darkness, and I crossed the room swiftly, still transfixed by the one idea of seeing my uncle.

His bed-room door beside the fireplace stood partly open, and I looked in.

Old Wyat, a white, high-cauled ghost, was pottering in her slippers in the shadow at the far side of the bed. The Doctor, a stout little bald man, with a paunch and a big bunch of seals, stood with his back to the fireplace, which corresponded with that in the next room, eyeing his patient through the curtains of the bed with a listless sort of importance.

The head of the large four-poster rested against the opposite wall. Its foot was presented toward the fireplace; but the curtains at the side, which alone I could see from my position, were closed.

The little Doctor knew me, and thinking me, I suppose, a person of consequence, removed his hands from behind him, suffering the skirts of his coat to fall forward, and with great celerity and gravity made me a low but important bow; then choosing more particularly to make my acquaintance he further advanced, and with another reverence he introduced himself as Doctor Jolks, in a murmured diapason.* He bowed me back again into my uncle's study, and the light of old Wyat's dreadful candle.

Doctor Jolks was suave and pompous. I longed for a fussy practitioner who would have got over the ground in half the time.

'Coma, madam, coma. Miss Ruthyn, your uncle, I may tell you has been in a very critical state; highly so. Coma of the most obstinate type. He would have sunk—he must have gone, in fact, had I not resorted to a very extreme remedy, and bled him freely, which happily told precisely as we could have wished. A wonderful constitution— a marvellous constitution—prodigious nervous fibre; the greatest pity in the world he won't give himself fair play. His habits, you know, are quite, I may say, destructive. We do our best—we do all we can, but if the patient won't co-operate it can't possibly end satisfactorily.'

And Jolks accompanied this with an awful shrug. 'Is there *any-thing*? Do you think change of air? What an awful complaint it is,' I exclaimed.

He smiled, mysteriously looking down, and shook his head undertaker-like.

'Why, we can hardly call it a *complaint*, Miss Ruthyn. I look upon it he has been poisoned—he has had, you understand me,' he pursued, observing my startled look, 'an overdose of opium; you know he takes opium habitually; he takes it in laudanum, he takes it in water, and most dangerous of all, he takes it solid, in lozenges. I've known people take it moderately. I've known people take it to excess, *but* they all were particular as to *measure*, and *that* is exactly the point I've tried to impress upon him. The habit, of course, you understand is formed, there's no uprooting that; but he won't *measure*—he goes by the eye and by sensation, which I need not tell you, Miss Ruthyn, is going by *chance*; and opium, as no doubt you are aware, is strictly a poison; a poison, no doubt, which habit will enable you to partake of, I may say, in considerable quantities, without fatal consequences, but still a poison; and to exhibit a poison *so*, is, I need scarcely tell you, to trifle with death. He has been so threatened, and for a time he changes his haphazard mode of dealing with it, and then returns; he may escape, of course, that is possible, but he may any day overdo the thing. I don't think the present crisis will result seriously. I am very glad, independently of the honour of making your acquaintance, Miss Ruthyn, that you and your cousin have returned; for, however zealous, I fear the servants are deficient in intelligence; and as in the event of a recurrence of the symptoms—which, however, is not probable—I would beg to inform you of their nature, and how exactly best to deal with them.'

So upon these points he delivered us a pompous little lecture, and begged that either Milly or I would remain in the room with the patient until his return at two or three o'clock in the morning; a reappearance of the coma 'might be very bad indeed.'

Of course Milly and I did as we were directed. We sat by the fire, scarcely daring to whisper. Uncle Silas, about whom a new and dreadful suspicion began to haunt me, lay still and motionless as if he were actually dead.

'Had he attempted to poison himself?'

If he believed his position to be as desperate as Lady Knollys had described it, was this, after all, improbable? There were strange wild theories, I had been told, mixed up in his religion.

Sometimes, at an hour's interval, a sign of life would come—a moan from that tall sheeted figure in the bed—a moan and a pattering of the lips. Was it prayer—*what* was it? who could guess what thoughts were passing behind that white-fillited forehead?

I had peeped at him: a white cloth steeped in vinegar and water was folded round his head; his great eyes were closed, so were his marble lips; his figure straight, thin, and long, dressed in a white dressing gown, looked like a corpse 'laid out' in the bed; his gaunt bandaged arm lay outside the sheet that covered his body.

With this awful image of death we kept our vigil, until poor Milly grew so sleepy that old Wyat proposed that she should take her place and watch with me.

Little as I liked the crone with the high-cauled cap, she would, at all events, keep awake, which Milly could not. And so at one o'clock this new arrangement began.

'Mr. Dudley Ruthyn is not at home?' I whispered to old Wyat.

'He went away wi' himself yesternight, to Cloperton, Miss, to see the wrestling; it was to come off this morning.'

'Was he sent for?'

'Not he.'

'And why not?'

'He would na' leave the sport for this, I'm thinking,' and the old woman grinned uglily.

'When is he to return?'

'When he wants money.'

So we grew silent, and again I thought of suicide, and of the unhappy old man, who just then whispered a sentence or two to himself with a sigh.

For the next hour he had been quite silent, and old Wyat informed me that she must go down for candles. Ours were already burnt down to the sockets.

'There's a candle in the next room,' I suggested, hating the idea of being left alone with the patient.

'Hoot! Miss. I *dare* na' set a candle but wax in his presence,' whispered the old woman, scornfully.

'I think if we were to stir the fire, and put on a little more coal, we should have a great deal of light.'

'He'll ha' the candles,' said Dame Wyat, doggedly; and she tottered from the chamber, muttering to herself; and I heard her take her candle from the next room and depart, shutting the outer door after her.

Here was I then alone, but for this unearthly companion, whom I feared inexpressibly, at two o'clock, in the vast old house of Bartram.

I stirred the fire. It was low, and would not blaze. I stood up, and with my hand on the mantelpiece, endeavoured to think of cheerful things. But it was a struggle against wind and tide—vain; and so I drifted away into haunted regions.

Uncle Silas was perfectly still. I would not suffer myself to think of the number of dark rooms and passages which now separated me from the other living tenants of the house. I awaited with a false composure the return of old Wyat.

Over the mantelpiece was a looking-glass. At another time this might have helped to entertain my solitary moments, but now I did not like to venture a peep. A small thick Bible lay on the chimney-piece, and leaning its back against the mirror, I began to read in it with a mind as attentively directed as I could. While so engaged in turning over the leaves, I lighted upon two or three odd-looking papers, which had been folded into it. One was a broad printed thing, with names and dates written into blank spaces, and was about the size of a quarter of a yard of very broad ribbon. The others were mere scraps, with 'Dudley Ruthyn' penned in my cousin's vulgar round-hand at the foot. While I folded and replaced these I really don't know what caused me to fancy that something was moving behind me, as I stood with my back toward the bed. I do not recollect any sound whatever; but instinctively I glanced into the mirror, and my eyes were instantly fixed by what I saw.

The figure of Uncle Silas rose up, and dressed in a long white morning gown, slid over the end of the bed, and with two or three swift noiseless steps, stood behind me, with a death-like scowl and a simper. Preternaturally tall and thin, he stood for a moment almost touching me, with the white bandage pinned across his forehead, his bandaged arm stiffly by his side, and diving over my shoulder, with his long thin hand he snatched the Bible, and whispered over my head—'The serpent beguiled her and she did eat;'* and after a momentary pause, he glided to the farthest window, and appeared to look out upon the midnight prospect.

It was cold, but he did not seem to feel it. With the same inflexible scowl and smile, he continued to look out for several minutes, and then with a great sigh, he sat down on the side of his bed, his face immovably turned toward me, with the same painful look.

It seemed to me an hour before old Wyat came back; and never was lover made happier at sight of his mistress than I to behold that withered crone.

You may be sure I did not prolong my watch. There was now plainly no risk of my uncle's relapsing into lethargy. I had a long hysterical fit of weeping when I got into my room, with honest Mary Quince by my side.

Whenever I closed my eyes, the face of Uncle Silas was before me, as I had seen it reflected in the glass. The sorceries of Bartram were enveloping me once more.

Next morning the Doctor said he was quite out of danger, but very weak. Milly and I saw him; and again in our afternoon walk we met the Doctor marching under the trees in the direction of the Windmill Wood.

'Going down to see that poor girl there?' he said, when he had made his salutation, prodding with his levelled stick in the direction. 'Hawke, or Hawkes, I think.'

'Beauty's sick, Maud,' exclaimed Milly.

'*Hawkes.* She's upon my dispensary list. Yes,' said the Doctor, looking into his little notebook—'Hawkes.'

'And what is her complaint?'

'Rheumatic fever.'

'Not infectious?'

'Not the least—no more, as we say, Miss Ruthyn, than a broken leg,' and he laughed obligingly.

So soon as the Doctor had departed, Milly and I agreed to follow to Hawkes' cottage and inquire more particularly how she was. To say truth, I am afraid it was rather for the sake of giving our walk a purpose and a point of termination, than for any very charitable interest we might have felt in the patient.

Over the inequalities of the upland slope, clumped with trees, we reached the gabled cottage, with its neglected little farm-yard. A rheumatic old woman was the only attendant; and, having turned her ear in an attitude of attention, which induced us in gradually exalted keys to inquire how Meg was, she informed us in very loud tones that she had long lost her hearing, and was perfectly deaf. And added considerately—

'When the man comes in 'appen he'll tell ye what ye want.'

Through the door of a small room at the further end of that in which we were, we could see a portion of the narrow apartment of the patient, and hear her moans and the Doctor's voice.

'We'll see him, Milly, when he comes out. Let us wait here.'

So we stood upon the door-stone awaiting him. The sounds of suffering had moved my compassion and interested us for the sick girl.

'Blest if here isn't Pegtop,' said Milly.

And the weather-stained red coat, the swarthy forbidding face and sooty locks of old Hawkes loomed in sight, as he stumped, steadying himself with his stick, over the uneven pavement of the yard. He touched his hat gruffly to me; but did not seem half to like our being where we were, for he looked surlily, and scratched his head under his wide-awake.

'Your daughter is very ill, I'm afraid,' said I.

'Ay—she'll be costin' me a handful, like her mother did,' said Pegtop.

'I hope her room is comfortable, poor thing.'

'Ay, that's it; she be comfortable enough, I warrant—more nor I. It be all Meg, and nout o' Dickon.'

'When did her illness commence?' I asked.

'Day the mare wor shod—*Saturday*. I talked a bit wi' the workus folk, but they won't gi'e nout—dang 'em—an' how be *I* to do't? It be all'ays hard bread wi' Silas, an' a deal harder now she' ta'en them pains. I won't stan' it much longer. Gammon! If she keeps on that way I'll just cut. See how the workus fellahs 'ill like *that*!'

'The Doctor gives his services for nothing,' I said.

'An' *does* nothin', bless him! ha, ha. No more nor that old deaf gammon there that costs me three tizzies a week, and haint worth a h'porth—no more nor Meg there, that's making all she can o' them pains. They be all a foolin' o' me, an' thinks I don't know't. Hey? *we*'ll see.'

All this time he was cutting a bit of tobacco into shreds on the window-stone.

'A workin' man be same as a hoss; if he baint cared, he can't work—'tisn't in him:' and with these words, having by this time stuffed his pipe with tobacco, he poked the deaf lady, who was pattering about with her back toward him, rather viciously with the point of his stick, and signed for a light.

'It bain't in him, you can't git it out o' 'im, no more nor ye'll draw smoke out o' this,' and he raised his pipe an inch or two, with his thumb on the bowl, 'without backy and fire. 'Tisn't in it.'

'Maybe I can be of some use?' I said, thinking.

'Maybe,' he rejoined.

By this time he received from the old deaf abagail* a flaming roll of brown paper, and, touching his hat to me, he withdrew, lighting his pipe and sending up little white puffs, like the salute of a departing ship.

So he did not care to hear how his daughter was, and had only come here to light his pipe!

Just then the Doctor emerged.

'We have been waiting to hear how your poor patient is to-day?' I said.

'Very ill, indeed, and utterly neglected, I fear. If she were equal to it—but she's not—I think she ought to be removed to the hospital immediately.'

'That poor old woman is quite deaf, and the man is so surly and selfish! Could you recommend a nurse who would stay here till she's better? I will pay her with pleasure, and anything you think might be good for the poor girl.'

So this was settled on the spot. Doctor Jolks was kind, like most men of his calling, and undertook to send the nurse from Feltram with a few comforts for the patient; and he called Dickon to the yard-gate, and I suppose told him of the arrangement; and Milly and I went to the poor girl's door and asked, 'May we come in?'

There was no answer. So with the conventional construction of silence, we entered. Her looks showed how ill she was. We adjusted her bed-clothes, and darkened the room, and did what we could for her—noting, beside, what her comfort chiefly required. She did not answer any questions. She did not thank us. I should almost have fancied that she had not perceived our presence, had I not observed her dark, sunken eyes once or twice turned up towards my face, with a dismal look of wonder and inquiry.

The girl was very ill, and we went every day to see her. Sometimes she would answer our questions—sometimes not. Thoughtful, obser-vant, surly, she seemed; and as people like to be thanked, I sometimes wonder that we continued to throw our bread upon these ungrateful waters. Milly was specially impatient under this treatment, and pro-tested against it, and finally refused to accompany me into poor Beauty's bed-room.

'I think, my good Meg,' said I one day, as I stood by her bed—she was now recovering with the sure reascent of youth—'that you ought to thank Miss Milly.'

'I'll *not* thank her,' said Beauty, doggedly.

'Very well, Meg, I only thought I'd ask you, for I think you ought.'

As I spoke, she very gently took just the tip of my finger, which hung close to her coverlet, in her fingers, and drew it beneath, and before I was aware, burying her head in the clothes, she suddenly clasped my hand in both hers to her lips, and kissed it passionately, again and again, sobbing. I felt her tears.

I tried to withdraw my hand, but she held it with an angry pull, continuing to weep and kiss it.

'Do you wish to say anything, my poor Meg?' I asked.

'Nout, Miss,' she sobbed gently; and she continued to kiss my hand and weep. But suddenly she said, 'I won't thank Milly, for it's a' *you*; it baint her, she hadn't the thought—no, no, it's a' you, Miss. I cried hearty in the dark last night, thinkin' o' the apples, and the way I knocked them awa' wi' a pur o' my foot, the day father rapped me ower the head wi' his stick; it was kind o' you and very bad o' me. I wish you'd beat me, Miss; ye're better to me than father or mother—better to me than a'; an' I wish I could die for you, Miss, for I'm not fit to look at you.'

I was surprised. I began to cry. I could have hugged poor Meg.

I did not know her history. I have never learned it since. She used to talk with the most utter self-abasement before me. It was no religious feeling—it was a kind of expression of her love and worship of me—all the more strange that she was naturally very proud. There was nothing she would not have borne from me except the slightest suspicion of her entire devotion, or that she could in the most trifling way wrong or deceive me.

I am not young now. I have had my sorrows, and with them all that wealth, virtually unlimited, can command; and through the retrospect a few bright and pure lights quiver along my life's dark stream—dark, but for them; and these are shed, not by the splendour of a splendid fortune, but by two or three of the simplest and kindest remembrances, such as the poorest and homeliest life may count up, and beside which, in the quiet hours of memory, all artificial triumphs pale, and disappear, for they are never quenched by time or distance, being founded on the affections, and so far, heavenly.

END OF VOL. II.

CHAPTER XLV

A CHAPTER-FULL OF LOVERS

WE had about this time a pleasant and quite unexpected visit from Lord Ilbury. He had come to pay his respects, understanding that my Uncle Silas was sufficiently recovered to see visitors. 'And I think I'll run up-stairs first, and see him, if he admits me, and then I have ever so long a message from my sister Mary, for you and Miss Millicent; but I had better dispose of my business first—don't you think so?—and I shall return in a few minutes.'

And as he spoke our tremulous old butler returned to say that Uncle Silas would be happy to see him. So he departed; and you can't think how pleasant our homely sitting-room looked with his coat and stick in it—guarantees of his return.

'Do you think, Milly, he is going to speak about the timber, you know, that Cousin Knollys spoke of? I do hope not.'

'So do I,' said Milly. 'I wish he'd stayed a bit longer with us first, for if he does, father will sure to turn him out of doors, and we'll see no more of him.'

'Exactly, my dear Milly; and he's so pleasant and good-natured.'

'And he likes you awful well, he does.'

'I'm sure he likes us both equally, Milly; he talked a great deal to you at Elverston, and used to ask you so often to sing those two pretty Lancashire ballads,' I said; 'but you know when you were at your controversies and religious exercises in the window, with that pillar of the church, the Rev. Spriggs Biddlepen—'

'Get awa' wi' your nonsense, Maud; how could I help answering when he dodged* me up and down my Testament and catechism?—an I, most hate him, I tell you, you and Cousin Knollys, you're such fools, I do. And whatever you say, the lord likes you uncommon, and well you know it, ye hussy.'

'I know no such thing; and you don't think it, *you* hussy, and I really don't care who likes me or who doesn't, except my relations; and I make the lord a present to you, if you'll have him.'

In this strain were we talking when he re-entered the room, a little sooner than we had expected to see him.

Milly, who, you are to recollect, was only in process of reformation, and still retained something of the Derbyshire dairymaid, gave me a little clandestine pinch on the arm just as he made his appearance.

'I just refused a present from her,' said odious Milly, in answer to his inquiring look, 'because I knew she could not spare it.'

The effect of all this was that I blushed one of my overpowering blushes. People told me they became me very much; I hope so, for the misfortune was frequent; and I think nature owed me that compensation.

'It places you both in a most becoming light,' said Lord Ilbury, quite innocently. 'I really don't know which most to admire—the generosity of the offer or of the refusal.'

'Well, it _was_ kind, if you but knew. I'm 'most tempted to tell him,' said Milly.

I checked her with a really angry look, and said 'Perhaps you have not observed it; but I really think, for a sensible person, my Cousin Milly here talks more nonsense than any twenty other girls.'

'A twenty-girl power! That's an immense compliment. I've the greatest respect for nonsense, I owe it so much; and I really think if nonsense were banished, the earth would grow insupportable.'

'Thank you, Lord Ilbury,' said Milly, who had grown quite easy in his company during our long visit at Elverston; 'and I tell you, Miss Maud, if you grow saucy, I'll accept your present, and what will you say then?'

'I really don't know; but just now I want to ask Lord Ilbury how he thinks my uncle looks; neither I nor Milly have seen him since his illness.'

'Very much weaker, I think; but he may be gaining strength. Still, as my business was not quite pleasant, I thought it better to postpone it, and if you think it would be right, I'll write to Doctor Bryerly to ask him to postpone the discussion for a little time.'

I at once assented, and thanked him; indeed if I had had my way, the subject should never have been mentioned, I felt so hard-hearted and rapacious; but Lord Ilbury explained that the trustees were constrained by the provisions of the will, and that I really had no power to release them; and I hoped that Uncle Silas also understood all this.

'And now,' said he, 'we've returned to Grange, my sister and I, and it is nearer than Elverston, so that we are really neighbours; and Mary wants Lady Knollys to fix a time—she owes us a visit, you know—and you really must come at the same time; it will be so very pleasant, the same party exactly meeting in a new scene; and we have not half explored our neighbourhood; and I've got down all those Spanish engravings I told you of, and the Venetian missals, and all the rest. I think I remember very accurately the things you were most interested by, and they're all there; and really you must promise, you and Miss Millicent Ruthyn. And I forgot to mention—you know you complained that you were ill supplied with books, so Mary thought you would allow her to share her supply—they are the new books, you know—and when you have read yours, you and she can exchange.'

What girl was ever quite frank about her likings? I don't think I was more of a cheat than others; but I never could tell of myself. It is quite true that this duplicity and reserve seldom deceives. Our hypocrisies are forced upon some of our sex by the acuteness and vigilance of all in this field of inquiry; but if we are sly we are also lynx-eyed, capital detectives, most ingenious in fitting together the bits and dovetails of a cumulative case; and in those affairs of love and liking, have a terrible exploratory instinct, and so, for the most part, when detected, we are found out not only to be in love, but to be rogues moreover.

Lady Mary was very kind; but had Lady Mary of her own mere motion, taken all this trouble? Was there no more energetic influence at the bottom of that welcome chest of books, which arrived only half an hour later? The circulating library of those days was not the epidemic and ubiquitous influence to which it has grown; and there were many places where it could not find you out.

Altogether that evening Bartram had acquired a peculiar beauty—a bright and mellow glow, in which, even its gate-posts and wheel-barrow were interesting, and next day came a little cloud— Dudley appeared.

'You may be sure he wants money,' said Milly. 'He and father had words this morning.'

He took a chair at our luncheon, found fault with everything in his own laconic dialect, ate a good deal notwithstanding, and was sulky, and with Milly, snappish. To me, on the contrary, when Milly went into the hall, he was mild and whimpering, and disposed to be confidential.

'There's the Governor says he hasn't a bob! Danged if I know how an old fellah in his bedroom muddles away money at that rate. I don't suppose he thinks I can git along without tin, and he knows them trustees won't gi'e me a tizzy till they gets what they calls an opinion—dang' 'em! Bryerly says he doubts it must all go under settlement. They'll settle me nicely if they do; and Governor knows all about it, and won't gi'e me a danged brass farthin', an' me wi' bills to pay an' lawyers—dang 'em—writing letters. He knows summat o' that hisself, does Governor; and he might ha' consideration a bit for his own flesh and blood, *I* say. But he never does nout for none but hisself. I'll sell his books and his jewels next fit he takes—that's how I'll fit him.'

This amiable young man, glowering, with his elbows on the table and his fingers in his great whiskers, followed his homily, where clergymen append the blessing, with a muttered variety of very different matter.

'Now, Maud,' said he, pathetically, leaning back suddenly in his chair, with all his conscious beauty and misfortunes in his face; 'is not it hard lines?'

I thought the appeal was going to shape itself into an application for money; but it did not.

'I never know'd a reel beauty—first-chop,* of course, I mean—that wasn't kind along of it, and I'm a fellah as can't git along without sympathy—that's why I say it—an' isn't it hard lines? Now, *say* it's hard lines—*haint* it, Maud?'

I did not know exactly what hard lines meant, but I said—

'I suppose it is very disagreeable.'

And with this concession, not caring to hear any more in the same vein, I rose, intending to take my departure.

'No, that's jest it. I knew ye'd say it, Maud. Ye're a kind lass—ye be—'tis in yer pretty face. I like ye awful, I do—there's not a handsomer lass in Liverpool nor Lunnon itself—*no* where.'

He had seized my hand, and trying to place his arm about my waist, essayed that salute which I had so narrowly escaped on my first introduction.

'*Don't*, sir,' I exclaimed, in high indignation, escaping at the same moment from his grasp.

'No offence, lass; no harm, Maud; you must not be so shy—we're cousins, ye know—an' I wouldn't hurt ye, Maud, no more nor I'd knock my head off. I wouldn't.'

I did not wait to hear the rest of his tender protestations; but, without showing how nervous I was, I glided out of the room quietly, making an orderly retreat, the more meritorious as I heard him call after me persuasively—

'Come back, Maud. What are ye afeard on, lass? Come back, I say—do now; there's a good wench.'

As Milly and I were taking our walk that day, in the direction of the Windmill Wood, to which, in consequence perhaps of some secret order, we had now free access, we saw Beauty, for the first time since her illness, in the little yard, throwing grain to the poultry.

'How do you find yourself to-day, Meg? I am *very* glad to see you able to be about again; but I hope it is not too soon.'

We were standing at the barred gate of the little enclosure, and quite close to Meg, who, however, did not choose to raise her head; but, continuing to shower her grain and potato skins among her hens and chickens, said in a low tone—

'Father baint in sight? Look jist round a bit and say if ye see him.'

But Dickon's dusky red costume was nowhere visible.

So Meg looked up, pale and thin, and with her old grave, observant eyes, and she said quietly—

''Tisn't that I'm not glad to see ye; but if father was to spy me talking friendly wi' ye, now that I'm hearty, and you havin' no more call to me, he'd be all'ays a watching and thinkin' I was tellin' o' tales, and 'appen he'd want me to worrit ye for money, Miss Maud; an' 'tisn't here he'd spend it, but in the Feltram pottusses,* he would, and we want for nothin' that's good for us. But that's how 'twould be, an' he'd all'ays be a jawing and a lickin' of I; so don't mind me, Miss Maud, and 'appen I might do ye a good turn some day.'

A few days after this little interview with Meg, as Milly and I were walking briskly—for it was a clear frosty day—along the pleasant slopes of the sheep-walk, we were overtaken by Dudley Ruthyn. It was not a pleasant surprise. There was this mitigation, however; we were on foot, and he driving in a dog-cart along the track leading to the moor, with his dogs and gun. He brought his horse for a moment to a walk, and with a careless nod to me, removing his short pipe from his mouth, he said—

'Governor's callin' for ye, Milly; and he told me to send you slick home to him if I saw you, and I think he'll gi'e ye some money; but ye better take him while he's in the humour, lass, or mayhap ye'll go long without.'

And with those words apparently intent on his game he nodded again, and, pipe in mouth, drove at a quick trot over the slope of the hill, and disappeared.

So I agreed to await Milly's return while she ran home, and rejoined me where I was. Away she ran, in high spirits, and I wandered listlessly about in search of some convenient spot to sit down upon, for I was a little tired.

She had not been gone five minutes, when I heard a step approaching, and looking round, saw the dog-cart close by, the horse browsing on the short grass, and Dudley Ruthyn within a few paces of me.

'Ye see, Maud, I've bin thinkin' why you're so vexed wi' me, an' I thought I'd jest come back an' ask ye what I may a' done to anger ye so; there's no sin in that, I think—is there?'

'I'm not angry. I did not say so. I hope that's enough,' I said, startled; and, notwithstanding my speech, *very* angry, for I felt instinctively that Milly's despatch homeward was a mere trick, and I the dupe of this coarse stratagem.

'Well then, if ye baint angry, so much the better, Maud. I only want to know why you're afeard o' me. I never struck a man foul, much less hurt a girl, in my days; besides, Maud, I likes ye too well to hurt ye. Dang it, lass, you're my cousin, ye know, and cousins is all'ays together and lovin' like, an' none says again it.'

'I've nothing to explain—there *is* nothing to explain. I've been quite friendly,' I said, hurriedly.

'*Friendly!* Well, if there baint a cram! How can ye think it friendly, Maud, when ye won't a'most shake hands wi' me? It's enough to make a fellah sware, or cry a'most. Why d'ye like aggravatin' a poor devil? Now baint ye an ill-natured little puss, Maud, an' I likin' ye so well? You're the prettiest lass in Derbyshire; there's nothin' I wouldn't do for ye.'

And he backed his declaration with an oath.

'Be so good, then, as to re-enter your dogcart and drive away,' I replied, very much incensed.

'Now, there it is again! Ye can't speak me civil. Another fella'd fly out, an' maybe kiss ye for spite; but I baint that sort, I'm all for coaxin' and kindness, an' ye won't let me. What *be* you drivin' at, Maud?'

'I think I've said very plainly, sir, that I wish to be alone. You've *nothing* to say, except utter nonsense, and I've heard quite enough. Once for all, I beg, sir, that you will be so good as to leave me.'

'Well, now, look here, Maud; I'll do anything you like—burn me if I don't—if you'll only jest be kind to me, like cousins should. What did I ever do to vex you? If you think I like any lass better than you—some fellah at Elverston's bin talkin', maybe—it's nout but lies an' nonsense. Not but there's lots o' wenches likes me well enough, though I be a plain lad, and speaks my mind straight out.'

'I can't see that you are so frank, sir, as you describe; you have just played a shabby trick to bring about this absurd and most disagreeable interview.'

'And supposin' I did send that fool, Milly, out o' the way, to talk a bit wi' you here, where's the harm? Dang it, lass, ye musn't be too hard. Didn't I say I'd do whatever ye wished?'

'And you *won't*,' said I.

'Ye mean to get along out o' this? Well, now, I *will*. There! No use, of course, askin' you to kiss and be friends, before I go, as cousins should. Well, don't be riled, lass, I'm not askin' it; only mind, I do like you awful, and 'appen I'll find ye in better humour another time. Good-by, Maud; I'll make ye like me at last.'

And with these words, to my comfort, he addressed himself to his horse and pipe, and was soon honestly on his way to the moor.

CHAPTER XLVI

THE RIVALS

ALL the time that Dudley chose to persecute me with his odious society, I continued to walk at a brisk pace toward home, so that I had nearly reached the house when Milly met me, with a note which had arrived for me by the post, in her hand.

'Here, Milly, are more verses. He is a very persevering poet, whoever he is.' So I broke the seal; but this time it was prose. And the first words were 'Captain Oakley!'

I confess to an odd sensation as these remarkable words met my eye. It might possibly be a proposal. I did not wait to speculate, however, but read these sentences traced in the identical handwriting which had copied the lines with which I had been twice favoured.

'Captain Oakley presents his compliments to Miss Ruthyn, and trusts she will excuse his venturing to ask whether, during his short stay in Feltram, he might be permitted to pay his respects at Bartram-Haugh. He has been making a short visit to his aunt, and could not find himself so near without at least attempting to renew an acquaintance which he has never ceased to cherish in memory. If Miss Ruthyn would be so very good as to favour him with ever so short a reply to the question he ventures most respectfully to ask, her decision would reach him at the Hall Hotel, Feltram.'

'Well, he's a round-about fellah, anyhow. Couldn't he come up and see you if he wanted to? They poeters, they do love writing long yarns—don't they?' And with this reflection, Milly took the note and read it through again.

'It's jolly polite anyhow, isn't it Maud?' said Milly, who had conned it over, and accepted it as a model composition.

I must have been, I think, naturally a rather shrewd girl; and considering how very little I had seen of the world—nothing in fact—I often wonder now at the sage conclusions at which I arrived.

Were I to answer this handsome and cunning fool according to his folly, in what position should I find myself? No doubt my reply would induce a rejoinder, and that compel another note from me, and that invite yet another from him; and however his might improve in warmth, they were sure not to abate. Was it his impertinent plan, with this show of respect and ceremony, to drag me into a clandestine correspondence? Inexperienced girl as I was, I fired at the idea of becoming his dupe, and fancying, perhaps, that there was more in merely answering his note than it would have amounted to, I said—

'That kind of thing may answer very well with button-makers, but ladies don't like it. What would your papa think of it if he found that I had been writing to him, and seeing him without his permission? If he wanted to see me he could have'—(I really did not know exactly what he could have done)—'he could have timed his visit to Lady Knollys differently; at all events, he has no right to place me in an embarrassing situation, and I am certain Cousin Knollys would say so; and I think his note both shabby and impertinent.'

Decision was not with me an intellectual process. When quite cool I was the most undecided of mortals, but once my feelings were excited I was prompt and bold.

'I'll give the note to Uncle Silas,' I said, quickening my pace toward home; 'he'll know what to do.'

But Milly, who, I fancy, had no objection to the little romance which the young officer proposed, told me that she could not see her father, that he was ill, and not speaking to anyone.

'And arn't ye making a plaguy row about nothin'? I lay a guinea if ye had never set eyes on Lord Ilbury you'd a told him to come, and see ye, an' welcome.'

'Don't talk like a fool, Milly. You never knew me do anything deceitful. Lord Ilbury has no more to do with it, you know very well, than the man in the moon.'

I was altogether very indignant. I did not speak another word to Milly. The proportions of the house are so great that it is a much longer walk than you would suppose from the hall-door to Uncle Silas's room. But I did not cool all that way; and it was not till I had just reached the lobby, and saw the sour, jealous face, and high caul of old Wyat, and felt the influence of that neighbourhood, that I paused to reconsider. I fancied there was a cool consciousness of success behind all the deferential phraseology of Captain Oakley, which nettled me extremely. No; there could be no doubt. I tapped softly at the door.

'What is it *now*, Miss?' snarled the querulous old woman, with her shrivelled fingers on the door-handle.

'Can I see my uncle for a moment?'

'He's tired, and not a word from him all day long.'

'Not ill, though?'

'Awful bad in the night,' said the old crone, with a sudden savage glare in my face, as if *I* had brought it about.

'Oh! I'm very sorry. I had not heard a word of it.'

'No one does but old Wyat. There's Milly there never asks neither—his own child!'

'Weakness, or what?'

'One o' them fits. He'll slide awa' in one o' them some day, and no one but old Wyat to know nor ask word about it; that's how 'twill be.'

'Will you please hand him this note, if he is well enough to look at it, and say I am at the door?'

She took it with a peevish nod and a grunt, closing the door in my face, and in a few minutes returned—

'Come in wi' ye,' said Dame Wyat, and I appeared.

Uncle Silas, who, after his nightly horror or vision, lay extended on a sofa, with his faded yellow silk dressing gown about him, his long white hair hanging toward the ground, and that wild and feeble smile lighting his face—a glimmer I feared to look upon—his long thin arms lay by his sides, with hands and fingers that stirred not, except when now and then, with a feeble motion, he wet his temples and forehead with eau de Cologne from a glass saucer placed beside him.

'Excellent girl! dutiful ward and niece!' murmured the oracle; 'heaven reward you—your frank dealing is your own safety and my peace. Sit you down, and say who is this Captain Oakley, when you made his acquaintance, what his age, fortune, and expectations, and who the aunt he mentions.'

Upon all these points I satisfied him as fully as I was able.

'Wyat—the white drops,'* he called in a thin, stern tone. 'I'll write a line presently. I can't see visitors, and, of course, you can't receive young captains before you've come out. Farewell! God bless you, dear.'

Wyat was dropping the 'white' restorative into a wine-glass and the room was redolent of ether. I was glad to escape. The figures and whole *mise en scène* were unearthly.

'Well, Milly,' I said, as I met her in the hall, 'your papa is going to write to him.'

I sometimes wonder whether Milly was right, and how I should have acted a few months earlier.

Next day whom should we meet in the Windmill Wood but Captain Oakley. The spot where this interesting *rencontre* occurred was near that ruinous bridge on my sketch of which I had received so many compliments. It was so great a surprise that I had not time to recollect my indignation, and, having received him very affably, I found it impossible, during our brief interview, to recover my lost altitude.

After our greetings were over, and some compliments neatly made, he said—

'I had such a curious note from Mr. Silas Ruthyn. I am sure he thinks me a very impertinent fellow, for it was really anything but inviting—extremely rude, in fact. But I could not quite see that because he does not want me to invade his bed-room—an incursion I never dreamed of—I was not to present myself to you, who had already honoured me with your acquaintance, with the sanction of those who were most interested in your welfare, and who were just as well qualified as he, I fancy, to say who were qualified for such an honour.'

'My uncle, Mr. Silas Ruthyn, you are aware, is my guardian; and this is my cousin, his daughter.'

This was an opportunity of becoming a little lofty, and I improved it. He raised his hat and bowed to Milly.

'I'm afraid I've been very rude and stupid. Mr. Ruthyn, of course, has a perfect right to—to—in fact, I was not the least aware that I had the honour of so near a relation's—a—a—and what exquisite scenery you have. I think this country round Feltram particularly fine; and this Bartram-Haugh is, I venture to say, about the very most beautiful spot in this beautiful region. I do assure you I am tempted beyond measure to make Feltram and the Hall Hotel my headquarters for at least a week. I only regret the foliage; but your trees show wonderfully, even in winter, so many of them have got that ivy about them. They say it spoils trees, but it certainly beautifies them. I have just ten days' leave unexpired; I wish I could induce you to advise me how to apply them. What shall I do, Miss Ruthyn?'

'I am the worst person in the world to make plans, even for myself, I find it so troublesome. What do you say? Suppose you try Wales or Scotland, and climb up some of those fine mountains that look so well in winter?'

'I should much prefer Feltram. I so wish you would recommend *it*. What is this pretty plant?'

'We call that Maud's myrtle. She planted it, and it's very pretty when it's full in blow,' said Milly.

Our visit to Elverston had been of immense use to us both.

'Oh! planted by *you*?' he said, very softly, with a momentary corresponding glance. 'May I—ever so little—just a leaf?'

And without waiting for permission, he held a sprig of it next his waistcoat.

'Yes, it goes very prettily with those buttons. They are *very* pretty buttons; are not they, Milly? A present, a souvenir, I dare say?'

This was a terrible hit at the button-maker, and I thought he looked a little oddly at me, but my countenance was so 'bewitchingly simple' that I suppose his suspicions were allayed.

Now, it was very odd of me, I must confess, to talk in this way, and to receive all those tender allusions from a gentleman about whom I had spoken and felt so sharply only the evening before. But Bartram was abominably lonely. A civilized person was a valuable waif or stray in that region of the picturesque and the brutal; and to my lady reader especially, because she will probably be hardest upon me, I put it—can you not recollect any such folly in your own past life? Can you not in as many minutes call to mind at least six similar inconsistencies of your own practising? For my part, I really can't see the advantage of being the weaker sex if we are always to be as strong as our masculine neighbours.

There was, indeed, no revival of the little sentiment which I had once experienced. When these things once expire I do believe they are as hard to revive as our dead lap-dogs, guinea-pigs and parrots. It was my perfect coolness which enabled me to chat, I flatter myself, so agreeably with the refined Captain, who plainly thought me his captive, and was probably now and then thinking what was to be done to utilize that little bit of Bartram, or to beautify some other, when he should see fit to become its master, as we rambled over these wild but beautiful grounds.

It was just about then that Milly nudged me rather vehemently, and whispered 'Look there!'

I followed with mine the direction of her eyes, and saw my odious cousin, Dudley, in a flagrant pair of cross-barred pegtops,* and what Milly before her reformation used to call other 'slops' of corresponding atrocity approaching our refined little party with great strides. I really think that Milly was very nearly ashamed of him.

I certainly was. I had no apprehension, however, of the scene which was imminent.

The charming Captain mistook him probably for some rustic servant of the place, for he continued his agreeable remarks up to the very moment when Dudley, whose face was pale with anger, and whose rapid advance had not served to cool him, without recollecting to salute either Milly or me, accosted our elegant companion as follows:—

'By your leave, Master, baint you summat in the wrong box* here, don't you think?'

He had planted himself directly in his front, and looked unmistakably menacing.

'May I speak to him? Will you excuse me?' said the Captain blandly.

'Ow—ay, they'll excuse ye ready enough, I dessay; you're to deal wi' me though. Baint ye in the wrong box now?'

'I'm not conscious, sir, of being in a box at all,' replied the Captain, with severe disdain. 'It strikes me you are disposed to get up a row. Let us, if you please, get a little apart from the ladies if that is your purpose.'

'I mean to turn you out o' this the way ye came. If you make a row so much the wuss for you, for I'll lick ye to fits.'

'Tell him not to fight,' whispered Milly; 'he'll a' no chance wi' Dudley.'

I saw Dickon Hawkes grinning over the paling on which he leaned.

'Mr. Hawkes,' I said, drawing Milly with me toward that unpromising meditator, 'pray prevent unpleasantness and go between them.'

'An' git licked o' both sides? Rather not, Miss, thank ye,' grinned Dickon, tranquilly.

'Who are you, sir?' demanded our romantic acquaintance, with military sternness.

'I'll tell you who you are—you're Oakley, as stops at the Hall, that Governor wrote, over night, not to dare show your nose inside the grounds. You're a half-starved cappen,* come down here to look for a wife, and—'

Before Dudley could finish his sentence, Captain Oakley, than whose face no regimentals could possibly have been more scarlet, at that moment, struck with his switch at Dudley's handsome features.

I don't know how it was done—by some 'devilish cantrip slight'.* A smack was heard, and the Captain lay on his back on the ground, with his mouth full of blood.

'How do ye like the taste o' that?' roared Dickon, from his post of observation.

In an instant Captain Oakley was on his feet again, hatless, looking quite frantic, and striking out at Dudley, who was ducking and dipping quite coolly, and again the same horrid sound, only this time it was double, like a quick postman's knock, and Captain Oakley was on the grass again.

'Tapped his smeller, by——,' thundered Dickon, with a roar of laughter.

'Come away, Milly, I'm growing ill,' said I.

'Drop it, Dudley, I tell ye; you'll kill him,' screamed Milly.

But the devoted Captain, whose nose and mouth and shirt-front formed now but one great patch of blood, and who was bleeding beside over one eye, dashed at him again.

I turned away. I felt quite faint, and on the point of crying, with mere horror.

'Hammer away at his knocker,' bellowed Dickon, in a frenzy of delight.

'He'll break it now, if it ain't already,' cried Milly, alluding, as I afterwards understood, to the Captain's Grecian nose.

'Brayvo, little 'un!' The Captain was considerably the taller.

Another smack, and, I suppose, Captain Oakley fell once more.

'Hooray! the dinner-service again, by ——,' roared Dickon. 'Stick to that. Over the same ground—subsoil, I say. He han't enough yet.'

In a perfect tremor of disgust, I was making as quick a retreat as I could, and as I did, I heard Captain Oakley shriek hoarsely—

'You're a d—— prizefighter; I can't box you.'

'I told ye I'd lick ye to fits,' hooted Dudley.

'But you're the son of a gentleman, and by —— you shall fight me *as* a gentleman.'

A yell of hooting laughter from Dudley and Dickon followed this sally.

'Gie my love to the Colonel, and think o' me when ye look in the glass—won't ye? An' so you're goin' arter all; well, follow what's left o' yer nose. Ye forgot some o' yer ivories*—didn't ye—on th' grass?'

These and many similar jibes followed the mangled Captain in his retreat.

NO ONE who has not experienced it can imagine the nervous disgust and horror which such a spectacle as we had been forced in part to witness, leaves upon the mind of a young person of my peculiar temperament.

It affected ever after my involuntary estimate of the principal actors in it. An exhibition of such thorough inferiority, accompanied by such a shock to the feminine sense of elegance, is not forgotten by any woman. Captain Oakley had been severely beaten by a smaller man. It was pitiable, but also undignified; and Milly's anxieties about his teeth and nose, though in a certain sense horrible, had also a painful suspicion of the absurd.

People say, on the other hand, that superior prowess, even in such barbarous contests, inspires in our sex an interest akin to admiration. I can positively say in my case it was quite the reverse. Dudley Ruthyn stood lower than ever in my estimation; for though I feared him more, it was by reason of these brutal and cold-blooded associations.

After this I lived in constant apprehension of being summoned to my uncle's room, and being called on for an explanation of my meeting with Captain Oakley, which, notwithstanding my perfect innocence, looked suspiciously, but no such inquisition resulted. Perhaps he did not suspect me; or, perhaps, he thought, not in his haste, all women are liars, and did not care to hear what I might say. I rather lean to the latter interpretation.

The exchequer just now, I suppose, by some means, was replenished, for next morning Dudley set off upon one of his fashionable excursions, as poor Milly thought them, to Wolverhampton. And the same day Doctor Bryerly arrived.

Milly and I, from my room window, saw him step from his vehicle to the court-yard.

A lean man with sandy hair and whiskers was in the chaise with him. Doctor Bryerly descended in the unchangeable black suit that always looked new and never fitted him.

The Doctor looked careworn, and older, I thought, by several years, than when I last saw him. He was not shown up to my uncle's room; on the contrary, Milly, who was more actively curious than I, ascertained that our tremulous butler informed him that my uncle was not sufficiently well for an interview. Whereupon Doctor Bryerly had pencilled a note the reply to which was a message from Uncle Silas, saying that he would be happy to see him in five minutes.

As Milly and I were conjecturing what it might mean, and before the five minutes had expired, Mary Quince entered.

'Wyat bid me tell you, Miss, your uncle wants you *this minute*.'

When I entered his room, Uncle Silas was seated at the table, with his desk before him. He looked up. Could anything be more dignified, suffering, and venerable?

'I sent for you, dear,' he said very gently, extending his thin, white hand, and taking mine, which he held affectionately while he spoke, 'because I desire to have no secrets, and wish you thoroughly to know all that concerns your own interests while subject to my guardianship; and I am happy to think, my beloved niece, that you requite my candour. Oh, here is the gentleman. Sit down, dear.'

Doctor Bryerly was advancing, as it seemed, to shake hands with Uncle Silas, who, however, rose with a severe and haughty air, not the least over-acted, and made him a slow, ceremonious bow. I wondered how the homely Doctor could confront so tranquilly that astounding statue of hauteur.

A faint and weary smile, rather sad than contemptuous, was the only sign he showed of feeling his repulse.

'How do *you* do, Miss?' he said, extending his hand, and greeting me after his ungallant fashion, as if it were an after-thought.

'I think I may as well take a chair, sir,' said Doctor Bryerly, sitting down serenely, near the table, and crossing his ungainly legs.

My uncle bowed.

'You understand the nature of the business, sir. Do you wish Miss Ruthyn to remain?' asked Doctor Bryerly.

'I *sent* for her, sir,' replied my uncle, in a very gentle and sarcastic tone, a smile on his thin lips, and his strangely-contorted eyebrows raised for a moment contemptuously. 'This gentleman, my dear Maud, thinks proper to insinuate that I am robbing you. It surprises me a little, and, no doubt, you—I've nothing to conceal, and wished you to be present while he favours me more particularly with his views. I'm right, I think, in describing it as *robbery*, sir?'

'Why,' said Doctor Bryerly thoughtfully, for he was treating the matter as one of right, and not of feeling, 'it would be, certainly, taking that which does not belong to you, and converting it to your own use; but, at the worst, it would more resemble *thieving*, I think, than robbery.'

I saw Uncle Silas's lip, eyelid, and thin cheek quiver and shrink, as if with a thrill of tic douloureux,* as Doctor Bryerly spoke this unconsciously insulting answer. My uncle had, however, the self-command which is learned at the gaming-table. He shrugged, with a chilly, sarcastic, little laugh, and a glance at me.

'Your note says *waste*,* I think, sir?'

'Yes, waste—the felling and sale of timber in the Windmill Wood, the selling of oak bark and burning of charcoal, as I'm informed,' said Bryerly, as sadly and quietly as a man might relate a piece of intelligence from the newspaper.

'Detectives? or private spies of your own?—or, perhaps, my servants, bribed with my poor brother's money? A very high-minded procedure.'

'Nothing of the kind, sir.'

My uncle sneered.

'I mean, sir, there has been no undue canvass for evidence, and the question is simply one of right; and it is our duty to see that this inexperienced young lady is not defrauded.'

'By her own uncle?'

'By anyone,' said Doctor Bryerly, with a natural impenetrability that excited my admiration.

'Of course you come armed with an opinion?' said my smiling uncle, insinuatingly.

'The case is before Mr. Sergeant Grinders. These bigwigs don't return their cases sometimes so quickly as we could wish.'

'Then you have *no* opinion?' smiled my uncle.

'My solicitor is quite clear upon it; and it seems to me there can be no question raised, but for form's sake.'

'Yes, for form's sake you take one, and in the meantime, upon a nice question of law, the surmises of a thick-headed attorney and of an ingenious apoth—I beg pardon, physician—are sufficient warrant for telling my niece and ward, in my presence, that I am defrauding her!'

My uncle leaned back in his chair, and smiled with a contemptuous patience over Doctor Bryerly's head, as he spoke.

'I don't know whether I used that expression, sir, but I am speaking merely in a technical sense. I mean to say, that, whether by mistake or otherwise, you are exercising a power which you don't lawfully possess, and that the effect of that is to impoverish the estate, and, by so much as it benefits you, to wrong this young lady.'

'I'm a technical defrauder, I see, and your manner conveys the rest. I thank my God, sir, I am a *very* different man from what I once was.' Uncle Silas was speaking in a low tone, and with extraordinary deliberation. 'I remember when I should have certainly knocked you down, sir, or *tried* it, at least, for a great deal less.'

'But seriously, sir, what *do* you propose?' asked Doctor Bryerly, sternly and a little flushed, for I think the old man* was stirred within him; and though he did not raise his voice, his manner was excited.

'I propose to defend my rights, sir,' murmured Uncle Silas very grim. 'I'm not without an opinion, though you are.'

'You seem to think, sir that I have a pleasure in annoying you; you are quite wrong. I hate annoying anyone—constitutionally—I *hate* it; but don't you see sir, the position I'm placed in? I wish I could please everyone, and do my duty.'

Uncle Silas bowed and smiled.

'I've brought with me the Scotch steward from Tolkingden, *your* estate, Miss, and if you let us we will visit the spot and make a note of what we observe, that is, assuming that you admit waste, and merely question our law.'

'If you please, sir, you and your Scotchman shall do *no such thing*; and, bearing in mind that I neither deny nor admit anything, you will please further never more to present yourself, under any pretext whatsoever, either in this house or on the grounds of Bartram-Haugh, during my lifetime.'

Uncle Silas rose up with the same glassy smile and scowl, in token that the interview was ended.

'Good-bye, sir,' said Doctor Bryerly, with a sad and thoughtful air, and hesitating for a moment, he said to me, 'Do you think, Miss, you could afford me a word in the hall?'

'Not a word, sir,' snarled Uncle Silas, with a white flash from his eyes.

There was a pause.

'Sit where you are, Maud.'

Another pause.

'If you have anything to say to my ward, sir, you will please to say it *here*.'

Doctor Bryerly's dark and homely face was turned on me with an expression of unspeakable compassion.

'I was going to say, that if you think of any way in which I can be of the least service, Miss, I'm ready to act, that's all; mind, *any* way.'

He hesitated, looking at me with the same expression as if he had something more to say; but he only repeated—

'That's all, Miss.'

'Won't you shake hands, Doctor Bryerly, before you go?' I said, eagerly approaching him.

Without a smile, with the same sad anxiety in his face, with his mind, as it seemed to me, on something else, and irresolute whether to speak it or be silent, he took my fingers in a very cold hand, and holding it so, and slowly shaking it, his grave and troubled glance unconsciously rested on Uncle Silas's face, while in a sad tone and absent way he said—

'Good-bye, Miss.'

From before that sad gaze my uncle averted his strange eyes quickly, and looked, oddly, to the window.

In a moment more Doctor Bryerly let my hand go with a sigh, and with an abrupt little nod to me, he left the room; and I heard that dismallest of sounds, the retreating footsteps of a true friend, *lost*.

'Lead us not into temptation; if we pray so we must not mock the eternal Majesty of Heaven by walking into temptation of our own accord.'

This oracular sentence was not uttered by my uncle until Doctor Bryerly had been gone at least five minutes.

'I've forbid him my house, Maud; first, because his perfectly unconscious insolence tries my patience nearly beyond endurance; and again, because I have heard unfavourable reports of him. On the question of right which he disputes, I am perfectly informed. I am your tenant, my dear niece; when I am gone you will learn how *scru-pulous* I have been; you will see how, under the pressure of the most agonizing pecuniary difficulties, the terrific penalty of a misspent youth, I have been careful never by a hair's breadth to transgress the strict line of my legal privileges; alike, as your tenant, Maud, and as your guardian; how, amid frightful agitations, I have kept myself, by the miraculous strength and grave vouchsafed me—*pure*.'

'The world,' he resumed after a short pause, 'has no faith in any man's conversion; it never forgets what he was, it never believes him anything better, it is an inexorable and stupid judge. What I was I will describe in blacker terms, and with more heartfelt detestation than my traducers—a reckless prodigal, a godless profligate. Such I was; what I am, I am. If I had no hope beyond this world, of all men most miserable; but with that hope, a sinner saved.'

Then he waxed eloquent and mystical. I think his Swedenborgian studies had crossed his notions of religion with strange lights. I never could follow him quite in these excursions into the region of symbolism. I only recollect that he talked of the deluge* and the waters of Mara,* and said, 'I am washed—I am sprinkled,'* and then pausing, bathed his thin temples and forehead with eau de Cologne, a process which was, perhaps, suggested by his imagery of sprinkling and so forth.

Thus refreshed, he sighed and smiled, and passed to the subject of Doctor Bryerly.

'Of Doctor Bryerly I know that he is sly, that he loves money, was born poor, and makes nothing by his profession. But he possesses many thousand pounds, under my poor brother's will, of *your money*; and he has glided with, of course a modest nolo episcopari,* into the acting trusteeship, with all its multitudinous opportunities, of your immense property. That is not doing so badly for a visionary Swedenborgian. Such a man *must* prosper. But if he expected to make money of me, he is disappointed. Money, however, he will make of his trusteeship, as you will see. It is a dangerous resolution. But if he will seek the life of Dives, the worst I wish him is to find the death of Lazarus.* But whether, like Lazarus, he be borne of angels into Abraham's bosom, or, like the rich man, only dies and is buried, and *the rest*, neither living nor dying do I desire his company.'

Uncle Silas here seemed suddenly overtaken by exhaustion. He leaned back with a ghastly look, and his lean features glistened with the dew of faintness. I screamed for Wyat. But he soon recovered sufficiently to smile his odd smile, and with it and his frown, nodded and waved me away.

CHAPTER XLVIII

QUESTION AND ANSWER

MY uncle, after all, was not ill that day, after the strange fashion of his malady, be it what it might. Old Wyat repeated in her sour laconic way that there was 'nothing to speak of amiss with him.' But there remained with me a sense of pain and fear. Doctor Bryerly, notwithstanding my uncle's sarcastic reflections, remained, in my estimation, a true and wise friend. I had all my life been accustomed to rely upon others, and here, haunted by many unavowed and ill-defined alarms and doubts, the disappearance of an active and able friend caused my heart to sink.

Still there remained my dear Cousin Monica and my pleasant and trusted friend, Lord Ilbury; and in less than a week arrived an invitation from Lady Mary to the Grange, for me and Milly, to meet Lady Knollys. It was accompanied, she told me, by a note from Lord Ilbury to my uncle, supporting her request; and in the afternoon I received a message to attend my uncle in his room.

'An invitation from Lady Mary Carysbroke for you and Milly to meet Monica Knollys; have you received it?' asked my uncle, so soon as I was seated. Answered in the affirmative, he continued—

'Now, Maud Ruthyn, I expect the truth from you; I have been frank, so shall you. Have you ever heard me spoken ill of by Lady Knollys?'

I was quite taken aback.

I felt my cheeks flushing. I was returning his fierce cold gaze with a stupid stare, and remained dumb.

'Yes, Maud, you *have*.'

I looked down in silence.

'I *know* it; but it is right you should answer; have you or have you not?'

I had to clear my voice twice or thrice. There was a kind of spasm in my throat.

'I am trying to recollect,' I said at last.

'*Do* recollect,' he replied imperiously.

There was a little interval of silence. I would have given the world to be, on any conditions, anywhere else in the world.

'Surely, Maud, you don't wish to deceive your guardian? Come, the question is a plain one, and I know the truth already. I ask you again—have you ever heard me spoken ill of by Lady Knollys?'

'Lady Knollys,' I said, hardly articulately, 'speaks very freely, and often half in jest; but,' I continued, observing something menacing in his face, 'I have heard her express disapprobation of some things you have done.'

'Come, Maud,' he continued, in a stern, though still a low key, 'did she not insinuate that charge—then, I suppose, in a state of incubation, the other day presented here full-fledged, with beak and claws, by that scheming apothecary—the statement that I was defrauding you by cutting down timber upon the grounds?'

'She certainly did mention the circumstance; but she also argued that it might have been through ignorance of the extent of your rights.'

'Come, come, Maud, you must not prevaricate, girl. I *will* have it. Does she not habitually speak disparagingly of me, in your presence, and *to* you? *Answer*.'

I hung my head.

'Yes or no?'

'Well, perhaps so—yes,' I faltered, and burst into tears.

'There, don't cry; it may well shock you. Did she not, to your knowledge, say the same things in presence of my child Millicent? I know it, I repeat—there is no use in hesitating; and I command you to answer.'

Sobbing, I told the truth.

'Now sit still, while I write my reply.'

He wrote, with the scowl and smile so painful to witness, as he looked down upon the paper, and then he placed the note before me—

'Read that, my dear.'

It began—

'MY DEAR LADY KNOLLYS,

'You have favoured me with a note, adding your request to that of Lord Ilbury, that I should permit my ward and my daughter to avail themselves of Lady Mary's invitation. Being perfectly cognizant of the ill-feeling you have always and unaccountably cherished toward me, and also of the terms in which you have had the delicacy and the conscience to speak of me before and to my child and my ward, I can only express my amazement at the modesty of your request, while peremptorily refusing it. And I shall conscientiously adopt effectual measures to prevent your ever again having an opportunity of endeavouring to destroy my influence and authority over my ward or my child, by direct or insinuated slander.

> 'Your defamed and injured kinsman,
> 'SILAS RUTHYN.'

I was stunned; yet what could I plead against the blow that was to isolate me? I wept aloud, with my hands clasped, looking on the marble face of the old man.

Without seeming to hear, he folded and sealed his note, and then proceeded to answer Lord Ilbury.

When that note was written, he placed it likewise before me, and I read it also through. It simply referred him to Lady Knollys 'for an explanation of the unhappy circumstances which compelled him to decline an invitation, which it would have made his niece and his daughter so happy to accept.'

'You see, my dear Maud, how frank I am with you,' he said, waving the open note, which I had just read, slightly before he folded it. 'I think I may ask you to reciprocate my candour.'

Dismissed from this interview, I ran to Milly, who burst into tears from sheer disappointment, so we wept and wailed together. But in my grief I think there was more reason.

I sat down to the dismal task of writing to my dear Lady Knollys. I implored her to make her peace with my uncle. I told her how frank he had been with me; and how he had shown me his sad reply to her letter. I told her of the interview to which he had himself invited me with Dr. Bryerly; how little disturbed he was by the accusation—no sign of guilt; quite the contrary, perfect confidence. I implored of her to think the best, and remembering my isolation, to accomplish a reconciliation with Uncle Silas. 'Only think,' I wrote, 'I only nineteen, and two years of solitude before me. What a separation!' No broken merchant ever signed the schedule of his bankruptcy with a heavier heart than did I this letter.

The griefs of youth are like the wounds of the gods—there is an ichor which heals the scars from which it flows: and thus Milly and

I consoled ourselves, and next day enjoyed our ramble, our talk and readings, with a wonderful resignation to the inevitable.

Milly and I stood in the relation of *Lord Duberly* to *Doctor Pangloss*.* I was to mend her 'cackleology', and the occupation amused us both. I think at the bottom of our submission to destiny lurked a hope that Uncle Silas, the inexorable, would relent, or that Cousin Monica, that siren, would win and melt him to her purpose.

Whatever comfort, however, I derived from the absence of Dudley was not to be of very long duration; for one morning, as I was amusing myself alone, with a piece of worsted work, thinking, and just at that moment not unpleasantly, of many things, my Cousin Dudley entered the room.

'Back again, like a bad halfpenny, ye see. And how a' ye bin ever since, lass? Purely, I warrant, be your looks. I'm jolly glad to see ye, I am; no cattle going like ye, Maud.'

'I think I must ask you to let go my hand, as I can't continue my work,' I said, very stiffly, hoping to chill his enthusiasm a little.

'Anything to pleasure ye, Maud, 'taint in my heart to refuse ye nout. I a' bin to Wolverhampton, lass—jolly row there—and run over to Leamington; a'most broke my neck, faith, wi' a borrowed horse arter the dogs; ye would na care, Maud, if I broke my neck, would ye? Well, 'appen, jest a little,' he good-naturedly supplied, as I was silent.

'Little over a week since I left here, by George; and to me it's half the almanac like; can ye guess the reason, Maud?'

'Have you seen your sister, Milly, or your father, since your return?' I asked coldly.

'*They'll* keep, Maud, never mind 'em; it be you I want to see—it be you I wor thinkin' on a' the time. I tell ye, lass, I'm all'ays a thinkin' on ye.'

'I think you ought to go and see your father; you have been away, you say, some time. I don't think it is respectful,' I said, a little sharply.

'If ye bid me go I'd a'most go, but I could na quite; there's nout on earth I would na do for you, Maud, excep' leaving you.'

'And that,' I said, with a petulant flush, 'is the only thing on earth I would ask you to do.'

'Blessed if you baint a blushin', Maud,' he drawled, with an odious grin.

His stupidity was proof against everything.

'It is *too* bad!' I muttered with an indignant little pat of my foot and mimic stamp.

'Well you lasses be queer cattle; ye're angry wi' me now, cos ye think I got into mischief—ye do, Maud; ye know't, ye buxsom little fool, down there at Wolverhampton; and jest for that ye're ready to turn off again the minute I come back; 'tisn't fair.'

'I don't *understand* you, sir; and I *beg* that you'll leave me.'

'Now, didn't I tell ye about leavin' ye, Maud; 'tis the only thing I can't compass for yer sake. I'm jest a child in yere hands, I am, ye know. I can lick a big fellah to pot as limp as a rag, by George!'—(his oaths were not really so mild)—'ye see summat o' that 'tother day. Well, don't be vexed, Maud; 'twas all along o' you; ye know, I wor a bit jealous, 'appen; but anyhow I can do it; and look at me here, jest a child, I say, in yer hands.'

'I wish you'd go away. Have you nothing to do, and no one to see? Why *can't* you leave me alone, sir?'

''Cos I can't, Maud, that's jest why; and I wonder, Maud, how can you be so ill-natured, when you see me like this; how can ye?'

'I wish Milly would come,' said I, peevishly, looking toward the door.

'Well, I'll tell you how it is, Maud. I may as well have it out. I like you better than any lass that ever I saw, a deal; you're nicer by chalks; there's none like ye—there isn't; and I wish you'd have me. I ha'n't much tin—father's run through a deal, he's pretty well up a tree, ye know; but though I baint so rich as some folk, I'm a better man, 'appen; and if ye'd take a tidy lad, that likes ye awful, and 'id die for your sake, why here he is.'

'What can you mean, sir?' I exclaimed, rising in indignant bewilderment.

'I mean, Maud, if ye'll marry me, you'll never ha' cause to complain; I'll never let ye want for nout, nor gie' ye a wry word.'

'Actually a proposal!' I ejaculated, like a person speaking in a dream.

I stood with my hand on the back of a chair, staring at Dudley, and looking, I dare say, as stupefied as I felt.

'There's a good lass, ye would na deny me,' said the odious creature, with one knee on the seat of the chair behind which I was standing, and attempting to place his arm lovingly round my neck.

This effectually roused me, and starting back, I stamped upon the ground with actual fury.

'What has there ever been, sir, in my conduct, words, or looks, to warrant this unparalleled audacity? But that you are as stupid as you are impertinent, brutal, and ugly, you must, long ago, sir, have seen how I dislike you. How dare you, sir? Don't presume to obstruct me; I'm going to my uncle.'

I had never spoken so violently to mortal before.

He in turn looked a little confounded; and I passed his extended but motionless arm with a quick and angry step.

He followed me a pace or two, however, before I reached the door, looking horridly angry, but stopped, and only swore after me some of these 'wry words', which I was never to have heard. I was myself, however, too much incensed, and moving at too rapid a pace to catch their import; and I had knocked at my uncle's door before I began to collect my thoughts.

'Come in,' replied my uncle's voice, clear, thin, and peevish.

I entered and confronted him.

'Your son, sir, has insulted me.'

He looked at me with a cold curiosity steadily for a few seconds, as I stood panting before him with flaming cheeks.

'Insulted you?' repeated he. 'Egad, you surprise me!'

The ejaculation savoured of 'the old man', to borrow his scriptural phrase, more than anything I had heard from him before.

'*How?*' he continued; 'how has Dudley *insulted* you, my dear child? Come, you're excited; sit down; take time, and tell me all about it. I did not know that Dudley was here.'

'I—he—it *is* an insult. He knew very well—he *must* know I dislike him; and he presumed to make a proposal of marriage to me.'

'O—o—oh!' exclaimed my uncle, with a prolonged intonation, which plainly said, is that the mighty matter?

He looked at me as he leaned back with the same steady curiosity, this time smiling, which somehow frightened me, and his countenance looked to me wicked, like the face of a witch, with a guilt I could not understand.

'And that is the amount of your complaint. He made you a formal proposal of marriage!'

'Yes; he proposed for me.'

As I cooled I began to feel just a very little disconcerted, and a suspicion was troubling me that possibly an indifferent person might think that, having no more to complain of, my language was perhaps a little exaggerated, and my demeanour a little too tempestuous.

My uncle, I dare say, saw some symptoms of this misgiving, for, smiling still, he said—

'My dear Maud, however just, you appear to me a little cruel; you don't seem to remember how much you are yourself to blame; you have one faithful friend at least, whom I advise your consulting—I mean your looking-glass. The foolish fellow is young, quite ignorant in the world's ways. He is in love—desperately enamoured—

"Aimer c'est craindre, et craindre c'est souffrir."*

And suffering prompts to desperate remedies. We must not be too hard on a rough but romantic young fool, who talks according to his folly and his pain.'

CHAPTER XLIX

AN APPARITION

'But, after all,' he suddenly resumed, as if a new thought had struck him, 'is it quite such folly, after all? It really strikes me, dear Maud, that the subject may be worth a second thought. No, no, you won't refuse to hear me,' he said, observing me on the point of protesting. 'I am, of course, assuming that you are fancy free. I am assuming, too, that you don't care twopence about Dudley, and even that you fancy you dislike him. You know in that pleasant play, poor Sheridan—delightful fellow!—all our fine spirits are dead—he makes Mrs. Malaprop* say there is nothing like beginning with a little aversion. Now, though in matrimony, of course, that is only a joke, yet in love, believe me, it is no such thing. His own marriage with Miss Ogle,* I *know*, was a case in point. She expressed a positive horror of him at their first acquaintance; and yet, I believe, she would, a few months later, have died rather than not have married him.'

I was again about to speak, but with a smile he beckoned me into silence.

'There are two or three points you must bear in mind. One of the happiest privileges of your fortune is that you may, without imprudence, marry simply for love. There are few men in England who could offer you an estate comparable with that you already possess; or, in fact, appreciably increase the splendour of your fortune. If, therefore, he were in all other respects eligible, I can't see that his poverty would be an objection to weigh for one moment. He is quite a rough diamond. He has been, like many young men of the highest rank, too much given up to athletic sports—to that society which constitutes the aristocracy of the ring and the turf, and all that kind of thing. You see, I am putting all the worst points first. But I have known so many young men in my day, after a madcap career of a few years among prize-fighters, wrestlers, and jockeys—learning their slang and affecting their manners—take up and cultivate the graces and the decencies. There was poor dear Newgate,* many degrees lower in that kind of frolic, who, when he grew tired of it, became one of the most elegant and accomplished men in the House of Peers. Poor Newgate, he's gone, too! I could reckon up fifty of my early friends who all began like Dudley, and all turned out, more or less, like Newgate.'

At this moment came a knock at the door, and Dudley put in his head most inopportunely for the vision of his future graces and accomplishments.

'My good fellow,' said his father, with a sharp sort of playfulness, 'I happen to be talking about my son, and should rather not be over-heard; you will, therefore, choose another time for your visit.'

Dudley hesitated gruffly at the door, but another look from his father dismissed him.

'And now, my dear, you are to remember that Dudley has fine qualities—the most affectionate son in his rough way that ever father was blessed with; most admirable qualities—indomitable courage, and a high sense of honour; and lastly, that he has the Ruthyn blood—the purest blood, I maintain it, in England.'

My uncle, as he said this, drew himself up a little, unconsciously, his thin hand laid lightly over his heart with a little patting motion, and his countenance looked so strangely dignified and melancholy, that in admiring contemplation of it I lost some sentences which followed next.

'Therefore, dear, naturally anxious that my boy should not be dis-missed from home—as he must be, should you persevere in rejecting his suit—I beg that you will reserve your decision to this day fort-night, when I will with much pleasure hear what you may have to say on the subject. But till then, observe me, not a word.'

That evening he and Dudley were closeted for a long time. I sus-pect that he lectured him on the psychology of ladies; for a bouquet was laid beside my plate every morning at breakfast, which it must have been troublesome to get, for the conservatory at Bartram was a desert. In a few days more an anonymous green parrot arrived, in a gilt cage, with a little note in a clerk's hand, addressed to 'Miss Ruthyn (of Knowl), Bartram-Haugh,' &c. It contained only 'Directions for caring green parrot', at the close of which, *underlined*, the words appeared—'The bird's name is Maud.'

The bouquets I invariably left on the tablecloth where I found them—the bird I insisted on Milly's keeping as her property. During the intervening fortnight Dudley never appeared, as he used some-times to do before, at luncheon, nor looked in at the window as we were at breakfast. He contented himself with one day placing himself in my way in the hall in his shooting accoutrements, and, with a clumsy, shuffling kind of respect, and hat in hand, he said—

'I think, Miss, I must a spoke uncivil t'other day. I was so awful put about, and didn't know no more nor a child what I was saying; and I wanted to tell ye I'm sorry for it, and I beg your pardon—very humble, I do.'

I did not know what to say. I therefore said nothing, but made a grave inclination, and passed on.

Two or three times Milly and I saw him at a little distance in our walks. He never attempted to join us. Once only he passed so near that some recognition was inevitable, and he stopped and in silence lifted his hat with an awkward respect. But although he did not approach us, he was ostentatious with a kind of telegraphic civility in the distance. He opened gates, he whistled his dogs to 'heel', he drove away cattle, and then himself withdrew. I really think he watched us occasionally to render these services, for in this distant way we encountered him decidedly oftener than we used to do before his flattering proposal of marriage.

You may be sure that we discussed, Milly and I, that occurrence pretty constantly in all sorts of moods. Limited as had been her experience of human society, she very clearly saw *now* how far below its presentable level was her hopeful brother.

The fortnight sped swiftly, as time always does when something we dislike and shrink from awaits us at its close. I never saw Uncle Silas during that period. It may seem odd to those who merely read the report of our last interview, in which his manner had been more playful and his talk more trifling than in any other, that from it I had carried away a profounder sense of fear and insecurity than from any other. It was with a foreboding of evil and an awful dejection that on a very dark day, in Milly's room, I awaited the summons which I was sure would reach me from my punctual guardian.

As I looked from the window upon the slanting rain and leaden sky, and thought of the hated interview that awaited me, I pressed my hand to my troubled heart, and murmured, 'Oh, that I had wings like a dove! then would I flee away, and be at rest.'

Just then the prattle of the parrot struck my ear. I looked round on the wire cage, and remembered the words, 'The bird's name is Maud.'

'Poor bird!' I said. 'I dare say, Milly, it longs to get out. If it were a native of this country, would not you like to open the window and then the door of that cruel cage, and let the poor thing fly away?'

'Master wants Miss Maud,' said Wyat's disagreeable tones, at the half-open door.

I followed in silence, with the pressure of a near alarm at my heart, like a person going to an operation.

When I entered the room my heart beat so fast that I could hardly speak. The tall form of Uncle Silas rose before me, and I made him a faltering reverence.

He darted from under his brows a wild, fierce glance at old Wyat, and pointed to the door imperiously with his skeleton finger. The door shut, and we were alone.

'A chair?' he said, pointing to a seat.

'Thank you, uncle, I prefer standing,' I faltered.

He also stood—his white head bowed forward, the phosphoric glare of his strange eyes shone upon me from under his brows—his finger-nails just rested on the table.

'You saw the luggage corded and addressed, as it stands ready for removal in the hall?' he asked.

I had. Milly and I had read the cards which dangled from the trunk-handles and gun-case. The address was—'Mr. Dudley R. Ruthyn, Paris, *via* Dover.'

'I am old—agitated—on the eve of a decision on which much depends. Pray relieve my suspense. Is my son to leave Bartram to-day in sorrow, or to remain in joy? Pray answer quickly.'

I stammered I know not what. I was incoherent—wild, perhaps; but somehow I expressed my meaning—my unalterable decision. I thought his lips grew whiter and his eyes shone brighter as I spoke.

When I had quite made an end he heaved a great sigh, and turning his eyes slowly to the right and the left, like a man in a helpless distraction, he whispered—

'God's will be done.'

I thought he was upon the point of fainting—a clay tint darkened the white of his face; and seeming to forget my presence, he sat down, looking with a despairing scowl on his ashy, old hand, as it lay upon the table.

I stood gazing at him, feeling almost as if I had murdered the old man—he still gazing askance, with an imbecile scowl, upon his hand.

'Shall I go, sir?' I at length found courage to whisper.

'*Go?*' he said, looking up suddenly; and it seemed to me as if a stream of cold sheet lightning had crossed and enveloped me for a moment.

'Go?—oh!—a—yes—*yes*, Maud—go. I must see poor Dudley before his departure,' he added, as it were, in soliloquy.

Trembling lest he should revoke his permission to depart, I glided quickly and noiselessly from the room.

Old Wyat was prowling outside, with a cloth in her hand, pretending to dust the carved doorcase. She frowned a stare of inquiry over her shrunken arm on me, as I passed. Milly, who had been on the watch, ran and met me. We heard my uncle's voice, as I shut the door, calling Dudley. He had been waiting probably in the adjoining room. I hurried into my chamber, with Milly at my side, and there my agitation found relief in tears, as that of girlhood naturally does.

A little while after we saw from the window Dudley, looking, I thought, very pale, get into a vehicle, on the top of which his luggage lay, and drive away from Bartram.

I began to take comfort. His departure was an inexpressible relief. His final departure! a distant journey!

We had tea in Milly's room that night. Firelight and candles are inspiring. In that red glow I always felt and feel more safe, as well as more comfortable, than in the daylight—quite irrationally, for we know the night is the appointed day of such as love the darkness better than light, and evil walks thereby. But so it is. Perhaps the very consciousness of external danger enhances the enjoyment of the well-lighted interior, just as the storm does that roars and hurtles over the roof.

While Milly and I were talking, very cosily, a knock came to the room door, and without waiting for an invitation to enter, old Wyat came in, and glowering at us, with her brown claw upon the door-handle, she said to Milly—

'Ye must leave your funnin', Miss Milly, and take your turn in your father's room.'

'Is he ill?' I asked.

She answered, addressing not me, but Milly—

'A wrought two hours in a fit arter Master Dudley went. 'Twill be the death o' him, I'm thinkin', poor old fellah. I wor sorry myself when I saw Master Dudley a going off in the moist to-day, poor fellah. There's trouble enough in the family without a' that; but 'twont be a family long, I'm thinkin'. Nout but trouble, nout but trouble, since late changes came.'

Judging by the sour glance she threw on me as she said this, I concluded that I represented those 'late changes' to which all the sorrows of the house were referred.

I felt unhappy under the ill-will even of this odious old woman, being one of those unhappily constructed mortals who cannot be indifferent when they reasonably ought, and always yearn after kindness, even that of the worthless.

'I must go. I wish you'd come wi' me, Maud, I'm so afraid all alone,' said Milly, imploringly.

'Certainly, Milly,' I answered, not liking it, you may be sure; 'you shan't sit there alone.'

So together we went, old Wyat cautioning us for our lives to make no noise.

We passed through the old man's sitting-room, where that day had occurred his brief but momentous interview with me, and his parting with his only son, and entered the bedroom at the further end.

A low fire burned in the grate. The room was in a sort of twilight. A dim lamp near the foot of the bed at the further side, was the only light burning there. Old Wyat whispered an injunction not to speak above our breaths, nor to leave the fireside unless the sick man called or showed signs of weariness. These were the directions of the Doctor, who had been there.

So Milly and I sat ourselves down near the hearth, and old Wyat left us to our resources. We could hear the patient breathe; but he was quite still. In whispers we talked; but our conversation flagged. I was, after my wont, upbraiding myself for the suffering I had inflicted. After about half an hour's desultory whispering, and intervals, growing longer and longer, of silence, it was plain that Milly was falling asleep.

She strove against it, and I tried hard to keep her talking; but it would not do, sleep overcame her; and I was the only person in that ghastly room in a state of perfect consciousness.

There were associations connected with my last vigil there to make my situation very nervous and disagreeable. Had I not had so much to occupy my mind of a distinctly practical kind, Dudley's audacious suit, my uncle's questionable toleration of it, and my own conduct throughout that most disagreeable period of my existence, I should have felt my present situation a great deal more.

As it was, I thought of my real troubles, and something of Cousin Knollys, and, I confess, a good deal of Lord Ilbury. When looking towards the door I thought I saw a human face, about the most terrible my fancy could have called up, looking fixedly into the room. It was only a 'three-quarter,'* and not the whole figure, the door hid that in a great measure, and I fancied I saw, too, a portion of the fingers. The face gazed toward the bed, and in the imperfect light looked like a livid mask, with chalky eyes.

I had so often been startled by similar apparitions formed by accidental lights and shadows disguising homely objects, that I stooped forward, expecting, though tremulously, to see this tremendous one in like manner dissolve itself into its harmless elements; and now, to my unspeakable terror, I became perfectly certain that I saw the countenance of Madame de la Rougierre.

With a cry, I started back, and shook Milly furiously from her trance.

'Look! look!' I cried. But the apparition or illusion was gone.

I clung so fast to Milly's arm, cowering behind her, that she could not rise.

'Milly! Milly! Milly! Milly!' I went on crying, like one struck with idiotcy, and unable to say anything else.

In a panic Milly, who had seen nothing, and could conjecture nothing of the cause of my terror, jumped up, and clinging to one another, we huddled together into the corner of the room, I still crying wildly, 'Milly! Milly! *Milly!*' and nothing else.

'What is it—where is it—what do you see?' cried Milly, clinging to me as I did to her.

'It will come again; it will come; oh, heaven!'

'What—what is it, Maud?'

'The face! the face!' I cried. 'Oh, Milly! Milly! Milly!'

We heard a step softly approaching the open door and in a horrible *sauve qui peut*, we rushed and stumbled together toward the light by Uncle Silas's bed. But old Wyat's voice and figure reassured us.

'Milly,' I said, so soon as, pale and very faint, I reached my apartment, 'no power on earth shall ever tempt me to enter that room again after dark.'

'Why, Maud, dear, what, in Heaven's name, did you see?' said Milly, scarcely less terrified.

'Oh, I can't; I can't; I *can't*, Milly. Never ask me. It is haunted. The room is haunted *horribly*.'

'Was it Charke?' whispered Milly, looking over her shoulder, all aghast.

'No, no—don't ask me; a fiend in a worse shape.' I was relieved at last by a long fit of weeping; and all night good Mary Quince sat by me, and Milly slept by my side. Starting and screaming, and drugged with sal-volatile, I got through that night of supernatural terror, and saw the blessed light of heaven again.

Doctor Jolks, when he came to see my uncle in the morning, visited me also. He pronounced me very hysterical, made minute inquiries respecting my hours and diet, asked what I had had for dinner yesterday. There was something a little comforting in his cool and confident pooh-poohing of the ghost theory. The result was a regimen which excluded tea, and imposed chocolate and porter, earlier hours, and I forget all beside; and he undertook to promise that, if I would but observe his directions, I should never see a ghost again.

CHAPTER L

MILLY'S FAREWELL

A FEW days' time saw me much better. Doctor Jolks was so contemptuously sturdy and positive on the point that I began to have comfortable doubts about the reality of my ghost; and having still a horror indescribable of the illusion, if such it were, the room in which it appeared, and everything concerning it, I would neither speak, nor, so far as I could, think of it.

So, though Bartram-Haugh was gloomy as well as beautiful, and some of its associations awful, and the solitude that reigned there sometimes almost terrible, yet early hours, bracing exercise, and the fine air that predominates that region, soon restored my nerves to a healthier tone.

But it seemed to me that Bartram-Haugh was to be to me a vale of tears; or rather, in my sad pilgrimage, that valley of the shadow of death through which poor Christian* fared alone and in the dark.

One day Milly ran into the parlour, pale, with wet cheeks, and, without saying a word, threw her arms about my neck, and burst into a paroxysm of weeping.

'What is it, Milly—what's the matter, dear—what is it?' I cried aghast; but returning her close embrace heartily.

'Oh! Maud—Maud darling, he's going to send me away.'

'Away, dear! *where* away? And leave me alone in this dreadful solitude, where he knows I shall die of fear and grief without you? Oh! no—no, it *must* be a mistake.'

'I'm going to France, Maud—I'm going away. Mrs. Jolks is going to London, day ar'ter to-morrow, and I'm to go wi' her; and an old French lady, he says, from the school will meet me there, and bring me the rest o' the way.'

'Oh—ho—ho—ho—ho—o—o—o!' cried poor Milly, hugging me closer still, with her head buried in my shoulder, and swaying me about like a wrestler, in her agony.

'I never wor away from home afore, except that little bit wi' you over there at Elverston; and you wor wi' me then, Maud; an' I love ye—better than Bartram—better than a'; an' I think I'll die, Maud, if they take me away.'

I was just as wild in my woe as poor Milly; and it was not until we had wept together for a full hour—sometimes standing—sometimes walking up and down the room—sometimes sitting and getting up in turns to fall on one another's necks—that Milly, plucking her hand-kerchief from her pocket, drew a note from it at the same time, which, as it fell upon the floor, she at once recollected to be one from Uncle Silas to me.

It was to this effect:—

'I wish to apprize my dear niece and ward of my plans. Milly pro-ceeds to an admirable French school, as a pensionnaire, and leaves this on Thursday next. If after three months' trial she finds it in any way objectionable, she returns to us. If, on the contrary, she finds it in all respects the charming residence it has been represented to me, you, on the expiration of that period, join her there, until the tempor-ary complication of my affairs shall have been so far adjusted as to enable me to receive you once more at Bartram. Hoping for happier days, and wishing to assure you that three months is the extreme limit of your separation from my poor Milly, I have written this, feeling, alas! unequal to seeing you at present.

'Bartram, Tuesday.

'P.S.—I can have no objection to your apprizing Monica Knollys of these arrangements. You will understand, of course, not a copy of this letter, but its substance.'

Over this document, scanning it as lawyers do a new Act of Parliament, we took comfort. After all, it was limited; a separation not to exceed three months, possibly much shorter. On the whole, too, I pleased myself with thinking Uncle Silas's note, though peremptory, was kind.

Our paroxysms subsided into sadness; a close correspondence was arranged. Something of the bustle and excitement of change super-vened. If it turned out to be, in truth, a 'charming residence', how very delightful our meeting in France, with the interest of foreign scenery, ways, and faces, would be!

So Thursday arrived—a new gush of sorrow—a new brightening up—and, amid regrets and anticipations, we parted at the gate at the further end of the Windmill Wood. Then, of course, were more good-byes, more embraces, and tearful smiles. Good Mrs. Jolks, who met us there, was in a huge fuss; I believe it was her first visit to the metropolis, and she was in proportion heated and important, and terrified about the train, so we had not many last words.

I watched poor Milly, whose head was stretched from the window, her hand waving many adieux, until the curve of the road, and the clump of old ash-trees, thick with ivy, hid Milly, carriage and all, from view. My eyes filled again with tears. I turned towards Bartram. At my side stood honest Mary Quince.

'Don't take on so, Miss; 'twont be no time passing; three months is nothing at all,' she said, smiling kindly.

I smiled through my tears and kissed the good creature, and so side by side we re-entered the gate.

The lithe young man in fustian, whom I had seen talking with Beauty on the morning of our first encounter with that youthful Amazon, was awaiting our re-entrance with the key in his hand. He stood half behind the open wicket. One lean brown cheek, one shy eye, and his sharp upturned nose, I saw as we passed. He was treating me to a stealthy scrutiny, and seemed to shun my glance, for he shut the door quickly, and busied himself locking it, and then began stubbing up some thistles which grew close by, with the toe of his thick shoe, his back to us all the time.

It struck me that I recognized his features, and I asked Mary Quince.

'Have you seen that young man before, Quince?'

'He brings up game for your uncle, sometimes, Miss, and lends a hand in the garden, I believe.'

'Do you know his name, Mary?'

'They call him Tom; I don't know what more, Miss.'

'Tom,' I called; 'please, Tom, come here for a moment.'

Tom turned about, and approached slowly. He was more civil than the Bartram people usually were, for he plucked off his shapeless cap of rabbit-skin with a clownish respect.

'Tom, what is your other name; Tom *what*, my good man?' I asked.

'Tom Brice, ma'am.'

'Haven't I seen you before, Tom Brice?' I pursued, for my curiosity was excited, and with it much graver feelings; for there certainly *was* a resemblance in Tom's features to those of the postilion who had looked so hard at me as I passed the carriage in the warren at Knowl, on the evening of the outrage which had scared that quiet place.

''Appen you may have, ma'am,' he answered, quite coolly, looking down the buttons of his gaiters.

'Are you a good whip—do you drive well?'

'I'll drive a plough wi' most lads hereabout,' answered Tom.

'Have you ever been to Knowl, Tom?'

Tom gaped very innocently.

'Anan,' he said.

'Here, Tom, is half-a-crown.'

He took it readily enough.

'That be very good,' said Tom, with a nod, having glanced sharply at the coin.

I can't say whether he applied that term to the coin, or to his luck, or to my generous self.

'Now, Tom, you'll tell me, have you ever been to Knowl?'

'Maught a' bin, ma'am, but I don't mind no sich place—no.'

As Tom spoke this with great deliberation, like a man who loves truth, putting a strain upon his memory for its sake, he spun the silver coin two or three times into the air and caught it, staring at it the while, with all his might.

'Now, Tom, recollect yourself, and tell me the truth, and I'll be a friend to you. Did you ride postilion to a carriage having a lady in it, and I think several gentlemen, which came to the grounds of Knowl, when the party had their luncheon on the grass, and there was a—a quarrel with the gamekeepers? Try, Tom, to recollect; you shall, upon my honour, have no trouble about it, and I'll try to serve you.'

Tom was silent, while with a vacant gape he watched the spin of his half-crown twice, and then catching it with a smack in his hand, which he thrust into his pocket, he said, still looking in the same direction—

'I never rid postilion in my days, ma'am. I know nout o' sich a place, though 'appen I maught a' bin there; Knowl, ye ca't. I was ne'er out o' Derbyshire but thrice to Warwick fair wi' horses be rail an twice to York.'

'You're certain, Tom?'

'Sartin sure, ma'am.'

And Tom made another loutish salute, and cut the conference short by turning off the path and beginning to hollo after some trespassing cattle.

I had not felt anything like so nearly sure in this essay at identification as I had in that of Dudley. Even of Dudley's identity with the Church Scarsdale man I had daily grown less confident; and, indeed, had it been proposed to bring it to the test of a wager, I do not think I should, in the language of sporting gentlemen, have cared to 'back' my original opinion. There was, however, a sufficient uncertainty to make me uncomfortable; and there was another uncertainty to enhance the unpleasant sense of ambiguity.

On our way back we passed the bleaching trunks and limbs of several ranks of barkless oaks lying side by side. Some squared by the hatchet, perhaps sold, for there were large letters and Roman numerals traced upon them in red chalk. I sighed as I passed them by, not because it was wrongfully done, for I really rather leaned to the belief that Uncle Silas was well advised in point of law. But alas! here lay low the grand old family decorations of Bartram-Haugh, not to be replaced for centuries to come, under whose spreading boughs the Ruthyns of three hundred years ago had hawked and hunted!

On the trunk of one of these I sat down to rest, Mary Quince meanwhile pattering about in unmeaning explorations. While thus listlessly seated, the girl, Meg Hawkes, walked by, carrying a basket.

'Hish!' she said quickly as she passed, without altering her pace or raising her eyes; 'don't ye speak nor look—fayther spies us; I'll tell ye next turn.'

'Next turn'—when was that? Well, she might be returning; and as she could not then say more than she had said, in merely passing without a pause, I concluded to wait for a short time and see what would come of it.

After a short time I looked about me a little, and I saw Dickon Hawkes—Pegtop, as poor Milly used to call him—with an axe in his hand, prowling luridly among the timber.

Observing that I saw him, he touched his hat sulkily, and by-and-by passed me, muttering to himself. He plainly could not understand what business I could have in that particular part of the Windmill Wood, and let me see it in his countenance.

His daughter did pass me again; but this time he was near, and she was silent. Her next transit occurred as he was questioning Mary Quince at some little distance; and as she passed precisely in the same way, she said—

'Don't you be alone wi' Master Dudley nowhere for the world's worth.'

The injunction was so startling that I was on the point of questioning the girl. But I recollected myself, and waited in the hope that in her future transits she might be more explicit. But one word more she did not utter, and the jealous eye of old Pegtop was so constantly upon us that I refrained.

There was vagueness and suggestion enough in the oracle to supply work for many an hour of anxious conjecture, and many a horrible vigil by night. Was I never to know peace at Bartram-Haugh?

Ten days of poor Milly's absence, and of my solitude, had already passed, when my uncle sent for me to his room.

When old Wyat stood at the door, mumbling and snarling her message, my heart died within me.

It was late—just that hour when dejected people feel their anxieties most—when the cold gray of twilight has deepened to its darkest shade, and before the cheerful candles are lighted, and the safe quiet of the night sets in.

When I entered my uncle's sitting-room—though his windowshutters were open and the wan streaks of sunset visible through them, like narrow lakes in the chasms of the dark western clouds—a pair of candles were burning; one stood upon the table by his desk, the other on the chimneypiece, before which his tall, thin figure stooped. His hand leaned on the mantelpiece, and the light from the candle just above his bowed head touched his silvery hair. He was looking, as it seemed, into the subsiding embers of the fire, and was a very statue of forsaken dejection and decay.

'Uncle!' I ventured to say, having stood for some time unperceived near his table.

'Ah, yes, Maud, my dear child—my *dear* child.'

He turned, and with the candle in his hand, smiling his silvery smile of suffering on me. He walked more feebly and stiffly, I thought, than I had ever seen him move before.

'Sit down, Maud—pray sit there.'

I took the chair he indicated

'In my misery and my solitude, Maud, I have invoked you like a spirit, and you appear.'

With his two hands leaning on the table he looked across at me, in a stooping attitude; he had not seated himself. I continued silent until it should be his pleasure to question or address me.

At last he said, raising himself and looking upward, with a wild adoration—his finger tips elevated and glimmering in the faint mixed light—

'No, I thank my Creator, I am not quite forsaken.'

Another silence, during which he looked stedfastly at me, and muttered, as if thinking aloud—

'My guardian angel!—my guardian angel! Maud, *you* have a heart.' He addressed me suddenly—'Listen, for a few moments, to the appeal of an old and broken-hearted man—your guardian—your uncle—your *suppliant*. I had resolved never to speak to you more on this subject. But I was wrong. It was pride that inspired me—mere pride.'

I felt myself growing pale, and flushed by turns during the pause that followed.

'I'm very miserable—very nearly desperate. What remains for me—what remains? Fortune has done her worst—thrown in the dust, her wheels rolled over me; and the servile world, who follow her chariot like a mob, stamp upon the mangled wretch. All this had passed over me, and left me scarred and bloodless in this solitude. It was not my fault, Maud—I say it was no fault of mine; I have no remorse, though more regrets than I can count, and all scored with fire. As people passed by Bartram, and looked upon its neglected grounds and smokeless chimneys, they thought my plight, I dare say, about the worst a proud man could be reduced to. They could not imagine one half its misery. But this old hectic*—this old epileptic— this old spectre of wrongs, calamities, and follies, had still one hope—my manly though untutored son—the last male scion of the Ruthyns. Maud, have I lost him? His fate—my fate—I may say *Milly's* fate;—we all await your sentence. He loves you, as none but the very young can love. And that once only in a life. He loves you desperately—a most affectionate nature—a Ruthyn, the best blood in England—the last man of the race; and I—if I lose him I lose all; and you will see me in my coffin, Maud, before many months. I stand before you in the attitude of a suppliant—shall I kneel?'

His eyes were fixed on me with the light of despair, his knotted hands clasped, his whole figure bowed toward me. I was inexpressibly shocked and pained.

'Oh, uncle! uncle!' I cried, and from very excitement I burst into tears.

I saw that his eyes were fixed on me with a dismal scrutiny. I think he divined the nature of my agitation; but he determined, notwithstanding, to press me while my helpless agitation continued.

'You see my suspense—you see my miserable and frightful suspense. You are kind, Maud; you love your father's memory; you pity your father's brother; you would not say no, and place a pistol at his head?'

'Oh! I must—I must—I *must* say no. Oh! spare me, uncle, for Heaven's sake. Don't question me—don't press me. I could not—I *could* not do what you ask.'

'I yield, Maud—I yield, my dear. I will *not* press you; you shall have time, your *own* time, to think. I will accept *no* answer now—no, *none*, Maud.'

He said this, raising his thin hand to silence me.

'There, Maud, enough. I have spoken, as I always do to you, frankly, perhaps too frankly; but agony and despair will speak out, and plead, even with the most obdurate and cruel.'

With these words Uncle Silas entered his bed-chamber, and shut the door, not violently, but with a resolute hand, and I thought I heard a cry.

I hastened to my own room. I threw myself on my knees, and thanked Heaven for the firmness vouchsafed me; I could not believe it to have been my own.

I was more miserable in consequence of this renewed suit on behalf of my odious cousin than I can describe. My uncle had taken such a line of importunity that it became a sort of agony to resist. I thought of the possibility of my hearing of his having made away with himself, and was every morning relieved when I heard that he was still as usual. I have often wondered since at my own firmness. In that dreadful interview with my uncle I had felt, in the whirl and horror of my mind, on the very point of submitting, just as nervous people are said to throw themselves over precipices through sheer dread of falling.

CHAPTER LI

SARAH MATILDA COMES TO LIGHT

SOME time after this interview, one day as I sat, sad enough, in my room, looking listlessly from the window, with good Mary Quince, whom, whether in the house or in my melancholy rambles, I always had by my side, I was startled by the sound of a loud and shrill female voice, in violent hysterical action, gabbling with great rapidity, sobbing, and very nearly screaming in a sort of fury.

I started up, staring at the door.

'Lord bless us!' cried honest Mary Quince, with round eyes and mouth agape, staring in the same direction.

'Mary—Mary, what can it be?'

'Are they beating some one down yonder? I don't know where it comes from,' gasped Quince.

'I will—I will—I'll see her. It's her I want. Oo—hoo—hoo—hoo—oo—o—Miss Maud Ruthyn of Knowl. Miss Ruthyn of Knowl. Hoo—hoo—hoo—hoo—oo!'

'What on earth can it be?' I exclaimed, in great bewilderment and terror.

It was now plainly very near indeed, and I heard the voice of our mild and shaky old butler evidently remonstrating with the distressed damsel.

'I'll see her,' she continued, pouring a torrent of vile abuse upon me, which stung me with a sudden sense of anger. What had I done to be afraid of any one? How dared any one in my uncle's house—in *my* house—mix my name up with her detestable scurrilities?

'For Heaven's sake, Miss, don't ye go out,' cried poor Quince; 'it's some drunken creature.'

But I was very angry, and, like a fool, as I was, I threw open the door, exclaiming in a loud and haughty key—

'Here is Miss Ruthyn of Knowl. Who wants to see her?'

A pink and white young lady, with black tresses, violent, weeping, shrill, voluble was flouncing up the last stair, and shook her dress out on the lobby; and poor old Giblets, as Milly used to call him, was following in her wake, with many small remonstrances and entreaties, perfectly unheeded.

The moment I looked at this person, it struck me that she was the identical lady whom I had seen in the carriage at Knowl Warren. The next moment I was in doubt; the next, still more so. She was decidedly thinner, and dressed by no means in such lady-like taste. Perhaps she was hardly like her at all. I began to distrust all these resemblances, and to fancy, with a shudder, that they originated, perhaps, only in my own sick brain.

On seeing me, this young lady—as it seemed to me, a good deal of the barmaid or lady's-maid species—dried her eyes fiercely, and, with a flaming countenance, called upon me peremptorily to produce her 'lawful husband'. Her loud, insolent, outrageous attack had the effect of enhancing my indignation, and I quite forget what I said to her, but I well remember that her manner became a good deal more decent. She was plainly under the impression that I wanted to appropriate her husband; or, at least, that he wanted to marry me; and she ran on at such a pace, and her harangue was so passionate, incoherent, and unintelligible, that I thought her out of her mind; she was far from it, however. I think if she had allowed me even a second for reflection, I should have hit upon her meaning. As it was, nothing could exceed my perplexity, until, plucking a soiled newspaper from her pocket, she indicated a particular paragraph, already sufficiently emphasized by double lines of red ink at its sides. It was a Lancashire paper, of about six weeks since, and very much worn and soiled for its age. I remember in particular a circular stain from the bottom of a vessel, either of coffee or brown stout. The paragraph was as follows, recording an event a year or more anterior to the date of the paper—

'MARRIAGE.—on Tuesday, August 7, 18— at Leatherwig Church, by the Rev. Arthur Hughes, Dudley R. Ruthyn, Esq., only son and heir of Silas Ruthyn, Esq., of Bartram-Haugh, Derbyshire, to Sarah Matilda, second daughter of John Mangles, Esq., of Wiggan, in this county.'

At first I read nothing but amazement in this announcement, but in another moment I felt how completely I was relieved; and showing, I believe, my intense satisfaction in my countenance—for the young lady eyed me with considerable surprise and curiosity—I said—

'This is extremely important. You must see Mr. Silas Ruthyn this moment. I am certain he knows nothing of it. I will conduct you to him.'

'No more he does. I know that myself,' she replied, following me with a self-asserting swagger, and a great rustling of cheap silk.

As we entered, Uncle Silas looked up from his sofa, and closed his *Revue des deux Mondes*.*

'What is all this?' he inquired, drily.

'This lady has brought with her a newspaper containing an extraordinary statement which affects our family,' I answered.

Uncle Silas raised himself, and looked with a hard, narrow scrutiny at the unknown young lady.

'A libel, I suppose, in the paper?' he said, extending his hand for it.

'No, uncle—no; only a marriage,' I answered.

'Not Monica?' he said, as he took it. 'Pah, it smells all over of tobacco and beer,' he added, throwing a little eau de Cologne over it.

He raised it with a mixture of curiosity and disgust, saying again 'pah', as he did so.

He read the paragraph, and as he did his face changed from white, all over, to lead colour. He raised his eyes, and looked steadily for some seconds at the young lady, who seemed a little awed by his strange presence.

'And you are, I suppose, the young lady, Sarah Matilda *née* Mangles, mentioned in this little paragraph?' he said, in a tone you would have called a sneer, were it not that it trembled.

Sarah Matilda assented.

'My son is, I dare say, within reach. It so happens that I wrote to arrest his journey, and summon him here, some days since—some days since—some days since,' he repeated slowly, like a person whose mind has wandered far away from the theme on which he is speaking.

He had rung his bell, and old Wyat, always hovering about his rooms, entered.

'I want my son, immediately. If not in the house, send Harry to the stables; if not there, let him be followed, instantly. Brice is an active fellow, and will know where to find him. If he is in Feltram, or at a distance, let Brice take a horse, and Master Dudley can ride it back. He must be here without the loss of one moment.'

There intervened nearly a quarter of an hour, during which, whenever he recollected her, Uncle Silas treated the young lady with a hyper-refined and ceremonious politeness, which appeared to make her uneasy, and even a little shy, and certainly prevented a renewal of those lamentations and invectives which he had heard faintly from the stair-head.

But for the most part Uncle Silas seemed to forget us and his book, and all that surrounded him, lying back in the corner of his sofa, his chin upon his breast, and such a fearful shade and carving on his features as made me prefer looking in any direction but his.

At length we heard the tread of Dudley's thick boots on the oak boards, and faint and muffled the sound of his voice as he cross-examined old Wyat before entering the chamber of audience.

I think he suspected quite another visitor, and had no expectation of seeing the particular young lady, who rose from her chair as he entered, in an opportune flood of tears, crying—

'Oh, Dudley, Dudley!—oh, Dudley, could you? Oh, Dudley, your own poor Sal! You could not—you would not—your lawful wife!'

This and a good deal more, with cheeks that streamed like a window-pane in a thunder shower, spoke Sarah Matilda with all her oratory, working his arm, which she clung to, up and down all the time, like the handle of a pump. But Dudley was, manifestly, confounded and dumb-foundered.* He stood for a long time gaping at his father, and stole just one sheepish glance at me; and, with red face and forehead, looked down at his boots, and then again at his father, who remained just in the attitude I have described, and with the same forbidding and dreary intensity in his strange face.

Like a quarrelsome man, worried in his sleep by a noise, Dudley suddenly woke up, as it were, with a start, in a half-suppressed exasperation, and shook her off with a jerk and a muttered curse, as she whisked involuntarily into a chair, with more violence than can have been pleasant.

'Judging by your looks and demeanour, Sir, I can almost anticipate your answers,' said my uncle, addressing him suddenly. 'Will you be good enough—pray, madame, (parenthetically to our visitor,) command yourself for a few moments. Is this young person the daughter of a Mr. Mangles, and is her name Sarah Matilda?'

'I dessay,' answered Dudley, hurriedly.

'Is she your wife?'

'Is she my wife?' repeated Dudley, ill at ease.

'Yes, Sir; it is a plain question.'

All this time Sarah Matilda was perpetually breaking into talk, and with difficulty silenced by my uncle.

'Well, 'appen she says I am—does she?' replied Dudley.

'Is she your wife, Sir?'

'Mayhap she so considers it, after a fashion,' he replied, with an impudent swagger, seating himself as he did so.

'What do *you* think, Sir?' persisted Uncle Silas.

'I don't think nout about it,' replied Dudley, surlily.

'Is that account true?' said my uncle, handing him the paper.

'They wishes us to believe so, at any rate.'

'Answer directly, Sir. We have our thoughts upon it. If it be true, it is capable of *every* proof. For expedition's sake I ask you. There is no use in prevaricating.'

'Who wants to deny it? It *is* true—there!'

'*There!* I knew he would,' screamed the young woman, hysterically, with a laugh of strange joy.

'Shut up, will ye?' growled Dudley, savagely.

'Oh, Dudley, Dudley, darling! what have I done?'

'Bin and ruined me, jest—that's all.'

'Oh! no, no, no, Dudley. Ye know I wouldn't. I could not—*could* not hurt ye, Dudley. No, no, no!'

He grinned at her, and, with a sharp side-nod, said—

'Wait a bit.'

'Oh, Dudley, don't be vexed, dear. I did not mean it. I would not hurt ye for all the world. Never.'

'Well, never mind. You and yours tricked me finely; and now you've got me—that's all.'

My uncle laughed a very odd laugh.

'I knew it, of course; and upon my word, madam, you and he make a very pretty couple,' sneered Uncle Silas.

Dudley made no answer, looking, however, very savage.

And with this poor young wife, so recently wedded, the low villain had actually solicited me to marry him!

I am quite certain that my uncle was as entirely ignorant as I of Dudley's connexion, and had, therefore, no participation in this appalling wickedness.

'And I have to congratulate you, my good fellow, on having secured the affections of a very suitable and vulgar young woman.'

'I baint the first o' the family as a' done the same,' retorted Dudley.

At this taunt the old man's fury for a moment overpowered him. In an instant he was on his feet, quivering from head to foot. I never saw such a countenance—like one of those demon-grotesques we see in the Gothic side-aisles and groinings*—a dreadful grimace, monkey-like and insane—and his thin hand caught up his ebony stick, and shook it paralytically in the air.

'If ye touch me wi' that, I'll smash ye, by ——!' shouted Dudley, furious, raising his hands and hitching his shoulder, just as I had seen him when he fought Captain Oakley.

For a moment this picture was suspended before me, and I screamed, I know not what, in my terror. But the old man, the veteran of many a scene of excitement, where men disguise their ferocity in calm tones, and varnish their fury with smiles, had not quite lost his self-command. He turned toward me and said—

'Does he know what he's saying?'

And with an icy laugh of contempt, his high, thin, forehead still flushed, he sat down trembling.

'If you want to say aught, I'll hear ye. Ye may jaw me all ye like, and I'll stan' it.'

'Oh, I may speak? Thank you,' sneered Uncle Silas, glancing slowly round at me, and breaking into a cold laugh.

'Ay, I don't mind cheek, not I; but you must not go for to do that, ye know. Gammon.* I won't stand a blow—I won't fro' *no* one.'

'Well, Sir, availing myself of your permission to speak, I may remark, without offence to the young lady, that I don't happen to recollect the name Mangles among the old families of England. I presume you have chosen her chiefly for her virtues and her graces.'

Mrs. Sarah Matilda, not apprehending this compliment quite as Uncle Silas meant it, dropped a courtesy, notwithstanding her agitation, and, wiping her eyes, said, with a blubbered smile—

'You're very kind, sure.'

'I hope, for both your sakes, she has got a little money. I don't see how you are to live else. You're too lazy for a gamekeeper; and I don't think you could keep a pot-house, you are so addicted to drinking and quarrelling. The only thing I am quite clear upon is, that you and your wife must find some other abode than this. You shall depart this evening; and now, Mr. and Mrs. Dudley Ruthyn, you may quit this room, if you please.'

Uncle Silas had risen, and made them one of his old courtly bows, smiling a death-like sneer, and pointing to the door with his trembling fingers.

'Come, will ye?' said Dudley, grinding his teeth. 'You're pretty well done here.'

Not half understanding the situation, but looking woefully bewildered, she dropped a farewell courtesy at the door.

'Will ye *cut*?' barked Dudley, in a tone that made her jump; and suddenly, without looking about, he strode after her from the room.

'Maud, how shall I recover this? The vulgar *villain*—the *fool*! What an abyss were we approaching! and for me the last hope gone—and for me utter, utter, irretrievable ruin.'

He was passing his fingers tremulously back and forward along the top of the mantelpiece, like a man in search of something, and continued so, looking along it, feebly and vacantly, although there was nothing there.

'I wish, uncle—you do not know how much I wish—I could be of any use to you. Maybe I can?'

He turned and looked at me sharply.

'Maybe you can,' he echoed slowly. 'Yes, maybe you can,' he repeated more briskly. 'Let us—let us see—let us think—that d— fellow!—my head!'

'You're not well, uncle?'

'Oh! yes, very well. We'll talk in the evening—I'll send for you.'

I found Wyat in the next room, and told her to hasten, as I thought he was ill. I hope it was not very selfish, but such had grown to be my horror of seeing him in one of his strange seizures, that I hastened from the room precipitately—partly to escape the risk of being asked to remain.

The walls of Bartram House are thick, and the recess at the doorway deep. As I closed my uncle's door I heard Dudley's voice on the stairs. I did not wish to be seen by him or by his 'lady', as his poor wife called herself, who was engaged in vehement dialogue with him as I emerged, and not caring either to re-enter my uncle's room, I remained quietly ensconced within the heavy door-case, in which position I overheard Dudley say with a savage snarl—

'You'll jest go back the way ye came. *I*'m not goin' wi'ye, if that's what ye be drivin' at—dang your impitins!'

'Oh! Dudley, dear, *what* have I done—what *have* I done—ye hate me so?'

'What a' ye done? ye vicious little beast, ye! You've got us turned out an' disinherited wi' yer d——d bosh, that's all; don't ye think it's enough?'

I could only hear her sobs and shrill tones in reply, for they were descending the stairs; and Mary Quince reported to me, in a horrified sort of way, that she saw him bundle her into the fly at the door, like a truss of hay into a hay-loft. And he stood with his head in at the window, scolding her, till it drove away.

'I knew he wor jawing her, poor thing! by the way he kep' waggin' his head—an' he had his fist inside, a shakin' in her face. I'm sure he looked wicked enough for anything; an' she a crying like a babby, an' lookin' back, an' wavin' her wet hankicher to him—poor thing!—and she so young! 'Tis a pity. Dear me! I often think, Miss, 'tis well for me I never was married. And see how we all would like to get husbands for all that, though so few is happy together. 'Tis a queer world, and them that's single is maybe the best off after all.'

CHAPTER LII

THE PICTURE OF A WOLF

I WENT down that evening to the sitting-room which had been assigned to Milly and me, in search of a book—my good Mary Quince always attending me. The door was a little open, and I was startled by the light of a candle proceeding from the fireside, together with a considerable aroma of tobacco and brandy.

On my little work-table, which he had drawn beside the hearth, lay Dudley's pipe, his brandy-flask, and an empty tumbler; and he was sitting with one foot on the fender, his elbow on his knee, and his head resting in his hand, weeping. His back being a little toward the door, he did not perceive us; and we saw him rub his knuckles in his eyes, and heard the sounds of his selfish lamentation.

Mary and I stole away quietly, leaving him in possession, wondering when he was to leave the house, according to the sentence which I had heard pronounced upon him.

I was delighted to see old 'Giblets' quietly strapping his luggage in the hall, and heard from him in a whisper that he was to leave that evening by rail—he did not know whither.

About half an hour afterwards Mary Quince, going out to reconnoitre, heard from old Wyat in the lobby that he had just started to meet the train.

Blessed be heaven for that deliverance! An evil spirit had been cast out, and the house looked lighter and happier. It was not until I sat down in the quiet of my room that the scenes and images of that agitating day began to move before my memory in orderly procession, and for the first time I appreciated, with a stunning sense of horror and a perfect rapture of thanksgiving, the value of my escape and the immensity of the danger which had threatened me. It may have been miserable weakness—I think it was. But I was young, nervous, and afflicted with a troublesome sort of conscience, which occasionally went mad, and insisted, in small things as well as great, upon sacrifices which my reason now assures me were absurd. Of Dudley I had a perfect horror; and yet had that system of solicitation, that dreadful and direct appeal to my compassion, that placing of my feeble girlhood in the seat of the arbiter of my aged uncle's hope or despair, been long persisted in, my resistance might have been worn out—who can tell?—and I self-sacrificed! Just as criminals in Germany* are teased, and watched, and cross-examined, year after year, incessantly, into a sort of madness; and worn out with the suspense, the iteration, the self-restraint, and insupportable fatigue, they at last cut all short, accuse themselves, and go infinitely relieved to the scaffold—you may guess, then, for me, nervous, self-diffident, and alone, how intense was the comfort of knowing that Dudley was actually married, and the harrowing importunity which had just commenced for ever silenced.

That night I saw my uncle. I pitied him, though I feared him. I was longing to tell him how anxious I was to help him, if only he could point out the way. It was in substance what I had already said, but now strongly urged. He brightened; he sat up perpendicularly in his chair with a countenance, not weak or fatuous now, but resolute and searching, and which contracted into dark thought or calculation as I talked.

I dare say I spoke confusedly enough. I was always nervous in his presence; there was, I fancy, something mesmeric in the odd sort of influence which, without effort, he exercised over my imagination.

Sometimes this grew into a dismal panic, and Uncle Silas—polished, mild—seemed unaccountably horrible to me. Then it was no longer an accidental fascination of electro-biology.* It was something more. His nature was incomprehensible by me. He was without the nobleness, without the freshness, without the softness, without the frivolities of such human nature as I had experienced, either within myself or in other persons. I instinctively felt that appeals to sympathies or feelings could no more affect him than a marble monument. He seemed to accommodate his conversation to the moral structure of others, just as spirits are said to assume the shape of mortals. There were the sensualities of the gourmet for his body, and there ended his human nature, as it seemed to me. Through that semi-transparent structure I thought I could now and then discern the light or the glare of his inner life. But I understood it not.

He never scoffed at what was good or noble—his hardest critic could not nail him to one such sentence; and yet, it seemed somehow to me, that his unknown nature was a systematic blasphemy against it all. If fiend he was, he was yet something higher than the garrulous, and withal feeble, demon of Goethe.* He assumed the limbs and features of our mortal nature. He shrouded his own, and was a profoundly reticent Mephistopheles. Gentle he had been to me—kindly he had nearly always spoken; but it seemed like the mild talk of one of those goblins of the desert, whom Asiatic superstition tells of, who appear in friendly shapes to stragglers from the caravan, beckon to them from afar, call them by their names, and lead them where they are found no more. Was, then, all his kindness but a phosphoric radiance covering something colder and more awful than the grave?

'It is very noble of you, Maud—it is angelic; your sympathy with a ruined and despairing old man. But I fear you will recoil. I tell you frankly that less than twenty thousand pounds will not extricate me from the quag of ruin in which I am entangled—lost.'

'Recoil! Far from it. I'll do it. There must be some way.'

'Enough, my fair young protectress—celestial enthusiast, enough. Though you do not, yet I recoil. I could not bring myself to accept this sacrifice. What signifies, even to me, my extrication. I lie a mangled wretch, with fifty mortal wounds on my crown; what avails the healing of one wound, when there are so many beyond all cure? Better to let me perish where I fall; and reserve your money for the worthier objects whom, perhaps, hereafter it may avail to save.'

'But I *will* do this. I must. I cannot see you suffer with the power in my hands unemployed to help you,' I exclaimed.

'Enough, dear Maud; the will is here—enough: there is balm in your compassion and good-will. Leave me, ministering angel, for the present I cannot. If you *will*, we can talk of it again. Good-night.'

And so we parted.

The attorney from Feltram, I afterwards heard, was with him nearly all that night, trying in vain to devise by their joint ingenuity any means by which I might tie myself up. But there were none. I could not bind myself.

I was myself full of the hope of helping him. What was this sum to me, great as it seemed? Truly nothing. I could have spared it, and never felt the loss.

I took up a large quarto with coloured prints, one of the few books I had brought with me from dear old Knowl. Too much excited to hope for sleep in bed, I opened it, and turned over the leaves, my mind still full of Uncle Silas and the sum I hoped to help him with.

Unaccountably one of those coloured engravings arrested my attention. It represented the solemn solitude of a lofty forest, a girl, in Swiss costume, was flying in terror, and as she fled flinging a piece of meat behind her which she had taken from a little market-basket hanging upon her arm. Through the glade a pack of wolves were pursuing her.

The narrative told, that on her return homeward with her marketing, she had been chased by wolves, and barely escaped by flying at her utmost speed, from time to time retarding, as she did so, the pursuit, by throwing, piece by piece, the contents of her basket, in her wake, to be devoured and fought for by the famished beasts of prey.

This print had seized my imagination. I looked with a curious interest on the print: something in the disposition of the trees, their great height, and rude boughs, interlacing, and the awful shadow beneath, reminded me of a portion of the Windmill Wood where Milly and I had often rambled. Then I looked at the figure of the poor girl, flying for her life, and glancing terrified over her shoulder. Then I gazed on the gaping, murderous pack, and the hoary brute that led the van; and then I leaned back in my chair, and I thought—perhaps some latent association suggested what seemed a thing so unlikely—of a fine print in my portfolio from Vandyke's noble picture of Belisarius.* Idly I traced with my pencil, as I leaned back, on an envelope that lay upon the table, this little inscription. It was mere fiddling; and, absurd as it looked, there was nothing but an honest meaning in it:—'£20,000. Date Obolum Belisario!' My dear father had translated the little Latin inscription for me, and I had written it down as a sort of exercise of memory; and also, perhaps, as expressive of that sort of compassion which my uncle's fall and miserable fate excited invariably in me. So I threw this queer little memorandum upon the open leaf of the book, and again the flight, the pursuit, and the bait to stay it, engaged my eye. And I heard a voice near the hearth-stone, as I thought, say, in a stern whisper, 'Fly the fangs of Belisarius!'

'What's that?' said I, turning sharply to Mary Quince.

Mary rose from her work at the fireside, staring at me with that odd sort of frown that accompanies fear and curiosity.

'You spoke? Did you speak?' I said, catching her by the arm, very much frightened myself.

'No, Miss; no, dear!' answered she, plainly, thinking that I was a little wrong in my head.

There could be no doubt it was a trick of the imagination, and yet to this hour I could recognize that clear stern voice among a thousand, were it to speak again.

Jaded after a night of broken sleep and much agitation I was summoned next morning to my uncle's room.

He received me *oddly*, I thought. His manner seemed changed, and made an uncomfortable impression upon me. He was gentle, kind, smiling, submissive, as usual; but it seemed to me that he experienced henceforth toward me the same half-superstitious repulsion which I had always felt from him. Dream, or voice, or vision—which had done it? There seemed to be an unconscious antipathy and fear. When he thought I was not looking, his eyes were sometimes grimly fixed for a moment upon me. When I looked at him, his eyes were upon the book before him; and when he spoke, a person not heeding what he uttered would have fancied that he was reading aloud from it.

There was nothing tangible but this shrinking from the encounter of our eyes. I said he was kind as usual. He was even more so. But there was this new sign of our silently repellant natures. Dislike it could not be. He knew I longed to serve him. Was it shame? Was there not a shade of horror in it?

'I have not slept,' said he. 'For me the night has passed in thought, and the fruit of it is this—I *cannot*, Maud, accept your noble offer.'

'I am *very* sorry,' exclaimed I, in all honesty.

'I know it, my dear niece, and appreciate your goodness; but there are many reasons—none of them, I trust—ignoble, and which together render it impossible. No. It would be misunderstood—my honour shall not be impugned.'

'But, Sir, that could not be; you have never proposed it. It would be all, from first to last, *my* doing.'

'True, dear Maud, but I know, alas! more of this evil and slanderous world than your happy inexperience can do. Who will receive our testimony? None—no, not one. The difficulty—the insuperable moral difficulty is this—that I should expose myself to the plausible imputation of having worked upon you, unduly, for this end; and more, that I could not hold myself quite free from blame. It is your voluntary goodness, Maud. But you are young, inexperienced; and it is, I hold it, my duty to stand between you and any dealing with your property at so unripe an age. Some people may call this Quixotic. In my mind it is an imperious mandate of conscience; and I peremptorily refuse to disobey it although within three weeks an execution* will be in this house!'

I did not quite know what an execution meant; but from two

harrowing novels, with whose distresses I was familiar, I knew that it indicated some direful process of legal torture and spoliation.

'Oh, uncle!—oh, Sir!—you cannot allow this to happen. What will people say of me? And—and there is poor Milly—and *everything*! Think what it will be.'

'It cannot be helped—*you* cannot help it, Maud. Listen to me. There will be an execution here, I cannot say exactly how soon; but I think in little more than a fortnight. I must provide for your comfort. You must leave. I have arranged that you shall join Milly, for the present, in France, till I have time to look about me. You had better, I think, write to your cousin, Lady Knollys. She, with all her oddities, has a heart. Can you say, Maud, that I have been kind?'

'You have never been anything but kind,' I exclaimed.

'That I've been self-denying when you made me a generous offer?' he continued. 'That I now act to spare you pain? You may tell her, not as a message from me, but as a fact, that I am seriously thinking of vacating my guardianship—that I feel I have done her an injustice, and that, so soon as my mind is a little less tortured, I shall endeavour to effect a reconciliation with her, and would wish ultimately to transfer the care of your person and education to *her*. You may say I have no longer an interest even in vindicating my name. My son has wrecked himself by a marriage. I forgot to tell you he stopped at Feltram, and this morning wrote to pray a parting interview. If I grant it, it shall be the last. I shall never see him or correspond with him more.'

The old man seemed much overcome, and held his handkerchief to his eyes.

'He and his wife are, I understand, about to emigrate; the sooner the better,' he resumed bitterly. 'Deeply, Maud, I regret having tolerated his suit to you, even for a moment. Had I thought it over, as I did the whole case last night, nothing could have induced me to permit it. But I have lived for so long like a monk in his cell, my wants and observation limited to the narrow compass of this chamber, that my knowledge of the world has died out with my youth and my hopes: and I did not, as I ought to have done, consider many objections. Therefore, dear Maud, on this one subject, I entreat, be silent; its discussion can effect nothing now. I was wrong, and frankly ask you to forget my mistake.'

I had been on the point of writing to Lady Knollys on this odious subject, when, happily, it was set at rest, by the disclosure of yesterday;

and, being so, I could have no difficulty in acceding to my uncle's request. He was conceding so much that I could not withhold so trifling a concession in return.

'I hope Monica will continue to be kind to poor Milly after I am gone.'

Here there were a few seconds of meditation.

'Maud, you will not, I think, refuse to convey the substance of what I have just said in a letter to Lady Knollys, and perhaps you would have no objection to let me see it when it is written. It will prevent the possibility of its containing any misconception of what I have just spoken; and, Maud, you won't forget to say whether I have been kind. It would be a satisfaction to me to know that Monica was assured that I never either teased or bullied my young ward.'

With these words he dismissed me; and forthwith I completed such a letter as would quite embody what he had said; and in my own glowing terms, being in high good-humour with Uncle Silas, recorded my estimate of his gentleness and good-nature; and when I submitted it to him he expressed his admiration of what he was pleased to call my cleverness in so exactly conveying what he wished, and his gratitude for the handsome terms in which I had spoken of my old guardian.

CHAPTER LIII

AN ODD PROPOSAL

As I and Mary Quince returned from our walk that day, and had entered the hall, I was surprised most disagreeably, by Dudley's emerging from the vestibule at the foot of the great staircase. He was, I suppose, in his travelling costume—a rather soiled white surtout,* a great coloured muffler in folds about his throat, his 'chimney-pot'* on, and his fur cap sticking out from his pocket. He had just descended, I suppose, from my uncle's room. On seeing me he stepped back, and stood with his shoulders to the wall, like a mummy in a museum.

I pretended to have a few words to say to Mary before leaving the hall, in the hope that, as he seemed to wish to escape me, he would take the opportunity of getting quickly off the scene.

But he had changed his mind, it would seem, in the interval; for when I glanced in that direction again he had moved toward us, and stood in the hall with his hat in his hand. I must do him the justice to say he looked horribly dismal, sulky, and frightened.

'Ye'll gie me a word, Miss—only a thing I ought to say—for your good; by ——, mind, it's for *your* good, Miss.'

Dudley stood a little way off, viewing me, with his hat in both hands and a 'glooming' countenance.

I detested the idea of either hearing or speaking to him; but I had not resolution to refuse, and only saying 'I can't imagine what you can wish to speak to me about,' I approached him. 'Wait there at the banister, Quince.'

There was a fragrance of alcohol about the flushed face and gaudy muffler of this odious cousin, which heightened the effect of his horribly dismal features. He was speaking, besides, a little thickly; but his manner was dejected, and he was treating me with an elaborate and discomfited respect which reassured me.

'I'm a bit up a tree, Miss,' he said, shuffling his feet on the oak floor. 'I behaved a d—— fool; but I baint one o' they sort. I'm a fellah as 'ill fight his man, an' stan' up to 'm fair, don't ye see? An' I *baint* one o' they sort—no, *dang* it, I baint.'

Dudley delivered his puzzling harangue with a good deal of under-toned vehemence, and was strangely agitated. He, too, had got an unpleasant way of avoiding my eye, and glancing along the floor from corner to corner as he spoke, which gave him a very hang-dog air.

He was twisting his fingers in his great sandy whisker, and pulling it roughly enough to drag his cheek about by that savage purchase; and with his other hand he was crushing and rubbing his hat against his knee.

'The old boy above there be half crazed, I think; he don't mean half as he says thof, not he. But I'm in a bad fix anyhow—a regular sell it's been, and I can't get a tizzy out of him. So, ye see, I'm up a tree, Miss; and he sich a one, he'll make it a wuss mull if I let him. He's as sharp wi' me as one o' them lawyer chaps, dang 'em, and he's a lot of I O's and rubbitch o' mine; and Bryerly writes to me he can't gie me my legacy, 'cause he's got a notice from Archer and Sleigh a warnin' him not to gie me as much as a bob; for I signed it away to governor, he says—which I believe's a lie. I may a' signed some writing—'appen I did—when I was a bit cut one night. But that's no way to catch a gentleman, and 'twon't stand. There's justice to be had, and 'twon't *stand*, I say; and I'm not in 's hands that way. Thof I may be a bit up the spout, too, I don't deny; only I baint a-goin' the whole hog all at once. I'm none o' they sort. He'll find I baint.'

Here Mary Quince coughed demurely from the foot of the stair to remind me that the conversation was protracted.

'I don't very well understand,' I said, gravely; 'and I am now going up-stairs.'

'Don't, jest a minute, Miss; it's only a word, ye see. We'll be goin' t' Australia, Sary Mangles an' me, aboard the *Seamew*, on the 5th. I'm for Liverpool to-night, and she'll meet me there, an'—an', please God Almighty, ye'll never see me more; an' I'd rather gie ye a lift, Maud, before I go; an' I tell ye what, if ye'll just gie me your written promise ye'll gie me that twenty thousand ye were offering to gie the Governor, I'll take ye cleverly out o' Bartram, and put ye wi' your Cousin Knollys, or anywhere ye like best.'

'Take me from Bartram—for twenty thousand pounds! Take me away from my guardian! You seem to forget, Sir,' my indignation rising as I spoke, 'that I can visit my cousin, Lady Knollys, whenever I please.'

'Well, that is as it may be,' he said, with a sulky deliberation scraping about a little bit of paper that lay on the floor with the toe of his boot.

'It *is* as it may be, and that is as I say, Sir; and considering how you have treated me—your mean, treacherous, and infamous suit, and your cruel treason to your poor wife, I am amazed at your effrontery.'

I turned to leave him, being, in truth, in one of my passions.

'Don't ye be a flyin' out,' he said peremptorily, and catching me roughly by the wrist, 'I baint a-going to vex ye. What a mouth you be, as can't see your way. Can't ye speak wi' common sense, like a woman—dang it—for once, and not keep brawling like a brat—can't ye see what I'm saying? I'll take ye out o' all this, and put ye wi' your cousin, or wheresoever you list, if ye'll gie me what I say.'

He was, for the first time, looking me in the face, but with contracted eyes, and a countenance very much agitated.

'Money?' said I, with a prompt disdain.

'Ay, money—twenty thousand pounds—*there*. On or off?' he replied, with an unpleasant sort of effort.

'You ask my promise for twenty thousand pounds, and you shan't have it.'

My cheeks were flaming, and I stamped on the ground as I spoke.

If he had known how to appeal to my better feelings I am sure I should have done, perhaps not quite that, all at once at least, but something handsome, to assist him. But this application was so shabby and insolent! What could he take me for? That I should suppose his placing me with Cousin Monica constituted her my guardian? Why, he must fancy me the merest baby. There was a kind of stupid cunning in this that disgusted my good-nature and outraged my self-importance.

'You won't gie me that then?' he said, looking down again, with a frown, and working his mouth and cheeks about as I could fancy a man rolling a piece of tobacco in his jaw.

'Certainly *not*, Sir,' I replied,

'*Take* it then,' he replied, still looking down, very black and discontented.

I joined Mary Quince, extremely angry. As I passed under the carved oak arch of the vestibule I saw his figure in the deepening twilight. The picture remains in its murky halo fixed in memory. Standing where he last spoke in the centre of the hall, not looking after me, but downward, and, as well as I could see, with the countenance of a man who has lost a game, and a ruinous wager too—that is black and desperate. I did not utter a syllable on the way up. When

I reached my room I began to reconsider the interview more at my leisure. I was, such were my ruminations, to have agreed at once to his preposterous offer, and to have been driven, while he smirked and grimaced behind my back at his acquaintances, through Feltram in his dog-cart to Elverston; and then, to the just indignation of my uncle, to have been delivered up to Lady Knollys' guardianship, and to have handed my driver, as I alighted, the handsome fare of £20,000! It required the impudence of Tony Lumpkin, without either his fun or his shrewdness, to have conceived such a prodigious practical joke.

'Maybe you'd like a little tea, Miss,' insinuated Mary Quince.

'What impertinence!' I exclaimed, with one of my angry stamps on the floor. 'Not you, dear old Quince,' I added. 'No—no tea just now.'

And I resumed my ruminations, which soon led me to this train of thought—'Stupid and insulting as Dudley's proposition was, it yet involved a great treason against my uncle. Should I be weak enough to be silent, may he not, wishing to forestal me, misrepresent all that has passed, so as to throw the blame altogether upon me.'

This idea seized upon me with a force which I could not withstand; and on the impulse of the moment I obtained admission to my uncle, and related exactly what had passed. When I had finished my narrative, which he listened to without once raising his eyes, my uncle cleared his throat once or twice, as if to speak. He was smiling—I thought with an effort, and with elevated brows. When I concluded he hummed one of those sliding notes, which a less refined man might have expressed by a whistle of surprise and contempt, and again he essayed to speak, but continued silent. The fact is, he seemed to me very much disconcerted. He rose from his seat, and shuffled about the room in his slippers, I believe affecting only to be in search of something, opening and shutting two or three drawers, and turning over some books and papers, and, at length, taking up some loose sheets of manuscript, he appeared to have found what he was looking for, and began to read them carelessly, with his back towards me, and with another effort to clear his voice, he said at last—

'And pray, what could the fool mean by all that?'

'I think he must have taken me for an idiot, Sir,' I answered.

'Not unlikely. He has lived in a stable, among horses and ostlers; he has always seemed to me something like a centaur—that is, a centaur composed not of man and horse, but of an ape and an ass.'

And upon this jibe he laughed, not coldly and sarcastically, as was his wont, but, I thought, flurriedly. And, continuing to look into his papers, he said, his back still toward me as he read—

'And he did not favour you with an exposition of his meaning, which, except in so far as it estimated his deserts at the modest sum you have named, appears to me too oracular to be interpreted without a kindred inspiration.'

And again he laughed. He was growing more like himself.

'As to your visiting your cousin, Lady Knollys, the stupid rogue had only five minutes before heard me express my wish that you should do so before leaving this. I am quite resolved you shall—that is, unless, dear Maud, you should yourself object; but, of course, we must wait for an invitation, which I conjecture will not be long in coming. In fact, your letter will naturally bring it about, and, I trust, open the way to a permanent residence with her. The more I think it over the more am I convinced, dear niece, that as things are likely to turn out, my roof would be no desirable shelter for you; and that, under all circumstances, hers would. Such were my motives, Maud, in opening, through your letter, a door of reconciliation between us.'

I felt that I ought to have kissed his hand—that he had indicated precisely the future that I most desired; and yet there was within me a vague feeling, akin to suspicion—akin to dismay, which chilled and overcast my soul.

'But, Maud,' he said, 'I am disquieted to think of that stupid jackanapes presuming to make you such an offer! A creditable situation truly—arriving in the dark at Elverston, under the solitary escort of that wild young man, with whom you would have fled from my guardianship! And, Maud, I tremble as I ask myself the question, would he have conducted you to Elverston at all? When you have lived as long in the world as I, you will appreciate its wickedness more justly.' Here there was a little pause.

'I know, my dear, that were he convinced of his legal marriage with that young woman,' he resumed, perceiving how startled I looked, 'such an idea, of course, would not have entered his head; but he does not believe any such thing. Contrary to fact and logic, he does honestly think that his hand is still at his disposal; and I certainly do suspect that he would have employed that excursion in endeavouring to persuade you to think as he does. Be that how it may, however, it is satisfactory to me to know that you shall never more be troubled by one word from that ill-regulated young man. I made him my adieux, such as they were, this evening; and never more shall he enter the walls of Bartram-Haugh while we two live.'

Uncle Silas replaced the papers which had ostensibly interested him so much, and returned. There was a vein which was visible near the angle of his lofty temple, and in moments of agitation stood out against the surrounding pallor in a knotted blue cord; and as he came back smiling askance, I saw this sign of inward tumult.

'We can, however, afford to despise the follies and knaveries of the world, Maud, so long as we act, as we have hitherto done, with perfect confidence in each other. Heaven bless you, dear Maud, your report troubled me, I believe, more than it need—troubled me a good deal; but reflection assures me it is nothing. He is gone. In a few days' time he will be on the sea. I will issue my orders to-morrow morning, and he will never more during his brief stay in England gain admission to Bartram-Haugh. Good-night, my good niece, I thank you.'

And so I returned to Mary Quince, on the whole happier than I had left her, but still with the confused and jarring vision I could not interpret perpetually rising before me; and as from time to time, shapeless anxieties agitated me, relieving them by appeals to Him who alone is wise and strong.

Next day brought me a good-natured gossiping letter from dear Milly, written in compulsory French, which was, in some places, very difficult to interpret. She gave me a very pleasant account of the place, and her opinion of the girls who were inmates, and mentioned some of the nuns with high commendation. The language plainly cramped poor Milly's genius; but although there was by no means so much fun as an honest English letter would have brought me, there could be no mistake about her liking the place, and she expressed her honest longing to see me in the most affectionate terms.

This letter came enclosed in one to my uncle, from the proper authority in the convent; and as there was neither address within, nor postmark without, I was as much in the dark as ever as to poor Milly's whereabouts.

Pencilled across the envelope of this letter, in my uncle's hand, were the words 'Let me have your answer when sealed, and I will transmit it.—S. R.'

When, accordingly, some days later, I did place my letter to Milly in my uncle's hands, he told me the reason of his reserve on the subject.

'I thought it best, dear Maud, not to plague you with a secret, and Milly's present address *is* one. It will in a few weeks become the rallying point of our diverse routes, when you shall meet her, and I join you both. Nobody, until the storm shall have blown over, must know where I am to be found, except my lawyer; and I think you would prefer ignorance to the trouble of keeping a secret on which so much may depend.'

This being reasonable, and even considerate, I acquiesced.

In that interval there reached me such a charming, gay, and affectionate letter—a very *long* letter, too—though the writer was scarcely seven miles away, from dear Cousin Monica, full of pleasant gossip, and rose-coloured and golden castles in the air, and the kindest interest in poor Milly, and the warmest affection for me.

One other incident varied that interval, if possible more pleasantly than those. It was the announcement, in a Liverpool paper, of the departure of the *Seamew*, bound for Melbourne; and among the passengers were reported 'Dudley Ruthyn, Esquire, of Bartram-H., and Mrs. D. Ruthyn.'

And now I began to breathe freely, I plainly saw the end of my probation approaching. A short excursion to France, a happy meeting with Milly, and then a delightful residence with Cousin Monica for the remainder of my nonage.

You will say, then, that my spirits and my serenity were quite restored. Not quite. How marvellously lie our anxieties, in filmy layers, one over the other! Take away that which has lain on the upper surface for so long—the care of cares—the only one, as it seemed to you, between your soul and the radiance of Heaven—and straight you find a new stratum there. As physical science tells us no fluid is without its skin, so does it seem with this fine medium of the soul, and these successive films of care that form upon its surface on mere contact with the upper air and light.

What was my new trouble? A very fantastic one you will say—the illusion of a self-tormentor. It was the face of Uncle Silas which haunted me. Notwithstanding the old pale smile, there was a shrinking grimness, and the always averted look.

Sometimes I fancied his mind was disordered. I could not account for the eerie lights and shadows that flickered on his face, except so. There was a look of shame and fear of me, amazing as that seems, in the sheen of his peaked smile.

I thought, 'Perhaps he blames himself for having tolerated Dudley's suit—for having urged it on grounds of personal distress—for having altogether lowered, though under sore temptation, both himself and his office; and he thinks that he has forfeited my respect.'

Such was my analysis; but in the *coup-d'œil* of that white face that dazzled me in darkness, and haunted my daily reveries with a faded light, there was an intangible character of the insidious and the terrible.

CHAPTER LIV

IN SEARCH OF MR. CHARKE'S SKELETON

ON the whole, however, I was unspeakably relieved. Dudley Ruthyn, Esq., and Mrs. D. Ruthyn, were now skimming the blue waves on the wings of the *Seamew*, and every morning widened the distance between us, which was to go on increasing until it measured a point on the antipodes. The Liverpool paper containing this golden line was carefully preserved in my room; and like the gentleman who, when much tried by the shrewish heiress whom he had married, used to retire to his closet and read over his marriage settlement, I used, when blue devils haunted me, to unfold my newspaper and read the paragraph concerning the *Seamew*.

The day I now speak of was a dismal one of sleety snow. My own room seemed to me cheerier than the lonely parlour, where I could not have had good Mary Quince so decorously.

A good fire, that kind and trusty face, the peep I had just indulged in at my favourite paragraph, and the certainty of soon seeing my dear Cousin Monica, and afterwards affectionate Milly, raised my spirits.

'So,' said I, 'as old Wyat, you say, is laid up with rheumatism, and can't turn up to scold me, I think, I'll run up stairs and make an exploration, and find poor Mr. Charke's skeleton in a closet.'

'Oh, law, Miss Maud, how can you say such things!' exclaimed good old Quince, lifting up her honest gray head and round eyes from her knitting.

I had grown so familiar with the frightful tradition of Mr. Charke and his suicide, that I could now afford to frighten old Quince with him.

'I am quite serious. I am going to have a ramble up-stairs and downstairs, like goosey-goosey-gander;* and if I do light upon his chamber it is all the more interesting. I feel so like Adelaide, in the "Romance of the Forest",* the book I was reading to you last night, when she commenced her delightful rambles through the interminable ruined abbey in the forest.'

'Shall I go with you, Miss?'

'No, Quince; stay there; keep a good fire, and make some tea. I suspect I shall lose heart and return very soon;' and with a shawl about me, cowl fashion, over my head, I stole up stairs.

I shall not recount with the particularity of the conscientious heroine of Mrs. Ann Radcliffe, all the suites of apartments, corridors, and lobbies, which I threaded in my ramble. It will be enough to mention that I lighted upon a door at the end of a long gallery, which, I think, ran parallel with the front of the house; it interested me because it had the air of having been very long undisturbed. There were two rusty bolts, which did not evidently belong to its original securities, and had been, though very long ago, somewhat clumsily superadded. Dusty and rusty they were, but I had no difficulty in drawing them back. There was a rusty key, I remember it well, with a crooked handle, in the lock; I tried to turn it, but could not. My curiosity was piqued. I was thinking of going back and getting Mary Quince's assistance. It struck me, however, that possibly it was not locked, so I pulled the door and it opened quite easily. I did not find myself in a strangely furnished suite of apartments, but at the entrance of a gallery, which diverged at right angles from that through which I had just passed; it was very imperfectly lighted, and ended in total darkness.

I began to think how far I had already come, and to consider whether I could retrace my steps with accuracy in case of a panic, and I had serious thoughts of returning.

The idea of Mr. Charke was growing unpleasantly sharp and menacing; and as I looked down the long space before me, losing itself among ambiguous shadows, lulled in a sinister silence, and as it were inviting my entrance like a trap, I was very near yielding to the cowardly impulse.

But I took heart of grace* and determined to see a little more. I opened a side-door, and entered a large room, where were, in a corner, some rusty and cobwebbed bird cages, but nothing more. It was a wainscoted room, but a white mildew stained the panels. I looked from the window: it commanded that dismal, weed-choked quadrangle into which I had once looked from another window. I opened a door at its further end, and entered another chamber, not quite so large, but equally dismal, with the same prison-like look-out, not very easily discerned through the grimy panes and the sleet that was falling thickly outside. The door through which I had entered made a little accidental creak, and with my heart at my lips, I gazed at it, expecting to see Charke, or the skeleton of which I had talked so lightly, stalk in at the half-open aperture. But I had an odd sort of courage which was always fighting against my cowardly nerves, and I walked to the door, and looking up and down the dismal passage, was reassured.

Well, one room more; just that whose deep-set door fronted me, with a melancholy frown, at the opposite end of the chamber. So to it I glided, shoved it open, advancing one step, and the great bony figure of Madame de la Rougierre was before me.

I could see nothing else.

The drowsy traveller who opens his sheets to slip into bed, and sees a scorpion coiled between them, may have experienced a shock the same in kind, but immeasurably less in degree.

She sat in a clumsy old arm-chair, with an ancient shawl about her, and her bare feet in a delft tub. She looked a thought more withered. Her wig shoved back disclosed her bald wrinkled forehead, and enhanced the ugly effect of her exaggerated features and the gaunt hollows of her face. With a sense of incredulity and terror I gazed, freezing, at this evil phantom, who returned my stare for a few seconds with a shrinking scowl, dismal and grim, as of an evil spirit detected.

The meeting, at least then and there, was as complete a surprise for her as for me. She could not tell how I might take it; but she quickly rallied, burst into a loud screeching laugh, and, with her old Walpurgis gaiety, danced some fantastic steps in her bare wet feet, tracking the floor with water, and holding out with finger and thumb, in dainty caricature, her slammakin old skirt, while she sang some of her nasal patois with an abominable hilarity and emphasis.

With a gasp, I too recovered from the fascination of the surprise. I could not speak though for some seconds, and Madame was first.

'Ah, dear Maud, what surprise! Are we not overjoy, dearest, and cannot speak? I am full of joy—quite charmed—*ravi*—of seeing you. So are you of me, your face betray. Ah! yes, thou dear little baboon! here is poor Madame once more! Who could have imagine?'

'I thought you were in France, Madame,' I said, with a dismal effort.

'And so I was, dear Maud; I 'av just arrive. Your Uncle Silas he wrote to the superioress for gouvernante to accompany a young lady—that is you, Maud—on her journey, and she send me; and so, ma chère, here is poor Madame arrive to charge herself of that affair.'

'How soon do we leave for France, Madame?' I asked.

'I do not know, but the old woman—wat is her name?'

'Wyat,' I suggested.

'Oh! oui, Waiatt;—she says two, three week. And who conduct you to poor Madame's apartment, my dear Maud?' she inquired, insinuatingly.

'No one,' I answered promptly: 'I reached it quite accidentally, and I can't imagine why you should conceal yourself.' Something like indignation kindled in my mind as I began to wonder at the sly strategy which had been practised upon me.

'I 'av not conceal myself, Mademoiselle,' retorted the governess. 'I 'av act precisally as I 'av been ordered. Your uncle, Mr. Silas Ruthyn, he is afraid, Waiat says, to be interrupted by his creditors, and everything must be done very quaitly. I have been commanded to avoid *me faire voir*, you know, and I must obey my employer—voilà tout!'

'And for how long have you been residing here?' I persisted, in the same resentful vein.

''Bout a week. It is soche triste* place! I am so glad to see you, Maud. I've been so isolée, you dear leetle fool.'

'You are *not* glad, Madame; you don't love me—you never did,' I exclaimed with sudden vehemence.

'Yes, I am *very* glad; you know not, chère petite *niaise*,* how I 'av desire to educate you a leetle more. Let us understand one another. You think I do not love you, Mademoiselle, because you have mentioned to your poor papa that little *dérèglement** in his library. I have repent very often that so great indiscretion of my life. I thought to find some letters of Doctor Braierly. I think that man was trying to get your property, my dear Maud, and if I had found something I would tell you all about. But it was very great *sottise*,* and you were very right to denounce me to Monsieur. Je n'ai point de rancune contre vous. No, no, none at all. On the contrary, I shall be your *gardien tutelaire*—wat you call?—guardian angel—ah, yes, that is it. You think I speak *par derision*, not at all. No, my dear cheaile, I do not speak *par moquerie*, unless perhaps the very least degree in the world.'

And with these words Madame laughed unpleasantly, showing the black caverns at the sides of her mouth, and with a cold, steady malignity in her gaze.

'Yes,' I said; 'I know what you mean, Madame—you *hate* me.'

'Oh! wat great ogly word! I am shock! *vous me faîtes honte.** Poor Madame, she never hate any one; she loves all her friends, and her enemies she leaves to heaven; while I am, as you see, more gay, more *joyeuse* than ever, they have not been 'appy—no, they have not been fortunate those others. Wen I return I find always some of my enemy they 'av die, and some they have put themselves into embarrassment, or there has arrived to them some misfortune,' and Madame shrugged and laughed a little scornfully.

A kind of horror chilled my rising anger, and I was silent.

'You see, my dear Maud, it is very natural you should think I hate you. When I was with Mr. Austin Ruthyn, at Knowl, you know you did not like a me—never. But in consequence of our intimacy I confide you that which I 'av of most dear in the world, my reputation. It is always so. The pupil can *calomniate*, without been discover, the *gouvernante*. 'Av I not been always kind to you, Maud? Which 'av I use of violence or of sweetness the most? I am, like other persons, *jalouse de ma reputation*; and it was difficult to suffer with patience the banishment which was invoked by you, because chiefly for your good, and for an indiscretion to which I was excited by motives the most pure and laudable. It was you who spied so cleverly—eh! and denounce me to Monsieur Ruthyn? Hélas! wat bad world it is!'

'I do not mean to speak at all about that occurrence, Madame; I will not discuss it. I dare say what you tell me of the cause of your engagement here is true, and I suppose we must travel, as you say, in company; but you must know that the less we see of each other while in this house the better.'

'I am not so sure of that, my sweet little *bête*; your education has been neglected, or rather entirely abandoned, since you 'av arrive at this place, I am told. You must not be a *bestiole*.* We must do, you and I, as we are ordered. Mr. Silas Ruthyn he will tell us.'

All this time Madame was pulling on her stockings, getting her boots on, and otherwise proceeding with her dowdy toilet. I do not know why I stood there talking to her. We often act very differently from what we would have done upon reflection. I had involved myself in a dialogue, as wiser generals than I have entangled themselves in a general action when they meant only an affair of outposts. I had grown a little angry, and would not betray the least symptom of fear, although I felt that sensation profoundly.

'My beloved father thought you so unfit a companion for me that he dismissed you at an hour's notice, and I am very sure that my uncle will think as he did; you are *not* a fit companion for me, and had my uncle known what had passed he would never have admitted you to this house—never!'

'Hélas! *Quelle disgrace!* And you really think so, my dear Maud,' exclaimed Madame, adjusting her wig before her glass, in the corner of which I could see half of her sly, grinning face, as she ogled herself in it.

'I do, and so do you, Madame,' I replied, growing more frightened.

'It may be—we shall see; but every one is not so cruel as you, *ma chère petite calomniatrice.*'

'You shan't call me those names,' I said, in an angry tremor.

'What name, dearest cheaile?'

'*Calomniatrice*—that is an insult.'

'Why, my most foolish little Maud, we may say rogue, and a thousand other little words in play which we do not say seriously.'

'You are not playing—you never play—you are angry, and you hate me,' I exclaimed vehemently.

'Oh, fie!—wat shame! Do you not perceive, dearest cheaile, how much education you still need? You are proud, little demoiselle; you must become, on the contrary, quaite humble. Je ferai baiser le babouin à vous, ha, ha, ha! I weel make a you to kees the monkey. You are too proud, my dear cheaile.'

'I am not such a fool as I was at Knowl,' I said, 'you shall not terrify me here. I will tell my uncle the whole truth,' I said.

'Well, it may be, that is the best,' she replied with provoking coolness.

'You think I don't mean it?'

'Of course you *do*,' she replied.

'And we shall see what my uncle thinks of it.'

'We shall see, my dear,' she replied, with an air of mock contrition.

'Adieu, Madame!'

'You are going to Monsieur Ruthyn?—very good!'

I made her no answer, but more agitated than I cared to show her, I left the room. I hurried along the twilight passage, and turned into the long gallery that opened from it at right angles. I had not gone half a dozen steps on my return when I heard a heavy tread and a rustling behind me.

'I am ready, my dear. I weel accompany you,' said the smirking phantom hurrying after me.

'Very well,' was my reply; and threading our way, with a few hesitations and mistakes, we reached and descended the stairs, and in a minute more stood at my uncle's door.

My uncle looked hard and strangely at us as we entered. He looked, indeed, as if his temper was violently excited, and glared and muttered to himself for a few seconds, and treating Madame to a stare of disgust, he asked peevishly—

'Why am I disturbed, pray?'

'Miss Maud a Ruthyn, she weel explain,' replied Madame with a great courtesy, like a boat going down in a ground swell.

'*Will* you explain, my dear?' he asked in his coldest and most sarcastic tone.

I was agitated, and I am sure my statement was confused. I succeeded, however, in saying what I wanted.

'Why, Madame, this is a grave charge! Do you admit it, pray?'

Madame with the coolest possible effrontery denied it all; with the most solemn asseverations, and with streaming eyes and clasped hands conjured me melodramatically to withdraw that intolerable story, and to do her justice. I stared at her for a while astounded, and turning suddenly to my uncle, as vehemently asserted the truth of every syllable I had related.

'You hear, my dear child, you hear her deny everything; what am I to think? You must excuse the bewilderment of my old head. Madame de la—that lady has arrived excellently recommended by the superioress of the place where dear Milly awaits you, and such persons are particular. It strikes me, my dear niece, that you must have made a mistake.'

I protested here. But he went on without seeming to hear the parenthesis—

'I know, my dear Maud, that you are quite incapable of wilfully deceiving any one; but you are liable to be deceived like other young people. You were, no doubt, very nervous and but half awake when you fancied you saw the occurrence you describe; and Madame de—de'—

'De la Rougierre,' I supplied.

'Yes, thank you—Madame de la Rougierre, who has arrived with excellent testimonials, strenuously denies the whole thing. Here is a conflict, my dear—in my mind a presumption of mistake. I confess I should prefer that theory to a peremptory assumption of guilt.'

I felt incredulous and amazed; it seemed as if a dream were being enacted before me. A transaction of the most serious import, which I had witnessed with my own eyes, and described with unexceptionable minuteness and consistency, is discredited by that strange and suspicious old man with an imbecile coolness. It was quite in vain my

reiterating my statement, backing it with the most earnest asseverations. I was beating the air. It did not seem to reach his mind. It was
all received with a simper of feeble incredulity.

He patted and smoothed my head—he laughed gently, and shook
his, while I insisted; and Madame protested her purity in now tranquil floods of innocent tears, and murmured mild and melancholy
prayers for my enlightenment and reformation. I felt as if I should
lose my reason.

'There now, dear Maud, we have heard enough; it is, I do believe,
a delusion. Madame de la Rougierre will be your companion, at the
utmost, for three or four weeks. Do exercise a little of your self-command
and good sense—you know how I am tortured. Do not, I entreat, add
to my perplexities. You may make yourself very happy with Madame
if you will, I have no doubt.'

'I propose to Mademoiselle,' said Madame, drying her eyes with
a gentle alacrity, 'to profit of my visit for her education. But she does
not seem to weesh wat I think is so useful.'

'She threatened me with some horrid French vulgarism—*de faire
baiser le babouin à moi,** whatever that means; and I know she hates
me,' I replied impetuously.

'Doucement—doucement!' said my uncle, with a smile at once
amused and compassionate. 'Doucement! ma chère.'

With her great hands and cunning eyes uplifted, Madame tear-
fully—for her tears came on short notice—again protested her absolute innocence. She had never in all her life so much as heard one so
villain phrase.

'You see, my dear, you have misheard; young people never attend.
You will do well to take advantage of Madame's short residence to get
up your French a little, and the more you are with her the better.'

'I understand then, Mr. Ruthyn, you weesh I should resume my
instructions?' asked Madame.

'Certainly; and converse all you can in French with Mademoiselle
Maud. You will be glad, my dear, that I've insisted on it,' he said,
turning to me, 'when you have reached France, where you will find
they speak nothing else And now, dear Maud—no, not a word
more—you must leave me. Farewell, Madame!'

And he waved us out a little impatiently; and I, without one look
toward Madame de la Rougierre, stunned and incensed, walked into
my room and shut the door.

CHAPTER LV

THE FOOT OF HERCULES

I STOOD at the window—still the same leaden sky and feathery sleet before me—trying to estimate the magnitude of the discovery I had just made. Gradually a kind of despair seized me, and I threw myself passionately on my bed, weeping aloud.

Good Mary Quince was, of course, beside me in a moment, with her pale, concerned face.

'Oh, Mary, Mary, she's come—that dreadful woman, Madame de la Rougierre, has come, to be my governess again; and Uncle Silas won't hear or believe anything about her. It is vain talking; he is prepossessed. Was ever so unfortunate a creature as I? who could have fancied or feared such a thing? Oh, Mary, Mary, what am I to do? what is to become of me? am I never to shake off that vindictive, terrible woman?'

Mary said all she could to console me. I was making too much of her. What was she after all more than a governess?—she could not hurt me. I was not a child no longer—she could not bully me now; and my uncle, though he might be deceived for a while, would not be long finding her out.

Thus and soforth did good Mary Quince declaim, and, at last, she did impress me a little, and I began to think that I had, perhaps, been making too much of Madame's visit. But still imagination, that instrument and mirror of prophecy, showed her formidable image always on its surface, with a terrible moving background of shadows.

In a few minutes there was a knock at my door, and Madame herself entered. She was in walking costume. There had been a brief clearing of the weather, and she proposed our making a promenade together.

On seeing Mary Quince she broke into a rapture of compliment and greeting, and took what Mr. Richardson* would have called her passive hand, and pressed it with wonderful tenderness.

Honest Mary suffered all this somewhat reluctantly, never smiling, and, on the contrary, looking rather ruefully at her feet.

'Weel you make a some tea? when I come back, dear Mary Quince, I 'av so much to tell you and dear Miss Maud of all my adventures while I 'av been away; it will make a you laugh ever so much. I was—what you theenk?—near, ever so near to be married!' And upon this she broke into a screeching laugh, and shook Mary Quince merrily by the shoulder.

I sullenly declined going out, or rising; and when she had gone away, I told Mary that I should confine myself to my room while Madame stayed.

But self-denying ordinances self-imposed are not always long observed by youth. Madame de la Rougierre laid herself out to be agreeable; she had no end of stories—more than half, no doubt, pure fictions—to tell, but all, in that triste place, amusing. Mary Quince began to entertain a better opinion of her. She actually helped to make beds, and tried to be in every way of use, and seemed to have quite turned over a new leaf; and so gradually she moved me, first to listen, and at last to talk.

On the whole these terms were better than a perpetual skirmish; but, notwithstanding all her gossip and friendliness, I continued to have a profound distrust and even terror of her.

She seemed curious about the Bartram-Haugh family, and all their ways, and listened darkly when I spoke. I told her, bit by bit, the whole story of Dudley, and she used, whenever there was news of the *Seamew*, to read the paragraph for my benefit; and in poor Milly's battered little atlas she used to trace the ship's course with a pencil, writing in, from point to point, the date at which the vessel was 'spoken' at sea. She seemed amused at the irrepressible satisfaction with which I received these minutes of his progress; and she used to calculate the distance;—on such a day he was two hundred and sixty miles, on such another five hundred; the last point was more than eight hundred—good, better, best—best of all would be those 'delee-cious antipode, w'ere he would so sooner promener on his head twelve thousand mile away;' and at the conceit she would fall into screams of laughter.

Laugh as she might, however, there was substantial comfort in thinking of the boundless stretch of blue wave that rolled between me and that villainous cousin.

I was now on very good terms with Madame. She had not relapsed into her favourite vein of oracular sarcasm and menace. She had, on the contrary, affected her good-humoured and genial vein. But I was not to be deceived by this. I carried in my heart that deep-seated fear of her which her unpleasant good-humour and gaiety never disturbed for a moment. I was very glad, therefore, when she went to Todcaster by rail, to make some purchases for the journey which we were daily expecting to commence; and happy in the opportunity of a walk, good old Mary Quince and I set forth for a little ramble.

As I wished to make some purchases in Feltram, I set out, with Mary Quince for my companion. On reaching the great gate we found it locked. The key, however, was in it, and as it required more than the strength of my hand to turn, Mary tried it. At the same moment old Crowle came out of the sombre lodge by its side, swallowing down a mouthful of his dinner in haste. No one, I believe, liked the long, suspicious face of the old man, seldom shorn or washed, and furrowed with great, grimy perpendicular wrinkles. Leering fiercely at Mary, not pretending to see me, he wiped his mouth hurriedly with the back of his hand, and growled—

'Drop it.'

'Open it, please, Mr. Crowle,' said Mary, renouncing the task.

Crowle wiped his mouth as before, looking inauspicious; shuffling to the spot, and, muttering to himself, he first satisfied himself that the lock was fast, and then lodged the key in his coat-pocket, and still muttering, retraced his steps.

'We want the gate open, please,' said Mary.

No answer.

'Miss Maud wants to go into the town,' she insisted.

'We wants many a thing we can't get,' he growled, stepping into his habitation.

'Please open the gate,' I said, advancing.

He half turned on his threshold, and made a dumb show of touching his hat, although he had none on.

'Can't ma'am; without an order from maister, no one goes out here.'

'You won't allow me and my maid to pass the gate?' I said.

''Tisn't *me*, ma'am,' said he; 'but I can't break orders, and no one goes out without the master allows.'

And without awaiting further parley, he entered, shutting his hatch behind him.

So Mary and I stood, looking very foolish at one another. This was the first restraint I had experienced since Milly and I had been refused a passage through the Windmill paling. The rule, however, on which

Crowle insisted I felt confident could not have been intended to apply to me. A word to Uncle Silas would set all right; and in the meantime I proposed to Mary that we should take a walk—my favourite ramble—into the Windmill Wood.

I looked toward Dickon's farmstead as we passed, thinking that Beauty might have been there. I did see the girl, who was plainly watching us. She stood in the doorway of the cottage, withdrawn into the shade, and, I fancied, anxious to escape observation. When we had passed on a little, I was confirmed in that belief by seeing her run down the footpath which led from the rear of the farm-yard in the direction contrary to that in which we were moving.

'So,' I thought, 'poor Meg falls from me!'

Mary Quince and I rambled on through the wood, till we reached the windmill itself, and seeing its low arched door open, we entered the chiaro-oscuro of its circular basement. As we did so I heard a rush and the creak of a plank, and looking up, I saw just a foot—no more—disappearing through the trap-door.

In the case of one we love or fear intensely, what feats of comparative anatomy will not the mind unconsciously perform? constructing the whole living animal from the turn of an elbow, the curl of a whisker, a segment of a hand. How instantaneous and unerring is the instinct!

'Oh, Mary, what have I seen!' I whispered, recovering from the fascination that held my gaze fast to the topmost rounds of the ladder, that disappeared in the darkness above the open door in the loft. 'Come, Mary—come away.'

At the same instant appeared the swarthy, sullen face of Dickon Hawkes in the shadow of the aperture. Having but one serviceable leg his descent was slow and awkward, and having got his head to the level of the loft he stopped to touch his hat to me and to hasp and lock the trap-door.

When this was done the man again touched his hat, and looked steadily and searchingly at me for a second or so, while he got the key into his pocket.

'These fellahs stores their flour too long 'ere, ma'am. There's a deal o' trouble a lookin' arter it. I'll talk wi' Silas, and settle that.'

By this time he had got upon the worn tiled floor, and touching his hat again he said—

'I'm a goin' to lock the door, ma'am!'

So with a start, and again whispering—

'Come, Mary—come away.'

With my arm fast in hers we made a swift departure.

'I feel very faint, Mary,' said I. 'Come quickly. There's nobody following us?'

'No, Miss, dear. That man with the wooden leg is putting a padlock on the door.'

'Come *very* fast,' I said; and when we had got a little further I said, 'Look again, and see whether any one is following.'

'No one, Miss,' answered Mary, plainly surprised. 'He's putting the key in his pocket, and standin' there a lookin' after us.'

'Oh, Mary, did not you see it?'

'What, Miss?' asked Mary, almost stopping.

'Come on, Mary. Don't pause. They will observe us,' I whispered, hurrying her forward.

'What did you see, Miss?' repeated Mary.

'*Mr. Dudley*,' I whispered with a terrified emphasis, not daring to turn my head as I spoke.

'Lawk, Miss!' remonstrated honest Quince, with a protracted intonation of wonder and incredulity, which plainly implied a suspicion that I was dreaming.

'Yes, Mary. When we went into that dreadful room—that dark, round place—I saw his foot on the ladder. *His* foot, Mary. I can't be mistaken. I *won't* be *questioned*. You'll *find* I'm right. He's *here*. He never went in that ship at all. A fraud has been practised on me. It is infamous—it is terrible. I'm frightened out of my life. For heaven's sake, look back again, and tell me what you see.'

'*Nothing*, Miss,' answered Mary, in contagious whispers, 'but that wooden-legged chap, standin' hard by the door.'

'And no one with him?'

'No one, Miss.'

We got without pursuit through the gate in the paling. I drew breath so soon as we had reached the cover of the thicket near the chestnut hollow, and I began to reflect that whoever the owner of the foot might be—and I was still instinctively certain that it was no other than Dudley—concealment was plainly his object. I need not, then, be at all uneasy lest he should pursue us.

As we walked slowly and in silence along the grassy footpath I heard a voice calling my name from behind. Mary Quince had not heard it at all, but I was quite certain.

It was repeated twice or thrice, and, looking in considerable doubt and trepidation under the hanging boughs, I saw Beauty, not ten yards away, standing warily among the underwood.

I remember how white the eyes and teeth of the swarthy girl looked, as with hand uplifted toward her ear she watched us while, as it seemed, listening for more distant sounds.

Beauty beckoned eagerly to me, advancing, with looks of great fear and anxiety, two or three short steps toward me.

'*She* baint to come,' said Beauty under her breath so soon as I had nearly reached her, pointing without raising her hand at Mary Quince.

'Tell her to sit on the ash-tree stump down yonder, and call ye as loud as she can if she sees any fellah a comin' this way, an' rin ye back to me;' and she impatiently beckoned me away on her errand.

When I returned, having made this disposition, I perceived how pale the girl was.

'Are you ill, Meg?' I asked.

'Never ye mind. Well enough. Listen, Miss; I must tell it all in a crack, an' if she calls, rin awa' to her, an' le' me to myself, for if fayther or t'other 'un wor to kotch me here, I think they'd kill me a'most. Hish!'

She paused a second, looking askance, in the direction where she fancied Mary Quince was. Then she resumed in a whisper——

'Now, lass, mind ye, ye'll keep what I say to yourself. You're not to tell that 'un nor any other for your life, mind, a word o' what I'm goin' to tell ye.'

'I'll not say a word. Go on.'

'Did ye see Dudley?'

'I think I saw him getting up the ladder.'

'In the mill? Ha! that's him. He never went beyond Todcaster. He staid in Feltram arter.'

It was my turn to look pale now. My worst conjecture was established.

CHAPTER LVI

I CONSPIRE

'THAT'S a bad 'un, he is—oh, Miss, Miss Maud! It's nout that's good as keeps him an' fayther—(mind, lass, ye promised you would not tell no one)—as keeps them two a talkin' and a smokin' secret-like together in the mill. An' fayther don't know I found him out. They don't let me into the town, but Brice tells me, and he knows it's Dudley; and it's nout that's good, but summat very bad. An' I reckon, Miss, it's all about you. Be ye frightened, Miss Maud?'

I felt on the point of fainting, but I rallied.

'Not much, Meg. Go on. For Heaven's sake, does Uncle Silas know he is here?'

'Well, Miss, they were with him, Brice told me, from eleven o'clock to nigh one o' Tuesday night, an' went in and come out like thieves, 'feard ye'd see 'em.'

'And how does Brice know it is anything bad?' I asked, with a strange freezing sensation creeping from my heels to my head and down again—I am sure deadly pale, but speaking very collectedly.

'Brice said, Miss, he saw Dudley a cryin' and lookin' awful black, and says he to fayther, "'Tisn't in my line nohow, an' I can't;" and says fayther to he, "No one likes they soart o' things, but how can ye help it? The old boy's behind ye wi' his pitchfork, and ye canna stop." An' wi' that he bethought him o' Brice, and says he, "What be ye a doin' there? Get ye down wi' the nags to blacksmith, do ye." An' oop gits Dudley, pullin' his hat ower his brows, an' says he, "I wish I was in the *Seamew*. I'm good for nout wi' this thing a hangin' ower me." An' that's all as Brice heard. An' he's afeard o' fayther and Dudley awful. Dudley could lick him to pot if he crossed him, and he and fayther u'd think nout o' havin' him afore the justices for poachin' and swearin' him into gaol.'

'But why does he think it's about *me*?'

'Hish!' said Meg, who fancied she heard a sound, but all was quiet. 'I can't stay—we're in danger, lass. I don't know why—but *he* does, an' so do I, an', for that matter, so do *ye*.'

'Meg, I'll leave Bartram.'

'Ye can't.'

'Can't. What do you mean, girl?'

'They won't let ye oot. The gates is all locked. They've dogs—they've bloodhounds, Brice says. Ye *can't* git oot, mind; put that oot o' your head.

'I tell ye what ye'll do. Write a bit o' a note to the lady yonder at Elverston; and though Brice be a wild fellah, and 'appen not ower good sometimes, he likes me, an' I'll make him take it. Fayther will be grindin' at mill to-morrow. Coom ye here about one o'clock—that's if ye see the mill sails a-turnin'—and me and Brice will meet ye here. Bring that old lass wi' ye. There's an old French 'un, though, that talks wi' Dudley. Mind ye, that 'un knows nout o' the matter. Brice be a kind lad to me, watsoe'er he be wi' others, and I think he won't split. Now, lass, I must go. God help ye; God bless ye; an', for the world's wealth, don't ye let one o' them see ye've got ought in your head, not even that 'un.'

Before I could say another word the girl had glided from me, with a wild gesture of silence, and a shake of her head.

I can't at all account for the state in which I was. There are resources both of energy and endurance in human nature which we never suspect until the tremendous voice of necessity summons them into play. Petrified with a totally new horror, but with something of the coldness and impassiveness of the transformation, I stood, spoke, and acted—a wonder, almost a terror, to myself.

I met Madame on my return as if nothing had happened. I heard her ugly gabble, and looked at the fruits of her hour's shopping, as I might hear, and see, and talk, and smile, in a dream.

But the night was dreadful. When Mary Quince and I were alone, I locked the door. I continued walking up and down the room, with my hands clasped, looking at the inexorable floor, the walls, the ceiling, with a sort of imploring despair. I was afraid to tell my dear old Mary. The least indiscretion would be failure, and failure destruction.

I answered her perplexed solicitudes by telling her that I was not very well—that I was uneasy; but I did not fail to extract from her a promise that she would not hint to mortal, either my suspicions about Dudley, or our rencontre with Meg Hawkes.

I remember how, when, after we had got, late at night, into bed, I sat up, shivering with horror, in mine, while honest Mary's tranquil breathing told how soundly she slept. I got up, and looked from the window, expecting to see some of those wolfish dogs which they had brought to the place prowling about the courtyard. Sometimes I prayed, and felt tranquillized, and fancied that I was perhaps to have a short interval of sleep. But the serenity was delusive, and all the time my nerves were strung hysterically. Sometimes I felt quite wild, and on the point of screaming. At length that dreadful night passed away. Morning came, and a less morbid, though hardly a less terrible state of mind. Madame paid me an early visit. A thought struck me. I knew that she loved shopping, and I said, quite carelessly—

'Your yesterday's shopping tempts me, Madame, and I must get a few things before we leave for France. Suppose we go into Feltram to-day, and make my purchases, you and I?'

She looked from the corner of her cunning eye in my face without answering. I did not blench, and she said—

'Vary good. I would be vary 'appy,' and again she looked oddly at me.

'Wat hour, my dear Maud? One o'clock? I think that weel do very well, eh?'

I assented, and she grew silent.

I wonder whether I did look as careless as I tried. I do not know. Through the whole of this awful period I was, I think, supernatural; and I even now look back with wonder upon my strange self-command.

Madame, I hoped, had heard nothing of the order which prohibited my exit from the place. She would herself conduct me to Feltram, and secure, by accompanying me, my free egress.

Once in Feltram, I would assert my freedom, and manage to reach my dear Cousin Knollys. Back to Bartram no power should convey me. My heart swelled and fluttered in the awful suspense of that hour.

Oh, Bartram-Haugh! how came you by those lofty walls? Which of my ancestors had begirt me with an impassable barrier in this horrible strait?

Suddenly I remembered my letter to Lady Knollys. If I were disappointed in effecting my escape through Feltram, all would depend upon it.

Having locked my door, I wrote as follows:—

'Oh, my beloved cousin, as you hope for comfort in *your* hour of fear, aid me now. Dudley has returned, and is secreted somewhere about the grounds. It is a *fraud*. They all pretend to me that he is gone away in the *Seamew*; and he or they had his name published as one of the passengers. Madame de la Rougierre has appeared! She is here, and my uncle insists on making her my close companion. I am at my wits' ends. I cannot escape—the walls are a prison; and I believe the eyes of my gaolers are always upon me. Dogs are kept for pursuit—yes, *dogs!* and the gates are locked against my escape. God help me! I don't know where to look, or whom to trust. I fear my uncle more than all. I think I could bear this better if I knew what their plans are, even the worst. If ever you loved or pitied me, dear cousin, I conjure you, help me in this extremity. Take me away from this. Oh, darling, for God's sake, take me away!'

'Your distracted and terrified cousin,

'MAUD.

'*Bartram-Haugh.*'

I sealed this letter jealously, as if the inanimate missive would burst its cerements, and proclaim my desperate appeal through all the chambers and passages of silent Bartram.

Old Quince, greatly to Cousin Monica's amusement, persisted in furnishing me with those capacious pockets which belonged to a former generation. I was glad of this old-world eccentricity now, and placed my guilty letter, that amidst all my hypocrisies, spoke out with such terrible frankness, deep in this receptacle, and having hid away the pen and ink, my accomplices, I opened the door, and resumed my careless looks, awaiting Madame's return.

'I was to demand to Mr. Ruthyn the permission to go to Feltram, and I think he will allow. He want to speak to you.'

With Madame I entered my uncle's room. He was reclining on a sofa, his back towards us, and his long white hair, as fine as spun glass, hung over the back of the couch.

'I was going to ask you, dear Maud, to execute two or three little commissions for me in Feltram.'

My dreadful letter felt lighter in my pocket, and my heart beat violently.

'But I have just recollected that this is a market-day, and Feltram will be full of doubtful characters and tipsy persons, so we must wait till to-morrow; and Madame says, very kindly, that she will, as she does not so much mind, make any little purchases to-day which cannot conveniently wait.'

Madame assented with a courtesy to Uncle Silas, and a great hollow smile to me.

By this time Uncle Silas had raised himself from his reclining posture, and was sitting, gaunt and white, upon the sofa.

'News of my prodigal to-day,' he said, with a peevish smile, drawing the newspaper towards him. 'The vessel has been spoken again. How many miles away, do you suppose?'

He spoke in a plaintive key, looking at me, with hungry eyes, and a horribly smiling countenance.

'How far do you suppose Dudley is to-day?' and he laid the palm of his hand on the paragraph as he spoke. '*Guess!*'

For a moment I fancied this was a theatric preparation to give point to the disclosure of Dudley's real whereabouts.

'It was a very long way. Guess!' he repeated.

So, stammering a little and pale, I performed the required hypocrisy, after which my uncle read aloud for my benefit the line or two in which were recorded the event, and the latitude and longitude of the vessel at the time, of which Madame made a note in her memory, for the purpose of making her usual tracing in poor Milly's atlas.

I cannot say how it really was, but I fancied that Uncle Silas was all the time reading my countenance, with a grim and practised scrutiny; but nothing came of it, and we were dismissed.

Madame loved shopping, even for its own sake, but shopping with opportunities of peculation still more. As she had had her luncheon, and was dressed for the excursion, she did precisely what I now most desired—she proposed to take charge of my commissions and my money, and thus intrusted, left me at liberty to keep tryst at the Chestnut Hollow.

So soon as I had seen Madame fairly off, I hurried Mary Quince, and got my things on quickly. We left the house by the side entrance, which I knew my uncle's windows did not command. Glad was I to feel a slight breeze, enough to make the mill-sails revolve; and as we got further into the grounds, and obtained a distant view of the picturesque old windmill, I felt inexpressibly relieved on seeing that it was actually working.

We were now in the Chestnut Hollow, and I sent Mary Quince to her old point of observation, which commanded a view of the path in the direction of the Windmill Wood, with her former order to call 'I've found it' as loudly as she could, in case she should see any one approaching.

I stopped at the point of our yesterday's meeting. I peered under the branches, and my heart beat fast as I saw Meg Hawkes awaiting me.

CHAPTER LVII

THE LETTER

'COME away, lass,' whispered Beauty, very pale; 'he's here—Tom Brice.'

And she led the way, shoving aside the leafless underwood, and we reached Tom. The slender youth, groom or poacher—he might answer for either—with his short coat and gaitered legs, was sitting on a low horizontal bough, with his shoulder against the trunk.

'*Don't* ye mind, sit ye still, lad,' said Meg, observing that he was preparing to rise, and had entangled his hat in the boughs. 'Sit ye still, and hark to the lady. He'll take it, Miss Maud, if he can; wi' na ye, lad?'

'E'es, I'll take it,' he replied, holding out his hand.

'Tom Brice, you won't deceive me?'

'Noa, sure,' said Tom and Meg nearly in the same breath.

'You are an honest English lad, Tom—you would not betray me?' I was speaking imploringly.

'Noa, sure,' repeated Tom.

There was something a little unsatisfactory in the countenance of this light-haired youth, with the sharpish up-turned nose. Throughout our interview he said next to nothing, and smiled lazily to himself, like a man listening to a child's solemn nonsense, and leading it on, with an amused irony, from one wise sally to another.

Thus it seemed to me that this young clown, without in the least intending to be offensive, was listening to me with a profound and lazy mockery.

I could not choose, however, and such as he was I must employ him or none.

'Now, Tom Brice, a great deal depends on this.'

'That's true for her, Tom Brice,' said Meg, who now and then confirmed my asseverations.

'I'll give you a pound *now*, Tom,' and I placed the coin and the letter together in his hand. 'And you are to give this letter to Lady Knollys at Elverston; you know Elverston, don't you?'

'He does, Miss. Don't ye, lad?'

'E'es.'

'Well, do so, Tom, and I'll be good to you so long as I live.'

'D'ye hear, lad?'

'E'es,' said Tom; 'it's very good.'

'You'll take the letter, Tom?' I said, in much greater trepidation as to his answer than I showed.

'E'es, I'll take the letter,' said he, rising, and turning it about in his fingers under his eye, like a curiosity.

'Tom Brice,' I said, 'if you can't be true to me, say so; but don't take the letter except to give it to Lady Knollys at Elverston. If you won't promise that, let me have the note back. Keep the pound; but tell me that you won't mention my having asked you to carry a letter to Elverston to any one.'

For the first time Tom looked perfectly serious. He twiddled the corner of my letter between his finger and thumb, and wore very much the countenance of a poacher about to be committed.

'I don't want to chouce ye, Miss; but I must take care o' myself, ye see. The letters goes all through Silas's fingers to the post, and he'd know damn well this worn't among 'em. They do say he opens 'em, and reads 'em before they go; an' that's his diversion. I don't know; but I do believe that's how it be; an' if this one turned up, they'd all know it went be hand, and I'd be spotted for't.'

'But you know who I am, Tom; and I'd save you,' said I, eagerly.

'Ye'd want savin' yerself, I'm thinkin', if that fell oot,' said Tom, cynically. 'I don't say, though, I'll not take it—only this—I won't run my head again a wall for no one.'

'Tom,' I said, with a sudden inspiration, 'give me back the letter, and take me out of Bartram; take me to Elverston; it will be the best thing—for *you*, Tom, I mean—it will indeed—that ever befell you.'

With this clown I was pleading, as for my life; my hand was on his sleeve. I was gazing imploringly in his face.

But it would not do; Tom Brice looked amused again, swung his head a little on one side, grinning sheepishly over his shoulder on the roots of the trees beside him, as if he were striving to keep himself from an uncivil fit of laughter.

'I'll do what a wise lad may, Miss; but ye don't know they lads; they baint that easy come over; and I won't get knocked on the head, nor sent to gaol 'appen, for no good to thee nor me. There's Meg there, she knows well enough. I could na manage that; so I won't try it, Miss, by no chance; no offence, Miss; but I'd rayther not, an I'll just try what I can make o' this; that's all I can do for ye.'

Tom Brice, with these words, stood up, and looked uneasily in the direction of the Windmill Wood.

'Mind ye, Miss, coom what will, ye'll not tell o' me?'

'Whar 'ill ye go now, Tom?' inquired Meg, uneasily.

'Never ye mind, lass,' answered he, breaking his way through the thicket, and soon disappearing.

'E'es, that 'ill be it—he'll git into the sheep-walk behind the mound. They're all down yonder; git ye back, Miss, to the hoose—be the side-door; mind ye, don't go round the corner; and I'll jest sit awhile among the bushes, and wait a good time for a start. And good-bye, Miss; and don't ye show like as if there was aught out o' common on your mind. Hish!'

There was a distant hallooing.

'That be fayther!' she whispered, with a very black countenance, and listened with her sunburnt hand to her ear.

''Tisn't me, only Davy he'll be callin',' she said, with a great sigh, and a joyless smile. 'Now git ye away i' God's name.'

So running lightly along the path, under cover of this thick wood, I recalled Mary Quince, and together we hastened back again to the house, and entered, as directed, by the side-door, which did not expose us to be seen from the Windmill Wood; and, like two criminals, we stole up by the back stairs, and so through the side gallery to my room; and there sat down to collect my wits, and try to estimate the exact effect of what had just occurred.

Madame had not returned. That was well; she always visited my room first, and everything was precisely as I had left it—a certain sign that her prying eyes and busy fingers had not been at work during my absence.

When she did appear, strange to say, it was to bring me unexpected comfort. She had in her hand a letter from my dear Lady Knollys—a gleam of sunlight from the free and happy outer world entered with it. The moment Madame left me to myself, I opened it and read as follows:—

'I am so happy, my dearest Maud, in the immediate prospect of seeing you. I have had a really kind letter from poor Silas—*poor*, I say, for I really compassionate his situation, about which he has been, I do believe, quite frank; at least, Ilbury says so—and somehow he happens to know. I have had quite an affecting, changed letter. I will tell you all when I see you. He wants me ultimately to undertake that which would afford me the most unmixed happiness—I mean the care of you, my dear girl. I only fear lest my too eager acceptance of the trust should excite that vein of opposition which is in most human beings, and induce him to think over his offer less favourably again. He says I must come to Bartram, and stay a night, and promises to lodge me comfortably; about which last, I honestly do not care a pin, when the chance of a comfortable evening's gossip with you is in view. Silas explains his sad situation, and must hold himself in readiness for early flight, if he would avoid the risk of losing his personal liberty. It is a sad thing that he should have so irretrievably ruined himself, that poor Austin's liberality seems to have positively precipitated his extremity. His great anxiety is that I should see you before you leave for your short stay in France. He thinks you must leave before a fort-night. I was thinking of asking you to come over here; I know you would be just as well at Elverston as in France; but perhaps, as he seems disposed to do what we all wish, it may be safer to let him set about it in his own way. The truth is I have so set my heart upon it that I fear to risk it by crossing him even in a trifle. He says I must fix an early day next week, and talks as if he meant to urge me to make a longer visit than he defined. I shall be only too happy. I begin, my dear Maud, to think that there is no use in trying to control events, and that things often turn out best, and most exactly to our wishes, by being left quite to themselves. I think it was Talleyrand* who praised the talent of *waiting* so much. In high spirits, and with my head brim-ful of plans, I remain, dearest Maud, ever your affectionate cousin,

'MONICA.'

Here was an inexplicable puzzle! A faint radiance of hope, however, began to overspread a landscape only a few minutes before darkened by total eclipse; but construct what theory I might, all were inconsist-ent with many well-established and awful incongruities, and their wrecks lay strown over the troubled waters of the gulf into which I gazed.

Why was Madame here? Why was Dudley concealed about the place? Why was I a prisoner within the walls? What were those dan-gers which Meg Hawkes seemed to think so great and so imminent as to induce her to risk her lover's safety for my deliverance? All these menacing facts stood grouped together against the dark certainty that never were men more deeply interested in making away with one human being, than were Uncle Silas and Dudley in removing me.

Sometimes to these dreadful evidences I abandoned my soul. Sometimes, reading Cousin Monica's sunny letter, the sky would clear, and my terrors melt away like nightmares in the morning. I never repented, however, that I had sent my letter by Tom Brice. Escape from Bartram-Haugh was my hourly longing.

That evening Madame invited herself to tea with me. I did not object. It was better just then to be on friendly relations with everybody if possible, even on their own terms. She was in one of her boisterous and hilarious moods, and there was a perfume of brandy.

She narrated some compliments paid her that morning in Feltram by that 'good crayature,' Mrs. Litheways, the silk mercer, and what ''ansom faylow' was her new foreman—(she intended plainly that I should 'queez' her)—and how 'he follow' her with his eyes wherever she went. I thought, perhaps, he fancied she might pocket some of his laces or gloves. And all the time her great wicked eyes were rolling and glancing according to her ideas of fascination, and her bony face grinning and flaming with the 'strong drink' in which she delighted. She sang twaddling chansons, and being, as was her wont, under such exhilarating influences in a vapouring mood, she vowed that I should have my carriage and horses immediately.

'I weel try what I can do weeth your Uncle Silas. We are very good old friends. Mr. Ruthyn and I,' she said with a leer which I did not understand, and which yet frightened me.

I never could quite understand why these Jezebels like to insinuate the dreadful truth against themselves; but they do. Is it the spirit of feminine triumph overcoming feminine shame, and making them vaunt their fall as an evidence of bygone fascination and existing power? Need we wonder? Have not women preferred hatred to indifference, and the reputation of witchcraft, with all its penalties, to absolute insignificance? Thus, as they enjoyed the fear inspired among simple neighbours by their imagined traffic with the father of ill, did Madame, I think, relish with a cynical vainglory the suspicion of her Satanic superiority.

Next morning Uncle Silas sent for me. He was seated at his table, and spoke his little French greeting, smiling as usual, pointing to a chair opposite.

'How far, I forget,' he said, carelessly laying his newspaper on the table, 'did you yesterday guess Dudley to be?'

Eleven hundred miles, I thought it was.

'Oh, yes, so it was;' and then there was an abstracted pause. 'I have been writing to Lord Ilbury, your trustee,' he resumed. 'I ventured to say, my dear Maud—(for having thoughts of a different arrangement for you, more suitable under my distressing circumstances, I do not wish to vacate without some expression of your estimate of my treatment of you while under my roof)— I ventured to say that you thought me kind, considerate, indulgent—may I say so?'

I assented. What could I say?

'I said you had enjoyed our poor way of living here—our rough ways and liberty. Was I right?'

Again, I assented.

'And in fact that you had nothing to object against your poor old uncle, except, indeed, his poverty, which you forgave. I think I said truth. Did I, dear Maud?'

Again, I acquiesced.

All this time he was fumbling among the papers in his coat-pocket.

'That is satisfactory. So I expected you to say,' he murmured. 'I expected no less.'

On a sudden a frightful change spread across his face. He rose like a spectre with a white scowl.

'Then how do you account for that?' he shrieked in a voice of thunder, and smiting my open letter to Lady Knollys, face upward, upon the table.

I stared at my uncle, unable to speak, until I seemed to lose sight of him; but his voice, like a bell, still yelled in my ears.

'There! young hypocrite and liar! explain that farrago of slander which you bribed my servant to place in the hands of my kinswoman, Lady Knollys.'

And so on and on it went, I gazing into darkness, until the voice itself became indistinct, grew into a buzz, and hummed away into silence.

I think I must have had a fit.

When I came to myself I was drenched with water, my hair, face, neck, and dress. I did not in the least know where I was. I thought my father was ill, and spoke to him. Uncle Silas was standing near the window looking unspeakably grim. Madame was seated beside me, and an open bottle of ether, one of Uncle Silas's restoratives, on the table before me.

'Who's that—who's ill—is any one dead?' I cried.

At last I was relieved by long paroxysms of weeping. When I was sufficiently recovered, I was conveyed into my own room.

CHAPTER LVIII

LADY KNOLLYS' CARRIAGE

NEXT morning, it was Sunday, I lay in my bed in my dressing-gown, dull, apathetic, with all my limbs sore, and, as I thought, rheumatic, and feeling so ill that I did not care to speak or lift my head. My recollection of what had passed in Uncle Silas's room was utterly confused, and it seemed to me as if my poor father had been there and taken a share—I could not remember how—in the conference.

I was too exhausted and stupid to clear up this horrible muddle, and merely lay with my face toward the wall, motionless and silent, except for a great sigh every now and then.

Good Mary Quince was in the room—there was some comfort in that; but I felt quite worn out, and had rather she did not speak to me; and indeed for the time I felt absolutely indifferent as to whether I lived or died.

Cousin Monica this morning, at pleasant Elverston, all unconscious of my sad plight, proposed to Lady Mary Carysbroke and Lord Ilbury, her guests, to drive over to church at Feltram, and then pay us a visit at Bartram-Haugh, to which they readily agreed.

Accordingly, at about two o'clock, this pleasant party of three arrived at Bartram. They walked, having left the carriage to follow when the horses were fed, and Madame de la Rougierre, who was in my uncle's room when little Giblets arrived to say that the party were in the parlour, whispered for a little with my uncle, who then said—

'Miss Maud Ruthyn has gone out to drive, but I shall be happy to see Lady Knollys here, if she will do me the favour to come up stairs, and see me for a few moments, and you can mention that I am very far from well.'

Madame followed him out upon the lobby, and added, holding him by the collar, and whispering earnestly in his ear—

'Bring hair ladysheep up by the back stairs—mind, the *back* stairs.'

And the next moment Madame entered my room, with long tiptoe steps, and looking, Mary Quince said, as if she were going to be hanged.

On entering she looked sharply round, and being satisfied of Mary Quince's presence, she turned the key in the door, and made some affectionate inquiries about me in a whisper; and then she stole to the window and peeped out, standing back some way; after which she came to my bedside, murmured some tender sentences, drew the curtain a little, and making some little fidgety adjustments about the room; among the rest she took the key from the lock, quietly, and put it into her pocket.

This was so odd a procedure that honest Mary Quince rose stoutly from her chair, pointing to the lock, with her frank little blue eyes fixed on Madame, and she whispered—

'Won't you put the key in the lock, please?'

'Oh, certainly, Mary Queence; but it is better it shall be locked, for I think her uncle he is coming to see her, and I am sure she would be very much frightened, for he is very much displease, don't you see? and we can tell him she is not well enough, or asleep, and so he weel go away again, without any trouble.'

I heard nothing of this, which was conducted in close whispers; and Mary, although she did not give Madame credit for caring whether I was frightened or not, and suspected her motives in everything, acquiesced grudgingly, fearing lest her alleged reason might possibly be the true one.

So Madame hovered about the door, uneasily; and of what went on elsewhere during that period Lady Knollys afterwards gave me the following account:–

'We were very much disappointed; but of course I was glad to see Silas, and your little hobgoblin butler led me upstairs to his room a different way, I think, from that I came before; but I don't know the house of Bartram well enough to speak positively. I only know that I was conducted quite across his bedroom, which I had not seen on my former visit, and so into his sitting-room, where I found him.

'He seemed very glad to see me, came forward smiling—I disliked his smile always—with both hands out, and shook mine with more warmth than I ever remembered in his greeting before, and said—

'"My dear, _dear_ Monica, how _very_ good of you—the very person I longed to see. I have been miserably ill, the sad consequence of still more miserable anxiety. Sit down, pray, for a moment."

'And he paid me some nice little French compliment in verse.

'"And where is Maud?" said I.

'"I think Maud is by this time about half-way to Elverston," said the old gentleman. "I persuaded her to take a drive, and advised a call there, which seemed to please her, so I conjecture she obeyed."

' "How *very* provoking!" cried I.

' "My poor Maud will be sadly disappointed, but you will console her by a visit—you have promised to come, and I shall try to make you comfortable. I shall be happier, Monica, with this proof of our perfect reconciliation. You won't deny me?"

' "Certainly not. I am only too glad to come," said I; "and I want to thank you, Silas."

' "For what?" said he.

' "For wishing to place Maud in my care. I am very much obliged to you."

' "I did not suggest it, I must say, Monica, with the least intention of obliging *you*," said Silas.

'I thought he was going to break into one of his ungracious moods.

' "But I *am* obliged to you—very much obliged to you, Silas; and you shan't refuse my thanks."

' "I am happy, at all events, Monica, in having won your good-will; we learn at last that in the affections only are our capacities for happiness; and how true is St. Paul's preference of love*—the principle that abideth! The affections, dear Monica, are eternal; and being so, celestial, divine, and consequently happy, deriving happiness, and bestowing it."

'I was always impatient of his or anybody else's metaphysics; but I controlled myself, and only said, with my customary impudence—

' "Well, dear Silas, and when do you wish me to come?"

' "The earlier the better," said he.

' "Lady Mary and Ilbury will be leaving me on Tuesday morning. I can come to you in the afternoon, if you think Tuesday a good day."

' "Thank you, dear Monica. I shall be, I trust, enlightened by that day as to my enemies' plans. It is a humiliating confession, Monica, but I am past feeling that. It is quite possible that an execution may be sent into this house to-morrow, and an end of all my schemes. It is not likely, however—hardly possible—before three weeks, my attorney tells me. I shall hear from him to-morrow morning, and then I shall ask you to name a very early day. If we are to have an unmolested fortnight certain, you shall hear, and name your own day."

'Then he asked me who had accompanied me, and lamented ever so much his not being able to go down to receive them, and he offered luncheon, with a sort of Ravenswood smile,* and a shrug, and I declined, telling him that we had but a few minutes, and that my companions were walking in the grounds near the house.

'I asked whether Maud was likely to return soon.

' "Certainly not before five o'clock." He thought we should probably meet her on our way back to Elverston; but could not be certain, as she might have changed her plans.

'So then came—no more remaining to be said—a very affectionate parting. I believe all about his legal dangers was strictly true. How he could, unless that horrid woman had deceived him, with so serene a countenance, tell me all those gross untruths about Maud, I can only admire.'

In the meantime, as I lay in my bed, Madame, gliding hither and thither, whispering sometimes, listening at others, I suddenly startled them both by saying—

'Whose carriage?'

'What carriage, dear?' inquired Quince, whose ears were not so sharp as mine.

Madame peeped from the window.

' 'Tis the physician, Doctor Jolks. He is come to see your uncle, my dear,' said Madame.

'But I hear a female voice,' I said, sitting up.

'No, my dear. There is only the doctor,' said Madame. 'He is come to your uncle. I tell you he is getting out of his carriage,' and she affected to watch the doctor's descent.

'The carriage is driving away!' I cried.

'Yes, it is draiving away,' she echoed.

But I had sprung from my bed, and was looking over her shoulder, before she perceived me.

'It is Lady Knollys!' I screamed, seizing the window-frame to force it up, and, vainly struggling to open it, I cried—

'I'm here, Cousin Monica, for God's sake! Cousin Monica—Cousin Monica!'

'You are mad, Meess, go back,' screamed Madame, exerting her superior strength to force me back.

But I saw deliverance and escape gliding away from my reach, and, strung to unnatural force by desperation, I pushed past her, and beat the window wildly with my hands, screaming—

'Save me—save me! Here, here, Monica, here! Cousin, Cousin, oh, save me!'

Madame had seized my wrists, and a wild struggle was going on. A window-pane was broken, and I was shrieking to stop the carriage.

The Frenchwoman looked black and haggard as a fury, as if she could have murdered me.

Nothing daunted—frantic—I screamed in my despair, seeing the carriage drive swiftly away—seeing Cousin Monica's bonnet, as she sat chatting with her *vis-à-vis*.

'Oh, oh, oh!' I shrieked, in vain and prolonged agony, as Madame, exerting her strength and matching her fury against my despair, forced me back in spite of my wild struggles, and pushed me sitting on the bed, where she held me fast, glaring in my face, and chuckling and panting over me.

I think I felt something of the despair of a lost spirit.

I remember the face of poor Mary Quince—its horror, its wonder—as she stood gaping into my face, over Madame's shoulder, and crying—

'What is it, Miss Maud? What is it, dear?' And turning fiercely on Madame, and striving to force her grasp from my wrists. 'Are you hurting the child? Let her go—let her go.'

'I *weel* let her go. Wat old fool are you, Mary Queence! She is mad, I think. She 'as lost hair head.'

'Oh, Mary, cry from the window. Stop the carriage!' I cried.

Mary looked out, but there was by this time, of course, nothing in sight.

'Wy don't a you stop the carriage?' sneered Madame. 'Call a the coachman and the postilion. W'ere is the footman? Bah! *elle a le cerveau mal timbré.*'*

'Oh, Mary, Mary, is it gone—is it gone? Is there nothing there?' cried I, rushing to the window, and turning to Madame, after a vain straining of my eyes, my face against the glass.

'Oh, cruel, cruel, wicked woman! why have you done this? What was it to you? Why do you persecute me? What good *can* you gain by my ruin?'

'Rueen! Par bleu! ma chère, you talk too fast. Did not a you see it, Mary Queence? It was the doctor's carriage, and Mrs. Jolks, and that eempudent faylow, young Jolks, staring up to the window, and Mademoiselle she come in soche shocking déshabille to show herself knocking at the window. 'Twould be very nice thing, Mary Queence, don't you think?'

I was sitting now on the bedside, crying in mere despair. I did not care to dispute or to resist. Oh, why had rescue come so near, only to prove that it could not reach me! So I went on crying, with a clasping of my hands and turning up of my eyes, in incoherent prayer. I was not thinking of Madame, or of Mary Quince, or any other person, only babbling my anguish and despair helplessly in the ear of heaven.

'I did not think there was soche fool. Wat *enfant gaté*! My dear cheaile, wat a can you *mean* by soche strange language and conduct? Wat for should a you weesh to display yourself in the window in soche 'orrible déshabille to the people in the doctor's coach?'

'It was *Cousin Knollys*—Cousin Knollys. Oh, Cousin Knollys! You're gone—you're gone—you're *gone*!'

'And if it was Lady Knollys' coach, there was certainly a coachman and a footman; and whoever has the coach there was young gentlemen in it. If it was Lady Knollys' carriage it would 'av been *worse* than the doctor.'

'It is no matter—it is all over. Oh, Cousin Monica, your poor Maud—where is she to turn? Is there no help?'

That evening Madame visited me again, in one of her sedate and moral moods. She found me dejected and passive, as she had left me.

'I think, Maud, there is news; but I am not certain.'

I raised my head and looked at her wistfully.

'I think there is letter of *bad* news from the attorney in London.'

'Oh!' I said, in a tone which I am sure implied the absolute indifference of dejection.

'But, my dear Maud, if 't be so, we shall go at once, you and me, to join Meess Millicent in France. La belle France! You weel like so moche! We shall be so gay. You cannot imagine there are such naice girl there. They all love a me so moche, you will be delight.'

'How soon do we go?' I asked.

'I do not know. Bote I was to bring in a case of eau de Cologne that came this evening, and he laid down a letter and say:—"The blow has descended, Madame! My niece must hold herself in readiness." I said, "For what, Monsieur?" *twice*; bote he did not answer. I am sure it is *un procés*. They 'av ruin him. Eh bien, my dear. I suppose we shall leave this triste place immediately. I am so rejoice. It appears to me *un cimetière*!'

'Yes, I should like to leave it,' I said, sitting up, with a great sigh and sunken eyes. It seemed to me that I had quite lost all sense of resentment towards Madame. A debility of feeling had supervened—the fatigue, I suppose, and prostration of the passions.

'I weel make excuse to go into his room again,' said Madame; 'and I weel endeavour to learn something more from him, and I weel come back again to you in half an hour.'

She departed. But in half an hour did not return. I had a dull longing to leave Bartram-Haugh. For me, since the departure of poor Milly, it had grown like the haunt of evil spirits, and to escape on any terms from it was a blessing unspeakable.

Another half-hour passed, and another, and I grew insufferably feverish. I sent Mary Quince to the lobby to try and see Madame, who, I feared, was probably to-ing and fro-ing in and out of Uncle Silas's room.

Mary returned to tell me that she had seen old Wyat, who told her that she thought Madame had gone to her bed half an hour before.

CHAPTER LIX

'MARY,' said I, 'I am miserably anxious to hear what Madame may have to tell; she knows the state I am in, and she would not take so much trouble as to look in at my door to say a word. Did you hear what she told me?'

'No, Miss Maud,' she answered, rising and drawing near.

'She thinks we are going to France immediately, and to leave this place perhaps for ever.'

'Heaven be praised for that, if it be so, Miss,' said Mary, with more energy than was common with her, 'for there is no luck about it, and I don't expect to see you ever well or happy in it.'

'You must take your candle, Mary, and make out her room, upstairs; I found it accidentally myself one evening.'

'But Wyat won't let us up-stairs.'

'Don't mind her, Mary; I tell you to go. You must try. I can't sleep till we hear.'

'What direction is her room in, Miss?' asked Mary.

'Somewhere in *that* direction, Mary,' I answered, pointing. 'I cannot describe the turns; but I think you will find it if you go along the great passage to your left, on getting to the top of the stairs, till you come to the cross galleries, and then turn to your left, and when you have passed four, or perhaps five doors, you must be very near it, and I am sure she will hear if you call.'

'But will she tell me—she *is* such a rum 'un, Miss?' suggested Mary.

'Tell her exactly what I have said to you, and when she learns that you already know as much as I do, she may—unless, indeed, she wishes to torture me. If she won't, perhaps at least you can persuade her to come to me for a moment. Try, dear Mary; we can but fail.'

'Will you be very lonely, Miss, while I am away?' asked Mary, uneasily, as she lighted her candle.

'I can't help it, Mary. Go. I think if I heard we were going, I could almost get up and dance and sing. I can't bear this dreadful uncertainty any longer.'

'If old Wyat is outside, I'll come back and wait here a bit, till she's out o' the way,' said Mary; 'and, anyhow, I'll make all the haste I can. The drops and the sal-volatile is here, Miss, by your hand.'

And with an anxious look at me, she made her exit, softly, and did not immediately return, by which I concluded that she had found the way clear, and had gained the upper story without interruption.

This little anxiety ended, its subsidence was followed by a sense of loneliness, and with it, of vague insecurity, which increased at last to such a pitch, that I wondered at my own madness in sending my companion away; and at last my terrors so grew, that I drew back into the furthest corner of the bed, with my shoulders to the wall, and my bed-clothes huddled about me, with only a point open to peep at.

At last the door opened gently.

'Who's there?' I cried, in extremity of horror, expecting I knew not whom.

'Me, Miss,' whispered Mary Quince, to my unutterable relief; and with her candle flared, and a wild and pallid face, Mary Quince glided into the room, locking the door as she entered.

I do not know how it was, but I found myself holding Mary fast with both my hands as we stood side by side on the floor.

'Mary, you are terrified; for God's sake, what is the matter?' I cried.

'No, Miss,' said Mary, faintly; 'not much.'

'I see it in your face. What is it?'

'Let me sit down, Miss. I'll tell you what I saw; only I'm just a bit queerish.'

Mary sat down by my bed.

'Get in, Miss, you'll take cold. Get into bed, and I'll tell you. It is not much.'

I did get into bed, and gazing on Mary's frightened face, I felt a corresponding horror.

'For mercy's sake, Mary, say what it is?'

So again assuring me 'it was not much,' she gave me in a somewhat diffuse and entangled narrative the following facts:—

On closing my door, she raised her candle above her head and surveyed the lobby, and seeing no one there, she ascended the stairs swiftly. She passed along the great gallery to the left, and paused a moment at the cross gallery, and then recollected my directions clearly, and followed the passage to the right.

There are doors at each side, and she had forgotten to ask me at which Madame's was. She opened several. In one room she was frightened by a bat, which had very nearly put her candle out. She went on a little, paused, and began to lose heart in the dismal solitude, when on a sudden, a few doors further on, she thought she heard Madame's voice.

She said that she knocked at the door, but receiving no answer, and hearing Madame still talking within, she opened it.

There was a candle on the chimney-piece, and another in a stable lantern near the window. Madame was conversing volubly on the hearth, with her face toward the window, the entire frame of which had been taken from its place; Dickon Hawkes, the Zamiel of the wooden leg, was supporting it with one hand, as it leaned imperfectly against the angle of the recess. There was a third figure standing, buttoned up in a surtout, with a bundle of tools under his arm, like a glazier, and, with a silent thrill of fear, she distinctly recognized the features as those of Dudley Ruthyn.

''Twas him, Miss, so sure as I sit here! Well, like that, they were as mute as mice; three pairs of eyes were on me. I don't know what made me so study like, but som'at told me I should not make as though I knew any but Madame; and so I made a courtesy, as well as I could, and I said might I speak a word wi' ye, please, on the lobby.

'Mr. Dudley was making belief be this time to look out at window, wi' his back to me, and I kept looking straight on Madame, and she said—"They're mendin' my broken glass, Mary," walking between them and me, and coming close up to me very quick; and so she marched me backward out o' the door, prating all the time.

'When we were on the lobby, she took my candle from my hand, shutting the door behind her, and she held the light a bit behind her ear; so 'twas full on my face, as she looked sharp into it; and, after a bit, she said again, in her queer lingo—there was two panes broke in her room, and men sent for to mend it.

'I was awful frightened when I saw Mr. Dudley, for I could not believe any such thing before, and I don't know how I could look her in the face as I did and not show it. I was as smooth and cool as yonder chimneypiece, and she has an awful evil eye to stan' against; but I never flinched, and I think she's puzzled, for as cunning as she is, whether I believe all she said, or knowed 'twas a pack o' stories. So I told her your message, and she said she had not heard another word since; but she did believe we had not many more days here, and would tell you if she heard to-night, when she brought his soup to your uncle, in half an hour's time.'

I asked her, so soon as I could speak, whether she was perfectly certain as to the fact that the man in the surtout was Dudley, and she made answer—

'I'd swear to him on that Bible, Miss.'

So far from any longer wishing Madame's return that night, I trembled at the idea of it. Who could tell who might enter the room with her, when the door opened to admit her?

Dudley, so soon as he recovered the surprise, had turned about, evidently anxious to prevent recognition; Dickon Hawkes stood glowering at her. Both might have hope of escaping recognition in the imperfect light, for the candle on the chimneypiece was flaring in the air, and the light from the lantern fell in spots, and was confusing.

What could that ruffian, Hawkes, be doing in the house? Why was Dudley there? Could a more ominous combination be imagined? I puzzled my distracted head over all Mary Quince's details, but could make nothing of their occupation. I know of nothing so terrifying as this kind of perpetual puzzling over ominous problems.

You may imagine how the long hours of that night passed, and how my heart beat at every fancied sound outside my door.

But morning came, and with its light some reassurance. Early, Madame de la Rougierre made her appearance; she searched my eyes darkly and shrewdly, but made no allusion to Mary Quince's visit. Perhaps she expected some question from me, and, hearing none, thought it as well to leave the subject at rest.

She had merely come in to say that she had heard nothing since, but was now going to make my uncle's chocolate, and that so soon as her interview was ended she would see me again, and let me hear anything she should have gleaned.

In a little while a knock came to my door, and Mary Quince was ordered by old Wyat into my uncle's room. She returned flushed, in a huge fuss, to say that I was to be up and dressed for a journey in half an hour, and to go straight, when dressed, to my uncle's room.

It was good news; at the same time it was a shock. I was glad. I was stunned. I jumped out of bed, and set about my toilet with an energy quite new to me. Good Mary Quince was busily packing my boxes, and consulting as to what I should take with me, and what not.

Was Mary Quince to accompany me? He had not said a word on that point; and I feared, from his silence, she was to remain. There was comfort, however, in this—that the separation would not be for long; I felt confident of that; and I was about to join Milly, whom I loved better than I could have believed before our separation; but whatsoever the conditions might be, it was an indescribable relief to have done with Bartram-Haugh, and leave behind me its sinister lines of circumvallation; its haunted recesses, and the awful spectres that had lately appeared within its walls.

I stood too much in awe of my uncle to fail in presenting myself punctually at the close of the half hour. I entered his sitting-room under the shadow of sour old Wyat's high-cauled cap; she closed the door behind me, and the conference commenced.

Madame de la Rougierre sat there, dressed and draped for a journey, and with a thick black lace veil on. My uncle rose, gaunt and venerable, and with a harsh and severe countenance. He did not offer his hand; he made me a kind of bow, more of repulsion than of respect. He remained in a standing position, supporting his crooked frame by his hand, which he leaned on a despatch-box; he glared on me steadily with his wild, phosphoric eyes, from under the dark brows I have described to you, now corrugated in lines indescribably stern.

'You shall join my daughter at the Pension, in France; Madame de la Rougierre shall accompany you,' said my uncle, delivering his directions with the stern monotony and the measured pauses of a person dictating an important despatch to a secretary. 'Old Mrs. Quince shall follow with me, or, if alone, in a week. You shall pass to-night in London; to-morrow night you proceed thence to Dover, and cross by the mail-packet. You shall now sit down and write a letter to your Cousin Monica Knollys, which I will first read and then despatch. To-morrow you shall write a note to Lady Knollys, from *London*, telling her how you have got over so much of your journey, and that you cannot write from Dover as you must instantly start by the packet on reaching it, and that until my affairs are a little settled, you cannot write to her from France, as it is of high importance to my safety that no clue should exist as to our address. Intelligence, however, shall reach her through my attorneys, Archer and Sleigh, and I trust we shall soon return. You will, please, submit that latter note to Madame de la Rougierre, who has my directions to see that it contains no *libels* upon my character. Now, sit down.'

So with those unpleasant words tingling in my ears, I obeyed.

'*Write*,' said he, when I was duly placed. 'You shall convey the substance of what I say in your own language. The imminent danger this morning announced of an execution—remember the word,' and he spelled it for me—'being put into this house either this afternoon or to-morrow, compels me to anticipate my plans, and despatch you for France this day. That you are starting with an attendant.' Here an uneasy movement from Madame, whose dignity was perhaps excited. 'An *attendant*,' he repeated, with a discordant emphasis; 'and you can, if you please—but I don't *solicit* that justice—say that you have been as kindly treated here as my unfortunate circumstances would permit. That is all. You have just fifteen minutes to write. Begin.'

I wrote accordingly. My hysterical state had made me far less combative than I might have proved some months since, for there was much that was insulting as well as formidable in his manner. I completed my letter, however, to his satisfaction in the prescribed time, and he said, as he laid it and its envelope on the table—

'Please to remember that this lady is not your attendant only, but that she has authority to direct every detail respecting your journey, and will make all the necessary payments on the way. You will, please, then, implicitly to comply with her directions. The carriage awaits you at the hall-door.'

Having thus spoken, with another grim bow, and 'I wish you a safe and pleasant journey,' he receded a step or two, and I, with an undefinable kind of melancholy, though also with a sense of relief, withdrew.

My letter, I afterwards found, reached Lady Knollys, accompanied by one from Uncle Silas, who said—'Dear Maud apprizes me that she has written to tell you something of our movements. A sudden crisis in my miserable affairs compels a break-up as sudden here. Maud joins my daughter at the Pension, in France. I purposely omit the address, because I mean to reside in its vicinity until this storm shall have blown over; and as the consequences of some of my unhappy entanglements might pursue me even there, I must only for the present spare you the pain and trouble of keeping a secret. I am sure for some little time you will excuse the girl's silence; in the mean-time you shall hear of them, and, perhaps, circuitously from me. Our dear Maud started this morning *en route* for her destination, very sorry, as am I, that she could not enjoy first a flying visit to Elverston; but in high spirits, notwithstanding, at the new life and sights before her.'

At the door my beloved old friend, Mary Quince, awaited me—

'Am I going with you, Miss Maud?'

I burst into tears and clasped her in my arms.

'I'm not,' said Mary, very sorrowfully; 'and I never was from you yet, Miss, since you wasn't the length of my arm.'

And kind old Mary began to cry with me.

'Bote you are coming in a few days, Mary Quince,' expostulated Madame. 'I wonder you are soche fool. What is two, three days. Bah! nonsense, girl.'

Another farewell to poor Mary Quince, quite bewildered at the suddenness of her bereavement. A serious and tremulous bow from our little old butler on the steps. Madame bawling through the open window to the driver to make good speed, and remember that we had but nineteen minutes to reach the station. Away we went. Old Crowle's iron *grille* rolled back before us. I looked on the receding landscape, the giant trees, the palatial, time-stained mansion. A strange conflict of feelings, sweet and bitter, rose and mingled in the reverie. Had I been too hard and suspicious with the inhabitants of that old house of my family? Was my uncle *justly* indignant? Was I ever again to know such pleasant rambles as some of those I had enjoyed with dear Millicent through the wild and beautiful woodlands I was leaving behind me? And there, with my latest glimpse of the front of Bartram-Haugh, I beheld dear old Mary Quince gazing after us. Again my tears flowed. I waved my handkerchief from the window; and now the park wall hid all from view, and at a great pace, through the steep wooded glen, with the rocky and precipitous character of a ravine, we glided; and when the road next emerged, Bartram-Haugh was a misty mass of forest and chimneys, slope and hollow, and we within a few minutes of the station.

CHAPTER LX
THE JOURNEY

WAITING for the train, as we stood upon the platform, I looked back again toward the wooded uplands of Bartram; and far behind, the fine range of mountains, azure and soft in the distance, beyond which lay beloved old Knowl, and my lost father and mother, and the scenes of my childhood, never embittered except by the sibyl who sat beside me.

Under happier circumstances I should have been, at my then early age, quite wild with pleasurable excitement on entering London for the first time. But black Care sat by me, with her pale hand in mine: a voice of fear and warning, whose words I could not catch, was always in my ear. We drove through London, amid the glare of lamps, toward the west-end, and for a little while the sense of novelty and curiosity overcame my despondency, and I peeped eagerly from the window; while Madame, who was in high good-humour, spite of the fatigues of our long railway flight, screeched scraps of topographic information in my ear; for London was a picture-book in which she was well read.

'That is Euston-square, my dear—Russell-square. Here is Oxford-street—Haymarket. See, there is the Opera House—hair Majesty's theatre. See all the carriages waiting;' and so on, till we reached at length a narrow street, which she told me was off Piccadilly, where we drew up before a private house, as it seemed to me—a family hotel—and I was glad to be at rest for the night.

Fatigued with the peculiar fatigue of railway travelling, dusty, a little chilly, with eyes aching and wearied, I ascended the stairs silently, our garrulous and bustling landlady leading the way, and telling her oft-told story of the house, its noble owner in old time, and how those fine drawing-rooms were taken every year during the session by the Bishop of Rochet-on-Copeley, and at last into our double-bedded room.

I would fain have been alone, but I was too tired and dejected to care very much for anything.

At tea, Madame expanded in spirit, like a giant refreshed, and chatted and sang; and at last, seeing that I was nodding, advised my going to bed, while she ran across the street to see 'her dear old friend, Mademoiselle St. Eloi, who was sure to be up, and would be offended if she failed to make her ever so short a call.'

I cared little what she did, and was glad to be rid of her even for a short time, and was soon fast asleep.

I saw her, I know not how much later, poking about the room, like a figure in a dream, and taking off her things.

She had her breakfast in bed next morning, and I was, to my comfort, left to take mine in solitary possession of our sitting-room; where I began to wonder how little annoyance I had as yet suffered from her company, and began to speculate upon the chances of my making the journey with tolerable comfort.

Our hostess gave me five minutes of her valuable time. Her talk ran chiefly upon nuns and convents, and her old acquaintance with Madame; and it seemed to me that she had at one time driven a kind of trade, no doubt profitable enough, in escorting young ladies to establishments on the Continent; and although I did not then quite understand the tone in which she spoke to me, I often thought afterwards that Madame had represented me as a young person destined for the holy vocation of the veil.

When she was gone I sat listlessly looking out of the window, and saw some chance equipages drive by, and now and then a fashionable pedestrian; and wondered if this quiet thorough-fare could really be one of the arteries so near the heart of the tumultuous capital.

I think my nervous vitality must have burnt very low just then, for I felt perfectly indifferent about all the novelty and world of wonders beyond, and should have hated to leave the dull tranquillity of my window for an excursion through the splendours of the unseen streets and palaces that surrounded me.

It was one o'clock before Madame joined me; and finding me in this dull mood, she did not press me to accompany her in her drive, no doubt well pleased to be rid of me.

After tea that evening, as we sat alone in our room, she entertained me with some very odd conversation—at the time unintelligible—but which acquired a tolerably distinct meaning from the events that followed.

Two or three times that day Madame appeared to me on the point of saying something of grave import, as she scanned me with her bleak wicked stare.

It was a peculiarity of hers, that whenever she was pressed upon by an anxiety that really troubled her, her countenance did not look sad or solicitous as other people's would, but simply wicked. Her great gaunt mouth was compressed and drawn down firmly at the corners, and her eyes glared with a dismal scowl.

At last she said suddenly—

'Are you ever grateful, Maud?'

'I hope so, Madame,' I answered.

'And how do you show your gratitude? For instance, would a you do great deal for a person who would run *risque* for your sake?'

It struck me all at once that she was sounding me about poor Meg Hawkes, whose fidelity, notwithstanding the treason or cowardice of her lover, Tom Brice, I never doubted; and I grew at once wary and reserved.

'I know of no opportunity, thank Heaven, for any such service, Madame. How can anyone serve me at present, by themselves incurring danger? What do you mean?'

'Do you like, for example, to go to that French Pension? Would you not like better some other arrangement?'

'Of course there are other arrangements I should like better; but I see no use in talking of them; they are not to be,' I answered.

'What other arrangements do you mean, my dear cheaile?' inquired Madame. 'You mean, I suppose, you would like better to go to Lady Knollys.'

'My uncle does not choose it at present; and except with his consent nothing can be done.'

'He weel never consent, dear cheaile.'

'But he *has* consented—not immediately indeed, but in a short time, when his affairs are settled.'

'*Lanternes!** They will never be settle,' said Madame.

'At all events, for the present I am to go to France. Milly seems very happy, and I dare say I shall like it too. I am very glad to leave Bartram-Haugh, at all events.'

'But your uncle weel bring you back there,' said Madame, drily.

'It is doubtful whether he will ever return to Bartram himself,' I said.

'Ah,' said Madame, with a long-drawn, nasal intonation, 'you theenk I hate you. You are quaite wrong, my dear Maud. I am, on the contrary very much interested for you—I am, I assure you, dear a cheaile.'

And she laid her great hand, with joints misshapen by old chilblains, upon the back of mine. I looked up in her face. She was not smiling. On the contrary, her wide mouth was drawn down at the corners ruefully, as before, and she gazed on my face with a scowl from her abysmal eyes.

I used to think the flare of that irony which lighted her face so often immeasurably worse than any other expression she could assume; but this lack-lustre stare and dismal collapse of feature was more wicked still.

'Suppose I should bring you to Lady Knollys, and place you in her charge, what would a you do then for poor Madame?' said this dark spectre.

I was inwardly startled at these words. I looked into her unsearchable face, but could draw thence nothing but fear. Had she made the same overture only two days since, I think I would have offered her half my fortune. But circumstances were altered. I was no longer in the panic of despair. The lesson I had received from Tom Brice was fresh in my mind, and my profound distrust of her was uppermost. I saw before me only a tempter and betrayer, and said—

'Do you mean to imply, Madame, that my guardian is not to be trusted, and that I ought to make my escape from him, and that you are really willing to aid me in doing so?'

This, you see, was turning the tables upon her. I looked her steadily in the face as I spoke. She returned my gaze with a strange stare and a gape, which haunted me long after; and it seemed as we sat in utter silence that each was rather horribly fascinated by the other's gaze.

At last she shut her mouth sternly, and eyed me with a more determined and meaning scowl, and then said in a low tone—

'I believe, Maud, that you are a cunning and wicked little thing.'

'Wisdom is not cunning, Madame; nor is it wicked to ask your meaning in explicit language,' I replied.

'And so, you clever cheaile, we two sit here, playing at a game of chess, over this little table, to decide which shall destroy the other—is it not so?'

'I will not allow you to destroy me,' I retorted, with a sudden flash.

Madame stood up, and rubbed her mouth with her open hand. She looked to me like some evil being seen in a dream. I was frightened.

'You are going to hurt me!' I ejaculated, scarce knowing what I said.

'If I were, you deserve it. You are very malicious, ma chère; or, it may be, only very stupid.'

A knock came to the door.

'Come in,' I cried, with a glad sense of relief.

A maid entered.

'A letter, please'm,' she said, handing it to me.

'For *me*,' snarled Madame, snatching it.

I had seen my uncle's hand and the Feltram postmark.

Madame broke the seal, and read. It seemed but a word, for she turned it about after the first momentary glance, and examined the interior of the envelope, and then returned to the line she had already read.

She folded the letter again, drawing her nails in a sharp pinch along the creases, as she stared in a blank, hesitating way at me.

'You stupid little ingrate, I am employ by Monsieur Ruthyn, and of course I am faithful to my employer. I do not want to talk to you. *There*, you may read that.'

She jerked the letter before me on the table. It contained but these words—

'BARTRAM-HAUGH,
'30th January, 1845.

'MY DEAR MADAME,

'Be so good as to take the half-past eight o'clock train to *Dover* to-night. Beds are prepared.

'Yours very truly,
'SILAS RUTHYN.'

I cannot say what it was in this short advice that struck me with fear. Was it the thick line beneath the word 'Dover' that was so uncalled for, and gave me a faint but terrible sense of something preconcerted?

I said to Madame—

'Why is "Dover" underlined?'

'I do not know, little fool, no more than you. How can I tell what is passing in your oncle's head when he make that a mark?'

'Has it not a meaning, Madame?'

'How can you talk like that?' she answered, more in her old way. 'You are either mocking of me, or you are becoming truly a fool!'

She rang the bell, called for our bill, saw our hostess; while I made a few hasty preparations in my room.

'You need not look after the trunks—they will follow us all right. Let us go, cheaile—we 'av half an hour only to reach the train.'

No one ever fussed like Madame when occasion offered. There was a cab at the door, into which she hurried me. I assumed that she would give all needful directions, and leaned back, very weary and sleepy already, though it was so early, listening to her farewell screamed from the cab-step, and seeing her black cloak flitting and flapping this way and that, like the wings of a raven disturbed over its prey.

In she got, and away we drove through a glare of lamps, and shop-windows, still open; gas everywhere, and cabs, busses, and carriages, still thundering through the streets. I was too tired and too depressed to look at those things. Madame, on the contrary, had her head out of the window till we reached the station.

'Where are the rest of the boxes?' I asked, as Madame placed me in charge of her box and my bag in the office of the terminus.

'They will follow with Boots in another cab, and will come safe with us in this train. Mind those two, we weel bring in the carriage with us.'

So into a carriage we got; in came Madame's box and my bag; Madame stood at the door, and, I think, frightened away intending passengers, by her size and shrillness.

At last the bell rang her into her place, the door clapt, the whistle sounded, and we were off.

CHAPTER LXI

OUR BED-CHAMBER

I HAD passed a miserable night, and, indeed, for many nights had not had my due proportion of sleep. Still I sometimes fancy that I may have swallowed something in my tea that helped to make me so irresistibly drowsy. It was a very dark night. No moon, and the stars soon hid by the gathering clouds. Madame sat silent, and ruminating in her place, with her rugs about her. I in my corner similarly enveloped I tried to keep awake. Madame plainly thought I was asleep already, for she stole a leather flask from her pocket, and applied it to her lips, causing an aroma of brandy.

But it was vain struggling against the influence that was stealing over me, and I was soon in a profound and dreamless slumber.

Madame awoke me at last, in a huge fuss. She had got out all our things and hurried them away to a close carriage which was awaiting us. It was still dark and starless. We got along the platform, I half asleep, the porter carrying our rugs, by the glare of a pair of gas jets in the wall, and out by a small door at the end.

I remember that Madame, contrary to her wont, gave the man some money. By the puzzling light of the carriage lamps we got in and took our seats.

'Go on,' screamed Madame, and drew up the window with a great chuck, and we were enclosed in dark and silence, the most favourable conditions for thought.

My sleep had not restored me as it might; I felt feverish, fatigued, and still very drowsy, though unable to sleep as I had done.

I dozed by fits and starts, and lay awake, or half awake sometimes, not thinking but in a way imagining what kind of a place Dover would be; but too tired and listless to ask Madame any questions, and merely seeing the hedges, gray in the lamp-light, glide backward into darkness, as I leaned back.

We turned off the main road, at right angles, and drew up.

'Get down and poosh it, it is open,' screamed Madame from the window.

A gate, I suppose, was thus passed, for when we resumed our brisk trot, Madame bawled across the carriage—

'We are now in the 'otel grounds.'

And so all again was darkness and silence, and I fell into another doze, from which, on waking, I found that we had come to a standstill, and Madame was standing on the low step of an open door, paying the driver. She, herself, pulled her box and the bag in. I was too tired to care what had become of the rest of our luggage.

I descended, glancing to the right and left, but there was nothing visible but a patch of light from the lamps on a paved ground and on the wall.

We stepped into the hall or vestibule, and Madame shut the door, and I thought I heard the key turn in it. We were in total darkness.

'Where are the lights, Madame—where are the people?' I asked, more awake than I had been.

''Tis pass three o'clock, cheaile, bote there is always light here.' She was groping at the side; and in a moment more lighted a lucifer match, and so a bed-room candle.

We were in a flagged lobby, under an archway at the right, and at the left of which opened long flagged passages, lost in darkness; a winding stair, barely wide enough to admit Madame, dragging her box, led upward under a doorway, in a corner at the right.

'Come, dear cheaile, take a your bag; don't mind the rugs, they are safe enough.'

'But where are we to go? There is no one!' I said, looking round in wonder. It certainly was a strange reception at a hotel.

'Never mind, my dear cheaile. They know me here, and I have always the same room ready when I write for it. Follow me quaitely.'

So she mounted, carrying the candle. The stair was steep, and the march long. We halted at the second landing, and entered a gaunt, grimy passage. All the way up we had not heard a single sound of life, nor seen a human being, nor so much as passed a gaslight.

'Voilà! here 'tis, my dear old room. Enter, dearest Maud.'

And so I did. The room was large and lofty, but shabby and dismal. There was a tall four-post bed, with its foot beside the window, hung with dark-green curtains, of some plush or velvet texture, that looked like a dusty pall. The remaining furniture was scant and old, and a ravelled square of threadbare carpet covered a patch of floor at the bed-side. The room was grim and large, and had a cold, vault-like atmosphere, as if long uninhabited; but there were cinders in the grate and under it. The imperfect light of our mutton-fat candle made all this look still more comfortless.

Madame placed the candle on the chimney-piece, locked the door, and put the key in her pocket.

'I always do so in '*otel*,' said she, with a wink at me.

And then with a long 'ha!' expressive of fatigue and relief, she threw herself into a chair.

'So 'ere we are at last!' said she; 'I'm glad. *There's* your bed, Maud. *Mine* is in the dressing-room.'

She took the candle, and I went in with her. A shabby press-bed, a chair, and table, were all its furniture; it was rather a closet than a dressing-room, and had no door except that through which we had entered. So we returned, and very tired, wondering, I sat down on the side of my bed, and yawned.

'I hope they will call us in time for the packet,' I said.

'Oh, yes, they never fail,' she answered, looking steadfastly on her box, which she was diligently uncording.

Uninviting as was my bed I was longing to lie down in it; and having made those ablutions which our journey rendered necessary, I at length lay down, having first religiously stuck my talismanic pin, with the head of sealing-wax, into the bolster.

Nothing escaped the restless eye of Madame.

'Wat is that, dear cheaile?' she inquired, drawing near and scrutinizing the head of the gipsy charm, which showed like a little ladybird newly lighted on the sheet.

'Nothing—a charm—folly. Pray, Madame, allow me to go to sleep.'

So, with another look and a little twiddle between her finger and thumb, she seemed satisfied; but, unhappily for me, she did not seem at all sleepy. She busied herself in unpacking and displaying over the back of the chair a whole series of London purchases. Silk dresses, a shawl, a sort of lace demi-coiffure, then in vogue, and a variety of other articles.

The vainest and most slammakin* of women. The merest slut at home, a milliner's lay figure* out of doors. She had one square foot of looking-glass upon the chimney-piece, and therein tried effects, and conjured up grotesque simpers upon her sinister and weary face.

I knew that the sure way to prolong this worry was to express my uneasiness under it, so I bore it as quietly as I could; and at last fell fast asleep with the gaunt image of Madame, with a festoon of gray silk with a cerise stripe, pinched up in her finger and thumb, and smiling over her shoulder across it into the little shaving-glass that stood on the chimney.

I awoke suddenly in the morning, and sat up in my bed, having for a moment forgotten all about our travelling. A moment more, however, brought all back again.

'Are we in time, Madame?'

'For the packet?' she inquired, with one of her charming smiles, and cutting a caper on the floor. 'To be sure; you don't suppose they would forget. We have two hours yet to wait.'

'Can we see the sea from the window?'

'No, dearest cheaile; you will see 't time enough.'

'I'd like to get up,' I said.

'Time enough, my dear Maud; you are fatigue; are you sure you feel quite well?'

'Well enough to get up; I should be better, I think, out of bed.'

'There is no hurry, you know; you need not even go by the next packet. Your uncle, he tell me, I may use my discretion.'

'Is there any water?'

'They will bring some.'

'Please, Madame, ring the bell.'

She pulled it with alacrity. I afterwards learnt that it did not ring.

'What has become of my gipsy pin?' I demanded, with an unaccountable sinking of the heart.

'Oh! the little pin with the red top? maybe it 'as fall on the ground; we weel find when you get up.'

I suspected that she had taken it merely to spite me. It would have been quite the thing she would have liked. I cannot describe to you how the loss of this little 'charm' depressed and excited me. I searched the bed; I turned over all the bed-clothes; I searched in and outside; at last I gave it up.

'How odious!' I cried; 'somebody has stolen it merely to vex me.'

And, like a fool as I was, I threw myself on my face on the bed and wept, partly in anger, partly in dismay.

After a time, however, this blew over. I had a hope of recovering it. If Madame had stolen it, it would turn up yet. But in the mean-time its disappearance troubled me like an omen.

'I am afraid, my dear cheaile, you are not very well. It is really very odd you should make such a fuss about a pin! Nobody would believe!

Do you not theenk it would be good plan to take a your breakfast in your bed?'

She continued to urge this point for some time. At last, however, having by this time quite recovered my self-command, and resolved to preserve ostensibly fair terms with Madame, who could contribute so essentially to make me wretched during the rest of my journey, and possibly to prejudice me very seriously on my arrival, I said quietly—

'Well, Madame, I know it is very silly; but I had kept that foolish little pin so long and so carefully, that I had grown quite fond of it; but I suppose it is lost, and I must content myself, though I cannot laugh as you do. So I will get up now, and dress.'

'I think you will do well to get all the repose you can,' answered Madame; 'but as you please,' she added, observing that I was getting up.

So soon as I had got some of my things on I said—

'Is there a pretty view from the window?'

'No,' said Madame.

I looked out and saw a dreary quadrangle of cut stone; in one side of which my window was placed. As I looked a dream rose up before me.

'This hotel,' I said, in a puzzled way. '*Is* it a hotel? Why this is just like—it *is* the inner court of Bartram-Haugh!'

Madame clapped her large hands together, made a fantastic *chassé* on the floor, burst into a great nasal laugh like the scream of a parrot, and then said—

'Well, dearest Maud, is not clever trick?'

I was so utterly confounded that I could only stare about me in stupid silence, a spectacle which renewed Madame's peals of laughter.

'We are at Bartram-Haugh!' I repeated in utter consternation. 'How was this done?'

I had no reply but shrieks of laughter, and one of those Walpurgis dances, in which she excelled.

'It is a mistake—is it? *What* is it?'

'All a mistake, of course. Bartram-Haugh, it is so like Dover, as all philosophers know.'

I sat down in total silence, looking out into the deep and dark enclosure, and trying to comprehend the reality and the meaning of all this.

'Well, Madame, I suppose you will be able to satisfy my uncle of your fidelity and intelligence. But to me it seems that his money has been ill spent, and his directions anything but well observed.'

'Ah ha! Never mind; I think he will forgive me,' laughed Madame.

Her tone frightened me. I began to think with a vague but over-powering sense of danger that she had acted under the Machiavelian directions of her superior.

'You have brought me back, then, by my uncle's orders.'

'Did I say so?'

'No; but what you have said can have no other meaning, though I can't believe it. And why have I been brought here? What is the object of all this duplicity and trick? I *will* know. It is not possible that my uncle, a gentleman and a kinsman, can be privy to so disreputable a manœuvre.'

'First you will eat your breakfast, dear Maud; next you can tell your story to your uncle, Monsieur Ruthyn; and then you shall hear what he thinks of my so terrible misconduct. What nonsense, cheaile! Can you not think how many things may 'appen to change a your uncle's plans? Is he not in danger to be arrest? Bah! You are cheaile still; you cannot have intelligence more than a cheaile. Dress yourself, and I will order breakfast.'

I could not comprehend the strategy which had been practised on me. Why had I been so shamelessly deceived? If it were decided that I should remain here, for what imaginable reason had I been sent so far on my journey to France? Why had I been conveyed back with such mystery? Why was I removed to this uncomfortable and desolate room, on the same floor with the apartment in which Charke had met his death, and with no window commanding the front of the house, and no view but the deep and weed-choked court, that looked like a deserted churchyard in a city?

'I suppose I may go to my own room?' I said.

'Not to-day, my dear cheaile, for it was all disarrange when we go 'way; 'twill be ready again in two three days.'

'Where is Mary Quince?' I asked.

'Mary Quince!—she has follow us to France,' said Madame, making what in Ireland they call a bull.*

'They are not sure where they will go or what will do for day or two more. I will go and get breakfast. Adieu for a moment.'

Madame was out of the door as she said this; and I thought I heard the key turn in the lock.

CHAPTER LXII

A WELL-KNOWN FACE LOOKS IN

You who have never experienced it can have no idea how angry and frightened you become under the sinister insult of being locked into a room, as on trying the door I found I was.

The key was in the lock; I could see it through the hole. I called after Madame, I shook at the solid oak door, beat upon it with my hands, kicked it—but all to no purpose.

I rushed into the next room, forgetting, if indeed I had observed it, that there was no door from it upon the gallery. I turned round in an angry and dismayed perplexity, and, like prisoners in romances, examined the windows.

I was shocked and affrighted on discovering in reality what they occasionally find—a series of iron bars crossing the window! They were firmly secured in the oak woodwork of the window frame, and each window was, besides, so compactly screwed down that it could not open. This bedroom was converted into a prison—a momentary hope flashed on me—perhaps all the windows were secured alike? But it was no such thing: these gaol-like precautions were confined to the windows to which I had access.

For a few minutes I felt quite distracted; but I bethought me that I must now, if ever, control my terrors and exert whatever faculties I possessed.

I stood upon a chair and examined the oak-work. I thought I detected marks of new chiselling here and there. The screws, too, looked new; and they and the scars on the wood-work were freshly smeared over with some coloured stuff by way of disguise.

While I was making these observations, I heard the key stealthily stirred. I suspect that Madame wished to surprise me. Her approaching step, indeed, was seldom audible. She had the soft tread of the feline tribe.

I was standing in the centre of the room confronting her when she entered.

'Why did you lock the door, Madame?' I demanded.

She slipped in suddenly, with an insidious smirk, and locked the door hastily.

'Hish!' whispered Madame, raising her broad palm, and then screwing in her cheeks, she made an ogle over her shoulder in the direction of the passage.

'Hish! be quiate, cheaile, weel you, and I weel tale you everything presently.'

She paused, with her ear laid to the door.

'Now I can speak, ma chère; I weel tale a you there is bailiff in the house, two, three, four soche impertinent fallows! They have another as bad as themselve to make a leest of the furniture, we most keep them out of these rooms, dear Maud.'

'You left the key in the door on the outside,' I retorted; 'that was not to keep them out, but me in, Madame.'

'*Deed* I leave a the key in the door?' ejaculated Madame, with both hands raised, and such a genuine look of consternation as for a moment shook me.

It was the nature of this woman's deceptions that they often puzzled, though they seldom convinced me.

'I re-ally think, Maud, all those so frequent changes and excitements they weel overturn my poor head.'

'And the windows are secured with iron bars—what are they for?' I whispered sternly, pointing with my finger at these grim securities.

'That is for more a than forty years, when Sir Phileep Aylmer was to reside here, and had this room for his children's nursery, and was afraid they should fall out.'

'But if you look you will find these bars have been put here very recently: the screws and marks are quite new.'

'*Eendeed!*' ejaculated Madame, with prolonged emphasis, in precisely the same consternation. 'Why, my dear, they told a me down stair what I have tell a you, when I ask the reason! Late a me see.'

And Madame mounted on a chair, and made her scrutiny with much curiosity; but could not agree with me as to the very recent date of the carpentry.

There is nothing, I think, so exasperating as that sort of falsehood which affects not to see what is quite palpable.

'Do you mean to say, Madame, that you really think those chisellings and screws are forty years old?'

'How can I tell, cheaile? What does signify whether it is forty or only fourteen years? Bah! we 'av other theeng to theenk about. Those villain men! I am glad to see bar and bolt, and lock and key, at least, to our room, to keep soche faylows out!'

At that moment a knock came to the door, and Madame's nasal, 'in moment,' answered promptly, and she opened the door stealthily popping out her head.

'Oh, that is all right; go you long, no ting more, go way.'

'Who's there?' I cried.

'Hold a your tongue,' said Madame, imperiously, to the visitor, whose voice I fancied I recognized, '*go* way.'

Out slipped Madame again, locking the door; but this time she returned immediately, bearing a tray with breakfast.

I think she fancied that I would perhaps attempt to break away and escape; but I had no such thought at that moment. She hastily set down the tray on the floor at the threshold, locking the door as before.

My share of breakfast was a little tea; but Madame's digestion was seldom disturbed by her sympathies, and she ate voraciously. During this process there was a silence unusual in her company; but when her meal was ended, she proposed a reconnaissance, professing much uncertainty as to whether my uncle had been arrested or not.

'And in case the poor old gentleman be poot in what you call stone jug,* where are *we* to go, my dear Maud—to Knowl or to Elverston? You most direct.'

And so she disappeared, turning the key in the door as before. It was an old custom of hers, locking herself in her room, and leaving the key in the lock, and the habit prevailed, for she left it there again.

With a heavy heart I completed my simple toilet, wondering all the while how much of Madame's story might be false and how much, if any, true. Then I looked out upon the dingy courtyard below, in its deep, damp shadow, and thought, 'how could an assassin have scaled that height in safety, and entered so noiselessly, as not to awaken the slumbering gamester?' Then there were the iron bars across my window. What a fool had I been to object to that security!

I was labouring hard to reassure myself, and keep all ghastly suspicions at arm's length. But I wished that my room had been to the front of the house, with some view less dismal.

Lost in these ruminations of fear, as I stood at the window, I was startled by the sound of a sharp tread on the lobby, and by the key turning in the lock of my door.

In a panic I sprang back into the corner, and stood with my eyes fixed upon the door. It opened a little, and the black head of Meg Hawkes was introduced.

'Oh, Meg!' I cried; 'thank God!'

'I guessed 'twas you, Miss Maud. I am feared, Miss.'

The miller's daughter was pale, and her eyes, I thought, were red and swollen.

'Oh, Meg! for God's sake, what is it all?'

'I darn't come in. The old un's gone down, and locked the cross-door, and left me to watch. They think I care nout about ye, no more nor themselves. I donna know all, but summat more nor her. They tell her nout, she's so gi'n to drink; they say she's not safe, an' awful quar-relsome. I hear a deal when fayther and Master Dudley be a-talking in the mill. They think, comin' in an' out, I don't mind; but I put one thing an' t'other together. And don't ye eat nor drink nout here, Miss; hide away this; it's black enough, but wholesome anyhow!' and she slipt a piece of a coarse loaf from under her apron. '*Hide* it mind. Drink nout but the water in the jug there—it's clean spring.'

'Oh, Meg! oh, Meg! I know what you mean,' said I, faintly.

'Ay, Miss, I'm feared they'll try it; they'll try to make away wi' ye somehow. I'm goin' to your friends arter dark; I darn't try it no sooner. I'll git awa' to Ellerston, to your lady cousin, and I'll bring 'em back wi' me in a rin; so keep a good hairt, lass. Meg Hawkes will stan' to ye. Ye were better to me than fayther and mother, and a',' and she clasped me round the waist, and buried her head in my dress; 'an' I'll gie my life for ye, darling, and if they hurt ye I'll kill myself.'

She recovered her sterner mood quickly.—

'Not a word lass,' she said, in her old tone. 'Don't ye try to git away—they'll *kill* ye—ye *can't* do't. Leave a' to me. It won't be, what-ever it is, till two or three o'clock in the morning. I'll ha'e them a' here long afore, so keep a brave heart—there's a darling.'

I suppose she heard, or fancied she heard a step approaching; for she said—

'Hish!'

Her pale, wild face vanished, the door shut quickly and softly, and the key turned again in the lock.

Meg, in her rude way, had spoken softly—almost under her breath; but no prophecy shrieked by the Pythoness* ever thundered so madly in the ears of the hearer. I dare say that Meg fancied I was marvellously little moved by her words. I felt my gaze grow intense, and my flesh and bones literally freeze. She did not know that every word she spoke seemed to burst like a blaze in my brain. She had delivered her frightful warning, and told her story coarsely and bluntly, which, in effect, means distinctly and concisely; and, I dare say, the announcement so made, like a quick, bold incision in surgery, was more tolerable than the slow, imperfect mangling, which falters, and recedes and equivocates with torture. Madame was long away. I sat down at the window, and tried to appreciate my dreadful situation. I was stupid—the imagery was all frightful; but I beheld it as we sometimes see horrors—heads cut off and houses burnt—in a dream, and without the corresponding emotions. It did not seem as if all this were really happening to me. I remember sitting at the window, and looking and blinking at the opposite side of the building, like a person unable, but striving, to see an object distinctly; and every minute pressing my hand to the side of my head and saying—

'Oh, it won't be—it won't be—oh, no!—never!—it could not be;' and in this stunned state Madame found me on her return.

But the valley of the shadow of death* has its varieties of dread. The 'horror of great darkness' is disturbed by voices, and illumed by sights. There are periods of incapacity and collapse, followed by paroxysms of active terror. Thus in my journey during those long hours I found it—agonies subsiding into lethargies, and these breaking again into frenzy. I sometimes wonder how I carried my reason safely through the ordeal.

Madame locked the door, and amused herself with her own business, without minding me, humming little nasal snatches of French airs, as she smirked on her silken purchases displayed in the daylight. Suddenly it struck me that it was very dark, considering how early it was. I looked at my watch. It seemed to me a great effort of concentration to understand it. Four o'clock, it said. Four o'clock! It would be dark at five—*night* in one hour!

'Madame, what o'clock is it? Is it evening?' I cried with my hand to my forehead, like a person puzzled.

'Two, three minutes past four. It had five minutes to four when I came upstairs,' answered she, without interrupting her examination of a piece of darned lace, which she was holding close to her eyes at the window.

'Oh, Madame! *Madame!* I'm frightened,' cried I, with a wild and piteous voice, grasping her arm, and looking up, as shipwrecked

people may their last to heaven, into her inexorable eyes. Madame
looked frightened too, I thought, as she stared into my face. At last she
said, rather angrily, and shaking her arm loose,

'What you mean, cheaile?'

'Oh save me, Madame!—oh, save me! oh, save me, Madame!'
I pleaded, with the wild monotony of perfect terror, grasping and
clinging to her dress, and looking up, with an agonized face, into the
eyes of that shadowy Atropos.*

'Save a you, indeed! Save! What *niaiserie*!'

'Oh, Madame! oh, *dear* Madame! for God's sake, only get me
away—get me from this, and I'll do everything you ask me all my
life—I will—*indeed*, Madame, I will! Oh, save me! save me! *save* me.'

I was clinging to Madame as to my guardian angel in my agony.

'And who told you cheaile, you are in any danger?' demanded
Madame, looking down on me, with a black and witch-like stare.

'I am, Madame—I am—in great danger! Oh, Madame, think of
me—take pity on me. I have none to help me—there is no one but
God and you!'

Madame all this time viewed me with the same dismal stare, like
a sorceress reading futurity in my face.

'Well, maybe you are—how can I tell? Maybe your uncle is
mad—maybe you are mad. You have been my enemy always—why
should I care?'

Again I burst into wild entreaty, and clasping her fast, poured forth
my supplications with the bitterness of death.

'I have no confidence in you, little Maud; you are little rogue—petite
traitresse! Reflect, if you can, how you 'av always treat Madame. You 'av
attempt to ruin me—you conspire with the bad domestics at Knowl to
destroy me; and you expect me here to take a your part! You would never
listen to me—you 'ad no mercy for me—you join to hunt me away from
your house like wolf. Well, what you expect to find me now? *Bah!*'

This terrific 'bah,' with a long, nasal yell of scorn, rang in my ears
like a clap of thunder.

'I say you are mad, petite insolente, to suppose I should care for
you more than the poor hare it will care for the hound—more than
the bird who has escape will love the oiseleur. I do not care. I ought
not care. It is your turn to suffer. Lie down on your bed there, and
suffer quaitely.'

CHAPTER LXIII

SPICED CLARET

I DID not lie down; but I despaired. I walked round and round the room, wringing my hands in utter distraction. I threw myself at the bed-side on my knees. I could not pray. I could only shiver and moan, with hands clasped, and eyes of horror turned up to heaven. I think Madame was, in her malignant way, perplexed. That some evil was intended me I am sure she was persuaded; but I dare say Meg Hawkes had said rightly in telling me that she was not fully in their secrets.

The first paroxysm of despair subsided into another state. All at once my mind was filled with the idea of Meg Hawkes, her enterprise, and my chances of escape. There is one point at which the road to Elverston makes a short ascent: there is a sudden curve there, two great ash-trees with a road-side stile between, at the right side, covered with ivy. Driving back and forward, I did not recollect having particularly remarked this point in the highway; but now it was before me, in the thin light of the thinnest segment of moon, and the figure of Meg Hawkes, her back toward me, always ascending slowly toward Elverston. It was constantly the same picture, the same motion without progress, the same dreadful suspense and impatience.

I was now sitting on the side of the bed, looking wistfully across the room. When I did not see Meg Hawkes, I beheld Madame darkly eyeing first one then another point of the chamber, evidently puzzling over some problem, and in one of her most savage moods—sometimes muttering to herself, sometimes protruding, and sometimes screwing up her great mouth.

She went into her own room, where she remained, I think, nearly ten minutes, and on her return there was that in the flash of her eyes, the glow of her face, and the peculiar fragrance that surrounded her, that showed she had been partaking of her favourite restorative.

I had not moved since she left my room.

She paused about the middle of the floor, and looked at me with what I can only describe as her wild-beast stare.

'You are a very secrete family, you Ruthyns, you are so coning; I hate the coning people. By my faith I weel see Mr. Silas Ruthyn, and ask wat he mean. I heard him tell old Wyat that Mr. Dudley is gone away to-night. He shall tell me everything, or else I will make echec et mat aussi vrai qua je vis.'*

Madame's words had hardly ceased, when I was again watching Meg Hawkes on the steep road, mounting, but never reaching, the top of the acclivity, on the way to Elverston, and mentally praying that she might be brought safely there. Vain prayer of an agonized heart! Meg's journey was already frustrated: she was not to reach Elverston in time.

Madame revisited her apartment, and returned, not, I think, improved in temper. She walked about the room, hustling the scanty furniture hither and thither as she encountered it. She kicked her empty box out of her way, with a horrid crash, and a curse in French. She strode and swaggered round the room, muttering all the way, and turning the corners of her course with a furious whisk. At last, out of the door she went. I think she fancied she had not been sufficiently taken into confidence as to what was intended for me.

It was now growing late, and yet no succour! I was seized, I remember, with a dreadful icy shivering.

I was listening for signals of deliverance. At every distant sound, half stifled with a palpitation, these sounds piercing my ear with a horrible and exaggerated distinctness—'Oh, Meg!—Oh, Cousin Monica!—oh, come! Oh, Heaven, have mercy!—Lord, have mercy!' I thought I heard a roaring and jangle of voices. Perhaps it came from Uncle Silas' room. It might be the tipsy violence of Madame. It might—merciful Heaven!—be the arrival of friends! I started to my feet. I listened, quivering with attention. Was it in my brain?—was it real? I was at the door, and it seemed to open of itself. Madame had forgot to lock it. She was losing her head a little by this time. The key stood in the gallery-door beyond. It, too, was open. I fled wildly. There was a subsiding sound of voices in my uncle's room. I was, I know not how, on the lobby at the great stair-head outside my uncle's apartment. My hand was on the banisters, my foot on the first step, when below me and against the faint light that glimmered through the great window on the landing, I saw a bulky human form ascending, and a voice said 'Hush!' I staggered back, and, at that instant, fancied with a thrill of conviction, Lady Knollys' voice in Uncle Silas' room!

I don't know how I entered the room; I was there like a ghost. I was frightened at my own state.

Lady Knollys was not there—no one but Madame and my guardian.

I can never forget the look that Uncle Silas fixed on me as he cowered, seemingly as appalled as I.

I think I must have looked like a phantom newly risen from the grave.

'What's that?—where do you come from?' whispered he.

'Death! death!' was my whispered answer as I froze with terror where I stood.

'What does she mean?—what does all this mean?' said Uncle Silas, recovering wonderfully, and turning with a withering sneer on Madame. 'Do you think it right to disobey my plain directions, and let her run about the house at this hour?'

'Death! death! Oh, pray to God for you and me!' I whispered in the same dreadful tones.

My uncle stared strangely at me again; and after several horrible seconds, in which he seemed to have recovered himself, he said, sternly and coolly—

'You give too much place to your imagination, niece. Your spirits are in an odd state—you ought to have advice.'

'Oh, uncle, pity me! Oh, uncle, you are good! you're kind; you're kind when you think. You could not—you could not—could not. Oh, think of your brother that was always so good to you. He sees me here. He sees us both. Oh, save me, uncle—save me—and I'll give up everything to you. I'll pray to God to bless you—I'll never forget your goodness and mercy. But don't keep me in doubt. If I'm to go, oh, for God's sake, shoot me now!'

'You were always odd, niece; I begin to fear you are insane,' he replied, in the same stern, icy tone:

'Oh, uncle—oh!—am I? Am I *mad*?'

'I hope not; but you'll conduct yourself like a sane person if you wish to enjoy the privileges of one.'

Then, with his finger pointing at me, he turned to Madame, and said, in a tone of suppressed ferocity—

'What's the meaning of this?—why is she here?'

Madame was gabbling volubly, but to me it was only a shrilly noise. My whole soul was concentrated in my uncle, the arbiter of my life, before whom I stood in the wildest agony of supplication.

That night was dreadful. The people I saw dizzily, made of smoke or shining vapour, smiling or frowning, I could have passed my hand through them. They were evil spirits.

'There's no ill intended you; by —— there's none,' said my uncle, for the first time violently agitated. 'Madame told you why we've changed your room. You told her about the bailiffs, did not you?' with a stamp of fury he demanded of Madame, whose nasal roullades of talk were running on like an accompaniment all the time. She had told me indeed, only a few hours since, and now it sounded to me like the echo of something heard a month ago or more.

'You can't go about the house, d——n it, with bailiffs in occupation. There now. There's the whole thing. Get to your room, Maud, and don't vex me. There's a good girl.'

He was trying to smile as he spoke these last words, and, with qua-vering soft tones, to quiet me; but the old scowl was there, the smile was corpselike and contorted, and the softness of his tones was more dreadful than another man's ferocity.

'There, Madame, she'll go quite gently, and you can call if you want help. Don't let it happen again.'

'Come, Maud,' said Madame, encircling, but not hurting my arm with her gripe, 'let us go, my friend.'

I did go, you will wonder, as well you may—as you may wonder at the docility with which strong men walk through the press-room* to the drop, and thank the people of the prison for their civility when they bid them good-bye, and facilitate the fixing of the rope and adjusting of the cap. Have you never wondered that they don't make a last battle for life, with the unscrupulous energy of terror, instead of surrendering it so gently in cold blood, on a silent calculation, the arithmetic of despair?

I went up stairs with Madame like a somnambulist. I rather quick-ened my step as I drew near my room. I went in and stood, a phantom, at the window, looking into the dark quadrangle. A thin glimmering crescent hung in the frosty sky, and all heaven was strewn with stars. Over the steep roof at the other side spread on the dark azure of the night this glorious blazonry of the unfathomable Creator. To me a dreadful scroll—inexorable eyes. The cloud of cruel witnesses look-ing down in freezing brightness on my prayers and agonies.*

I turned about and sat down, leaning my head upon my arms. Then, suddenly, I sat up, as for the first time the picture of Uncle Silas's littered room, and the travelling bags and black boxes piled on the floor by his table; the desk, hat-case, umbrella, coats, rugs, and mufflers, all ready for a journey, reached my brain and suggested thought. The *mise en scène* had remained in every detail fixed upon my retina; and how I wondered—'When is he going—how soon? Is he going to carry me away and place me in a mad-house?'

'Am I—am I mad?' I began to think. 'Is this all a dream, or is it real?'

I remembered how a thin, polite gentleman, with a tall grizzled head and a black velvet waistcoat, came into the carriage on our journey, and said a few words to me; how Madame whispered him something, and he murmured 'Oh!' very gently, with raised eyebrows, and a glance at me, and thenceforward spoke no more to me, only to Madame, and at the next station carried his hat and other travelling chattels into another carriage. Had she told him I was mad?

These horrid bars! Madame always with me! The direful hints that dropt from my uncle! My own terrific sensations! All these evidences revolved in my brain, and presented themselves in turn like writings on a wheel of fire.

There came a knock to the door—

Oh, Meg! Was it she? No; old Wyat whispered Madame something about her room.

So Madame re-entered with a little silver tray and flagon in her hands, and a glass. Nothing came from Uncle Silas in ungentleman-like fashion.

'Drink, Maud,' said Madame, raising the cover, and evidently enjoying the fragrant steam.

I could not. I might have done so had I been able to swallow anything—for I was too distracted to think of Meg's warning.

Madame suddenly recollected her mistake of that evening, and tried the door; but it was duly locked. She took the key from her pocket and placed it in her breast.

'You weel 'av these rooms to yourself, ma chère. I shall sleep down stairs to-night.'

She poured out some of the hot claret into the glass abstractedly, and drank it off.

''Tis very good—I drank without theenk. Bote 'tis very good. Why don't a you drink some?'

'I could not,' I repeated. And Madame boldly helped herself.

'Vary polite, certally, to Madame was it to send nothing at all for *hair*' (so she pronounced 'her'); 'bote is all same thing.' And so she ran on in her tipsy vein, which was loud and sarcastic, with a fierce laugh now and then.

Afterwards I heard that they were afraid of Madame, who was given to cross purposes, and violent in her cups. She had been noisy and quarrelsome down-stairs. She was under the delusion that I was to be conveyed away that night to a remote and safe place, and she was to be handsomely compensated for services and evidence to be afterwards given. She was not to be trusted, however, with the truth. That was to be known but to three persons on earth.

I never knew, but I believe that the spiced claret which Madame drank was drugged. She was a person who could, I have been told, drink a great deal without exhibiting any change from it but an inflamed colour and furious temper. I can only state for certain what I saw, and that was, that shortly after she had finished the claret, she lay down upon my bed, and, I now know, fell asleep. I then thought she was *feigning* sleep only, and that she was really watching me.

About an hour after this I suddenly heard a little *clink* in the yard beneath. I peeped out, but saw nothing. The sound was repeated, however—sometimes more frequently, sometimes at long intervals. At last, in the deep shadow next the further wall, I thought I could discover a figure sometimes erect, sometimes stooping and bowing toward the earth. I could see this figure only in the rudest outline mingling with the dark.

Like a thunderbolt it smote my brain, 'They are making my grave.'

After the first dreadful stun, I grew quite wild, and ran up and down the room wringing my hands and gasping prayers to heaven. Then a calm stole over me—such a dreadful calm as I could fancy glide over one who floated in a boat under the shadow of the 'Traitors' Gate,'* leaving life, and hope, and trouble behind.

Shortly after there came a very low tap at my door; then another, like a tiny post-knock. I could never understand why it was I made no answer. Had I done so, and thus shown that I was awake, it might have sealed my fate. I was standing in the middle of the floor staring at the door, which I expected to see open and admit I knew not what troop of spectres.

CHAPTER LXIV

THE HOUR OF DEATH

It was a very still night and frosty. My candle had long burnt out. There was still a faint moonlight, which fell in a square of yellow on the floor near the window, leaving the rest of the room in what, to an eye less accustomed than mine had become to that faint light, would have been total darkness. Now, I am sure, I heard a soft whispering outside my door. I knew that I was in a state of siege! The crisis was come, and, strange to say, I felt myself grow all at once resolute and self-possessed. It was not a subsidence, however, of the dreadful excitement, but a sudden screwing up of my nerves to a pitch such as I cannot describe.

I suppose the people outside moved with great caution; and the perfect solidity of the floor, which had not anywhere a creaking board in it, favoured their noiseless movements. It was well for me that there were in the house three persons whom it was part of their plan to mystify respecting my fate. This alone compelled the extreme caution of their proceedings. They suspected that I had placed furniture against the door, and were afraid to force it, lest a crash, a scream, perhaps a long and shrilly struggle, might follow.

I remained for a space which I cannot pretend to estimate in the same posture, afraid to stir—afraid to move my eye from the door.

A very peculiar grating sound above my head startled me from my watch—something of the character of sawing, only more crunching, and with a faint, continued rumble in it—utterly inexplicable. It sounded over that portion of the roof which was furthest from the door, toward which I now glided; and as I took my stand under cover of the projecting angle of a clumsy old press* that stood close by it, I perceived the room a little darkened, and I saw a man descend and take his stand upon the window-stone. He let go a rope, which, however, was still fast round his body, and employed both his hands, with apparently some exertion, about something at the side of the window, which in a moment more, in one mass, bars and all, swung noiselessly open, admitting the frosty night air, and the man, whom I now distinctly saw to be Dudley Ruthyn, kneeled on the sill, and stept, after a moment's listening, into the room. His foot made no sound upon the floor; his head was bare, and he wore his usual short shooting jacket.

I cowered to the ground in my post of observation. He stood, as it seemed to me, irresolutely for a moment, and then drew from his pocket an instrument which I distinctly saw against the faint moonlight. Imagine a hammer, one end of which had been beaten out into a longish tapering spike, with a handle something longer than usual. He drew stealthily to the window, and seemed to examine this hurriedly, and tested its strength with a twist or two of his hand. And then he adjusted it very carefully in his grasp, and made two or three little experimental picks with it in the air.

I remained perfectly still, with a terrible composure, crouched in my hiding-place, my teeth clenched, and prepared to struggle like a tigress for my life when discovered. I thought his next measure would be to light a match. I saw a lantern, I fancied, on the window-sill. But this was not his plan. He stole, in a groping way, which seemed strange to me, who could distinguish objects in this light, to the side of my bed, the exact position of which he evidently knew; he stooped over it. Madame was breathing in the deep respiration of heavy sleep. Suddenly, but softly, he laid, as it seemed to me, his left hand over her face, and nearly at the same instant there came a scrunching blow; an unnatural shriek, beginning small and swelling for two or three seconds into a yell such as are imagined in haunted houses, accompanied by a convulsive sound, as of the motion of running, and the arms drumming on the bed; and then another blow—and with a horrid gasp he recoiled a step or two, and stood perfectly still. I heard a horrible tremor quivering through the joints and curtains of the bedstead, the convulsion of the murdered woman. It was a dreadful sound, like the shaking of a tree and rustling of leaves. Then once more he stept to the side of the bed, and I heard another of those horrid blows—and silence—and another—and more silence—and the diabolical surgery was ended. For a few seconds, I think, I was on the point of fainting; but a gentle stir outside the door, close to my ear, startled me, and proved that there had been a watcher posted outside. There was a little tapping at the door.

'Who's that?' whispered Dudley, hoarsely.

'A friend,' answered a sweet voice.

And a key was introduced, the door quickly unlocked, and Uncle Silas entered. I saw that frail, tall, white figure, the venerable silver

locks that resembled those upon the honoured head of John Wesley,*
and his thin white hand, the back of which hung so close to my face
that I feared to breathe. I could see his fingers twitching nervously.
The smell of perfumes and of ether entered the room with him.

Dudley was trembling now like a man in an ague-fit.

'Look what you made me do!' he said, maniacally.

'Steady, sir!' said the old man, close beside me.

'Yes, you damned old murderer; I've a mind to do for you.'

'There, Dudley, like a dear boy, don't give way; it's done. Right or
wrong we can't help it. You must be quiet,' said the old man, with
a stern gentleness.

Dudley groaned.

'Whoever advised it, you're a gainer, Dudley,' said Uncle Silas.

Then there was a pause.

'I hope that was not heard,' said Uncle Silas.

Dudley walked to the window and stood there.

'Come, Dudley, you and Hawkes must use expedition. You know
you must get that out of the way.'

'I've done too much. I won't do nout. I'll not touch it. I wish my
hand was off first. I wish I was a soger. Do as ye like, you an' Hawkes.
I won't go nigh it; damn ye both—and *that*!' and he hurled the hammer with all his force upon the floor.

'Come, come, be reasonable, Dudley, dear boy. There's nothing to
fear but your own folly. You won't make a noise?'

'Oh, oh, my God!' said Dudley, hoarsely, and he wiped his forehead with his open hand.

'There now, you'll be all well in a minute,' continued the old man.

'You said 'twouldn't hurt her. If I'd a known she'd a screeched like
that I'd never a done it. 'Twas a damn lie. You're the damndest villain
on earth.'

'Come, Dudley!' said the old man under his breath, but very
sternly, 'make up your mind. If you don't choose to go on, it can't be
helped; only it's a pity you began. For *you* it is a good deal—it does
not much matter for *me*.'

'Ay, for *you*!' echoed Dudley, through his set teeth. 'The old talk!'

'Well, sir,' snarled the old man, in the same low tones, 'you should
have thought of all this before. It's only taking leave of the world
a year or two sooner; but a year or two's something. I'll leave you to do
as you please.'

'Stop, will you? Stop here. I know it's a fixt thing now. If a fella does a thing he's damned for, you might let him talk a bit anyhow. I don't care much if I was shot.'

'There now—*there*—just stick to that, and don't run off again. There's a box and a bag here, we must change the direction, and take them away. The box has some jewels. Can you see them? I wish we had a light.'

'No, I'd rayther not; I can see well enough. I wish we were out o' this. *Here's* the box.'

'Pull it to the window,' said the old man, to my inexpressible relief advancing at last a few steps.

Coolness was given me in that dreadful moment; and I knew that all depended on my being prompt and resolute. I stood up swiftly. I often thought if I had happened to wear silk instead of the cachmere I had on that night, its rustle would have betrayed me.

I distinctly saw the tall stooping figure of my uncle, and the outline of his venerable tresses, as he stood between me and the dull light of the window, like a shape cut out in card.

He was saying 'just to *there*,' and pointing with his long arm at that contracting patch of moonlight which lay squared upon the floor. The door was about a quarter open, and just as Dudley began to drag Madame's heavy box, with my jewel case in it, across the floor from her room, inhaling a great breath—with a mental prayer for help—I glided on tiptoe from the room, and found myself on the gallery floor.

I turned to my right, simply by chance, and followed a long gallery in the dark, not running—I was too fearful of making the least noise—but walking with the tiptoe-swiftness of terror. At the termination of this was a cross gallery, one end of which, that to my left, terminated in a great window, through which the dusky night-view was visible. With the instinct of terror I chose the darker, and turned again to my right: hurrying through this long and nearly dark passage I was terrified by a light about thirty feet before me, emerging from the ceiling. In spotted patches this light fell through the door and sides of a stable lantern, and showed me a ladder, down which, from an open skylight, I suppose, for the cool night-air floated in my face, came Dickon Hawkes, notwithstanding his maimed condition, with so much celerity as to leave me hardly a moment for consideration.

He sat on the last round of the ladder, and tightened the straps of his wooden leg.

At my left was a door-case open, but no door. I entered; it was a short passage about six feet long, leading perhaps to a back-stair, but the door at the end was locked.

I was forced to stand in this recess, then, which afforded no shelter, while Pegtop stumped by with his lantern in his hand. I fancy he had some idea of listening to his master unperceived, for he stopped close to my hiding-place, blew out the candle, and pinched the long snuff with his horny finger and thumb.

Having listened for a few seconds, he stumped stealthily along the gallery which I had just traversed, and turned the corner in the direction of the chamber where the crime had just been committed, and the discovery was impending. I could see him against the broad window which in the day-time lighted this long passage, and the moment he had passed the corner I resumed my flight.

I descended a stair corresponding with that back stair, as I am told, up which Madame had led me only the night before. I tried the outer door. To my wild surprise it was open. In a moment I was upon the step, in the free air, and as instantaneously was seized by the arm in the gripe of a man.

It was Tom Brice, who had already betrayed me, and who was now in surtout and hat, waiting to drive the carriage with the guilty father and son from the scene of their abhorred outrage.

CHAPTER LXV

IN THE OAK PARLOUR

So it was vain—I was trapped, and all was over.

I stood before him on the step, the white moon shining on my face. I was trembling so that I wonder I could stand, my helpless hands raised towards him, and I looking up in his face. A long, shuddering moan—'Oh—oh—oh!' was all I uttered.

The man, still holding my arm, looked, I thought, frightened, into my white, dumb face.

Suddenly he said, in a wild, fierce whisper—

'Never say another word.' (I had not uttered one). 'They shan't hurt ye, Miss; git ye in, I don't care a damn!'

It was an uncouth speech. To me it was the voice of an angel. With a burst of gratitude that sounded in my own ears like a laugh, I thanked God for those blessed words.

In a moment more he had placed me in the carriage, and almost instantly we were in motion—very cautiously while crossing the court, until he had got the wheels upon the grass, and then at a rapid pace, improving his speed as the distance increased. He drove along the side of the back approach to the house, keeping on the grass; so that our progress, though swaying like that of a ship in a swell, was very nearly as noiseless.

The gate had been left unlocked—he swung it open, and remounted the box. And we were now beyond the spell of Bartram-Haugh, thundering—Heaven be praised!—along the Queen's highway, right in the route to Elverston. It was literally a gallop. Through the chariot windows I saw Tom stand as he drove, and every now and then throw an awful glance over his shoulder. Were we pursued? Never was agony of prayer like mine, as with clasped hands and wild stare I gazed through the windows on the road, whose trees, and hedges, and gabled cottages, were chasing one another backward at so giddy a speed.

We were now ascending that identical steep with the giant ash-trees at the right and the stile between, which my vision of Meg Hawkes had presented all that night, when my excited eye detected a running figure within the hedge. I saw the head of some one crossing the stile in pursuit, and heard Brice's name shrieked.

'Drive on—on—!' I screamed.

But Brice pulled up. I was on my knees on the floor of the carriage, with clasped hands, expecting capture, when the door opened, and Meg Hawkes, pale as death, her cloak drawn over her black tresses, looked in.

'Oh!—ho!—ho!—thank God!' she screamed. 'Shake hands, lass. Tom, yer a good 'un! He's a good lad, Tom.'

'Come in, Meg—you must sit by me,' I said, recovering all at once.

Meg made no demur. 'Take my hand,' I said, offering mine to her disengaged one.

'I can't, Miss—my arm's broke.'

And so it was, poor thing! She had been espied and overtaken in her errand of mercy for me, and her ruffian father had felled her with his cudgel, and then locked her into the cottage, whence, however she had contrived to escape, and was now flying to Elverston, having tried in vain to get a hearing in Feltram, whose people had been for hours in bed.

The door being shut upon Meg, the steaming horses were instantly at a gallop again.

Tom was still watching as before, with many an anxious glance to rearward, for pursuit. Again he pulled up, and came to the window.

'Oh, what is it?' cried I.

''Bout that letter, Miss; I couldn't help. 'Twas Dickon, he found it in my pocket. That's a'.'

'Oh, yes!—no matter—thank you—thank Heaven! Are we near Elverston?'

''Twill be a mile, Miss: and please'm to mind I had no finger in't.'

'Thanks—thank you—you're very good—I shall *always* thank you, Tom, as long as I live!'

At length we entered Elverston. I think I was half wild. I don't know how I got into the hall. I was in the oak-parlour, I believe, when I saw Cousin Monica. I was standing, my arms extended. I could not speak; but I ran with a loud, long scream into her arms. I forget a great deal after that.

Oh, my beloved Cousin Monica! Thank Heaven, you are living still; and younger, I think, than I in all things but in years.

And Milly, my dear companion, she is now the happy wife of that good little clergyman, Sprigge Biddlepen. It has been in my power to be of use to them, and he shall have the next presentation to Dawling.

Meg Hawkes, proud and wayward, and the most affectionate creature on earth, was married to Tom Brice a few months after these events; and as both wished to emigrate, I furnished them with the capital; and I am told they are likely to be rich. I hear from my kind Meg often; and she seems very happy.

My dear old friends, Mary Quince and Mrs. Rusk, are, alas! growing old, but living with me, and very happy. And after long solicitation, I persuaded Doctor Bryerly, the best and truest of ministers, with my dearest friend's concurrence, to undertake the management of the Derbyshire estates. In this I have been most fortunate. He is the very person for such a charge—so punctual, so laborious, so kind, and so shrewd.

In compliance with medical advice, Cousin Monica hurried me away to the Continent, where she would never permit me to allude to the terrific scenes which remain branded so awfully on my brain. It needed no constraint. It is a sort of agony to me even now to think of them.

The plan was craftily devised. Neither old Wyat nor Giles, the butler, had a suspicion that I had returned to Bartram. Had I been put to death, the secret of my fate would have been deposited in the keeping of four persons only—the two Ruthyns, Hawkes, and ultimately Madame. My dear Cousin Monica had been artfully led to believe in my departure for France, and prepared for my silence. Suspicion might not have been excited for a year after my death; and then would never, in all probability, have pointed to Bartram as the scene of the crime. The weeds would have grown over me, and I should have lain in that deep grave where the corpse of Madame de la Rougierre was unearthed in the darksome quadrangle of Bartram-Haugh.

It was more than two years after that I heard what had befallen at Bartram after my flight. Old Wyat, who went early to Uncle Silas' room, to her surprise, for he had told her that he was that night to accompany his son, who had to meet the mail train to Derby at five o'clock in the morning, saw her old master lying on the sofa, much in his usual position.

'There was nout much strange about him,' old Wyat said; 'but that his scent bottle was spilt, on its side, over on the table, and he dead.'

She thought he was not quite cold when she found him, and she sent the old butler for Doctor Jolks, who said he died of too much 'loddlum.'

Of my wretched uncle's religion what am I to say? Was it utter hypocrisy, or had it at any time a vein of sincerity in it? I cannot say. I don't believe that he had any heart left for religion, which is the highest form of affection, to take hold of. Perhaps he was a sceptic with misgivings about the future, but past the time for finding anything reliable in it. The devil approached the citadel of his heart by stealth, with many zigzags and parallels. The idea of marrying me to his son by fair means, then by foul; and when that wicked chance was gone, then the design of seizing all by murder, supervened. I dare say that Uncle Silas thought for a while that he was a righteous man. He wished to have Heaven and to escape Hell, if there were such places. But there were other things whose existence was not speculative, of which some he coveted, and some he dreaded more, and temptation came. 'Now if any man build upon this foundation, gold, silver, precious stones, wood, hay, stubble; every man's work shall be made manifest; for the day shall declare it, because it shall be revealed by fire; and the fire shall try every man's work of what sort it is.'* There comes with old age a time when the heart is no longer fusible or malleable, and must retain the form in which it has cooled down. 'He that is unjust, let him be unjust still; he which is filthy, let him be filthy still.'*

Dudley had disappeared; but in one of her letters, Meg, writing from her Australian farm, says—'There's a fella in toon as calls hiself Colbroke, wi' a good hoose o' wood, 15 foot length, and as hy 'bout as silling o' the pearler o' Bartram—only lots o' rats, they do say, my lady—a bying and sellin' of goold back and forred wi' the diggin' foke and the marchants. His chick and mouth be wry wi' scar o' burns or vitterel, an' no wiskers, bless you; but my Tom ee tolt him he knowed him for Master Doodley. I ant seed him; but he sade ad shute Tom soon is look at 'im, an' denide it, wi' moathful o' curses and oaf. Tom baint right shure; if I seed 'un wons i'd no for sartin; but 'appen, 'twil best be let be.' This was all.

Old Hawkes stood his ground, relying on the profound cunning with which their actual proceedings had been concealed even from the suspicions of the two inmates of the house, and on the mystery that habitually shrouded Bartram-Haugh and all its belongings from the eyes of the outer world.

Strangely enough, he fancied that I had made my escape long before the room was entered, and even if he were arrested, there was no evidence he was certain, to connect *him* with the murder, all knowledge of which, he would stoutly deny.

There was an inquest on the body of my uncle, and Dr. Jolks was the chief witness. They found that his death was caused by 'an excessive dose of laudanum, accidentally administered by himself.'

It was not until nearly a year after the dreadful occurrences at Bartram that Dickon Hawkes was arrested on a very awful charge, and placed in gaol. It was an old crime, committed in Lancashire, that had found him out. After his conviction, as a last chance, he tried a disclosure of all the circumstances of the unsuspected death of the Frenchwoman. Her body was discovered buried, where he indicated, in the inner court of Bartram-Haugh, and, after due legal inquiry, was interred in the churchyard of Feltram.

Thus I escaped the horrors of the witness-box, or the far worse torture of a dreadful secret.

Doctor Bryerly, shortly after Lady Knollys had described to him the manner in which Dudley entered my room, visited the house of Bartram-Haugh, and minutely examined the windows of the room in which Mr. Charke had slept on the night of his murder. One of these he found provided with powerful steel hinges, very craftily sunk and concealed in the timber of the window-frame, which was secured by an iron pin outside, and swung open on its removal. This was the room in which they had placed me, and this the contrivance by means of which the room had been entered. The problem of Mr. Charke's murder was solved.

*

I have penned it. I sit for a moment breathless. My hands are cold and damp. I rise with a great sigh, and look out on the sweet green landscape and pastoral hills, and see the flowers and birds, and the waving boughs of glorious trees—all images of liberty and safety; and as the tremendous nightmare of my youth melts into air, I lift my eyes in boundless gratitude to the God of all comfort, whose mighty hand and outstretched arm delivered me. When I lower my eyes and unclasp my hands, my cheeks are wet with tears. A tiny voice is calling me 'Mamma!' and a beloved smiling face, with his dear father's silken brown tresses, peeps in.

'Yes, darling, our walk. Come away!'

I am Lady Ilbury, happy in the affection of a beloved and noble-hearted husband, The shy, useless girl you have known is now a mother—trying to be a good one; and this, the last pledge, has lived.

I am not going to tell of sorrows—how brief has been my pride of early maternity, or how beloved were those whom the Lord gave and the Lord has taken away. But sometimes as, smiling on my little boy, the tears gather in my eyes, and he wonders, I can see, why they come. I am thinking—and trembling while I smile, to think—how strong is love, how frail is life; and rejoicing while I tremble, that in the death-less love of those who mourn, the Lord of Life, who never gave a pang in vain, conveys the sweet and ennobling promise of a compensation by eternal reunion. So, through my sorrows, I have heard a voice from heaven say, 'Write, from henceforth blessed are the dead that die in the Lord.'*

This world is a parable—the habitation of symbols—the phantoms of spiritual things immortal shown in material shape. May the blessed second-sight be mine—to recognize under these beautiful forms of earth the ANGELS who wear them;* for I am sure we may walk with them if we will, and hear them speak.

THE END.

EXPLANATORY NOTES

3 'Passage . . . an Irish Countess' . . . altered title: 'Passage in the Secret History of an Irish Countess' appeared anonymously in the Dublin University Magazine for November 1838 and was reprinted as 'The Murdered Cousin' in Le Fanu's anonymous collection Ghost Stories and Tales of Mystery (Dublin, 1851).

5 COUNTESS OF GIFFORD: Helen Selina, countess of Gifford (née Sheridan), 1807–67, was a cousin of Le Fanu's, to whom he became particularly close after his mother's death in 1861.

8 Chateaubriand's father in . . . Château de Combourg: see the first section of Mémoires d'outre-tombe by Vicomte Francois-René de Chateaubriand (1768–1843) for the great Romantic's account of his parental home in Brittany.

Swedenborgian: a follower of the mystic Emanuel Swedenborg (1688–1772).

'a cloud without water . . . darkness': cf. Jude 12–13.

9 à la Wouvermans: in the style of Philips Wouvermans (1619–68), Dutch painter of landscapes, and marine and hunting scenes.

10 Some one said that Doctor Johnson . . . speak: see Boswell's Life of Johnson, v. The Tour to the Hebrides and The Journey into North Wales (Second Edition), ed. George Birkbeck Norman Hill, and L. F. Powell (Oxford: Oxford University Press, 1964). 'Tom Tyers described me best. He once said to me, "Sir, you are like a ghost: you never speak till you are spoken to"', p. x.

18 Caen stone steps: the use of a light yellow building stone from near Caen in Normandy was not uncommon in country houses.

20 translated: to translate = to take or convey (a living or deceased person, a soul, etc.) to heaven or the afterlife (OED, definitions 8 and 10).

Hagar: Abraham's concubine, mother of Ishmael, banished to the wilderness; see Genesis 21:12–21.

magic-lantern: an early optical device that used slides to display a magnified image on a screen or wall in a darkened room.

24 'Je vous expliquerai tout cela à fond': (Fr.) 'I will explain it all to you thoroughly.'

25 Eleusinian priestess on the vase: Demeter found her daughter, Persephone, at Eleusis, a scene depicted on classical vases.

26 'link-man': servant who carried a torch from the carriage door to the house door.

35 at hugger-mugger: involved in secret or clandestine business.

37 Bretagne ballad . . . punishment coming: no original has ever been traced for this and M. R. James's suggestion that Le Fanu himself composed it is borne out by Jan Bondenson's research in The Two Headed Boy, and other

Medical Marvels (2000). Tales of 'Hog-faced Gentlewomen' were collected from the seventeenth century in Britain and the Netherlands. The legend gained currency in early nineteenth-century Dublin when Griselda Steevens, foundress (in effect) of Dr Steevens's Hospital in Dublin, displayed her profile in a window to scotch rumours that she had the features of a pig. Le Fanu's cousin, the Revd William Peter Hume Dobbin, was chaplain to the Hospital in the 1860s, and it is likely that Le Fanu drew on such traditions for his pastiche. The reference to a 'Bretagne ballad' suggests knowledge of Théodore Hersart de la Villmarqué's *Barzaz Breiz: Chants populaires de Bretagen* (1839; new enlarged edn 1845).

39 *Ma foi—wat mauvais goût*: (Fr.) Indeed—what tasteless behaviour.

Walpurgis: strictly, the name of a saint. Like Halloween (31 October) and St John's Eve (23 June) in Ireland, Walpurgis Night (30 April) in German folkore is associated with the tradition that witches gathered from across the land at a central mountain summit.

40 *a jerry hat*: a round felt hat; the *OED* gives 1841 as the first recorded written use.

Curl's Divan: divan is a name sometimes given to a smoking shop with lounges; the *OED* dates its first use in this context to Dickens's *Dombey and Son* in 1847.

47 *death unto death*: cf. 1 John 5:16.

Lilliputian: in Jonathan Swift's *Gulliver's Travels*, Lilliput is the kingdom of a tiny but tyrannical people.

48 *Fifth-Monarchy-man*: in the seventeenth century, one who believed that the millennium was at hand; a violent sectarian enthusiast.

49 *"What is't ye do? . . . without a name!"*: cf. *Macbeth* IV. i. 49.

51 *oblige des bontés, ma chère, que vous avez tout pour moi*: (Fr.), Obliged by that good disposition you all have for me.

52 *Fron-de-Boeufs*: in Fr. the phrase as such does not appear to exist; *fron de bœuf* would literally mean bull's brow, forehead, etc., and might be thought to be cognate with *teste de bœuf*, defined in Randle Cotgrave's 1611 dictionary as 'a joulthead . . . one whose wit is as little as his head is great'. Sir Walter Scott, in *Ivanhoe*, has a character Sir Reginald Front-de-Boeuf, a Norman baron of Torquilstone, and in his 1830 introduction to the novel writes that 'a roll of Norman warriors, occurring in the Auchinleck Manuscript [now in Nat. Lib. Scotland] gave him the formidable name of Front-de-Boeuf'. Le Fanu's source was probably *Ivanhoe*.

56 *dreamt of in your philosophy*: see *Hamlet* I. v. 166–7.

59 *courtesy*: curtsy or curtsey; Le Fanu's formalized spelling occurs throughout the novel.

63 *he had two boroughs*: prior to 1832, many parliamentary seats were controlled by great landowners—these were sometimes known as 'rotten boroughs' as they contained virtually no electors; the allusion here serves to date Silas's offence as earlier than the 1832 Reform Act.

67 *the Albums, the Souvenirs, the Keepsakes*: moderately priced literary jour-
nals that appeared seasonally, aimed at a middle-class audience and often
associated with women readers.

68 *"Twas on a widow's . . . stand.'*: no source has been traced. Perhaps the lines
are by Le Fanu himself; they are *not* by Swift, a likely source in the circumstances of Le Fanu's family traditions.

69 *swallowed up alive like Jonah*: in the Old Testament (Jonah 1–2) the
prophet Jonah was swallowed by a whale and spewed up three days later.

74 *la grâce*: a game played, *c.*1842, with hoops and slender rods.

calisthenics: gymnastic exercises for girls (1847).

Cenerentola: opera by Gioachino Rossini (1792–1868), based on the
Cinderella story.

75 *I'm no Quixote, to draw my sword on illusions*: the familiar English view of
Cervantes's eponymous hero.

76 *salamanders*: lizard-like animals reputedly able to withstand fire.

80 *griped*: to gripe = to make a grasp, to clutch at.

83 *'blarney'*: smooth talk, blandishment, cajolery; after the stone at Blarney,
Co. Cork, said to bestow eloquence on all who kiss it.

88 *Woodward*: George Moutard Woodward (1760?–1809), caricaturist.

89 *Punch*: satirical literary magazine famous for its cartoons; published
weekly in London from 1841.

90 *curaçoa*: curaçao is a generic term for liqueurs flavoured with sweet or
bitter oranges, its name derived from a Dutch island off the coast of
Venezuela formerly colonized by Spain. Thomas Moore's rhyme in his
Intercepted Letters (1812) ('And it pleased me to think at a house that you
know | Were such good mutton cutlets and strong curaçoa') indicates the
common nineteenth-century pronunciation of the word.

93 *Pandemonium*: strictly, the assembly of demons or devils; cf. *Paradise Lost*
i. 752–98.

98 *the deceived husband in the 'Arabian Nights'*: *The Arabian Nights'
Entertainment* or *The Thousand and One Nights* is a collection of about 200
folk tales from Arabia, Egypt, India, Persia, and other countries, written in
Arabic in the 1500s and translated into French by Jean Antoine Galland in
the early 1700s. Numerous English translations followed, including edi-
tions aimed at children along with magazine extracts. The story referred
to here may be 'The Tale of the Husband and the Parrot' in which a man
discovers his wife's adultery.

99 *a mare's nest*: an illusory discovery; a complex situation.

104 *carogne* (Fr.): jade, hussy.

106 *ubi lapsus, quid feci*: (Lat.) 'Whither have I fallen? What have I done?', the
second and less familiar motto of the Courtenay family (earls of Devon).
In 1585, Sir William Courtenay (13th de jure earl of Devon) 'was one of

the undertakers to send over settlers for the better planting of Ireland, and thus laid the foundation of the prodigious estate in that kingdom enjoyed by his posterity' (Burke's *Peerage* (1893), 414). The Courtenay family seats included The Castle, Newcastle, County Limerick.

107 *time—edax rerum*: cf. Ovid, *Metamorphoses* xv. 234 (*Tempus edax rerum* (Lat.) = 'Time, the destroyer of all things').

To whom much is committed, of him will much be required: cf. Luke 12:48.

109 *a saint; not . . . in the Popish sense*: in Catholic doctrine, saints are formally recognized as deserving veneration by the faithful for whom they may intercede in heaven; the Anglican Church holds to a more restricted definition.

110 *the ravens who supplied the prophet*: cf. 1 Kings 17:4–6; the prophet was Elijah.

he is Church: i.e. he is an orthodox member of the Established Church of England.

111 *Dissenters*: Nonconformists, Protestants of Low Church attitudes.

Tractarians: an Anglican group (*c.*1830s) of High Church and (in some instances) Romish tendencies; the implication is that Fairfield is unutterably middle-of-the-road.

'ordeal': ancient mode of trial in which a suspect's truthfulness or integrity was tested under physical pain.

113 *"C, 15"*: a library shelf mark, and so indicative of the house's status.

116 *sten*: a leap or bound, variant of 'stend'; in Scottish use only.

119 *litera scripta*: (Lat.) the written letter; i.e. the written word, documentary evidence.

doxology: a short and formalized address of praise to God.

120 *a child of the Sphinx*: a riddle, an enigma, with ominous overtones.

122 *distich*: two lines of verse, usually complete in themselves, a couplet.

ciel . . . l'amour: (Fr.) sky . . . love.

129 *apaugasma*: (late Gr.) see Hebrews 1:3 where the word is translated as 'brightness' in a passage describing Christ's ascent into glory on the right hand of God after his triumph over death; by what is probably coincidence and no more, a form of the same word is used in Heliodorus' (3rd century AD) erotic writings.

the ladder of Jacob: see Genesis 28:10–15.

131 *As the sparks fly upwards*: see Job 5:7.

He will give His angels charge over us: see Psalm 91:11.

139 *devises*: clauses in a will, leaving property to somebody.

144 *Lord Chancellor*: the legal officer who presides in the Courts of Chancery where cases involving inheritance, title, etc., are heard.

145 *duty to your neighbour*: the last six of the Ten Commandments, summarized and defined thus in the Anglican catechism.

146 *Oh, Death, king of terrors!*: the phrase comes from Edmund Burke, *A Philosophical Enquiry into Our Ideas of the Sublime and Beautiful* (1757).

the broken vault . . . the Star of Bethlehem: the references are to the Bible as filtered through the language and imagery of Swedenborg's *Heaven and Hell* (1758).

149 *"wolving"*: giving forth a hollow sound, like a wolf.

151 *the tabernacle . . . from heaven*: cf. II Corinthians 5:1–4.

153 *to prove the marriage bad*: to prove that the marriage (contract) was invalid, or improperly conducted.

I am told that Welsh women often do: an 1847 government enquiry into the state of education in Wales (known as the Blue Books Reports) remarked on the immorality of Welsh women; its controversial findings were widely circulated in the national press.

163 *chapletted*: a chaplet is a wreath of flowers worn on the head.

164 *bating*: restraining.

166 *"Thou fool . . . thee"*: cf. Luke 12:20.

176 *a wonderful old curiosity shop*: Charles Dickens's *Old Curiosity Shop* was published in 1841.

180 *the doctrine of correspondents*: Swedenborg taught that there exists a comprehensive and accessible system of relations or correspondences between the material and spiritual worlds; see his *Heaven and Hell*, paras. 87–115.

182 *picquet*: a picquet may be a party of soldiers, sentries, or picketers who guard an outpost, etc.—thus 'more than travelling picquet' may mean 'better than travelling as a sentinel etc.'; however, the card game may also be intended here.

190 *puck*: a sprite or imp; cf. Irish *púca*, a fairy or bogeyman.

Coburg: a thin fabric (from the town in Germany) used in women's dresses.

191 *the prints of the Bavarian broom girls*: typical nineteenth-century illustrations of rustic German maidens.

Lammermoor: Scott's *The Bride of Lammermoor* (1819) provided the plot for Gaetano Donizetti's (1797–1848) opera *Lucia di Lammermoor*.

195 *a finely painted Dutch portrait*: the Netherlands saw a golden age in portraiture in the 17th century with notable achievements in the realist depiction of human figures achieved by artists including Rembrandt.

196 *Miranda . . . Caliban . . . Prospero*: characters in William Shakespeare's *The Tempest*.

Miss Hoyden: the type of ill-educated, roistering woman; Richard Brinsley Sheridan uses the term for a character in *A Trip to Scarborough* (1777).

198 *chased repeater*: engraved or embossed watch.

201 *'roughing it'*: a reference to Susanna Moodie's *Roughing it in the Bush* (1852), an account of British settler migration to Upper Canada.

202 *Mrs. Radcliffe's romance . . . family of La Mote*: Ann Radcliffe's *Romance of the Forest* (1791); the family correctly is La Motte.

203 *the erl-king*: a German goblin who haunts the Black Forest luring humans to destruction.

204 *drugget*: a coarse woollen cloth.

208 *German folk-lore*: the folklorists Jacob and Wilhelm Grimm published their collection of traditional fairy tales between 1812 and 1822; it was first translated into English in 1823.

Der Freischütz: opera by Carl Maria von Weber (1786–1826), largely set in woodland; like *Uncle Silas* it has a character called Zamiel, the Black Ranger, alias the Devil. In the 1864 three-decker first edition, the text of this paragraph was scrambled by the printer: W. J. McCormack restored it by reference to the serial in the *Dublin University Magazine*. Zamiel, the Arch Fiend, appears in Charles M. Barras's melodramatic musical spectacle, *The Black Crook*, which played in Broadway, New York, in 1866.

211 *Beauty . . . Beast*: a fairy tale common in Europe, Africa, the Middle East, and Asia; given its first European literary treatment as *La Belle et la Bête* in 1740 and widely adapted, illustrated, and retold in the eighteenth and nineteenth centuries.

212 *fought the Philistines . . . an ass*: cf. Judges 15:15.

213 *fishing-book*: a notebook, often of water-resistant material, for recording weights, etc.

217 *a labour of Hercules*: the greatest hero of the Greek world was known for his twelve feats of strength, known as 'The Labours of Hercules'.

218 *Bluebeard*: in the classic fairy story, Captain Bluebeard murders his wives successively; in a curious letter, probably of August 1842, Le Fanu refers to Susanna Bennett when noting the similarity between 'my *character* & that of Bluebeard, & between Susy's style of beauty & that of *Mrs.* Bluebeard'; he married Susanna Bennett fifteen months later. See W. J. McCormack, *Sheridan Le Fanu and Victorian Ireland* (Oxford: Clarendon Press, 1980), 113.

223 *Banbury cake*: a small flat cake made from puff pastry with a spicy currant filling.

taffy: an American chewy candy made with sugar, molasses or corn syrup, butter, and assorted flavourings.

225 *an epileptic*: nineteenth-century neuroanatomists and neurophysiologists advanced new scientific understandings of how the brain worked and began to distinguish epilepsy from other convulsive disorders including hysteria.

neuralgia: intense pain in the area served by a nerve; a term first used in the early nineteenth century.

he be like Saint Paul . . . day: cf. 1 Corinthians 15:31.

paralytic: associated with loss of muscle function, paralysis was one of a group of disorders investigated by neuroanatomists and neurophysiologists in the nineteenth century; often associated with hysteria.

as mad as bedlam: a corruption of Bethlehem, applied to the Hospital of St Mary of Bethlehem, just outside Bishopsgate, London; a hospital for the mentally ill.

226 *laudlum*: laudanum.

232 *Æsculapius*: Roman god of medicine.

233 *Chaulieu's sweet lines . . . l'inquiétude* (Oh night oh sorrowful night, oh dawn so late. | Are you coming? Will you come? Are you far away still?): see opening stanza of 'Sur Fontenai en 1710', *Œuvres de L'Abbé Chaulieu* (Paris, 1757), ii. 142; the Abbé Chaulieu (Guillaume Amfrye, 1639–1720) moved from voluptuary to libertine to reconverted Christian, the last state thought by some to include a tincture of hypocrisy.

234 *"Judge not . . . judged"*: see Matthew 7:1.

longo intervallo: (Lat.) after a great delay.

"O nuit . . . loin encore" (Oh night oh sorrowful night, oh dawn so late. | Are you coming? Will you come? Are you far away still?): opening couplet of 'Elegy xxiii' by André Chenier (1762–94), who was guillotined three days before the fall of Robespierre.

235 *Heaven and Hell*: first published in London in 1758 and the best known of Swedenborg's writings; written in a simple style, it describes conversations with angels and understands death as an encounter, in the spirit world, with a replica of the self.

237 *the "Opium Eater"*: Thomas De Quincey's *Confessions of an English Opium Eater* began as articles in the *London Magazine* in 1821, was published in book form in 1822, and substantially revised for a new edition in 1856.

240 *apropos des bottes*: (Fr.) about nothing, irrelevantly; here, for no reason at all.

crams: lies (slang term from 1842).

241 *struldbrug*: one of the beings who, in the third book of *Gulliver's Travels* are immortal in that they endure perpetual old age.

All Hallows E'en: Halloween (31 October); originated in the Celtic festival of Samhain when the spirits of the dead were believed to return to this world.

242 *Hebe*: personification of youth in Greek mythology.

243 *the Picts and Ancient Britons*: historical ancient people of the British Isles, perhaps the earliest to speak any form of a Celtic language, named as Picts by the Romans.

one of the cakes baked by King Alfred: the king of Wessex, 871–99, generally known as Alfred the Great, who led the Saxons to victory over Danish invaders; associated with the legend that, when in hiding in Somerset, he forgot to watch a peasant woman's cakes, as he had been asked to do, with the result that they burnt.

Danish beer in a skull: evidently a blurred allusion to the gravediggers' scene in *Hamlet* (v. i) in which there are passing references to drink, etc.; there may be some unidentified intermediary source.

244 *angels and ministers of grace!*: William Shakespeare, *Hamlet* I. iv.

delirium tremens: (Lat.) an extreme state of hallucination and tremor caused by prolonged addiction to alcohol, drugs, etc.

246 *Sir Tunbelly Clumsy*: character in Sheridan's *A Trip to Scarborough*.

circumvallation: encirclement by walls.

249 *bogle*: a phantom, a mere phantom or bugbear (a form of bogy from northern England).

256 *'Barnaby Rudge'*: historical novel of 1841 by Charles Dickens; the original illustrations were by Halbot K. Browne ('Phiz') and George Cattermole (1800–68); Browne (1815–82) also illustrated Le Fanu's second novel, *The Fortunes of Colonel Torlogh O'Brien* (1847).

259 *Walter Scott's poems*: *The Poetical Works of Walter Scott* were published in a collected edition by J. G. Lockhart in 1833 and appeared regularly throughout the nineteenth century.

261 *Tony Lumpkin*: the ill-educated, happy-go-lucky hero of Oliver Goldsmith's *She Stoops to Conquer* (1773).

cases of turtle from Liverpool: turtles were imported to Britain from the West Indies from the mid-eighteenth century; by the mid-nineteenth century turtle meat was considered an expensive delicacy.

262 *Moore's lines . . . live*: the opening of 'Oh ye Dead!' by the Irish poet Thomas Moore (1779–1852).

Woman of Endor: cf. 1 Samuel 28:7–25 for the story of the Witch of Endor's conjuring up of the figure of Samuel.

264 *Michael Scott*: see Walter Scott's 'Lay of the Last Minstrel', XI. xiii–xxii.

"Lay of the Last Minstrel": a poem or metrical romance in six cantos by Walter Scott, published in 1805; features the mysterious medieval wizard Michael Scott and his book of spells.

265 *Falstaff's billet-doux*: cf. Shakespeare's *Merry Wives of Windsor*, II. i, etc., where Falstaff woos both Mistress Page and Mistress Ford.

267 *dryades*: wood-nymphs, native spirits of the woods.

268 *il en est épris*: (Fr.) he is smitten with her, is in love with her.

"Whoso findeth . . . obtaineth favour": see Proverbs 18:22.

269 *Van Diemen's Land*: Tasmania.

274 *the refrain is not that of Sterne's*: see Laurence Sterne's *A Sentimental Journey* (1768), especially 'The Passport; the Hotel at Paris' in which a caged starling prompts the narrator to discourse on slavery.

275 *as Chaulieu so prettily says*: probably intended as a rough synopsis of 'Épîtres xxi' (*Œuvres*, ii. 289–90) addressed to the Marquise de Lassai.

277 *Saint Kevin*: Irish medieval monk.

281 *diapason*: combination of notes in swelling harmony.

284 *'The serpent beguiled her and she did eat;'*: cf. Genesis 3:13.

286 *abagail*: Abigail, Nabal's wife in 1 Samuel 25; the type of faithful waiting-woman.

289 *dodged*: baffled by artfulness.

292 *first-chop*: first class.

293 *pottusses*: pothouses, public houses.

298 *the white drops*: laudanum.

300 *pegtops*: trousers, very wide at the hips and narrow at the ankles.

301 *in the wrong box*: in a difficult position, at a disadvantage.

   cappen: captain.

   'devilish cantrip slight': cantrip = necromantic spell, a witch's trick; the phrase occurs in Robert Burns's 'Tam O'Shanter'.

302 *ivories*: teeth.

305 *tic douloureux*: (Fr.) facial neuralgia.

   waste: see Frederick Pollock's *The Law of Torts* (Philadelphia, 1887), 222; (in law) 'any unauthorized act of a tenant for a freehold estate not of inheritance, or for any lesser interest, which tends to the destruction of the tenement, or otherwise to the injury of the inheritance'.

306 *the old man*: see Romans 6:6 and Ephesians 4:22 where the corrupt state of the soul before Redemption, or before conversion to Christianity, is thus metaphorically described.

308 *the deluge*: the Flood in which all but Noah and his ark was destroyed; see Genesis 7:17, etc.

   the waters of Mara: see Exodus 15:23 where the children of Israel in the desert come upon a well of bitter undrinkable water.

   'I am washed. I am sprinkled': an echo of Ezekiel 36:25.

   nolo episcopari: (late Lat.) 'I do not wish to be a bishop'; an avoidance of responsibility, tinged with false modesty.

   Dives . . . Lazarus: see Luke 16:19–31 for the parable of the rich man (Dives) in hell and the beggar (Lazarus) in heaven.

312 *Lord Duberly . . . Doctor Pangloss*: characters in 'The Heir at Law' by George Colman, the Younger (1762–1836); Duberly (alias Daniel Dowlas) has until recently been a shopkeeper in Gosport—the theme of an aristocracy with 'low' associations is echoed in Dudley Ruthyn, and his father's obscure marriage. George Colman the Elder was a friend of the novelist's grandfather, Joseph Le Fanu; a portrait of George Colman the Younger is said to have provided a model for the description of Uncle Silas's portrait in Ch. II.

315 *"Aimer c'est craindre, et craindre c'est soufrir."*: (Fr.) the meaning is familiar— 'to love is to fear, to fear is to suffer'—but no precise source has been

traced; cf. Mme de Scudéry (1607–1701) 'C'est un grand malheur de se faire aimer, avant qu'on ait assez de raison pour se faire craindre', and Jean Racine (1639–99) 'Las de se faire aimer, il veut se faire craindre' (*Brittanicus* 1:1).

316 *Mrs. Malaprop*: character in Sheridan's *The Rivals* (1777) famous for the ludicrous misuse of words.

Miss Ogle: Esther Ogle, Sheridan's second wife.

Newgate: there was never a peer of this name or title in either the UK or Irish House of Lords; Le Fanu may be echoing the career of Thomas Gleadowe-*Newcomen*, viscount Newcomen and baron Newcomen of Mosstown (1776–1825); Newcomen, a Dublin banker by profession, died unmarried, all his honours became extinct, and he left all his property to eight illegitimate children.

322 *a 'three-quarter'*: portrait showing the body from the hips upward only.

324 *Christian*: hero of John Bunyan's *Pilgrim's Progress* (1678).

330 *hectic*: Le Fanu uses the adjective elliptically to mean 'someone who is (constitutionally) fevered or excited'.

334 *Revue des deux Mondes*: the premier French journal of ideas, founded 1825.

335 *dumb-foundered*: a legitimate compound word, used by Charlotte Brontë in *Jane Eyre*.

336 *groinings*: the edges formed by the intersection of two vaults, usually on a roof interior, or the lines of stone or wood covering such edges.

337 *Gammon*: humbug.

341 *criminals in Germany*: the reference negatively points up the virtues of the British provision of habeas corpus, whereby a prisoner could not be kept indefinitely in confinement before trial; in the nineteenth century the right to habeas corpus was periodically suspended in Ireland under various Coercion Acts.

electro-biology: a branch of biology which deals with electrical phenomena in living organisms; the term was in use from the 1840s and was associated with debates about mesmerism or states of hypnotic suggestibility.

demon of Goethe: Mephistopheles in *Faust*, by J. W. von Goethe (1749–1832).

343 *Vandyke's noble picture of Belisarius*: entitled 'Date Obulum Belisario' (i.e. 'Give a penny to Belisarius'), the picture shows the great Roman general, blinded, begging by the roadside; Le Fanu may have seen the engraving by Gerard-Jean-Baptiste Scotin, or read a description of the original in John Smith's *Catalogue Raisonné of the Works of the Most Eminent Dutch, Flemish, and French Painters . . .* (London, 1831)—see iii. 80–1.

344 *execution*: (in law) the enforcement of the judgment of a court.

347 *surtout*: a greatcoat.

'chimney-pot': a hat resembling a chimney-pot in shape.

355 *goosey-goosey-gander*: a popular nursery rhyme.

the "*Romance of the Forest*": Ann Radcliffe's Gothic novel from 1791.

356 *took heart of grace*: took courage (origin obscure).

358 *triste*: (Fr.) sad.

niaise: (Fr.) a foolish girl.

dérèglement: (Fr.) disturbance.

sottise: (Fr.) foolishness.

vous me faîtes honte: (Fr.) you make me ashamed

359 *bestiole*: (Fr.) critter.

362 *de faire baiser le babouin à moi*: (Fr.) Kissing a baboon, implying forced submission to an unpleasant encounter or act.

363 *Mr. Richardson*: Samuel Richardson (1689–1761), author of *Clarissa*, etc.

377 *Talleyrand*: Charles-Maurice de Tallyrand-Perigord (1754–1838), French statesman and diplomat, served successively the Revolution, the Empire, and the restored monarchy.

383 *St. Paul's preference of love*: see 1 Corinthians 13:13.

Ravenswood smile: in the manner of Edgar Ravenswood, hero of Scott's *Bride of Lammermoor*.

385 *elle a le cerveau mal timbré*: (Fr.) she's a bit off her head.

397 *Lanternes!*: (Fr.) literally 'lamp-posts', used also to mean dawdlers, slow-moving people, etc.; 'à la lanterne' was used during the Revolution to mean 'Hang him!' (i.e. hang him from the lamp-post).

403 *slammakin*: a slovenly woman, a slattern.

lay figure: a jointed wooden dummy, used by drapers (or artists) as a model.

406 *what in Ireland they call a bull*: a bull is 'a self-contradictory proposition' or 'an expression involving a ludicrous inconsistency unperceived by the speaker'; see Maria Edgeworth's *An Essay on Irish Bulls* (1802).

409 *stone jug*: nineteenth-century slang for prison; cf. present-day 'in the jug'.

410 *the Pythoness*: in Greek myth, a priestess at Delphi.

411 *the valley of the shadow of death*: Psalm 23:4.

412 *Atropos*: in Greek myth, one of the Fates; Le Fanu may have built up a more dreadful image of the figure by drawing on John Milton's account of her in 'Lycidas' as 'the blind Fury with th' abhorred shears'.

414 '*I will make echec et mat aussi vrai que je vis*': (Fr.) 'I will put a stop to everything.'

416 *the press-room*: in the nineteenth century, the area through which condemned prisoners passed on their way to the gallows was called the press room (or, more often, the press yard); the origin of the term lay in the medieval practice of pressing with heavy weights prisoners who refused to speak.

The cloud of cruel witnesses . . . my prayers and agonies: cf. 'so great a cloud of witness' (Hebrews 12:1); Maud's biblical echo is quite at variance with St Paul's phrase.

418 *'Traitor's Gate'*: the gateway in the Tower of London under which condemned prisoners passed.

419 *press*: (Ireland and Scotland) cupboard.

421 *the honoured head of John Wesley*: the founder of Methodism, Wesley (1703–91), may strike readers as an unexpected comparison for Silas.

427 *'Now if any man build . . . what sort it is.'*: 1 Corinthians 3:12–13.

'He that is unjust . . . filthy still.': Revelation 22:11.

429 *'Write . . . that die in the Lord.'*: Revelation 14:13.

to recognize under these beautiful forms of earth the angels who wear them: see Swedenborg's *Heaven and Hell*, para. 74.